AFTER DUNKIRK

AFTER DUNKIRK

MILENA McGRAW

HOUGHTON MIFFLIN COMPANY

BOSTON   NEW YORK

1998

Copyright © 1998 by Milena McGraw

For information about permission to reproduce
selections from this book, write to Permissions,
Houghton Mifflin Company, 215 Park Avenue South,
New York, New York 10003.

Library of Congress Cataloging-in-Publication Data
McGraw, Milena.
    After Dunkirk / Milena McGraw.
        p.   cm.
    ISBN 0-395-86885-8
        1. World War, 1939–1945 — Great Britain —
Fiction. 2. Britain, Battle of, 1940 — Fiction.   I. Title
PS3563.C3676A69   1998
813'.54 — dc21   97-49148   CIP

Printed in the United States of America

QUM 10 9 8 7 6 5 4 3 2 1

Book design by Melodie Wertelet

ACKNOWLEDGMENTS

My gratitude and appreciation to Molly Malone
Cook, my agent, and John Radziewicz, my editor,
whose efforts made it possible for this book to
reach an audience.

BOOK I

PART ONE

1

I

When the war broke out, I joined the RAF.

Then I went home, and waited for them to call me. There was not much point in doing anything else, really.

I was paid five pounds a week for staying at home and waiting.

The sky was as blue as a child's painting of it, and there was a fragility about everything.

Apples hung on the trees, ripening slowly in the sun of early autumn, and almost every day, almost every morning, my father and I walked through the orchard — round and round and round and round we went. We leaned against the fence and stared at the apples.

One day my father had to go to London. It's the time of Harley Street specialists for him, and I don't like it. Every now and then I can catch a glimpse of my grandfather's death mask in his face — I loved the old man, my grandfather.

He took me fishing once, my grandfather.

I was twelve that summer he took me fishing — it was my first summer in England after I'd arrived from India. My grandfather was almost eighty then, but he still walked like a much younger man.

My grandmother had had Mrs. Simmonds pack us a supply of sandwiches: "In case you don't catch anything."

"We'll catch something," my grandfather said.

We didn't catch anything.

We had tea and ate the sandwiches; we drank our tea out of metal folding cups. My grandfather put a spoon in his cup and drank like that, the spoon in the cup: the handle sticking past his mustache, past his cheek like a third ear. Shocking manners.

He gave a slurp, quite deliberately.

My dignified grandfather, in his beautifully tailored tweeds.

I looked at him, slurped back.

He slurped.

I was twelve, not quite thirteen. When one is twelve, one does like a slurping contest on occasion.

My grandfather: commandingly large ears, a handlebar mustache.

Well, my father had to go to London.

Breakfast. My mother sipping at her Lapsang souchong; my father always has Darjeeling.

As for me, I usually drink coffee for breakfast: I am the new generation. It's black as all the sins of the world, that coffee, but that's how I like it; I put three lumps of sugar in it, to take the bitterness away.

Breakfast. My mother: "Philip, you'll miss your train."

I looked at my father. "Oh no, he won't."

My mother: "Of course, it's far better to miss the train than . . ." Well, God in heaven, woman!

My mother has never been an ordinary mother. On 3rd September, 1939, she became a painfully ordinary mother. There is nothing like a good war to make a mother realize that she loves her only son, after all.

I said, "Well, I'll bring the car around."

I have been something of a fighter pilot driver ever since I turned fifteen — have always suffered from overreliance on the rear-view mirror. Well, that's what they tell you: "Look in the mirror. Keep looking in the mirror." So, I keep looking in the mirror, and so long as there is nobody behind me — in this case the local constabulary — I keep going, and I am reasonably confident that whatever may be ahead of me or to the sides of me will either take care of itself or I can take care of it. No, my driving is perfectly safe, actually. I am fairly responsible, I think, for my age.

So, there we were. My father in his nice, subdued going-to-London clothes; as usual, I had on my lamb's-wool, my old gray lamb's-wool sweater worn thin at the elbows. The morning was warm, though: I took off the lamb's-wool, tied it by the sleeves around my neck. It's like me, I think, that old lamb's-wool tied around the neck: both homey and dashing.

My sunglasses. They are enormous: they make me look positively sinister. Mysterious and all that. I pilot that battleship of a (somewhat) elderly Bentley about; I can pretend it's a brand-new MG.

I gave my father one of my best grins.

Slowly, at a stately and majestic pace, we rolled down the drive, in case my mother should be watching from behind a curtain. Then, past the hedge, where the lawn stops and the meadows begin, I put my foot down. And we went.

The Bentley *is* a bit on in years, there is no doubt about it. But my grandfather kept it in beautiful working order. My father has also kept it in good condition. It's a powerful beast — oh, absolutely. It hadn't rained in several days, and as we went, we raised a dust storm in the gentle morning: the morning that, inside, smelled of the Bentley upholstery: well-cared-for leather; and outside, of apples.

And slowly, my father returned my grin.

A thin-faced man, a sallow-faced man, a man who looked unwell; an old man, his adventures confined to trusting his nineteen-year-old son to get him to the railway station at breakneck speed in time to catch the 8:25 for London.

Well, God in heaven, there are times when I hope I die young.

I was five. This was in India. I remember mornings.

Swish swish went the broom on the steps. Then, the sound of water being poured on the warm steps — not hot, yet: warm — and then, swish swish again.

My father came up behind me as I stood on the verandah, and scooped me up and held me aloft. "Well, I'm off, then, little son. I'll see you tonight. Be good, won't you." And silently we surveyed our domain. It was awfully brown, our domain, I remember: a season of brownness? Anything from hazel to dark chocolate, with only a few splotches of green to relieve the sameness. In the distance, in the morning air, a large dark bird circled — a vulture? — far from us: oh, quite far from us. In silence, we watched.

Strong arms around me.

In the morning, my father's skin smelled of soap, warm water, and general well-being.

Swish swish went the broom and, for a few moments, time stood still for both of us.

Well, that's what he liked, I think — time standing still. He probably wasn't much of a one for adventures, anyway, my father: forty-four years old when I was born; a childless widower of almost ten years when he met my mother. My mother was nineteen.

So, now I looked at him and I realized that, in spite of his grin, neither of us was enjoying the ride very much. We used to enjoy it — he enjoyed it: my daredevil act. But now it all seemed very wrong, somehow.

I wanted to slow down, but I'd promised he wouldn't miss his train. So, I kept going, and didn't slow down till the first houses of the village came into view.

We got to the station with two minutes to spare by my absolutely brand-new Rolex Oyster. "Well, go and buy your ticket," I said. "And if the train comes in the meantime, I'll throw myself in front of the engine."

But the train was late, almost ten minutes late. We stood there, talked. "I think I'll have a go at the rain gutters today," I announced. "Climb up on the roof . . . it really must be done, you know. All the pipes, all the spouts cleaned out before the bad weather comes —"

My father said immediately: "It's dangerous."

"Well, other people have done it for us for years." Is it my fault that, now, all of a sudden, nobody seems interested in climbing up on other people's roofs, even if good money is offered to do it? "I can do it." I grinned. "A piece of cake, really."

But he still didn't like it. He's like my mother. "It *is* very high."

Four storeys high, including the attic.

"I'll wear rubber-soled shoes," I promised. Well, how high does a Spitfire or Hurricane fly? Oh yes, he was thinking of that. And yet, I've been flying since I was sixteen: I finally soloed two days before going back to school after the summer of my sixteenth year. And he never minded. He never said he minded.

Then, thank God, the train came, and I handed him in. He had no luggage, of course: just his *Times,* to read on the train, and his umbrella; but he limps, a bit. So, I handed him in, and he didn't protest. And that, too, seemed rather wrong, in a vague way: I mean, the fact that he was going, if only for a day, and I'd stay.

"All right, it's the 4:33 on the way back," I said. "I'll be here," I said, as reassuring as I could make it: I am not going anywhere, yet.

He smiled. "Don't forget, now."

Then he settled himself in his compartment and pressed his face to the window, like a child. I have no idea what was in his mind: did he believe that I couldn't see him? But he stared at me and stared, at all six feet four inches of me standing on the platform (my legs are rather badly double-jointed, and so I appear an inch or two shorter, but I am six feet four); and I shriveled to nothingness under his love.

So, when the train finally pulled out, I gave a perfunctory little wave, and then, when the chug-chugging of the engine died in the distance, I walked slowly back to the Bentley.

I walked, not paying much attention to anything, and something wrapped itself around my forehead: I'd destroyed a spider web in the morning, a little thing with dewdrops on it.

And we waited, day after day after day.

But that was eleven months ago, and since then many things have happened.

This, of necessity, will have to be written in fits and starts, but if I put my mind to it, I assume some semblance of a whole will emerge.

Who I am:

My name is Wayne Robert George Henry Luthie. It's a mouthful.

Robert and George Henry were my uncles, my father's younger brothers.

My grandfather called George Henry "George"; my grandmother called him "Harry."

Roberta is my mother's name.

My mother named me Wayne. My father should not have permitted it.

God has put me on this earth to fly aeroplanes. However, if God had meant for me to be a soldier, he'd not have given me, among other things, my double-jointed legs. For example, to stand at attention, I must bring my knees forward a bit, bend them a little: in effect, I have to stand in a half-crouch; only then is my double-jointedness masked, and I appear properly ramrod straight. It is extremely difficult for me to remember this at all times.

For better or worse, I am myself.

Myself.

And nothing and nobody can ever change me.

My grandfather looked like the rhinoceros in the Kipling story.

I mean, he didn't really *look* like a rhino: he was tall and thin — like my father, like myself (*and* like my uncles, in old photographs: from the Great War, the First War; as far back as photographs exist, almost all Luthie men had been tall and thin) — but his old skin hung on him very large.

"Them that eats cakes that Parsee-man bakes makes dreadful mistakes."

I was five years old. Bedtime. My father always read a bedtime story to me. When I was five years old, I had a thin cotton dressing gown: it was white, with red and blue stripes. But we read our bedtime stories while sitting on the sofa in my father's study; and the sofa was tweedy and scratchy: little prickly hairs always made their way through the thin cotton, and I rubbed my back against the tweed to get rid of them. And I wiggled my toes inside my slippers.

Then I settled down. And it was hot.

My father said: "Now that was a good story, wasn't it?"

"Them that eats cakes . . ."

And I sounded *exactly* like my father: well, I had put a lot of effort into it, oh, absolutely — (imitation) Cockney, although I had no idea that it was called Cockney.

There is an old picture postcard of good old S.S. *City of Bagora,* which was the ship that brought my parents to India.

In the summer of my sixteenth year, I played God in the attic. My father had written that he and my mother were coming home for good (actually, it took them two years; never mind), and he had charged me with clearing the attic in preparation for their own trunks, boxes: the debris of their lives.

"I am confident that I can trust your judgment." Well, here was my father, all mock formal. (We had corresponded frequently — my weekly letters from school — and we knew each other fairly well still.)

"You'll know what to do with all that rubbish. But sort through it carefully."

Here was my father, bestowing the responsibility of adulthood upon me: I was sixteen, my grandfather was dead, and I was the only male of the family in the house.

I played God. My great-aunt Maude's love letters to and from the man she eventually did not marry: what to do with those?

My great-aunt Maude had made a dreadful nuisance of herself at the time of my grandfather's funeral. She and my great-uncle William. My great-uncle William's handkerchiefs: enormous handkerchiefs, like sails on a man-of-war. He kept losing them. My great-aunt Maude kept insisting, sweetly, gently, helplessly, and firmly ("My dear child . . . would you mind . . . there's a good boy") that I should mount search expeditions for them. But God in heaven, I had other matters to attend to! My father was in India — well, on his way from India: Imperial Airways, four and a half days, four nights. My grandfather was dead, and I had the funeral to arrange. ("No flowers," I announced. "Beechwood branches.")

Well, that's what I would like, if I were dead: beechwood branches.

Why are so many clergymen so fond of sherry? Here was the Reverend Dr. Stibbs: decorous, his nose in his third glass. But he said, gently, "It's too early in the year for beechwood branches, I'm afraid."

Oh.

"Evergreens?"

And he put his hand on my shoulder, gently; gave my back a single gentle and comforting pat. He was most dreadfully gentle. "A trifle too much like Christmas, perhaps."

Quite. My grandfather liked Christmas carols.

"Evergreens," I decided. And that was final.)

And it rained. Rain, rain — God, it rained during that week my grandfather died! It was like a monsoon, only this rain was perishingly cold. Well, it was late March. Late March, and the beginning of April.

Umbrellas. Galoshes. Mackintoshes. The wipers on the Bentley slapping as it braved the mud and the puddles to ferry ancient relatives to and from the station.

Cocoa. Tea. Brandy. Warm milk at bedtime for my great-aunt Genevieve. Hot-water bottles for everybody.

Late at night, I sat in the kitchen with Mrs. Simmonds, and with Janet the parlor maid, and with Mr. Parrish, who was — is — the butler; we drank our own cocoa and told jokes and laughed. My grandfather was dead, and we were laughing!

I slept with Emmeline. Emmeline the Third came, her tail a graceful half-moon, making her look somehow very deserving; she settled on my chest and purred up my nose.

And through all that week, I had to keep my tie from slipping: in those days, when I was sixteen, my tie was always at half-mast. But this was a new tie: black, my mourning tie; and it really looked quite disrespectful at half-mast.

"Young Robert . . ." said my great-uncle William, fixing my tie with disapproving eyes. (I didn't even tell him my name was not Robert.)

Now here were my great-aunt Maude's love letters to and from the man she did not marry. And she herself was dead now: had died barely two months after my grandfather. Oh, I could make her disappear completely! Throw the letters into the dustbin — and not a trace would be left of her! She would be truly dead! Oh, I was powerful, indeed!

I retied the letters (they were tied with pink ribbons, several stacks of those letters); found a brand-new box for them: the very last shirts of my grandfather's had come from the shirtmaker's in that box. I labeled the box in my small, neat handwriting (at that time, my handwriting was very neat).

The attic: vast dark. Well, here was Martin the Moth-eaten Moose (stuffed). Somebody — who? — must have brought him — when? — from . . . from Canada?

And there was the album that my grandparents must have put together once and then abandoned. Good old S.S. *City of Bagora*.

Two funnels; 13,500 tons.

I probably was conceived on good old S.S. *City of Bagora*: nobody in the family denies it. My father certainly does not deny it.

Hot. The fans whirring, stirring the hot air. Slowly.

Well, wake me when it's over. (Truly, one wanted to sleep through the whole voyage.)

Slow. Slow. Slow.

I know: good old S.S. *City of Bagora*, repainted on the outside, refurbished on the inside, also was the ship that, some thirteen years later, brought me back to England.

My father trusted her.

But there is no postcard of good old S.S. *And So On And So On* as she was when I traveled on her.

II

About my childhood:

I remember Sada the Ayah in a blue sari. Blue was Ayah's favorite: blue saris of different hues, different patterns in the fabric.

Breakfast. "Eat your kedgeree, pet. My pet, are you eating? Pet . . . ?!"

Ayah smelled of the silver polish in which she dipped her bracelets, necklaces, and earrings, and of perfume that was vaguely like the scent of roses.

Afternoons. After lunch, every day, including on Sundays and holidays, I was sent to bed. My task: to take a nap.

And the air shimmered, as . . . as it shimmers over the flame in the dentist's office, when the dentist sterilizes the metal beak of that little balloon with which he then drives hot air into the tooth before filling it.

(I am an absolute coward about dentists.)

Hot thoughts. Hot. Lazy. And at the same time frantic: darting to and fro.

And I lay there, in my more than Oriental splendor: stark naked underneath the crisp, starched, rustly sheets (and then limp sheets: limp with my sleep-sweat); Ayah always made me put on my pajama bottoms, but as soon as she closed the door, I wiggled out of them.

The ceiling overhead was blindingly white. The mosquito netting over my bed: that was white, too.

This probably is one of my earliest memories:

One day, there was a lizard in my room. (And many others after that, and many more before, I am sure; but this is the first one I remember.) Purposefully, its feet made dry scratching noises. Up and down the wall just opposite my bed, down and up again. Marching. Not marching, really: lizards do not march. Scurrying, then. A bit like my thoughts.

The walls of my room: white as the ceiling (that was a bit out of the ordinary, really; in most English houses in India the walls are cream-colored, I seem to remember); the lizard: a nice brown, like Cadbury's milk chocolate with dried fruits and nuts.

Then it — he — stopped scurrying. Was he looking at me?

Slowly, very slowly, I raised the netting.

Slowly, very slowly, I pulled down the sheets.

I remember getting up. The bed creaked: I held my breath. Every muscle in my body tensed. My neck sitting stiff and still on my drawn-up shoulders.

First one foot down on the ground, cautiously; then the other. I crept forward. I wanted to touch him. I've no idea why I wanted to touch him.

Perhaps my father had said that lizards' skins were dry, not slimy, and rough to the touch. (Dry as the sound of *this* lizard's feet? Dry as the wood for the kitchen fire?)

(But perhaps it was later that my father had said this, and it was about snakes.)

Still, as I went forth, I spoke to the milk-chocolate lizard on my wall. I spoke in Punjabi. "Here, little lizard. Do not be afraid. Well, can you hear me, then? What is your name?"

I knew, of course, that lizards hadn't got names; but that was the first thing that came into my mind. If I spoke long enough, and in the *proper* voice, perhaps he'd realize that I was friendly.

"Are you a woman lizard, then?" In English: "Liz the Lizard." I liked that. "Liz . . . Liz . . ." I called out. Softly.

Was he — she? — playing dead now?

We eyed each other: I, in my more than Oriental splendor, naked as a jaybird, and jabbering away in a mixture of Punjabi and accented English, with a singsong to the voice. (Later, much later — I was quite grown up, actually; it wasn't so long ago; not long before Dunkirk, really — my father told me that when I was four, five, six years old, I'd had an Indian singsong to my voice.) We eyed each other, I and a small brown lizard, opaque-lidded, on a white wall.

I was four years old, probably. I was unprotected, barefoot.

"Little son, never go outdoors without your shoes." (My father.)

Ayah: "I am thinking there are splinters in the floor, pet. And nasty beasties. They may bite you."

Splinters in *our* floors? We had carpets. Lots of them. And thick ones. And underneath the carpets, the floors were beautifully polished.

Beasties? Scorpions.

Snakes! *Tigers!!!* And lizards.

But there *was* a splinter in the floor, where there was no carpet.

I didn't scream: oh, most certainly I didn't. I didn't cry out: I was afraid to cry out, to frighten the creature off. I remember only a sharp intake of breath, as my eyes filled with tears.

The lizard scurried away, frightened off.

Never mind.

I had playmates. We went to auctions.

There is an auction when somebody one's known all one's life is going Home: to England. (And after the auction, the somebody's house is quite empty. Well, full, actually: full of boxes, crates, valises — I've always liked that word, *valises.* Grips — *grips, gr-r-rips!* Portmanteaux . . . Ah! *Port-man-teaux.* I was six years old.)

For children, auctions are better than birthday parties. Sweets. Sweets. Sweets. Honey cakes. Jam tarts. Ginger squares: cut in the middle, filled with vanilla cream; vanilla cream overflowing. Lemonade.

And Sunday-best shoes raising dust the color of fresh cow dung. My shoes became untied sometimes. "I'll race you to the gate."

"I won."

"No, I did."

"He won."

"Well, *he did not.*"

"Aw . . . let's go swing on Harriet's swing."

Grown-ups went about their grown-up auction business; we snatched the last of the ginger squares and went to swing on Harriet's swing. I remember: running . . .

Jimmy Clarke. Dennis Kirby-Green. (Good God, I haven't thought of those names in years!) All of us running. "Luthie-e-e, hurry up. Well . . . Luthie-e-e . . . are you coming?"

A jam tart between my teeth like a pirate dagger. Like a Gurkha's *kukri*.

Harriet's swing was seventy years old. The wooden seat was, that is. Not the ropes, of course.

"It's a *hundred* and seventy years old."

"It is not."

"It came on a sailing ship and it took two years to get here."

Harriet. A *girl:* silly, frilly girl-frocks. Harriet's Ayah: always brushing Harriet's hair. We used to stand there and wait for Harriet's Ayah to finish brushing Harriet's hair. Silken hair flowing down her back; but part of the hair was caught by a ribbon: sometimes the ribbon was pale green, and sometimes pink, or sometimes, on those rare very dress-up occasions, it was white; and the ribbon was tied into a huge, silly-looking bow. A *girl*.

A liar. Oh, a daring liar! A liar of great courage. A liar of stout heart. Oh, absolutely. "Stout heart." It must have come from one of my bedtime stories. The story has long since been lost to memory, but to this day I can remember saying, thinking, "stout heart" a lot. Turning it over in my mind.

Now Mrs. Holloway, for example: she was said to be "stout." She was *fat*.

A *stout* heart? . . . I thought of hearts with little rolls of flab, such as Mrs. Holloway had around her middle.

Fascinating.

Repulsive, a bit.

Interesting. Definitely. Never mind.

Said Harriet: "Well, Daddy said so: the swing is *two hundred* years old. You can ask him. My Daddy never lies. . . . It came from . . . Harrods," Harriet said.

I remember standing there, honey from a honey cake dripping between my fingers. It was hot. A slightly sweetish nausea rising in me from eating all those jam tarts. "There was no Harrods then," I said with conviction, and then . . . wavered. Was it true? Was I a liar? If so, then I was rather . . . drab liar, not nearly quite so . . . interesting a liar as Harriet.

The seat of the swing certainly looked old, though. Seventy years old. That was old.

I had asked Harriet's father once when Harriet wasn't present; when she was having her hair brushed again, no doubt. "How old is the swing?" I said. I felt uneasy. Guilty? When all was said and done, I didn't want to hear, really. (I felt unchivalrous, I suppose.)

"Sixty-five . . . seventy years," Harriet's father said.

The wood was beautifully smooth. No splinters there to drive themselves into our bottoms. It was well polished: years and years of varnish, transparent, so that the grain of the wood was still exposed. Many layers, coats. That's what the word is: *coats*.

"Harriet's great-grandfather brought it. For her grandmother."

Great-grandfather! Awe.

I am twenty years old now. I assume I can say that it was the awe of permanence. Tradition. In India, the rains are the permanence, I suppose; and things untended, unattended rot.

The seat of the swing shone. It was like a mirror.

"I can see my face in it."

"Luthie, you cannot."

Four faces. Four pairs of hands pushing, shoving. "Well, let me see, I want to see."

I sat in the swing. The smooth wood felt cool. I slid the backs of my bare legs against the smoothness; began to slide, from side to side, then back and forth, back and forth. It felt good.

I sat, quiet, contented, thinking my own thoughts.

Harriet: "Luthie, get off."

I gave myself a good push with my feet, and went high, and then swooped down again, and swung higher and higher, my legs pumping furiously.

Harriet said, reverently: "Luthie can swing higher than *anyone* in the *world!*"

And I could, of course.

. . .

That is how I am.

. . .

That is how I was.

I write this at home: the luxury of time!

After Dunkirk.

III

Both my father's brothers — my uncle George Henry and my uncle Robert — were killed on the Somme, in the summer of 1916, three years before I was born, within two days of each other.

My grandparents learned of both deaths on the same day: one telegram arrived in the morning, one in the afternoon. My grandmother — it must have been my grandmother — saved both telegrams. (Only about a year ago my father discovered them in the "secret" compartment of her little spindly-legged, rosewood-and-ivory-inlaid writing desk. The message in both is written out by hand.)

Christ God!

My father is a pacifist.

Quietly, reasonably, and with all that is in his heart.

With an old man's helpless resignation.

IV

Two months ago — it *was* almost two months ago: the end of May, the time of Dunkirk — my father the pacifist gave me a knife.

I've filled up the rest of my notebook. Only a few lines left.

Sturdy, serviceable covers of some sort of dark cloth; good prewar paper; ink decently dark blue; my conscientious handwriting (in those days, as I've said, my handwriting was neat in the extreme): and not much of importance is written in that notebook, really. Actually, the first two-thirds or so of the entries are simply reminders to myself of Things to Do Tomorrow and such, jotted down during the months of the *Sitzkrieg*.

There are a few drawings — sketches: some deliberately hurried (a few quick lines), some truly done in haste — that's all.

I'd save a good deal of space, I suppose, if I stopped pretending that this is a *real book* I'm writing, divided into *real chapters*.

V

And so I wake up, and it is morning.

I get up, get rid of the blackout: very early morning. A small rain is falling, and the grass glistens.

It is July, and days go on forever. God . . . if you exist . . . God, please make my days go on forever.

I stand in the coolness of the morning, in my more than Oriental splendor: naked as a jaybird —

> Well, world, here I am!
> Well, world, look at me!
> All magnificent six feet four of me!
> Oh yes: legs very comfortably double-jointed.
> (Rejoice, O Young Man, In Thy Youth — and all that?)
> Sheer — God forgive me — joy and love of life!

A good stretch, and a yawn. I am still sleepy. And so I fall back into bed . . . I burrow about: my body seeks warmth; my head searches for a fresh, uncrumpled, *cool* spot on the pillow. And now there is a most delicious coolness at the base of my skull, where the hair ends and bare skin begins . . .

God, if you exist . . . God, please grant me thoughts as small and peaceful as the leaves of the old plum tree outside the window!

(Apples are our livelihood, for the most part; but we've a few plum trees: they are the slightly elongated type of plum, not very juicy, but firm-fleshed and sweet.)

A terrified heart hammering against the rib cage.

(Quiet, Luthie. *Qui-et.*

Luthie, this is not the hour when ghosts walk! — Ghosts walk at midnight?

Wrong! As a rule, ghosts walk at about three or four in the morning.)

And so, after a while, I get up again. I wrap myself in my old, well-worn brown corduroy dressing gown: comforting warmth! I tighten the sash, pad to the window on leather-slippered feet. Open the window.

A small rain is falling; a breeze in the trees. It is . . . well, it is like . . . like a woman's hand touching one's face.

I lean out of the window, lean my face into the morning . . . and think a woman-hungry man's thoughts.

Rain on the grass; a breeze in the dark leaves of the old plum tree.

To be touched by a woman in tenderness!

Well . . . yes . . . in passion, of course.

(This is a brand-new notebook, by the way.)

I bicycled to the village yesterday afternoon to buy it.

I took my hands off the handlebars, and I went:

Sheer bravado!

I waved my arms about:

Sheer exuberance!

On the days when it doesn't rain, I cut the grass: there is special sweetness to all very early in the morning.

(Tom, the gardener — and Janet's husband — is in the navy now: "Well, he counts blankets in stores, Mr. Wayne! He's in charge of a whole storage room!" And needless to say, Janet is happy.

And Janet is pregnant — well, God in heaven, woman! After years of waiting, at last!

Tom was home on leave . . . was it at the end of March?

She suffers from the morning sickness, badly.)

In Tom's absence, I cut the grass: push the mowing machine about with ferocious determination; but for all my efforts, the lawn hardly looks carefully tended to.

The grass dries in the sun, and I sneeze. And sneeze again. And laugh.

I squint and grin up at the sun; and the sun is warm on my face, and on my Adam's apple, and all over.

Off with my shirt!

And by and by, I wave to Mrs. Simmonds, a basket over her arm, on her way to the kitchen garden to inspect lettuces and perhaps provide us

with a few carrots at lunch; and then I wave to my mother, a large straw
hat on her head, on her way to putter among the roses.

Sweat running between my shoulder blades.

Well, as soon as the south section of the lawn is cropped and tidy,
I'll draw a bathtubful of warm water for myself. No, I'll go for a swim in
the pond!

In the afternoon, for about an hour each day, I help my father with the accounts: I do the home farm, which includes the orchard; he does the rents.

"A sip of sherry, son?" (Not *little son*. Never *little son* — not ever
again.)

"Well, I don't mind if I do." (This was . . . last Tuesday? We broke
out the sherry bottle at about two in the afternoon! A lovely oloroso.)
And we sipped, judiciously.

My father: "I've spent the morning on the telephone, making arrangements for the harvest." (Almost all able-bodied men from the village are gone by now.) "From pillar to post, and back again. It took me
three hours. . . . At last they said they might send me . . . Germans. Do
you mind? . . . We'll have to provide shelter for them for the duration, I
suppose. They will be under . . . supervision, I assume."

And I sat, quietly, pondered that one over. "No, of course not. No,
not at all. No, I don't mind."

These days, my father lives on nitro tablets under his tongue as I lived
on Benzedrine at the time of Dunkirk. And he is quite skillful about it.
Oh, he is skillful! He yawns: he pretends to yawn: hand in his pocket;
then he covers his mouth with his hand, politely; and he slips a tablet under his tongue; then he finishes his yawn.

There was anxiety in his eyes. (These days, both he and my mother
follow me with their eyes as if they wanted to touch me all the time; they
look at me with gratitude and wonder; with fear: as if their hands might
go right through me — if ever they did touch me — as through thin air.)
"You truly don't mind?"

"No, of course not."

And we sat, and then we sipped, judiciously; then went back to work.
Our pencils virtually silent: his more so than mine, of course. I bear
down harder: well, my hand is generally clumsy.

My father: "Bloody hell!"

I said, "I've discovered a mistake. Five quid. In our favor."

My father: "I need five hundred."

"Sorry, the next time I'll try to provide five thousand."

"Wayne, do not joke! This is not a joke!" With a fine show of temper.
With his old temper! (And, for a few moments, he was his old self again.
Oh, I well remember: that fine temper he used to exhibit when I was
small and had misbehaved.

"Go *immediately* and apologize to Ayah *at once!*" . . . And so on and so on.

Now we looked at each other. Anxiety in both our faces, I suppose: are our finances really so precarious?

We sat in silence.

Companionship.

We drained our glasses, judiciously.

Happiness!???

Now Emmeline the Fourth — cinnamon-and-sugar on ginger; large ears; small head; and a still adolescent, inelegant tail — Emmeline, then, is cautiously making her way up the rain-darkened, white-sanded footpath, avoiding the wet grass, heading for home.

> Emmeline . . .
> Where have you been? Where have you been?
> I've been to London to see the Queen,
> And she says my hands are *perfickly* clean!

Permanence. Tradition: Emmeline the Fourth. There has always been an Emmeline in the family.

It was my uncle Robert, actually, who named the very first Emmeline. I think.

I go before the RAF Medical Board in two days' time.

VI

Here is a ghost story, of sorts. Ghost Story, Part I:

"On ran Dingo. Yellow Dog Dingo . . . always hungry. *Hungry in the sunshine. Grinning like a coal scuttle.*" I was five years old.

And I stopped wiggling my toes inside my slippers, and I stopped rubbing my back against the prickly-scratchy sofa; and as my father put more and more drama into his voice, I sat still, hardly breathing, really.

Oh, it was a terrible thing to be *hungry in the sunshine!*

Coal's cuttle. What was a *coal's cuttle?* A *grinning* coal's cuttle?

Grinning like a coal's cuttle.

And then I was in bed, under the mosquito netting, and in the night-dark, outside my window — when I was four or five years old — bats were on the wing, large and plump; and insects rubbed their legs together — or their wings, I'm not sure which; but they *talked,* the insects did, I know that much: I could hear them when I listened closely, and they said dry words, like paper being crumpled. *Amritsar,* they said, for example, *Amritsar* (well, Amritsar is a town, and nothing menacing

about it, really, is there? But it was a chills-down-one's-spine word, nevertheless: more about that later?); and pi-dogs fought, snarling, somewhere
in the distance — oh, far from us: quite far from us! And Jimmy Clarke's
mother played the piano: plink plink plink. Familiar sights. Familiar
sounds.

The air was heavy with the grown-ups' dinner: lamb and coriander.

Beyond this known darkness, in the *deepest* darkness, *coal's cuttles* lurked.

I am a man who loves words. And so it seems utterly appropriate —
typical of me, no doubt about it — that words should have been my
childhood nightmare.

VII

The Med. Board.

Routine. Nothing unusual.

They had me out of there — stripped; poked and prodded; my lungs
listened to; my hand and finger exercises done; and then dressed again —
within a quarter of an hour, perhaps twenty minutes.

"Pilot Officer . . . Well, Pilot Officer . . ."

But then the short, bald one — there were four medicos in all — the
one whose head looked like a large pink beach ball, the one with the
round wire-rimmed spectacles: he looked up from his files at last, spotted
the full stripe on my sleeve.

"So sorry. *Flying Officer.*" With exquisite courtesy. "You see, our
paperwork never catches up to the events, I'm afraid. You see, it says
Pilot Officer in our paperwork, I'm afraid." He sighed. He removed
his specs, rubbed the root of his nose. He said: "Our sincere congratulations, *Flying Officer.*" With exquisite courtesy. . . . "Ne-e-ext!!!" Without
courtesy.

And so I drove home, pronounced right as rain and fit as a fiddle, of
course.

(My *personal motorcar,* by the way, is a black Austin 7 with somewhat
tattered upholstery of a singularly unattractive shade. I bought her very
much secondhand last February, the day after my Wings Exam, to celebrate. Not a fighter pilot's car — oh, most definitely not! But she was
paid for with my very own earnings, not with family money.)

Three days later. Tonight: *last night,* actually. The telephone rang: at
midnight — well, almost. Dramatically. Well, such is Hanmer.

"Luthie, you bag of misery!" Ah, Hanmer, Hanmer! No exquisite
courtesy for him. Well, such is Hanmer.

Hanmer and I are friends unto death. (One tries, of course, not to
have friends in wartime.)

"Luthie, tonight our *commanding officer* delivered himself of a speech at dinner. Well, you know how Old Man Hammett is. . . . No, you don't, actually, do you? You didn't get to know him very well. Good old Hurry-up. . . . *'Ahem . . . Gentlemen. . . . Uh-huh . . . Gentlemen. . . .'* Well, that's why they call him *Hurry-up Hammett* — because he talks so wonderfully *fast*. . . . Luthie, you miserable . . ."

I said: "Hanmer, what do you want? Are you at a call box, by the way? If so, may I remind you your time will be up soon?"

But Hanmer was laughing like a madman. "Not to worry, old bean. No lowly, *bourgeois* call boxes for me! This communication is coming to you from the squadron's *most exalted* Signals Section! But the dragon will be here soon. What's her name?" And there was a muffled mutter mutter. "Corporal, love, what's your boss's name? . . . Hah! Tunnard-Jones, Luthie. The dragon's name is Section Officer Tunnard-Jones, Luthie." Mutter mutter. "Corporal, love, in your debt. Forever. . . . The dragon's name is *N. M.* Tunnard-Jones. . . . *Norma Margaret,* perhaps? She *looks* like a Norma Margaret, you know."

I said: "Hanmer —"

"Red hair. *N. M.* Tunnard-Jones. But the hair is not permitted to touch her collar, of course . . . So she's got it pulled back into a . . . bun. Is it a bun? Well, I think it looks like a tumor at the nape of her neck. Honest! And she is away at the moment — gone off to the loo, I presume . . ." And there were WAAFs giggling in the background.

"Hanmer . . . Make sense."

And Hanmer said: "Well, Old Man Hammett said tonight at dinner: 'Uh-huh . . . Gentlemen. When Mr. . . . uh-huh . . . Luthie . . .' Well, that's how he said it. Do you know what he said? He said: 'If any of you . . . uh-huh . . . gentlemen . . . *remembers* Mr. Luthie . . .' And then he went: laugh laugh. Witty. Witty. Witty.

"Whereupon cried Newby . . ." And here Hanmer paused for effect.

But the effect was delayed; the effect was diluted, of course. Well, such is Hanmer. Instead of the effect, he prattled on: "Well, *you* remember Newby, Luthie, don't you? Big nose, big ears. Good old Newby R. Roy F. Newby. Frederick? Or Francis? I *must* ask him, sometime. . . . Well, said Hurry-up: 'If any of you . . . gentlemen . . . *remembers* Mr. Luthie . . .' And good old Roy N. cried . . ." And here came the effect at last. "Cried Roy N.: *'The man with the dogshit Austin!'* Sorry, Corporal, my eternal love. Just say the word; I'll clean up my language." Actually, Hanmer's language was uncommonly clean, already, because of the WAAFs. "So, Newby, R., cried: 'The kid with the dogshit Austin!' Whereupon came this brilliant repartee from yours truly: 'Newby, you bag of misery, go to the dais and collect your medal. The Charing Cross, Third Class.'"

And the WAAFs were giggling. And I was silent. I felt protective of my Austin. (The upholstery *is,* of course, of a singularly unattractive shade.)

The man with the dogshit Austin. . . . I endured.

"So, says Old Hurry-up" — Hanmer continued — "the CO says: 'When Mr. . . . uh-huh . . . Luthie rejoins us . . . uh-huh . . . next week, we'll start building . . . uh-huh . . . our B Flight again.' And he — the CO — was chewing on his pipe . . . Well, he stopped smoking a week ago: doctor's orders . . ."

"Hanmer," I said, "Hanmer, take a deep breath. Hanmer, you're drunk."

"No, not really. Not much. Not to worry, old bean." And Hanmer was laughing. "So, he stopped smoking, and now he *salivates* into his pipe . . . Ah, it's to laugh! The man is suffering so because he can't smoke! . . . Luthie, the squadron's been at half-strength ever since Dunkirk. Strictly Flight A only. No Flight B. . . . Not that we need a B Flight. It's quiet as a grave here. We're *Somewhere in Scotland* . . . sounds ever so grand. Right *ro-mantic*."

God Christ, Hanmer!

"We protect the shipping —"

Shut up, Hanmer!

But there was a bare heartbeat of silence, and then, all of a sudden, Hanmer turned serious. "Luthie, I demand to know. Pukka gen, now. What's all this about? *'When Mr. Luthie . . . uh-huh . . . rejoins us next week . . . uh-huh . . . we'll start building our B Flight again . . . uh-huh.'*

"Luthie, you bag of misery, what do *you* know? . . . Or do you know anything? . . . There's nothing to do here, and so everyone gossips. *Why wait for you to start 'building the B Flight'?* . . . Luthie, rumors are afoot. Luthie, rumors are abroad. Rumors are rampant. This is a proper mystery! . . . And so Colin said tonight after dinner . . . You do remember good Colin K., now, Luthie, don't you? Colin Kenley —"

"I say, Hanmer . . . Hanmer, in heaven's name!"

But, in reply, Hanmer only swore. And then exclaimed: "My God, the dragon N. M. Tunnard-Jones is back!" And the line went dead.

(Needless to say, it is strictly forbidden to use the Signals Section telephones for private conversation. Ah, Hanmer, Hanmer.)

Yes, I *am* to rejoin the squadron next week: right as rain, and fit as a fiddle (and so on and so on). Well, yes, I expected that — I *knew* I'd be going back — when (and even before) I went before the Med. Board.

But Christ God, what *did* Hanmer mean? What in the world *was* that midnight telephone call about?

Ah, Hanmer, Hanmer.

One tries, of course, not to have friends in wartime. (Hanmer and I knew each other for exactly four days at the time of Dunkirk.)

It's a peculiar name: Hanmer. But his family name is Acklington.

(Flight Lieutenant Acklington now. He was Flying Officer Acklington, then, when I first met him.

He still — again — outranks me.)

He is Flight A commander now. He is two years older than I.

I remember trying to sketch Hanmer one afternoon — on one of those four afternoons (the time of Dunkirk): Hanmer sprawled in the grass, sound asleep (Hanmer puffing in his sleep — Hanmer doesn't snore: he puffs). The Adj. — the Squadron Adjutant, *Uncle Dixon:* for some reason, almost every squadron has an *Uncle* . . . needs an Uncle? . . . of one sort or another (the squadron leader himself, the intelligence officer . . . they're the ones called *Uncle,* usually) — the Adj. was trying to wake Hanmer, because we had to cross the Channel one more time that day, Hanmer and I, for the third time that day, before the light failed. (Well, we went out in pairs then, at the time of Dunkirk, our squadron did: not enough of us for larger sections; a patrol of one would have been suicidal.)

(Hanmer: his fine shark's teeth looking fit and sharp. They are small teeth, but positively knifelike. By contrast, for example, even my milk teeth were enormous when I was a child. My famous Luthie grin is a grin of huge teeth.)

(Hanmer goes into combat with his tie carefully and beautifully knotted. This is a man who *goes out to get shot at in a tie,* in heaven's name! A freshly pressed tunic underneath his Mae West. A professional: a Cranwell type? No, no, he merely is a fop! We met: he took one look at my well-worn roll-neck — the equivalent of my trusty lamb's-wool: sleeves comfortably sagging at the elbows, the collar jauntily frayed — he took one look, and I knew at once what he thought of me.)

Well, I was four years old once: Ayah fed me cod-liver oil; I didn't want to take it. That is what Hanmer looked like, sprawled in the grass, not wanting to wake up.

And then, later, I never returned to the sketch, to work on it again, to build on it, whatever. It didn't turn out very well, anyway, I'm afraid. My sketches probably aren't as good as I think they are. . . . Never mind.

VIII

When I was thirteen, fourteen, fifteen, I created worlds. (One often does when one is thirteen, fourteen, fifteen — create worlds, I mean.

England was new to me — and I was new to England — when I was thirteen; and besides, at that age one often is lonely but doesn't want to let on.)

And so when I was at school: instead of doing my Latin prep, I drew maps, of places both real and imaginary. They were beautiful maps. Lovely maps. Spectacular maps — oh, absolutely! Carefully thought-out, painstakingly and precisely executed; joyful, caution-to-the-winds, flights-of-fancy; true to reality but faithful to the truth of my imagination . . .

Color. Squalor. (Oh God, yes! India is my home.) Crowds. Crowds. Crowds.

English evenings. Grass under my feet. Trees to shade me. Roads for me to follow.

Gallia est omnis divisa in partes tres?

These were the landscapes of my own choosing!

Night. It is very late. If I do not go to bed soon, it will be morning.

But I scribble, scribble, to improve my handwriting. I practice my signature. I've covered a whole page with my signature: W. R. Luthie W. R. Luthie W. R. Luthie. The W is very large; the R a bit smaller; and then the L in *Luthie* comes good and big and strong.

I am myself.

And Emmeline the Fourth, my silly paperweight cat, sits on my desk. And her purring — oh, enthusiastic! — is like tiny ratchets, badly in need of oiling, working overtime.

She gets up and stretches: her tail up majestically, but scrawny and in-elegant. And she rubs her furry forehead against my hand. Then she rubs her forehead against my wrist. Thank you, Emmeline!

The cuffs of my shirtsleeves hide the scars.

Thank you, Emmeline.

Christ God, how can I ever touch a woman with the hands that grow out of those scars?!

With a lover's touch, I mean.

In all her secret places.

IX

1 August 40

My Dear People:

As you can see, I arrived safely. No, I did not drive straight through from 4 a.m. onward: at about 7 o'clock I did pull off the road and have my breakfast. Then the coffee and the cocoa in the thermos flasks lasted through the rest of the journey. I mixed it in the cup: half-coffee, half-cocoa. It is good, it really is: the cocoa to keep one warm, the coffee to keep one awake.

Mother, you couldn't wear a hat here — or you'd have to tie it down with one of those filmy, gauzy scarves. You know, the beginning of the century: ladies went motoring, they tied their hats down. Grandmother had one of those — there is a photograph of her up in the attic. Grandfather looks like me, like a skinned rabbit: a leather helmet, goggles.

Here there always is the wind: it's in the grass, and in the heather, and in people's bones; and I rather think every now and then a morning will come that will be bone-achingly cold.

Speaking of skinned rabbits in helmets: herewith the snapshot. It is old, of course: taken in May; but Hanmer only recently had it developed. I realized you had never seen me in full war paint. Are my hands really so very bony? The little "snake-things" I am twirling in my fingers — the ones running to my helmet — are the R/T leads. Radio-telephone. R/T. The oxygen mask is sort of hanging from my ear. By my ear. When one pulls it over one's face — it fastens on the other side, too — one looks like a harem girl. No, it is peculiar, truly: one's eyes suddenly seem to look all different when one puts that silly mask on. What I mean to say, I suppose, is that one begins to notice people's eyes more when the rest of their faces are covered. Said one of the WAAFs from Parachutes that from the eyes on up, everyone seems simply <u>heartbreakingly</u> handsome. Including myself!?

I am well.

Please send more cocoa; and also those fancy mixed fruits from Fortnum's, if possible. The kind with a lot of pineapple. Here they've only got tinned cherries.

Do take care of yourselves.

As ever,

Your Prodigal Son,
Wayne

2

I

Ashley straddled his motorcycle, the engine idling.

The WAAF in the window by the gate had nothing to do and was mothering him. She wasn't flirting with him: she was mothering. He knew the difference.

She was old, really. Twenty-five? After a certain age — once they were past twenty or so — it was difficult for Ashley to tell about women. About men, too, actually.

The WAAF said: "Have a honey bun, then, Sergeant. Heather honey. You buy it in the shops here, heather honey. A place called *Campbell's*. And a witch of a woman there was in the shop. Mrs. Campbell. Well, she looked at me . . . at my *uniform* . . . she looked at me as if I might not be all *respectable*, like . . . Well, you know wot a woman wot is not respectable is, Sergeant. You're grown up . . ."

Was she mothering him or not? In confusion, Ashley managed to blush scarlet (and despised himself for it); then he cut the engine: this was going to take a long time.

"But I gave her my recipe for honey buns. 'Mrs. Campbell,' I said. I had no idea: she may not have been Mrs. Campbell at all; but 'Mrs. Campbell,' I said; and she was. 'Your honey in my honey buns . . . We're a team, Mrs. Campbell.' But she still looked through me, like. But, I talked. And by the time I left, I had her eating out of my hand, I did. . . . Have a honey bun, then, Sergeant. I made them myself."

And a plate appeared, at last, from within the depths of the WAAF's cubicle: a chipped plate, with red roses on the china underneath the honey buns; it came . . . from inside a *drawer?* Her *secret* honey buns? She pushed the plate through the window.

"Thank you," Ashley said politely, and some heather honey immediately dripped on his chin, embarrassing him, but — nonchalantly — he managed not to show it.

The WAAF said: "Sergeant . . . Well, it's a shame, really. You know, the h-officers . . . in that big house. Ever so posh, the house: well, at the end of that road goes past the fence, you know. With real bathtubs, on big brass feet, like claws. So, they're the ones have got the kitchen, too, the . . . officers. It's a shame, really: they don't cook; they drink.

"But Pilot Officer Kenley . . . he's a good man, ever so nice, for all he's a h-officer . . . he smuggled me in, like. Yesterday. Well, there's nobody there, not a soul, all day. Not till evening.

"And so I fired up the stove . . . I like to sing when I cook. And soon . . . soon . . . Ah, those buns . . . they perfumed the air. Sergeant, eat."

Obediently, Ashley stuffed half a honey bun into his mouth.

"And then I thought," said the WAAF, "I thought, I'll nip over, see what the drawing room is like. Well, the furniture that was there is gone, you know . . . But there I was, on the stairs . . . tiptoeing . . . tiptoeing . . . and, all suddenly . . . the door opens. So, I ducked into the broom cupboard. And I peeked out . . .

"Well, who do you think? The squadron leader. Himself!

"And he stood in the hall. . . . And in the oven, the honey buns were baking . . . and it was like *real* perfume. So, he was sniffing the air, like.

"And my heart was up in my throat. Because if he found me . . . and Colin — I mean, Pilot Officer Kenley — it would be bad for him.

"But he never did come down to the kitchen, the squadron leader. He just shook his head, and then he bit down on that pipe of his, he did, and he went on up the stairs, up to where the bedrooms are. He didn't believe wot he was smelling! Men are so silly, don't you think?"

Then she stopped, realizing (probably) that Ashley was a man, too: though probably the trouble was that he was not old enough to qualify as a real man for someone as old as she was.

"Well, do you like my honey buns?" she said eagerly. "It's heather honey." Did she sound too eager?

He chewed with determination. Swallowed. "Thank you." Politely: his best manners.

A diplomat: that's what the word was.

Well, had the honey buns been better when they "perfumed the air"? They certainly were heavy on the honey: the glaze ran between his fingers, and it was all over his teeth, finding its way unerringly to the one and only cavity of his life . . . He really should have it taken care of.

She said, "You'll like it here." Sadly? Disappointed. (Had she detected he didn't like the honey buns?)

Brightly: "You'll like it here. It's ever so nice here."

Well, if it's so nice, why are you babbling so much?

And Ashley's eyes swept over the cheerless landscape under the pale, cold sun: if he had to stay here for any length of time, he'd start babbling, too. Poor woman!

Nice chestnut hair (though it was too short: regulation short); and she *was* old.

And not much between the ears, that was for certain.

Her breasts were too big, too, for Ashley's taste. But then, some people liked big breasts.

(Well, that was what most of the talk had been about, through the long months of training: *sex*. At *real* stations, such as this one — as opposed to training stations, or so the rumor went — there were women and there was *sex*.

"But it's guarded, where the WAAFs live. Like a bloody prison. Like bloody nunneries. Because they want the bloody places to be like bloody monasteries."

But there was a chap, his name was Grant. He said: "Well, do you know what monasteries were like in . . . in the Middle Ages? All the monks and nuns at it. All the time. Day and night.")

Now, here there was an officer — what was his name? Kenley — and . . . and a lowly aircraftswoman? Unlikely. Most unlikely. But then, why not? Oh, it would be a most dreadful scandal, though — hah! — should it be discovered.

But it seemed to Ashley that he could sense in the woman something that was almost like loneliness. Was she confiding in him somehow?

That made him feel older. Truly grown up, really.

So, he chewed, bravely: too much tough dough to sink one's teeth into.

She was eyeing his motorcycle. Now if she says, "It's ever so nice," I'll . . . I'll . . . I don't know what I'll do, thought Ashley.

She said: "A Husqvarna?" She pronounced it right, too. "Well, it's not a Harley, is it, now?"

He almost choked. Well, people always surprised one!

"Uh-huh," he nodded; and at last, the honey bun was finished, and he could speak like a human being. *Now* they had something to talk about! Oh, he was willing to talk about his motorcycle! But he never got the chance.

She whipped out a map. "So, you go this way: that's where you leave the motorbike. And then around here . . ." And her pencil flew, weaving around buildings and dashing through empty spaces. "And this is where you live.

"But come back and talk to me. If ever you're homesick. It's ever so nice here . . ."

Not just cheerless: bleak. Must be dreadfully depressing in November. (And December. And January. And . . .)

"Come for more buns. You did like them, didn't you?"

Ashley said: "Uh-huh."

But her voice was definitely mothering him now; and it felt safe. Ashley felt young, too, again: not grown up; but he didn't like *that*.

She said, "The name's Mary Ann."

"Mine's Ashley."

"Well, you silly goose, Sergeant, I know it's Ashley."

"George," said Ashley, "George."

"Well, I never . . . A cousin of mine is George."

And about half the rest of the world!

"George Bevil," he said, forcefully.

"Sounds grand, really. Ever so nice," she said. "All la di da. Just like some of the . . . officers."

God damn the woman. Not much between the ears, that was as clear as day. But now she was laughing at him!

Well, was she mothering him, or was she flirting? The trouble with women was that they had no more idea how to treat him than he knew how to treat them.

And then she dropped her bombshell. "Well, run along, then, Sergeant. George. Bevil. Ashley. You're the last one, you know. The rest of them, they came in yesterday; and some of them the day before. So, he's been asking about you, Flying Officer Luthie was. And I said, 'Sir.' I like to chat. But he was impatient, like. He's ever so anxious to get his hands on you people . . ."

God damn the woman.

To tell the truth, Ashley's ambition in life was to be safely in the middle: to disappear in the crowd.

But, because his name began with an A, he usually was the first on any list; and because of that, he was the one people remembered. (For example, the first day of any term at school: "Who knows the answer?" And, rustle rustle: the master searching through the names. "Ashley? . . .") And now, as luck would have it, he was the *last* one. But, singled out again.

Ashley's ambition in life was to be a watcher, an observer; not the one observed. But somehow, he wasn't made that way.

Well, God damn it all!

And so, hurriedly — in some panic, really — he started his motor-cycle, kicked it into life. He pulled his goggles down.

She cried after him: "Well, take another honey bun, then, Sergeant. Save it for tea."

He didn't even turn his head. Into the wind that tore the words from his mouth, he called: "Some other time." (Only later it occurred to him that perhaps he should have been polite one more time, adding: "Thank you.")

And, her map in his gloved hand — the paper flapping in the wind, so that he could hardly see the writing — he rode off in search of the place to park his motorcycle, and then, in some panic, he ran to report to Flying Officer Luthie.

II

Ashley was unpacking: his socks, his camera . . .

His *portfolio*.

Where in the devil should he stow that? No place large and flat enough, naturally.

Under the bed? Not secure enough. They swept under the beds occasionally, didn't they? Jesus. Filthy broom bristles raking through his pictures . . .

He sat down on the bed, surrounded by half-folded underclothes and by his photographs.

On either side of him, there were more beds, with iron bedsteads. Like his dormitory at school.

Like . . . like a hospital ward. That was more like it.

No sick people, though; no wounded. Ashley the watcher, the observer had set out with his camera to record Wartime. What he had in his *portfolio* so far could, for want of a better word, be called Ordinary Life.

There was a cigarette burn in his blanket. Well, that certainly was unlike school. At school, if you were caught with a cigarette burn in your blanket . . . horrible things would start happening. And here they'd issued him a blanket with a hole in it.

This was . . . grown up.

He stuck his finger through the cigarette burn, waggled it several times with pleasure; then began to contemplate whether he should try to return the blanket to Stores and exchange it for one without a hole.

Ordinary Life: a group of people passing under the window, talking in loud voices. ("And so I said to her . . .")

"And what did she say?")

Ashley looked out the window, but they were gone, by now: he could only see their backs, disappearing. Some distance away, three or four people were kicking a football.

As far as the eye could see: long, low buildings, painted the color of the grass, so that they'd blend in. The grass growing the color of the buildings, so that it would blend in. Dull. Dull. Dull.

His pictures: well, here was the one that had won the prize. The third prize and five guineas.

It was the picture of the letter lying on the breakfast table, two days before the war started. But nobody knew then that the war would start in exactly two days.

The letter on the breakfast table, the envelope ripped open down the middle — that was how Ashley's father always opened letters: with brute force, if the flap wouldn't give way at first try.

(And Ashley had said impudently, "*Daddy,* I gave you a letter opener for Christmas, remember?"

Ashley's mother: she'd taken a big gulp of tea. Blinking her eyes, nervously. But in no way was Ashley's mother afraid of her husband, the father of her sons. "Eddie . . . Edward . . . dear . . . did you hear? Georgie gave you a letter opener last Christmas. Edward, why don't you use Georgie's nice letter opener?" Ashley's father resolutely tore the envelope limb from limb.)

Then breakfast was over. The letter lay there. Father's teacup was empty; his plate still held a half piece of toast. The crumpled napkin had marmalade stains on it. So, before the dishes were cleared away, Ashley sneaked downstairs again and snapped the picture.

A picture of loneliness, born out of — what did one call it? — indifference. The letter was from Ashley's brother John. John had disobeyed, displeased, and disappointed *them,* and *they* — well, mainly Father — they'd stopped liking John.

It was a picture of Ordinary Life; but it was an interesting picture. It told a story. But supply your own story.

A tired old housewife writing to her husband, telling him that she was leaving him forever after a thirty-years' marriage? Oh yes, it could be. (After all, Mrs. Manvers, their next-door neighbor, she'd left after *forty* years!) The Bixbys' kitchen girl telling her young man that she was going to have a baby? Oh, there could be a hundred stories!

Well, that was why it made such a good picture.

The third prize and five guineas.

But what a dull letter!

"Dear Mummy and Daddy, How are you? All is well with me. Georgie — or is it *George* now? — so, summer is over and it is school for you, again, old boy. When?"

But then, John was an RAF navigator, not a writer of novels. (Nor Father's *assistant, learning so that he might continue what Father had built with his sweat.*)

It was a Wartime picture: the war came barely two days later, and four days after that, John was dead, shot down on a reconnaissance flight in . . . "in operations over Enemy Territory." (So, Ashley couldn't even look it up on a map.)

"There never was a man died that another man would not be happy." John used to say that.

And so Ashley had won the third prize and five guineas.

And Ashley inherited his brother's motorcycle.

(In his *portfolio* there was one photograph which had been taken by the chap named Grant when they were training. Ashley straddling the motorcycle, with a big smile, the smile of ownership, the smile of pride. There was a field near the little railway station which served the village where they were training: Ashley used to make it his destination because the road that led there was full of serpentine curves, and that was where his riding skill could be properly displayed. In the middle of the field there stood a tree. This was in spring: the tree was leafing out. Ashley on his motorcycle, under the tree.

It is spring, and I am happy and I am on my way. Where? I've no idea. My hair slicked down with Brylcreem. And I look stupid, sitting here like this.

But the chap named Grant had taken the picture on Ashley's orders because Ashley wanted to show his dead brother that the motorcycle was in top condition.)

Ashley's father had short, fat fingers. Ughhh!

And so now Ashley picked himself up and shoved his *portfolio* under the bed, after all, and then decided to give the B Flight office and Flying Officer Luthie another try.

The first time, he had found the door locked. Above the doorknob, there was stuck with tape a piece of paper, pulled out of a loose-leaf notebook. BACK AT ELEVEN, it said, in big block letters.

In parentheses: (I HOPE).

The signature: WRL. A big W, a much smaller R, a very large L.

I hope?

Well, what kind of a flight commander was that?

Grenfeld:

Well, he had happened to be passing by just then, as Ashley was inspecting the locked B Flight office door.

"Grenfeld," he introduced himself, his hand outstretched. "Grenfeld, Jeremy. . . . And if you're looking for Him" — and with his thumb he indicated the locked door — "He's taking somebody Upstairs . . . Cartwright, I think."

One took a single glance at Grenfeld and saw a darkened cinema. The screen flickering. The swell of music. And the names of the actors rolling.

"And introducing . . . Jeremy Grenfeld . . . as . . . Don Diego de Garcia!"

Well, *Grenfeld* and *de Garcia* didn't quite go together, actually.

But there was no acne on Grenfeld's face. Not one single pimple!

Jeremy Grenfeld . . . Jesus, he should not be wearing flying boots! Nothing like ordinary flying boots should do for somebody like Grenfeld! Those fisherman's wading boots that the three musketeers wore in the sixteenth . . . or was it the seventeenth? . . . century (only they weren't really like fisherman's hip boots; they folded down somewhere around the knees — how did people walk in those things? Everybody must have been bowlegged): that was what he should have on.

A castle burning. (The image on the screen flickering.)

And Jeremy Grenfeld . . . Don Diego de Something . . . striding through the flames, head thrown back proudly, unconcerned; beams falling around him; a swooned blonde in his arms. The swooned blonde's swooned breasts pointing at Grenfeld's teeth.

Not a pimple on him! The sword at his side . . . the rapier . . . whatever . . . clinking on the pavement. (Or was there pavement in castles?)

Then Grenfeld said in an everyday, plain voice, "Your bed is next to mine, isn't it? At least that was the only one that was empty last night."

"Uh-huh," said Ashley.

Grenfeld said, looking at his watch, "I'm sorry, but I must be off now. I'll see you later. . . . And if He" — again a nod toward the door — "if He takes you upstairs this afternoon — mind you, He may not have time — but if He does, I want to hear about it. I'll tell you about mine." Unsmiling. He didn't smile once.

He certainly looked like a film star. He didn't walk like a film star.

He walked like . . . like . . . Ashley the observer watched him.

He walked like somebody older than his age — that was it. And no play-acting about it. Not really grown up: just older. There was a difference. (But he probably was about Ashley's age.)

"I say . . . Wait . . . Grenfeld . . . Jeremy . . ." Ashley called after him. "What's He like? Wait . . ."

But Grenfeld was moving at a good fast clip; and there was the wind blowing, and the grass rustled. He probably couldn't hear, or chose not to hear.

God knows where he was going with such a sense of purpose.

5

I

I am fairly responsible, I think, for my age.

II

How we live:

One of the many resident (half-wild?) cats sharpening its claws on a tire of Roy Newby's Spit.

Corporal Rossiter (he is one of the armorers): "Beast! Off with you! Off! Beast!"

The grass smells of petrol fumes and other people's boots: it's always other people's boots that the grass smells of, never one's own.

I arrived here, and went straight to work.

III

The squadron leader's office (the afternoon of the day of my arrival):

Huge photographs of his children hang on the wall behind his desk.

"Ah! Mr. . . . uh-huh . . . Luthie. Do sit down. I shan't be . . . uh-huh . . . a minute." But on he goes: scribble scribble scribble.

(Are the smaller — more modest — versions of the photos on the desk, where he might feast his eyes upon them at all times? No no. Only these enormous things: open the door, and here they are!)

The girl: by God, she most definitely is staring at the world in a *stouthearted* manner! (Six or seven years old?) A white ribbon in her hair. (Thus she looks like Harriet, somewhat, of my childhood.) Her brother seems two or three years younger. Summer. The seashore. Sand. (An enlargement — grainy — of a snapshot.) And — barefoot, on his haunches — with awe (how gratifying for a parent! probably); with some bemusement (it seems) he is contemplating the most enormous . . . no, wait: there is more! . . . the most *elaborate* (absolutely!) sandcastle on the face of this earth. Turrets. Battlements. And donjons. Drawbridges. Courtyards. And . . . dungeons? (There always are dungeons in castles.) A miniature paper Union Jack flying, without a care in the world, from the battlements.

Ah, it cannot be a bad life — not at all, I'm sure! — to be the offspring of *Old Hurry-up*.

(*Hurry-up* Hammett. Because he speaks so very slowly.)

"Mr. . . . uh-huh . . . Luthie. Sorry. . . . Uh-huh . . . Bear with me."

(I do not know him well at all, of course. It is a bit like meeting him for the first time, really.)

Large, powerful hands; but they are pampered hands: he slathers hand cream on lavishly, it seems. Scribble scribble scribble.

He bites down on his — unlit — pipe, morosely.

But then he looks up; smiles to himself: the cat who ate all the cream — he knows that all those who enter cannot fail but see those photographs at once.

"There. Uh-huh . . . finished. My . . . uh-huh . . . profound apologies." A regretful — oh, courteous! — incline of the head. "I have requested that you should . . . uh-huh . . . attend me. I do sincerely hope you have had enough time to . . . uh-huh . . . wash the dust of the road off your feet. Literally or . . . uh-huh . . . figuratively."

"Thank you, sir. . . . I'm quite all right, sir."

"May you this time stay with us . . . uh-huh . . . longer."

"Thank you, sir."

Well, God in heaven! He doesn't know what to do with me.

(I've no idea what to say to him.)

(And afternoon sunlight streams into the room; on the photographs.)

Well, we did shake hands once — another afternoon — in late May, almost three months ago, the time of Dunkirk, when I first arrived to join the squadron. He stank of sweat then and his eyes were red-rimmed. I particularly remember that irresolute voice of his. But he said at once then: "Mr. . . . uh-huh . . . Acklington will take care of you." That is called *delegating*.

(I'd guess his age at . . . twenty-eight, perhaps? . . . Must have married young. Now he is old.)

(Hanmer has put me in the picture: "Well, watch him *salivating* into that pipe. The thing is awash in his spit!" But last winter — and it was a harsh winter, oh absolutely!, one of the worst on record, truly it was — last winter, before I met him, Old Hurry-up Hammett had been ill off and on, or so Hanmer says. Recurring respiratory problems — a smoker's cough; and in the spring — or so Hanmer says — he'd sometimes get winded just running for his kite. That is why the medical profession's advice to eschew cigarettes, switch to the pipe, be sparing with the pipe.)

And he bites down on the — unlit — pipe; frowns, rather unhappily.

But the children are beautiful, no doubt about it! (The photos are behind him: somehow, they are between us.)

And he leans forward, then quickly back in his chair again — well, *he is trying to read my mind!;* and his eyes make me feel . . . ten years old! six years old! — not a grown man, that is what I mean; then he smiles to himself, again: in quiet amusement? A smile of pride: the cat who ate all the cream just before teatime. He is a man fulfilled in his manhood.

(*And you, Mr. . . . uh-huh . . . Luthie, you are not:* that is what that smile seems to be saying.)

Oh you . . . you . . . !

But says Old Hurry-up: "Mr. . . . uh-huh . . . Luthie. Well, you look most . . . uh-huh . . . wonderfully fit, I must say. If the . . . uh-huh . . . circumstances did not . . . uh-huh . . . warrant otherwise, I'd be tempted to say you got that splendid . . . uh-huh . . . tan of yours on the . . . Riviera."

Well, does he fancy himself to possess a sense of humor, now?

His eyes are steely blue. Resolute? The eyes of a man of determination — the eyes of a leader of men? But wait — wait! There seems to be a spark of warmth in those eyes now — oh, a good deal of warmth, actually: so, that is what he lets his children see, no doubt. Yes, it must be.

"Sir . . . I only cut the grass at home, before my leave was up."

"Sounds like . . . uh-huh . . . work." And this *is* a joke now! (*Cluck cluck:* of sympathy . . . But his voice, when he says the word "work": it sounds as if he were dangling a particularly smelly sock from his fingertips! And laughing about it: a childlike — childish — laugh, almost; and good-natured.) Oh, this very well may be a man who builds sandcastles from which little paper flags fly without a care in the world!

I laugh, too. "Actually . . . I enjoyed it, sir."

"Good. Good, Capital. . . . With your . . . uh-huh . . . permission, I'll say a few words at dinner to welcome you . . . officially."

"Thank you, sir. Actually, the . . . officers of Flight A — for all they know me only slightly — they've already given me a rather raucous welcome."

"Mr. . . . uh-huh . . . Luthie. We'll work well together." Friendly.

"Yes. . . . *Uh-huh* . . ." Well, God in heaven! "Thank you for your confidence in me, sir."

"Mr. . . . uh-huh . . . Luthie. . . . You are feeling . . . uh-huh . . . fit, aren't you?" Fatherly. With genuine concern? He looks old.

Well, he is much older than I.

"Yes, sir. I'm quite recovered. . . . Had to get up early this morning, of course. I'll get a good night's sleep tonight."

And so we sit there.

The photographs are on the wall behind him. *Behind* him . . . but he's staring ahead, and yet he seems to see them. (That is the thought that flashes through my mind.)

Large hands: powerful. Pampered hands. Fingers in a steeple in front of his nose; his — unlit — pipe on the desk in front of him.

And he gives me a quick glance . . . What in the name of heaven and hell is in those eyes *now?*

. . .

Well. Yes. My watchband is too tight. All right, loosen it, you idiot.

And I am breathing: a good, steady, regular *in and out, in and out* . . . There is an itch somewhere: where? I need to scratch, though.

In short, I observe myself being alive.

. . .

And he seems distant: very far away; but he looks satisfied. With himself? *Smug?* A man at peace . . . not with the world! Most definitely not.

A man at peace with *himself?*

In possession of something that I do not possess? And secure in that knowledge?

And so his little daughter in the picture continues to remind me of Harriet, of my childhood. The little boy is squatting on his haunches by his sandcastle.

Bloody hell! Well, there, on display, for all to see: hanging from two hooks (and in black and white), is that silly man parading his *immortality?*

And he did say a few words that evening at dinner. Introduced me: "Please welcome Mr. . . . uh-huh . . . Luthie: back by . . . popular demand!" As if I were an actor, on the stage.

Laugh laugh laugh.

Witty witty witty.

There are three WAAF officers. Two of them: they were *evaluating* me quite frankly — oh good God, yes: shamelessly! The third continued to eat her dinner, *neatly.*

Red hair. A very small woman.

W. R. Luthie: *Flight B commander.* That's me. From this day forward . . . And so on and so on. Good God!

Well, I had a good night's sleep. (Went to bed early, anyway.)

I went to work.

How we live:

My Dear People:

This certainly is a beautiful old house that they have billeted us in. Six <u>*real*</u> *bathrooms — no wartime-haste, yesterday-built showers; six enormous bathtubs on huge brass feet, like claws. Badly in need of polishing, the claws. And if Janet saw them, she'd want to go to work at once with her Brasso.*

The wallpaper in my room is all flowers-of-the-field. Very red poppies; very blue bluebells . . . This was a woman's room once, obviously. A young woman's, probably: a girl's? A very young girl's: eleven . . . twelve years old, perhaps? Sometimes I can almost feel her presence. Well, she got up in the morning; put a warm headscarf on. Wore wellies. Went to feed rabbits in their rabbit hutches.

. . .

Rabbits? . . . Rabbits!

Luthie, go to sleep.

Stub out your cigarette and go to sleep.
Pour out the rest of your drink and go to sleep.

We've rabbits at home. I was the one to feed them when I was at home.

"Hullo, Brunnhilde. Good morning, Brunnhilde." (And so on and so on.) (Needless to say, Brunnhilde is a very large rabbit.)

"I'll shut the gate;" — the hutches are inside a little enclosure — "you may hop about while I clean your cage. . . . Ah, your cage will be as spotless as Lady Chadha's syce's turban on Durbar Day!"
. . .

Lady Chadha: betrousered; bejeweled. (Sikh women wear trousers, not saris.)

Sir Prabhjot Chadha: jolly; jowly. Carried sweets about him in a scarlet silk pouch with a scarlet drawstring. ("Young Luthie . . . Good for the tum, what?" Always "tum," never "tummy.")

They had a son, Surjit — about five months older than I.
. . .

Well, Brunnhilde's nose goes: *twitch twitch twitch.*
"You silly rabbit. Move. Exercise."
Twitch twitch twitch.

Her ears: extremely large, like the horns on Brunnhilde's helmet; but they are soft inside, and warm, unlike the horns on Brunnhilde's helmet.

Ah, life is good!

The rabbits were one of my father's *wartime* ideas: rabbit stew — feed the family. Sell the skins, perhaps . . . Well, it was seeing Mrs. Simmonds one day in her winter jacket had given him the thought: she boasts a magnificently cozy rabbit skin sewn inside the back of that jacket!

But there is nobody at home now to kill the rabbits. My father: ha! He is a pacifist; and has seen enough slaughter in his time: he's no taste for slitting the throats of furry creatures — though he could do it, I'm sure, with quite a surgical precision. And Mr. Parrish . . . ? Too old. Tom . . . He used to do the honors. But Tom is in the navy and counts blankets in Stores. And the capable men of the village are in the Forces, too, now — every manjack of them, it seems.

I . . . I pleaded wounds not yet healed, when I was at home. With great dignity: a modest dignity.

Life is good.

My Dear People:
Please do send the cocoa. I bought some shortbread biscuits in town yesterday: four large tins of them, not bad. A place called Campbell's.

*Dignified black lettering — edged in gold, by God!; the gold is peeling off
in places. Mrs. Campbell is a sourpuss.
. . . I do hope all is well with you.*

That's how we live.
    I wonder:
    The small girl of my imagination, feeding *her* rabbits: did her family
offer this house to us for the duration — or was it suggested to them, politely but firmly?

IV

In the morning:
    The Spitfires — in the morning — in a row in front of what would
soon become the Flight B Pilots' Room.
    The wind is honey-scented, sometimes — heather-scented, I suppose,
but in the morning it is only cold. A fighter pilot's day begins abomi-
nably early, usually. A thermos-flask: half-coffee, half-cocoa inside —
my own invention, my very own personal recipe; and the cocoa keeps me
warm, the coffee keeps me awake. The air is clear, and one can see forever. Outside the fence there are lichen-covered boulders. They are outside the fence, not inside: when the airfield was being built — when the
ground was leveled — workmen must have . . . dynamited? then carted a
lot of those boulders away. Not a job of work I'd like to have done. But
it's a good field, really: good drainage. And that is what matters in an airfield: drainage.
    Never mind.
    The boulders are like huge felt hats left by a forgotten people.

Work.
    "My parachute on the tail, please.
    "The helmet inside the kite, the leads connected. Yes, both the R/T
and the oxygen.
    "Thank you, Sergeant. . . . Would you please relay this and all other
requests to Corporal Lansing and Corporal Dunaway?"

Well, look at those wings!
    The Spitfire is absolutely the most beautiful aeroplane ever built.
    The wings alone are a work of art: as in sculpture — that kind of work
of art. I mean it. Aesthetically pleasing — and so on and so on.
    "A name for her, sir?" Now this *is* Corporal Dunaway. "Now Mr.
Acklington, sir . . . he's got a nice Dragonslayer, sir. In nice red letters,
sir." Obsequious: our Corporal Dunaway?
    "Yes. I see."
    Dragonslayer. How very like Hanmer!

"I think I'll wait for a bit. A name may come to me." I am a deliberate man. My very first kite — my very first Spitfire (the time of Dunkirk, more than two months ago): her name was Rocinante.

("A Rosi-*what*, sir?"

And I could see them exchanging glances: that day more than two months ago; the time of Dunkirk. The screwdriver-between-the-teeth people — the fitters, the armorers — were exchanging glances. I was absolutely brand-new to the squadron then: had arrived not half an hour before. I'd traveled by train to a base in the Midlands to pick up the Spit, then had flown myself to Kent.)

Who am I to be a Rocinante's master?

"Yes. I'll wait, I think."

Corporal Dunaway: pouting.

Well, so be it.

Why *does* a fighter pilot's day begin so miserably early? My eyelids feel as if there are grains of sand behind them.

"Sir."

And I come awake with a start. . . . "I beg your pardon, Sergeant?"

Sergeant Bennett. His name is Sergeant Bennett.

(There is Corporal Lansing. There is Corporal Dunaway. But Sergeant Bennett is the man of importance.) Gingery whiskers: fierce, proud, like one of the (half-wild) cats'; and, if married young, he could be my father in age.

Polished shoes.

Polished shoes looking . . . predatory. Oh good God, yes!

(Sergeant . . . Yes, I am awake now.)

Ah, *dangerous* shoes, really — *gleaming* dangerously — as dangerous as all the devils of hell! The shiniest shoes I have ever seen in my life. Absolutely!

(My flying boots are clean and polished, too, of course; but they've seen better days, no doubt about it.)

(Sergeant . . . I most definitely am awake.)

"Sergeant . . . And I'd be much obliged if the same . . . the brollies on the tail, the helmets . . . could be done for all pilots of B Flight, once they begin to arrive. At all times. . . . It's not terribly important here, of course — not at the moment; but once we go south . . . Might as well keep in practice, I suppose. All parties involved."

Conscientious is my middle name. One of my many middle names.

Babbling too much?

. . .

And it seemed to me then that the fierce, proud whiskers twitched: as Brunnhilde's nose twitches. But in displeasure.

And so I stood before him, and I brought my knees forward a bit, bent them a little, so as not to appear so terribly double-jointed: not only does one then look properly soldierly; it makes one feel less vulnerable, somehow.

Then, with rather insane bravery, I slammed my knees back home. *Sergeant* . . .
I am who I am.
I am myself.
· · ·

His eyes at infinity: *respectfully*.
· · ·

Did the whiskers twitch again: in amusement?

And I got ready to take the kite up:
God has put me on this earth to fly aeroplanes.
The Spitfire is absolutely the most beautiful aeroplane ever built.
Yes, I've missed this.

You . . . you machine. So many pounds of metal with wings.

I hoisted myself into the cockpit; leaned my head against the headrest; looked about. Well, yes. The white paint on the undercarriage handle had peeled off in places, with time; but the handle itself: clean as if *washed* clean.

A brand-new rear-view mirror, buffed to a quite resplendent shine with a nice chamois cloth; but what ho! (and all that): what is it hiding behind the mirror? The fact that the mirror itself was installed in a somewhat elderly mount. (But it works. It works very well.)

A lady of *experience,* this Spit? No doubt about it. Made even before the war, perhaps? Has seen a few things? Oh, definitely! Well, I am not complaining. She's as good as new, really, under the cowling: brought down to zero hours, under the cowling.

Tanks full. . . . Airscrew in fine pitch. . . . (And so on and so on.)

They say the good Mr. Mitchell — the man who designed the Spit — saw but a few test flights of his creation. He used to sit just outside the fence in his old white Rolls-Royce: a gaunt, dying man. Everybody — including himself, of course — knew that he was dying.

He was forty-two years old when he died. Cancer.
That means he was two years older than my mother is now.
In a few weeks it will be my father's sixty-fifth birthday.

Well, let's go, shall we?
My gloved palm under the brake lever. A gentle pressure . . . Go.
· · ·

Christ, I've missed this! . . . Go.
· · ·

Off the ground. Up up up. My stomach — all my insides — pressing against my backbone; trying to get out into the world through the backbone. A fighter pilot's body takes a tremendous amount of punishment, no doubt about it.

But here we are. Ten thousand feet . . . and climbing.

Level off . . . Feet off the rudder pedals — oh, I can trim her without my feet on the rudder pedals! (Now try to do *that* in a Messerschmitt . . . hah!) And searching the airwaves for the kind of music I like . . . Cannot find the BBC Third Programme. But here . . . here's a sprightly little tune.

Sheer bravado!

End of music, abruptly.

All right . . . A half-roll. Diving diving.

A controlled spin . . . which in a Spit is quite difficult to do.

Sheer exuberance!

Here I go, in splendid solitude, being *absolutely* competent! Oh yes.

(I was back.

"Thank you, Sergeant."

A sepulchral voice: "Very well, sir. . . . Will there be anything else, sir?"

Well, God in heaven! The man sounds like a butler in a detective novel.

"No. No. Not at the moment. Thank you, Sergeant. . . . Thank you very much. . . . If there is anything else at all, I'll let you know, of course. . . . Thank you."

. . .

Ah, well done, Luthie!

. . .

One "thank you" too many, though. I think.)

. . .

Work.

("Sir."

"Yes, Sergeant."

"Am I correct in assuming, sir, that the . . . pilots of Flight B will begin to arrive three days from today?"

Well, he even talks like a butler! *Am I correct in assuming . . .*

He will not say "the gentlemen of Flight B": the men of B Flight will be sergeants, too, and he knows it: the very first sergeant pilots in the history of the squadron. Yet, in some respects, at least, it will be in their power to *request his cooperation*. And he doesn't like it.

A-a-a-argh! as they say.

If married young, he could be my father in age.

"Yes, you are correct, Sergeant."

Work.)

V

How I learned to fly: . . . ?
    No.
    . . .

How my father came to marry my mother: he was almost forty-four
years old; she was nineteen . . . ?
    No. (Peculiar thoughts come to one late at night, very early in the
morning.)
    (God! How I wish I could fall into bed at bedtime and sleep till the
sun rises . . . till my alarm clock wakes me . . . and so on.)

Amritsar? *Amritsar,* then: a town whose name sounds like paper being
crumpled.
    Night . . . Whispering . . . Whispering at night, after I was in bed —
grown-ups whispering (and outside my window bats were on the wing,
large and plump): "It will be another Amritsar . . ."
    I remember: a column of smoke rising — not far from us, not far from
us at all! (daylight); (well, there had been a most horrific explosion, and
then a column of smoke rising); and we were running, Ayah and I.
"Make haste, pet. . . . Hurry." (The *pet* in English; the rest in Hindustani.) Her sandals went slap slap in the dust.
    And the street was empty. Sun and silence sat astride the rooftops.
    And I understood that everyone at home — my father, of course —
would be most dreadfully worried if we didn't get home very quickly.
    Ayah reached out for me and picked me up and held me.
    I was . . . six years old? Too old to be picked up like a small baby. Too
heavy to carry. Too fast a runner for Ayah, really. *I had to wait for her* —
because she couldn't run fast at all in her sandals; in her sari. Slap slap
went the sandals.
    Her hair was braided; and slap slap went the heavy braid against her
back.
    But she caught up to me and gathered me up in her arms and held me.
I rode her hip.
    She smelled of her silver polish and of the perfume that was vaguely like
the scent of roses. She was pressing my head against her shoulder — my
face was almost hidden under her armpit, really. Under Ayah's armpit it
smelled of sweat and her perfume: better than the silver polish, actually.
    She ran.
    She put me down, panting.
    The street was empty and everything was silent. Black smoke rising.

To reassure her, I said, "Everyone is inside, having their tea." I knew, of course, that it wasn't teatime.

(In those days I thought of Ayah as *very old*. She was probably a woman in her mid-twenties when I was five or six or thereabouts.)

("Another Amritsar" never came.

The *real* Amritsar events had occurred in April 1919. My mother was about four months pregnant when Amritsar happened: no doubt it was just barely becoming visible to the outside world that there I was, growing inside her.)

More about that later?

. . .

Peculiar thoughts.

There are photographs of Ayah and myself.

The two of us poring over a picture-book together, for example.

W. R. Luthie — that's me — helping Ayah polish her bracelets, necklaces, and earrings. The silver polish came in large blue bottles. *Bright's,* it said on the bottle in fancy large white letters. *Since . . . 1895 . . . By ap-point-ment . . .* I read, moving my finger along with my lips — or was it the other way round? . . . *Ap-point-ment!* Almost as good a word as *port-man-teau!*

I remember the *music* of the place when I was very small.

Khamsamah — the cook — scolding: always scolding somebody.

Ali: a breeze of white robes. Gliding by. A sigh of white robes. Ali carried trays: clearing away my father's breakfast dishes, for example; Ali hugged bundles of sun-fragrant towels — handed them to Ayah. It was Ayah who prepared my after-breakfast bath.

Bees buzzing. And Ayah's bracelets sounded like tiny wind-bells . . .

Warmth. Heat. . . . Oh, I remember!

Sleepy. Sleep.

And everything was peaceful.

Peace.

A peaceful childhood, then. Most of the time.

Nighttime thoughts.

One day I should try to explain why I've decided to write all this down.

I've no idea, really, why I've decided to write all this down.

At first it was meant to be but an exercise, nothing else: a hand and finger exercise to improve my handwriting, my coordination. Strengthen the muscles. Whatever.

Presumptuous of me, I suppose. Scribbling scribbling scribbling.

Damned cheek, really, I suppose: to want to leave a record of how I lived.

How *we* live: the Old Man from Intelligence has got his little table set up in the grass, under a little striped awning; two paperweights on the table, to prevent his papers from being carried away by the wind. One of the paperweights says "A Souvenir of Brighton"; the other is a rock, a souvenir of a stone wall some two hundred yards away.

The IO: his paunch strains against his belt.

A very small woman: red hair . . . copper-colored hair, pulled back into a *chignon;* a woman of about my age: small-boned . . . gray eyes . . . are they gray?: serious . . . behind the wheel of a blue Hillman.

She is the woman who eats her dinner *neatly.*

My Dear People:
   I have been given an office of my own.
   (Failed to post yesterday's letter. Herewith, letter con't. Why don't you write? Well, no news is good news, I assume. And besides, the post probably is woefully slow these days.)
   When I was still at home, you said you wanted to hear everything, *were interested in every smallest detail. Well, here goes. The office is the size of a better-grade coffin. The building which contains the office is the size of a* deluxe *coffin. The very first morning after my arrival: the office door was locked. No key to be found anywhere. I ran from pillar to post and back again, as Father would say. Begged and cajoled and flirted with various WAAFs. (There was one — mightily peroxided —* young person *in particular: sitting at her post, knitting little mittens for her small twin nieces. Christmas presents: in August! Still, they were attractive little mittens — definitely!; and I told her so, several times, in words flattering to a high degree.) But to no avail. "Well, you see, sir . . . the B Flight office was never ever used, sir — not since* this *squadron was rotated here. As you know, we hadn't a B Flight before you arrived, sir. . . . Sorry, sir. . . . Well, you might try one of the fitters: they might know how to make a new key . . . might oblige you."*
   At last I climbed in through the window.
   Do you really want to hear every smallest detail?
   People had gathered in the meantime, of course: the people of Flight A, of course.
   Colin Kenley:
         "I'd rather stand around
         Piccadilly Underground . . ."
   (Not all of this ditty is suitable for Mother's ears, by the way — for Mother's eyes, should I write the rest of it down.)
   Caw, caw, caw.
   Cackle, cackle, cackle.
   I said, "Well, shall I pick *the lock?"*
   Hanmer: "Breaking and entering, Luthie. Breaking and entering. . . . And on the date in question, he did unlawfully pick the lock . . ."

"Shall I shoot out the lock?"

"*Defacing and/or otherwise willfully violating the property of the Royal Air Force . . .*" Well, you know how Hanmer is: I have told you enough about him, haven't I?

There were seven of us in all, I think. Seven intrepid officers of the Royal Air Force, all ready to do battle with the door. <u>Per</u> <u>ardua</u> <u>ad</u> <u>astra</u> and all that. With us, the fun is in the doing, not in the deed done.

Well, I climbed in through the window. (Hanmer: "*Displaying idiocy beyond the call of duty . . .*" and so on and so on.) It was not a difficult operation at all, though: the window was not latched from the inside, gave way with a single push. That whole ramshackle little building: huff and puff and blow the house down. Only the lock on the door was fit for a bank vault, you see.

Details. More details. For example, the air inside the office — once I got in — smelled like very stale bread. And piles . . . well, they were <u>mountains</u> . . . of dead-looking paper everywhere: on the desk, and on the solitary desk-chair, and on the floor, and on top of the little pot-bellied stove . . . There also was a half-empty (half-full?) teacup on the desk, but in all honesty I cannot tell you whether it was half full of tea or coffee: growing inside there was enough mold to start a . . . a scientific laboratory! (Well, I've heard about a medical bloke making a study of this: whether mold might actually cure diseases.)

The people outside were calling to me. Catcalling and all that.

I stood there.

I remember thinking: <u>This</u> <u>is</u> <u>the place</u> <u>from</u> <u>which</u> <u>I</u> <u>am</u> <u>to</u> <u>conduct</u> <u>the</u> <u>affairs</u> <u>of</u> <u>Flight</u> <u>B.</u> Christ God!

(But after some moments of deliberation, I crossed out the *Christ God*. Not because my people are the kind who would be offended by my taking the Supreme Being's name in vain; but because it sounded a bit . . . unrestrained. They might take the little exclamation and twist it and turn it in their minds: they'd begin to worry.)

I was quiet for too long a time to suit the Flight A people, I suppose. Hanmer: "*Luthie . . . misery . . . Stop being quiet!*" And so on and so on.

And so resolutely I unlocked the door from the inside. I forgot to mention that this was very early in the morning, now didn't I? In the morning — the sun barely rising — one can almost <u>taste</u> the wind: it tastes wonderfully clean on the tongue.

Caw, caw, caw.

Cackle, cackle, cackle. (If one should listen to us with a complete objectivity, one could say, I suppose, we sound like choking chickens. Ravens with laryngitis.)

"*Hip hip hurrah, Luthie! Three cheers for Luthie!*"

"Veni . . . Crawled in through the window . . . Vici."

"Luthie, you —" — *unsuitable for Mother's eyes/ears, I suppose* — "do a victory roll."

And so, resolutely, I threw myself into the grass and rolled over. They applauded.

I lay in the grass. Cold grass. Wet grass. For a moment, it was like drinking from a summer well.

That is how we live.

Friendship.

Do write, will you.

(For some reason, I never sent this letter.)

And it turned out later that Hanmer's key — the key to the Flight A office — would open my door, too. And it probably fits the squadron leader's office; and the office of the Old Man from Intelligence, where all the dreadful secrets are kept; and the office of the Old Man from Accounts *and* his safe, where all the lovely money is kept just before pay parade, and . . . and . . .

But nobody knows this; only Hanmer.

Well, I had a copy of Hanmer's key made.

And I lock my door, defiantly; it is a private joke, of sorts.

My Dear People,

Rec'd your missive this afternoon. It did take unconscionably long for it to reach me. Good to hear all's well.

And I've also summoned an aircraftsman orderly and directed him, quite firmly, to have the Flight B office cleaned out *please*.

(But so far, only the mold-laden teacup has disappeared; and the untidy piles of paper have been coaxed into tidy piles.)

Two more days.

Then they'll be here, Flight B. The *Nine Days' Wonders*.

Quite inevitably — and without a known culprit: a collective action, then? — the Flight A people have dubbed Flight B *Luthie's Nine Days' Wonders*.

This, of necessity, will have to be written in fits and starts.

I do not want them   I don't   I don't   I don't

VI

I traveled the road (the time of Dunkirk); and I was as a lowly homing pigeon: home home home home home.

There, ahead of me, the sky was burning; so, that was the west: that was where I had to go.

How far to go? I had no idea. And I sang to myself inside my head,

> I'd rather stand around
> Piccadilly Underground —

And I cursed to myself inside my head: horrible words, really.

There were dead bodies in the night along the road; and I had a fever; and I put one foot in front of the other.

Out of the night shadows a shadow came. (The shadows were dark red with the distant fires, I seem to remember.)

I cried out in fear. In more than fear: in terror, really. I gave a little yelp (I seem to remember). Then I whispered, "God . . . Please . . ."

The shadow wagged his tail and squatted down on his haunches in the middle of the road. A dog not too large and not too small.

"Well, hullo, boy," I said. "How are you, boy?" (Somehow, I knew that this was a male dog, though I could not see. It was a dark night. The stars were obscured by the smoke from the fires, I remember.)

And I went down on my knees there in the middle of the road (wondering all the while whether I'd be able to get up again: I had a fever and felt giddy); and I said, "Well, it's all right, then, do you see. Here, boy, here . . ." I said.

But he shied away from me.

He seemed afraid of me.

I said, "It's not my blood you are smelling. It's another's. . . . So, that's all right, then. . . . You needn't let me touch you. I understand. . . . The blood will dry, of course. On my clothes and all . . . All over me. . . . Please let me pass. And I'll be on my way."

(It is almost three months later now. Looking back, I think even at the time I probably was aware that I was suffering from a most horrible fatigue of the soul.)

And slowly — very slowly — I got to my feet; and I backed away from him, to the edge of the road; and then I continued on my journey.

And I sang to myself inside my head:

> I'd rather stand around
> Piccadilly Underground . . .

But the dog came with me. Sometimes he lagged behind, and then caught up to me; and sometimes he ran ahead and then returned.

And I had no idea where I was, really, or how far to go.

> I'd rather stand around . . .

I said to the dog when, suddenly, he once again appeared by my side: "Well," I said, "what is your name?" But he couldn't understand me, of course.

I repeated it in French. And then in German. Well, people around Dunkirk speak Flemish — many of them; and Flemish is like Dutch; and Dutch is a bit like German.

Dogs are in this world to be named.

"I'll name you Shadow," I said. "From now on, your name is Shadow."

But he didn't care. He ran on ahead.

And when he returned (though through all this he'd still kept his distance: still wary of me; but he'd come back — always: so he must think he needed me), I said, "My wrists are damaged. My right hand is damaged. So, I couldn't touch you even if you let me. . . . It hurts rather badly, you see," I said. "Oh, I hurt all over," I said.

But, once it was said, the pain lessened. And I began to feel joyful.

The burning sky seemed beautiful.

(I needed him.)

And when the dog Shadow came back yet once again, I said, "I'm very tired. I must rest. I need to sleep. I am ill, you see. . . . If I found a place safe . . . dark . . . peaceful . . . would you stand guard over me, so that nothing bad would happen to me?" But he wanted to keep going. And so we kept going.

But then the dog suddenly died, and I was left alone. He had simply wandered off; did not return.

It was getting on toward dawn, I remember: a fire ahead of me; a fire behind me.

And at first I was sure he'd be back, and I waited for him: I stood there, in the middle of the road, waiting waiting waiting. Then I called out, softly, into the silence of the breaking dawn, "Shadow . . . Shadow . . ."

But he didn't come; and I retraced my steps.

He lay there, by the side of the road, as if in a sound sleep. But he was dead.

I accepted it then. It did not surprise me. I did not wonder how it had happened.

I had a fever.

(Can a dog die of sudden heart failure? A stroke, perhaps? Or was it . . . poison of some sort, perhaps? I wonder about it now, and it frightens me. But it did not frighten me at all then. I had a fever. It seemed quite normal that a dog should die; that we all should die. That I deserved this: to have this dog die.)

Still, I lowered myself into the grass there by the side of the road (with some difficulty, I must say). Shall I touch him at last — with my "good" hand? The fur looked coarse-soft, I remember. And it would be warm, still, of course: warmer than the coolness of the passing night. Fawn-colored fur: I had not noticed this before. Well, would it be disrespectful to touch him now, when in life he had not wanted me to do it?

I said, "I'd have taken you home with me. We'd have become friends. . . . I'll get home, you'll see. And all this will be as if it had never happened. Once I am home, I'll be the man I've always been. You'd have liked me then. . . . We'd have become friends."

(I think I was suffering from a most horrible numbness of the senses. Mine was the oddest of sorrows, really.)

I did not bury him, of course. That would have been silly.

Besides, I was not at all certain I had enough strength for the task.

There were dead bodies along the road. There was a corpse of a middle-aged man lying in the ditch by the road. And, with some difficulty, I dragged the dog Shadow to the ditch, and I left the two of them together, to keep one another company.

And then I walked on.

I'd rather stand around . . .

And so on and so on. Over and over.

And I wept, I think, in my loneliness and in my sorrow.

It was almost morning. I must get off the road, I thought. I must hide.

I had a fever.

Ghost Story: Part . . . ?

4

Said one of them — and, to tell the truth, it was difficult for Ashley to remember all their names all at once — said the one with the blue eyes and with his eyebrows coming together at the root of his nose: "Well, how many times did He *kill* you?"

And then they all waited. Flight B. They waited like . . . well, like vultures.

Ashley was being tested.

Ashley was being judged.

5

I

My Dear People:
I'll be doing a good bit of training.

My Dear People:
I'll be doing a spot of training, I suppose.

My Dear People:
It's perfectly normal — it stands to reason — that one might have to do a spot of training.

My Dear People:
Thank you for the cocoa.

II

Stanhope. He is one of mine.
Flight B.
He has never sat inside a Spit.
Never. Not once. EVER!!!

III

I was born.
(That is how one begins a proper memoir.
That is how I should have begun, I suppose. Well, too late to start over now.)

I was born at Lahore, in the Punjab, in September 1919.
Lahore is a city made of redstone and shade trees.
(Christ, this is not a memoir I am writing: it is a hodgepodge!)
(I am a man who loves words.
I am a man who knows how to use words.
But my thoughts are *disorganized* . . .)

(Quiet, Luthie. Qui-et.
Lie back. Stretch out. Take off your boots. Change your socks, Luthie. . . . It's simply amazing what a nice, clean pair of socks will do for a man.
It is evening, Luthie. The day is over. . . . Actually, it is late afternoon.
Now feed the cats. Here . . . there are some table scraps here, wrapped in a piece of very greasy paper. Simply put them outside, paper and all; the cats will discover them quickly enough.
"Well, Harry Hammett, hurry up!" The — half-wild — cat Harry Hammett's name is Harry Hammett because his favorite sleeping place is under the squadron leader's car. He himself is as black as a motorcar tire.
Six o'clock. Not a soul about. They all are gathered in the mess ante-room, no doubt: Flight A; drinking. Dinner at seven. Well, pour yourself a large gin, Luthie. Lie back . . . stretch out.

The furniture in the room is RAF-issue, every stick of it, by way of the Salvation Army. The sofa . . . not uncomfortable, though. The upholstery may have seen better days, but there is only one coil threatening to jab a recumbent man between the shoulder blades.

Shift your position, Luthie. Light a cigarette. Wiggle your toes inside nice, clean socks . . . A-a-a-ah!)

IV

Earlier in the afternoon:

"Mr. . . . uh-huh . . . Luthie. Well, come in. Come in. . . . You have . . . uh-huh . . . requested that I should . . . uh-huh . . . see you. How may I be of . . . uh-huh . . . assistance?" Scribble scribble scribble. And dust motes danced in the sunlit air.

I took a deep breath. "Yes, sir. Thank you, sir. Thank you for your time, sir. Thank you for agreeing to see me so promptly, sir. I appreciate it deeply, sir."
· · ·

Bloody hell! Luthie . . . How many "sirs"? . . . Too many "sirs."
· · ·

I pulled myself together. "I need a Miles Master, sir. Now. Immediately. Today. Yesterday." (The Miles Master is a trainer most closely resembling the Spitfire.)

Little specks of dust danced in the sunlight.

Scribble scribble scribble.

The CO of the squadron to Flight B commander: "Mr. Luthie, *muddle through.*"

Well, God in heaven! (Please note: Not Mr. . . . *uh-huh* . . . Luthie.)

His little daughter in the huge photograph behind his back is looking out at the world in a most definitely *stouthearted* manner.

Ah, that poor child!
· · ·

He didn't quite say "muddle through" in so many words, of course.

Outside, the mid-afternoon sunlight was dark golden; a stiff breeze blowing, of course; under the half-open window someone — Colin Kenley? — Kenley, then, was . . . singing, I suppose.

> There will be blackbirds over
> The white cliffs of Dover . . .

Caw, caw, caw. Vera Lynn herself could not do it better!
(And, under the window, somebody else — little fat Geoffrey Thomas?

— said: "Kenley, it's not *blackbirds,* actually, you know." A voice neat and tidy.

Ah, such is our good little Geoff Thomas: a man neat and tidy! And it rather interferes, at times, with his sense of humor, I'm afraid . . .)

Kenley: Caw. Caw. Caw.

Cackle. Cackle. Cackle.

And the squadron leader, out into the world through the open window: laughing laughing laughing. That good-natured laughter of his. (Outside, there was a shocked silence.)

Old Hurry-up Hammett to W. R. Luthie: "Mr. . . . uh-huh . . . Luthie. *Wayne.* . . . May I call you . . . Wayne?"

· · ·

Well, is he dangling another smelly sock from his fingertips, now? That was what I thought.

· · ·

That almost childlike laughter of his. *Wayne Wayne Wayne.* As if my name were a joke. (Obviously, he does not like my name much.)

· · ·

"If you so wish, sir."

· · ·

(Well, I do not like my name overmuch, either.)

"Wayne. By the time I shall have succeeded in . . . securing a Miles Master for you . . . by that time you will no longer . . . need it." Resolutely. In a voice that inspires confidence, in general. In a voice that absolutely *radiated* at me his faith and confidence in me.

Well, God in heaven!

He seems so much older than I: in appearance; in . . . everything.

Then, for a few fractions of a second, he sat very still: was he looking within himself? I believe so.

But this time he wasn't searching his soul for the image of his children: I am sure of it. Oh, absolutely!

He looked within himself: did he fail me?

· · ·

The photographs of his children on the wall behind him.

The sunlight had shifted; and dust motes no longer danced. And, with the passing of the sunlight, it was somewhat colder in the room.

He bit down on his — unlit — pipe, morosely.

But, on the whole, he seemed satisfied.

He knows what is good for me.

This was our second interview since the time I arrived here: *in addition* to the one on the very first afternoon after my arrival . . . well, more about that later?; and he seemed impatient now for this particular meeting to end.

He smiled at me: friendly, fatherly.

"Mr. . . . uh-huh . . . Luthie. . . . Wayne . . ."

(I'll muddle through.)

(I've collected the Wonders' logbooks:
Burning the midnight oil and all that.)

V

My Dear People:
This place is full of the gentleness of life.

(Crumple up the piece of paper; take aim at the wastepaper basket.)

VI

(Well, where was I? Oh yes, the logbooks.

Grenfeld, Jeremy. A Jew: Grenfeld, Jeremy? Good looks that are rather *Mediterranean*, I suppose; and not a single pimple . . .)

"Acklington . . . I'm busy, you see."

Hanmer in the door.

Well, that is how it invariably goes when one is trying to burn the midnight oil and all that.

I looked up. "Hanmer . . . I say . . . Is anything the matter? Out with it."

Hanmer. Bloody hell. I AM BUSY.

Hanmer: his fine shark's teeth gleaming fit and sharp. Hanmer: working somewhat hard, it seemed, at making his shark's teeth gleam fit and sharp.

"Acklington, if there is anything . . ."

I'll give you ten minutes. I'll give you a quarter of an hour. Well, thirty minutes.

Flight A are the operational half of the squadron. They do go out and shoot at Germans on occasion. The Germans do shoot back on occasion.

Flight A: they protect the shipping. The water is out there. We cannot see it. Every now and then, the wind brings with it a whiff of . . . something. It's out there, the water. As the Spit flies, it is very close.

•

"Han-mer . . . Sit down, will you? You look bloody silly standing here like a bloody monk with a bloody begging bowl."

But he was staring now at all the ashes and all my cigarette stubs accumulated — accumulating — inside the lid from one of those large jars of fancy mixed fruits from Fortnum's: I use the lids as ashtrays. And he gave a little sigh of . . . well, it was resignation, I suppose: a resolve to push away . . . whatever it was; for the moment. Then he said: "Luthie . . . Misery," in . . . in a *mother's voice?* And with a . . . *mother's fingers* ("Here are your mittens, dear. And your woolly hat and galoshes . . .") he produced a matchbox out of his pocket, grubbed about, fished a Benzedrine tablet out of the matchbox, and with a flourish and a cackle most *un-motherlike* — well, such is Hanmer!: with a grand gesture, then, but with a laugh somewhat subdued for all that, he deposited the tablet on my desk.

Then, out of the other pocket, he produced a hip flask full of brandy. Well, God in heaven!

(Well, where was I? Oh yes. Grenfeld, Jeremy. The logbook. . . . Here we are.

And I had barely caught a glimpse of it, really, just before Hanmer knocked on my door — the very last page: he's had a . . . full five hours in a Spit. Grenfeld, Jeremy. *A full five hours.*

Oh, it would make a man's heart soar!)

And so: "Acklington," I said. "Don't be daft," I said, indicating the Benzedrine tablet. "I do not want this. I do not need this to help me through the night. I haven't touched these since the time of Dunkirk. I am not about to begin now." I was prim and proper as you please!

But Hanmer unscrewed the top of the brandy bottle; took a big gulp. "Well, Death to the Enemy," he said; and we both giggled, like two girls. He handed the hip flask to me. Hanmer's brandy is not just everyday, ordinary stuff. Oh, it smelled — tasted — felt good, going down!

I said: "Death to the Enemy!" And we both giggled. And we both were comforted. I think.

This place is full of the gentleness of life.

And then Hanmer took himself off, leaving both the Benzedrine and the brandy with me.

We are friends, Hanmer and I. We truly are.

I've no idea, of course, what really was on his mind and why he had come to see me.

Well, the logbooks: Brown. . . . Which one is Brown?

Bloody hell! I should have arranged these by alphabet.

Brown: nondescript. That's the best description.

The obligatory Harvard . . . Well, it *is* a modern aeroplane, the Harvard, trainer or not. Then he flew Gladiators. Glads. Well, Christ God! Well, it is a bloody biplane! . . . But wait. Wait. *Seven* — a lucky seven? — *seven hours in Hurricanes.* God . . . Thank you, God.

We'll muddle through. Oh yes, we'll muddle through. . . . and so on and so on.

Burning the midnight oil.

Why is this happening to me? A punishment from On High? For my sins?

Well, surely not.(???)

A punishment for being as a lowly homing pigeon: home home home home home?

I was in hospital, of course, after Dunkirk. And then, for a short time (which seemed long, nevertheless), at one of those RAF convalescent places: now this was a posh place, very posh — leather armchairs and green plants everywhere — and they were large plants and *masculine-looking:* leaves as tough as boiled beef. (The torture chambers — therapy rooms and all that — were hidden in the cellar, quite appropriately: in the dungeon. A creaky lift took there those who couldn't walk.)

My parents came visiting, of course.

And then I was released into the care of my family.

My good father the pacifist: in all this time he never asked me once what happened to his knife. Was he — is he — waiting for me to tell him? Ha!

(I have not taken the Benzedrine.

I have not touched the brandy.

I only am very, very tired.

· · ·

I have devoured two tinfuls of shortbread biscuits. There are crumbs everywhere. Including my bed. God, it feels awful: trying to lie down in the middle of that mess!

But I have come up with a detailed plan and schedule for each and every wretch of a Wonder for the remainder of the week. Then I'll plan for the next week: try to make a team of them and so on. . . . Have I got two weeks?)

VII

This place is full of the gentleness of life:

I was feeding the cats . . . LACW Robison came pedaling down the path on her bicycle. She is the one who knits. Little mittens for her little nieces.

She slowed down; stopped; dismounted. I watched: how clumsy and ugly those Service shoes are! Her neatly painted red claws gripped the handlebars securely. Well, *lovingly* painted — oh good God, yes! — little red claws on the handlebars.

"I'm feeding the cats," I said.

"Oh, I see, sir."

She's the one who knits.

I said, "Well, how are the kitten-mittens coming?"

"Oh, go on with you, sir. Kitten-mittens. The idea! I've told you, sir. They're for the twins, sir. Molly and Dolly, sir." *Molly and Dolly!!!*

Her nose is quite small. Why does it look so prominent, then? Because it is so carefully . . . elaborately! . . . powdered?

Peroxided hair: LACW Robison.

I said: "Those sound like kittens' names to me." (Or do they?)

"Kittens

      "Kittens

            "Kittens."

"Sir . . . Oh, do stop, sir." Nice, white, even teeth.

When I first arrived here, she was all official and officious with me; now I've been accepted. I think she rather likes me.

She is a bit plump; somewhat stuffed into her uniform. Red claws, lovingly painted. Comfortably, her hands gripped the handlebars. The face open, friendly.

I gave her a very large Luthie grin.

"Kittens

      "Kittens

            "Kittens."

She almost stuck her tongue out at me; in the very last heartbeat of a second she remembered I was an officer.

The privilege of rank: I stuck my tongue out at her. "Kittens."

And we both burst out laughing. When we were finished laughing, she climbed on her bicycle again; continued on her way down the path, heading for the little stone cottage — a lodge, in former times? — a guest house? — where all the WAAFs live regardless of rank (because there are so few of them).

(Half-wild) cats crouched, looking half-wild, as she passed.

. . .

Ah, life is good!

. . .

I do prefer natural fingernails on a woman, of course.

VIII

Woke up. Pearl buttons on a white blouse.

White. White as the coolness of the mornings at Simla.

Hair the color of copper. A small — small-boned — woman.
I have never seen her wear a white blouse with small pearl buttons.
(I should not be writing this down. I should not.)

Ghosts walk at about three or four in the morning, usually.
(But she is the woman who eats her dinner *neatly;* not a ghost.)
. . .

Serious, terribly serious gray eyes. Beautiful eyebrows.
Beautiful collarbones. (But in the waking world, I have never seen her collarbones, of course.)

(I should not be writing this down at all.
We'll be sent south.
And I may go west then, courtesy of some zealous German. And then good old Uncle Dixon, the Adj. — the Squadron Adjutant — Uncle will go riffling through the earthly goods I'll have left behind: it is one of his many duties to be the effects officer, and one of the effects officer's odious tasks is to "remove all materials" — letters to married men from women not their wives, for example; photographs and/or books or magazines of *unseemly* subject matter, for example — "which might cause embarrassment and/or anguish to the deceased's family.")

(Uncle Dixon: an old man's teeth — bridgework.)
(A man of . . . maturity, then? Our good Uncle Dixon. A man of . . . decency?)

Dear Uncle Dixon:
If I should cease to exist, please do not simply tear out these pages and then proceed to entertain all and sundry with selected readings from them in the mess anteroom before dinner.
Thank you.

W. R. Luthie

I dreamt about her, then.
A girl, running: in a pleated skirt. (I have never seen her run in a pleated skirt.)
In the dream: the pleated skirt flying . . .

About Simla:
I was seven years old when I went away to prep school at Simla. A sheltered life, and not one of freedom.
But I grew: I was ten years old; I was twelve years old.
And families were encouraged to visit on Games Days and such: we went for walks, my father and I. Sometimes.
But I was *twelve years old* — a man grown! — almost ready now to

leave for Home, for England. And so I forged ahead. Left him far behind.

Solitude. A rather splendid loneliness, I remember.

A carpet of fir needles on the path, I remember. Water dripped somewhere: cool . . . drip . . . drip . . . cool . . . *extravagant*. (Well, I had been born and brought up on the plains!) Fog swirled through the trees.

Rhododendrons . . . *Rho-do-dendrons*.

And I continued climbing; and then the fog parted, and the trees parted; and there . . . there before me . . . there they were: the mountains. And those mountains were the Himalayas!

A wonderful solitude and a splendid loneliness within me, and yearning. I was twelve years old.

And I wanted to run then . . . run, run never stop . . . spread my hands . . . feel the ribbons of wind between my fingers . . .

But I had no idea, really, where it was that I wanted to run. I was twelve years old. *A man grown.*

She is N. M. Tunnard-Jones, from Signals. Hanmer's *Dragon* N. M. Tunnard-Jones. Yes. Yes, she is.

Here there always is the wind.

(And I think back — I think of yesterday.)

N. M. Tunnard-Jones. And Hanmer.

N. M. Tunnard-Jones and Hanmer: those two standing on the path together, the path from the Med. Section to Signals; those two silhouetted against the late-afternoon sky together. (Ah, the wind!) The wind, tearing at Hanmer's hair. Oh my God, they look romantic!

And the wind has driven her skirt straight between her legs. She . . . she . . . well, it is as if she were stark naked! (For a moment.)

And Hanmer is feasting his eyes. Pretending not to be feasting.

· · ·

Acklington . . . I'll break every bone in your miserable body.

· · ·

She advances on Hanmer, pushes a sheaf of papers at him.

Hanmer takes a step back: he doesn't want the papers; and he is gesturing at her like a tenor in an Italian opera. The villain. (Actually, in opera the tenor never is the villain. Well, in *Rigoletto* he is the villain. The evil Duke of Mantua . . . Never mind.)

She *forces* him to take the papers; and they part. And they no longer look romantic.

Hanmer: trudging through the grass, hugging the papers to himself; and he looks disgruntled.

Good. Good.

N. M. Tunnard-Jones: she leans her small body into the wind, calmly.
Oh, you *woman of character*. Oh, absolutely!

In the dream, I opened my arms . . .
She was running toward me.

(Two evenings ago, at dinner, I passed the salt to her.
"Miss Tunnard-Jones . . ."
"Thank you, Mr. Luthie."
On the way to breakfast, this morning, I held the door open for her.
"Miss Tunnard-Jones . . ."
"Thank you, Mr. Luthie."
A soft voice; but something echoes in it. Serious, terribly serious gray
eyes: N. M. Tunnard-Jones. Gray eyes. So very serious.
There is something a bit odd about her.)

In the dream, she had on a white blouse with small pearl buttons.

Small, sweet, firm breasts underneath the blouse.
Oh, good God, yes! Lovely breasts.
Oh my love. Love   Love

Natural fingernails: N. M. Tunnard-Jones.

And so I woke up about an hour ago.
And I hold a pencil: clumsily . . . clumsily . . . a few quick lines . . . a
sketch.
God . . . if you exist . . . God . . . God, thank you! I am healed. I can
do it still! (Or again, as the case may be: I am healed.)
*See, these are your eyebrows, N. M. Tunnard-Jones. . . . And one day
I'll show you how I do it.*
. . .
Here you are, running in a pleated skirt.

And, in the dream, I reached out . . . slowly, very slowly . . . to touch one
of those little pearl buttons on her white blouse: to unbutton it. To un-
button all of them.
Sweet, small, firm breasts.
But this was a dream, of course; and, in the dream, she was far away,
of course: a woman not to be touched. She is the kind of woman whose
hair, no doubt, smells faintly of apples, like the orchard in high autumn.
She was running toward me . . . And I ran to meet her.
But she is a woman who is far away.
Then she was in my bed, naked. I, too, was naked.

She wanted me to lie between her legs.

And I woke up.

And now — in the moonlight: no blackout; the window of my room thrown wide open — in the moonlight, then, there are cats. Caterwauling.

Other windows opening. Horrible language to be heard. Boots and other objects descending from the windows on the hapless cats.

. . .

"Uh-huh . . . gentlemen. Please . . . gentlemen."

. . .

And there is silence: well, as if we were schoolboys, reprimanded by the master!

And now, in the moonlight, there is Victoria. And Victoria is a cat of dignity: unlike Emmeline's, her tail is elegant.

(There is an Albert, too. He is ginger-colored, with large whiskers.)

Victoria on the path, proud and sure-footed and — oh good God, yes! — queenly in the moonlight: she's got a most magnificent white ruff about her neck and a little white widow's peak on her forehead; Victoria on the path, heading for . . .

Has she got a home?

6

I

The chap named Grenfeld played the piano.

(Ashley observed: he was an Observer.)

The chap named Grenfeld announced that the piano in sergeants' mess was very badly in need of professional attention.

(And as the others jostled closer, Ashley moved in, too: a part of the group.

A part of the crowd: well, that was his ambition, wasn't it?)

Well stop staring at me, then (he thought).

(The one with the freckles . . . Stanhope? He was staring at him, now. And before that, somebody else. And before . . .

And Ashley was worried.)

Well, the piano was badly in need of professional attention.

"That's because Cartwright played it with his feet yesterday!"

"I did not."

"You bloody well did."

"Well, bugger off."

And Stanhope said, "Aw, come on! Let's have a tune!" And he buried all ten fingers in the keys. "Now that wasn't so bad, was it?" He sounded

nervous. He bit into a peppermint: he didn't suck on his peppermints —
he crunched on them. Crunch crunch crunch. It wasn't his piano, but he
seemed anxious for it to be a *good* piano. (As in, *Good dog, Spot, good
dog.*)

Grenfeld announced that he would play something called "The
Minute Waltz."

"Gentlemen, synchronize your watches," commanded the one whose
eyebrows came together at the root of his nose: his name was McGregor.

There was a bit of squabbling about the watches; but not much.

"Ready?" McGregor inquired, in an it-is-possible-for-*you*-to-be ready-
because-everybody-else-is voice. McGregor had piercingly blue eyes.

Grenfeld gave the ready-for-takeoff sign. (Grave-looking. Unsmiling.
He did not smile once.)

Then he poised his fingers above the keyboard.

"Three . . . two . . . one . . . GO!"

Grenfeld began to play, very fast.

"Twenty-five seconds!" McGregor cried. "Thirty-two . . . three . . .
four!"

And Grenfeld's fingers cooked all together. His face seemed to have
gone pale with the effort.

"Forty-five . . . ! Six! . . . Seven!"

And Grenfeld had to start a part of the piece over, losing much
valuable time. But then desperately he rushed on. And on. Till the finish
line.

"That was *one hundred and eleven seconds,*" said McGregor. And he
did not sound disgusted, exactly, but he seemed to be putting Grenfeld
on notice that it certainly was possible to do better. With practice, perhaps. With . . . encouragement?

(And Ashley concluded that McGregor was not bad at all at handling
people.)

(But *somebody* — Cartwright, this time? Or was it Farrell? — *somebody*
was staring at Ashley, again.)

But then Cartwright said, "No, it wasn't one hundred and eleven. It
was one hundred and nine."

"One hundred and twelve!"

"Thirteen!"

There was a lot of squabbling.

Grenfeld sat, pale, breathing to himself. Aloof. As if it did not concern
him at all, really. And yet, obviously — Ashley was sure of it — he had
tried very hard to show them that he could play the piece called "The
Minute Waltz" . . . in one minute? (Was it possible to play it in one
minute?) He wanted to impress them. He wanted to be one of them.

He *was* one of them.

Wasn't he?

And as if it did not concern him at all, really, Grenfeld began to play again. Not fast, this time: slowly. Softly. Just running his fingers over the keyboard idly, with unconcern.

Was this to be a place full of music?

II

And time began to crawl. An afternoon; night; morning; and then afternoon again (since Ashley's arrival): my God, it even sounded long!

In the morning, the B Flight commander, Flying Officer Luthie, had "borrowed" two officers from A Flight. Two men . . . ungracious.

Well, they had not been on Ready; that was how it happened that he might "borrow" them.

They had not even been on Available.

If not for the fact that the B Flight commander had *requested their assistance* and the squadron CO . . . what was his name? Yes, Hammett . . . had issued an order, they would have been on Released.

But one went upstairs with Grenfeld; the other took Farrell.

Officers. "La-di-da blokes."

"So bloody . . . polite, aren't they?" What was the word? *Disdainful* politeness.

Two men bursting with uppity correctness. Their names were Pilot Officer Newby and Pilot Officer Something-or-Other: Kenley. Well, up yours!

Now Flying Officer Luthie was a mere flying officer: *not* a flight lieutenant. An *acting* flight lieutenant only, obviously.

Didn't the men of B Flight rate a *real* flight lieutenant?

And McGregor — well, several voices, actually — grumbled about it.

Flying Officer Luthie had conferred with the two snobby blokes from Flight A there in the grass, some little distance away from the men of Flight B. At least the two appeared to treat him with some respect! — and with a show of patient suffering.

"But they're *seething!*" Farrell reported; and he seemed to enjoy the word. "They're ready to *kill* him!" he reported. And he lingered lovingly over the word.

Farrell. Did he, too, consider himself something of an observer?

Well, it was interesting to observe how officers were with one another in public. They did not squabble.

But how would life be for the men of B Flight? No one spoke of it, Ashley observed.

Now it was afternoon.

"When he keeps his hands in cold water, those scars turn white."

"Say again?" Flying Officer Luthie had scars on his wrists!

"One of the kiwis said so." The ground crews: the erks. The *kiwis:* the flightless ones. . . . Interesting.

"Well, how white?" The scars. "Are they white-white? . . . How would a bloody kiwi know?"

"Haven't the foggiest."

Grenfeld was not present. Grenfeld had been sent off on an oxygen climb: 30,000 feet, up up up, in ever-widening circles.

(Upstairs *twice* in one day? Odd. Odd. Odd. Peculiar. But Grenfeld had not complained.)

Stanhope was not present. Flying Officer Luthie had spent most of the morning with Stanhope. Now — five minutes ago? ten? — Stanhope had once again reported to the Flight B office. (And the men of Flight B waited.)

The office door opened; Stanhope emerged.

Then Flying Officer Luthie appeared, and he reached back *with his foot;* hooked the door *with his foot!* Pulled it closer *WITH HIS FOOT!* And only then did his hand grab the doorknob. He tested the lock. (The men of B Flight exchanged glances, uncertain. A trifle undignified, that whole exercise?)

Well, here was Stanhope, on his way, his parachute slung over his shoulder.

Flying Officer Luthie carried no parachute.

Stanhope had his flying boots on. Flying Officer Luthie hadn't: he wore shoes. Comfortable. He *looked* comfortable. Stanhope didn't.

Stanhope had his helmet on.

Flying Officer Luthie's skiff was at a rakish angle. A nice scarf about his neck. Very nice. It would be silk, of course. And Flying Officer Luthie stopped and began to unwind his scarf, all six feet of it; then, carefully, he rearranged it about his neck again — all six feet of it. In the meantime, Stanhope waited.

Flying Officer Luthie looked so *bloody comfortable!* His legs slightly apart. His legs were double-jointed (Ashley noticed).

And out of one of his many pockets, Flying Officer Luthie produced a pair of sunglasses, with round — *owlish* — extremely large lenses. The sunglasses made him look . . . mysterious? Well, when he put the silly things on, no one could tell what he was thinking (probably). That was why he wore them (probably).

(The men of Flight B exchanged looks: resentful?)

"He'll prang the kite." Stanhope would. For certain.

Whose voice? . . . Anxious. Or was the voice . . . excited?

"Ashley! Will you let me borrow your motorbike tomorrow?"

"It's out of juice." That was the first thing that came into Ashley's mind. It was a lie, of course. God, what a coward he was! Couldn't he simply make an announcement that his motorcycle was off-limits to all ranks and that was final?

"Those scars. Why do they turn white? Anything to do with blood circulation?"
"Ask me another."

And the men of Flight B tagged along behind Stanhope and Flying Officer Luthie, at a respectful — respectable — distance.
Then Stanhope sat inside the Spit; Flying Officer Luthie knelt on the wing. Talking talking talking. And time crawled. A long, long time passed.
"Well, this is boring."
"This is *suspenseful*. . . . He'll prang 'er."
"Shut up." Cartwright's voice: full of . . . terror, now?
And Ashley, too, suddenly hugged himself as if the wind had bitten into him.

"White scars. *White*. Ughhh!"
"Shut up."

"Brown's socks stink. . . . Brown, do you plan to wear clean socks tomorrow?"
There was a wail of rage and outrage from Brown.

And then, suddenly, Stanhope was off.
The Spit trundled through the filthy grass — grass trampled: *murdered,* really — by so many rolling wheels of so many aeroplanes.
(But the little group of men of Flight B sat in nice, high grass.)
Surely the kite must now be up to takeoff speed!
"Well, come on . . . Come on. Stanhope. Get your arse off the ground."
And Stanhope was off.

"Not, bad. Not bad. . . . A beginner's luck."

And Flying Officer Luthie settled himself in the grass, too — a hundred or so yards away from Flight B.
He looked so . . . so . . . oh, so *comfortable!* His sinister sunglasses on.
His legs stretched out in front of him, the toes of his comfortable shoes pointing up at the sky, comfortably.
But Sergeant — what was his name, now? — the one whose voice sounded as if he were . . . well, making a speech at a funeral: the be-whiskered man — he of the shoes that shone like *a hundred mirrors put*

together! — Sergeant Bennett was standing up. And he towered over Flying Officer Luthie, of course. His shoes hidden from view of the men of Flight B at the moment, of course. But, all of a sudden, it came to Ashley that those polished shoes might be made to look damned disapproving! Oh yes, nasty. Bad. Nasty, indeed.

And Flying Officer Luthie raised his head and said something to Sergeant Bennett. Flying Officer Luthie must have told him to sit down. He must have said it rather sharply: Sergeant Bennett seemed rather displeased. Well, Sergeant Bennett somehow was not the kind of person who ever was *meant* to be sitting down. But, suddenly, he was sitting down.

And the men of Flight B exchanged glances: heartened? Well, this was how one dealt with the Sergeant Bennetts of this world!

"White scars. . . . Does anyone know how he got them?"

"Tried to kill himself, probably. Because of a woman, probably."

It sounded quite romantic.

Then Stanhope was landing.

"He'll prang 'er." And it was like a prayer, now, to ensure the opposite? All eyes on Stanhope.

"Je-e-e-sus!"

"Well, back on the stick, you idiot! Back . . . He'll prang 'er."

But Ashley was watching Flying Officer Luthie.

Now Sergeant Bennett: he was halfway out of the grass already. Ready to jump up. Ready to run.

Luthie? . . . He *lay back.*

Well, he really had overdone it, this time! He was stretched out *on his back,* in the grass: comfortably. (And, for some reason, he had taken off his sunglasses. He was staring the world in the face with bare, naked, unprotected eyes.) Only the tips of his comfy shoes, pointing up at the sky: only the toes of the shoes suddenly looked . . . *tense.* My God, he really was overdoing it! (But no one else was looking at him.)

And Stanhope barely cleared the fence.

But yes, he had raised the kite's nose . . . too much? Just enough. Then did he push the stick forward . . . too much? Or just enough? (The Spitfire's airscrew is very long.) The kite touched down.

A nasty swing to the tail . . .

But Stanhope had done it. And Stanhope was off again.

Well, had Luthie given him the standard four bumps, four circuits?

Stanhope hadn't pranged.

Stanhope would not prang. *(He would not. Would not.)*

"When we go south . . . in a scrap . . . remind me to stay clear of the bugger." Stay clear of Stanhope. (Cartwright's voice? Calm. Very calm now.)

And Cartwright picked himself up: it was his turn to report to Flying

Officer Luthie. At fifteen hundred hours. Well, he had more than enough time to collect his brolly from the Parachutes Section.

And by and by, Grenfeld was back, from his oxygen climb. Looking tired. From now on, life would settle into a routine (probably).

That evening, Flying Officer Luthie and Flight Lieutenant Acklington were seen swinging on the gate.

(The gate no longer served any purpose, really.) A weathered notice, put up by the owner of the pasture a long time ago, proclaimed to all who might pass along the path: NOTIS: PLEASE SHUT GATE THANK YOU. (But the gate — the notice — no longer served a purpose.) The gate was between two low stone walls.

Luthie and Acklington took a running start. Jumped on the lowest wooden slat. There they went, as if on one of those playground merry-go-rounds! Then, *slam* the gate went against the stone wall. A bone-shaking, teeth-rattling bang. Luthie and Acklington's bones shook and teeth rattled — from five miles off one could have seen that! (Well, perhaps not *five* miles . . .) Luthie and Acklington laughed like two bloody madmen.

And they took a running start . . . Laughing laughing laughing.

The men of Flight B exchanged looks.

"When he sits in his kite, his knees are by his ears. . . . Looks bloody ridiculous, if you ask me." It was McGregor said this.

"His legs must cramp."

"His . . . his maps fall between his legs."

Flying Officer — *not* Flight Lieutenant! — Luthie did not look very much like a fighter pilot, really.

The men of Flight B exchanged glances: uncertain? Actually, it rather seemed to Ashley that the men of B Flight were uncertain about many things.

But later that evening, Flying Officer Luthie gathered them together, made a little speech. Said ordinary things, such as, "If there is anything — a problem, a question — come to me. Anytime. Any question. I am available." And so on and so on. That sort of thing. Ordinary things.

Life would settle into a routine.

"Well, how many times did He *kill* you?"

It was McGregor had asked that. And Ashley had put his hands in his pockets: so long, long ago now — yesterday evening.

And he had kept them in his pockets. And, inside his pockets, his hands had balled themselves up into fists.

A good, deep breath, now: he had heard somewhere that one should always take a good big whiff of oxygen just as the command "Going in" or "Going down" came. It made one feel better.

And he could see them waiting. Waiting . . . like vultures.

"Twice," he said. "Twice." It sounded plausible.

But ever since then, they'd been giving him odd little sidelong glances.

Was *twice* too many or too few?

Now Grenfeld. Grenfeld, for example: how many times had He *killed* Grenfeld?

(And it seemed to Ashley that, in order to blend in — to become part of this group — he should like all these people.

But he wasn't at all certain whether he liked them or not. He knew that he viewed the world rather differently from the others; and a thought nagged at him that perhaps this should be a source of pride to him.

But instead — for the moment, at least — it only filled him with anxiety.)

7

What do I want for my miserable wretches the Nine Days' Wonders?

8

How Ashley had met Flying Officer Luthie that very, very first day — the afternoon after his arrival (and time was passing; he could not forget).

The wireless had been on inside the Flight B office, the volume on maximum loud. One of those Bachs or Beethovens or whatnot — the BBC Third Programme (Ashley had recognized it at once).

Well, was this to be a place full of music? . . . And was this Flying Officer Luthie's very own, personal set, brought from home, perhaps? (The notice gone from the office door. BACK SOON. I HOPE. . . . What kind of a flight commander was this: I HOPE?! . . . The window half open.)

Beginnings always were exciting! But they also were like watching a picture in the cinema, for example, and not being able to guess the next twist in the plot.

Or they were like huddling in bed at school after the lights had been turned out: a small electric torch and a book under the blanket: hurry hurry, how will this turn out? But in the rather airless space under the blanket — in the dark darkness of the night under the blanket — one didn't really feel suspense: that was what uncertainty was like.

Well, at least he had something to write home about!
("Dear Mummy:" . . . *NO!!!*
"Dear Mum:" . . . No.
"Dear Mater:" . . . N-no.)

An hour or so earlier — at lunch: he'd sat chewing and working very hard at answering a thousand the-new-boy-at-school kind of questions — it had occurred to him, suddenly, that perhaps he should drop a line to his mother, tell her he had arrived safely.

"Dear Mother: The flight commander is terribly keen on the kind of music one gets dressed up for." (And something told Ashley that, although his mother never got dressed up to listen to any kind of music, she might be reassured by this information and wouldn't worry quite so much.)

The wireless had been on, then.

The windows: too high — much too high (Ashley'd *observed*) — to stand up on tiptoes and peek inside.

But under the window — by the door, actually, a few feet away — there was . . . yes, a deck chair: such as one might find on an excursion boat, for example; on it: stacked neatly, blank . . . combat report forms, several medium-sized stones weighing them down. The word "Secret" was printed in the upper left-hand corner of each form. But wait . . . wait . . . *somebody* had drawn a pair of elephant's ears — floppy, in pencil — over the *t* in "Secret" on the topmost form! Well, well, well.

("Dear — :"

Dear Chap Named Grant!

"The flight commander is eccentric in quite interesting ways. He draws elephants' ears on combat reports."

The chap named Grant: he who had taken the picture of Ashley on his motorcycle. The very same one who used to speculate with Ashley about what life would be like at a real station, as opposed to a training station . . . The chap named Grant had been posted to Army Cooperation, not a fighter squadron. A true *eccentric* Fighter Command–type flight commander . . . the chap named Grant would die with envy!)

But: was there a . . . a rightness to it? Was it . . . grown up, really, to draw elephants' ears on combat reports? And what if it had not been Flying Officer Luthie, after all, who had drawn the elephants' ears?

And so, carefully, Ashley lifted the sheaf of papers off the chair; carefully he placed them in the grass. He positioned the chair directly under the window. Scrambled up on the chair. Glanced about.

Danger excitement. (What if somebody came along and caught him?)

Danger excitement. (He rather liked *danger excitement,* on the whole.)

(And a lorry rumbled along the unpaved road in the middle distance, and then one of those very elderly Hillmans, painted an RAF blue, and then . . . nothing: this was a place boring boring boring. And a group of people sprawled in the grass in the middle distance, but they appeared to be absorbed in something terribly important.)

Inside the Flight B office: Flying Officer Luthie, Ashley's very first flight commander (now this was a beginning — a new life: wasn't it? wasn't it? And it was Ashley's first flight commander, none other — right? right! — because, after all, this was the Flight B office) — Ashley's flight commander, facing the wireless set, his back to Ashley — Flying Officer Luthie was conducting the orchestra.

> Tum taa   de da   dum taa
> De da   dum taa

My God! Weighty music.

Weighty. (Was that the right word?) Heavy, too, in a way: like enormous hammers pounding. And now that he truly began to listen to it, Ashley knew at once he didn't quite like it.

Didn't like it?! To tell the truth, he was afraid of it! A bit.

What a piece! What a piece! Pounding pounding pounding. But underneath the pounding of the hammers, there seemed to be a current of some sort, like a dark river muttering angrily at night. Was Flying Officer Luthie afraid of it, too? No way to tell! (And Ashley shifted his weight from one foot to the other: the chair creaked. He swallowed hard. But nothing happened.)

Well, Flying Officer Luthie certainly was throwing himself into the business of conducting! Arms — hands — down: pushing pushing on something — or someone. Arms rising, slowly, in exultation? *Exaltation?* He cued in an instrument: a trumpet of some sort. A horn. Something that one blew into, anyway. And then, as the music swelled — as it broke clear: free, all abruptly (the man who had written the piece must suddenly have decided to celebrate a glorious victory of some sort; but, really, it made Ashley's ears hurt) — as all those instruments continued celebrating and rejoicing (but rather solemnly, it seemed: without the true wildness of joy), the man stood there, waving his arms about, majestically. Well, my God!

Well, altogether silly-looking: Flying Officer Luthie. Yes, he was.

("Dear — :" . . . "Dear — :" . . . *"Dear John:"*

Ashley's brother John. John: dead now . . . for almost a year . . . !

Well, why should he suddenly think of John?

Actually, Ashley thought of John rather often.

"Dear John . . . You know all about flight commanders, now don't you? I want to ask you . . . I need your advice . . .")

(And then it came to Ashley, all of a sudden: well, it was *obscene,* that's what! It was . . . it was *disrespectful* of John's memory: of the memory of all those who were dead, that's what! — to draw elephants' ears on combat reports! Wicked wicked *irresponsible.* So, there! No matter Flying Officer Luthie had had no idea John had ever existed.

If it had been he who had drawn the elephants' ears. So, there!)

•

A door slammed somewhere. Hard.

Flying Officer Luthie jumped as if he had been shot.

And Ashley jumped, too; almost fell off the chair: almost. (Actually, one would hardly have noticed that door slamming, really, over the trumpeting and the pounding of the music; but it shook the flimsy little building, and the shock wave traveled and traveled, like an earthquake . . .)

Then, silence. What to do now? A perfectly dead silence, inside: Flying Officer Luthie had switched off the wireless.

Silence. Had it merely been the confounded wind had slammed the door?

And Ashley glanced about. Careful . . . Look *normal,* now. Look as if you're *not* looking . . . *Danger excitement* . . . Whew! What a close call!

(But there they still were, that same cluster of people, some distance away; and if they had *observed* him, they didn't seem to care.)

(And then . . . a Spit landing! . . . Well, the very first one Ashley had seen — heard — since his arrival! And his eyes followed it — her. *Her* . . . She skimmed the fence . . . His heart — not the music — pounding, pounding now.)

("Dear — :" . . .

But there was nobody else left to tell about it. He had taken care of all of them.

Well, of course, he never wrote letters to his father, for example — never. Not once: since joining up, he hadn't written to him one single time.

And he felt free. Free!)

Beginnings always were exciting.

However, if the truth be known, the art of observation mainly was the art of knowing when to run.

Well, was it time to run, now? . . . Well, past the time, really.

But, quite against his better judgment, Ashley stood up on tiptoes on the chair again. Idiot!

Well, was he perhaps trying to delay his having to report to Flying Officer Luthie, to postpone the new beginning? No no no. Unlikely. Most unlikely. . . . Well, what was the point, then, in working oneself up into a state about it?

And when he peered into the half-gloom of the Flight B office yet once again, he saw the shoulders of a disappointed man (slumped shoulders: perhaps the piece had been almost over?); then, with some reluctance — with a good deal of reluctance (it seemed to Ashley) — Flying Officer Luthie turned away from the wireless and neatly folded himself like . . . like some skinny-legged but not too badly coordinated insect into a chair. (Was the room tiny, or was the man very tall? . . . God, what long legs!)

Feet up on the desk; feet off the desk.

Rummage rummage through some — tidily stacked — papers; and then: a pencil in his hand; feet up, again: he lit a cigarette; juggled cigarette, pencil, and the papers (no, not combat reports — surely not!); and he began to read . . . and underline . . . make notations in the margins . . . He no longer looked silly, as he had when conducting the orchestra: he looked diligent, and Ashley liked that.

But by and by, the shoulders sagged; the head fell back . . . back . . . a sharp Adam's apple outlined against the dirty-white wall. And the arms hung down over the chair's armrests, the hands almost touching the floor . . . He'll set the place on fire!

(But the cigarette ashes fell; and finally, the cigarette went out.)

The hands . . . my God, lifeless! The man looked *dead*.

My God, was he dead? (The papers on his stomach; the pencil had rolled away.)

And Ashley knew frustration: there was a picture here — of his sleeping flight commander. But no camera. Damn! Well, he couldn't shoot into the room, anyway. Not the right light: too dark . . . God damn it all!

Thus Sleep the Brave: that was what he would name the picture. (Well, had he read or heard these words somewhere, or were they all his own? It did not matter.)

(And second prize, this time; and ten . . . ten! . . . pounds?)

(Was Flying Officer Luthie brave? . . . It did not matter.

It would be a good picture. . . . And supply your own story!)

But something stirred within him, quite unbidden — all unexpected and rather new, really (and it stayed with him for but a fleeting moment, not much longer): pity for the bone-weary man?

My God, why was he bone-weary?

Was *observing* people perhaps not . . . quite the thing (sometimes)?

Well, was it bad form, really? No rightness to it. . . . Un-grown-up?

But truly, pity was the last thing one wanted to feel for a man who one day — very, very soon (Ashley assumed) — would lead one into combat! (And he was very frightened then.)

Then, suddenly, from within the room the voice came: "Whoever you are standing on the chair under the window, come in."

My God! (Well, things like this were always happening to Ashley.)

Now he couldn't run! (And his heart was pounding in fear.)

Danger excitement — hah! (Who needs *danger excitement?* To be part of the crowd; not to get himself into scrapes: that was what he was after.)

And so, slowly, his head low, his feet clumsy — they always went all clumsy when something like this happened — he climbed down from the chair and made his way to the door of the Flight B office. He composed himself: not a good job at all — he was aware of it. He knocked.

"Yes. . . . Yes."

He entered. He drew himself up. Smartly. His cap in his hand. "Sir." Very smartly. His eyes at infinity. Good. Good. Extremely good. Wizard. Stunning. Smashing.

Silence. It stretched on.

Well, God damn it all, one couldn't keep one's eyes at infinity forever! (Outside, the wind suddenly rattled the pane of the open window.)

And Ashley's eyes strayed, cautiously.

Flying Officer Luthie's feet were no longer on the desk: he had hauled himself up into a sitting position, as a proper flight commander should.

A homely face. Not ugly, really, not at all: merely homely.

Eyes: light brown? Hazel. Was that the word? Hazel.

And they were a fighter pilot's eyes: quick quick quick bright — Ashley was very very sure they never ever missed anything, those eyes studying his face (and yet they had missed his peering in through the window for such a long time, by God!) They were quick eyes, then: lively, animated. But at the same time — a contrast: almost a contradiction, wasn't it? — those eyes studying Ashley with such unabashed, and puzzled, interest were quiet, reasonable. Reasonable!

And at that — at least for that moment — the butterflies in Ashley's stomach gratefully folded their wings.

(And so Ashley knew things that the other men of Flight B didn't. And he viewed the world a bit differently.

But that had happened . . . well, two days ago.)

9

I

I've bought a scrawny thing, a potted plant.

1) Water the plant. (Things to Do Tomorrow.)

The wretch Stanhope is still among the living. He acquitted himself creditably! (And the day is done. Celebrate!)

Two children came selling the plants, past teatime — two small Scottish heads: red; two small Scottish voices. (Were not permitted past the gate, of course; but they stood there, stalwart: waited, stalwart, for people to gather.
 . . .

"Well, have you grown the plants yourselves?"

Nods of the heads: half proud, half bashful.

"A grand little wagon, that!"

They pulled a little toy wagon, most unbashfully painted a bright bright bright green. The plants in the wagon, in little earthenware pots.)

And so, see the squadron leader, himself, in person, buy a potted plant. (But he would, of course.) Well, surprises beyond belief: Sergeant Bennett bought one! And Corporal Rossiter — he is one of the armorers — he bought *four*.

My Wonders. My poor poor poor Wonders.

Bloody hell! *Wonders* . . . I eat, drink, sleep nothing but the Wonders.

Tomorrow afternoon: formation attacks for the very first time with selected Wonders. The Enemy: Geoff Thomas and Roy Newby, led by Hanmer.

(And so: I'd like to wave a magic wand . . . Clap my hands.

> *Abracadabra. Presto change-o. Open Shazaam*
> *Voilà!* No more Wonders.)

Hanmer most definitely has got his predatory shark's teeth at the ready. "Luthie . . . You misery . . . You poor benighted soul old bean . . . When we're through with you tomorrow, you're dead meat."

No doubt.

But Hanmer and I must plan the show as we wolf down our bacon and eggs so very early in the morning, all at the break of day and all that, tomorrow: Hanmer goes on duty at six o'clock. In the morning. Six hundred hours. I am taking Ashley upstairs at seven. This will be his — Ashley's — second time with me, will it not?

(About the eggs: they're powdered here. . . . The time of Dunkirk: they fed us real eggs, not powdered. Yellow and fluffy as a gosling's down.)

Ashley: the Nosy Parker . . . *adolescent*. Squirrel teeth.

Stanhope. With a name like that he should look like an equestrian statue of a general: Stanhope. He doesn't, of course. Stanhope is freckle-nosed, crunches on peppermints, and whines. The peppermints are the red, white, and green kind: they look like Christmas. Smell like Christmas. Stanhope carries Christmas with him wherever he goes.

And at one point, I almost invited myself to sample one of those peppermints. "I say, Sergeant. . . . I'm a colonial, you see. Born and brought up in the East. And when I was five or six years old, my grandmother — in England — used to send me toffees in tins with pictures of the Houses of Parliament on them and such . . . And peppermints that looked very similar."

But then I didn't say it. Should I have?

How would he have taken it? I wonder.

(Ashley: that Nosy Parker adolescent.)

•

I have spoken to Hanmer already, very briefly, about tomorrow.

Hanmer: "You propose to do *what?* The *Schwarm?* The Finger Four formation? *Jerry tactics?* . . . My lips are sealed. Cemented. Plastered over. . . . If Old Hurry-up got wind of this, you know, he'd have you shot, you know. . . . For treason. . . . On the spot. . . . At sunrise. . . . He'd personally head the firing squad. 'Uh-huh . . . Fire!'"

"Oh, shut up, Hanmer."

"He'd have you drawn and quartered —"

"I said shut up!" (Well, I used rather stronger language, actually.)

(Ah! Would our good old squadron leader . . . uh-huh . . . disapprove? Well, would he?)

But I am feeling almost reckless. The wretch Stanhope is still among the living: will anything I do from now on turn out all right in the end? Will it?

Besides, the Finger Four formation is definitely superior to our Vic and a line astern. In my opinion. And easier to maintain: well, that is why the Fritzes do it. It is safer for the Wonders. I think.

Enough! Enough, already! (Enough of the thrice-confounded Wonders.)

About the *stalwart* plant-sellers.

My poor poor poor Wonders. They are too young, I suppose, to know how to act unembarrassed when buying little green plants from children. And so they didn't buy any — not one man of them.

But the children departed satisfied.

. . .

"How much is the one with the spotted leaves, then?"

"A threepenny bit, sir." The *r*'s rolling.

. . .

They went away happy. The girl cast a look of victory at her . . . brother? *I told you they'd buy!* The shrewd businesswoman.

1) Water the plant.

Things to Do Right Now: (Ha!)
   1) Put feet up on desk.
   2) Shut eyes. Doze off.

No. No.

To work, Luthie, to work. (The Air Ministry visits paperwork upon us.)

But I rather feel, at the moment, as if I've just finished a glass of warm milk. As if I have soaked for a good, long time in water . . . well, not scalding hot, exactly, but not merely *tepid*. (I haven't, of course.)

N. M. Tunnard-Jones.

Not beautiful: lovely.

Copper-colored hair: N. M. Tunnard-Jones. Hair cascading down down to her shoulders: it must be like watching a waterfall through a setting sun!

(I have never seen her with her hair free of her *chignon*. That, I believe, is the charitable way of putting it: *chignon*. Well, Hanmer is right, for a change: it does look a bit like a tumor at the nape of her neck. And the uniform cap intersects it. Uniforms were not made for women. Or perhaps somebody ought to redesign them.

But: lovely copper-colored hair. N. M. Tunnard-Jones.)

Beautiful eyebrows: N. M. Tunnard-Jones.

Gray eyes. Sad? Or simply the eyes of *a woman of an unusual mind?*

Sweet, lovely breasts.

Natural fingernails: N. M. Tunnard-Jones.

Hands innocent of all adornment: no engagement ring, for example. No wedding band — oh, absolutely not!

My Dear People:
  The weather has been fine,
  I've bought a potted plant, a scrawny thing

Replenish paper in my notebook . . .
  Tear the band that binds the new pages together . . .

My Dear People:
  As you can see, this is wartime paper. Looks as if trying (unsuccessfully) to recover from jaundice: has made it all the way to yellow-gray.
  The paper does make the ink fuzzy, rather. Sorry about the splotches. Can you read this?
  Life

TOM IS DEAD.

Janet has lost the baby.

Tom. Our gardener. Janet's husband. Tom — in the navy — who counted blankets in Stores. The depot where he did his blanket-counting was bombed. Janet has suffered a miscarriage. She is quite ill.

(My mother has telephoned.)
  . . .

(I remember:

I left home — how many days ago? I went off, to rejoin the squadron: I gave Ms. Simmonds a big hug; and she snuffled.

From Mr. Parrish: an old man's manly handshake.

Janet: thick-waisted.

"Well, take care of the little one," I said. And, on an impulse, I grabbed her by the shoulders; on an impulse, I kissed her on the cheek.

Janet: no bulge yet. But heavy-waisted. And so we brushed against one another — oh, purely by accident, I swear! . . . Definitely unpremeditated on my part, my word of honor!: her belly against mine. But it excited me.

And then I felt . . . not guilty, exactly; nor embarrassed; but . . .)

Tom is dead.
Dear Janet:

My Dear Janet:
Please do get well

Yes. Quite.

Janet Dear:
I think of Tom. My heart goes to you. Well, I remember Tom.

Went to see Hanmer.
Hanmer not there.

Dear Janet:
Oh, I remember Christmases!

My mother *telephoned* to impart to me the news about Tom's death and Janet's misfortune.

And thereby hangs a tale!

II

Why I went to war:?
No.
Why I *volunteered* to go to war:?
Christ God. *Not now!* . . . This is not the time.

What do I want for my wretched Wonders?

III

And so:
On ran Dingo, Yellow Dog Dingo . . . Always hungry. Hungry in the sunshine.
Grinning like a coal's cuttle.

Never mind. A ghost story.
Never mind.

10

How Ashley had met Flying Officer Luthie that very, very first time (and it was difficult simply to let time pass: he kept turning it over and over in his mind).

There he had stood, inside the Flight B office. (The reasonable — well, trustworthy, really! — eyes upon him: two days ago.)

And then Flying Officer Luthie had said, "Hullo, Victoria."

Vic- . . . Victoria . . . ???!

But Flying Officer Luthie was staring somewhere beyond Ashley — beyond Ashley's feet, to be exact.

Well, was one permitted to turn around, to turn one's back on one's flight commander?

Well, God damn it all! Well, the man — after all — seemed to be introducing? Ashley to . . . to Victoria.

Ashley turned around. And there, in the door (which he had failed to shut behind him): on the threshold, half in and half out of the room, there sat — crouched — a cat. My God, what a massive cat! — especially if this was a female cat: Victoria. . . . A cat . . . well, not distrustful, really. Was she a cat . . . dissatisfied? Was Ashley, the stranger, not to her liking? Well, cats here should be accustomed to people coming and going all the time! So, there. . . . And the cat was gray, all gray, save for a meticulously white bib under her chin and a little white spot on her forehead.

And Flying Officer Luthie grinned at Victoria. (*Not* at Ashley? . . . Actually, if the truth be known, Flying Officer Luthie seemed to be avoiding Ashley's eyes, now.) He grinned. (And Ashley thought: Oh. *Oh, Grandmother, what big teeth you have!* What a grin!)

Said Flying Officer Luthie: "Here, Vicky . . . Puss puss."

Vicky.

And at once it was obvious that the cat Victoria took a dim view of it. No no, she would not tolerate it: being called Vicky — not even from an officer, by God! And slowly, she unfurled herself from her crouch. Then, very slowly, she departed . . . *I've nothing but contempt for those who might want to make me depart quickly!* (that was what she seemed to be saying). Only once — twice? — did she glance back, a furtive glance.

And Flying Officer Luthie laughed: an easy laugh. Then he frowned, to himself. But then, or so it seemed to Ashley, he squared his shoulders: resolutely, as if steeling himself for a task; and Flying Officer Luthie grinned: at Ashley.

Oh, Ashley liked Flying Officer Luthie!

Not in all his years at school, most certainly not in all the months since he had stumbled his way into joining the air force after Jon's death: really, not in his whole life had he ever met anyone *in authority* who was so willing to overlook — to accept? — the fact that Ashley was by nature a watcher, an Observer; was so ready to come to terms with the fact that, every now and then, Ashley was likely to get himself into scrapes! (But if the man was simply ignoring it all, then Ashley had not got himself into a scrape, now had he?)

Oh, Ashley was of light heart and good cheer!

How he had come to join the Royal Air Force:

There had never been a proper funeral for John, since there was no body to bury. (Had John been buried in Germany? . . . Well, did *anyone* know, really? They had simply received the telegram: "Killed in operations" — and so on and so on; and then the letter confirming the telegram.)

But the memorial service: that had been nice, very nice. Dignified. (And even before the service had begun, Mrs. Bixby, their next-door neighbor, had put her arms around Ashley's mother, murmuring, "Such lovely flowers, dear," and then, later, was overheard exclaiming to Mrs. Manvers, "So very lovely!"; and she should know because her roses always won prizes.)

But then the service was over, and they all were home again: Father, Mother, and their one remaining son: Ashley himself; and Bridget, the kitchen girl, too, of course — but Bridget headed for the kitchen straight away. And the rest of them stood in the hall and were rather at a loss what to do next.

Ashley remembered: late-afternoon sunlight pouring in, past and around the two powerfully antlered stags etched into the glass panels of the door (the light making the stags seem even larger and more powerful than they would otherwise have been); and his mother stared and stared at her face in the gilt-framed mirror on the wall — but she didn't seem to see anything. But then at last she made as if to begin to take off her hat with its enormous mourning veil; and she said: "I hope Bridget has put the kettle on"; and then she said to George Bevil Ashley, her son: "Georgie . . . Go and pack your things, darling. I'll call you for tea. . . . Daddy says it's best to catch the six-twenty tomorrow . . . you'll have to get up early . . . well, you've missed nearly a week of school, darling. And the fees so dear . . ." And she sounded almost like herself: almost. Even to the point of calling him *darling:* one of the crosses that Ashley had to bear.

But it was then that Ashley took a big gulp of air *(always take a good whiff of oxygen when the command "Going in" or "Going down" comes);* and it was then he announced that no, he would not be returning to school tomorrow — that . . . well, actually, he had gone yesterday morning and had signed his name on a piece of paper that said . . . well, it said, in a manner of speaking, that he would follow in his brother's footsteps . . .

Now Ashley's mother still hadn't taken off her hat. She still had the hat on, the long veil and all.

Ashley's mother was short and . . . the word was *plump*. Not fat, really. Well, she waddled a bit when she walked.

But now . . . uh-oh, there she came: she flew — flew! — across the hall, a tight little ball of black, and the silly veil streaming behind her . . . *A black comet. Bearing no-good tidings.* And she slapped — slapped! — her one remaining son across the face. A resounding slap. . . . Well, perhaps she hadn't meant it to hurt quite so much, really. Perhaps she hadn't. But her little plump hand had caught him right on the nose. And Ashley's nose began to bleed. And he snuffled.

But Ashley's father . . . There was a blue-upholstered chair in the hall: faded, worn-looking pink flowers on the dark blue. Every evening: Ashley's father came home; with a deep grunt of relief — of satisfaction — he lowered himself into the chair . . . untied his shoes . . . put on his carpet slippers.

Now, slowly, he *sank* down into the chair. Without a word. Without a word! Defeated. (Now neither of his sons would be there to be commanded to learn *in order to continue what he* — Ashley's father — *had built with his sweat!*)

But, somehow, this wasn't quite the way Ashley had imagined his father's defeat. (But that had happened a long time ago.)

Well, God damn it all! Not much one could do about it anymore . . . Well, was there?

(It had happened a long time ago.)

Now. The present.
Flight B. Flying Officer Luthie.

The cat Victoria . . . (Actually, that very same afternoon, after his meeting with Flying Officer Luthie, Ashley had managed to snap a picture of the cat Victoria.)

("Dear —" He paused. But then, in his mind, he continued writing: the picture developed, in his mind's eye — and it had turned out well and was ready to be sealed in an envelope. "Dear Everybody: The cat is named Victoria. She is all gray. In the other pictures: the chap with his cheeks bulging is Stanhope — he is chewing on a peppermint. The foot in the right-hand corner is the flight commander's . . .")

Flying Officer Luthie.

His teeth were *huge.*

And there he had been, two days ago . . . well, he'd seemed to be trying to put Ashley at his ease . . . Ah! Wizard.

Stunning. Smashing. A new life: beginnings were exciting!

A man of eyes that were calm and steady — a man who made one feel calm, steady, and safe: this was a man who . . . who knew himself.

And so, in his good cheer and in joyful gratitude, Ashley had blurted out: "Sir . . . That was Beethoven you were playing on the wireless, sir, wasn't it?"

(Never speak unless first spoken to. But Flying Officer Luthie had already spoken to him — so that was all right, wasn't it?)

(Ah, it would be easy not to get himself into scrapes with Flying Officer Luthie!)

"Beethoven on the wireless —" . . . But as soon as the words were out, he could have bitten off his tongue.

The reasonable eyes: the trustworthy eyes . . . they widened. Darkened? (That was what they said in books: *His eyes darkened.*) Well, in a fraction of a second it must have come to Flying Officer Luthie that he had been observed for quite some time. His conducting the orchestra and all . . .

My God, what to do now?

(It would be easy not to get into scrapes???!)

Flying Officer Luthie's face (rather homely): it had been an open book, there for Ashley to read. The book snapped shut.

But then, not another muscle moved in that face: Flying Officer Luthie bore the pain of his embarrassment with . . . gallantry.

There was silence, of course. (My God, would it always be so: Ashley committing an act of idiocy; and then . . . silence?)

And once again the silence stretched on.

My God, the man was counting to ten! . . . to twenty? thirty? . . . to a hundred?! . . . How angry was he? Was he furious with Ashley? And would he take revenge: would he promptly visit some sort of a perfectly legal but nevertheless fiendish punishment on Ashley?

Then, at last, at long last, Flying Officer Luthie gave a little sigh: a sigh such as a long-suffering man might give; but he caught himself in the middle of it. Drew in his breath sharply.

A man of very good self-control.

(Well, did he for some reason — because he was flight commander? — did he think he could not *permit* himself a sigh?

Well, Ashley permitted himself a sigh. Of relief.)

And Flying Officer Luthie said: "Beethoven . . . Beethoven?" And he really looked as if he would much rather be thinking of something else. But dutifully he met Ashley's gaze. "Yes. Beethoven. . . . Quite."

And Ashley knew at once then that he was lying. (Well, it was there: in the face. No problem reading the face now: a piece of cake, really!)

This was a man of tremendous . . . kindness. Of . . . of superhuman kindness! (Or was he?)

And, all of a sudden — but why? Why? God damn it all, he himself could not quite grasp the reason — all at once, Ashley rejected the kindness. Oh no: no no no, he would not have it! From anybody! Nobody's kindness! He simply would not have it. From *anybody!*

Well, Flying Officer bloody Luthie: he must know that Ashley couldn't tell bloody Beethoven from Bridget the scullery girl's mixing pans! Well, did he think that Ashley wasn't *worth* being told the truth? What business had this man to pity Ashley? (But Ashley had pitied him, now hadn't he?: two — three — minutes ago. . . . No. No. Those two matters were entirely separate; very, very different.) What business had this man to be so . . . patronizing?

And Flying Officer Luthie's eyes still were on Ashley, but it was obvious he must have realized he'd made a mistake.

And, for the smallest of moments, he hesitated; then . . . he compounded his mistake: he put on a determined look . . . and reversed himself.

"No, it was Sibelius, actually. The Second Symphony, actually."

Well, *Sibbeh*-who? What?

On this man — one day soon — Ashley's *life* might depend?! (And Ashley's brother John had lost his life. He was dead dead dead. And Ashley was afraid of dying.) Well, *Flying Officer bloody Luthie*. First he said one thing, and then another! A man who couldn't make up his mind!

A man who did *not* make one feel safe.

And Ashley's throat felt dry, his knees weak and his heart was somewhere where one's tonsils usually are: pounding, panic-stricken.

Then, after a few moments, Flying Officer Luthie said, with some enthusiasm: "Well, it's a marvelous piece, isn't it? . . . Oh, absolutely!"

Absolutely.??? Oh yes.

(And, in that moment, Ashley rather wished that one would be permitted to sneer at one's flight commander.)

But of course Flying Officer Luthie wasn't being patronizing — that was pure nonsense: he was trying to be friendly, he really was; and, in a quiet voice, he said: "Well, it seems to be all about Fate, rather, that music, isn't it?" Of course he spoke — acted — as if Ashley were his equal. My God, the *reasonable* eyes: a book — well, God damn it all! — a book, but written in a language that Ashley could not understand? Well, Ashley had never ever met anyone like this in all his life; though, really, Flying Officer Luthie seemed to be now talking mainly to himself.

But, of course, Ashley had long since lost all faith in him.

PART TWO

11

I

I was born.

Nighttime thoughts.
    Forsake all others.

Wonders Wonders Wonders: daytime thoughts.
    Are they my punishment from On High: the Wonders? . . .

I was born at Lahore: September 1919.
    (That is how one should begin a proper memoir.
    Let us rectify some omissions. Now, at once. Now. There may not be
much time.)

I never lived there — at Lahore; but we traveled there frequently, my fa-
ther and I, in those years of my childhood before I was sent away to
Simla. We traveled by train. I had a stuffed bear whose name was
Brighton. (A good, stuffy name, I thought, for a stuffed bear.)
    I packed *my own personal luggage* whenever we traveled to Lahore.
One Brighton: end of packing. (Ayah did the rest.)
    In my memory, Lahore is a city made of redstone and shade trees.

The museum. At Lahore.
    ("Little son . . . What shall we do in the afternoon, when my ap-
pointments are done?" . . . The Shalimar Gardens? The Lawrence Gardens?
    "The museum," I said, resolutely.
    "Little son . . . Imagine. The father of the man who wrote the story
about the Parsee-man and the rhino was the very first curator here!")

The museum was a cool place, and thus well suited to exuberance; but it was a quiet place, and one was not permitted to run there.
. . .
Curator Cu-ra-tor. CURATOR!!!
CURATOR CURATOR CURATOR
("Little son, do be quiet.")
. . .
Cu-ra-tor!
Cu-ra-tor!
Cu-ra-tor! I tried to teach Brighton to say the word *curator*.
("Sahib . . . Your grandson seems a right merry young chap, I am thinking. Jolly good. If it is possible to say jolly word *curator* in a voice quiet and peaceable, it is a difficulty then not at all.")
I remember: the museum guard — is that what he was? — had a most magnificent red turban; the rest of him was a rustly starched white.
(My father, his voice meek: "Yes. Of course. I am sorry.")
(My father, his head high: "This is not my grandson; he is my son.")
My father, to me, his temper rising: "Wayne Robert!"
When my father called me "Wayne Robert," I knew it was time to be quiet.
. . .
Cu-ra-tor . . .
Cu-ra-tor . . .
Cu-ra-tor . . . (Very softly.)

Nighttime thoughts? . . . Peaceful?
. . .
(I remember that my father, too, spoke in a sort of half-voice for the rest of that afternoon. At the time I found it odd. Peculiar.)

My father is not an apple-grower by choice or inclination: he has had duty thrust upon him. He was the eldest son.
But after the death of his first wife (dark hair: his first wife — in photographs; very much like my mother's hair) — after her death (or so I understand) he had at one point decided to sign away his birthright in favor of my uncle Robert, the only one among the three brothers with a true farmer's love of the place. But then both my uncle Robert and my uncle George Henry were killed on the Somme, three years before I was born; and in his time — but I was sixteen by then — my grandfather died, too. My father has had duty thrust upon him.
He is a medical man by training, though — also trained as a surgeon, actually: that is how I know that he could slit the throats of all those furry rabbit-creatures at home (Brunnhilde: the very large rabbit — ears proud as the horns on Brunnhilde's helmet, but soft, unlike the horns on

Brunnhilde's helmet; rabbit stew: feed the family and all that): he could dispatch them with an unwavering precision if he so chose. But he does not choose. My father the pacifist (who had given me the knife: the time of Dunkirk).

After the death of his first wife he returned to India, where he had been born and done his growing up, the first eight years of it; and for a time he had a moderately successful practice at Lahore: gall bladders, appendectomies, that sort of thing — so very routine! But caught by the First War in England, he dutifully offered his services to King and Country and spent the next four years trying to put together what others had torn apart. For three of those four years he was in France. He, too, was on the Somme. (My father the pacifist.)

And when, after the war, he sailed for India yet once again — with his new wife, brand-new wife: my mother — it was as a pen-pusher he went, an administrator; and to my knowledge, he never touched a patient with a surgeon's hand: not ever again. Through all the years of my growing up he was head of a tiny mission hospital in our Godforsaken little town in the Punjab: St. Joseph's was the name of the hospital.

And we traveled to Lahore, my father and I, when I was a child, and he had appointments with Important People to make his reports on the hospital; and he visited Powerful People to beg for money. Back at home, he spent much of his time writing letters to Important and Powerful People, many of them in England. My father can write a mean begging letter.

(But when we traveled to Lahore. I waited for him: all morning, after breakfast. Sat at a table just my size.

. . .

"Brighton, I am drawing a picture of you. Your fur is very brown."

. . .

And I drew pictures of . . . apricot trees: apricot trees . . . apricot trees . . . as far as the eye could see — out of the train window, the previous day.

. . .

"Brighton, this is millet. . . . *Millet*."

I had seen that, too, from the train window: fields of millet.

. . .

"*Ir-ri-gation, Brighton. . . . Ir-ri-gation*."

. . .

And Mrs. McGinty, of McGinty's Family Hotel, dusted and did her ironing.

Well, that was where we always stayed: McGinty's Family Hotel.)

(Mrs. McGinty: one two three four chins. When she laughed, the chins quivered — and she laughed often; but she was thin: well, usually, it was the *stout* people who had many chins, it seemed to me.

And she dusted. All the time. I mean this. Because it was a very small hotel, and only two bearers to do the work.)

About the hospital: St. Joseph's. In our dusty little town.

The hospital, too, was made of redstone.

And cannas grew in front: big red RED *ENORMOUS!* Hibiscus in the back.

Inside, a most wonderful organized chaos reigned. And the whole place smelled of *doctor* and coriander.

(Nighttime thoughts.)
   (Forsake all others.)

This, of necessity, will have to be written in scratches and patches, in fits and starts.
   · · ·

One must understand the past in order to understand the present.

To understand . . . Accept. To forgive?

Not long ago, at home, I'd set out to record the story of my life, to make a record of my past.

But the present — and the future, by God! — keep interfering; keep intruding.

Herewith my resolve: I'll not turn my mind to other matters — I'll not write down *Wonders Wonders Wonders* again — till I've finished . . . what?

(There may not be much time.)

For my sixth birthday I was given a pony. Named her Apricot. (Well, shut your eyes; touch her flanks: it was like touching the furry coat of an apricot, or perhaps a peach. But she was apricot-colored, somewhat.) A patient and most gentle soul.

We went to the bazaar, Apricot and I.
   · · ·

Dark clouds gathering. The monsoon touches the Punjab but lightly; still, it comes.

Black clouds gathering.

(And already there is an interruption: our good Colin K. in the doorway. He is *soliciting contributions* to purchase good things to drink at Roy Newby's soon-to-come birthday party.
   · · ·

This place: oh dear God yes! — full of the gentleness of life. And life is good. And so on and so on.

God . . . if you exist . . . God, do not let me die in terror.
God, do not let me die in pain.
· · ·

I said to Colin, "Right. Right. Tell Miller" — the barman in the mess
— "to add my part to my bill. . . . *He does not give credit for parties?!*"
Bloody hell!
"My wallet is here somewhere. . . . Yes, on the nightstand. Take however much you need. How much did Hanmer give?"

It is Roy Newby's twenty-second birthday. He will be an old man.)

Black clouds gathering.
"And has your mother many fine sons like you?" (I was six years old.)
I took a deep breath.
(The vendor-woman of sweets: wrapped from head to foot in grubby
green.)
(I had dismounted, led Apricot by the reins: we'd pushed our way
through the crowd, and my white linen cap with the stiff green bill was
on my head, firmly: "Little son, never go outdoors without your cap!" —
and I never did; and quietly, I sweated.)
I took a deep breath. "Yes. Many sons. I've come to buy sugared al-
monds. Enough for my hands . . . both hands, I am thinking . . ." And I
cupped my hands, but did not let go of Apricot's reins.
"Many sons! A woman blessed, your mother! Your mother is a happy
woman, then. . . . *Capital* almonds!" (*Capital,* in English.)
"The sweetest sugar," said the vendor-woman. "Bite. You do not pay."
(And I bit; tasted; and it tasted good.)
"And many daughters? Beautiful daughters?"
"Yes. Many daughters."
The clouds were coming. (And, after the rain, the hibiscus at St.
Joseph's, for example: it would steam; and the roses in the garden at
home would steam; and the mud everywhere; and oh God, yes: people's
necks would steam!)
And Apricot nuzzled my ear, softly. She snorted. Her nostrils quiv-
ered. Because of the coming storm?
No no. Because of the almonds!
Apricot was exceedingly fond of sugared almonds.

(A peaceful childhood?)
· · ·
(Nighttime thoughts.)

The vendor-woman said then, "Your mother is a woman doubly blessed.
Sons *and* daughters. . . . Shall I fill that pretty box for you?"
Well, I'd brought a small tin for my almonds. At one time, the tin had

held toffees. Pictures, in color, on the tin. (And my grandfather and grandmother also sent me books: "On ran Dingo, Yellow Dog Dingo . . . *Always hungry . . . hungry in the sunshine . . .*"; and knee-high stockings knitted by my grandmother . . .

My Dearest Darling Grandson:
 . . . Our New Emmeline [this was Emmeline the Third] *the New Emmeline is about to bring the Very First Litter of Kittens into the world. And do you know where she wants her little Nest to be? Why, in the Library — the west wall, the third shelf up from the bottom, between Mill on the Floss and the Milton! Your grandfather is at a loss — completely! — what to do.*

And the vendor-woman of sugared almonds brought the tin very close to her eyes; examined it. "Ah, the wonders of the world!"
 But then she let a delicate silence fall. "I am trusting there is rich dowry in the house."
 "Yes. Dowry for everyone." And I pushed my cap off my forehead, impatiently, resolutely. "O Mother of Many Sons . . ." My best manners! "I am trusting that your children are a joy to you in your old age."
 "They are a mother's joy. . . . And I am thankful for your asking." And at last I had said the proper thing: she seemed satisfied. "Now these are most jolly good almonds. I can make a mountain high as the peaks of Kashmir. As high as Nanga Parbat!"
 (And Apricot snorted once again.)
 Then I bargained for a while, but so as to show that I was not really bargaining; and I got my "mountain high as the peaks of Kashmir," and she added five almonds to the mountain, and gave me two anna in change.
 She was all wrapped in grubby green: faintly scented with cardamom, I seem to remember. Smiling, I remember: squinting at me, as people who wear specs do when they take off their specs. Only this woman had no specs.
 The clouds were upon us.
 She was still smiling. Her teeth: black. Brown. Well, dark yellow, actually: from chewing betel?
 And I gave her my very best grin. I was quite certain she could see the grin, for all she had no specs. "O Mother of Many Sons," I said, "I'll come again tomorrow."
 And then, utterly competent — oh, absolutely! I felt so very competent! — I led Apricot through the throng: we breathed our way through the thick, damp air.
 "Apricot, hurry."
 The clouds were upon us.

•

But the present does keep intruding.

. . .

"Sir. With the squadron leader's compliments, sir."

. . .

The Air Ministry visits paperwork upon us, in triplicate. And I'd failed to press hard enough for my writing to come through the two layers of copies.

Old Hurry-up:

Wayne,
Hate to be a bother at this late hour, but would you mind giving a glancing attention to these silly details in the future?

HH

Well, God in heaven! (No *uh-huh* comes through in writing, of course.)

Sir,
Error corrected. Sorry, sir.

WRL

A-a-a-argh! (as they say). How dare he? Well, God in heaven! (He seemed a much more *complicated* man when I first arrived here — not one who would so easily succumb to this simple-minded fussiness.)

"To the squadron leader, with my compliments, Corporal."

. . .

Did I simply fail to press hard enough, or does my hand still fail me, on occasion?

Luthie . . . Ah, Luthie! Luthie, *you are healed.*

Well, here's a *very good* little sketch of N. M. Tunnard-Jones: those rather widely spaced eyes, the exquisite eyebrows . . . lips slightly parted. I've pinned the little drawing on the wall right opposite my so miserably chaste-looking bed. (Is it the future now intruding? . . . I *will* speak to her.)

Well, where was I?

Yes. Oh yes. The almonds. Sugared almonds! Well, two for me, and one for Apricot. And one for me, and two for Apricot. And three for me . . .

I had no mother.

From the time I was not quite two years old till the time I was almost seven and ready to be sent away to Simla, my mother was not with us. All through that time my mother was gone.

•

Nighttime thoughts.
. . .

(If I put my mind to it, a semblance of a whole may emerge, one day.)

(Things to Do Right Now:
Keep mind on task at hand.)

How my father came to marry my mother (he a childless widower for ten years: forty-four years old; she a full twenty-five years younger than he):

My mother married him because it was the autumn of 1918: the Great War — the First War — the First Great War — was ending: there were no young men left.

(It was autumn. A glorious show: leaves turning. Children flying kites on Hampstead Heath: little boys in sailor suits; little girls in coats with soft black velvet collars. No young *men* left.)

The one young man of her acquaintance who still was among the living and with whom she was very much in love: he had gone off; married someone else. He was an American man, I understand.
. . .

When I was born, my mother named me Wayne.

My father should not have permitted it. (But of course, he truly had no idea at the time of the other man's existence.)
. . .

(No. No. It is not at all what one might think: I was born *ten months after the wedding to the day*. Conceived on good old S.S. *City of Bagora*. Yes, I was. I was. No one in the family denies it.)

(And my mother was about four months pregnant when the events of Amritsar happened.

Am-rit-sar. Am-rit-sar: the town whose name sounds like paper being crumpled.)
. . .

My mother had asked my father to marry her. *She did the asking.*

(She was the daughter of a friend of my father's: a Friend-of-War.)

He said no at first, my father did — full of yearning to say yes yes yes; then, a fortnight later, *he* did the asking.

He married her because it was the autumn of 1918, and he had survived but his two brothers hadn't; the Great War was ending: a fatigue of the soul, a dreadful weariness . . . and all that; but suddenly it became important to him that he should continue living. (Children flying kites on Hampstead Heath and all that.)

(Well, that was where my mother had done her asking: Hampstead Heath. Her parents — my "other" grandparents, long dead now — they were Hampstead people: a house not too large and not too small; a garden with roses climbing up white-painted trellises. So I have heard.)

So, my father was just like good Old Hurry-up, I suppose: seeking . . . *immortality?*

But time presses on me.

The formation attacks . . . We'll keep trying. Again. And again. *Practice makes perfect.???*

Will everything I do from now on turn out all right in the end, after all?

. . .

Beam attacks with Grenfeld and Brown today . . . Difficult to do, no doubt about it. *Practice makes perfect.*

Upstairs with Ashley, Farrell, and McGregor. I gave each of them the standard forty minutes of my time — and a postmortem, of course (no pun intended?) — a detailed analysis of their performance. What do I want for my wretched Wonders?

Why did I volunteer to go to war?

Bloody hell! Did I not promise myself not to say the word *Wonders?*

Quite.

What do I want for the men of Flight B? There. I have not said the word *Wonders.*

(The news from the south is rather desperate. Till now, I chose to ignore it. . . . Well, I kept pushing it and pushing it to the very back of my mind.)

(And I have just reread — ah, barely glanced at, actually! — the first five or six pages of this account: how orderly! how organized! how . . . leisurely! how . . . calm! When did my style of writing begin to change?)

How I arrived in England (I was twelve years old, not quite thirteen):

. . .

About my grandfather: he looked like the rhinoceros in the Kipling story. Well, his shape was different, of course: he was tall and thin like my father, like myself — like most Luthie men.

Now in the story about the Parsee-man and the rhino, the rhino takes off his skin — unbuttons all the little buttons on it — and goes for a swim. But the Parsee-man is lying in wait. And he sprinkles cake crumbs and raisins all over the skin, so that when the rhino puts it on again, it tickles; it chafes; it feels scratchy. And the rhino rolls and rolls about on the ground to get rid of the tickly-scratchy feeling — and his skin gets larger and larger. But the raisins and cake crumbs and whatnot are still there, still showing underneath the skin.

Raisins and cake crumbs underneath the skin? Cake crumbs and raisins?

I was five years old when my father first read the story to me.

How I arrived in England:

Good old S.S. *City of Bagora* smelled of the unknown. (Some thirteen years after she had — presumably — brought me to India; she was now carrying me Home: with a capital H.)

I made the journey with some people named Price, friends — professional acquaintances, really — of my father's: he had asked them to look after me. (My mother by then was once again my mother and my father's wife, and at first she had been almost adamant that she should be the one to come with me; but then, after a while, the subject was dropped. Was my father afraid she'd never come back?)

About the Prices:
"Lambkin . . ."
Lambkin!!!
"Lambkin . . . Look at yourself, kitten. Where have you been?"
In the engine room. (A *top secret* visit: the chief engineer must not know. Well, I had made friends with one of the engine-room people.)
The Prices: even at the time I'd probably have said that they treated me as if I were a basket of eggs. (And by the time we reached Suez, I was ready to jump ship.)

Good old S.S. *And So On And So On.*
Yes. Oh yes! Fans whirring, stirring the air ver . . . ry slow . . . ly . . . And the ship smelled . . . well, of the sea itself — of the voyage: most certainly not of home (home with a small h. Well, India *is* my home: I was born there, by God! Wasn't I?).
It rather gave one shivers down the spine.
Water. Water. It seemed very dark.
"Guess How Far the Ship Has Traveled Since Noon Yesterday." And just once my guess was better than all the other passengers', and my prize was a box of chocolates. I devoured them forthwith.
An exciting time. Disquieting, too. Well, exciting, mostly (and disquieting only at night, really, when I lay in bed — it was a nice and comfortable bed).

Liverpool.
Said Mrs. Price, "You are to stay here, little lambkin." In my cabin.
Lambkin! Lambkin! Lambkin!!!
And good old S.S. *And So On And So On* smelled of damp cold, of cold rain, and something else . . .
Mr. Price was coughing. (He had never coughed before, not even when he was Feeling Poorly.
Well, that was why they were going Home: because of Mr. Price's health. And they both were very sad about it. Such sad people!)
Mrs. Price: she sniffed the air and sighed. "It's coal dust, that horrid smell," she said.

And my bare knees (I still wore short trousers in those days — ah, the very, very last days of childhood: how I hated my short trousers!): were my bare knees slowly turning *blue?*

I sat in an armchair. Mr. and Mr. Price insisted on standing, flanking me: guarding me?; and outside the door there were many voices. All those people who had become friends during the voyage — they were shouting farewells to one another and invitations to visit at Christmas or Friday-till-Monday two months hence . . .

We waited for my grandparents.

And the door opened. In strode my grandfather. (He strode: he did not walk. He moved in a way a much younger man would!) He opened his arms. "Here he is! Oh, Beatrice . . . look!" he cried. (My grandmother: two steps, or three, behind him: clutching a photograph of me. And she glanced at me, and then she looked at the photograph . . . And she looked at me . . .

Christ! I'll never forget! The very first words my grandmother said — oh, not to me: most definitely not! — but to whom, then? Well, God in heaven, was she speaking to herself? My grandmother said, and she sounded breathless, "In the picture he doesn't look like Robert."

. . .

Robert? . . . Robert? Who?
My *uncle Robert* . . . dead . . . on the Somme . . . before I was born?

. . .

A look of dreadful grief passed then over my grandfather's face, very very briefly. Then, something much like . . . well, like annoyance, (anger? God, at whom? At *me?!* For looking like my uncle Robert?! *Not at me:* at my grandmother?!); then, a sadness; then, calm. He squared his shoulders. "Beatrice . . . Beatrice . . . Look at him," he said, very calmly. "The very image of Philip!" My father.

And *he* continued gazing at me. Staring at me. (And my grandmother stood there, stiff-backed. *Stiff-backed!*) I was frightened.

His ears were extremely large, I remember. My grandfather: commandingly large ears. Extremely *old* ears.

Old　Old　Old　Old　Old

He moved as a much younger man would. But his skin hung on him very loose. Very large.

And . . . *Raisins and cake crumbs! Cake crumbs and raisins* . . . all over him, by God! Old-age spots all over him!

Burnt, dry, old cake crumbs; and raisins; shriveled up. Very, very old raisins.

Old　Old　Old　Old　Old

And I drew back: repelled, I suppose.

And I knew my grandfather had seen it.

•

And then I sat in the chair. I sat sat sat sat sat. Blood must have rushed away from my face: I *felt* pale. Oh, I remember! I remember!

. . .

Well, do something, Luthie.

Up, up with you, Luthie!

. . .

How do you do, sir. I am Wayne Luthie, sir. I mean . . . your grandson, sir. I am sorry, sir. I didn't mean it, sir.

. . .

And slowly — reluctantly? — my grandfather once again opened his arms and then waited: to see whether I'd dare venture near enough to be embraced? And should I? Did he truly want me to? Or would he prefer for me not to? I did come to him. Through his waistcoat and his shirt I could feel the old body trembling.

His waistcoat smelled of pipe tobacco: he and my father must have smoked the same kind.

(My father could blow perfect smoke rings. When I was very small, sometimes those smoke rings were the Battle of Trafalgar: poof poof — the ships shooting at one another.)

And then, several hours later: at last!, after confirming the arrangements for my trunk . . . my valises . . . my grips . . . my *portmanteaux;* after expressing our thanks and undying gratitude to the Prices — we were on our way home. Not Home: another home with a small h.

Mr. Parrish driving. The wipers on the Bentley slapping. Dark city streets. And the Bentley heading for the open road. . . . I sat in the back, between my grandparents. There was only the sound of the motor.

The sound of rain. Rain. The end of May: it was a very cold rain.

We overtook a bus. There was an advertisement on the side of the bus. *"Chiver's!"* I shouted.

And my grandmother flinched; she turned to me, but remained silent.

And I gave myself over to despair.

It took a very long time before I said, "When I was . . . small, Ayah bought Chiver's marmalade for my breakfast. It is made at Cambridge, isn't it? I have seen similar advertisements at Lahore —" Christ, I sounded *well behaved!* "And at Simla . . . advertisements for Chiver's marmalade."

And this time my grandfather did not hesitate: he quickly helped himself to my hand and gave it a gentle squeeze. Well, God in heaven!

(Nighttime thoughts. Do not think others.

I had a happy childhood.)

Dear Janet:

My Dear Janet:

Please get well.

I remember

Oh, I remember Christmases! (In England.)

Mr. Willson — double *l* — played — still plays — the organ.

My grandfather liked to sing Christmas carols. My grandmother was like tea with warm milk: tea-colored cardigans, tea-colored blouses of soft, soft stuff (silk?), tweedy skirts the color of my father's personal Darjeeling. And her hair was like Devon cream.

O Come Let Us Adore Him
O Come Let Us Adore Him

St. Crispin's — the village church — is colder than Siberia at Christmastime. One sits there; watches rheumatism grow in people's bones.

"Did you see? Did you see? Mr. Willson *wore gloves* when playing the organ!" This was my very first Christmas in England. . . . Fingerless gloves, of course; still, they were gloves. Gray knitted gloves, to prevent his hands from seizing up in the cold.

And my grandmother laughed! Now *her* old skin was soft: as a blanket underneath which one may spend many peaceful nights. She laughed, for just a moment; but then she put her finger to her lips: hush. Hush, child.

And thus I discovered that Mr. Willson's wearing of the gloves while playing the organ was considered a weakness on his part, a human failing — quite akin to an otherwise *upright* man's excessive fondness for port or sherry, for example — and was therefore out of . . . charity (?) not usually mentioned in public. Ah, the wonders of the world!

But that was why, no doubt, Mr. Willson hit so many wrong notes!

Hark, the Herald Angels Sing . . .

because of those gloves.

I remember!

We returned from church: it was well past midnight; at home, Janet waited with a hot toddy on a tray.

Mrs. Simmonds waited: her apron smelled of cinnamon and spotlessness.

Mr. Parrish waited. And Tom.

(Mr. Parrish and Mrs. Simmonds had been to the afternoon service; Tom and Janet would go very early the next morning.)

About my grandmother:

"His hair is like Robert's. He walks like Robert. . . . And his flights of fancy: Robin was the fanciful one." (Sometimes she called him Robbie or Robin.) "He's Robin, come back." In a sweet voice of a woman sad who is feeling joyful.

My uncle Robert had been her youngest by far and her favorite.

(But my grandfather, upon first seeing me, had said that I looked very much like my father.)

Well, God in heaven! I am my own man. I am myself.

(Actually, my grandparents seldom mentioned my father.)

Never mind.

(I wondered about it?) I *tried* not to wonder. . . . Well, I was thirteen, fourteen years old: new to England; and my grandfather had taken me fishing; and my grandmother had had Mrs. Simmonds make us a supply of sandwiches; and my grandfather had given me a bicycle (more about that later?); and my grandmother had a rather beautiful laugh . . .

Never mind.

I remember:

My very first Christmas in England — I was brushing my teeth before going to bed on Christmas Eve — there, on the bathroom window, frost had painted a white garden, full of flowers of *outlandish* beauty. And I shivered in my flannel pajamas: none of my more-than-Oriental splendor in those days!; and I was terribly homesick for India. And yet I stared at the window in fascination (my toothbrush between my teeth: like a pirate dagger, or a Gurkha's *kukri*); and my heart was beating very fast: I was so filled with wonder.

Then I slipped between the sheets: Janet had warmed the bed with a charcoal bed-warmer. And she had placed a hot-water bottle where she had guessed my feet would be.

Janet seldom called me "Master Wayne," as Mr. Parrish invariably did. She never said I reminded her of my uncle Robert. "Mouse," she called me sometimes. "Tall mouse."

And I remember how I wrapped the warmth of the sheets and the blankets and the quilted eiderdown about me.

I was thirteen years old, and Janet was pretty; and this was the time when I was afraid of pretty women.

Mouse. Well, God in heaven!

Well . . . *Tall mouse.* It was better than *lambkin*, wasn't it?

And, into the darkness of the English winter night, I sent a rather happy large-toothed Luthie grin, I seem to remember.

Merry Christmas.

But time presses on me. There may not be much time.

The Wonders: so woefully undertrained. Christ! For all my efforts, it simply is not possible for them to improve much in just a few short days!

The news coming from the south is not good.

I went to see Hanmer.

II

Hanmer sprawled on his bed.

. . .

Acklington . . . I would speak with thee (as W. Shakespeare would say).

. . .

Hanmer: a dog-eared paperbound book on his stomach. *Rogue Male.* "A chap . . . he's English . . . goes out to kill Hitler because Hitler has killed his girl. But one doesn't really know it's Hitler and one doesn't really know he killed the girl . . . not till the end, you know . . . well, one *never* knows it's Hitler. This is complicated. . . ."

Yes!

(Well, that is the way we live.)

Hanmer: a brand-new dressing gown on over not-so-new pajama bottoms. Black silk, of course, the dressing gown: black as all the sins of the world; black as my morning coffee. (But I put three lumps of sugar in my coffee, to take the bitterness away!)

And he got down from the bed and he flapped about the room like a giant bat bleeding to death. "How do I look?" (The dressing gown is lined in red-light-district scarlet.)

. . .

Acklington, I would speak . . .

. . .

I said, "Well, go and sink your mighty canines into some innocent young thing's neck."

And Hanmer exclaimed, "Quite the idea! Yes, I think I'll go," he said: a musing voice. "I am on my way!" Hanmer announced. "*Sans* the pajama bottoms, of course." And Hanmer said, "I'll go and bite N. M. Tunnard-Jones." And I threw myself at him.

But he fled down the hall. He fled into *my* room.

I fell against the door. Managed to wedge my foot in the door.

Hanmer very nearly crushed my foot.

And . . . Roy Newby and Geoff Thomas, in the hall: *Lu-thie! Lu-thie! Lu-thie!*

Encouragement. (And oh God, it felt good!)

People gathering. *Lu-thie! Lu-thie! Lu-thie!*

(That is how we live.

Friendship. And all that.)

. . .

And Hanmer let go of the door, and I fell inside; and we grappled, struggled. Fell on my bed in a heap. Shaking with laughter.

Then after a while we stopped laughing; sat up; looked at each other.

And so I began to play host. (Brought out the brandy bottle . . .)

And a bit later, I said, "You know . . . When Mater was on the blower to me, two days ago . . . the other day . . . you know . . ."

And Hanmer nodded, *sagely*. He looked *sagacious*. "They *will* do frightening things, will they not. One's . . . progenitors."

(Well, my mother *had telephoned* to impart the news about Tom's death and Janet's misfortune. And thereby hangs a tale!)

But first I told him about Tom. "A bit of a cold fish, actually, our Tom. Hoarded his laughter. A perfectionist. Hedges clipped just so. Boys from the village used to come to help him in the summer: tweed caps. They had to doff their caps to him, every morning. He was most particular about this manifestation of *respect*."

. . .

My grandfather had said once that Tom was a young man quite painfully shy.

His marriage to Janet had been so absolutely obviously a most happy one. Oh, definitely!

. . .

And I mentioned the miscarriage to Hanmer.

(Are we a family *blighted* by war? . . . Pompous ass, Luthie.)

But Hanmer said only, "Rotten luck, that." And now he looked positively *owlish:* well, he must already have drunk quite a bit before dinner; and at dinner; and after dinner, too, probably.

But we drank some more. Sat in silence. Finally, I said, "But when Mater was on the blower to me . . ."

. . .

Ah, Hanmer Acklington! A man of uncommon perception! He is quick: quick as a darting fish! He did not wait for me to finish. "Well, your Pater . . . You thought . . . Didn't you?" It was said quickly: mumble mumble mumble.

And I nodded, quickly: *not* looking owlish? (Bloody hell, of course I had thought: I had thought she was telephoning to say that my father was dead!

. . .

And thereby hangs a tale!

. . .

Well, that *is* the tale.
An anticlimax?)

. . .

One does not telephone lightly.

The Signals Section will not accept private calls for any airbase personnel; but they will relay a message. *One most certainly does not telephone lightly.*

I said to Hanmer, "Well, I was not in the office, you see. I'd gone for a walk. Just ten minutes — not more. It was such an exceptionally fine night, remember? And I was feeling rather hopeful just then: well, about the Wonders and all . . . But I never left the base. They shoved one of those message slips under the B Flight office door."

. . .

The message: *Contact your mother ASAP.*

. . .

(Contact your mother. Mother.
Mother. Mother.
Not: family. My father: not mentioned. Not mentioned at all.)

One tries not to have friends in wartime.
Why should one not have friends in wartime?
Hanmer is a friend.
(Still, I hesitated now. And then I really told him very little.
And he did not pry. Nor did he waste his time patting me on the back in support or sympathy. We are two unsentimental men.)

Hanmer: "Well, they will do frightening things, will they not? Mothers. . . ." And then, after a while, he said, "How did you learn it wasn't true? Were you in the dark till you actually spoke to her?" (When it is important, he does not pry; but it is his nature — human nature, really! — to be inquisitive.)

"N. M. Tunnard-Jones told me." Well, that miserable slip of paper had been folded into thirds. And I had unfolded it at last . . . "In the lower fold there was a scrawl, in different hand: 'Your immediate family all right, but there is bad news, I'm afraid. N. M. Tunnard-Jones.'"

And Hanmer — his shark's teeth looking sharp — Hanmer threw his head back and laughed and laughed and laughed.

. . .

"Shut up, Acklington."

. . .

N. M. Tunnard-Jones: You woman of kindness! Oh, absolutely.

. . .

Hanmer: that persistent bastard! His nose twitching with excitement. "And *then* what did you do?"

"Put my feet up on the desk, lit a cigarette. All those papers, you know . . . So neatly stacked. They *were* neatly stacked. . . . And I spread my feet. Rustle rustle swish thud. Papers, on the floor. And I contemplated my feet — with some pleasure, I must say. But then I remembered that the note said 'Bad news,' and so I ran to Signals to put a call through to my people." (It is forbidden to use the Signals Section telephones for private conversations.)

But Hanmer: there was a *sage* nod, from Hanmer.

Thus, I let some air into my lungs. Opened my heart to him: "N. M. Tunnard-Jones had gone off duty by then. Christ God! I've been trying to see her ever since. I want to thank her. Sent her a note tonight. Asked to see her . . . at her convenience."

And Hanmer . . . Ah, Hanmer! He howled with laughter. "*You made an appointment!* . . . All that red hair!" he said (and seemed to be choking). "She's probably red between her legs, too. . . . Luthie," Hanmer said, looking sagacious, "do you want to stuff a woman who's red between her legs?"

. . .

Acklington, I'll break every bone in your miserable body.

. . .

Hanmer said, "Sorry. I'll not say that again."

"If you do, I'll break every bone in your body."

And then it turned out that I happened to be in possession of some of those abominable honey buns, periodically inflicted upon us by ACW Mary Ann: protégée (?!) of good old Colin K.; and so we disposed of the buns, every one of them. We also finished the brandy.

Hanmer: grubbing about with his fingers for bits of pineapple inside one of those jars of fancy mixed fruits from Fortnum's. There was engine oil on his fingers. Well, in the name of heaven and hell! Hadn't the man *bathed?* . . . (Actually, the fruit was a bit fermented, anyway.)

And then after a while he took himself off, looking not a well man: "Luthie . . . You bag of misery. Tummy all skew-wiff." Yes. Well.

We are two completely unsentimental men.

(When Hanmer had come to me, the other day — when he had needed me to listen — I had been too busy to hear him out.

So, a debt of sorts still exists.)

Grinning   grinning   grinning like a coal's cuttle . . .

Four of them. Four.

Four grinning coal's cuttles. The time of Dunkirk.

And I recognized them at once: they were *hungry in the sunshine* . . .

Thus there are things that one will keep private — secret — hidden.

(And one does meet, in the end, one's childhood nightmare.

The time of Dunkirk: the end of May, a hot day: unseasonably hot weather, the time of Dunkirk — my father the pacifist had given me a knife.)

III

My hands bound behind my back.

They forced me to my knees.

Blood poured down my palms, between my fingers: soaked the seat of my trousers.

A peculiar sound . . . What is it? What is it? My own breath.

Breathe   breathe   gulp for air. (Perhaps if I breathe deeply enough, I can carry that breath with me through eternity.)

Sweat poured from me. (Well, it was a hot day.)

And there was a slight breeze in the treetops.

Silence. No, there was no silence: one of them shifted his weight from one foot to the other; and there was that breeze in the trees.

They pressed the muzzle of my own Colt .45 — my very own — to the base of my skull.

Well, I'd handed it over.

That had been the first — and only — thing I'd handed over.

But they had my father's knife, of course.

And they pressed the gun — very firmly — where the hair ends and bare skin begins: it feels cool. It's as cool a feeling as . . . as a fresh pillow in the evening. God Christ, this is true! I swear it is true!

And sweat poured from me.

And there was silence. No. Not silence. Click: and the gun was off safety.

Through the sandy soil, in front of my eyes, an ant was making its way purposefully, struggling with a burden of . . . a crumb of bread?

And I hated. Hated. Hated hated hated.

I hated . . . the ant.

Hated   Hated   Hated

In hatred, I closed my eyes on the world.

God, please accept me.

Then into the darkness I whispered — and I put absolutely the very last shreds of what remained of myself into those three words — I whispered: "I am ready."

God . . . if you exist . . . God, please help me. End it.

God, quite properly, didn't care.

They laughed, and they spared me.

I fainted.

PART THREE

12

My Dear People:
  This is to inform you

Let us start over.

  My Dear People:
  Yes, I accept your rebuke that I have of late become an unsatisfactorily sporadic correspondent. But the chief purpose of this missive is to inform you that I have quite suddenly entered a period of an uncommon buoyancy of spirit.

13

Intoned Cartwright:

> "There was a young lady of fashion —"

A few snickers. And then Farrell chimed in:

> "Who had oodles and oodles of passion."

All right. All together, now.

> "To her lover she said
> As they jumped into bed —"

And Grenfeld looked . . . the way Grenfeld always looked: as if he very much wanted to join in; still, he remained aloof.

But Ashley plunged in. (Without a moment's hesitation?) He could hear himself sounding enthusiastic!

"Well, here's one thing the bastards can't ration."

And they laughed. They hooted with laughter.

14

Dear Uncle Dixon:
In the Event of my Death please do not present a reading from these
pages in the mess anteroom before or after dinner.
I know I can trust you. Thank you.

W. R. Luthie

My Dear People:
I have entered a period of contentment.

15

Somebody said, "See Luthie chatting up the popsy? . . . Afternoon.
Teatime."
"Luthie and crumpet."
"The judy from Signals."
"She's the *section officer* from Signals."
They laughed. They hooted. They crowed.

It was after dinner; they were sated, feeling lazy.
And said McGregor — the voice of a man who finds it easy to *have his*
sources, "It should be possible to get the gen why Luthie is not on tomorrow after lunch."
And they sat up; stopped feeling lazy at once.
Yes, yes, Luthie would be taking the afternoon off. But before the
afternoon of that day to come, he would by turn take Brown and Farrell
up; and Ashley and McGregor and Cartwright and Grenfeld had been
instructed to go out in pairs after lunch, to engage in attempts to "shoot"
each other down; and then, quite late in the afternoon, Brown would
once again go, this time with Pilot Officer Thomas, and Stanhope with
Flight Lieutenant Acklington. In addition, for some time now, Luthie
had been threatening a sneak EA — enemy aircraft — recognition test:
thus, they really should study their pictures of EA's . . . A life busy. As
usual. As usual. But . . .
No doubt about it, they were not a little resentful of Luthie for taking
the afternoon off.
McGregor said, sounding very very competent, "I will find out."

And . . . should they be resentful of McGregor?

Well, the bastard knew, didn't he, what Luthie would be doing! He knew!

But, as Ashley watched — as he observed — instead of resentment there seemed to be rather a feeling . . . no, not of suspense, but anticipation . . .

They knew — suspected — what Luthie would be doing, didn't they?

McGregor said, "The kiwis are working on my kite. But Dunaway *informs* me it will not be ready till 1500." And did he make it sound now as if he'd arranged it specially for the kite not to be ready till 1500?

"Grenfeld and Farrell," McGregor said, "you don't have to log your forty minutes' worth till 1600, now do you?" And yes, he did sound *most thoroughly* competent: well, whatever it was that was about to happen would happen *before* 1500, wouldn't it? Oh yes, McGregor was in complete charge of everything.

And so — as Ashley watched: as he observed — there was (or at least there seemed to be) a sudden release of tension. Some of the feeling of being adrift that had hung over them from the first moments of their arrival here — that seemed to be gone. (They needed a leader. They needed . . . yes, an anchor. Had they found an anchor?) (Well, *some* of the feeling was gone — a good deal of it, actually; but not all of it.)

They sat; and after a while they began to tell filthy jokes, and they laughed. They hooted. They crowed.

And Ashley hesitated for but a brief moment; then joined in.

16

I

1) Blanket. (The one from my bed will suffice.)

2) Tea. (She'll preside over the tea-things . . . A picnic!)

(One thermos; two metal mess-kit cups. *Are those tea-things?!*)

(Unobtainable here: wine — even sherry — of drinkable quality.)

(Brandy? Whisky? Gin? Inappropriate.)

3) Sandwiches. (Bought several tins of potted meat at Campbell's in town the other day; then forgot I had them. . . . Serendipity! Thy name is . . . Mrs. Sourpuss Campbell!

Bread for the sandwiches: I'll beg, borrow, or steal from the mess.)

Today! Today she is coming with me: *this afternoon!* (It is past midnight now.) Yesterday: yesterday I spoke to her.

Yesterday! Well, down the little path we trotted (*before* I asked her to come for a walk with me today) — we trotted from Signals past the Med. Section to Parachutes — she said she wanted to stop at Parachutes, had to see someone (whoever it was) there.

When we get to Parachutes, I'll be dismissed.

Wind blowing.

That woman's smile . . . well, when at last I said what I had come to say — in well-rehearsed words (few words, but carefully chosen: I am a man who knows how to use words) — when I thanked her for that little note: "Bad news, I'm afraid, but . . ." That woman's smile! A *clean* smile. Like a drink of water on a summer's day.

No female wiles and guiles. A smile . . . straightforward. A smile full of pleasure.

Serious gray eyes. God!

. . .

The smile of a woman who . . . who has not smiled in pleasure in . . . in quite some time?

(Silly ass, Luthie.)

Is there something a bit odd about her?

(Silly ass, Luthie.)

My Dear People:

No. (Would they *really* understand my elation?)

I remember: yesterday. The sky was very slowly going to evening.

Adrenalin pumping: fight or flight? Oh, I'll fight to win her! I'll fight.

"The sunsets here . . . they're quite nice, aren't they?"

Quite nice. . . . Luthie, go to ten thousand feet and let yourself fall without a parachute!

As soon as we get to the Parachutes Section, I'll be dismissed.

I tugged down the sleeves of my roll-neck, of my tunic. Are the scars hidden? They were hidden.

I do not want a woman to gentle my wounds.

I do not want a woman to be repelled by my wounds.

"Miss Tunnard-Jones . . ."

"Mr. Luthie." Curtly? (Or just the opposite, perhaps? Did she make my name sound as if she knew I was a good man?)

When we get to Parachutes . . .

(We'd passed the Med. Section already.)

Look at me. Look at me, N. M. Tunnard-Jones.

Oh, I looked good!

(I am not good-looking.)

A nice, clean roll-neck. . . . Look at me! A dandyish thing, the roll-neck: very much like something Hanmer would wear — if Hanmer did not insist on going even into combat with his tie beautifully knotted. . . . Look at me, will you, N. M. Tunnard-Jones. The roll-neck: the black yarn is wool, the white silk. It would feel soft on a woman's skin if she should choose to rest her face against my chest!

(I had brand-new underclothes on, never before worn. . . . Luthie, you idiot!)

My flying gloves stuffed inside my boots, the finger part showing: flapping. Quite the thing! (Well, anything goes inside those boots: paper-work mostly, maps . . . The more the better: a man of importance. It is one of those RAF affectations.)

(Another affectation: keeping the top button of one's tunic unbuttoned. *I am a fighter pilot!* — that is what that button undone proclaims to the world. But I had not done that, of course. Not for her. Not her! I had not taken complete leave of my senses.)

She was leaning that delicate body of hers into the wind, calmly.

And I had to put absolutely everything I had into not trembling at the nearness of her.

Dear Uncle Dixon: etc. etc.

(I should not be writing this down, of course.)

I said, "Miss Tunnard-Jones . . . Well, do you like it here?"

Brilliant. Brilliant.

And she thought about it. Considered it. She said, "Yes, I do now. . . . I've never lived anywhere but London, really, you see — school the only exception. This is so very different. . . . Of course at first . . ." And what was it she was about to say then? Was she about to say something . . . about herself? But then she didn't.

(That is her privilege. Oh, absolutely! Why should she be telling me about herself? No reason whatsoever. . . . After all, she knows not a thing about *me*. And so it is her right to change her mind and not to finish sentences. It is her right! Most definitely.)

There was a small silence between us. Then she said, with emphasis — and of course, she said it instead of whatever she had meant to say — "I do like London."

Oh. And I had hoped she was like me!

London has never been one of my favorite places.

. . .

N. M. Tunnard-Jones, these days London looks like a French cemetery on All Hallows' Eve. At night, I mean. All that darkness.

And those little yellow lights over the bomb-shelter entrances, under their little pointed roofs, so that the lights would not shine up at the sky . . . they're like candles in a graveyard — in remembrance . . . of something, N. M. Tunnard-Jones. And people's faces swim out of that darkness, then recede again, like . . . like wraiths. Sallow spirits.

A ghost story all its own, by God! — on a winter's night? That most wonderful tingling down one's spine? Exciting feeling of . . . uneasiness? Oh good God yes, I have been to London lately, N. M. Tunnard-Jones! But after a while, it is not exciting. Pity takes over. Grief. Sorrow, N. M. Tunnard-Jones. All that reflecting tape on the lampposts, for example! Almost gaudy! Rather brave. Well, that's what I mean about French cemeteries: brave and gaudy, French cemeteries. Candles burning, flowers growing: nice bright flower beds . . . All rather defiant of the darkness, really. But one feels grief: perhaps because it looks so very brave.

Do you like London, N. M. Tunnard-Jones? I disagree with you, N. M. Tunnard-Jones. And I'll tell you so, if you ask me. Oh, I'll tell you . . . tell you! And I'll stand my ground. Try me.
· · ·

The love affair of the century: why shouldn't it begin with a quarrel?!
· · ·

And she said — a soft voice, but something echoes in it — she said it very very quickly, and once it was said, she was almost breathless: "Of course, these days it's a bit like walking through one of those stories that one thinks one might want to hear on a dark and rainy night in November. But afterward one rather wishes one hadn't heard it."

Well, God in heaven, woman!

Well, what did I do then? I did not do anything, of course. Say anything. One cannot. We merely continued down the path together. Wind blowing, naturally.

We stopped in front of Parachutes.

A stillness about her: those gray eyes. A woman who is far away? A woman not to be touched?

And I myself did not dare move. I knew she understood well that something had happened between us.

But then, when I asked her, it was so terribly obvious that there was a certainty in the very core of her being that she *shouldn't* want to come for a walk with me. Not that she *didn't* want to come; but she shouldn't.
· · ·

Love   My love   Well, what is it, love? Do tell me, love.
· · ·

Women: they always assess a man. (Well, such is the privilege of women.) And her eyes were on me: a gaze . . . straightforward. Naturally. No female wiles and guiles.

But — well, God in heaven — she seemed to be assessing herself! (What is it, love?)

And I brought my knees forward a bit, bent them a little, so as not to seem so double-jointed; but, unlike with good old Sergeant Bennett, not so long ago, I did not then immediately slam them back home, in defiance: *I am who I am. I am myself,* and so on. I stood before her, not double-jointed: impressively straight-backed, all magnificent six feet four inches of me; I stood, in supplication. (*I am myself?* Ha!)

. . .

Oh my love   Love   I want to trace your eyebrows with my fingers. (And quickly, I tugged down the sleeves of my roll-neck.)

. . .

"Mr. Luthie . . ." she said; and now — by God! — she did make it sound as if she knew that I was a good man, and wanted to let *me* know she knew.

. . .

Oh my love   Love
There will be a day you'll wake up with your head on my pillow!

. . .

She said, "I'll come only this once" — and it was a quiet voice.
"I am honored," I said. (Stupid ass, Luthie.)
Once?!
We'll see!

Today. *Today!* At two o'clock in the afternoon — 1400 hours — she is coming.

(But I must be back by 2000. One of those sessions on tactics with the Wonders at 2000. They are called lectures, actually, those sessions; the Nissen hut in which they take place is "the lecture room."
How does one Spit confront fifteen Messerschmitts, shoot down two, damage one, and escape unscathed? With little diagrams. . . . Never mind.)

And her hair does not smell of apples: it smells of chamomile! (Does she wash her hair in chamomile?)

Ah, the woman who comes to a man in his dreams: a white blouse with small pearl buttons!

Lovely, sweet, small breasts.

II

My Dear People:
    I am so very glad the new doctor seems to be good for Father!

(That is the letter I'll send, I think.)

•

And I fall into bed; and there is a most *delicious* coolness at the base of my skull, where the hair ends and bare skin begins . . .

(That was where they placed the muzzle of my gun. It is a cool feeling.)

No. I will not think about it.

(And I . . . hated —)

NO, NO.
Never mind. I am myself.

Victoria . . . Vicky . . . Puss puss . . . I've a proposition: I provide a warm bed; you purr up my nose.

God! I am in love with N. M. Tunnard-Jones.

17

I

And the next day, ten minutes before L-Hour (Luthie-Hour): Luthie-and-the-section-officer-from-Signals-Hour), the men of Flight B sprawled on their bellies in the grass, the sun warming their hides.

McGregor had brought two pairs of field glasses. ("I can see the IO picking his teeth!" Stanhope cried. The intelligence officer picking his teeth!!! My God! Powerful field glasses, then.)

From behind one of those lichen-covered boulders the men of Flight B peered down the gentle slop toward the gate with the notice on it that said: NOTIS. (Well, neither Luthie nor the girl were expecting . . . spies; and they would not be scanning the horizon, would they? Well, would they? No.)

McGregor was issuing instructions. "Take turns. Two minutes each." McGregor sounded thoroughly un-Scottish, in spite of his so very Scottish name (Ashley decided). A bland (well, so it seemed to Ashley) and colorless and most terribly careful RP — Received Pronunciation — hammered into his head . . . his tongue . . . his very vocal cords . . . at school, no doubt; it gave no clue whatsoever as to where his home might be. (But that rather made McGregor something of a man of mystery, now didn't it?)

They waited.
"If he doesn't hurry up, he'll be late."
They waited.
"Tallyho! Here he comes!"
"Well, let me see. *Let me bloody well see.*"

But McGregor was in full command. "Quie-e-et! The wind might shift, and he might hear us."

Flying Officer Luthie had tan corduroy (?) trousers on, a brown tweed jacket; a tweedy cap. He carried a haversack: it seemed heavy.

"Gentlemen, there's enough food there for the whole squadron for a week —"

"He'll stuff her with food first, and then he'll stuff her . . ."

(For he's a jolly good fellow . . . for he's a jolly good fellow . . . McGregor.)

Why had they come here? Because McGregor had told them to.

And because they hoped to see some French kissing. . . . Companions. Friends: together.

Hip hip hurrah for McGregor! And all that.

McGregor: he knew how to handle people. A man of mystery. . . .

But Luthie, too, was something of a mystery — so Ashley thought.

The men of Flight B liked McGregor, though.

Did Ashley like McGregor?

What did it matter? McGregor knew how to handle people.

Somebody said, "*She's* late." And they waited.

"What's he doing?"

"Lighting a cigarette." (And Flying Officer Luthie had slipped the haversack off his shoulders.)

"And now . . . now . . . he's eating . . . a peppermint?!" To make his breath sweet?

"She is not coming."

(And the sun warmed their hides.)

(Then, for a minute or so, they were distracted by three Spits taking off: Pilot Officer Newby and Flight Lieutenant Acklington — by the code letters on their kites — and . . . my God! . . . well, leading, of course . . . the squadron leader, himself! Up . . . up . . . up; and they headed out: out west where the water was. They disappeared.)

"She'll leave him standing there till midnight."

"Till tomorrow morning!"

And a scuffle broke out over the field glasses. "Well, give here —"

"Bugger off."

"I want to see. I want to see. Well, does Luthie look . . . well, you know . . . disappointed?"

Then at last it was Ashley's turn. (God, almost every time these days he asked himself whether it was proper to watch people! Watch: observe; to record . . . *Preserve* a record: in pictures or in one's memory . . . God damn it all, no one had the right to make him feel it was not proper!) He adjusted the glasses . . . Luthie: *disappointed?* The man was in anguish! The man was in pain. She was not coming, and he was clearly hurting.

Well, would they — should they — laugh, Flight B, in malice? (Actually, it was comforting, rather, Ashley thought, to see another man being hurt. It almost gave one a feeling of safety: *bad things are happening to him; nothing bad is happening to me*.)

Why had they come here?

To see some French kissing.

They wouldn't see any. Had McGregor failed them? Would they laugh at McGregor?

"She is not coming."

But she came. More than a quarter of an hour late, but hurrying, hurrying. A small figure. In the distance. Tiny. Hurrying.

"Gentlemen . . . A tweed skirt . . . A cardigan . . . Whitish . . ." Large. Bulky: she seemed lost in it; it cocooned her. (And both pairs of field glasses and all eyes were on her.)

"It covers her bum, that sweater." And someone giggled.

"She borrowed it from LACW Robison!" (The one who knitted: little mittens.) LACW Robison was . . . bulky.

"Covers her tits, too. A chap wants to see a popsy's tits . . ."

On her head a whitish knitted hat — a beret-type hat, but with a large tassel. And the tassel bobbed, as she hurried: with each step it jumped like . . . like a live thing.

"Nice tassel." Grenfeld . . . breathed it out. (*Grenfeld,* of all people! Leaving himself so open to ridicule, and so on?!)

(And — in embarrassment? probably — Farrell began to roil up the earth with the tips of his boots. Stanhope snatched the field glasses from Grenfeld. And Grenfeld did not protest: Grenfeld looked embarrassed.)

"Nice tassel," Stanhope said, smacking his lips. (For once, there was no crunch crunch of peppermints.) (Stanhope — Stanhope?! He of the whiny voice — smacking his lips?)

But yes, it *was* a nice tassel; and the men of Flight B were quite capable of appreciating the good things of life. (And thus — as Ashley looked about, as he listened — there only were a few grunts of satisfaction.)

"Gentlemen . . . Luthie on the move."

Well, my God — God damn it all — they'd forgotten Luthie completely!

"Gentlemen . . ." Luthie running.

Running. He had doffed his silly cap to her. Held it in his hand. His arms outstretched. And my God, how he ran!

And she took a flying leap: over a ditch; there she was, on the path . . . the heavy tweed skirt flying . . . the tassel flying . . . And her hair was spilling out . . . spilling out . . . from underneath the stupid knitted hat . . . No ugly bun today. God damn it all!

(What would Flight B do now?) Well, not a single word was then said. Not one single word need be said. Oh, it was the most beautiful sight in the world — it was! oh it was! — that red . . . no: copper-colored . . . hair against the green grass, the white sweater, the white hat!

"Let me see. Let me see." And name-calling began. Ended.

Ah, when those two running people came together!

They didn't.

They stopped. She lowered her head: in shyness? Luthie's arms fell by his sides. Well, these clearly were two people who didn't know each other very well! *(Really, if the truth be known — they hardly knew one another at all!)*

But then her head went up again; and he took a step toward her. Yes yes yes . . . but did they *want* to get to know each other! (He had taken a step toward her. Did she truly want to get to know him?)

(Well, they were men, too. Flight B, weren't they? They did know a thing or two, didn't they? . . . And what they didn't know, they could guess. . . . They watched.)

Luthie. Two or three swift steps — very swift. Ah, Flying Officer Luthie: here was a man who could not help himself! (Anyone could see: no field glasses needed. Well, they were men, too, Flight B. They knew things.)

And Luthie hugged her. Hugged her. (Not a lover's embrace. It was a hug: full of joy. Joy overflowing. Joy impossible to contain. This was a man suffering from a . . . from a . . . Ashley reached for the word and found it and liked it: a *surfeit* of happiness.)

"A-a-a-ah!" said somebody. A voice full of jealousy and envy.

Of a male body hurting.

"What are they doing? . . . What are they doing?"

"Laughing. Talking."

And Flying Officer Luthie tugged at her tassel.

She stood up on tiptoes: what a small woman! She jumped: a small jump (the tassel bobbed). She snatched the cap from his head (how had the cap found its way back on his head?) and she ran with it.

"Not bad. Not bad. Did she run cross-country at school, do you think?"

"Too big, that sweater. Covers her bum."

No one said anything about tits.

But she was no match for Luthie's stork's legs. (Besides, she wanted to be caught, no doubt.)

(Luthie must have found it difficult to run, though: painful. . . . Women. They knew nothing about men.)

(And somebody giggled.)

He caught her.

"What are they doing now? Give here. Let me see. Let me see."

"They're laughing like two bloody madmen, both of them."

"Gentlemen . . . He'll pull up her bloody skirt right here. Throw her on the ground . . ."

Stanhope? . . . Again?

And abruptly, there was a silence. (Ashley glanced about.) *Bad form, Stanhope?*

But then several people did laugh, of course. They crowed. Softly and carefully they hooted, so they'd not be heard if the wind should shift. And they did say some things that Ashley truly thought should not be said about a man and a woman one *actually knew*. (*Actually knowing* them made a difference, somehow.) But still it seemed to him they all were laughing because they thought it was expected of them to hoot with laughter. (Nobody chastised Stanhope, of course.)

"Whose turn now? Whose turn?" Politely — well-disciplined men of good manners — they passed the field glasses about.

And she returned the cap; and Luthie shoved it on his head. They stood; two statues, rooted to the spot — looking dumb, daft, stupid, idiotic; but then at last he parted from her, trotted back to the gate to retrieve his haversack.

She waited. He rejoined her.

And together, they started down the path, toward the road; turning their backs on the airfield. They walked side by side.

Suddenly, Luthie held out his hand. And a collective groan went up. As if they had rehearsed it.

(Well, what an ass! *Oh, absolutely!* Well, grab her hand: one quick act of courage — the prize in hand! — so to speak.)

(God, this *hesitating, unforceful*, well, *unmasterful* . . . this *idiot* would one day — very soon — take them into battle?!

God, this *innocent* was worse by far than even Grenfeld moaning over the bloody tassel!)

(And my God, how Ashley agreed! Oh, he agreed!)

And somebody said, "Well, will she do it? Will she hold hands with him? Five bob she won't."

Because a man and a woman holding hands — that was serious — more serious by far than laughing laughing laughing and chasing after tweed caps all over the fair countryside! More important even than being hugged. (And it had been a hug: not a lovers' embrace.)

Well, a woman *placing* her hand in a man's . . .

If she should ignore the hand — if she should reject him — would they laugh: Flight B? Would they laugh in malice?

•

The hand stayed there. All alone. Forlorn.

Somebody growled. In anger? In frustration?

But those two continued walking: marching forward. The girl stared straight ahead, apparently: in shyness?

"Bloody women!" Was it Farrell's voice?

(*They knew nothing about men: women didn't. Why did they then seem to take delight in hurting them?*)

"Wait! . . . Wait! . . . Gentlemen . . . Atten-shun . . . Gentlemen . . ."

And slowly — *well, just like a woman: taking her time about it!* — her hand went out.

Fingers intertwining. (No field glasses needed: they all could see it, in their minds' eyes.)

"A-a-a-ah!" Several voices now, in unison. Had they rehearsed it? Well, they hadn't, of course. Jealousy. Envy. And so many male bodies hurting. (But was it also the equivalent of Three Cheers for Luthie?)

"Can she see the scars?"

A hush fell.

But the girl's head was up now: she seemed to be . . . searching the man's face.

"Did the scars scare her? Give here. Let me see."

And Ashley spoke for the first time that afternoon — and his voice sounded rusty to him, from disuse. "She looks calm," he said. Had Luthie *wanted* her to see the scars?

And so the show was over.

Why had they come here? Because McGregor had told them to. And because they had hoped to see some French kissing. They hadn't seen any, but were grateful to McGregor, nevertheless. (For he's a jolly good fellow, for he's a jolly good fellow . . .)

(At some point during the proceedings, McGregor had simply faded into the background, fallen silent. No one had noticed when; no one had noticed how — not even Ashley.

But they did need a leader. They needed . . . oh yes, an *anchor*.)

And so it occurred to Ashley to wonder: How did they — Flight B — view Luthie now? What did they think about him? (They were laughing and joking — at Luthie's expense, mostly: no malice, though: good-natured. They didn't see him as a man of mystery. They saw him as a source of . . . entertainment.)

But McGregor had at some point begun to look disgruntled, Ashley now observed. Well, had anything changed, then?

(But then somebody — Cartwright? — slapped McGregor on the back, in approval. Several other people expressed their approval.

And McGregor ceased looking disgruntled — he looked his usual self: competent. After a while, McGregor began to look . . . thoughtful. McGregor was lost in deep thought.)

Ashley turned back, peered once again through the field glasses.

Those two were ill-matched: Flying Officer Luthie and the section officer from Signals. Looked ridiculous together, really: he so very tall, and she so tiny.

But, as Ashley watched, Luthie paused; and then adjusted his . . . his giant insect's stride to her. (And the girl's tassel bobbed: jumped like a live thing, with each step.)

Did she lengthen her step now, the smallest bit? She did. Yes, she did. There was no doubt about it. And so their strides matched.

Now this was grown up!

And Ashley was seized with a dreadful sadness and a terrible yearning.

Overhead, there was the good, familiar sound of thunder: the squadron leader and Newby and Acklington were coming back.

One. Two. Three. They all were coming back.

Comforting.

Somebody called out: "Ashley! Well, are you coming? . . . Ashley . . . Move!" And, with some reluctance, Ashley ran to catch up.

Did he like these people?

Did it matter?

It was better to be with them than to be alone.

II

Yes, Ashley knew things that other people didn't.

Yesterday morning — or the day before yesterday (well, it was past midnight now: a new day?) — yesterday morning, then, Ashley had "killed" Flying Officer Luthie.

A fraction of a second's inattention on Luthie's part . . . But then Luthie was running running.

(Ashley had gone: "Takatakataka!"

And: "Christ!" Luthie had said, and then he was running running.)

Well, actually, Luthie had kicked the rudder even before Ashley was half finished with his "takatakataka": my God, nothing wrong with his reflexes, now was there! Wizard — stunning — smashing! Well, he did not go for a half-roll, for example (as Ashley would have done, for example) — he went for a controlled spin. Luthie: nowhere to be seen. Out of Ashley's reach. Well, completely! Ashley had lost him. But still too late: if it had been *real life,* he'd not have been running.

And Ashley shouted in senseless glee and went on screaming, "You are dead! You are dead! You are dead!"

What now? A victory roll! A *beautifully* executed victory roll! At last. . . . He was good! Good good good. "You are dead! You are dead!"

And for a long time, there was but static in his ears, over the R/T. Then Flying Officer Luthie . . . well, laughed. "Nothing personal, I hope, in that jubilation."

And so Ashley stopped screaming "You are dead! You are dead!"

Some twenty minutes later, they went home. And Luthie let himself down from his kite; took off his helmet; ran his hand through his hair; then he spoke to Corporal Lansing and Corporal Dunaway for perhaps a minute — or less; ran his hand through his hair again; rubbed the bridge of his nose; and he walked toward Ashley.

"Yes, I feel dead." And he sent one of those enormous-toothed Luthie grins out at Ashley. He held himself rigid. "Most thoroughly dead. . . ." He grinned again.

And: "Well done," he said. He actually said it!

Then he said, "Sergeant, if I were you, I'd give that victory roll a miss. If I had really been a Fritz . . . Well, for example: while you are engaged in celebrations, there is a Jerry version of Flight Lieutenant Acklington lining you up in his sights, more than eager to avenge my inglorious passing. Understood?"

And Ashley said, "Yes, sir."

But Luthie was peering into the middle distance.

(Why? Well, simply, because a NAAFI van was coming.)

"Ah! Here comes a NAAFI van. Jam tarts again today, do you think, Sergeant? Cut along, now. Queue up, have a cup of tea. A strawberry jam tart? . . . I'll be along later. And we'll do our postmortem."

(Postmortem! What a daft way of putting it!)

But Ashley said, "Yes, sir." And obediently, he ran to queue up for the NAAFI van.

(Well, once again: to look or not to look?)

And so it was some little while before he dared glance in Luthie's direction.

Flying Officer Luthie still stood in the grass, looking . . . *not* double-jointed. (And Ashley knew from previous observations that Luthie's legs were very double-jointed.) Now Luthie was holding himself straight and rigid. But then, suddenly, he went into a half-crouch, picked up . . . a pebble? Threw it. There it went, through the air! He followed its progress with his eyes — and Ashley followed the pebble with his eyes. And the grass closed over the pebble. End of pebble. Flying Officer Luthie lit a cigarette. But a few moments later he, too, joined the queue, and bought a strawberry jam tart: there were no others — no apricot, no black currant, no plum. And by and by he and Ashley had their postmortem.

(Well, *sir* . . . well, this is what it is all about, now isn't it? *Sir*.

Being able to kill one's . . . opponent. That's what you've been teaching us, haven't you? *Sir*.

And I've done it. Done it! I've done it, by God! So, there.)

. . .

(Ashley's brother was dead.

Ashley had at last learned to avenge his brother.

. . .

Flying Officer Luthie was not the kind of man who should lead *anybody* into combat: so Ashley thought.

But somehow, it had never before occurred to Ashley to think of Luthie as being mortal.)

Ashley had, at last, learned to avenge his brother.

Why, then, late at night, did he feel like blubbering . . . bawling?

(My God, he could not tell anybody about the things he knew!

No matter how hard he tried, there was no place for him.)

18

I

I'll kill that bastard McGregor! Squeeze the life out of him . . .

One of those reckless buggers — knows no fear: a one-man Charge of the Light Brigade . . .

Christ! I did not suspect anything. I'd no inkling, no . . . premonition!

Well, it began . . . Well, good old Colin K.: he always seems to be at my door, these days. And so — *no premonition!* — I said to Kenley: "Well, if it's about Newby's birthday, I'll be in later. Soon. Sorry. . . . Paperwork, you know." Well, a blinding headache, actually. (And a *heaviness of heart* sat on me like a winter coat. . . . More about that later?)

(Kenley: Cackle. Cackle.) That is how it began.

I'll kill the bastard McGregor!

(A compelling sort of face: the monster McGregor. Black hair: *black;* forget-me-not *blue* eyes. Those interesting eyebrows, joined over the root of his nose . . . A compelling face, no doubt about it.)

Kenley (important — imparting *mysterious* information): "Three little Wonders downstairs, in the hall. Next time tell them to use the tradesmen's entrance. But they look . . . *in terrorem,* you know. Scared shitless, you know. *In terrorem.* They do." (Well, God in heaven! Colin K. . . . he's *educated,* is he? *In terrorem.*)

Kenley (alarmed, now): "Luthie . . . Wait. God's blood! Put your shoes on. Comb your hair . . . Whatever. Wouldn't do at all . . . well, would it, now . . . for the *children* under your command to see you in disarray . . ."

"Kenley . . . What time is it?" (Yes, I had taken off my watch. The watchband does bother my wrist sometimes.)

"Twenty to midnight."

Christ! I rammed my feet into my flying boots; pounded down the stairs.

One of the Wonders has got hold of Ashley's infernal motorcycle; has crashed the hellish machine. (That was my first thought.)

One of the Wonders has been stricken with some horrible disease.

One of the Wonders has got hold of Ashley's thrice-cursed motorcycle, has taken it to town, knocked down . . . injured . . . killed! . . . someone. An elderly lady. Then fled the scene. Soon the constabulary will be here.

The Wonders have gone . . . stealing apples from a poor widow's orchard. The constabulary will be here. (Luthie . . . No apple orchards here!)

(The . . . beast McGregor. That supermeticulous speech of his! As if at one time he had set out to obliterate all traces of who he really was. Is.
. . .

Oh, let's not get melodramatic, Luthie!)
I'll kill him.

Well, I paused at the bottom of the stairs. In the hall: McGregor. Farrell. . . . Ashley. *In terrorem.*

(How does it go, in books? *Blood froze in my veins.*)

(Ashley . . . Squirrel teeth. The Nosy Parker. . . . He of the camera . . . The *journalist:* always looks as if inside that round head of his he is storing it all for posterity. But now he was just . . . nervous. Terrified? As the others, he was afraid.

Yes, it's something to do with the bloody motorcycle! Definitely!)

I said, "Well, let's go in, shall we?" (Into what used to be the drawing room. And upstairs, the party was really getting raucous. It had begun at eleven. Old Hurry-up, himself, was the host. God! The Wonders: wide-eyed; wild-eyed at the din.)

"Sit down. Out with it." And my poor head was pounding pounding. (Sinus headaches are an occupational disease of fighter pilots; but this wasn't like that at all.) I was so bloody tired! And a sadness sat on me. (More about that later?)

But I must cope. *Defend them.*

Cope. *Confront the problem.*

Cope. *Comfort them — yes, comfort them* (if that is what is needed).

(W. R. Luthie: ready for anything.)

(And Farrell . . . did that little *weasel* Farrell think he was invisible? That I couldn't hear him? White-faced, he tugged at McGregor's sleeve. "Let's blow . . ." Run. Run. "Let's blow." The smallest of whispers. *Let's get out*.) But McGregor: wild-eyed, he threw himself on the spear of the enemy. "Sir . . . We were studying our EA's tonight, sir. Prepping, sir . . ."

Oh, they were, were they?

. . .

(But . . . Well . . . The bad news?)

"I see." (W. R. Luthie: calm.)

(And upstairs: suddenly, there was a crash. And they jumped. I jumped.

Upstairs: laughter. Then another crash.

In hell's name, be quiet! Cease and desist!)

And McGregor looked as if a math exam at school were about to begin — or the gun to go off for an important race. But after the crash upstairs, he almost smirked. Smirked?! (And warning bells should have pealed inside my head! He was trying not to look nervous — or insolent. "We were prepping for tomorrow, sir. A . . . a spirited discussion, sir." And now he managed to make himself look deserving: well, in the way cats look deserving, lapping up their milk. He took a breath. "Sir, what will the weather be like tomorrow?"

What will the weather . . . ? "I . . . I . . ." And dear Jesus, I know I looked — not just sounded — stupid! (Well, it was midnight, after all. Late.) "I'm afraid . . ."

What . . . will . . . the weather . . . be . . . like . . . tomorrow . . . ?!

Oh, you bastard! How dare you   How dare you

This is a prank. A dare? A practical joke. A dare, to test me . . .

Oh, you . . . ! *They'd been prepping for tomorrow . . .* Ha!

Where do the wretches think they are? Well, at school, still?

What will the weather . . . ?

And it came to me then. Not in a flash. *Slowly. Very slowly.* Out of the fog in my brain it swam out — *most miserably slowly*. And I did not believe it at first; then I did. Well, I had told them — upon their arrival: so long ago! (how many days ago?) — "If there is a problem, or a question, come to see me. Anytime. Any question."

Anytime. Any question. Well, one of those things one says! (A matter of some importance: that is what's understood.) And then, of course, I'd forgotten all about it. You little . . . beasts!

. . .

What will Luthie do if we ask him a trivial, unimportant, silly question at midnight?

(And so they'd disguised it a bit — oh, so clumsily! — to give it the polish, a veneer — ha! cracked! — of legitimacy. *Such diligent people — prepping and all that! They are absolutely burning — dying — to know what the weather will be like tomorrow.* Ha!)

(God, I might have been asleep, for all they knew! Would they have requested that I should be awakened?)

How dare you! (But I can see through you. I, too, have been at school not so long ago, do you see? I know how it is.)

I'll . . . kill all of you!

They have done this childish . . . immature . . . and rather monstrous thing because they hold me in contempt.

And it hit me. *They feel contempt for me.*

Christ! What to do now?

I stood there. I'm afraid I brought my hands up to my face, for a moment; covered my face, for a moment. Fought back . . . tears? Bloody hell!

What to do now?   God   What shall I do now?

Bring them up on charges. For . . . disrespect to an officer.

(Oh dear God, no!)

A two-pound fine for each of them, to be taken out of their pay.

(Yes. Strike where it hurts.)

Confine them to base for the duration. Till we are sent south.

(Can I do that? For the duration. . . . Ah Luthie, Luthie!

And I felt most dreadfully sorry for myself.)

And McGregor: there still was in those blue eyes the fire of a madman capable of either great valor or great cruelty. How the bastard must have worked to steel himself for this . . . this act of silly childishness! But: had he done it precisely because he *is* cruel? Well, God in heaven!

Well, he must have known I'd come running! *In terrorem* (yes!), worried, at the least. Had he also guessed that I'd come running desperate to help them; ready to protect them; eager to offer . . . comfort?! He must have known! . . . Guessed. . . . Hoped.

And he had done this not only to make me appear foolish. He'd done it to hurt me.

. . .

Could they . . . did they now see my hurt? My fury? Oh you little . . . (And my head was aching.)

Well, W. R. Luthie: ready for anything.

(And stop that infernal noise upstairs, now will you?)

(And were the little monsters *exchanging glances? Smirking* at the din: the officers making idiots of themselves?)

I said — steady, now, steady — I said, calmly, "The weather? . . . If it should become relevant, you'll learn tomorrow. For details contact the Met. people. . . . It's a bit late now, though. Wait till the morning."

Steady, now. Steady. I said, very quietly — did not trust my voice; but still I said it with some force (I hope): "Sergeant McGregor . . . Sergeant Farrell . . . Sergeant Ashley . . . You have my *permission* to leave now."

And so they went. (A small push: Farrell will keel over, in his fright. The gutless villain! The miserable wretch!)

(But while McGregor's . . . performance was on, I'd forgotten about Farrell and Ashley: I'd been concentrating on McGregor.)

Ashley: he seemed most thoroughly . . . ashamed. Ashamed?! Of lending himself to this idiocy? The Nosy Parker! The . . . adolescent! Or was the shame not for himself but for McGregor, for thinking it up?

Christ God! Ashley: feeling compassion for me? Pity? Oh how dare you how dare you. Oh go away.

. . .

Stop *gazing* at me with those doglike eyes. Well, and so you "killed" me the other day.

Oh you . . . What do you think this is? A . . . game, of some sort? (Was I as they are now — naive — when I was that age?) Ah, Ashley, Ashley! *And now I live; and now my life is done.*

. . .

(God . . . do not let me die in terror. Do not let me die in pain.)

. . .

Ashley . . . you had better become accustomed to this.

McGregor said, "Thank you, sir." (Thank you for what?) But now there was no insolence about him. That brave child! There was a rather mad — insane — dignity about him. A one-man Charge of the Light Brigade. Ah, to squeeze the life out of him!

And so they went. What do I do now?

Upstairs, the party was most horribly raucous. A conga line snaking down the hall . . . (*Doing the Lambeth Walk* and all that. They were . . . singing, I suppose.) I'd left my cigarettes upstairs.

And I was all alone in what used to be the drawing room. Felt light-headed. Almost ill. I shivered. (A heaviness of spirit sitting on me.)

Why did they do it? Why? Why? *What do they want from me?* (And I keep asking myself: What do I want for them?) *What do they want from me?* (I'd never asked that before.)

Why the . . . contempt?

(And had they . . . well, drawn lots, for example, to determine who else would come with the beast McGregor?)

Why? Why hurt a man who has never done them any harm?

I've done my best. Acted responsibly. (I am fairly responsible, I think, for my age.) *Conscientious* is my middle name! I simply cannot do any better.

Now McGregor wants to be their leader — win their admiration — by causing me pain. The clever bugger. Cunning bastard. *Well, punish them, Luthie — punish them.* And so . . . they would have been punished. But in some way, I'd have lost face. Shown myself as . . . petty. Diminished myself. Lost my . . . dignity. That clever man!

Have I won this round of the bout? Was it a draw? Perhaps. I do not think so. But . . . what happens next? What do they want from me?

Well, there was nothing for it now but go and retrieve my cigarettes. (The party: most horribly raucous.) My head aching.

I said to myself: I'll go for a walk.

Written later:

Instead, I joined the party and got very very very very drunk.

Overslept this morning. Missed breakfast: no time for breakfast.

Took Brown upstairs at half past seven. Oh, I felt rotten! Every other second, it seemed, I grayed myself out.

Brown: nondescript. That's the best description.

No. No. Brown is brown, by God! Brown hair, brown eyes. A sharp little nose. Little pink ears set close to the head. He looks like a field mouse.

Oh, definitely! No doubt about it! A mouse in a children's story — the kind of story in which animals wear clothes and act like people.

Flight B. The bloody . . . Wonders. Sent for my sins from On High.

Well . . . whatever my sins: this is enough! Whoever you are — On High — take back the bastards! Now. At once. Hurry. Chop-chop.

I do not want them.

. . .

(Did I not say something similar before they arrived here?

Yes, I did. Didn't I? I did. But it seems to me that what I meant then was simply the idea: the abstract idea of lives depending on me.)

Well, I do not want these *particular lives*. I don't   I don't   I don't. Take back the bastards; I've had enough.

II

But life goes on.

III

Colin Kenley is dead.

IV

1) *Cackle. Cackle. Cackle.*

(Let us remember Colin Kenley.)

2) He organized Newby's birthday party. (They were friends, he and Newby, as Hanmer and I are friends, weren't they?)

(One should not have friends in wartime?)

(Old Hurry-up himself was the official host for the birthday party, though.)

3) Colin used to terrify the Fritzes.

Well, they've got inflatable life rafts, the Fritzes. And a Do-17 . . . or an He-111: one of those goes into the drink; the raft — *poof!* Like one of those puffball mushrooms. (We've only our Mae Wests to keep us from drowning; our skins to protect our insides from the numbing coldness of the water. The water: *very* cold. So I understand. . . . No inflatable life rafts for us. Well, that's how we live.)

And the Fritzes, in their little life rafts: waving. *Help us! Help us! Radio our position. Send a rescue boat.* And here comes our Colin! (Used to worry Hanmer a bit, I think. He is — well, he was — Kenley's flight commander.)

"Luthie . . . Misery . . ." (Hanmer: well, chuckling.) "His airscrew is practically whipping the water! And his guns: he's had them set for a murderously close range . . ." (Hanmer: chortling. Hanmer: *cackle cackle?*)

"The Fritzes screaming!" (But no one can hear them. One may catch a glimpse of their open mouths.) And the Fritzes fighting, among themselves: hide   run   escape   hide. (But there are no hiding places, of course.) *You on top; me on the bottom.* . . . And Colin is coming.

The beautiful, fine-tuned, 1,000-hp Merlin is coming.

And the eight nice Brownings, all sitting pretty in their gunports.

"Luthie . . . What a sight!" (Hanmer: laughing laughing.) "At the very last moment . . . up he goes. Up up up. And we can hear him . . ."

(But the Germans cannot: not possessing the proper equipment in their life rafts.)

Ta dum tada taa daa
Ta dum tada taa daa

It's the *Ride of the Valkyries.*

(It used to worry Hanmer a bit, I think.)

Colin is dead.

The Wonders need me.

About five minutes after Kenley's name was erased from the board (the Adj. Uncle Dixon did the honors), Old Hurry-up had emerged from his lair.

"Mr. . . . uh-huh . . . Dixon." But then: no more uh-huh's. "Please send a signal at once that a replacement is needed.

"Mr. . . . Luthie. Please stand ready to become operational as of eleven hundred hours. Until further . . . notice. I am confident that you will successfully rearrange Flight B's schedule." And he sounded confident — oh God, yes! — absolutely beamed at me in approval. "Mr. . . . Luthie, you have done a splendid job so far. Splendid." He looked dubious.

(Oh, how dare you!)

He turned . . . inward: peered *within* himself? (Did he then give me a glance full of vague distaste? Of anxiety? Distrust? Of *dis*approval?

. . .

(How dare you! How dare you!)

. . .

"Splendid."

"Thank you, sir."

"Carry on, Mr. Luthie. . . . Splendid." And he withdrew back into his lair, to safety: to the photographs of his children on the wall.

I rearranged the Wonders' schedule. (Took myself off the schedule.)

Those *creatures* need me. (Oh you hateful creatures!)

My kite being loaded with live ammo; armor-piercing; incendiary; tracer . . .

Wonders, be gone! *Shoo*. Go. You're being bothersome.

Stop pretending that you are *not* staring at me. Stop pretending that you are *not* following my every move.

Go and look . . . *baffled*. (Well, all day yesterday. *A.M.* — *After McGregor* — they looked baffled. Did not seem embarrassed. No. Not at all! Did not seem to suffer from guilt. The little monsters. By God, they do not feel guilty! Unlike Ashley, they are not shamefaced.)

Go and look *baffled Baff Baff* — a-a-a-a-rgh!

(Yesterday, all day, they seemed uncertain. But then, they always seem uncertain: how can one tell the difference?)

(From the very beginning they've seemed uncertain. I never paid much attention to it. Never tried to do anything about it.

Not much one can do about it, of course. Things are as they are.)

You . . . miseries. Stop pretending you are not *excited*. (*Danger excitement:* live ammo — armor-piercing; incendiary; tracer . . .) Stop pretending you are not *impressed*.

Stop pretending you are not scared out of your wits. You are. I know you are. *You had better become accustomed to this.*

Kenley is dead.

They need me. The Wonders: huddled together.

Well, go and huddle about the bastard McGregor.
(Where is he, anyway? Is he baffled? Smug?)
The Wonders: *together.* Huddled about Grenfeld and Stanhope, actually. Stanhope and Grenfeld: playing — pretending to be playing — chess. One of those portable, folding little chessboards. Stanhope and Grenfeld poring — pretending to be poring — over the chessboard. (And Cartwright and Farrell: out there somewhere, trying to shoot each other down.)

Kenley is dead. Killed quite early in the morning. Then, at a quarter to eleven: Flight A called upon to scramble again. Two of the three came back. Newby: overdue. Well, it never rains but it pours!

I sat with Flight A, of course, as we waited.
    "What's for lunch, I wonder." (Voices calm, measured.)
    "Roast beef? For a change. Leftovers from yesterday? Sandwiches?" (Voices calm, measured.)
    "Roast beef is no good without chutney on it."
    "Luthie . . . stop being such a bloody colonial! And *nautch* girls, huh? An elephant with a howdah. Wouldn't mind a *nautch* girl, myself."
    Newby: overdue.
    Voices: very calm. "Ah . . . A year of my life for strawberries and bubbly!"
    "Shut up, Thomas!"

Waiting for Roy Newby.
    I sat with Flight A.
    I belong with them. I do. Well, God in heaven, I do! I do   I do
    (Well, I was operational, of course: twenty-five minutes past 1100. That was another reason why I sat with them.)
    The Wonders: still huddled together? (Luthie . . . Do not let them see you watching them!) (But Cartwright and Farrell had come back.) Now they all were supposed to be studying their little mimeographed sheets on tactics. (Grenfeld, Stanhope: studying the chessboard.)
    Not my province. Do what you will, you little . . . children.
    Not my responsibility. I am operational. I do not want you.

Waiting for Roy Newby.

Newby: gliding in on the last drops of juice. *Brake, God damn it. Brake   Brake* (And the blood wagon was at the ready; fire engines and all that . . .) But he did brake at last; and he taxied up; cut the engine; slid the hood back; let himself down . . . See Roy Newby.
    See Newby running. Dropping sweat-soaked clothes as he runs. His Mae West . . . His leather flying jacket . . . His tunic . . . His roll-neck . . .

See Newby's roll-neck flapping like a flag in the breeze, as he tries to dry it. But then a sudden gust of wind lays a whip across Newby's bare flesh; and he scurries back for the comfort of the sweat-soaked roll-neck.

Nobody said anything. No one asked a single question.

(Well, when he is ready — if he is ready — he will tell us.)

(He must tell the IO all about it, anyway, at the debriefing.)

And by and by lunch came. Mutton. (Not roast beef.) And Brussels sprouts. The ubiquitous Brussels sprouts. The ubiquitous Brussels sprouts swam in the gray sea of congealed mutton fat like shriveled beach balls. The Royal Air Force fly on Brussels sprouts.

. . .

"Gentlemen . . . Luthie is drinking apple juice! Good for the family coffers . . . He's an apple baron, Luthie. Luthie is a war profiteer . . ."

"Shut up, Thomas. You're not making sense."

After lunch, one stretches out in the grass: the smell of petrol fumes and other people's boots. The wind barely skims over the body.

I was dropping off to sleep . . . Something hit me in the stomach: Newby! (Well, my stomach will do for a pillow.) After a while he said, "Luthie, your bloody hipbones are too bloody sharp. You're too thin, you know. It's uncomfortable."

"Well, try Geoff Thomas. He's got . . . padding."

(Roy Newby and our good Colin K. — dead — used to be friends. As Hanmer and I are. Hanmer did not mourn me, I'm sure: the time of Dunkirk.)

You miserable Wonders . . . You had better become accustomed to this.

And my people were presented with the dreaded Air Ministry telegram: the time of Dunkirk. "We regret to inform you . . . Missing presumed to have lost his life . . ." (Hanmer had reported *no parachute:* that was why the presumed-to-have-lost-his-life version. Ah, Hanmer, Hanmer! God damn you, Acklington! . . . Hanmer and I are friends.) "Inquiries will be made through the Red Cross as to his fate and/or possible where-abouts . . ." Those things take bloody months! "A letter will follow to confirm this telegram."

(Such were my thoughts as I lay there dropping off to sleep.)

Mr. Parrish: he brought in the telegram — on the same tray he uses to bring in the post. Then he retreated, but paused on the stairs — so I have heard. Would he be needed? He knew what was in the telegram! A man of some reticence: Mr. Parrish. *Do not intrude on their grief.* A stern man, a man of moral rectitude, Mr. Parrish — good God, yes! — he'd handed the telegram to my father, not to my mother. *A man must accept his burden; shield the woman.* And then Mr. Parrish began to weep for me — so Mrs. Simmonds has told me. He is a very old man.

And my father read the message in the telegram aloud, in a calm voice. He was standing — so I understand. And then he fell down: he had fainted.

And thus my mother, for a time, was deprived of grieving. Her son may be dead — but far away. Her husband lay — dead? — at her feet. She had to cope.

Well, I fell asleep now.

The afternoon dragged on. Grenfeld and Stanhope went out; and then Ashley and Brown and Farrell and McGregor, together — as I had instructed. And when not otherwise engaged, they all were supposed to be studying their EA pictures. It is important. Happens all the time: someone mistakes one of our own kites for a bandit and opens fire.

. . .

Well, do what you will, little Wonders. Not my responsibility. If a "flap" comes, I'll go out with little fat Geoff Thomas and a chap named Jennings, whom I do not know very well. (I'll be shot at, and I'll shoot back. . . . We protect the shipping.)

"Well, who is winning?" Shall I say it?
The bloody chess game. It dragged on and on; the afternoon dragged on.
"Grenfeld, sir."
Oh yes. In any game of *intellect,* I'd put my money on Grenfeld. (But I did not say anything. If I asked them, they'd probably say quite deliberately that Stanhope was winning.)
And thus the afternoon passed uneventfully. This is a quiet place.

Old Hurry-up Hammett, after dinner: "Mr. . . . uh-huh . . . Luthie. My . . . uh-huh . . . profound thanks. The replacement will be on the . . . uh-huh . . . train that arrives just before midnight. Swift. Efficient. I am . . . uh-huh . . . pleased." And he was chewing on his — unlit — pipe.

The Wonders need me.
The Wonders: huddled together. Huddled about . . . yes, that bastard McGregor. About the peppermint-cruncher Stanhope and about the *oh-so-quiet* (rather unnaturally quiet, most of the time?) Grenfeld.

. . .

Well, tomorrow is another day.
Ah, do what you will, you little . . .

Kenley: *Cackle. Cackle.* (Let us remember Colin Kenley.)
A blackness of spirit sitting on me. My heart heavy. (And so on and so on.)

•

Nim. N. M.

Nim. Love. Getting to know each other!

V

"I like orange marmalade."

"So do I! Chiver's." (Two days ago. Yes, it was two days ago: getting to know each other.)

So . . . carefree she came! (It overwhelmed me.)
. . .

Was she determinedly carefree? (But why should I question her change of mind from her erstwhile reluctance? I did not want to question.)
. . .

Getting to know each other:

Ninotchka. Well, it had been on at the little cinema in the village. "Have you gone to see it?"

"No. . . . Have you?"

"No."

"I hear now they've made a film of *Gone with the Wind.*" She said, "I've enjoyed the book. The picture won't be nearly so good, I'm sure."

Me — I've only heard about the book; have not read it: heard *a lot* — an exceeding amount of information — about it. "Actually," I said, "after one's been through the burning of Dunkirk," I said — a witticism(!?): whatever possessed me(?!) — "one can give the burning of Atlanta a miss."

No no no no no. It really is not like me at all to . . . well, draw attention to myself. (And to be so flippant. Something of a . . . curmudgeon?)
. . .

I do not want a woman to gentle my wounds.

I do not want a woman to be repelled by my wounds. (And yet I had put those miserable scars on exhibit for her.)
. . .

Serious gray eyes: Nim. (Oh, bloody hell!)

Never mind. She looked up at me, and we burst out laughing.

(There is a painting by . . . da Vinci, I think. A woman . . . well, a noblewoman, I presume — it being da Vinci: copper-colored hair, like Nim's. Looks so wonderfully self-contained, like Nim. But it is so absolutely obvious that there is a great deal of emotion underneath.

Nim?

My very own. My love.)

(Getting to know each other.)
. . .

("Well, have you read . . . ?"

"No. . . . Have *you read* . . . ?"

"Rather! . . . Not bad by half! Awfully good, actually, I thought.")

We came to a farmhouse, after a time. "Is this a *croft,* do you think?"
(A country foreign: we're having an adventure.)
We bought some milk for our tea. "What if it is sheep's milk?" (Giggle giggle giggle.)
"No, it's cow's milk." A nice, cream-colored layer of cream on top. Serendipity! I had an extra metal mess-kit cup, to put the milk in. (W. R. Luthie: ready for anything.)
"Now we must carry it like this till teatime. It'll spill."
"Give here."
"Did you *understand* that farmer's wife?"
"The *crofter's* wife. . . . *Och, nae.*"
(This is a foreign country; we are explorers.)

Teatime. And she looked *regal* presiding over the tea-things.
And we went: Prattle prattle prattle . . . The weather . . . This and that. . . . My potted meat sandwiches — the verdict: *excellent.* . . . The general shape of the landscape. . . . This and that. Music. Et cetera. . . . Bach. . . . Oh.
But Bach is so . . . so . . . bloody bloodless! . . . Well, I think I even *look* like someone who likes the Romantics!
And she took one of those — Cadbury's — milk chocolate bars with dried fruits and nuts from me; unwrapped it, with *precise* fingers; broke it in two halves — never had I seen it done with such *precision!*
"It is *precise* music, of course," I said. "Bach. It is."
(And: crunch crunch went the dried fruits and nuts between our teeth. Like miniature explosions. We burst out laughing.)

She is a very *precise* person.
(But, some time before, as we'd tramped together over hill and dale in search of our perfect picnic spot, I had watched her for a time: she had walked ahead of me — not much leg showing; sensible walking shoes; ugly wartime stockings.
A precise person. And so the seam on the left stocking was straight as an arrow. But on the right one it was a bit . . . askew. Well, God in heaven!
Now there's music for you! Bach? Ha! God, the tenderness I felt for her because of that tiny imperfection! Well, inside me: it was . . . well, like the very last bit of the last movement of the Dvořák cello concerto — absolutely! The cello alone, you know . . . sweet; bittersweet . . . God, yes. But I didn't think of it that way at the time: I only was breathless with tenderness for her.)
(Getting to know each other.
"Two lumps of sugar in your tea?" And so on and so on.)

And I told her about myself and mine . . . all the way down to Emmeline. The Fourth. "A cat of an inelegant tail."

Ah, that woman's smile! Her laugh! (Well, more about music?) She must have a beautiful singing voice.

But she did not say anything.

I told her about myself. I said: "When I was very small, there were lizards on the walls of my room — now and then. Ayah sent me to bed for my nap, but instead I watched them. *They* were like Cadbury's milk chocolate with dried fruits and nuts. Nice and brown."

"Oh, you were born in the East, then? . . . Lizards! I should have liked that." And she clapped her hands, childlike. . . . Oh, she was carefree!

(A woman who has not felt carefree in a very long time?)
· · ·

My love. Love. . . . Serious gray eyes. . . . You are so very lovely.

After tea we lay on the blanket, in the grass: it's an old man's sky, overhead — it seems *experienced*, as if it has seen everything. We fell silent. And I . . . well, I ached, of course, with my need for her; but, at the same time, I knew a quite wonderful tranquility.

After a while, she suddenly fell asleep. Trusting.

(Beautiful eyebrows.)

And so, after a while, I rolled off my part of the blanket; wrapped her in the warmth my body had left (she stirred; mumbled something; but did not wake up); and then faithfully I guarded her sleep.
· · ·

Now touch the eyebrows. *Now* trace them with your fingers. (Well, after all, I had already hugged her: held her in my arms, so to speak! And also, we had come here holding hands!) But she was asleep, and she was trusting; and so I did not touch her at all. (I only imagined that she was quite naked underneath that blanket.) And I touched — I stroked with one finger — that silly little tassel on her hat. . . . She had taken off the hat; it lay in the grass.
· · ·

But then at last that vast sky, the cool grass, and her quiet breathing — her hair scented with chamomile . . . (God, I do get tired: those miserable Wonders! But this was Before McGregor, of course: B.M.) Anyway I, too, fell asleep. And when I woke up, she was watching *me*.

I felt chilled (wind blowing and all that), and I think I looked not a little bedraggled, and I was embarrassed.

She said, "You needed to rest." A no-nonsense, practical woman.

"You always look preoccupied," she said. (So, she had noticed me before! Had she been watching me all along? . . . Ah, the woman who eats her dinner *neatly;* quietly and calmly avoiding men's eyes!)

She said, "You looked peaceful in your sleep." Now what a nice thing
to say!

(And she *had* seen the scars, of course. . . . Calm gray eyes on me.)

So, I blurted out, "Oh, you are so absolutely lovely!"

Was she ready to be kissed now?

. . .

There she was, a stillness about her.

. . .

No. No. Not yet.

Dare I ask for a parting kiss at the end of the afternoon?

. . .

Love   Love   Please. There is not much time.

As the sun hung low on the horizon, we walked back, subdued; it was on
my mind that she had said she would come only once.

We both were quiet. "Tired?" I said.

"A bit." Well, we had done a good deal of walking!

"I'll carry you." A Luthie grin. We laughed.

"Don't be silly." We laughed.

The air was honey-scented: heather-scented; clear. We met a man on
a bicycle: only the third . . . fourth . . . human being we'd seen all afternoon, save for the farmer and his wife from whom we'd bought the milk.

. . .

N. M. Tunnard-Jones . . . You'll like me. I am a silly, gentle creature.

. . .

You'll like me. I am a virile man; and woman-starved.

And after the bicycle rider disappeared in the distance, I stopped; and
she stopped; and she looked up at me, and I kissed her. (Did not ask her
permission.)

She is so small; and seemed so . . . far away. And thus it was a kiss . . .
oh, quite akin to . . . well, to a hand (for example) trying to touch — not
capture! — a butterfly (for example).

And she was very, very silent. But she let herself be kissed.

Well, it was then I at last took her face in my hands and traced her
eyebrows. Her eyelids. Her nose. Mouth.

. . .

(How can I ever touch a woman with the hands that grow out of those
scars? . . . Oh, easily! Luthie, you are healed!)

. . .

I kissed her again. A very small breath caught in her throat.

Yes, that's better. Better.

. . .

Oh, you'll like me!

I am a good man.

· · ·

And she relaxed. God, I could feel it! A . . . a tenseness of some sort leaving her; and suddenly, she folded herself against me — but her face hidden from me, against my shoulder; and there she was: small. It was as if she were shutting out the world. Seeking . . . peace? With me? From fire and brimstone and pestilence and all evils amen?

· · ·

Oh my love   Love   I'll protect you.
No, I cannot protect you. . . . I'll cherish you.

· · ·

And this time she responded to my kiss. Well, God in heaven!
God Christ, what a woman!
Oh, N. M. Tunnard-Jones   Nim   My love   I am grateful.

· · ·

You'll like me.
I'm not good-looking.
I *am* a good man.
You'll like me. . . . Oh, you do like me, don't you?

· · ·

I love you. I'm in love with you. You are lovely.
Nim   *You woman of character   You woman of beautiful eyebrows*
You are lovely   (And so on and so on.)
And so we stood there, in the middle of the road, and for some time we were quite lost to the world. (And so on and so on.)

Then it was almost eight o'clock, and I was alone again; and I barely had time to change into my uniform: the Wonders were waiting, shuffling their feet impatiently when I walked into the "lecture room" (late).

They stared at me: *glances* and all that; acted oddly.

This was Before McGregor, of course: B.M. Were they even then planning their little caper? (But at the time I had merely thought: do they — can they, somehow — *see* her kisses?) And I managed to get through the session, looking composed — just barely.

Flight B office afterward: to work, Luthie . . . more work.

And so it was quite late when finally I made my way to the house and up to my room; but still I could taste her lips on mine (or so I thought).

Must I brush my teeth? (Luthie . . . You idiot.)

· · ·

Switch on the light . . . I took a step back.

"Acklington — *what are you doing here?*"

Hanmer: in my bed; on my bed. (No blanket: the blanket still in the haversack which I had dropped by the door.) Hanmer, curled up: asleep. His asinine tie on. Shoes: *on my sheets.* Bloody hell!

"Acklington . . ." (And quite distinctly I remembered locking that door; but nothing stops him, of course.)

(Hanmer . . . ah, Hanmer! I remember trying to sketch Hanmer — the time of Dunkirk! — the Adj. trying to wake him. Hanmer looked then like an affronted child, not wanting to give up his slumber.) Hanmer, now: from a deep sleep to full wakefulness in . . . five seconds? He smiled — a beatific smile. "Did the widow show you a good time?"

And some time passed then.

I said, "What are you talking about?" Cautiously. And time seemed to stretch.

Hanmer: "Luthie . . . Misery . . . I lost a full guinea! I'd bet she'd stand you up. . . . Well, others had tried before you, you know — before you came here. . . . There is not much choice here. . . . She refused all. *She was mourning.* . . . Tomorrow, Geoff Thomas is a rich man: wins it all. An astute judge of the human soul . . . and body . . . is our Geoff Thomas. The *tidy* bastard."

"Acklington . . ." *I'll strangle you.*

But I said, stupidly, "I looked at her hands . . . No wedding ring . . ."

Hanmer: a shrug. . . . *Acklington, I'll . . . I'll . . .*

(Well, I had wormed her age out of Uncle Dixon. I had asked him what the N.M. stood for. I had not asked . . .)

Hanmer: he shook his head, sadly. "And so she'll go for the arty type, every time."

"But I'm not —" (A voice reasonable, in a crazy sort of way.)

"Ah, Luthie . . . All that drawing . . . scribbling . . ."

"I'm not —"(Voice rising.) *I simply know how to use words. (???)*

Hanmer said, "She was some sort of plink-plink . . . studied to be a music teacher of some sort . . . piano? singing? . . . before the war, you know. Her dear departed was a budding sculptor, you know. Lately of the RAF, of course. A training accident: pranged a Maggy — would you credit it?" A Miles Master, a beginner's trainer. "Took his instructor with him." Couldn't have been a very good instructor: serves him right. "But there goes the sculptor. Happened seven months ago or so."

Hanmer knew all this! The bastard knew.

. . .

"Well, you could have asked Uncle Dixon. He'd have told you."

. . .

Everybody knew! But quite deliberately, they did not tell me.

They were placing bets on me!

I said, very, very quietly (I seem to remember), "Acklington, I thought we were friends." (What a bloody maudlin thing to say!)

Hanmer: his shark's teeth, in a smile *angelic.* (Well, a smile good-natured, and all that.) "I lost the damned guinea, didn't I? You woke the

Ice Matron. Had a good time doing it, I hope. Congratulations. *Is* she red between her legs, by the way?"
    . . .
Hanmer, I'll kill you.
    . . .
    But with that, the shock(?) of it . . . the numbness . . . suddenly, it was gone. "Acklington . . . *Why did you tell me now?*"
    And I took a deep breath. *"Out!"* I roared.
    Then, with some dignity, I said, "Hanmer, please leave. Or I'll throw you out."
    Hanmer looked two-thirds amused; one-third offended. He went.

She never told me.
    (A . . . a *deep secret*. God God God God God.
    That was why she would not talk about herself.)
    . . .
    So wonderfully carefree she came running! Toward me.
    Not toward me. Toward a dead man?
    . . .
She'll only come once. Ha!
    Did she use me?
    So carefree she came! (Had refused all others.)
    Did she use me because I seemed *safe* to her? *Innocent?*
    A . . . a substitute. But *safe. Innocent.*
    And so she let me provide the touch of a man's hand. A man's voice whispering endearments. A moment's comfort. A moment's *safe* solace.
    Never told me. . . . Ah, the woman who comes to a man in his dreams! Serious gray eyes. Beautiful eyebrows.
    She knew I'd not make demands.
    If she cared about me, if she cared for me, she'd have told me. She would have been open — sincere — with me. Truthful. Trusting.
    . . .
    Was she comparing me to him?

(God, it's only been seven months! Of course she is mourning.)

She'll only come once.

Her name is Nimuë. What a bloody awful name for parents to visit upon an unsuspecting child! *Nimuë Tunnard-Jones.* Oh heaven and hell, every piece of paper she signs, that signature reads N. M. Tunnard-Jones! (Is Tunnard-Jones her married name?)
    I've no idea what the *M.* stands for. I asked, "What may I call you?"
    "Nim."

Love.

. . .

Nimuë. The downfall of Merlin the Magician.
Nimuë. . . . The downfall of all men?
(Bloody hell! Luthie, you idiot.)

. . .

She is not beautiful. She is lovely.

This happened . . . the day before yesterday? (Before McGregor: B.M.)
I have not seen her since.

Have hoped to see her by chance. At breakfast? Dinner? She has not
been at breakfast or dinner at the same time I have.

This was two days ago. Only now I can bring myself to write it down.
My heart . . . well . . . yes . . . heavy.

19

Ashley was in town with Grenfeld, buying shortbread biscuits at Campbell's Provisions.

ACW Mary Ann and her honey buns . . . (Well, all of a sudden the
thought had popped into his head: ACW Mary Ann had bought the honey
for her dreadful — and dreaded — honey buns at Campbell's.)

Ashley had never gone back for more dreaded buns.

Well, there was still time. She'd be nicer to him — by far! — than
that old witch Mrs. Campbell, for example.

(And how nice it would be to be treated nicely! To tell the truth, Ashley was sick — fed up — deathly tired of feeling vaguely out of sorts and
of being unsure . . . groping, groping for he knew not what. To tell the
truth, he was in bad need of something to make him feel . . . comfortable.)

(But this was a small town, of *small* people; and they seemed to have
but little liking for the strangers whom the war had dropped in their
midst.)

"No. I said five *large* tins. *Five. Large tins. I said,*" Ashley said to Mrs.
Campbell in a voice — in a manner — that he was quite sure his mother
(for example) would find unacceptable.

Mrs. Campbell looked glum. Climbed on her stepstool; reached . . .
reached . . . very high . . . with a great deal of effort, grunting. Her arms
were quite short. And she was fat. (And old.)

(Well, here the tins came: all five of them! Take evasive action . . .
They crash-landed on the counter, all five of them: wizard prang! Mrs.
Campbell glared at Ashley: disapproving.)

Grenfeld had bought six large tins of biscuits.

Ashley thought (his arm full): *How are we going to open the door?*

•

And the door opened. (The bell overhead tinkled.)

A girl had opened the door. (And the bell stopped tinkling.)

Ashley . . . well, panic seized him. He had never felt so frantic in all his life. I'll drop the lot, he thought. I'll make an ass of myself. I'll drop it. (And some time passed then.)

She was holding the door open for Ashley! (And for Grenfeld.)

She had reddish hair. A bit like the section officer from Signals. But she was prettier — well, wasn't she? wasn't she? — than the section officer from Signals. Wasn't she? She was about Ashley's age. (Not *old* like ACW Mary Ann, for example.)

She held the door open for Ashley! (And for Grenfeld.)

Ashley clutched at his five tins of shortbread biscuits; felt them slipping . . . Tried to balance them. In despair.

And she smiled at Ashley. It was a nice smile. Not too shy; but it was not forward. Not brazen — not anything like that.

And Ashley sailed through the door, with his burden of shortbread biscuits: a miracle of miracles! How did it happen? Was it at all possible? Well, he was through the door; and that burden of biscuits suddenly no longer was a burden! (Grenfeld followed.)

"Thank you," said Ashley to the girl. "Oh, thanks awfully. Very kind."

She said something, too. But the door had shut behind her, and he could not hear what it was. ("Do not mention it."(?) "Not at all."(?) Something like that?)

Ashley stood outside the shop. Stared at her through the glass. Her hair was *this* long, and her ankles were *this* little. She glanced over her shoulder — very, very briefly; smiled again — very, very briefly. She smiled at Ashley. (And the world — suddenly — seemed a *somewhat* better place.)

Grenfeld said, "Let's go."

And so Ashley turned to Grenfeld, in triumph: well, Grenfeld was the one who was as good-looking as a film star!

But she had smiled at Ashley!

(Grenfeld seemed uncomfortable. Not jealous, really. . . . Sad?)

Cartwright came pedaling down the street on one of those bicycles from the base that seemed to belong to everyone and no one. Pedaling, pedaling with all his might.

He braked hard; very nearly fell off. "Here you are!" he cried. "Luthie sent me." He was out of breath. "All leaves canceled. . . . A signal came we're being made operational. . . . Everybody return to base. Start packing. . . . We're moving south." He still was out of breath. "D'you know where Brown is?"

Ashley said, "Haven't the foggiest."

Then Ashley just stood there. A new beginning.

Another new beginning. A new life.

Well, this was what *true* panic felt like: he'd never see the girl again! He turned to Grenfeld. Grenfeld seemed . . . happy. Eager.

20

I

I travel light.

II

How my father came to give me the knife — the time of Dunkirk:
  (No. Not enough time. It's a long story.)
  (Actually, not much packing, though. I travel light: well, in the literal sense of the word!)

Why did I go to war? Why did I *volunteer* to go to war?

The Wonders are *still* woefully undertrained.
  A tally:
  Stanhope. Probably the most talented of the lot. (Not the best; but it comes easily to him.) After that so inauspicious beginning has continued to improve steadily and speedily, our peppermint-cruncher.
  Grenfeld. Very little feel for flying. Strives to prevail through sheer tenacity. A terribly hard worker. Hasn't done him much good so far, though.
  Cartwright. So-so.
  Ashley. So-so.
  Brown. A disaster.
  Ah, Luthie Luthie

About Amritsar: my mother was about four months pregnant when Amritsar happened.
  (Nighttime thoughts.)
  (But I'll never finish, at this rate: clearing my desk, packing . . .
  I must not forget my little wireless set, in the Flight B office. I should tidy up a bit, in the office. Time permitting. I must not permit my thoughts to wander. Keep mind on task at hand.)

Dear Janet:

My dear Janet:

(Right! A draft. Well, several drafts, many drafts, of my letter to Janet. . . . Take aim at the wastepaper basket . . .)

My people say she's still very ill. They say she seems to *refuse* to get better.

And so I sit here; I try to summon up anger.

(When the war broke out, I joined the RAF.)

(Anger against those who did this to Janet?)

Fury? No no no no no. Blood lust? Oh no no no no.

I sit; I summon up anger. (No. Back to packing.)

My father gave me the knife at the railway station at Manchester.

III

How Hanmer and I became friends (Part I):

A human being burning to death sounds like . . . like hot oil in a pan sizzling? . . . Meat roasting? . . . Bacon frying? Yes, exactly like bacon frying! This is true. True! I swear it's true!

(Sunday: and Mrs. Simmonds in her starched white apron . . . Bacon frying.)

I never harmed that German. I never so much as touched a hair on his head. Absolutely not! Hanmer takes the honors for that one. (The time of Dunkirk, of course.)

And the German had his R/T on Send all the way down, so that we could hear it. Well, it does happen — not often, not rarely — the frequencies coincide . . .

At first he screamed for help: in German, of course. Then he just screamed. And then he stopped screaming: he no longer knew what was happening, I suppose. And the flames must have reached his face.

Ghost Story, Part II?

No, this one stands all alone, actually. It isn't part of anything. (It is a story about how Hanmer and I became friends: Part I.)

(Sunday morning: breakfast cooking, tiny globules of fat playing jumping jacks . . . spattering the stove. They'll be wiped away, scoured away later.)

(Our good old Colin K. — when he was still among the living — used to terrify the Fritzes. I think it worried Hanmer a bit.)

The Wonders are undertrained.

IV

The night before I went over Dunkirk for the very first time: I sat down, wrote letters to my people — one to each. I knew that the following morning I'd travel by train to a base in the Midlands, pick up a Spitfire for myself, fly her to Kent. And then I'd be sent over Dunkirk.

And when I arrived at my Kentish destination, I gave the letters to good old Uncle Dixon: "If you wouldn't mind . . . A silly thing, really . . . Much obliged . . ." God: miserably shy! (After all, I did not know Uncle Dixon at all then.) The letters: *To Be Delivered in the Event of My Death.*

(It is not unusual in the least, though, actually. Many people do it. Leave letters, I mean.)

Then, after Dunkirk, when I was at one of those RAF convalescent places — oh, a posh place! Very posh — Uncle Dixon returned them. (Suggested, almost in passing, that things may now be rather different for me and my family both, and thus the next time I might want to write something different.)

I've kept the letters. What do I do with them now? (Finish your packing, Luthie.)

What do I do with the letters?

To Be Delivered in the Event of My Death:
Dear N. M. Tunnard-Jones,
Thank you for saying that I looked peaceful in my sleep.

Well, take your cigarette lighter to that one, Luthie! Oh, absolutely.

And now I live; and now my life is done.
(Chidiock Tichborne. Was he about my age — or a bit older? Wrote this — it's a part of poem, a refrain, repeats itself over and over — he wrote it while awaiting death, in the Tower. After a failed plot to free Mary Queen of Scots.)

Why did *I* go to war of my own will? (And so on and so on. . . . Ah, you pompous, posturing fool, Luthie.)

I do not travel light.

Corporal Rossiter — one of the armorers, the one who bought four potted plants from the plant-selling children — Corporal Rossiter is driving my car, my dogshit Austin.

One sizeable suitcase will go in the car; one sturdy box. (And the potted plant, of course: my potted plant — so far it has survived.) The box — the wireless set is in it, among other things — the box is *quite heavy.* I most definitely do not travel light.

I am taking my whole life with me.

(Pompous ass, Luthie.)

But yes, I *have* kept my . . . yes . . . sense of . . . proportion? (My sense of humor?! Yes!)

I am myself.

The Wonders are undertrained.

BOOK II

INTERLUDE

21

And so Ashley had to make arrangements for his motorcycle in a hurry.

God damn it all! He should have thought of it earlier. Not enough time, now. No time at all. He should be packing.

The various kiwis:

"Sorry, Sergeant. It's the squadron leader's Jag I am driving."

". . . Flight Lieutenant Acklington's MG."

"Och, lad. Must stay wi' the lorries, ye know."

Would Corporal Dunaway *condescend* to do it? (The one who always fawned on Luthie. On all the officers.) How did it happen he was not *reserved*, too? (Because, well, nobody liked him?) Would he treat the Husqvarna in the manner it deserved to be treated?

But at last the matter was settled; and excitement took over.

"Grenfeld . . . Jeremy . . . Are you packing the big warm roll-neck to take with you?" — in the aftercockpit of the Spit: the rest of their kit would follow later.

"It's hot down south. In Kent. Swimming weather."

"Swimming . . . Do you like fishing, Stanhope?"

"And it'll be a big place, gentlemen. Not like here. A big place. Real pubs in the evening, gentlemen . . . And real popsies in real summer dresses . . ."

Nobody could sleep.

"It takes five kills!" — to become an ace.

"Five *confirmed* kills."

"But some of the blokes from Intelligence . . . one can rake up kills with them the way a gardener rakes up leaves in autumn. . . . Well, I know a chap knows a chap was in France from the beginning. And he

says . . . some of the IOs: they can't tell the airscrew from the tail. Former schoolmasters and all, you know."

They all laughed at that. Schoolmasters!

But . . . their IO? Well, Ashley thought about it; and it seemed to him
that even after all this time they knew but little about their own IO.

Everybody kept trotting to the bog. (Ashley's stomach churned.)

But they all seemed terribly, dreadfully hungry. As far as Ashley had
been able to observe, though, they all had eaten their fill at dinner.

"Ashley, give here." Ashley's shortbread biscuits. Then they devoured Grenfeld's biscuits, too. And Cartwright's mother had sent him
a cake not long ago, and so they ate that, too, though they all agreed —
including Cartwright — that is wasn't very good, really.

"Swimming weather . . ."

"Five kills . . ."

At last McGregor said, in his resolute voice, "We *must* go to sleep now."

But when Ashley at last fell asleep, he dreamt . . . that his camera was
missing. And so, in his dream, he raced through — empty — rooms and
in a frantic haste peered under beds and opened desk drawers; and all
those rooms — empty of people! — were supposed to be known: familiar
to him; but as it often is in dreams they both were and they weren't.

Where was the sodding camera? Had somebody stolen it? Well,
Luthie had it! He had borrowed it to . . . to take a picture of the section
officer from Signals, of course! He had . . . everything of Ashley's. . . .
No, it was not true. It could not be true. It was a dream. (And tomorrow
Luthie would lead them into combat.) It was a dream. It all was thor-
oughly confusing.

Then he dreamt that he was on his motorcycle and it was night, and
he was on his way. He could feel the wind against his face, and he was
happy — felt triumphant, really — because the girl he had met at Campbell's was prettier by far than the section officer from Signals. Wasn't
she? Wasn't she? He'd stop by Campbell's and see her again. But suddenly he realized that he was past Campbell's without having really
passed the shop; and it was night and he was on his way.

The worry about the motorcycle was still with him: now Corporal
Dunaway . . . he wouldn't . . . well, *prang* it or anything, now would he?
But by and by it occurred to Ashley, in his dream, that his motorcycle —
his brother's motorcycle! — was a bit of a nuisance, really. And he felt
guilty, and woke up.

His stomach churned, and he got up to go to the bog.

Then he lay in his bed, waiting waiting waiting for the morning: he
very much wanted to be on his way. But then, after a while, he really did
not want to go anywhere.

It all was most *thoroughly* confusing.

22

I

20th Aug 1940

My Dear People:

(Written in the wee hours of the morning, after I was at last finished packing: to be posted . . . whenever.)

My Dear People:
   Father being called "Guv"! Imagine! What fun! (Rec'd yrs. about <u>addition to household!</u> yesterday p.m.: it's the wee hours of the morning now; read yr. letter rather on the run. I am hereby notifying you: we are moving south.)
   Yes, I <u>am</u> glad — very glad — you have taken in the children. Five of them! <u>Cor!</u> Quite right: E. London no place for children these days. (The rest of the city: spared so far? So I hear. We've held them off? — good show!)
   The presence of the <u>evacuees</u> — bloody hell!: (sorry): the children: how is Mrs. Simmonds managing? Mr. Parrish? Janet?!!! Advise.
   Of course, they — the children — may help themselves to any and all things of mine left from the olden days: books and suchlike. Of course, I was quite a bit older than they when I first arrived in England: my books may not be right for them. ("Of course" twice close together, I see. Sorry. Not much of a stylist these days, I'm afraid.)
   There <u>are</u> two large boxes of very, very old toys up in the attic, by the way. I still remember from the days when I played God in the attic, after Grandfather died. Ah, Martin the Moth-eaten Moose! (though not a toy, strictly speaking): old Martin would make a splendid . . . well, not a rocking horse, but a steed of some sort to carry a child to faraway lands. But you probably have no idea I once named that stuffed beast in the attic Martin. (This was long before your time, of course: before you came Home.) It is possible you have no idea that there is a <u>real</u> <u>genuine moose: stuffed,</u> up in the attic. Somebody in the family — who? — must have brought him — when? — from . . . Canada? There are quite a few things, I suppose, we've never told each other. Perhaps one day we'll sit down and tell stories to each other.
   I love you.
   If you do not hear otherwise, assume the best.
   Take care of yourselves.

(Rewrite the letter: leave out the "I love you"? No.)

Yours,

Will this do in lieu of a letter *In the Event of My Death?* Probably not.

II

(And, for the sake of *neatness* —
· · ·

This actually was written not long after Tom's death and Janet's miscarriage — along with some of the other stories about my childhood and arrival in England — on scraps of paper separate from my note-book; lost in the Flight B office under the piles of . . . work and rediscov-ered as I was packing. For the sake of . . . well, *tidiness,* then, I suppose: of *not leaving anything of myself behind . . .*)

How I became accustomed to living in England:
When I was sixteen, my grandfather died. I was called home from school, of course. The railway station in the village has not got a covered platform. It rained.
Rain   Rain   It rained! I splashed through night-dark puddles (*squish squish* the water in my shoes); my beautiful — ah! *a-quiet-man-of-the-world* elegant; leather — overnight case *slap slap* against my leg. . . . That overnight case had been my grandparents' birthday present to me the previous September.
"Mr. Mannington . . . Mr. Mannington . . ." Mr. Mannington the stationmaster. "Would you please ring and tell Mr. Parrish I am here?" (I had not been certain by which train I might be arriving, and so the arrangement was that I should telephone from the station.)

About Mr. Mannington:
When I was twelve years old — not quite thirteen — well, the very next day after my arrival in England: my grandfather had given me a bi-cycle, a nice brand-new Raleigh, black and shiny. For the rest of that spring and the whole summer, my bicycle and I were inseparable.
J. R. ODELL
BOOKSELLER STATIONER
· · ·
Yes. Yes. I'll return to Mr. Mannington.
· · ·
Well, time presses on me, of course.
· · ·
Well, I'll not let it press on me, by God!
· · ·
Never mind.
BOOKSELLER STATIONER
Miss Odell. Miss Josephine Odell.
(And instead of a bell tinkling overhead — when one opened the door of the shop — *Collie Cibber* gave two short barks: never one, never three.
· · ·

"Hullo, Collie. . . . How are you, Collie?"

And *thump thump* went Collie's tail against the floor. . . . Collie Cibber was a very old dog.

. . .

Inside the shop it smelled of . . . well, books, of course!; and . . . and of dried flower petals: Miss Odell kept little bowls of dried flower petals everywhere; and of wood, polished.)

"Miss Odell . . . Miss Odell . . . Have you got any new John Buchan?"

In John Buchan's books, people said things such as . . . well, about the trenches — the Great War, the First War: "Oh, I thrive on it, sir. Sleep like a top, sir." I could not understand it, and it rather filled me with wonder.

Miss Odell did not think much of my fascination with John Buchan.

And I did outgrow those books, by and by.

One would rather expect that Miss Odell herself would look a bit like a dried flower petal — whatever in the world do I mean?: prim blouses, sensible shoes, and a fragile teacup in the afternoon? But Miss Odell wore . . . *shawls.* Black. With long, black, silky fringes. And, oh yes, there were flowers on the shawls: enormous *red* . . . peonies? — whatever; bright bright green leaves — a green that almost hurt one's eyes: garish; and yellow flowers of some sort . . . Those shawls were unlike anything anybody else in the village wore. *Eccentric,* my grandmother called them, in a voice usually reserved for Mr. Willson the wearer of gloves at Christmastime: "Hark the Herald Angels Sing," etc., etc. (My grandmother, like tea with warm milk: was there a wistful kind of excitement in that voice whenever she said the word *eccentric?*) Well, for myself: I was accustomed to color. But those shawls were unlike anything *I* had ever seen! "My *Hungarian Gypsy* shawls," Miss Odell said.

Hungarian Gypsy! Well, God in heaven!

. . .

She liked to listen to Sibelius on the wireless, and Mahler. (It was from her I first heard the names.)

I used to climb a small hill on the way between the house and the village. (Left the bicycle leaning against a tree by the road.)

From the top of the hill: now *there* was green! Green as far as the eye could see.

(The gray stone belfry of St. Crispin's in the middle distance.)

Well, green . . . green . . .

A *sharp* green? It hurt one's eyes, by God! An irritating green. A garish green? *Bloody* green! ("Bloody" was a most terrible word to me then.) Bloody bloody bloody bloody green!

Well, Simla, for example, had been green, too. Grass . . . trees . . . oh yes. Yes. Definitely! (And in the morning, fog wandered through those

trees, sometimes . . .) But . . . a *different* green: at Simla, for example?!
Oh, *absolutely! Absolutely!*

. . .

I was homesick.

I stood there, on top of the hill, feeling homesick.

. . .

And I spread my arms then and launched myself down the hill. Run
Run   Never stop . . . Feel the ribbons of wind between the fingers . . .

I ran toward . . . something. Not loneliness within me, really, but
aloneness and a . . . well, yearning . . . (Well, I do it still — sometimes —
whenever I am home.

And I am a man grown and have killed people.)

About Mr. Mannington:

I was twelve years old — not quite thirteen; I bicycled to the station.
Sat on the bench and waited for trains.

I was . . . homesick? Well, everything was so very new: England.
Walk down High Street — pedal down High Street — listen to the
voices, to all the sounds: well, the *music* of the place was so very very different! And so the trains would come and then be gone again. I sat on the
bench. Watched sparrows quarreling. Watched Mr. Mannington putter-
ing about: potting and repotting his geraniums.

Then a train did arrive. And Mr. Mannington . . . ah, Mr. Mannington! Well, God in heaven . . . Mr. Mannington!

(His mustache almost rivaled my grandfather's. But his ears, of
course, were not *commanding* ears.)

Well well, Mr. Mannington! Mr. Mannington became somebody entirely different when a train arrived! Well, it was as if he were ushering in
a duchess who had come to tea!

I watched. I was not homesick.

And after the duchess had departed, huffing and puffing, Mr. Mannington gave me a wink.

He'd invite me to step into his *inner sanctum* now and then. The kettle
was always on in his *inner sanctum*. His teacups had pictures of . . . dragoons on them. . . . Hussars? They were dragoons. (There is a difference, I suppose.) And the dragoons: now *these* were mustaches!

Thus I became accustomed to living in England.

My grandfather had given me the bicycle. Watched me straddle it in
Mr. Ryder's shop that very first day after my arrival: the right size? Yes,
it was the right size.

"He is long-legged," he said, some days later: teatime, I remember —
he said it to my grandmother. "He's long-legged, like Philip." Like my
father.

(But my father's name was seldom mentioned, really.)

And my grandmother was silent. Well, God in heaven! Her *silences:* a few heartbeats of silence. But then she smiled: that sweet smile of a woman sad who is feeling joyful. And she reached out with her small old hand and ruffled my hair. Well, God in heaven! I was almost thirteen! I did not and did like to have my hair ruffled.

Thus I became accustomed to living in England.
    It is not my home. India is my home. . . . Well, never mind.

(This, then, for the sake of *neatness:* I am taking my whole life with me.)
    (Actually, all this does rather belong right here, in the story. It may happen that I'll have to lay down my life for the place.)

2 5

And the day dawned.
    Fueling vans rumbled about.
    Let's go. Let's go. We are no longer of this place.
    Where do we belong? By tonight we must belong somewhere.
    "What in bloody hell are we waiting for?"
    "For the replacements to get here, idiot."
    No, it would not do at all well, would it now, to leave the base not manned — unprotected.
    People milled about; people shouted. "Mickey! Hey, Mick! Give us a hand."
    "Just a tick."
    "Coming through. . . . Make way. Coming through."
    Ashley's camera hung about his neck by its strap, securely.
    "We'll shake all the windows off their hinges today. Wizard!"
    "Stunning. Smashing." (All the teacups would dance in the cupboards.)
    Luthie ran about like a rather clumsy greyhound. (Well, greyhounds did not carry clipboards, usually. And colored pencils. And maps. And . . . and . . . a thermos cup: half-coffee, half-cocoa. No accounting for taste. . . . "Bloody hell! I've spilled it.")

"Did you see what Luthie named his kite?"
    Yes. *Aunt Millicent.* My God! Well, my God! (The name freshly painted: overnight.) An aircraft — *the* aircraft — the very very best, most magnificent fighter aircraft in the world, named *Aunt Millicent?!*
    (Well, Acklington's Spit, for example, was named *Dragonslayer.* And Ashley had named his *Matchless,* after much thought: well, among other things, Matchless was a make of motorcycle, though of course not of Ashley's motorcycle. And Cartwright, for example, had named his kite *Viperous.* It sounded more like a navy ship, actually — a destroyer, but . . .)

Aunt Millicent!

"Almost named her Great-aunt Maude at first." This was Farrell who had piped up. "That corporal of the fitters — the one who sounds like he's soaping his hands when he talks to officers: lathery-slathery . . ." Ah, Corporal Dunaway! (Yes, Farrell was a good observer. And, admitting it to himself, Ashley felt jealous.) "He overheard Luthie talking to Acklington. Luthie said he'd had a royal pain in the arse of a great-aunt Maude once. Used to say, 'Dear boy . . . Find Great-uncle . . . Somebody's handkerchiefs . . .' Well, the fitter corporal heard him say it! . . . But the old girl's dead. Luthie told Acklington he thought it might be a bit . . . disrespectful to name the kite for her. Well, Aunt Millicent is the same idea, you know — so he said. Said his kite was an old lady —" Farrell paused. "All done up in . . . *corsets, with innocent blue eyes and a sharp tongue.* He and Acklington were laughing about it."

Well, my God! My God!

But Farrell was not finished. "Now Luthie's first kite — the one he left at Dunkirk — was named a Rosie-something."

A Rosie . . . ? (!!!) "A popsy!" (Yes, that was more like it.)

"No, it was a horse."

A horse? (!!!) "A racehorse!?"

"Some ruddy foreign-sounding bloke's horse."

Grenfeld said, "Rocinante."

And everybody turned to stare at Grenfeld. Grenfeld plainly was excited. At the same time, he appeared to be dreadfully embarrassed by the attention. At the same time — for the very first time since Ashley knew him — Grenfeld managed to look snotty.

Farrell quickly snatched the spotlight from Grenfeld. "Well, Luthie said to Acklington *Aunt Millicent* was a more . . . humble name . . ." But now his voice trailed off, uncertainly.

(Still, Farrell clearly was proud of himself. Bringer of *interesting information:* his very self-respect — and McGregor's respect, above all? — seemed to have been restored to him after his less-than-admirable performance during the expedition to ask Luthie what the weather would be like tomorrow.)

The men of Flight B were laughing at Luthie, in malice. Well, did they laugh in malice (so it occurred to Ashley, but he would never say it aloud) — did they laugh because they felt robbed by Luthie of what was rightfully theirs: namely, a flight commander just like any other flight commander?

Let's go.

"Where *is* the ruddy relief squadron, then?"

"The Jerries have eaten them."

"Shut up."

"Well, you shut up. . . . Shut up shut up shut up."

A new life? But all these . . . *things:* feelings . . . emotions unresolved . . . all those they were bringing with them! (So Ashley thought;
but then he decided that, on the whole, he would prefer not to think
about it.)

Let's go. (But Luthie was conferring with the squadron leader.)

(And somebody — an officer, of course — had brought a gramophone
out; and an aircraftsman had been put to work cranking the handle . . .
Tada tadaaa — tada tadaaa *Alex-ander's Rag-time Band* . . . And then:
Silver Wings. Very loudly.)

But Brown was frowning. Worried. Downright anxious. "The hood of
my kite doesn't slide well. It sticks."

"Well, go and tell good old Bennett." Ha-ha! Good old Sergeant Bennett ate little Browns for breakfast.

"Complain to . . . Luthie." Interesting. Interesting. Would Luthie attempt to eat Sergeant Bennett for breakfast?

And so Brown waited, frowning: downright anxious; he waited for
Luthie to finish his powwow with the squadron leader . . . And yes,
Luthie then did take Sergeant Bennett aside; and there he was: *his legs
did not look double-jointed!* And the men of Flight B would gladly have
given up a week's pay to hear what was being said or to see Bennett's
face. But Sergeant Bennett had his back turned to them. And it was too
far to see Luthie's face well.

(Said Stanhope, "The field glasses . . . Has anyone brought —?" No.)

But not more than five — ten? — seconds after Luthie let Sergeant
Bennett go, various kiwis came swarming: *out of nowhere!* And they set
to work with metal files and machine oil and worked frantically hard; and
then Luthie sat inside Brown's kite — knees at the ears: well, ridiculous!
He always looked ridiculous inside a Spit: McGregor had been right
about that from the beginning — and he worked the hood back and
forth, back and forth, till he was *absolutely* certain; and then he had
Brown do the same. And when finally he went away, his every muscle
seemed taut, and he held his head high, and he did not look . . . well, out-
rageous or unusual, for example, as one would expect a man to look who
named his Spitfire *Aunt Millicent:* he looked . . . *forbidding.* (Well, he
looked forbidding all the time these days: ever since McGregor's . . .
Farrell's . . . Ashley's! *expedition.*)

(And somebody — the fat PO Thomas — shouted something at him,
laughing.

And Luthie answered, laughing. He seemed excited and sounded —
what was the word? — *brittle.*)

(Well, oh my God! All these matters *uncertain* — all the things one
sometimes thought about before falling asleep at night — they'd carry
those with them!

Let's go. Let's go.
"The bloody relief people . . ."

"Ashley, take a picture. Take a picture of me."
"Of me." "Me." "Me!" "Me."
"A picture of all of us! Together."
And Grenfeld said then, rather quietly: "Shouldn't we have Luthie in the picture, too? He's the flight commander, after all."
What a peculiar . . . well, courageous! . . . man Grenfeld was.
A picture with Luthie . . . ? "Must we have him?"
"Who's going to ask him?"
"Let Ashley ask him. He's the one with the camera —"
"Why in bloody hell —? I'm not going!" But even before it was out, Ashley could see it: McGregor's mouth about to open . . . McGregor would *suggest* that Ashley should go. (McGregor never *ordered:* he *suggested.*) And from the night of their "expedition" forward, Ashley would never ever again do McGregor's bidding. He would stand alone. Without needs. His own man. Alone. Not part of any group. *Not belonging anywhere.* Alone. . . . But to defy McGregor? He glanced about . . . Not the proper time. "I'll go," he said, quickly, and realized that yes, he was doing McGregor's bidding.

Ashley went to ask Flying Officer Luthie to be in the picture.
Luthie was now sitting in the grass, drinking his half-coffee, half-cocoa. The gray-furred cat Victoria was with him.
Where were the other cats? In hiding? Waiting out the disturbance? My God, Flight B would not then say good-bye to the cats! (There were things that they would leave behind.)
And the idiotic gramophone was bleating: "I am stepping out with a memory tonight . . ." God damn it all!
Luthie looked forbidding but was scrupulously courteous when Ashley asked him to be in the picture. "Yes. Yes. I'll come." He left Victoria sitting there in the grass. He left his clipboard and his colored pencils and his maps and his thermos cup in the grass.
Luthie looked most dreadfully forbidding. But then he grinned. "Well, let's give it a good sprint, shall we?" And he and Ashley gave it a good sprint.

They lined up; posed.
Luthie said, sounding worried, "Sergeant Ashley will not be able to be in the picture." Yes. Yes. Well, Ashley hadn't got a delay timer!
(God, there was a kindness to the man: no other officer was like him!)
And Luthie called out to Pilot Officer Peterson — the new one, the replacement for the dead PO Kenley — and asked him to take the picture.
And Peterson said, "*Do* something. Don't stand like bloody statues."

And so then something happened that the men of Flight B would never ever forget: well, on the right-hand side of Luthie, Ashley heard McGregor gasp: well, my God, as if he were choking!

My God, what was happening?

Luthie had thrown his arm about McGregor's shoulders: a gesture of . . . easy camaraderie?! Actually, his arm was about McGregor's neck: in . . . camaraderie?! He was pulling pulling McGregor to him, almost throttling him . . . well, mock throttling him: in camaraderie! (This was unheard-of!) Luthie grinning. McGregor gagging on the . . . honor.

And so somebody began to laugh, nervously. Then they all were laughing. As if a dam had broken.

(To tell the truth, they all had hoped that after the "expedition" Luthie would bite McGregor's head off for him: do something . . . *forceful*. But he hadn't.

And they hadn't ridiculed him for that, really. Not for *that*.

But McGregor had become their leader.)

Now they all were laughing: high-pitched laughter. Hysterical — almost — in excitement? *What was happening? What was it?*

And Peterson snapped the picture. "Another one," he said.

And . . . who had thought of it? Nobody and everybody: all of them together, at the same time. And so they all linked arms, on one another's shoulders. Including Luthie's. (And he was an officer! *Would one dare touch an officer?* Ashley observed: somebody's hand — Stanhope's? — reached out, tentative . . .) And then they all kicked out, in their booted feet: as if doing the cancan! — chorus girls in the West End and all that. Laughing Laughing Laughing.

And Peterson snapped the picture.

They were doing the cancan and laughing.

And there was the wind blowing, of course, but it would be a warm day, probably. (Swimming weather: here?)

And so they would be there like that forever, in the picture.

Companions. Friends. Together.

(But for all that — even if one excluded Luthie — they still didn't know one another terribly well, so Ashley thought.)

And: "Here they are!" somebody cried. The new squadron. The relief squadron. The replacement squadron.

And the section officer from Signals came running. A tiny figure. Tiny. A betrousered tiny figure.

"Gentlemen, they're Hurris." Hurricanes — not Spitfires. The relief squadron.

And the girl — the woman — was running running . . . "Flying Officer . . ." she said. "Flying Officer . . . A message for you, Flying Officer."

A message for Luthie? Well, a likely story! Why would a section officer come running with an ordinary message? She'd send somebody else: an underling!

And she was breathing breathing as if she had been running for a night and a day. (A white envelope — *sealed!* — in her hand.)

(Her copper hair: braided, this time. The braid stuffed under her cap. And her neck was small, small: delicate. It made one's own — well, Ashley's — lungs feel . . . inadequate.)

Her eyes the biggest thing about her — at the moment. Oh my God, what eyes!

"Gentlemen . . . They're coming in. They're coming in." The Hurricanes.

Luthie's *mistress*. My God, what a word! What a taste it left on one's tongue, even if one didn't say it aloud! She had brought her *lover* a love letter to take with him to battle. *Mistress. Lover.* What words! (And somebody giggled: the smallest of giggles; but a giggle that could not be helped in the middle of all that excitement. Stanhope grunted: in pain? Somebody — Farrell, next to him? — must have kicked him in the ankle; in the shin.)

In the meantime, the Hurricanes were down. There, in front of Flight A and Flight B Pilots' Rooms.

It took five kills to become an ace. How many of these people were . . . aces?

Well, what *odd* people, the Hurricane pilots! They did not gather into a group, even. There they were, all the way across the field . . .

And the ground crews milled about: yes, even Sergeant Bennett, for example. But the pilots of the new squadron, the relief squadron, the replacement squadron: they stood, looking about — in wonder? — but mostly they stood, each as if alone. Well, their shoulders seemed to be the shoulders of tired men. Still, it all was distinctly odd!

And: "Flying Officer," the woman kept saying. "Flying Officer . . ."

And . . . and . . . well, the *naked despair* on her face. . . . This was grown up. This was *too* grown up. Ashley had never ever seen anything like it in all his life! Not even on his mother's face. Never. Ever.

Did she know something? What did she know? Did she know something that Ashley didn't want to know? That no man in Flight B wanted to know? She must be aware of the men of Flight B; of the world. She chose not to see the men of Flight B; ignored the world.

And Luthie . . . What a spectacle!

He took a few steps toward her; held his hand out — slowly, very slowly — to accept the letter . . . *He* chose to ignore the world.

"Thank you," he said. "Thank you very much." An ordinary, normal, everyday voice.

Well, what had happened?

Nothing had happened.

Everything had happened.

She'd brought him a "message"; he'd said "thank you." That was all.

But yet there they were, two *adults* together. They knew something . . . Luthie *understood* her.

The men of Flight B could not see Luthie's face. But from the very way he walked they could tell that he *understood* this woman . . . (Well, they were not daft, were they: the men of Flight B!)

And the squadron leader, too, had noticed the little scene; and he seemed startled. Not pleased.

Conduct unbecoming? Ah!

"Thank you," Luthie said again. An ordinary, everyday voice.

What had happened? Under the letter — under the envelope — their fingers had met.

Ashley could see it! Had everyone seen it?

With my body I thee worship . . . This was too grown up.

Well, go away, you two. God damn you both.

Ashley would never ever see the girl from Campbell's again! (God! So many things they would bring with them. But so many things they'd leave behind . . . *Ashley did not want to leave the girl from Campbell's behind!* He felt like bawling.)

"Thank you," Luthie said one last time.

And the woman . . . did she try to give him a small smile? She failed. And she turned and began to walk away. Her back straight. But then . . . she looked back. And *now* — well, finally! at last! — she suddenly seemed to see them all. But she was not in the least embarrassed.

What enormous serious eyes she had! And, terribly serious of face, she raised her clasped hands above her head, slowly, in a gesture wishing them good luck. Then she went.

And Ashley snapped a picture of her: the woman leaving.

Well, not just of her: Luthie was in the picture, too, watching her go; and one or two of the others, watching her go.

The woman leaving.

Ashley had set out with his camera to record Wartime. This was both

Wartime and Ordinary Life. (And everyone was so intent on watching her go that not a single one of them had noticed Ashley taking the picture.)

An orderly came running up to Luthie. "Sir . . . Takeoff in five minutes, sir."

"Takeoff in five minutes," Flying Officer Luthie said to the men of Flight B.

The gramophone was blaring one of the *Pomp and Circumstance* marches.

Let's go.

And so they went. And when, halfway through their journey, they came down to refuel, Luthie requested permission for a formation landing.

And so they landed in formation — my God, what a tight formation! (Ashley's heart thumping in his throat all the way down: in excitement — exhilaration; fear; *danger excitement*.) My God, Luthie was a brave man!

Then, as they sat — in chairs! at little folding tables! — drinking tea and wolfing down scrambled eggs: from plates! — a second breakfast! all these luxuries their hosts had provided — as they worked their way through the breakfast, Luthie had a conference with the squadron leader. Then he pored over his maps and scribbled in his notebook. But then, quite suddenly, he disappeared: to have *privacy* to read the woman's letter?! Then at last he came over and stood there and he seemed proud of them.

Ashley wondered whether he truly was proud of them or only pretended. (Had he ever seemed proud of them before? No, he hadn't. Most certainly he hadn't.)

Had the others noticed he now seemed proud of them? Yes, they had.

And so, when the time came to leave again, they sauntered to their kites. No need to run: this was not an order to scramble . . . They sauntered.

McGregor said, "Let's go get the Fritzes." Sounding self-possessed again and competent. (McGregor was a man to admire, really.)

They sauntered to their kites, proud.

24

I

19th August — no, 20th August 1940

Wayne,

Night is a time of honesty. When you go away tomorrow — today! — my heart and my soul and everything that I am will go with you. There. I've been honest.

I have never written a real letter to you (only that hastily scribbled note)

— am not much good at writing anything & thus I am careful with every word. I tend to think in snatches of music — honestly! not in words. Perhaps you have heard (people here do enjoy their gossip) — no doubt you've heard that that was what my life's work was going to be: music. The cello, actually: I've studied it for years and years and have become quite good, I think, tho I know that I am not good enough to be truly truly good (if you know what I mean). But I carry music inside my head — I paint pictures inside my head with music. Am not good at words. I wish I had told you more about myself when we were together.

But I digress — mainly because writing this is so very difficult. Not a year ago I married a man — was very much in love with a man — and I'd meant it to last a lifetime. We were friends, too, not just lovers, David and I, and at the time he died, I loved him more than ever. The sense of disloyalty I now have to live with is rather difficult to bear. But I also question whether I ever really did love him. And am I then capable of loving anybody? The <u>uncertainty</u> is rather terrible to bear — especially since I've never been an uncertain person. Until now I had always thought I knew myself quite well: not only my limitations, but also my strengths.

David was seven years older than I. By the time our two months together were ended, I naturally was an altogether different person from the girl of my wedding day. But after he died, I felt very old. Very very old. (By the way, Tunnard-Jones <u>is</u> my maiden name, in case you wondered. Not that I am terribly fond of it, but at one point, in desperation, I simply decided to make an effort to bring back who I once was. It didn't work, of course.)

In quite a few ways you seem even older than David, tho you are six months younger than I — our birthdays <u>are</u> on the same day of the month! (Yes, Intelligence Work!) It does seem most terribly unfair — to you more than to me, I suppose — that it should be a source of anguish to me to know that being with you made me feel <u>just right.</u> Our walk & the picnic & talking & laughing together. And being kissed by you — & my own kisses. I am being honest.

I am not at all sure I am in love with you.

Yes, I am in love with you.

What I mean to say is that I am not certain whether I want to be in love with you.

I do want to be in love with you. (I hope I know you well enough: you will not be taken aback by my honesty, nor take it amiss.)

I know I should say that perhaps our separation will be for the best, for the time being. Yes, there is much thinking I must do. I do not want to be separated from you. I do not want you to go away.

It is quite senseless, of course, to pray for your safety. I am certain that even now some poor German woman somewhere must be praying that all <u>her</u> wishes should be granted. The whole thing is rather mad, really. And *would it truly be so wonderful if there did exist a living — & <u>kind</u> — force of some sort, capable of helping us in our need? I do not know. Sometimes I do wish it were so. The truth is that it will never be so.*

    Take care of yourself. Be careful. Look after yourself.

N.

    I think of you tracing my eyebrows with your fingers.

God God God God God

tho & & tho. Ha — an affectation!
    (Getting to know each other.)
    Christ, it makes me feel the same way I did that time when I walked behind her, and the seam on her stocking was crooked. Tenderness. Choking with tenderness. Oh, it is much like listening to the very last part of the last movement of the Dvořák cello concerto! Tenderness.
    I feel . . . well, humble, I think.
    Oh, life is so good!

II

Nim   Nim
My love

Nim   Love
All is well so far.
They're gorging themselves on scrambled eggs, peacefully.

BOOK III

PART ONE

25

I

And so they arrived.

II

There was a portable chemical toilet at Dispersal.

My God! No more furtive pissing under the open sky — hurry hurry: any WAAFs about? This *was* a big place.

"Runways!"

One took off and landed on a runway, not on grass.

"Smashing!"

"Wizard! . . . Stunning!"

Four squadrons: three all Hurricanes, one Spits. (And they, the men of Flight B, the officers of Flight A — they were the Spitfire squadron!)

A satellite field some twenty-five miles distant: another squadron of Spits. All sharing a headquarters.

A big place.

III

Flying Officer Luthie said, mildly, as he nodded (and with his hand gave a little wave) toward the chemical bog, "Actually, I recommend —" And, to lead by example, he pulled the door open and stepped inside. He shut the door slowly, *neatly:* to show them how — *un-self-conscious* (!) he was, he rattled the lock, testing it.

Well, my God! My God! What was it he was intimating? This was an insult!

Well, yesterday — last night — it was then they'd kept trotting to the bog!

(And Ashley looked about. Yes, each and every one of them *clearly* considered it an insult!)

How did Ashley's innards feel? (Well, of course he needed to go to the bog! Was it . . . shameful?)

Well, God damn it! Was the man Luthie truly telling them he thought that if they didn't — *empty* themselves now, they might . . . *let loose* later?

Somebody laughed.

Snickered. . . . Giggled? Were they laughing at Luthie or at themselves? (Well, McGregor was not laughing. McGregor's face was ugly with fury.)

IV

But this was a much *nicer* place than the one they'd left only this morning.

The grass was greener here. Trees in the distance: yes, trees — that was what made the difference: trees green . . . green . . . Well, an end-of-the-summer green: rather dark; but *green,* by God! *Green.* A . . . cozy green. Green as far as the eye could see.

A *nice* place.

"When are they going to show us to our billets?"

"They'd better. They bloody well must."

(But the ground crews were at work, diligent: a turnaround on a Spit takes about thirty minutes. Not their own ground crews: *foreign* ground crews: their own ground people weren't here yet, of course.)

Both flights had been directed to unload their luggage.

"Well, where are we supposed to put the stuff?"

And Ashley glanced at his watch. It was just half past noon: time for lunch. (Or had they missed lunch?)

V

SECRET (no elephants' ears over the T!)   Form F
                    COMBAT REPORT
Sector Serial No._____(A)_____

"Never mind that, lad. I'll fill some of those things in later." And the IO's voice boomed in Ashley's ears (Ashley's ears hurting; his head hurting). So, this was what it was like, by God!: a . . . a *debriefing* after a . . . yes, a *scrap!* God damn it all! (The IO had begun the debriefing: "Have a good trip, lad? Tell me about it lad." And so Ashley talked; and the IO wrote; and the IO read aloud to Ashley what he was writing.)

Serial No. of Order detailing Flight
or Squadron to Patrol _____ (B) _____
Date _____ (C) ___ 20 August 40 _____
Flight, Squadron _____ (D) Flight: B Sqdn.: 125 __
Number of Enemy Aircraft _____ (E) _25 Do 17 50 Me 109 __
Type of Enemy Aircraft _____ (F) ___ 10 ME 110 _____
Time Attack Delivered _____ (G) _____ 13.25 _____
Place Attack Delivered _____ (H) _ SE edge of London __
Height of Enemy _____ (J) ___ 18,000' _____
Enemy Casualties _____ (K) _____
Our Casualties   Aircraft _____ (L) _____ NIL _____
           Personnel _____ (M) ____ NIL _____
GENERAL REPORT _____ (R) _____
I was in No. 2 position, Red Section. The Enemy A/C came from SSE. OC (Fl. B) FO W.R. Luthie positioned the flight between the sun and the Do's, at the same time also providing us with the advantage of height.

"Well, it's good to hear he did a nice job," said the IO. He looked cool — did not sweat at all, because the awning over his table (a new awning! a different awning! camouflage-colored, not gaily striped) shaded him." It *is* his job, lad. . . . He'd be pleased to hear, though, that you appreciate his efforts, I'm sure.

From our position approximately one thousand feet above the leading Do's, we attacked from the sun. I brought my sights onto one of the Do's and broke away downwards and sideways to make it difficult for the enemy rear gunner —

"Wait. Wait just a minute. Never mind the Fritz rear gunner. Did you fire?"
"Uh-huh. . . . One does, doesn't one?"
"Right-o. 'I . . . gave . . . a . . . quick . . . burst. . . .'"

but did not see the outcome. I climbed into the sun and saw a Zerstoerer . . .

"Z-E-R . . . Lad, it's easier to call a kettle a kettle. An Me-110 will do nicely, lad."
(Now Flying Officer Luthie would know how to spell Zerstoerer! Ashley thought. But Flying Officer Luthie was not present.)

. . . and I brought him into my sights and fired. I again broke downwards, but by the time I pulled up, the formation had scattered and I could not see *anything*.

"The formation . . . had . . . scattered. Full stop. . . . Always be concise, lad."

> Later on I attacked three Me-109s, each time closing almost to two
> hundred yards, but again there I did not have time to observe the
> outcome.

"All right. Sign, lad," said the IO; and he sounded . . . patient. He handed
Ashley a beautiful *beautiful* — well, dandyish, really!, but in a dignified
way — a truly beautiful Waterman fountain pen.
    Ashley breathed in; breathed out; signed, after a fashion.

He stared and stared at the fine print, at the very bottom of the page.
The tiny print.
    Numbers. For no reason at all, it suddenly seemed terribly important
to know what all those odd — peculiar — numbers meant. *Wt. 27885-
2553* . . . The weight of the *paper? 850 Pads 9/39* . . . Eight hundred and
fifty pads of this stuff, printed in September 1939? *Form 1151*. Ashley
stared and stared.

On the IO's table there were his paperweights: *A Souvenir of Brighton,*
and a large stone. My God, had he brought even the stone with him?
    How had the IO got here, anyway? Taken the train, last night?
    Driven all night, last night?
    Ashley kept staring.
    The IO said, sounding very patient, "Go and have a nice cup of tea,
lad. And send the next one . . . the lad Brown . . . to me, will you."
    Ashley went in search of a cup of tea. After a while he put his hands in
his pockets, so that nobody could see that his hands were shaking. (And
his knees felt the way one's knees sometimes feel when one is very hungry; but he was not hungry. His guts churned. Well, he had not *let loose.*
But, for some reason, the knowledge brought him only a small comfort.)

On the walls inside the Ready Room there were pictures of German aircraft and of women really really naked: breasts really . . . exposed and all,
but the legs were crossed.
    On the far wall, there was *My Dog Flufy.*
    F-l-u-f-y!
    This is My Cat Snowball.
    (And all those naked women. But the sturdy, round-bellied stove in
the middle of the room looked rather like a comfortable grandmother.
Nice.)
    F-l-u-f-y!
    (God, it was hot! Air all *breathed out:* inside. Outside, the sky was a
pale blue hot sky: swimming weather. The sun high and hot and glary.)
    Chairs: tattered armchairs. In the Ready Room. One cot. Magazines

on a table: *Punch, Razzle, For Men Only.* A week-old *Times,* three fresh copies of the *Daily Mirror.*

This is My Cat Snowball. Our House. Mummy and I. Form IIa, Miss Kittredge. June 1940. *Our Very Best to the Pilots* . . . My God! Well, just like little pieces of now faded but once both white and colorful laundry: the children's drawings! Strung on a bit of rope along that far wall: just like laundry.

Flying Officer Luthie had said about an hour ago . . . or two hours ago . . . three-quarters of an hour ago? Well, *before the scrap* — that's when it had been — Flying Officer Luthie had said . . . Ashley now stared at My Cat Snowball.

Try not to think about Flying Officer Luthie!

Well, he had walked into the Ready Room, Flying Officer Luthie had, after a . . . chat? — a *conference* — with the wing commander(!); his eyes had swept over the naked women, taken in the children's drawings. "Oh in Christ's name!" he'd said, upon seeing the children's drawings. (And he had laughed. . . . *Brittle? Bitter?* Who would understand him? A peculiar man.)

But then he'd walked over: moved from one little picture to the next (and all eyes had been on him: well, Ashley'd *observed* him peering at the pictures: *My Angel-Fish ~~There~~ Their Names Are Hark and ~~Harold~~ Herald*); and by and by, he — Luthie — had rubbed the root of his nose, as if his eyes were tired. His wrists in plain view. (Well, it *was* hot. He had taken off his flying jacket, shrugged out of his tunic, put his Mae West on over his shirt; opened his collar; rolled up his sleeves to just below the elbows. His wrists in plain view.) After a while, as if lost in thought about . . . something, he absent-mindedly rubbed the scar underneath his watchband: it must be itching. Finally, he settled himself in one of the armchairs. His wrists in plain view. He kept glancing at the children's drawings.

"And so we know what we're fighting for," he said. And he laughed again. *(Well, did one say such things aloud? — if one really meant them, that is, took them seriously?)* But oh, what an . . . *unforbidding?* laugh?! (a small laugh). An *open, friendly* laugh?! (a small laugh). "I do hate to be nagged into it, don't you?" he said. And he was laughing. (An I-cannot-help-it-that-I-am-so-very-different-from-you-but-still-I-am-like-you kind of laugh?) Well, who could understand him!

(But then they sat and sat. Waited. Waited. Waited. . . . Nobody would come to show them to their billets. . . . They waited for . . . the telephone in the Ready Room to ring?; for the loudspeaker to spit and crackle and announce . . . Well, would it shout "Scra-a-a-amble"? And,

after a while, a little sigh escaped Flying Officer Luthie. And, a while after that, he said, quietly, speaking at no one in particular? to himself?
well, to the Germans! "Well, come on, you bastards. Come on Come on
Let's get it over." Well, should a flight commander permit himself a
sigh? Should he permit himself to talk aloud to himself? Was Luthie
breaking down? Well, Ashley had been very frightened then.)

Now — the scrap over — Ashley stared and stared at *My Dog Flufy*. And
he drew some snot back up into his nose; wiped his nose with the back of
his hand (well, he had . . . snuffled); and his legs still were weak, but the
rest of his body felt as if it were three times its normal weight. After a
while the thought came to him that the picture didn't look very much
like a dog, really, let alone a fluffy one.

Stanhope, next to him, said, "My grandmother had a cat named
Snowball. She died." The cat Snowball? Stanhope's grandmother?

Grenfeld came into the Ready Room. Not running, not sauntering: he
came. *Nonchalant?* "He's on his way," he said. "Telephoned in. Acklington announced it. He had to land at . . . what's the name of that satellite
field? They fueled him up. He'll be here. . . . Five minutes."

(Flying Officer Luthie had been overdue!)

VI

At night, mice played . . . hide-and-seek? inside the walls of the camouflage-painted building that was their sleeping quarters.

2 6

My Dear People:
  How we live:
  *I share a room with Hanmer. (The place where we were before, we each
had our own room.) The men of Flight B are bedded down in an adjacent
building.* <u>Adjacent:</u> *a quarter of a mile away or so.*
  (You always say you're interested in hearing every smallest detail.)

2 7

In the bed next to Ashley's, Grenfeld said, in his sleep, "Splendid. Splendid." Then he turned over, roiled up the covers with his feet, slept on.

His voice must have awakened McGregor and Stanhope, who began
to whisper in the corner about . . . food.

"Trifle, Stanhope. Trifle!" McGregor's voice: was there . . . longing (!) in it?

"And gooseberry tarts," said Stanhope.

Beginnings . . .
How different were they from the way one had expected them to be?

28

I

Nim:
  Combat

(I'll never send this letter. It's not a letter, really.)

Why I've decided to write all this down:

(Nim, I am tired.)

Why I've decided to make a written record of my life:
  I was at one of those RAF convalescent places — after Dunkirk; after hospital: dark leather armchairs, well-polished brass doorknobs, green plants with leaves as tough as boiled beef. Young men like old dogs dozing in the sunshine.
  Hanmer came visiting the infirm.

My only love,
  Now   Night
  Beyond the perimeter of the base: lorries rumbling. A very long convoy. Heavy armor: tanks? . . . the sound of an earthquake? And then they are gone and silence falls . . . I am very very very very tired.

Well, light a cigarette, Luthie! Change your socks, Luthie? It's amazing what a nice fresh pair of socks will do for a tired man!
  (Cannot sleep. Tried counting sheep, but it did not work. The night is young yet, of course.
  · · ·
  Well, I slept like one dead: earlier, after coming down from ops. We'd gone out three times this afternoon to . . . *Repel The Enemy.*)
  No socks to change. Bare feet.
  · · ·
  In absence of socks, contemplate bare feet, Luthie.
  (Christ! Clip your toenails, Luthie. Absolutely! . . . That's better.)

•

Nim   Combat

Well, <u>after</u> <u>combat,</u> actually — <u>after</u> ops. — <u>after</u> the first scrap, this afternoon — <u>after</u> <u>my</u> <u>very</u> <u>first</u> <u>time</u> <u>out</u> <u>with</u> <u>the</u> <u>Wonders,</u> this afternoon:
Well done, Luthie!
Well, I acquitted myself creditably, this afternoon. I think.
. . .

Cartwright: "Sir . . . Sir . . . And one of the fitters says my rudder cable was <u>very</u> <u>nearly</u> <u>severed!</u>"
<u>Sir</u> — that's me — W. R. Luthie — the Flight B commander: "Don't worry about it. Do not think about it. When it mattered, you didn't know about it — now it no longer matters. Don't think about it."
Well done!
        ???
<u>You</u> <u>child.</u> <u>Cartwright.</u>
<u>Yes,</u> <u>your</u> <u>terror</u> <u>is</u> <u>important</u> <u>to</u> <u>me.</u>
Is mine important to him? Oh, bloody hell! (Sorry, Nim. . . . I'll not send this, of course. It's not a real letter.)

Nim, I hurt.

Well, my <u>tongue</u> is hurting! Well, it is so very silly, really: I bit my tongue this afternoon — no idea when exactly, really, but sometime in the middle of <u>Repelling</u> <u>The</u> <u>Enemy.</u> It hurts like the devil.

About the convalescent place: Hanmer came visiting. He suddenly popped up from behind one of those beef-leaf plants: the very jack-in-the-box. "Luthie . . . You bag of misery! Up. Up with you! Wake up!"
We had not seen one another since the time of Dunkirk.
We are two completely unsentimental men.
"Luthie . . . No wonder you look as if Goering Himself had kicked you in the balls. If they locked *me* up in this place, I'd be *dead* by now."

(This is not a letter to be sent at all, Nim.
No need, then, to beg your indulgence for the language? Quite.)

Well, God damn you, Hanmer!
(For example: "No parachute," Hanmer had reported upon his return — the time of Dunkirk; without me. "No parachute." *An honest mistake. In the heat of the moment — in the . . . emotion of the moment — well, he could see my kite going down . . . he'd somehow failed to see the brolly.* And thus that very evening my poor people would be presented with the *Missing-Presumed-to-Have-Lost-His-Life* version of the dreaded Air Ministry telegram.
. . .

But, of course, you know nothing of this, Nim.
. . .

Acklington, I'll never forgive you.

. . .

Has never apologized, the wretch. Not when he came to see me at that convalescent place; not since. The subject has never come up between us.

. . .

Acklington, I'll never forgive you.

. . .

We are friends, Hanmer and I. We really are.)

He said, a beef-leaf dangling from his fingertips, "This place *stinks*. Of furniture polish."

I ignored his . . . uncouthness. I said, mildly, "There are wild strawberries in the woods. Acres and acres of woods, you know. And I and a few others: almost hale and hearty. The nurses send us out in the morning to gather wild strawberries. . . . *Pick* strawberries? Whatever. It's very peaceful. Oh, a fierce rivalry, you know! Nothing more warlike to do here but compete: which of us will be the first to return bearing a cupful. We eat them for lunch, the strawberries. All mixed with . . . beaten egg whites, I think. And sugar, I presume. Perhaps it isn't real sugar. But the whole concoction is . . . well, foamy, you know. Strawberry foam. Not bad." And I gave him a grin. A Luthie grin. A crooked grin? (I do not remember.)

Hanmer was laughing.

(At present, Hanmer is away from the room. Taking a shower. . . . Well, it has been a *very long* shower. Hanmer was quite drunk when he went to take his shower.)

. . .

Footsteps outside the door . . . but they passed by.

(Will there be more or fewer interruptions here than when we were Somewhere in Scotland?)

Nim My only love

If I were home — if you were home with me — I'd put on my lamb's-wool — my old gray lamb's-wool sweater worn thin at the elbows — and we'd go walking through the cool night grass.

Do you know how to eat a freshly picked apple, Nim? You roll it about in the palms of your hands. Then . . . you sniff the palm of your hand. Inhale: like this. <u>Then</u> you bite into the apple. Christ! There are times when it's as close to heaven as one can get! (Well, Mahler's Eighth Symphony gives one a similar feeling, though in an <u>entirely</u> different way, of course. . . . In your letter you said you painted pictures inside your head with music.) My grandfather taught me about apples.

Nim Combat (well, after combat):

Ashley, don't even think of taking my picture as I drink my . . . civilized
tea. (I'd helped myself to a cup of tea: one of those metal mess-kit cups.)
(Ashley's camera: on the IO's table. We'd not even had time to be
shown to our billets, to unpack: we were in the thick of it!
Ashley: casting his eyes in the direction of the IO's table?)
Don't even think of it, you little bugger.
(I'll not send this letter, of course.)

Ashley seems so very determined . . . God in heaven! What does the child
want, besides recording it all for posterity?! To tell the truth, I don't know
much about any of them.
    (What do I want for them? — etc. etc.
    What do they want from me?)
    A man of some . . . compassion: our Ashley? Of some . . . maturity?
The little Nosy Parker adolescent.
    Ashley, learn to distinguish when it is proper and when it's not to . . . to
intrude upon a fellow human being. (Pompous ass, Luthie.)
    Ashley, let me drink my civilized tea and learn . . . civilization! (Tea
mixed with blood. "Not bad. Not bad. . . . Quite good, actually." I said
that to the Wonders. The Wonders gaping gawping watching me spit
blood. "Oh, in hell's holy name!" I said. "I'm not dying. Not yet." . . .
God, what an idiot you are, Luthie!)
    Nim, I hurt.
    Well, it is such a small *small* thing: biting one's tongue.
    I'm not dying.

The convalescent place: all the nurses wore street clothes, not nurses'
uniforms. They called us by our given names. We called them *Siobhan.*
Muriel. And all that. (Good for the morale! And all that.)
    (Now *Muriel* is such a homely name. But she was truly truly beautiful.)
    I remember saying to Hanmer, "A lovely name: *Siobhan,* isn't it? She
isn't. Plain in the extreme, actually, Siobhan. . . . One of the physios,
you know: tortures me every morning from ten till half past. . . . There is
a chap here has lost both his legs. He's very concerned she may never
find a husband. He's convinced he'd make a fine husband. And it's his
hope they'd be good together: a girl plain in the extreme and a crip-
ple. . . . I've counseled caution. 'Proceed,' I said, 'but proceed with caution.' A very lovely Irish voice, Siobhan."
    Hanmer was laughing. And staring at me. Both at the same time.
(Well, I didn't really sound quite like myself, I suppose.)
    Hanmer: "Luthie . . . Put your bonnet on." (Well, it turned out he
had come to take me out of that place, for an evening.) "I've popsies
waiting, Luthie! Two popsies: one for you, one for me. . . . Well, they're
rather *popsies-of-the-moment,* you know: nothing special. . . . I'm on

leave at the moment, you know. Basking in the bosom of the family. . . .
I've borrowed Pater's Daimler, you know." And so we'd go in style.

We went. And the girls *were* rather girls-of-the-moment: Doris. Mandy.
(I think.)
 Gladys? Daphne?
 · · ·
 No, mine was Doris, I remember. (Oh, Nim . . . This was a long, long
time before I ever knew you! Absolutely. . . . Nim, love, I am being
straightforward: honest with you.)
 Well, nothing very wrong with Doris, really. Only a trifle too much
lipstick; and the lipstick was a shade too bright, for my taste.
 Did I not quite . . . fit in? Oh, not really.
 Did I feel out of place, just a bit? Not terribly so . . .
 Well, God in heaven, God Christ: the world rather felt as if . . . as if
I'd just stepped outdoors after a spring rain!
 (I remember: I was twelve years old once. Not quite thirteen. My first
summer in England. I was on my way home from the village on my nice
new Raleigh, black and shiny — a wire basket on the handlebars. I remember a small rain falling, gentle. And it would be some time then — a
few years — but in the end I did come to love England. It is not my
home. India is my home.
 Well, never mind. . . . A small rain.)
 And so the world felt as if washed clean and all rather new, that
time — how many months ago? — after Dunkirk; after hospital; after
several days of that convalescent place. It was as if I were seeing it all for
the very first time, really. (And for that I was grateful to Hanmer.)

Dinner. The cinema — *Wuthering Heights* — afterward. (*"Heath-cli-i-iff!"*
and all that.)
 (Dinner. A curry of some sort for me, I remember: no need to cut up
the meat, I remember. My wrists — my right hand — still bandaged,
very lightly. I displayed dainty table manners, though.)
 Wuthering Heights. The lights dimmed. Doris's hand on my knee, in-
stantly. (Nim, I am being truthful.) Well, God in heaven!
 (Well, it felt not bad, actually. In the darkness, in the flickering light
from the screen, her profile was rather nice, actually. One did not see the
thick layer of bright lipstick at all.)
 · · ·
 (*How can I ever touch a woman . . . ?* And so on and so on.)
 · · ·
 (Nim. She knows nothing of this, of course: *I do not want a woman to
gentle my wounds. I do not want a woman to be repelled by my wounds.*)
 · · ·

Well, I sat there, let Doris touch me. Hand on my . . . knee. I sat there, tried to determine whether I felt . . . happy (being quit — though for only an evening — of that place of boiled-beef-leaf plants and wild strawberries, where people who could not sleep at night dozed in the sunshine).

An interruption. What is happening?! A quarrel has broken out in the hall. A row. Well, God Christ! Will they come to blows?

Voices I do not recognize. Voices . . . failing under the strain of the dreadful fury.

Terrible language. Words hurtful beyond belief. Will they come to blows?

A door slamming. Another door slamming.

Somebody . . . laughing. A laugh like the short bark of a dog.

Then, an uneasy quiet.

(There *will* be interruptions here, no doubt about it.)

But back to the story:

There was a newsreel. One of those Pathé things.

A Spit with a camera under her wings had really got lucky. Oh yes! (Usually, those pictures are dreadfully grainy: smudgy; and the layman would get but a small idea of what is happening. But this one was first-class, no doubt about it.)

An Me-109. A little . . . cloud appeared at his wing root.

The Spit's camera rolling: the cloud grew bigger, very very quickly. And then — poof! Ah, a most magnificent fireball! No more Me-109.

The newsreel announcer intoned something smug, sonorously. Was drowned out, though: the audience in the cinema stomping cheering laughing whistling clapping.

Doris's hand . . . gone. She was stomping cheering whistling clapping.

And I looked at Hanmer, in the darkness. Hanmer looked . . . at me?: in the darkness. He seemed uncertain.

. . .

(How Hanmer and I Became Friends . . . ?: Part One.)

(One of my Ghost Stories: Part . . . Whatever.)

. . .

Then Hanmer evidently reached a decision, and he began to laugh with the rest of them.

. . .

(When the war broke out, I joined the RAF. Why did I go to war of my own free will?)

. . .

Well, this was after Dunkirk: this cinema visit. And things had become so very . . . yes, *simple* after Dunkirk — well, for most people.

Now it is August. And things absolutely are *simple* now — oh, definitely! *Things are so very desperate.* An hour of need . . . I am frightened. But it makes me feel rather solemn. I think.

. . .

Pompous ass, Luthie.

. . .

Well, at one point yesterday — last night: only last night! (before we arrived here) at one point I said, in these pages, that I may have to *lay down my life* for England!

How very — oh, thoroughly! — maudlin.

. . .

Silly ass, Luthie.

The audience in the cinema: cheering whistling etc. etc. . . . Who can blame them?

. . .

Nim   I've killed people. And will do so again.

(Before I went over Dunkirk, my father had given me a knife.

. . .

What do I want . . . for my Wonders? No: *for myself?* Oh, bloody hell!

. . .

I've killed people and must do so again.)

But a thought came to me then: struck me, suddenly, as I sat there, in that cinema. *This Fritz has been dead for a week(?) . . . ten days(?).*

(The developing of the film itself is very fast. But it must take some time for the film to get to the newsreel people and for the announcer to record the text. So I assume. *The Fritz has been dead for some time.*)

And yet, here he's dying all over again (the thought struck me). (The people cheering etc. etc.) And tomorrow evening he will die again. And on Saturday, for the matinee. And then again on Sunday, in the evening. Till the newsreel's been changed.

Nim   Nim . . .

And so my fear is this: one day, an Me-109 — or perhaps a 110 — will record the manner of my passing. And then I'll be able to die over and over. A fortnight from now. Ten . . . *years* from now?

Twenty years? . . . Fifty? (Well, for as long as the film shall live.) (Christ, what an absolutely terrifying thought!)

And those who then watch — Ashley-types: record keepers? Historians: Nosy Parkers? — those *interested* in seeing events with their own eyes, as they really happened — they'll no longer cheer clap stomp their feet (I hope): what made people do so once will no longer matter. (That is an even more terrifying thought: all this will have been resolved one way or the other, and years from now it may no longer matter.)

But, if they so choose, people may watch me die.

But nobody will know how I lived.

(I've no idea why I've decided to write all this down. Well, it is an exercise — it began as an exercise — to improve my handwriting . . . ?)

I know bloody well why I've decided to write all this down. Christ! I was sixteen once — played God in the attic — *and I did not destroy my great-aunt Maude's love letters to the man she eventually did not marry!* (She would have disappeared forever. . . . Well, throw the letters in the dust-bin — she would be truly dead. Oh, I was powerful, indeed!)

Am I now playing God with myself?

Do not forget me, N. M. Tunnard-Jones.

Hanmer! At last!

II

How we live:

(Colin K.: he used to interrupt. Now Hanmer has to do the honors: Colin K. is no longer with us.)

. . .

(After today, little fat Geoff Thomas is no longer with us.)

Hanmer: only *half*-drunk, now. Hanmer: morose. (Well, our Geoff Thomas is no longer with us, and Hanmer was his flight commander, of course.) "The bastard Peterson borrowed my comb this evening. On his way to get drunk. . . . Said he'd lent his to the bastard Thomas . . ." (Geoff is alive, though — *still* alive; but he was burned very, very badly, I understand; is in hospital. So, that's where Peterson's comb is, pre-sumably.)

> God, do not let me die in terror.
> God, do not let me —

Hanmer: stark naked. A towel over his shoulder. Steam rising from his half-boiled, newborn-piglet-pink skin.

Hanmer: morose. "Luthie . . . switch off that light, will you? Now. *Toot sweet.* Now, God damn you! I want to sleep."

Hanmer: stark naked; putting on his pajamas. He buttons the jacket to the last button — looks prim and proper: suddenly, for just a moment, he seems younger than my Wonders, although he is older than I.

"Luthie . . . Want a drink?" A brandy bottle emerging from under the bed.

We drink. Light cigarettes. Drink.

Hanmer, in a fit of temper: "Luthie, *switch off that light!*"

Hanmer: fast asleep. Puff Puff Puff. (Hanmer doesn't snore; he puffs.)

How we live:

Clean sheets. Blackout curtains. The room holds the heat of the day.

My sketch of Nim's face will go on the wall opposite my bed as soon as the rest of our kit has arrived. Those eyes — those eyebrows: the first thing I'll see when I wake up. (Tried to telephone her earlier. At last wormed out of someone the *secret* information that she was away from the base: back tomorrow.) (Began a *real* letter to her: did not get very far.)

. . .

N. M. Tunnard-Jones, if you were here, I'd bury my face in your hair scented with chamomile.

. . .

A little framed photograph of my parents on the bedside table. My potted plant on the bedside table.

Hanmer and I share not just the room; we share a batman: in the evening, the batman lays out one's pajamas, folded neatly, on one's bed. (Unlike Hanmer, I do not sleep in pajamas, as a rule; I sleep in my more-than-Oriental splendor. . . . Never mind. The pajamas, laid out on the bed.)

A dog-eared paperbound book on the bedside table. Dorothy Sayers: *Gaudy Night.* It takes place at Oxford.

Nim's face on the wall opposite my bed.

My bed. *Mine. My* side of the room. (Hanmer can do whatever he wants with his.)

Outside, on the road, beyond the perimeter of the base: lorries rumbling.

I had a *very* close call this afternoon, that very first time out with the Wonders.

But, all's well that ends well. (My miserable tongue is hurting, though.)

(Ah, here's an interesting bit of information!: *Did You Know That . . .* churches have been forbidden to ring their bells — so I understand. The pealing of church bells has henceforth been designated to mean one thing only: Invasion.)

I am frightened.

Combat:

(Well, *after* combat, actually — after that very first scrap of ours — before the next . . . *installment* of combat):

We sit, my . . . young men and I. (The IO kept calling them my *young men.*)

The IO: a man of superhuman patience. Starts every debriefing: "Have a good trip, lad?" I kept tripping over my tongue (no pun intended). Well, I was hurting.

.   .   .

The IO: his small paunch strains against his belt.

Waiting waiting . . . We waited for the next installment of combat. (But one must watch the ground crews like a hawk: in the morning, the hood of Brown's kite would not slide properly.)

Waiting. Waiting. (After a while, a Spit landing. Spewing glycol all over the countryside. And it's . . . yes, Peterson — yes, definitely: the replacement for poor old C. Kenley. He's the one took the pictures of us this morning: Peterson. We watch. The Spit manages the landing.)

And we sit, waiting; and the men of Flight B: they are somewhere where I have never been — each in his own place.

They must know that I am where they will never go.

We sit.

"Oh, do get rid of the jackets. Absolutely! Sergeant Stanhope, you have not my permission to take off your boots, though. Nobody in Flight B will scramble barefoot. Bare feet slip on the rudder pedals."

"Sir . . . Have you tried it, sir? Flying barefoot?"

.   .   .

Oh you . . . *impertinent* little bugger! You . . . *courageous* beast: Farrell.

.   .   .

"I have tried it." (I have not.)

We wait.

Well done, Luthie! (I've acquitted myself well, so far. I think.)

.   .   .

(What do they — my young men the Wonders — think?)

I had a *very* close call this afternoon.

29

I

And the next day — the day after their arrival — what happened that day?

The base was bombed: sirens shrieking; the ack-ack firing.

Flying Officer Luthie shouting. "Let's go. Let's go." Take the kites up. So that they'd not become sitting targets on the ground.

(But what did it matter?)

Ashley was most terribly tired.

"Dear Everybody," Ashley wrote that evening. (*Everybody?* Now that would include his father, too, of course, wouldn't it?! . . . Well, who else in the family would "everybody" include now that John was dead? Well, Bridget the scullery girl, perhaps.)

"We engaged The Enemy," he wrote; counted on his fingers *one two three* (inside his head); added one finger (inside his head), "four times today. On the whole a satisfying day."

There. That would show his father.

. . .

Ashley was dog-tired.

"Dear Mother," he wrote, "The flight commander —" (What should he say about Flying Officer Luthie?) "The flight commander is *incredibly brave*. He *sings* when he leads us into combat!"

But then, dimly, a thought came to him; and when it came, he abruptly *understood* his mother — for a moment; but whether the *understanding* made him feel grown up or not, or whether it was the kind of "grown up" he had once wanted, he was not sure. The thought was that his mother might not find it a comfort, after all, to be told that her son's flight commander sang on his way to combat.

Well, God damn it all! Things were so very complicated.

Ashley was thoroughly, thoroughly tired. (Did it matter?)

II

And on that very same day, the second day of their new life: well, not on the first day (nor on the third: the third would no longer be a beginning, really, would it? — the new life would no longer be new; nor on the fourth day: ha! — well, by the fourth day that place whence they had come would cease to exist in their minds at all: Ashley was sure of it) — on the second day, then, in the morning, they had sat and waited: for the telephone in the Ready Room to ring, for the loudspeaker to spit and crackle. And, *in the presence of all,* Flying Officer Luthie had read — reread, actually!: the envelope carefully slit open — he'd reread (so Ashley would remember) the letter from the section officer from Signals. (But what did it matter?)

My God, now there was a brave man! What trust! (Did it matter?)

Well, he'd positioned himself in the doorway of the Ready Room hut — with his back turned to the men of Flight B, of course (and it was

hot — most frightfully hot — though only about ten in the morning).
His back was turned, then, but he . . . he trusted them not to *titter;* he
trusted them to treat his privacy with . . . well, how would one say it?
(Ashley rummaged for the words in the far corners of his mind, but
when at last he found them, for some reason his pleasure in them was
only about half of what it used to be) — with an *adultness of face.* What
a man!

(Or was it really the letter from the section officer from Signals? Or
some other letter? No way to tell! And did it matter?)

With my body I thee worship —

Well, Ashley knew he would never ever see the girl from Campbell's
again.

What was her name? *Buttercup.*

Buttercup?! He had never learned her name, actually. . . . *Buttercup.*
. . .

The men of Flight B *observed* Luthie's shoulders as he read his letter.
Two pages? Three . . . four! (Did it matter?)
. . .

Buttercup was a yellow word: like sunlight streaming in through the
glass of the door at home (Ashley thought) — the door with the stags
etched into the glass.

(Ashley's stomach churned, and he wanted to go home.)

He would never see the girl again.

At last Luthie was finished reading, and carefully he folded the letter.
And he turned to face the men of Flight B. My God, what courage!

He was being rather casual about the whole thing, really. As if he
thought nothing of it. What trust! (Or was he pretending to be casual,
deliberately *showing* them that he trusted them?)

Well, he held his head high, and his face was . . . proud.

And, clumsy oaf that he was, he dropped the letter.

And McGregor dove forward. (McGregor! Had he been in hiding, all
this time?! — since yesterday, since the time Luthie had throttled him in
camaraderie! Had he been in . . . ambush? Biding his time? Plotting . . .
my God! . . . *revenge?*) Now he threw himself forward. Picked up the
letter. Well, he must see . . . be able to read it: a word here and there! At
the very least, he'd see the handwriting! And politely — a gentleman of
manners — he handed the letter to Luthie: "Here you are, sir."

Luthie said, "Thank you, Sergeant," in a voice small and terrible.
And Luthie was . . . blushing. Blood rushing into his face. In rage? In
humiliation?
. . .

Oh go away, both of you, Ashley thought. McGregor, bugger off.
What did all these . . . *silly games* matter? Nothing mattered.

Where did the men of Flight B belong? . . . Who cared?!

Ha! The feelings . . . the *emotions* unresolved they had brought with them. Well, it didn't even matter whether Ashley would find . . . he could not even remember any longer what it was he had wanted to find! (His thoughts upon him like a heavy blanket at night when one is having nightmares. Ashley felt . . . oh, not grown up at all, now, but somehow older than his age. Like . . . like Grenfeld? No. No. Grenfeld seemed to be a man with a purpose. Ashley wasn't.)

Go away.

Ashley wanted to go home.

. . .

But the others — Farrell, first, and then the others of Flight B — well, did they somehow *draw closer* to McGregor (without actually doing so)? And would Luthie flee? Walk out of the Ready Room, slam the door behind him? No, he would not.

Very, very carefully, he smoothed the letter (*dusting* it: trying to clean away every trace of McGregor's paws?). He slipped it back into its envelope and put it in his shirt pocket — *next to his heart!* — and then he sat down. With a rather desperate dignity he folded himself into one of the tattered armchairs, his insect legs drawn up — not stretched out — and he buried his nose in an old issue of *Punch*.

. . .

So what was changed? Nothing was changed. Did it matter?

Ashley wanted to go home.

After a while, Brown said, "The jam we had at breakfast . . . the strawberry jam . . . it was off. Old. Moldy. No bloody good. Rotten. It was off."

And then, a minute or so later, Flight Lieutenant Acklington appeared, and he and Luthie put their heads together. Mutter. Mutter. Whispering together.

Well, was it serious? Did they look serious? What if it was something very serious? Well, God damn Luthie and Acklington: whisper whisper whispering together. Nobody could tell what they were saying.

Well, it probably was nothing important! But whispering like this should not be permitted: it made people nervous.

Brown said, "The bloody strawberry jam was no bloody good. The jam was off."

They waited for the loudspeaker to cough and crackle.

It was hot: quietly, they sweated. (Ashley most desperately wanted to go home.)

And then the loudspeaker did cough, spit, and crackle: on that second — yes, the second, not the first, nor the third — on the second day. And

almost at the same time, the telephone inside the Ready Room began
to ring.

Sir. Do not answer it, sir.

*Well, wasn't there supposed to be an orderly — or somebody? Must the
flight commander himself answer the Ready Room telephone?*

Do not answer it, sir. Let it ring, sir. Ple-e-ease . . .

. . .

But they knew, of course, that that would not happen.

(And yes, there Luthie was, pointing. *Out. Run.*)

And so they went: they *ran.*

Cartwright . . . crossed himself. Well, he hadn't done that the day before, on the first day . . . had he?

My God, was Cartwright a Catholic?

McGregor shouted, "Let's go get the Fritzes." He always shouted
"Let's go get the Fritzes." McGregor was a man of tremendous courage,
but Ashley rather wished he wouldn't always shout "Let's go get the
Fritzes."

Ashley's stomach hurt. (He quite badly needed to go to the bog.)

Grenfeld was the very first one out the door. McGregor might shout,
but Grenfeld always was the first one out the door. (Grenfeld: a man
with a purpose?)

Luthie was waiting just outside the door.

And beyond Ashley, Brown gave a little gasp, a little strangled cry,
and then began to spew forth his strawberry jam and bacon and eggs and
the rest of his breakfast.

Ashley collided in the door with Luthie: upon hearing Brown, Luthie had
turned back.

And so now they stared at each other, Luthie and Ashley. And Luthie
stared at Brown. And he didn't know what to do: *which* to do.

A man who could not make up his mind: Luthie. Oh, he knew very well
where his loyalty lay! . . . He just could not decide where his duty lay.
(But Ashley had known this about Luthie all along: *a man who could not
make up his mind.*)

(But what did it matter?)

And they stared and stared at each other; and Brown went on and on
puking and puking: there was enough . . . disgusting stuff inside him
to . . . to flood the world; and Luthie's eyes were full of horror as he
stared at Brown. But then, every time he looked at Ashley again, it was as
if he were pleading with Ashley for . . . something; and they . . . Ashley
and he . . . they understood each other. (But what did it matter?)

Then Luthie finally moved. He pushed Ashley outside: roughly; very
roughly. "Go! Run!"

So Ashley ran. And behind him Luthie was running; and he must be
dragging Brown . . . by the hand? And he was breathing breathing . . .

well, like a man running, and gasping for breath; screaming at Brown. "Don't ever . . . do this . . . ever . . . again. Do you know . . . what they'll . . . do to you . . . if you . . . do not . . . take off? Now get in your kite . . . and take off. Do you know . . . what they'll . . . do to you? Don't ever do this . . . to me . . . again. Don't ever . . . do this . . . to yourself again. I don't care what you do . . . once you get up there —"

My God!

"— but get in your kite . . . and take . . . off."

And Brown was still retching and sniveling, blubbering about the jam that had been moldy . . . rotten . . . *off. "The jam was off!"*

And so they went. And this time the controller vectoring them on to The Enemy was a man: code name Ice cream!

The day before: that very first day — the very first time — the controller had been a woman: code name Buttercup. She wore a yellow dress. Had dark eyes: black. Well, just like a real buttercup. Well, "buttercup" was a yellow word: sounded yellow. Weren't buttercups yellow, with black in the middle? For God's sake!

She wore a uniform, didn't she? Just like everybody else.

(What daft ideas came into one's head! — so Ashley had thought. And it had been on that very very first day, the very first time — not on the second day.)

She'd had a la-di-da voice (even over the static; on that first day). A la-di-da accent. Just like Luthie's.

Ashley detested la-di-da accents. . . . Well, Luthie's wasn't too bad.

And Ashley could hear himself breathing (on that very first day, the very first time). And he could hear somebody else's breath — Luthie's — over the R/T, and Luthie's voice, as he talked to Buttercup: a steady, reasonable voice.

And the engine: sweet, strong, altogether *healthy*.

Well, he was not then afraid of anything (on that very first day). Suddenly, he was not even nervous! (His throttle hand working overtime.)

Until all at once there was silence over the R/T. (Well, silence and static, of course.) And he could hear the fear in Luthie's silence.

"Repeat . . ." Luthie then said. "Say again. How many?"

And Buttercup repeated in her precise — yes, *officious* — voice how many *bandits* were coming at them.

And again that silence. Then Luthie said: "Say again."

She repeated and sounded annoyed.

And *then* Ashley was afraid.

And: Luthie's voice — small, but not even terribly off-key . . . Well, my God, the man was . . . what was he doing? *Singing!!!*

> And it's home, dearie, home
> Oh, it's home I want to be . . .

And he was laughing. Laughing at his fear.

Ashley was most terribly afraid.

But Buttercup stopped sounding *officious,* and in a voice that was like any human voice — oh God, a *nice* voice! — she wished them all good luck.

Well, this was a most terrible breach of procedure! Somebody would have Luthie's head for it. Somebody would have Buttercup's head for it.

But, for a moment, Ashley felt a bit better.

Then, for some reason, he remembered the rest of that idiotic song.

> But my topsails are hoisted
> And I must out to sea,
> Though the oak and the ash and the bonnie birchen tree
> They're all a-growing green in the North Countree . . .
> Oh, it's home, dearie, home.

And suddenly, Ashley was most thoroughly homesick for that North Countree he had never seen: the one with the oak and the ash and all that stuff. God damn Luthie! God damn him. Ashley's goggles were most thoroughly fogged up; and so he pushed them up on his forehead. (Well, that had been that very first day.)

Now Ashley also remembered having, at last, a Do-17 in his sights. And he'd braced himself: both feet on the rudder pedals . . . back firmly against the seat . . . clear your mind of everything . . . Well, that was what Luthie had taught them.

He pushed the Fire button on the stick. And . . . nothing happened. *Because he had forgotten to take his guns off Safety.*

And Luthie's voice: "Break! Break! For Christ's sake, go go go go go. Get out! Get out! Break!"

And so he kicked the rudder and was running running. And something thudded into him — into his kite — against the kite; and he screamed and screamed — could hear himself screaming; but he was running.

(That had been that very first time, on the first day.)

After that . . . well, staying alive was the only thing that mattered.

Would there come a time when everything would settle into a routine?

50

My Dear People:
For some reason, they talk about food a lot, my Wonders.

What copycats they are!

My Dear People:
They are copycats, my Wonders. For example: I massage Roy Newby's

neck and shoulders. (Have I mentioned this before? A stiff neck, stiff shoulders, sinus headaches: occupational diseases of fighter pilots.) And so I give Newby's neck and shoulders a good rubdown. They watch from afar, the Wonders. Then, after a while: Cartwright massaging Stanhope's neck and shoulders. Stanhope massaging Cartwright's back and shoulders.

(Cartwright: asleep, the poor sod. Cartwright's compact little body sagging, *sinking* into the grass, into the very earth. Oh, absolutely! Cartwright in a dead-to-the-world sleep: the poor sod.)

Nim   My love
   How we live:
   Oh, life is so good!

(No, it is not good: it hurts so much to be without her.)

Nim   My only love
   (This is not a real letter.)
   This place is full of the gentleness of life.
   They disobey me — the little beasts! Well, a NAAFI van came this afternoon, selling — three guesses! — ice cream on a stick. Stanhope: his boots off. (I've forbidden them to take off their boots. They disobey me!
   Well, this place is full of the most wonderful ordinariness of life.)
   Stanhope: his ice cream over his bare feet. The ice cream melts . . . slowly . . . slowly . . . drips over Stanhope's feet. God in heaven! Nim, you should see the sight! Ughh! Disgusting! (It really is.)
   Stanhope: a look of fierce concentration on his face. (Remember Stanhope the Frecklenose: the Once and Forever Peppermint-Cruncher? His peppermints look like Christmas; smell like Christmas. He carries Christmas with him wherever he goes.) And Stanhope: he is cooling his hot, swollen feet. (Performing a scientific experiment? Ah, that ferocious concentration!) Every time an ice cream drop goes splat against his flesh, he flinches.
   The men of Flight B watch with interest. With . . . relish. They make faces: Ughh! Disgusting!!! . . . Nim, this place is full

(And McGregor: our eyes met. Bloody hell!
   He looked away, quickly. His face . . . oh yes, *pious*. Ah, he knows Stanhope has disobeyed me. Bloody hell!
   McGregor: following the ice-cream-melting proceedings not only with interest, but with — God damn it! — with approval? Encouragement? Yes! Egging Stanhope on? . . . They disobey me? Bloody hell!)
      . . .

   This place is full of the . . . delicate uneasiness of ordinary life. (In other words, life goes on.) I am being compelled to absorb a great many emotions. I think. (Well God Christ, I did not come here *traveling light:* I have brought my whole life with me.)

How we live:

My Dear People:
   The Germans come and bomb us.

No.

My Dear People:
   There is a well at Dispersal — a water pump, actually. The water tastes brackish but is safe to drink.

(The Wonders: are they taking *things* in stride? I've no idea, really.
   . . .
   The Germans come and bomb us.
   A Hurri squadron armorer was killed today, I understand.)

My Dear People:
   Here's an interesting story about one of the Hurricanes. This afternoon one of the Hurris   Sorry. A longish story. My alarm clock's gone off: I'd set it so that I'd not have to keep looking at my watch. Meeting w. Wonders — 5 min. Finish this later —

(That is how we live.)

31

Ashley observed — he was an Observer:
   A Hurricane coming in for a landing.
   (Ashley stuffed a boiled sweet in his mouth and observed, idly.)
   It was afternoon; they had been out only once that day — so far — since coming on duty at 1400.
   The Hurri was down; had taxied up. The man inside cut the engine.
   The Hurricane stood there. The hood did not open.
   Inside, there was a man . . . slumped. Head fallen forward — a dark blur; the shoulders held back by the harness.
   People running: the ground crews running. The blood wagon on its way, bell clanging.
   The Hurri did not appear to have been *severely* hit: just, well, the usual — the usual.
   The men of Flight B broke into a run, too. But then they slowed down; stopped, one after another: well, they had not yet seen a man . . . dead.

Ashley had never seen a man dead: he had not even seen his brother dead. His poor brother John had simply . . . disappeared, of course. Pilot Office Kenley, too, had . . . disappeared.

They had never seen a man severely wounded . . . dripping blood!

Someone pried the hood open. There were too many people — difficult to see what was going on.

But then, quite suddenly: was that . . . *was that the Hurri pilot?* Yes! Walking!

Looking . . . embarrassed? Sheepish?

Somebody said, "The bastard. Gave me a fright, he did. He was asleep in there! Snoring!"

(And by and by, Ashley's tongue began to search for his boiled sweet. . . . He must have swallowed it whole without noticing it. Well, God damn it all!

Resolutely, he stuffed another boiled sweet in his mouth. He did not like boiled sweets, as a rule; but this tasted delicious.)

There was a well with a pump at Dispersal. One pumped the water into a large bucket . . .

That same afternoon — after the Hurricane incident — they sat in the grass and waited waited waited; and a man came running — another of the Hurri pilots. Well, he must be very, very thirsty! He pumped the bucket full; then . . . he plunged his head into the bucket. The water splashed out, but he held his head inside the bucket, under whatever water there remained.

And time passed then. My God, he'll drown!

But at last the man came up and shook himself off the way a wet dog does. He had very blond hair — almost white (so Ashley observed). And water dripped down his neck, soaked his shirt; but he stood there and seemed to be listening . . . to something inside him. Was he looking for something within?

Ashley watched. Flying Officer Luthie (his nose in his thermos cup full of half-coffee, half-cocoa): was he watching, too?

And finally, the man . . . well, he *woke up*. And as he went away, he and Luthie exchanged looks. Glances. No, not a grin, really. A . . . smirk? *Had the man managed to wash off whatever it was he had wanted to wash off? But one never managed to wash off whatever it was one wanted to wash off.* Was that what it all meant?

Well, my God! My God! (But Ashley decided that he would think about it later.)

And . . . Flying Officer Luthie was rubbing Pilot Officer Newby's neck and shoulders.

Stanhope rubbing Cartwright's neck and shoulders.

Cartwright: asleep, a quiet exhaustion on his face — the very same

kind of exhaustion Ashley had glimpsed on the face of the Hurri pilot
who had *snored* inside his cockpit.

(Would life settle into a routine?)

Before the afternoon was over, they had scrambled three times.

Every time, McGregor would shout, "Let's go get the Fritzes!"

Cartwright shouted, "Let's go get the Fritzes!" . . . Cartwright? Cartwright: he who had crossed himself the other day?

Not to be outdone, Farrell shouted, "Let's go get the Fritzes!"

Well, what a *thoroughly unusual* man McGregor was, really!

The base was bombed again, the next morning.

Did it matter?

5 2

I

Dear Mr. and

Dear Mr. and Mrs.

Dear Mr. and Mrs. McGregor:
  As the commanding officer of your son's flight

Dear Mr. and Mrs. McGregor:
  I am well aware that whatever I say cannot diminish

Bloody hell! This is old Hurry-up's business, not mine. His responsibility. The commander of the squadron writes the letter!

(The bastard Hammett: Wayne . . . uh-huh . . . would you mind . . .
uh-huh . . . taking over this . . . uh-huh . . . onerous task? A mil-
lion . . . uh-huh . . . things I must do. . . . Your . . . uh-huh . . . understanding is greatly . . . uh-huh . . . appreciated.")

My Dear People:
  All is well with me.

Nim   Love
  *I am well. It is quiet here tonight. (This is a noisy place, usually.) If I
were home — if you were home with me*

Dear Mr. and Mrs.

●

Dear Mr. and Mrs. McGregor:

Your son was a nasty little piece of baggage, and there were times when I hated him from the bottom of my heart.

There.

I do not want to think about it.

II

There was a . . . house: the time of Dunkirk.

(I do not want to think about it.)

There was a house. I had a fever.

(Well, this was after the dog Shadow was dead. Remember the dog Shadow? I remember. I'll never forget.)

It was . . . late morning when I came upon the house. The sun quite high.

(Remember the dog Shadow? Out of the night shadows he had come; and we'd traveled the road together: the time of Dunkirk.

Dogs are in this world to be named. "I'll name you Shadow," I had said.

But then the dog suddenly died, and I was left alone. And I'd said to him, as he lay there, dead, by the side of the road, "I'd have taken you home with me. . . . Oh, I'll get home. You'll see. And when I get home, I'll be the man I've always been. All this will be as if it had never been. . . . I'd have taken you with me, and we'd have become friends."

But he was dead; and so I left him there, and I traveled the road.)

I had a fever.

There was a house.

And smoke rising . . . rising . . . reaching out for the sky but never quite succeeding: smoke from . . . the chimney! Not from rubble.

(I had a fever.)

There were window boxes: flower boxes. Red flowers in the flower boxes. But the plaster was peeling here and there; and the windows were . . . well, as if *blind:* not clean, I suppose — they did not gleam, spotless, in the sunshine.

(I had a fever. I felt lightheaded.)

Not half an hour before, I had been strafed by a Ju-87, a Stuka.

I remember: running running. But it was difficult to run. I could not breathe. I ran.

Now the Ju-87 has got, well, one might call them whistles, for want of a better word. Yes, sirens. On the wings. One on each. Metal pipes. As the aircraft dives in for the kill, air rushes through the pipes. I am a man who knows how to use words. But words fail me. I cannot describe the sound. The only purpose these devices serve is to terrify the human beings who are about to be killed or maimed. It is most admirably effective.

I ran.

There was a . . . cart in the middle of the road — a wagon, once drawn by horses: the horses long gone. I threw myself under the wagon. Tried to break my fall — tried to *direct* it — well, with my hands, of course. My poor wounded hands. I lost consciousness in pain and in terror.

When I came to, the wagon — what was left of it — was . . . well, perhaps two hundred yards away. The impact had set it rolling, cartwheeling (no pun intended!), and two wheels were missing . . .

I lay in the middle of the road, at peace.

After a while, there was nothing for it but pick myself up and be on my way. (And there, ahead of me, the sky was burning: smoke rising, reaching out for the sky . . . So that was the west: that was where I had to go.)

I had a fever.

This was the time of Dunkirk.

There was a house.

And there was . . . laundry . . . bed sheets, pillowcases, nice and white; a yellow . . . tablecloth(?) . . . all on the fresh spring green grass in the back of the house. A watering can in the grass. (I was most dreadfully thirsty.)

I lay in the ditch by the side of the road and watched the house.

And an old woman came out, by and by — a woman dressed all in black: a black frock and apron; black stockings; a black scarf. A black crow of a woman. An old raven of a woman: birdlike steps.

But that is how old Frenchwomen are.

A Flemish woman? . . . So many people around Dunkirk are Flemish.

Wooden shoes. Not black, of course: the only thing about her that was not black. She was a woman made small by age. Her wooden shoes seemed the biggest thing about her. And yet her steps were birdlike. Her bent shoulders — the way she held her head — made her seem birdlike. And she picked up the watering can and began to sprinkle the laundry.

(Not half an hour before, I had been strafed by a Stuka.)

(I had a fever.)

(I was most frightfully thirsty. And hungry, too — God!
. . .

Well, they had fed me the night before . . . the Germans. *Ah, the grinning coal's cuttles!*)

(*On ran Dingo, Yellow Dog Dingo*. And so on and so on.

Grinning grinning *grinning like a coal's cuttle.*)

(No, the . . . Germans had fed me: the *coal's cuttles* had been gone by then. But I, well . . . I was haunted. *Cool. A cool feeling. My own .45 at the base of my skull: a cool feeling. An ant struggling struggling with a crumb of bread.*

And I hated

Hated

I could not eat, the night before the day I found the house. Besides — well, at the time: the night before the day I found the house — it had seemed to me, at that time . . . it had seemed very nearly impossible even to hold a spoon with those hands! The night before the day I found the house.

Now I was hungry. And oh God, thirsty!)

And she — dressed all in black — she was watering her laundry; and then her black scarf slipped, and I saw that she had beautiful white hair. No, not *white,* really: more like . . . old silver, just before it is in need of . . . of Ayah's silver polish. Hair the color of Devon cream . . .

(I do not want to think about it.)

I'll be the man I've always —

I am myself.

Dear Mr. and Mrs.

3 3

I

They sat on the steps on the camouflage-painted building that was their sleeping quarters; and as the evening closed in, a wind rose from the river.

McGregor had been their leader.

Now he was gone.

. . .

They sat; and the gray-furred cat Victoria came.

(Well, the cat Victoria: Corporal — what was his name? — Rossiter — one of the armorers — he had brought her, in Luthie's dogshit Austin. In a basket.

On Luthie's orders? Luthie's whim? On his own whim?)

Well, transportation was provided for cats — no problem! Cats traveled in comfort!

But Ashley, for example, Ashley had had trouble making arrangements for his motorcycle in a hurry! And thus, at one point — in his dream — it had even occurred to him that the motorcycle — his *brother's* motorcycle! — was something of a nuisance, really. And he had been made to feel guilty!

This was . . . *dreadful.*

. . .

Well, even now he felt guilty. Were things beginning to matter once again?

. . .

Corporal Rossiter: he had brought two baskets. Victoria, and the ginger-whiskered Albert: the married couple.

Now Victoria the cat came; settled herself down, matronly and large; and she *observed* them: serene; dignified.

Farrell threw a stone at her.

Victoria lost her dignity and ran.

"For Christ's sake, it's only a cat," said Grenfeld, who seldom spoke, really, though he always was the first one when the order came to scramble.

Farrell said, "Bloody cat."

And as the wind rose from the river, they began to shiver with a terrible sense of loss.

II

Where was the sodding bastard Luthie?

. . .

It was quite late: Luthie came.

. . .

Well, bugger Luthie!
We can do without him!

. . .

(No. No.
Make us feel better . . . SIR. Now. Quickly. Now. Now. At once.)

It was dark *dark* by then (well, the stars were out; the moon low: huge and yellow — it was *light*). Luthie came. Folded his insect legs; sat, cross-legged. *Like a Hindoo.*

Well, he had bathed, clearly: showered!

Cleanliness about him (so Ashley thought).

3 4

I got them drunk.
    I had to do something!

3 5

And after that, the past had an *odd* way of becoming the past (it seemed to Ashley): hours long as days; hours swift as seconds.
    That was how it went.

3 6

I

How I came into manhood.
    When I was sixteen, my grandfather died.

II

Dear Mr. and Mrs. McGregor

(A full twenty-four hours have passed: haven't finished the thrice-cursed letter yet.)

What *do* they want from me, the miserable Wonders?
    (I had to do something: I got them drunk.)
    They are so . . . without *knowledge.*
    (Pompous ass, Luthie.)
    · · ·
    You . . . children   My Wonders
    Men   Soldiers!   ???
    My Wonders
    You had better become accustomed to this!
    · · ·
(They're without knowledge.)
    · · ·
    Well, they sat there (last night, in the grass); and their hatred of me (because McGregor their leader — and my enemy? — was gone forever), and their need of me (because McGregor their hero was gone forever: who would be their hero now?! Christ, they must have a hero, mustn't they?): well, they sat there and it was like an electric field. (Ah, it

almost made the air *crackle!*) And the only thing important to them was their own grief.

Bloody hell! I only matter to them because they have to call me sir!
   (What do they know about me? . . . What do they care?
   · · ·
   No knowledge.)

I remember: I sat with them, last night (the moon bright); a breeze had come up from the river; I felt very very very very old.

III

I was sixteen; my grandfather died.

(Organize — *marshal* — your thoughts, Luthie.)

Dear Mr. and Mrs.
   · · ·
   My grandfather died. Upstairs, my grandmother lay — propped up on pillows. Etc. etc. (The story — it rather wants to *pour out,* all of a sudden.)

Dear Mr. and

Why I am writing all this down:
   Well, if tomorrow, for example, I should follow McGregor into that *ultimate darkness* . . . ah, maudlin again? Being maudlin, Luthie? . . . Nobody would know how I lived.
   · · ·
   Do not forget me, N. M. Tunnard-Jones etc. etc.)

(Still, there are things about me that I do not want her to know.)
   Tried to telephone her again yesterday evening: late afternoon? — well, early evening: the evening of the day McGregor . . . *bought it.* (McGregor: gone from this world not long before noon.)
   I had left several messages for Nim in the past two or three days or so. Not a word from her. Is she avoiding me?
   No. No. There is that letter of hers, isn't there? And for all she is a woman given to a fierce kind of privacy . . . yes! — to omissions, perhaps? — she would never be given to lies.
   But: do I need her love more than she needs mine?
   No! I remember: she folded herself against me as if seeking . . . *surcease* from fire brimstone pestilence and all evils of the world amen: she sought peace with me!
   · · ·

N. M. Tunnard-Jones, I cannot protect you.
. . .

Nim, my only love
I'll cherish you.

Well, where was I? . . .
    The story wants out.
    . . .

My grandfather died. I was called home from school.

Mr. Mannington the stationmaster telephoned Mr. Parrish upon my arrival — and God God God, it rained! (And the little stove in Mr. Mannington's *inner sanctum:* stone cold. Well, this had been the last train of the day, and he had got out of bed to meet it, planning to go back to bed directly.

"No, no. Mr. Mannington, please do not bother to light a fire." Mr. Parrish would be here soon. Wouldn't he? *Wouldn't he?*
    . . .

Ah, Mr. Parrish: a damnably slow and cautious driver!)

The kitchen: afterward.

Mrs. Simmonds: a cup of cocoa.

Mr. Parrish: a glass of brandy.

Mrs. Simmonds (staring down Mr. Parrish): *Brandy! The idea! The child needs comfort.* (And the cocoa — it steamed; ah, it foamed!: she had whipped it with a little whisk, swirled a few drops of vanilla in it . . .)

Mr. Parrish: *He is a man now. There is a man's work awaiting him.* (And the glass was made of cut crystal, and it was on a silver tray . . .)

Well, God in heaven! *Somebody . . . please help me. I am cold and soaked to the skin.* (Yes, I was a child.) (And my grandfather was dead — and the whole universe had gone topsy-turvy! I had never seen those two old people like this: *competing* with each other.)

And my teeth began to chatter. "I'll have some cocoa first, I think," I said. "Then, a bath. *Then* a drop of brandy. . . . And a good night's sleep. I think I'll be glad tomorrow to have had a good night's rest. I am tired." (I was not a child.) And my striped school scarf hung about my neck like a dead snake.
    . . .

And, Mr. Parrish and Mrs. Simmonds became their old selves again, by and by. Well, I could not have managed the next few days without them! And without Janet. I had the funeral to arrange — and other matters: all those ancient relatives descending upon us. And my father: on his way from India — Imperial Airways, four and a half days, four nights . . .

Upstairs, my grandmother lay.

•

Yes, this *is* a story — well, one of the stories, I suppose — about how I came into manhood.

Dear Mr. and
Dear Mr. and Mrs.

God, what a debauch — last night! God, were they drunk, the Wonders, last night!
Drunk drunk drunk. Blotto.

About yesterday (last night? late afternoon? early evening? the evening of the day McGregor *bought it*) . . . the following things happened yesterday evening:
    Dear Mr. and Mrs.
               (I tried to write the letter: yesterday evening)
    "Hanmer . . . God's blood! Hanmer . . . ! What is the matter? . . ."
GEOFF THOMAS IS DEAD. DIED IN HOSPITAL.
               (And news of it came yesterday evening,
               and Hanmer came to tell me yesterday evening.)
When I was sixteen, my grandfather died.
Upstairs, my grandmother lay — etc. etc.
               (I thought nighttime thoughts, yesterday evening.)
    Tried to telephone Nim. She was not there. Again.
            (yesterday evening)
Dear Mr. and Mrs.
               (Again and again. *Keep mind on task at hand —*
               yesterday evening.)
    Should go see the Wonders. Have put it off long enough. Keep putting it off and putting it off.
         (yesterday evening)
    Well, that's how *I* live, by God! What do those wretched *children* know? The miserable . . . the ever-present . . . the *men* of Flight B: never-to-be-rid-of . . . what do they care?

Well, fate has rid me of McGregor, hasn't she! (Is fate a she?)

(This is a story about my coming into manhood.?)

And Hanmer said then, yesterday evening, "Happens. Happens." (Geoff Thomas was dead. *We all have to die,* Hanmer was saying.)
    "Oh, absolutely!" I said. And calmly, we drank: Hanmer's brandy. Oh, it smelled, felt, tasted wonderful as it went down!

An interruption.

Roy Newby stopped by, to chat for a while. About nothing special. About how best to kill Germans. . . . He is gone now.

Let us remember our little fat Geoff Thomas: he who died yesterday evening.
(He had been blinded, so I understand: his face had been burned away. Most of his upper body had been burned . . . *to a crisp?*)
· · ·

(*A human being burning sounds like . . . meat roasting over a campfire???:* How Hanmer and I became friends — Part Two.
One of my ghost stories — Part . . . Whatever.)
· · ·

Let us remember Geoffrey Thomas.
What I remember: Kenley singing — that is what I remember.

> There will be blackbirds over
> The white cliffs of Dover —

Geoff: "Kenley, it's not *blackbirds,* actually, you know." A man neat and tidy, our Geoffrey Thomas. It interfered somewhat with his sense of humor, I suppose . . .)
(Colin Kenley is dead, too, of course.)

Well, where was I?

How I came into manhood:
My grandmother: like tea with warm milk — tea-colored blouses; tea-colored cardigans; skirts the rich brown of my father's personal Darjeeling; her hair the color of Devon cream. Well, her hair was like Ayah's bracelets, necklaces, and earrings, just barely on the verge of needing a dose of silver polish!

Nim   Love
(I'll not telephone again.)

Nim, I know nothing about you. How you grew up.
(She said once that she was from London.)
A flat? All the rooms dark — dignified and proper: Victorian? All the rooms light and airy? Or fussy: flowery . . . suffused with a pinkish light . . . cushions everywhere . . . chintzes . . . and . . . and a Persian cat?
· · ·

I think you grew up in rooms light and airy!

I'll not telephone again . . . *This is not a real letter, Nim.*

●

I remember: my grandmother's bedroom. A lamp by her bedside; tiny crystal prisms on the lampshade: teardrops. And when the door opened — if the window happened to be open, too — the teardrops quivered: tiny wind-bells speaking from far away. (When I was twelve years old, it rather gave me the shivers.)

(I am almost twenty-one years old now. I think I can say that it was a sound that only those who are lonely would crave when the need was upon them to be filled with an even greater loneliness.)

. . .

(Well, when I was lonely I created worlds! . . . Fourteen, fifteen — at that age one often is lonely but will not let on. . . . I drew maps. And they were maps painstakingly and precisely executed; but joyful: caution-to-the-winds flights of fancy; true to reality but faithful to the truth of my imagination! They were the landscapes of my own choosing!

That is how I am. That is how I was.)

I'll never send this.
This is not a real letter, Nim.

My grandfather died suddenly, unexpectedly (a stroke: a swift way to go — painless?); and upstairs my grandmother lay in her great big bed and would not let anyone in but me.

(Well, she would not let me in, either. . . . Of course, she could have locked the door if she hadn't wanted anyone to come in; but she hadn't locked it. People knocked. She said, "Go away," in a voice that no one dare disobey.

But I was her grandson: I could do things that other people couldn't. I knocked. She said, "Go away." I went in, anyway.)

"Grandmama, lunch. Here's some nice curry." And the curry was made from scratch, too: not leftovers, the way curry-for-lunch usually is. "A nice glass of white wine . . . A nice poached pear."

I put the tray down; kissed her on the cheek. Oh, she was a beautiful old woman!

I had loved the old man my grandfather.

I sought comfort from her. She could not give it.

"Grandmama, here's the curry."

(I remember: a tea-colored bed jacket. A pearl necklace — *choker?* — several strands of pearls — tight about her neck. Those pearls had been my grandfather's gift to her on their wedding day.)

She drank all the wine. Would not touch the curry.

I fed her. It was undignified.

"Robert," she said. "Robin, read the obituary in the *Times* again."

And so I read my grandfather's obituary to her again and again: well, it was not very long at all — my grandfather had not been an important man.

"Robin . . . Robbie . . . Robert . . ."

Shall I say it? Well, shall I? (How long before at last I said it?) "Grand-mama, I am not Robert. Robert was my uncle." Dead on the Somme. Three years before I was born: 1916. "I am your grandson. I am your eldest son Philip's son."

. . .

This is a story of how I came into manhood.

. . .

"Philip always knew how to take care of himself."

. . .

???

. . .

"Grandmama . . . Why did you say that?"

(Christ, the . . . venom in her voice!)

(No. No. It probably had been venom . . . once; now it was a . . . grudge. Held for long, long years.)

"Grandmama . . . Why?"

. . .

(Well, God in heaven! . . . And something did come together then, though really it didn't:

Well, there had been a time once: I was new to England . . . Through all those years since I was twelve — new to England — my father's name had rarely been mentioned.

And I'd *tried* not to wonder about it — well, let us be honest:

My grandfather: he took me fishing once! . . . my first summer in England . . . And he had given me the beautiful brand-new Raleigh, black and shiny. . . . And I had then worked most frightfully hard at becoming accustomed to living in England.

And my grandmother: her old skin was like an old blanket underneath which a child may spend many peaceful nights!

I was new to England.

And thus my fear . . . of what? Had I been afraid of more than the *newness?* My fear had *forbidden* me to wonder why my father's name was rarely mentioned. ???)

. . .

"Yes. Oh yes," she said now. "Philip's son. My grandson. . . . You've always looked very much like my poor Robin." In a voice of a well-brought-up child politely giving up a favorite toy. "Read the obituary. Please." In a sweet voice of a woman sad.

And so I read the bloody obituary over and over; and she wept. Once she said, "Now I am all alone." And she sounded utterly utterly desolate.

Well, I was only sixteen. God, I was afraid of her! Stood in awe of her: of her rather . . . bottomless grief.

I found it tiresome, of course, after a while.

Felt sorry for myself: I sought comfort from her; she would not give it.

I felt heroic: I fed her and kept her alive. (She wanted to die, of course. But I was only sixteen.)

I felt smug: I could do things that other people couldn't. I kept her alive. (At night, after my grandmother was asleep, Janet would go in and tidy up the room.)

I felt wonderfully competent: the responsibilities of adulthood on me.

(And I remember: I slept with Emmeline. Emmeline the Third came, her tail a graceful half-moon; she settled on my chest and purred up my nose.)

Then my father came home.

Dear Mr. and Mrs.

(Can I manage to scribble a few lines at last, and be quit of it?)

Another interruption.

Hanmer, Newby, Peterson: going out. "For a pint. . . . Two. Three. Luthie, are you coming?"

Oh God, I felt tempted! "Well, I'd have to get dressed all over again. . . . Definitely count on me tomorrow."

(I assume Peterson has acquired a new comb. . . . He's the one who lent his comb to Geoff Thomas.)

Beyond the perimeter of the base, lorries rumbling rumbling. A long convoy: rumbling.

My father came home. Had taken a taxi all the way from the Croydon aerodrome. Suddenly, there he was, standing in the hall. "Little son . . . Little son . . ." We had not seen each other in four years. (Does this truly belong in the story?)

Well, I was sixteen; six feet and one inch tall. Ah, enormous — but not *commanding* — ears! (My grandfather's ears had been *commanding*.) Huge teeth. Sharp knees. A body *unfinished*.

At the sight of me, something caught in my father's throat. (Does this belong in the story?: How I came into manhood.)

(And all the ancient relatives: ah! Great-aunt Maude and Great-uncle William: he of the handkerchiefs — sails on a man-of-war . . . my great-aunt Genevieve . . . she who always wanted warm milk at bedtime: they seemed to be peering from around the corners surreptitiously. *Philip is here. Philip is home. After . . . how many years?*

And Mrs. Simmonds hurrying hurrying, up from the kitchen. And poor old Mr. Parrish also hurrying hurrying, as fast as his old legs could carry him. And Janet. *Master is here. Master is home. After . . . how many years?*

Because the house and everything in it was my father's, now.)

And, a small child, I flew to him. And folded myself against him. *My father was home, and the universe would never again be topsy-turvy! Oh, absolutely not!* (This does belong in the story.)

But by and by it came to me — slowly I realized — that it was not I who was being held: I was holding him, wasn't I? And a dreadful pang of disappointment shot through me — a sense of betrayal: I was being betrayed.

I looked at him. He was ashen-faced. Very, very very tired. (Imperial Airways: four and a half days, four nights.) And so there we were, holding each other up. (This most definitely belongs in the story.)

(And the ancient relatives were gathered in various corners, peering peeking.

And Mrs. Simmonds, Mr. Parrish, Tom, and Janet in a row: shoulders back, stomach in — Mrs. Simmonds, Mr. Parrish, Tom, and Janet on parade.)

And my father took it all in — a single glance — but he looked about yet once again. He gave *me* a questioning look, and said, "Where is Mother?"

A dam broke then: I blurted out *absolutely everything* — well, about the past few days, I mean.

And my father said — well, he did not say: "God in heaven!" or anything like that — he uttered a most horrible oath. A *horrible* oath. God! Well . . . *Venom in his voice?!* Well, surely not! And there he was, racing up the stairs.

"Philip!" Great-aunt Maude cried, shocked, from her corner.

"A-a-a-ah!" said Great-uncle William, enjoying himself; and he blew his nose into one of those enormous handkerchiefs.

I waited for a door upstairs to slam.

Everybody waited for a door to slam. It never did. My father must have shut the door *extremely* softly: nobody heard a thing. Such was my father's homecoming after . . . how many years? (Well, that is a *very important* part of, well, the *fabric* of the story.)

And that very evening, the evening before the funeral, my grandmother rose from her bed and put on her widow's weeds; and the next day she walked behind the coffin, in her widow's weeds. Dignified: oh good God, yes! My father's arm about her, protective: supporting her. I walked on her left side, holding her elbow: supporting her.

And it had stopped raining.

Then my father stayed for six weeks, *to take care of things;* and he visited me at school at weekends, and it was altogether different from the way we used to know each other when I was four, five, six, or twelve years old: well yes, he still was my father, of course, and we knew each other fairly well, still (my weekly letters from school); but now we were also learning to be, well, equals: two grown men together.

Then, his six weeks up, he left again. I went to see him off at Croydon. The aeroplane: an HP-42, the Heracles! Thirty-eight passenger seats: a big beast. (Only five had been built. The cost: 20,000 pounds each!)

My father: he did not want to go — he did not want to leave me. But he was anxious to be gone; although he dreaded the going.

And so, rather desperately, I was reassuring. (Oh, quite competently I was reassuring!) "The engines are very, very reliable, you know. Bristol Jupiters. *Not* water-cooled: air-cooled. . . . She's got a wingspan of one hundred and thirty feet. . . . The wings flex a distance of eight feet at the tips in bad weather . . ." *Do not mention bad weather. Nor flexing wings, in God's name!* "She is very sturdy. Strong and stable."

And once again something caught in his throat.

(Well, in those five weekends we'd had together, the subject of aeroplanes had not really come up, not in a *major* way: oh, there were so many things we'd not had time to tell each other! Now it must have come to him all over again. Christ, we both had missed much by our having been apart for so many years! . . . An important part of *my* life story.)

"We'll come back," he said. "We'll come Home." He and my mother both. (But it would take them two years — though I did not know it then.)

Well, the aeroplane: a Handley Page 42. A heavy brute.

Rolling down the runway. Shaking.

Up   Up   Help me   Concentrate

(The most luxuriously appointed passenger aeroplane in the world, I understand. In the cockpit: rudder pedals big enough for an elephant's feet, so I have heard. The exalted creatures of Imperial Airways who flew her joked about it. But I have never been on board.)

Help me   Help me get off the ground

And then — oh, there she was — a thing of beauty. In her own element. And I waved and waved, my heart in my throat.

(So, there are these various threads of my life: laid down, side by side?
. . .

A whole *will* emerge, though: if I work at it. And if I live.)

Croydon. Le Bourget. By rail to Brindisi: Mussolini would not grant Imperial Airways the right of overflight of Italian territory. By air again to Athens, and on to Crete. Alexandria, Cairo, Gaza. Rutbah Wells. Baghdad, Basra, Kuwait, and Bahrein. Sharjah. Gwadar. Karachi. Jodhpur. And Delhi. Then, my father took another train. (I remember all the stops very well.)

•

My grandmother died not quite two years later. In that time left to her, she would never again call me Robert; Robin. (Of course, in those days I did not come home from school very often; and she did spend most of her time in her room, in bed.) But whenever she did speak to me, she sounded . . . well, like a woman sad, of course (but I was accustomed to that, wasn't I?): one who had given up a . . . treasure? She had grown very frail, and was quite confused, really. Well, nothing had been right with her . . . universe in a long time. (I had understood it all along, in a way: since the time I was twelve years old, new to England . . .)

My father did not come for the funeral (Delhi, Jodhpur, Karachi . . .) But not two months after the funeral, both he and my mother came home.

There are other stories of my coming into manhood, I suppose.
    (I do not want to think about it.?)

Dear Mr. and Mrs.

Nim, I miss you . . . I'll not telephone again.

IV

Dear Mr. and Mrs. McGregor:
    I cannot offer comfort.
    Your son was in my unit for only a short time. But his resourcefulness, inventiveness, and initiative were admired by many; and — a bold young man, and courageous — he was well liked by his peers.
    Of course, these days many of us die before having had a chance to become adults. It saddens me. I must say it rather frightens me.
    I feel for you. Thank you for reading this letter. I want to assure you once again that the men of Flight B will remember Hugh with fondness and will miss him.
                            Yours sincerely,
                                W. R. Luthie, F/O
                                O.C. Fl. B, 125 Sqd.

There. (*That* is how we live.)
    Slap a three-penny George on the letter, Luthie; post it.

(Dear Mr. and Mrs. McGregor:
    Your son was a nasty little piece of baggage.)

God damn the Wonders!

Fate has rid me of McGregor.

5 7

And the replacement for McGregor was a man named . . . Randall?
He arrived in time for lunch; was dead by teatime.

The next day, Cartwright was overdue.
Suck suck suck. Stanhope sucked on his thumb as they sat . . . waited: waited to hear what had happened to Cartwright. *Suck suck suck.* (Not *crunch crunch.* Had Stanhope run out of peppermints?) *Suck suck suck.*
"Shut up!"
Brown? Brown!
"Shut up. You sound like a bloody fish in a bloody aquarium at bloody feeding time!"
And the men of Flight B turned to stare at Brown. Brown . . . well, Brown was one of those people who almost never raise their voices (Ashley knew that! Everybody knew that); people of Brown's kind usually have voices raised at them!
Then somebody chuckled — heh heh heh. Somebody laughed. Then they all were laughing — ha ha ha. *Fish in an aquarium at feeding time!* They liked that, didn't they? They were laughing at Stanhope . . . in malice?
It went beyond malice. They were laughing in . . . viciousness?
They wanted to see somebody — *anybody* — pounded into a fine white powder! It would feel good to see somebody — *anybody* — pounded into a fine white powder.

They sat.
(Flying Officer Luthie had begun to scribble something, filling in a form of some sort the Adj. had given him: about . . . well, for example . . . the dead man Randall? Then he stopped scribbling and just stared into space — not sucking on his pencil! but tapping it against his teeth, *tap tap tap.*)

Ashley's loneliness was quite difficult to bear.

Then they had to scramble again — without learning first what had become of Cartwright.

5 8

I

"Hanmer, bugger off, will you. Leave me alone."

•

A bad ride, this afternoon. Very bad. A terrible ride this afternoon, with my Wonders.

(Well, all our trips are somewhat suicidal: was this one so very different, really? Oh yes, it was.) My fault. My mistake. My blunder. I'd miscalculated — oh, *grievously!* They should have shot *me* down, the Wonders.
. . .

I do not want to think about it?

"All right, Hanmer. What is it you want?"

He wanted me to read — and rewrite! — his letter to Geoff Thomas's family. And so we spent some time working on it: together.

Then, painstakingly, Hanmer wrote out the final copy, forced it on me for one last perusal — and I discovered two errors in spelling (well, only one, actually: *recieve* instead of *receive,* but twice); advised Hanmer simple to scribble in the corrections, but he insisted on recopying the letter from the beginning.

Now he has at last gone to post the bloody letter: well, to get it off his hands, anyway (does Old Hurry-up truly censor all our correspondence?); when he — Hanmer — returns, we'll go out and get drunk. (No. A correction. A reminder from Newby that this morning Hanmer had called a meeting of Flight A for 2000 to discuss how best to kill Germans. We are not going to get drunk.)

My Dear People:
It is so good to hear that the presence of the children seems to have a good effect on Janet.
I was rather afraid the opposite might be the case

Then I slept for a while: took a nap.

N. M. Tunnard-Jones,
I dreamt I woke up: your head was on my pillow.
I thought: A day will come I'll kiss away the sleep-creases from your face!

Nim,
I'll not telephone again.

(Perhaps she has written a letter. The post is *most dreadfully* slow these days.)

II

How Hanmer and I became friends (Part Two) — the time of Dunkirk:
Well, the German who had sounded like meat roasting — like bacon

frying: he was finished burning; and we went home. *Pushing our kites through the gate,* I remember. My Rocinante (Christ, what a presumptuous . . . *innocent* . . . little bastard I was in those days!; but now I am a chastened man of wisdom, of course: Who am I to be a Rocinante's master?) — my poor Rocinante straining, shuddering. Hanmer (over the R/T): "Home. Home. Let's go home. Home." I've no idea why he had to say it so many times.

And we landed and ran to one another and Hanmer threw his arms about me and I threw my arms about him: like . . . like a pair of lovers — well, God in heaven!; and, clutching one another like a pair of lovers, we staggered some little way away from our kites, and there we spewed our scrambled eggs out into the grass: real eggs — *real!:* not at all powdered — yellow and fluffy as a gosling's down (well, yellow and fluffy *once upon a time,* before they had been *received* into our stomachs — *received: ei.* The food: *excellent,* the time of Dunkirk).

I remember trying to clean Hanmer up afterward. A brand-new handkerchief — good Irish linen (my mother had sent me half a dozen not long before). I remember Hanmer's stricken face when suddenly he realized he could not perform the same service for me. The fop! The dandy! But he does not carry handkerchiefs. Too disorganized. Such is Hanmer.

"Well, that's all right," I remember I said — and kept saying it over and over. "That's all right, *Hanmer,*" I said, trying his given name on for size.

We hardly knew one another in those days, Hanmer and I: the time of Dunkirk.

Hanmer's eyes: cunning. . . . *Cunning?!* God yes, the man was white as . . . *death,* I suppose; the man was trembling! But his eyes were . . . cunning. "Luthie, we'll claim this one together. Both of us. Together. Half you half me. Don't you want a half-claim on your record?" Wheedling. "It's good to have a claim or two . . . Helps a chap get established." (I was so new to the squadron then!)

. . .

I was being asked to claim a share in that dreadful death?!

. . .

God! The memories that sizzling sound had brought!

Mrs. Simmonds in her Sunday apron . . . Little globules of fat spattering the stove: they'll be wiped away, scoured away later.

Little globules of fat playing jumping jacks.

. . .

I'd never so much as touched that German! Had not so much as harmed a hair on his head! *I'll have none of that death!*

. . .

"Sir," I said, cautiously. (Hanmer outranked me. He still does, of course. And we hardly knew one another at all in those days.) "Sir, false claims . . ."

Hanmer's eyes: pleading. *(Help me Help me carry that horrible burden. . . . Help me forget that terrible sound. Help me forgive myself — now! now! And I don't mean forever* . . . and his eyes were those of a man in pain: a man willing to do anything to ease the pain . . . *help me forgive myself for just a moment.)* Eyes: pleading.

But his words came harsh: "Don't you *sir* me. *Pilot Officer,* you keep your big teeth in. I'll do the talking! We roasted the bastard Fritz together."

. . .

I'd never harmed that German, though! . . . *How dare you How dare you*

"Go to hell!" I screamed.

. . .

I should not have looked at him then, of course. Had I not looked at him, I'd not have seen those eyes again, of course.

And so there *is* a false half-claim on my record. Yes, officially and in writing, I do carry one half of Hanmer's guilt. That is what binds us.

God! What a bloody idiot Hanmer Acklington is — absolutely! It did not *really* ease his conscience, did it? Well, did it?

(A fleeting thought, now: Would it have eased his conscience if we had never mentioned the *roasted* — *fried* — German: if, officially and in writing —

SECRET   Form F
                    COMBAT REPORT

— the German had never died?)

The other day — two days ago: it was only two days ago? — the day before yesterday, then, I was the one, of course, to receive — *ei* — the news that McGregor's kite had been found.

The . . . remains inside.

The telephone connection: excellent; but the man on the other end was shouting. I held the receiver away from my ear.

The code letters on the kite, etc., etc.: did everything match? It all matched.

Needless to say, the kite had burned. The . . . remains inside.

Oh, I sounded perfectly coherent!: calm and collected. Nobody would have been able to guess that I did not feel well.

What do those miserable children know?

Bloody hell! Why should I have to prove to them that I grieved for McGregor?!

(They'll never read this, of course. I hope.)

•

What do I want for the Wonders?
(I keep repeating it: an incantation.)

And today we waited for Cartwright. But before we had a chance to learn whether he was still among the living, there was a *flap:* we had to go out again.
A terrible ride. I took them on a dreadful ride, this afternoon.

Cartwright is fine. Fine.
(Randall — was that his name: Randall? — he is not fine, of course.)

And I remember the evening of the day McGregor *bought it:* the very same evening the news arrived of Geoff Thomas's demise —
I remember Hanmer: defiant.
"That bastard Hurry-up had better not ask *me* to write The Letter." To Thomas's family, that is. "He can write it himself, the bastard. Luthie, are you really writing The Letter to the bastard McGregor's people?"
I nodded. Shrugged. "Happens. Happens."
Hanmer: "Luthie, you're daft."
And calmly, we drank. Hanmer's brandy.
We are friends. We really are.
Acklington, grow up.

Well, I remember: later in the evening — that very evening, two evenings ago:
Hanmer: *primping* in front of the mirror.
Hanmer: morose. Hanmer: mourning Geoff Thomas. Hanmer: *primping;* retying his idiotic tie, over and over. "Do I look all right? . . . I don't. I know I don't. . . . Shall I comb my hair over the forehead? . . . The cap on straight or at an angle?"
Hanmer was going out to meet his Belgian woman.
. . .

Oh good God yes! Hanmer's Belgian woman! How did it happen I did not mention her earlier?
Too many things happening. (I do not want to have so many things happening. All at once. Too many emotions.)
My style of writing is probably different yet once again from the way it was when I last took notice of such matters.
Well, never mind.
. . .

About Hanmer's *très charmant* — his words — Belgian woman. It was Hanmer's MG that had met the Belgian woman: she was driving on the wrong side of the road. For all of Hanmer's fighter pilot's instincts, the MG had not emerged unscathed from the encounter. Now my dogshit Austin — and Hanmer — were on their way to meet the Belgian woman.

. . .

Hanmer: morose. Hanmer: mourning Geoff Thomas.

Then, Hanmer: *"Très charmant!"* His shark's teeth gleaming.

Door slamming behind Hanmer.

But he probably got no farther than halfway down the hall; came back. And he said, calmly — a responsible man: "I'll write The Letter . . . later. When I've the time." A responsible man. A . . . mature man. I nodded.

Hanmer said, very calmly, "That bastard Hammett — he'd never write The Letter. Not the balls to do it. He leads the squadron from behind his desk. His bloody *progeny* leads the squadron, you know. *'Little Gloria . . . uh-huh . . . plays the piano. She can span an octave between her . . . uh-huh . . . thumb and her second finger . . .'"*

And, for some reason, we both burst out laughing. We fell on Hanmer's bed and laughed and laughed and laughed.

Then, soberly — ha! — we drank. And drank and drank: deeply. And, for a few moments, we were rather . . . happy in our aloneness: together. . . . Aloneness! Outside there was the usual din — people shouting, doors slamming. But we were happy, drinking. It was . . . well, cozy . . . for we all felt abandoned by the whole world.

Acklington, Luthie, grow up.

Then Hanmer brushed his teeth, *very* thoroughly; puffed a big puff of breath into my face; I nodded my approval: no alcohol on his breath; and he departed yet once again.

I went and got the Wonders drunk.

We are friends, Hanmer and I. We really are.

The time of Dunkirk: the ground crews had watched us spewing. I was so very new to the squadron then. It was Hanmer's reputation saved *my* reputation, I think. His reputation for . . . fearlessness? *Valor?* Hanmer Acklington the Debonair. Hanmer Acklington of the Stout Heart.

. . .

"Well, they were overexcited," the ground people said then. "Everyone is overexcited once in a while."

. . .

That is what binds us.

God, oh God, things are so very complicated!

. . .

Brown, for example, spilling his strawberry jam all over the Ready Room floor the other day . . . What will they say — are they saying — about him?

On the other hand, Brown seems to have gained some popularity to-day when he began to shout at Stanhope.

Everything is so terribly complicated!

III

And this afternoon, I led the Wonders —

. . .

My fault. My mistake: my miscalculation (the understatement of the century).

. . .

The controllers . . . they vector us; I interpret their mumbo-jumbo and then do my very best to plot out a textbook case of interception. *Wizard! Stunning! Smashing! Well done, Luthie!* (*Conscientious* is one of my many middle names, isn't it?)

. . .

There are times when it is less *well done*. Today . . . Well, God Christ!

(Grenfeld was the first to call out: "Tallyho!" . . . Grenfeld: eyes as sharp as Hanmer's teeth are sharp.)

And at first I could not believe it. There the Fritzes were: with ab-solutely every advantage. (Including numbers, of course. There always are the numbers, of course.) The only thing worse would have been to get jumped out of the blue — no warning whatsoever, no idea where they had come from.

My first feeling: embarrassment. Mortification. Oh, utter *utter* shame!

My first impulse: turn tail and run. Run Run Get out Never come back. *I do not run.*

. . .

Well, shout at the Wonders to run and never come back. *We do not run.*

It is about six or seven hours later now.

I think about it. *W. R. Luthie does not run.* Is that cowardice — or is it courage?

Well, this is what happened then: I took a good big whiff of oxygen, to make myself feel better. (I could only hope the Wonders did the same.)

Time slowed down, then. Time . . . it stood absolutely still. Well, that is what fear does: makes time slow down. And one is so very much aware of every smallest detail of *absolutely everything. We do not run.*

(And it is our task to try to get the bombers. Ignore the fighters . . . ? Go and get the bombers. But the 109s had spotted us long since and were coming coming coming *down* upon us . . .)

(Most of our trips are rather suicidal: was this so terribly different? Yes, it was. It was.)

"Let's go," I said. "Let's go. . . . Going in." *Going in???*

(Let's get the bloody bombers. Let's try to get the bombers. They're the ones do the most damage, after all.)

. . .

The rest of it truly does not bear repeating: I already told the IO about it at the debriefing.

"Lad," he said. "Lad, let's . . . you know . . . do it over: a word here and there . . . ?"

"Let's edit it?"

"Quite," he said. "Right. Right."

The IO: a man of experience. Some of them — I hear — they can't tell the airscrew from the tail. He flew in the First War, the Great War.

His name is Jimmy. *Not* Jim — it is Jimmy. His small paunch strains against his belt.

. . .

What I did not tell *Jimmy:*

It happens often — though not always — that I am the last one to land, after a scrap.

This time, I most certainly did not expect all the Wonders to be there, intact (minus Cartwright, of course — I still had no idea at that time what had become of Cartwright).

But they were there.

And we all dripped with sweat, of course. Our clothes: soaked with sweat. We stank of sweat. All the Wonders' hair looked *black,* I remember. (Most of them had got rid of their helmets. Their hair, sweat-soaked, plastered to their skulls. Their hair . . . drying in the breeze.) Grimy faces. The men of Flight B: so many little mounds of filth. The ground crews: they with their hands — and all their clothes — forever stained with engine oil: they were the clean ones! . . .

And the Wonders were rather desperately puffing on their cigarettes, I remember. Farrell: his hands shaking.

Stanhope: his hands shaking; his teeth chattering.

Ashley: his teeth chattering; his hands shaking.

I did not feel well.

I gave them a brazen Luthie grin. "Sorry," I said, humbly.

They did not seem to blame me!

. . .

Dark smudges — circles — under their eyes. But there was a fire in those eyes. The eyes of men — well, God in heaven! — the eyes of men capable of either great cruelty or great courage. The eyes of men capable of a great viciousness or great courage. They appeared . . . satisfied.

And so I stood there. Rather desperately, I puffed on my cigarette, I remember.

That was the last time we had to go out this afternoon.

•

Cartwright is fine. Fine.

Came back not long before dinner, in the passenger seat of a battered little Morris: a village vicar's wife? (so I understand: a gorgeous creature!) driving.

Life goes on:

Is Stanhope trying to grow a mustache? One of those lush, ridiculous-looking RAF mustaches?

. . .

It's another RAF affectation, that mustache — along with the top button on the tunic unbuttoned: *I am a fighter pilot!* that top button undone proclaims to the world; also the maps and paperwork in general sticking out of one's boots: the more the better — *a man of importance.*

. . .

Ah. Stanhope, Stanhope! God in heaven!

Can he manage to grow a true, lush, ridiculous RAF mustache?

Life goes on.

IV

About Hanmer and me:

It's a peculiar thing, really: neither of us has any trouble eating bacon, really.

59

And the next day — so Ashley would remember — Farrell discovered on his final approach that he could not put his undercarriage down. Around and around Farrell went: one two three four circuits. The tower trying to talk him down.

"He'll prang 'er."

"He won't."

"He'll prang 'er."

(Flying Officer Luthie had not landed yet. Luthie would not learn about the . . . incident till it was over.)

Was Farrell's breakfast — curdled — all the way back up in his mouth, again (in fear)? Was he feeling *really really* lonely (as Ashley often felt lonely, in fear)?

Stanhope: "Well, take 'er up and send her . . . somewhere." (Where there were no houses? But where was there a place here where one could be *ab-*

solutely sure there would be no houses?!) "Send 'er somewhere and bail out."

"He'll prang."

But then, on the fifth attempt, the U/C just as suddenly did go down; and Farrell came in. He let himself down from his kite and began to walk around in circles. Flapping his arms: a very very large bird — a bloody *swan?* But his teeth sounded as if he had *too many* teeth: his teeth chattering (and swans hadn't got any teeth, now had they?) "Leave me alone . . . Well, bugger off, will you? Leave me alone."

By then Flying Officer Luthie had come in. Well, there he was! And what did he do? He pushed a brandy flask between Farrell's teeth. "Here. . . . No more, though. . . . Enough, I said. *Enough!* Come come," said Luthie to Farrell, and he sounded . . . well, my God! resolute and self-assured, "these things happen. You aren't the first or the last."

And all at once, Farrell's face was full of rage and . . . hurt. (But he stopped flapping his arms about, and he stopped guzzling the brandy as if it were the last in the world.)

Flying Officer Luthie said, in a quiet voice, "Sergeant Farrell, go to the Med. Section. That is an order. Tell them you need to sleep. Somebody . . ." Ah, somebody would be *delegated* to go with Farrell! Flying Officer Luthie looked about. . . . Well, Farrell would be going to the Med. Section: he was out of the fray. And Brown had been stung by a bumblebee earlier that morning, and by now his right hand was the size of . . . of . . . well, *almost* the size of one of those barrage balloons one saw over London — all the cities — these days. Brown was in bed! — *an invalid!* (And whatever respect he may have gained by telling Stanhope that he sounded like a fish at feeding time: that respect was gone now. They laughed at him in viciousness and malice.)

Could Luthie spare a man to accompany Farrell? Send one of the ground crew, perhaps? (Or the blood wagon people: yes, yes, there had been a blood wagon at the ready, and a fire engine, too; but they all were gone now because Farrell after all was not bleeding or anything.) My God, would Luthie *dishonor* Farrell — would he? — by having him *nursemaided* by a kiwi?! (Ashley watched.)

Luthie grinned. "You're all right. Just go."

And so Farrell departed, his shoulders sagging in . . . resignation: God yes, he himself knew by now that he was in bad need of some good *artificial* sleep.

But then, quite suddenly, he squared his shoulders: he most certainly was strong enough to get there under his own power!

The rest of Flight B exchanged looks, uncertain, seeking agreement: well . . . had Luthie done a decent job of it?

The men of Flight B settled down in the grass and waited: for the loudspeaker to crackle; for the telephone in the Ready Room to ring.

They would be going off ops. at 1500 hours.
Please, God, let there not be a "flap" before 1500 hours.

Life had settled into a routine.
(Did it matter?)

40

A morning of blessings:
Nobody I know was killed yesterday.

How my father the pacifist became a pacifist:
How I came into manhood(?)
. . .

Not now? (Because it is a story full of hurt? . . . And this is a beautiful morning.)
. . .

Well, having launched into the storytelling the other day, must I now go on — on and on and on? And will anything of importance have happened — anything of significance been achieved — once all the story-telling is finished . . . if I finish?
. . .

And now I live and now my life is done, etc., etc. Time presses on me. But that is what drives me forward. . . . Why *am* I writing all this down?

Morning. The luxury of time, the luxury of splendid solitude. (Hanmer and Flight A: ops. till 1400. I am blessedly alone.)
We bicker, Hanmer and I. The man of untidy! (The fop? The dandy?) I do not think I am *fanatically* neat; still . . . the luxury of solitude.

My Dear People
Sibelius on the wireless — the Second Symphony

. . . again: the one Ashley the Nosy Parker had — probably? — caught me "conducting." This time I shall finish listening.

My Dear People:
It occurs to me, by the way, that lately I've had no news from you re harvest: the pearmains should be ready to pick soon.

(Our apples: Cox's orange pippins, mainly; some Worcester pearmains.)

•

And it is morning. I *know* there will be a letter from Nim in the post.
(I sit in bittersweet solitude. . . . Nobody I know was killed yesterday.)

How my father the pacifist became a pacifist:
Has had duty thrust upon him (I've said that before, haven't I?) — he is not an apple-grower by choice or inclination. A medical man by training, my father (I've said that before), and trained as a surgeon; and in 1916 he was on the Somme.

Not just my uncle Robert was killed in the Somme: my uncle George Henry, too. My grandparents learned about both deaths on the same day: one telegram in the morning, one in the afternoon. Christ! (And afterward, everyone called it the Great War. Now it is simply the First War.) The present war began on a Sunday, almost a year ago.

Oh God God God. Poor old Farrell, yesterday: arms flapping like a grounded duck . . .
And my mind turns to Ashley. Is there more to him than meets the eye? A kindred spirit, of sorts? God in heaven!

HANMER IS MISSING.

(Later.)
Hanmer's called in. Is without a scratch. Well, with scratches — but not *large* scratches. He bailed out. Must take the train back.

Shall I put my last-but-one jar of mixed fruits from Fortnum's on his bedside table: a welcome-home present? (The man loves the stuff.) (The Wonders and I: ops. at 1300; thus, I'll not be here when he arrives.)

(One should not have friends in wartime. One should not. But there are ties that bind us.)

Evening.
Again! Again!!! No one I know was killed today!!! Peterson: shot down not long after Hanmer, but is all right.

Hanmer: at the Med. Section *for observation*. A blinding headache, but he is fine. Fine. I took my welcome-home present there. Hanmer: grubbing about with his fingers for bits of pineapple. Hanmer's shark's teeth: demolishing the pineapple.

Solitude. (No letter from Nim, of course. . . . Well, perhaps she writes them, but then she does not send them — as I have done with all of mine.)
(But I've left all those telephone messages for her, now haven't I?)

About combat:
I come back from ops. and empty my mind of the *actual events* of

combat. I try to think about something else. Took my usual beauty nap, after dinner: exhausted. . . . Ah, healthful, invigorating sleep — no dreams!: this time. I did not dream about Nim at all, this time.

N. M. Tunnard-Jones . . . You woman of exquisite eyebrows . . .

Colin Kenley is dead.
   A Flight A chap named Jennings is dead. (I did not know him well.)
   Our little Geoff Thomas is dead. . . . McGregor is dead.
   And that poor devil Randall: stayed with us for barely four hours . . .

The present war began on a Sunday.
   (Having begun the storytelling, I must finish.)
   · · ·

What do I want for the men of Flight B?
   (I began the storytelling the other day. I must finish.)

The present war . . .
   (How I came into manhood.)
   Well, that Saturday evening: we sat (after dinner) reading: my father read his book, and my mother read hers, and I read my book.
   (But during the day on Saturday: business as usual — I'd been packing: the summer over; and by Tuesday I'd be off: Cambridge.
   Well, God in heaven! Have I mentioned this before? Well, perhaps once the war was on, it no longer seemed important, really. But, oh yes, I've had one year at Cambridge — not a well-known college at all, though. And I'll never have the second year, now, I suppose; nor the third. Well, for all my being in love with words; for all my pushing of pencils across paper: drawings, sketches — for all that, I've grown too old now for lectures, I think, and for *wise* discussions with tutors. And even then, at the time . . .
   God has put me on this earth to fly aeroplanes: to me, the best part of being at Cambridge was the CU Air Squadron.)
   · · ·
   Saturday, then. After a while I shut the book; made my way downstairs — at the kitchen table Mrs. Simmonds knitting, looking cross . . . because she kept dropping her *purls? stitches!* She could not see: dabbing at her nose, her eyes, with a hanky, now and then. And Mr. Parrish still held forth, as he had all day: "They'll back down, mark my words. They'll not want to tangle with us again." Well, in the afternoon my father had at last snapped at him, though I had never before heard my father say an unkind word to Mr. Parrish. But still Mr. Parrish held forth, now; and Tom and Janet simply looked glum, and soon they quietly went off to bed in the gardener's cottage where they lived. That was the Saturday.
   · · ·

(Tom is dead now, of course.)

I had no trouble sleeping in those days.

Still, that night: well, it was the time when *ghosts are done walking* — four o'clock? — when finally I hurtled into sleep as a stone does into water. And in the morning, my people let me sleep: the good old stiff upper lip, God damn it! — business as usual. And after I finally woke up, I took a good, long soaking bath — oh, it felt wonderful! God damn it. And thus I never heard The Fateful Words on the wireless: "Therefore . . . Britain is at war with Germany." (In London, the air raid sirens sounded almost at once, I understand — though of course no air raid came then. For us . . . for me . . . Birds chirping: the bathroom window was open. Apples ripening in the orchard. And so on and so on.)

Finally, my father could stand it no longer; knocked on the door.

I said, "Come in." He came in. Looked at me in my nakedness. Rather stared.

Shall I cover myself?

. . .

Well, take a look. Keep looking.

I *am* your flesh.

. . .

And he kept staring. At last, he sat down — heavily — on the rim of the bathtub: his leg clearly was bothering him. He did not look a well man. I said, after a while, "I'll go tomorrow. Sign up." And he did not say anything. Then, a few moments later, he turned the tap on; ran some more hot water into the bathtub.

Steam rising.

I remember: my father leaning forward, elbows on knees; his fingers in a steeple in front of his face. He began to talk. Steam rising.

(This is how I came into manhood — etc., etc.)

And now, what in the —! (An interruption . . . Resumed later.)

The bloody Germans!

Well, suddenly, there were windows rattling. (One's very bones rattling.) No, *not* lorries rumbling. *Not* tanks, out on the road.

. . .

People pouring out into the hall. I ran out into the hall.

And we ran outside. . . . . We are the Royal Air Force: be-pajama'd; be-dressing-gowned. Barefoot. Oh yes, helpless.

And here . . . there: the . . . Huns. Up above us. In the darkness. But yes, we can see them — oh, we can *feel* them! Shadows — shadows. Where are they going? Do they know we are down here? How many of them? *So many!* It makes one's bones rattle.

And no sirens had wailed: no alert! (Well, nothing we could have done about it, anyway: this base does not possess night-fighting capability.) And so they are unopposed. No ack-ack. (It makes one's bones rattle.)

And then . . . a single straggler. An He-111, by the sound. His engines badly synchronized. The poor sod!

Well, for a while we talked about what we'd do to the straggler should he find himself among us. It does not make a pleasant tale to tell. Not hatred, really, but . . . *scientific fervor:* the very same fierce concentration Stanhope had exhibited when letting melted ice cream drip on his bare feet. *No:* the fervor of nine-year-olds pulling wings off a fly.

And a good time was had by all. The Fritzes gone, we rather relished the sound of our voices — and our plans: *Ughh . . . Disgusting!*

By and by I returned to my room.

Hubbub out in the hall; then hubbub fading. Single voice; more hubbub; voices fading.

(And now here is Nim's face: looking at me. It's the drawing I've pinned to the wall.)

Before I went over Dunkirk for the very first time, my father the pacifist had given me a knife.

(My wrists: my watchband *still* is a bother, sometimes. I take the watch off, now and again. . . . Well, what time is it? *Time to go to sleep.* Never mind.)

I am frightened.

I remember:

God, they looked so . . . comical, the Wonders, descending into their drunkenness with such a . . . *desperate* gusto! (after McGregor, that is).

. . .

But life goes on: Stanhope most definitely is trying to grow a mustache!

My father was on the Somme. (Had offered his services to King and Country: I've said that before.)

Slaughter: the Somme. Everyone knows that. He worked day and night. (Red-rimmed eyes. Sand behind the eyelids.) Trying to put together what others had torn apart. He and those with him worked without rest. (And all that.) And he had long since stopped looking at the faces of the men on the operating table before him. Never ever looked at their faces. (A terrible fatigue of the soul. And all that.) Until one afternoon? evening? morning? "Well, it was the body that was familiar, actually." So he said to me (and he sat there on the edge of the bathtub that first day . . . Sunday . . . of the present war; shifted his weight: his leg must be bothering him). "There was not much left of the body, actually. But one knows. . . . It was the hand, actually. He was all draped, you know . . . all ready for me . . . and the hand slipped out. I knew. Well, we'd grown up together, after all. Three brothers. . . . No need to look. . . . I looked. And the face was unmarred. The face was untouched."

(My father: after his first wife's death — *without issue* — he had at one time considered giving up his birthright — the house and all that comes with it — in favor of my uncle Robert.

My uncle Robert: the only one of the three brothers with a true *farmer's* love of the place.)

Well, my father said then, that time on the Somme, "I do need a rest. I . . . I'm dizzy, I think. A bit faint. Tired. Cannot go on. Need a rest. Please . . . Somebody. Would you take over for just a minute, just till I've had a rest? . . . I'm about to . . . faint," said my father.

And somebody — a kind soul — said, "Do have a lie-down, Luthie. . . . Have a cig. Whatever. . . . Have a nip. I'll take over."

And so my father walked out of the tent that was the operating room, and leaned against a tree trunk: leaned his face against the bark ("And to my dying day I'll not forget how . . . how much it hurt, rubbing my cheek against that bark. Well, that was what I wanted, actually, you know: to have some part of my body hurting, so that my . . . my . . . soul would not hurt; I wanted to hate the tree for hurting me, so that my hatred of people would not overwhelm me."); and my uncle Robert died.

And I'll not forget (though nearly a year has passed since he told me): Steam rising. (*I* ran some hot water into the bathtub.)
. . .

Luthie . . . Don't ask, "Did you tell them?" My grandparents.
. . .

(I'll not forget: it was a beautiful day, outside. The sky blue as a child's painting of it. A true Sunday-type Sunday. Et cetera.)

There was silence between us. What does one say?

"She didn't *really* hate you, you know." My grandmother. "Toward the end I think she'd forgotten, in a way . . . well, not *forgotten,* but all those feelings were rather . . . worn-out: tired. Do you know what I mean?"

(Would that *matter* to him?)
. . .

(Drip. Drip. Water dripping.)
. . .

"She simply held a monstrous . . . terrible . . . a bad grudge."
(Tell the truth.)
. . .

(Water dripping.

And my father's fingers: still in a steeple in front of his face. His *still* are a surgeon's hands, by God! Suddenly, he bit down on both his thumbs. Hard.)

. . .

"But Grandfather," I hurried on, "he spoke of you — sometimes. Not unkindly. You two were very much alike, you know. . . . And so my uncle Robert may have been Grandmother's favorite . . . when you were children. But you most definitely used to be his. I think. Well, you *remained* his favorite! I swear. And I was terribly fond of him, you know. He seemed to be . . . well, at peace with himself and the world — as much as one can be, under the circumstances. . . . But there was a *reasonableness* about him. Oh, absolutely! He took me fishing once. We did not catch anything. Drank tea out of little folding cups: we had a slurping contest. . . . I must have written to you about it in a letter."

And at that, my father shrugged; then he gave a wave of the hand: well, that letter had been a long time ago.

(Birds chirping outside. A breeze in the trees.

. . .

God . . . if you exist . . . God, please grant me thoughts as small and peaceful as the leaves of those trees outside the window.)

"They both loved me!" (I almost cried it out.) "Well, *she* loved me — after her own fashion! She did not hold it against *me* at all that I looked like my uncle Robert. . . . And she never spoke against you in my presence, you know — not till she got really . . . old. She simply seldom mentioned you. Now that is true." (Tell the truth.)

"It did make me wonder, of course. I *tried* not to wonder. Mainly, it made me uncomfortable to be compared to my uncle Robert all the time. But she did not hold it against you, you know, that you . . . well, *produced* a child who looked like my uncle Robert and then . . . well, one day *presented* her with a *twelve-year-old Robert!* She simply permitted herself . . . well, she let it bring her comfort."

(God in heaven, I was defending her! Was that what he wanted to hear?)

"And even before that! Do you remember all those toffees? Little tins. Pictures on them. The Brighton Pavilion. A Cottage. . . . All those knee stockings, all hand-knitted. 'My Dearest Darling Grandson: Emmeline has decided to have her kittens in the Library, between *Mill on the Floss* and the Milton.' That was Emmeline the Second."

"Well, I read those letters to you, didn't I?" And my father sounded . . . well, bitter. "*I* wrote letters to them. They wrote back. We all were civilized together." And he exploded: "Bloody hell! I came to my father's funeral, didn't I? It very nearly bankrupted me. Us. You. I very nearly . . . *mortgaged* your . . . *future.*"

. . .

Well, yes. We are not what one would call wealthy people.

Imperial Airways . . . etc. etc.: a journey frightfully expensive, no doubt about it.

Never before had I thought of it that way.

(I remember: there was a fly in the room. An end-of-the-summer fly: old; undercarriage in poor working order. Heavy . . . wallowing . . . it came in for a landing on the edge of the bathtub. Sat, resting. I stared at it.)

After a while, my father said, "God, you weren't there when I told them. I don't know why I told them. The blame is on me: I should not have told them. I wanted absolution. And when I didn't get it, I didn't like it. . . . I wanted punishment. And when I got it, I didn't like it. I wanted absolution, but I hurt them. I must have been mad. I delivered . . . what a blow! They never stopped blaming me. He said I should have *tried* to stay with him and save him. She said I *should have saved him.* She did call me her son's murderer. Not my brother's: her son's. And she meant it. . . . He said I should have *tried* to save him."

"Well, you could not have done it." (What does one say?)

. . .

Bloody hell! Did it really come out — could it be *construed* as coming out — a question?

. . .

Shall I say, "I swear to God I didn't mean it to come out a question?"

. . .

Christ! Would he strike me?

He didn't, of course.

"No, I could not save him." His voice was even, by God!

(And I remember: the fly, startled — frightened? — by the sudden movement of his hand — would he strike me? He didn't, of course — the fly swung nose into wind, wearily, and took off again, in a resigned fashion.)

My father the pacifist. For him, no cause is rightful or righteous enough to justify a war.

But my God, what did he expect me to do (on that first morning of the first day of the present war)? *To say, "No, I will not go and sign up tomorrow. Something similarly dreadful may happen to my . . . soul?"*

. . .

Dreadful things happen in war. (I was a year younger then, of course. Older than the Wonders are now, though.)

. . .

I do not want the Wonders! I don't want them!

. . .

I did not want them.

I remember:

When I first arrived in Scotland — when I first learned that the command of Flight B had been visited upon me — well, I sat down that very evening — I am a man who knows how to use words — and I wrote a letter to the Air Ministry — passionate words, but carefully chosen — I wrote a letter refusing the command.

The very next afternoon, Old Hurry-up called me in. "Mr. . . . uh-huh . . . Luthie . . . Would you . . . uh-huh . . . come with me?"

And we went. *To the bog!*

A trick of magic — a sleight of hand: my letter in his *hand-cream-pampered paws!* And he tore the letter into little pieces, and he flushed the scraps down the loo.

"Mr. Luthie, you may go now." *No* "uh-huh." . . . Well, God in heaven!
. . .

But at the time, I barely mentioned in these pages an encounter with Hammett other than the one concerning a Miles Master for Stanhope. *More about that later?* I'd said, merely: because, at that time, I'd meant to write about the letter incident at much greater length, someday?! — when I'd gathered my thoughts together, when I could explain it all clearly.

It was most terribly important to me then. Now, suddenly, it no longer seems to matter much.
. . .

I am fairly responsible, I think, for my age.
. . .

The Wonders: my punishment from On High?
. . .

How I came into manhood . . .)

Well, after the war — the Great War — my father left for India again: with his second wife, my mother; and it was as a pen-pusher he went, an administrator: the head of a tiny mission hospital in a Godforsaken town in the Punjab. (And cannas grew in front of the hospital — big *red* RED *ENORMOUS;* hibiscus in the back.) My father never touched a patient with a surgeon's hand — not ever again.

Before I went over Dunkirk for the very first time, my father gave me the knife — he gave it to me in the Gents of the railway station at Manchester. Pushing this vicious thing at me. "Here. Take it. Take it. Before somebody comes sees us." One of those cunning weapons: press on a spring; the blade slides out. "It saved my life once. In the First War, you know."

(But medical personnel are not supposed to carry weapons.)

I did not say anything.

(One discovers things about people that one didn't know were there.)

In memory of that Sunday, I took the knife.

(How I came into manhood.)
. . .

But what had he expected me to do on that Sunday?
(I've no time to think about it, really.)

(And to this day, I've no idea what my father said to my grandmother to make her rise from her bed on the eve of my grandfather's funeral.)

There are things that hurt.

Ah, the Wonders!
    Their eyes: the eyes of men capable of either great cruelty or great valor . . .
    . . .
    And Farrell: flapping his arms, gulping the brandy, yesterday . . . (It was to laugh — as Hanmer would say. A dog would laugh.)

Are we a family blighted: by war?
    (Ha! Permanence. Tradition. Emmeline the Fourth.
    It was my uncle Robert, I think, named the very first Emmeline.)

Nim's face . . .

41

And so they had emptied themselves of McGregor. McGregor seemed to be forgotten.
    (The chap named Randall had not stayed long enough to be remembered, let alone forgotten. Time was passing both slowly and quickly.)
    Was Ashley the only one who remembered? Was he the only one who still — every now and then: not very often, mind you — thought about that night after the day McGregor died? (But this was not the time for thinking, really — only reacting.)

What Ashley remembered: He had been the only one who hadn't got drunk that night Luthie had taken them to get drunk.
    My God! Luthie: what a clever man!
    Cleanliness about him.
    Had commandeered a lorry that night. "LACW [Whatever-Her-Name] has kindly agreed to give us a lift into town. We'll have to walk back, though. Unfortunately. . . . She is going to the station to pick up . . . flour? No, sugar." (Under the stupid cover of bloody darkness. Darkness. Darkness. Ordinary Life was lived in darkness these days.)

Did they want to get drunk? They didn't want to get drunk. Well, they rather resented being dragged to get drunk, didn't they? Oh, they hated being dragged to get drunk! They hated Luthie: hated hated hated. Because . . . because . . . Why?

They went to get drunk. (The *sheep:* so Ashley thought then.

The *sheep:* so Ashley thought now.)

(But how did one say no to an officer? To one's flight commander? Would that be . . . *mutiny?*)

Luthie: ah, that *shrewd* man! (For example, *a lift into town!*: well, at that time not a single one of them had so much as set foot in the town yet — nobody'd *seen* the town yet, except from the air. Did they want to see the town: McGregor or no McGregor?)

· · ·

They went to get drunk.

And Ashley remembered: the bed of the lorry had smelled not of flour or sugar: not of things baked — and sweet; it'd smelled of . . . earth; dust: things . . . sad. No. . . . Of potatoes?

Somebody — Brown — began to sneeze, so Ashley remembered.

They went to get drunk.

· · ·

This had happened how long ago? not long ago? Well, the past had an altogether *odd* way of becoming the past, hadn't it?

The present:

The replacement for the chap named Randall arrived: his name was Peploe-Webb.

And Stanhope was shot down, but came back; and that evening at dinner he sat next to Cartwright: *the only two men in Flight B to have been shot down and lived to tell about it — an exclusive club.* . . . But Cartwright and Stanhope did not talk about it: talked about other things.

Well, who would tell Ashley what it had been like — *really* like — after McGregor had been shot down, that is; on the night Luthie had taken them to get drunk? "You know, downing all those pints one after another . . . being blotto . . . *was it different from any other time?*" Who *could* tell him? Grenfeld? Well, Grenfeld seldom spoke, these days. Grenfeld was . . . well my God, fairly obsessed! True, it was the very quietest obsession Ashley had ever seen in his life, but obsession nevertheless with killing his first German (he had not succeeded yet).

And the others? Did they know themselves well enough to be able to answer the question? (Now Grenfeld from the very start had seemed to know himself well enough. What would he say if he ever did start talking?)

· · ·

And so they had found a pub (that night Luthie had taken them to get drunk). A rather crowded place, the pub.

Did they want to get drunk? They proceeded to get drunk.

They drank in silence. They drank and began to talk. They drank and began to shout. They shouted very loudly. Screamed. Shrieked. . . . Laughed.

(Ah, there had been a lot of other people in the pub! But then . . . there weren't: everybody had left. Well, had they all left because, for some reason — why? — they hadn't wanted to be with them: with the men of Flight B? Because they'd . . . well, *reached a conclusion* that, all in all, it would be *better* — *safer* — my God! . . . to leave them alone?

(But Ashley thought about it only now.)

(Actually, try as he might, Ashley could not remember what the publican had looked like. He couldn't remember the name of the pub! He couldn't remember *anything about the town!*)

"Grenfeld! Hey, Grenfeld . . . Jeremy."

But it was only inside his head that he would sometimes begin these . . . conversations with Grenfeld, when, in the middle of the night, he would come awake with a start (at three in the morning?). And yes, he'd been dreaming . . . oh, not about being drunk; not about Do-17s, He-111s, or Ju-88s; nor about . . . tracer, for example: see it coming at you . . . sit there and do nothing . . . watch it coming coming . . . like a rabbit *mesmerized* by a snake . . . scared scared scared. Actually, he had dreamt about . . . the girl from Campbell's, again? But in the dream the girl had looked like Buttercup — she who vectored them on to The Enemy; but Ashley had never really seen Buttercup, and thus the girl in the dream looked rather the way Ashley *thought* Buttercup would look: it all was very confusing, and Ashley's poor male body was hurting; and he could not get to sleep again.

"Well, I *mourned* McGregor," Ashley said (to Grenfeld), and felt righteous.

Grenfeld (inside Ashley's head) did not ask: "Why?" (Grenfeld — inside Ashley's head — never asked: "Why?")

(Now John — Ashley's brother John — dead now for a *long* time: he could not comprehend anything unless it was explained to him three times.) And it came to Ashley that for the first time in his life he was thinking unkindly about his dead brother. Did he feel as guilty now as he had that time when in one of his dreams it had occurred to him that his motorcycle — *once his brother's motorcycle* — was something of a nuisance, really? Should he feel guilty?

"I sat and didn't get drunk. Well, had a pint or two. . . . Watched old Yellow Brown sneezing and sneezing in his beer. *He* got blotto."

(*Yellow* Brown: that had been the last thing McGregor had left with them. *Yellow* Brown. *Yellowbelly Brown.* Brown — who, in his fear, had spewed his strawberry jam all over the Ready Room floor.

Well, it had been rather unlike McGregor, really: well, my God, *unsubtle!* And Ashley had despised him — hated him — for it.)

But *somebody* had to mourn McGregor. Somebody had to do it.
It was a noble thing to do.

. . .

(God! Had a sixth sense of some sort told McGregor that sooner or later he was bound to lose his tug-of-war with Luthie? Was that why he'd become so . . . unsubtle, desperate: *Yellow* Brown and all that?

And, for just a moment, Ashley felt sorry for McGregor. All the others had emptied themselves of McGregor.)

The *sheep,* so Ashley thought. Herded by the *sheepdog:* by Luthie.

"Luthie wasn't drunk," Ashley said (to Grenfeld). (And mercifully, Grenfeld, inside Ashley's head, did not say: "How so?") "Luthie was not drunk."

And Ashley's and Luthie's eyes had met.

Luthie's eyes: startled. Wide. Wide. Startled.

My God! *Did he think Ashley was just like the rest of them?* (All eager to be . . . manipulated? My God!) *Well, Flying Officer Bloody Luthie had another think coming!*

The man's eyes: so quiet and reasonable when Ashley had first met him. Actually, now they were simply . . . determined.

Startled. Shocked? . . . Determined.

Yes, Luthie was *manipulating* them: the *men* of Flight B.

And so they stared at each other, Ashley and Luthie; and they understood each other. . . . Was Luthie pleading once again for Ashley's understanding — as he had that time when Brown had started spewing? No no. Well, quiet and reasonable — and determined — he simply seemed to be offering himself for . . . examination: *This is how things are. This is how I am. Take it or leave it. McGregor is gone, and this is my chance. Take it or leave it.* Luthie was . . . changing. My God, Luthie was changed!

He grinned at Ashley: a rather small and . . . *tight* grin. A grin . . . defiant? No, merely determined. Then he relaxed; and it was a *nice* grin. Open. With a hint of . . . well, God damn it all! . . . a hint of compassion . . . God damn it all! . . . *compassion for Ashley?*

What should Ashley do?

(Well, here they all were, Flight B — all of them blotto, and all of them empty of all emotions — empty of McGregor forever, and of fear of death for the time being. And so Ashley felt terribly alone. And oh my God, it mattered so that he felt alone! . . . Yes, most certainly things mattered once again.)

Very, very cautiously, Ashley grinned back. Tried to make his grin . . . *cynical.* Tried. Tried. And so here they were, grinning at each other: two . . . conspirators together.

But Ashley was not sure at all that he liked it. Oh my God, he did not like it! (And it mattered that he didn't like it.)

•

And then they did walk home: more or less. (Luthie running, prancing about like a clumsy greyhound. No: like a real *sheepdog* herding *sheep*. Barking; nipping at their heels. *Cleanliness* about him.) They had to stop and wait twice: once while Stanhope spewed his beer and his dinner right there on the gravel in the middle of the road; once when Cartwright did the same into the grass by the side of the road.

But by the next afternoon, when they were up for ops. again, their heads were remarkably clear.

Then time began to pass both very slowly and very quickly.
   "Gooseberry tarts, gentlemen . . . And trifle, gentlemen. Trifle . . ."
   (The men of Flight B: each as if alone.
   Luthie watching over them all.)

4 2

I

I am myself. Nobody and nothing can change me.

Why I went to war of my own free will:
   (No, not this time. I'll not think about it.)

Combat:
   (When the day is done, sometimes it is not possible to remove oneself altogether from the actual events of combat.)
   Over the R/T one hears commands, mostly, and the most foul language imaginable. In two languages, sometimes.
   What one sees: well, a sky empty . . . suddenly. And one hears silence. (There is the engine, of course; but that is not an *outside* sound: it is an inseparable part of one's very being.)
   Clear sky. And one is so wonderfully, terribly alone!
   Somebody breathing: over the R/T.
   Christ! A *German* breathing?!: over the R/T.
   · · ·

   Well, go ahead and breathe. Go home and breathe.
   · · ·

   Oh no you don't, you bastard. Bastard bastard bastard. (Blood lust. And all that.)

There are commands, over the R/T; and the most foul language one can imagine. People die in middle of an utterance they never would *choose* as their dying words. (Or would they?)
   I am myself.
   · · ·

The sound of bacon frying . . . *That's enough!*

(When the day is done, sometimes it is not possible to remove oneself from the events — think about something else: thoughts small and *ordinary.*)

I had *another* very close call today. My second since we arrived here. An *exceedingly* close call. . . . Never mind.

II

Why I *volunteered* to go to war:

(This story definitely belongs with the other two. How I came into manhood, etc., etc.)
  · · ·

Why I went to war:

November. (Yes. Flying training. November. The war, of course, had begun some two months before; it was November now.) I was billeted in the house of an elderly couple. (She made wonderful scones. He drank.) November.

God! This afternoon I had a very *very* dicey time of it! A miserably close call.

But now I flex my fingers; shift my weight in my chair . . .

A living being: W. R. Luthie. Ah . . . yawning!
  · · ·

Hanmer: asleep. Was asleep when I returned from dinner: a note on my pillow asking me to wake him at 2100. Well, his *très charmant* Belgian, again: she comes all the way from London to meet him! He showed me a photo of her last night: oh, a striking woman — most definitely! Not beautiful, really, but rather . . . *extravagantly* handsome. Just the kind of woman Hanmer would like. Her eyes . . . well, I may be mistaken, but they seem to be the eyes of a thoroughly *nice* person. . . . A thoroughly levelheaded person? Just the kind of woman Hanmer needs.

Bless you, my children!

For me: Nim's silence — an ever-present dull ache. Oh, absolutely!

But: am I settling into resignation? Bloody hell!
  · · ·

I seem to have reached a plateau of sorts: after a period of rather too many emotions, I now feel all . . . calm inside, well don't I? — and quite without peaks and valleys of strong feelings. (The Wonders and I: Have we reached this plateau together, at the same time?) And yet I am restless. Bloody hell!
  · · ·

(I sit now — tap my pencil against my teeth; I listen: puff puff puff. Hanmer puffing away in his sleep, as usual. He, too, has had an uneasy time: shot down again. His second time.)

•

Why I went to war:

Well, when I was training, there was a chap . . .

. . .

November.

Frost on the ground; tree branches: white lacework . . . I arrived: the beginning of flying training; my home for the duration: a *sedate*-looking small house in a sedate-looking village. "There will be three of you young gentlemen upstairs," the landlady said. And in the small room under the eaves, the middle bed was crumpled up already. On the one by the window a woebegone-looking moonface sat. (Ah, Luthie, Luthie! It's the bed by the stove for you. Oh God!: the plains of India in midsummer when that miserable stove gets going!)

. . .

Well, I advanced on Moonface, hand outstretched. "Luthie, W. R."

Moonface looked woebegone. (But he had snagged the best bed in the house.) "Jiří Vřešťala," he said. (Well, that is how it is spelled.)

Monkeys chattering! "Say again . . ." I said.

And a head appeared in the door. "His name is George. . . . That's what it means: ruddy *George* — that . . . that . . . first word."

Moonface looked woebegone.

The man to whom the head belonged was named Blair, I learned later.

And I remember: "Say it again . . . Ji . . . rzhi . . . *Christ!*"

"Ruddy *George!*"

"Wait. . . . Wait. Ji . . . rzhi . . . Vrzh- . . ."

"Why bother? . . . *George*. It's easy."

. . .

Oh, go and . . .

. . .

"Polish?" I said.

"It is Czech." Moonface: woebegone. "It not matters," he said.

I wanted to say, "Stop looking woebegone." I said, "It matters."

Blair: "*George* is easy."

I said, "This is a bet. Five bob. I'll learn it by tomorrow morning."

Well, Blair was not a bad sort, really — merely a man of a lazy mind. "You're on," he said; and he sounded eager. He *knew* he'd win.

Jiří Vřešťala.

(Well, it was a good thing, actually, to have it to worry through the night the way a dog worries a bone; to wrap my mind around it the way a tongue wraps itself around a sore tooth. Because . . . well, the beginning of flying training: the whole thing was *real* now — the war. God yes.)

Jiří Vřešťala. Jiří Vřešťala. (Ha! W. R. Luthie: Famous Linguist.

Punjabi Hindustani. Also, a smattering of Gujerati. Four years of

French at school; but only two of German. Latin. Greek. W. R. Luthie: an educated man!)

. . .

Jiří Vřešťala! Success! A Czech — a Bohemian? — born and bred could not do it better! *Bohemian:* It sounds so wonderfully rakish; debonair. (Moonface looked neither debonair nor rakish, of course.)

. . .

Jiří Vřešťala! (A Bohemian born *could* do it better, actually.
But from under the window, there was a big big sigh. Of . . . happiness?)
(From that day on, Jiří Vřešťala attached himself to me like a leech.)

. . .

He is dead now. . . . Well, never mind.
I did not like him very much, really.
In times sad or merry, he looked woebegone. Called me *Lucy:* never got the *th* right. Everybody started calling me Lucy, including the instructors. Oh, I hated it! Absolutely! It rather seemed he expected me simply to *take care of him* from this day forward, till death do us part . . . sorry. Well, for example, he felt but little need to work at improving his English so long as I was there (he spoke fluent German, with a dreadful accent; my German: awful). Gods! Had the Luftwaffe been listening, they'd have laughed themselves to death. No more war!!! What a thought! (The instructors simply rolled their eyes. . . . But I worked most frightfully hard at *interpreting* for him!)
Then, at last, about a fortnight later, Vřešťala and I had a flaming row about . . . something utterly trivial; and among other things I told him to go find himself another nursemaid — somehow made him understand what "nursemaid" meant; and lo and behold! this turned out to be a very good thing for Vřešťala because instead of finding himself another nursemaid, he began to try to stand on his own two feet.

. . .

Well done, Luthie. Well done.
(God, what an exhilarating time! Oh, I was so far ahead of the others! — well, in the actual *flying* part of the flight training. And there were times when it was easy to forget why I was doing it all, really.
The instructors: I did not fit at all into their lesson plans, of course; it rather made them tear their hair. But ah, *Lucy* — a-a-a-argh! — the teachers' pet: how far how fast can he go? . . . It was as exciting — exhilarating — for them, I suppose, as it was for me; though I did tend to make an ass of myself on occasion in Armaments and other courses of that nature.

. . .

I finally took my wings exam by special arrangement ahead of the others. . . . Never mind.)

•

I am myself. Nobody can change me.

I did not want to die, this afternoon. (Well, never mind.)

Nim. Is she . . . ill, perhaps?

Has something . . . happened to her?

. . .

Luthie, settle into resignation, will you! And tell the story. Set the strands down one next to the other . . .

December rolled around. (A long time still till my wings exam.)

December. This was how it was: cold, crisp air; a cold, sparkling sky — perfect flying weather. (To the south, England was all but paralyzed by storms.)

Mid-morning in early December: I'd had my forty minutes in the air, then returned to the room. Sunlight on Vřešťala's bed. The room itself was teeth-chatteringly cold. I sprawled on Vřešťala's bed, in the sunlight.

(Oh, that confounded stove! At bedtime, I'd fall asleep stark naked, all covers in a heap at the foot of the bed. A few hours later . . . W. R. Luthie: wide-awake, giant icicles for arms and legs. . . . Three blankets and an eiderdown on top of me. A-a-ah! Blessed warmth.)

After a while, Vřešťala came in. I made to vacate the bed, but he simply sat down. Began to conduct a search of his pockets. "You have a fag?" And so I gave him a cigarette. He continued the search. "No matches." He looked woebegone. Well, God in heaven! I threw my lighter at him; then lit a cigarette for myself.

Vřešťala, a few moments later: "Lucy . . . you're rich, don't you know."

Continentals!: they are so . . . *uncircumspect.* "No, I don't know."

(*Don't you know.* Yes, yes: he was trying to learn English; but his English sometimes went . . . sideways.) I said: "How much do you need? Ten bob till next pay parade?"

"No. No." And then, quite suddenly, it . . . well, it came *gushing* out. Pouring out: as, these days, *my* story is pouring out of me. . . . It was half in German — well, more than half: his English was not up to it.

"Slowly!" I kept shouting at him. "Slowly. *Langsam,* damn it!"

The whole thing was most dreadfully painful.

Well, they'd left Prague: Vřešťala's father, mother, and two younger sisters — they'd escaped, and they'd brought with them . . . things. Several suitcases — boxes — full of things. Tablecloths.

"Tablecloths!"

"Beautiful tablecloths."

"What did you say? . . . Does that word mean . . . *embroidered?*"

We looked at each other helplessly. Shrugged. . . . And so on. (I worked very hard at understanding him: a very difficult conversation.)

Silverware. Things made of gold. Jewelry.

And that was how they lived now: a great part of their livelihood — selling off their beautiful possessions. But there was a war on, and nobody was buying. The whole thing was most dreadfully painful.

"Bohemian crystal wine goblets," said Vřešťala. "A dozen. . . . Lucy, do you want to buy Bohemian crystal wine goblets?" He looked woebegone.

What in bloody hell do I do with Bohemian crystal wine goblets?

"Christmas," said Vřešťala. And he looked . . . shrewd. And woebegone. Then he straightened his chubby narrow shoulders, and — for the first time since I knew him — he looked dignified, by God! A somewhat desperate dignity: well, naturally. A . . . pathetic dignity. God Christ! *This was painful.*

"Quite. . . . I see. You're absolutely right. Oh, absolutely! . . . A grand idea. A capital idea! A simply splendid Christmas present for my mother. . . . Well, give me your people's phone number, will you."

"We are not on telephone," said Vřešťala. "We are poor."

God damn you! *I know you are poor.*

"Well, you arrange it," I said. "I'd want to see the goblets first, of course . . . and all that. I've some leave coming . . ."

And Vřešťala arranged it.

I went.

(And Hanmer, now: laughing in his sleep! Hanmer thrashing about. Well, a laughter . . . disquieting to those who hear it, no doubt about it.
. . .

"Hanmer . . . It's all right . . . all right. . . . Was it a bad dream? Acklington . . . Time! Time! . . . Up, up."
. . .

Well, let him sleep. He'll simply have to hurry later. Hanmer: puffing away in his sleep. At peace.)

(Hanmer said to me last night, "Luthie, you need a woman. Then you'll stop this bloody scribbling. And *you'll* sleep better. Misery . . . Your going to sleep, waking up, going to sleep — it's driving me insane."

"*Inane.*"

"Shut up, Luthie. Buy LACW Gilhooly a drink." Ah, a woman with a *reputation!* "The rest will follow," Hanmer said. "If *she who is red between her legs* wants to weep for a dead man and spurns such a magnificent specimen of a live one . . ."

But I was in no mood for him last night, I fear. We quarreled. Bitterly. Hanmer and I.)

Well, the story . . . Well, *who* am I writing it for? Bloody hell! (And the strands: when they, in the end, come together . . . Can I truly expect — *do I want* — a resolution? . . . I am unburdening myself.)
. . .

I went.

"Mrs. . . . Vřešťala . . ."

"Mr. Luthie." She had the *th* perfectly!

I blushed. Oh, she was incredibly beautiful! Dark, *dark* eyes: the loveliest I have ever seen, including Nim's. About my mother's age — which means quite young, really, to have a son who is all grown up. Well, she was *not* my mother. Oh, she was beautiful!

The flat: dingy.

"Mrs. Vřešťala . . ." (And outside, snow was falling: dirty snow. Dirty sleet. London.)

She had on a . . . silk? dress. Gray. A bit too formal for the occasion? Probably. The dress: a small *décolletage* — oh, nothing improper, of course! *Womanly* breasts.

Shall I wake Hanmer now, after all?

God, he looks peaceful!

About Mrs. Vřešťala:

I continued blushing. *(Luthie, pull yourself together. Idiot!)*

In the V of the dress, on a gold chain, a large Star of David rested.

I took a step back.

. . .

Well, it's a bit like . . . like standing at attention by a grave: the feeling one gets when meeting a Jew these days, isn't it?

. . .

(Grenfeld: Grenfeld is Jewish, isn't he? . . . Never mind.)

. . .

Well, *Vřešťala!* I'd had no idea, of course! *Vřešťala.* Well, his name wasn't *Goldberg* or *Moskowitz* or anything! Or: was it only she who was Jewish; her husband was not? . . . Oh, I felt young and so terribly ignorant! (I'd never asked Old Moonface about his family, of course . . . One waits for information to be freely given.

. . .

Well, I did not like him very much. That was the problem.)

And yet . . . that Star of David: was she *pushing* it at me? (As a woman of . . . another sort *would* push her breasts at me, for example?) Well, God in heaven! I mean . . . *I'd* never be so very obvious, so . . . ostentatious about who I was!

And she took my greatcoat; then she led the way: yes, the place was one of those dreadful bed-sitters.

I cleared my throat. "Mrs. . . . Vřešťala." (For the *third* time!) But she remained silent. An old brownish sweater on, over her formal silk dress: a sweater thin at the elbows. (Now my lamb's-wool-worn-thin-at-the-elbows is comfortable. Hers was . . . threadbare.) Well, which was she flaunting: her present poverty or her former wealth?

The table was set. Ah, one of those tablecloths Old Moonface had mentioned! Ah, a thing of beauty! (Am I expected to offer to buy the tablecloth? I'd emptied my miserable savings to come on this Mission of Mercy: I'd been saving my meager wages to buy a motorcar all my own — with my own funds, not family money. Well, I did buy my Austin, in the end.)

The tablecloth: beautiful, then. But the china: Woolworth's quality. (Had they sold their good china already?)

Vřešťala's mother: much, much too silent.

"Ah! The goblets. Here they are!" I exclaimed, happily. On the table, but away from the teapot and the cups and so on. They were red, the goblets. I had not expected them to be red. Oh.

"May I?" And I picked one up; took it to the window. A miserable day outside: mid-afternoon. Sleet; gray snow, wind-driven. Gray sky. But suddenly — a quirk of light, for but a moment: the red glass caught something, for a moment . . . Oh my God!

And I held the thing: held it aloft — well, as if it were a sacred vessel of some sort! A chalice. Oh, absolutely! I tried and tried to duplicate the moment.

"There is not a flaw in it." In German.

Well, of course I did not understand! Not one word. Naturally! (Only later I . . . well, surmised the meaning.)

But the voice: a whip across my face. A blow. A slap. And it hurt. God, it hurt — somewhere deep inside me.

Rather in terror, I stared at her. "I beg —"

She paraphrased it, speaking very slowly. "It — is — not — broken." Every word a dagger. As if by holding the thing to the light I had some-how . . . well, *stained* her honor.

"No no no. Of course not. I did not mean . . . It is so very beautiful. . . . I'll take them, of course."

"Will you have some tea?" she said, politely. The word *tea:* an insult. An insult? God's name! She must have thought that she was *ridicul-ing* me . . . mocking me: ah!, *wounding* me, really, in my very . . . yes, Englishness.
. . .

This woman hates me. Does not know a thing about me: hates me.

Because . . . because I am in my own country? Because I've enough money to buy her beautiful things?
. . .

Well, it's a bit like standing at attention by a grave, these days, when one meets a Jew.

What kind of a grave am I standing over?

(And I stood, clutching the silly goblet. *Easy, Luthie . . . Easy. You'll break it.*)
. . .

There was a cake on the table. (Had it been there all along? I'd not noticed.) An altogether prewar type of cake! And she cut a *huge* piece; handed it to me on a plate. "God, how delicious!" I said, miserably. (And it was. Well, the kind of cake one gets in Vienna; Germany! *Decadent*. The tea, on the other hand, was awful. Warm, though: thank God! The room: frigid. She huddled in her ratty old brown sweater.)

And we made — one-sided — *polite* conversation (my spirits being so very low, and my German so utterly awful); and she was beautiful — oh God, she was beautiful! (Not my mother: she most definitely was not my mother!, though she was an unhappy woman, obviously.) And the Star of David sat between her breasts; and she stared at me with contempt as desperately I gorged myself on cake and valiantly gulped down the tea; and there was enough hatred in those eyes to kill the universe.

She hated me.

I began to hate her.

Well, I was four five six seven years old once. Went to the bazaar with Ayah. Went to the bazaar with Apricot. (For my sixth birthday I'd been given a pony; named her Apricot.) I know the ways of the bazaar!

. . .

(I'd emptied my miserable savings to come on this Mission of Mercy.)

. . .

But now I . . . bargained.

(And though almost . . . nine? months have passed since then, I remember — oh, I remember!: well, it was . . . amusing, really, after a fashion: a well-brought-up young Englishman of good family using the wily ways of shopkeepers from a Godforsaken corner of the Punjab to best a once-distinguished Jewess from . . . Bohemia. It *is* called Bohemia, isn't it? Bargaining in . . . German: her native language! (I could tell. She did not sound like her son at all. It was her native tongue. And she put up resistance: tried some . . . negotiating of her own. Was quite good at it, too. But no match for me — in spite of my dire handicap of language.)

. . .

Well, she did not have to sell if she didn't like the terms.

But she did sell.

She was near tears. (After I was gone, she did cry, I'm sure.)

. . .

"Would you wrap them for me, please?" I said, finally.

And she wrapped the goblets — *very carefully* — in layers and layers of old copies of the *Times*. Tied the package with a piece of string.

Her hands shaking. In rage: hatred. In grief. In . . . humiliation.

Christ, I hate London!

I remember: I ran down the street. And snow, snow was falling: compact tiny snowflakes, sharp as miniature knives.

I remember: I did pause at last, my newspaper-wrapped burden at my feet. I lit a cigarette. *My* hands shaking: with shame? One always discovers things about oneself that one didn't know were there. It is rather terrible, really, that I went to war for the sake of people like Vřešťala's mother. (Dreadful things happen in war.)

(And *that* is how I came into manhood.)

Vřešťala's mother never — apparently — did tell her son what had happened. Old Moonface acted grateful. Bloody hell!

(But he was learning to stand on his own two feet.)

(He is dead now. A training accident: like Nim's husband. *David,* his name was — Nim's husband's name. *David.*)

Has something terrible happened to Nim?

Please, God . . . No. No.

Vřešťala had no feel for flying, really. No talent. He was just terribly, terribly earnest about it: like . . . Grenfeld.

What do I want for my Wonders? (Again and again I keep repeating it.)

And: *where do I want my storytelling to lead me?* (Never mind. I am unburdening myself, that is all.)

(There are things that hurt.)

(There are things one would keep private, secret, hidden.)

"Hanmer . . . Up. Up with you! You'll miss your . . . assignation as surely as . . . as . . . well, I don't know."

Hanmer: awake at once. Hanmer: vaulting out of bed. "You bastard. This is your fault."

"It's not. I tried to wake you."

"Well, it is, too."

(And I feel guilty, of course.)

We do not quarrel: we bicker.

I am myself.

III

"Nim . . ." On the telephone.

"Love! Oh my love . . ." (Joy in that voice!!! She has not been avoiding me!)

Then, silence. (Had it slipped out, without thinking — that "Love! Oh my love"?)

Silence. What in the world do I say? "Nim, I've tried to write a letter to you. Several letters. . . . After reading yours, I felt . . . well, humble . . ."

"Hush."
What do I say? "Nim . . . I am most desperately in love with you."
"Hush."
Silence. Then she said, "You sound tired."
"I'm fine. Fine . . . I'd like to bring you home with me. A place full of
apples, you know: home. Cox's orange pippins. Some Worcester pearmains. The pearmains should be ready to pick soon. Father said — this
was some time ago — he said we'd be getting . . . Germans to help with
the harvest: whoever it is sends them. . . . Nim, do you know how to eat
a freshly picked apple? You roll it about in the palms of your hands . . ."
(And so on and so on.)
More silence. The connection was excellent, though. I could hear her
breathing. A quiet, even breath . . . Was she picturing herself eating one
of our apples?
What do I say? "The pearmains must be got to market quickly. They're
a good and sweet — juicy — dessert apple. Don't keep well, though. The
skin becomes greasy if they're stored too long. And they lose their flavor."
Silence. Then she said: "Oh!"
And we burst out laughing. Both of us laughing.
"Now the pippins —"
"Spare me."
"They account for 55 percent of all apples grown commercially in
Britain."
"Spare me."
Laughing. Laughing.
. . .
"Nim . . . I love you."
"Hush."
"Nim . . . Are you from Kensington? I mean . . . is that where you
lived as a child . . . Kensington?" A Londoner born and bred: she'd said
that herself.
(Well, in God's name! Still learning mere *things* about each other?!)
. . .
In my mind, I've known *her* for a long, long time.
. . .
We do not know *things* about each other.
. . .
Getting to know *things* about each other.
. . .
There are things one would keep private . . . secret . . . hidden?
. . .
What peculiar times these are, really!
"Kensington. Y-yes. . . . How did you —"
"Well, you look like Kensington. Sound like Kensington. . . . You're
not Mayfair. Definitely not!"

"And you said you didn't like London! You . . . country bumpkin!"

"I am proud to be a country bumpkin." Laughing. "I do not like London. That does not mean I do not know anything about it."

"Stop sounding as if you were *instructing* me." Laughing. "Is that what you'd have become if not for the war: a teacher . . . a schoolmaster? Is that what you'll be when this is over?"

. . .

A schoolmaster? . . . A *schoolmaster?!* Well, God in heaven!

. . .

"Nim, Nim, you do know the Dvořák cello concerto, don't you?" (Well, poor old Moonface Vřešťala had taught me how to pronounce it! Do not think of Vřešťala now: things secret and hidden.) "You do know it, I'm sure. Naturally."

"Yes. Oh yes. . . . Why?" (Getting to know each other.)

"Whenever I think of you, I think of that very last bit of the last movement of the Dvořák cello concerto."

Silence. Not: *Hush*. (Getting to know each other.)

"Nim . . . I am not tired anymore."

"Good." Briskly. No nonsense. She is a practical woman. "Wayne . . ." A soft voice: something echoes in it when she says my name. "Wayne, I must go now. I am sorry. . . . I'm on duty. I've work to do."

"Right."

Silence.

"Wayne . . . Wayne . . . I love you."

. . .

Oh, strike up the bands!!!

(*Oh, N. M. Tunnard-Jones, you woman of character!* You woman of beautiful eyebrows! You woman of serious gray eyes. . . .

Her voice: a soft voice. But determined. Defiant, almost. Oh, I could see her eyes — I could see them when she said *I love you!*)

. . .

In a rush, sounding almost breathless, she said, "The evening before last I went to Edinburgh." She said, "Had dinner with . . . well, I've always called him *Uncle*. An old school friend of my father's, you know."

Yes! Yes! And the bloke is bishop of Edinburgh, isn't he? And she had gone to ask him to marry us! Hadn't she?

. . .

Then silence. Well, confound the woman! Confound her silences! (It is her right, of course. Her privilege. Oh, absolutely! . . . Christ, what do I know about her — and about the dead man who haunts her dreams? . . . or her waking hours? . . . Things secret: hidden.

What miserable times we live in!)

. . .

Nim. A soft voice — something echoes in it. "I miss you."

"God, I miss *you*."

"Well, I did try not to think about you." (So, she *had* been trying to avoid me!) "I said in the letter, didn't I? I had a lot of thinking to do. But at first I rather put off the thinking. I tried to forget you."
. . .

Do not forget me, N. M. Tunnard-Jones.
. . .

"I said to myself, 'If I put off the thinking, I may forget him.'"
"Love . . . Do not forget me. Love . . . I love you."
"I love you." Barely audibly; but resolutely. With conviction. With self-assurance. Definitely! ". . . Good night."
"Good night, love."
"Good night."
"Good night."
"Good night."
Oh, unquiet dreams to you, N. M. Tunnard-Jones (when finally you lie in your bed . . . this morning)! Dream about me!
. . .

Christ, what an idiot Hanmer is! I do not need just *any* woman!
. . .

"Nim . . . Nim . . . When I see you again, I'll trace your eyebrows with my fingers." (But the line had gone dead.)

I AM HAPPY!!!
I am tired. (Before, I had been feeling low; not tired.)
God, I am so very happy!!! (I am most dreadfully tired. . . . Never been happier in my life!) *I am tired.* So happy! . . . Tired. . . . Happy.

Things most definitely had been dicey for a while this afternoon.
I did not tell her, of course. I'll never tell her.
. . .

Getting killed is what happens to other people — not to me: each and every man thinks that of himself.
. . .

I was over water.
NO KNOWN GRAVE, I kept thinking.
NO KNOWN GRAVE.
. . .

Why should I care whether I've a grave?
. . .

But I panted like a dog, in my fear.
. . .

(My poor *Aunt Millicent* did bring me home, though — rather the worse for wear, but all's well that ends well. Getting killed is what happens to other people.)

•

What if *they* win? Christ! What would happen to Nim? (What would they do to . . . women in uniform?) It is unthinkable!

(Luthie, go to sleep.)

What would happen to me? What would happen to Nim? to us?

(God has put me on this earth to fly aeroplanes — etc., etc.)

What would they do to me?

Nim. I want to protect her! I cannot protect her.

It is idiotic to make long-range plans.

. . .

A schoolmaster? I . . . a schoolmaster!?

Well, before the war it had been in my mind to go home to India — after meekly taking my degree at Cambridge (to please my people: at one time my people considered a degree frightfully important). I'd fly the mails — that kind of thing. Do good deeds. . . . How very like Wayne Luthie!

. . .

Ah, Luthie, Luthie!

. . .

Perhaps . . . God! have a flying service of my own: well, one plane, one man — and a contract with a medical mission of some sort: fly doctors, nurses — people of that nature — to places where a doctor's foot does not tread very often.

Ah, W. R. Luthie coming around Nanga Parbat. On his final approach into Gilgit.

And those mountains are the Himalayas!

. . .

Then — when duty at last was thrust upon me — then I'd grow apples.

. . .

Well, never mind.

(Go to sleep.)

It *is* idiotic to have long-range plans.

(A woman who studies the cello; a man who wants to fly around Nanga Parbat: how do they build a life together? . . . It is useless to have — long-range plans.)

. . .

A schoolmaster . . . ?!! *A schoolmaster???*

. . .

I want to fly without killing people!

(But one of these days all this will no longer matter: the *future* — now distant — will be the *present,* and it will not make one whit of difference in the lives of ordinary people who won or lost this war. . . . Or will it?

Bloody hell! It matters to me!)

Now, music — somewhere in the building. A violin. Well, in Peterson's room, actually: old Peterson *practicing*. Very, very very softly.
Well, he really has gone too far, this time! (What time is it?)
. . .

(He is not terribly good, really; but, rather uncharacteristically, our little . . . *community* has been charitable: forbearing: very, very very patient. He is apologetic about his playing, usually. A shy chap, really. . . . Well, overly hearty, sometimes: trying to mask the shyness.)
. . .

He really has overstepped his bounds, though (this time).
Doors opening. Curses flying.
Peterson's apologetic voice. . . . Silence.

43

And the very day of Peploe-Webb's arrival (he was the replacement for McGregor and the chap Randall): in the afternoon — so Ashley would remember — the men of Flight B moved (an army of occupation!) to claim the deck chairs. There were deck chairs — lawn chairs — at Dispersal.
"That's called a *chaise longue*," Peploe-Webb said.
Well, la-di-da! *Chaises longue? Chaises longues? Chaise longues?*
"They're *chairs*," said Cartwright.
. . .

Peploe-Webb was *St. Lawrence College*.

Flight A officers sat in the chairs, usually. (Prattle prattle: Women. Cars. Cars. And women. They ignored the men of Flight B. Some things never change!)
This time, the gray-furred cat Victoria was present.
Digby was present: the official mascot of one of the Hurri squadrons. (Once upon a time — so the tale went — Digby had belonged to one man only. But the man had been killed — or merely wounded? No one could so much as recall his name! And so now Digby was the squadron's. A runty, floppy-eared, *yippy-yappy* dog-dog: not any particular breed.)
Victoria was grooming — beautifying — her face, looking grave. Digby was running himself ragged, and dizzy: racing in circles around her. *Yapping.*
Victoria looked up, left front paw poised; said "Heh!" in contempt, wrinkling her nose and baring her incisors; returned to beautifying her face. Digby plopped down on his haunches — not frightened, but . . . puzzled.

Laughter. *Everybody* laughed: Flight A, Flight B, the kiwis. And at that, thoroughly dishonored, Digby took himself off, looking hurt and *unappreciated*. Victoria merely looked unperturbed.

There was more laughter.

After a while, Cartwright said: "She's preggers. Look at her. . . . Gentlemen, we'll have bloody kittens!"

"Wizard."

"Stunning. . . . When? How long does it take?" But nobody was sure.

"Sir . . . Sir . . ." Stanhope said to Flying Officer Luthie, politely — *Do not speak unless spoken to* (but if you sound as polite as Stanhope, can anyone take offense?) — "Sir, do you happen to know how long it takes for kittens to be born?"

Luthie had just finished a discussion of some sort with the Adj.; was heading for the IO's table. "About two months."

He knew . . . so many things. (Did *everyone* stand rather in awe of him? Ashley wondered. *The sheep!* thought Ashley.)

Two months!

Two months stretched before them. What would happen before the two months were over?

"Well, it's not two months from now," Cartwright said, happily. "If she's showing already!"

Well, what would happen before however-long-it-*would*-be was over?

There were lawn chairs at Dispersal.

The loudspeaker spat and crackled . . . Not for them. (A brace of Hurricanes scrambled.)

Pilot Officer Newby got up, by and by: yes, the Adj. was calling to him. And they went off together, the Adj. and Newby.

There was an empty chair at Dispersal.

Minutes ticked.

And it was . . . Grenfeld who moved. (Grenfeld the Obsessed. Well, he had taken to sleeping *in the cockpit of his kite* between sorties! Said it made for a quicker getaway when the next flap came. But this time he'd been sitting in the grass.) He stood up and stretched, slowly. And then he crossed over to the empty chair: its canvas seat was dun-colored; camouflage-colored. (And Grenfeld looked as if it did not concern him, really: as if any *possible consequences* did not concern him — were none of his business, really; nor anyone else's.)

He sat down.

(Not a single pimple on his face. No acne whatsoever. And he seemed not *grown up,* exactly; but somehow older than his age.)

(But, of course, everyone in Flight B was accustomed by now to Grenfeld being like that.)

He sat.

Well, *there*. They were as good as anybody else. *Equal to any officer!* So *there*.

Pilot Officer Peterson — the replacement for the dead PO Kenley — Peterson opened his mouth; shut it. He cast a quick glance at Flight Lieutenant Acklington; and Flight Lieutenant Acklington's mouth was open already, as if he were about to say something — but then *he* shut it, having obviously changed his mind, abruptly.

(Well, sirs . . . say something . . . COMMANDING. . . . Something sharp.

Try. Just try. Dare.

Well, was there a rule that said a sergeant pilot could not sit in a lawn chair? Was there? . . . Ha! There wasn't.)

. . .

But what would happen when PO Newby came back?

Newby came back.

My God! Oh my God! *He* opened his mouth; shut it. Incredible! Well, it had been his lawn chair! . . . No, not *his* lawn chair; but he had sat in it first. Had he the right to claim it? The men of Flight B pondered that one over. They moved closer to the chairs and to Grenfeld, as if to aid, succor, and support him, should he need support.

Pilot Officer Newby looked very, very angry. His neck and his ears had gone red. (His ears were very large.) His nose had gone red! (He had a very large nose.) He stared: at Flight Lieutenant Acklington? No — he was peering about: for Luthie?! (Flight Lieutenant Acklington seemed . . . amused.) Both Acklington and Newby were staring at Luthie.

(Well, he had not said, upon leaving — Newby hadn't: *"Save the chair for me."* Had he?)

And what would Luthie do? *Was he one of them?* (One of Flight B, that is: not one of The Others.)

Luthie seemed to be paying no attention. He was . . . drinking tea. *Out of a real cup, yet!* (Well, it was the IO who was known to all as a man of . . . civilization: kept a supply — two or three — *real cups* and *real saucers*. And what did it matter that they did not match! He kept them in a deep desk-type drawer under his table. He must have offered the tea to Luthie: the IO, whose paunch strained against his belt.)

Flying Officer Luthie was drinking tea.

Ashley the Observer *observed*. And, in a single moment, he forgot all else. *My God . . . bring me my camera, God*. What a picture!

A shot from the shoulders up. Just the head: the face. And the hands, naturally: one holding the cup, bringing it up to the man's lips; the other clutching the saucer. God, what a . . . homey picture!

The cup covering most of the lower face now: the man was sipping the tea carefully — *not gulping it down.* Only the eyes visible above the rim of the cup, now.

A homey picture of a home that was . . . uncomplicated. A picture of a home simple.

Home. A simple life.

Home. Drinking tea. That was all.

. . .

And suddenly, Ashley's loneliness was not only difficult, but impossible to bear. Because . . . my God, life was so terribly complicated! Because . . . Ashley felt grown up only when taking pictures!

(What? What in the world did he mean?! . . . The thought barely flashed through his mind: it startled him. He did not understand it — and he tried to dismiss it.)

What would Luthie do now? (Yes, he only *seemed* to be not paying attention.)

The eyes above the cup were alert; wary. And Luthie's legs *did not look double-jointed.* (And *everyone* knew by now that bending his knees so as not to appear double-jointed was Officer Luthie's armor against the cruel world.)

And so, had Ashley taken the picture, the picture would have lied. Well, the *homeyness* of it would have been a lie.

Why were things so seldom as they seemed to be?

. . .

What would Luthie do?

He did not do anything. It was rather obvious that quite deliberately he did not do anything. (And . . . and there was something about those eyes . . . Nonsense! so Ashley told himself. . . . But they were . . . *knowing* eyes. It was as if Luthie knew something about . . . *life?!* . . . that the others didn't. . . . Nonsense!)

Well, Luthie continued to drink his tea.

Let them sort it out.

Suddenly, the sirens began to wail. And the loudspeakers began to blare — but of course, nobody could hear what they were saying, though everybody knew what they were saying.

Luthie shouting, as usual, "Well, let's go. Let's go."

Let's go get them. Let's try to get them. (Take the kites up and try to get the bombers.)

(Fear grabbing at the belly. The old and familiar fear. Well, it really was more like nervousness: such as one gets before an exam at school, for example. The *cold terror* came only in the air; on occasion — and then at night: most frequently at night — when one thought about the day past and then about the day to come . . . That was how it went. Ashley had

become accustomed to it. They all had become accustomed to it. . . .
They had never yet had to sit out an air raid on the ground. But they'd
heard that it was a thoroughly nasty experience.)

And so they went: Flight B and Flight A both. But too late, really: not
nearly enough warning! And so Pilot Officer Newby . . . well, he'd
barely got off the ground. . . . Was he hit, then? He fell back like a rock.

And it wasn't till they were permitted to land again that the rest of
them could learn what had happened: he'd fallen back like a rock — his
Spit had stood up on her nose, actually: then fallen over on her back, the
broken airscrew still spinning, crazily. Newby had hung there in his harness, head down, till the air raid was over. By the time the medicos had
got to him, he was unconscious.

That rather spoiled the victory of the lawn chairs, didn't it?

(Well, he was all right, really: before the day was done he was back
from the Med. Section, though he would be off ops. till the next day.)

After the air raid: *machinery* of all sorts rumbled about — and lorries
with loads of gravel; and various civilians were at work with shovels,
glancing up at the sky every other second: were more bombers coming?
The civilians glared at the men of Flight B and the officers of Flight A
with . . . hostility.

(At the beginning of the war the base had *signed a contract* with two
dozen or so men from town to perform bomb damage repair — so Ashley had heard. And every day, from the very start, these men would report for duty and be paid wages — a *retainer,* it was called; but not till
July or so had they had to do any *real work* — so Ashley had heard.
"They sat on their arses and played cards," that was what was said about
them. "Remember? One of them" — gone now — "he . . . whittled."
Farm animals: horses, cows, sheep . . . Did not value his work, though, it
seemed: every so often somebody would let out a curse as he stepped on
a fragile wooden pig or rooster left lying in the grass — so Ashley had
heard. Now all these civilians seemed to view those in uniform with hostility: "They run away. Leave us here. Bloody cowards. They leave us here."

Well, God damn them! They had not been left *unprotected!* The Bo-
fors guns protected them: the ack-ack. So, there!

Well . . . yes . . . But the men of Flight B, for example, had never yet had
to sit through an air raid on the ground.

But these people — the bloody civilians — they were staring at them
with *hatred!*)

The world had become an unpleasant and complicated place.

No doubt about it, all the men of Flight B were becoming obsessed
with killing Germans.

•

They went out twice more that day; and were bombed one more time. This time, the runways had been cratered; and they were directed to land at the satellite field. Spent the night there, baby-sitting their kites; and what with the sleeping quarters cramped hardly anybody slept.

They had been driven from their home.

(Ashley, too, was becoming obsessed with killing Germans.)

But that evening, at the satellite field, Grenfeld and Stanhope settled in the grass after dinner, poring over a chessboard. (Not Grenfeld's own portable chessboard: they must have borrowed one.) Pilot Officer Peterson came. Squatted down. Observed without saying a word, till it got too dark to play. That was the very first time an officer of Flight A had openly exhibited an interest in the men of Flight B.

And so, from that day on, sometimes the men of Flight B sat in the lawn chairs; and sometimes they didn't.

Companions. Friends? Together. (Luthie *not* watching over them all? Ashley observed.)

Now that *was* a victory of sorts, wasn't it?

And another thing that did not change and yet somehow did change: with their move south, Luthie's "lectures" — the gatherings to discuss tactics and such — did not end.

"Never fly on a straight course for more than two or three seconds."

"A quick burst — and then out. In and out. Never never wait around to see the results of your . . . efforts." He pounded and pounded it into their brains.

. . .

How does one Spitfire attack fifteen Me's, shoot down two, damage one, and escape unscathed?

Luthie gave a little sigh. But then his chalk fairly flew across the blackboard.

My God! A . . . picture. A picture of a Spit. A . . . cat in the cockpit. The ginger-whiskered Albert! His battle-scarred ears sticking through the helmet: that was how they knew it was Albert — because of the ears. No, in all other respects, too, this cat looked like Albert.

Good old Albert, looking warlike. A tremendously long . . . silk? scarf streaming behind him. The code letters on his kite: CAT.

Well, Luthie clearly was a man of some talent!

Luthie grinned. "Here is Albert, on his way to perform imbecilic feats of valor. Please note the ears: too many imbecilic feats of valor. . . . Now every time before you go out to perform feats of valor, please touch your own ears." Everybody laughing.

Well, the man was balmy; but they laughed like madmen.

Luthie was laughing. Then he did make a few suggestions, though — oh yes, they always were *suggestions:* he drew little diagrams showing how one Spitfire would go about attacking fifteen Me's. "Looks a lot easier on paper, of course — on the blackboard — than in reality."

"As long as you know how to run, you're all right." He always said that.

And Ashley remembered: Luthie yelling, screaming at Brown that time Brown had started spewing his strawberry jam . . . "Now get in your kite and take off. I don't care what you do once you get up there —"

My God! Had he really meant it?

Yes, they were obsessed with killing Germans: talked about nothing else, almost.

Surely Luthie must know they were obsessed with killing Germans!: Luthie, who himself killed Germans, of course, and spoke about it quite freely.

. . .

At some point, Ashley had suddenly realized that yes, he did trust Luthie now to lead them into combat. He and everyone else in Flight B: they all had somehow begun to develop a faith in Luthie always to come back. No matter how battered his kite, he'd come back: he would not abandon them.

But, Ashley wondered, was Luthie really the kind of man who would want them to be *obsessed* with killing anybody?

44

I

I am The Expert:
How Does One Spit Confront Fifteen Me's?
The gestation period of kittens.
I am The Expert.

(The Germans come and bomb us.)

II

My Dear People:
I seem to have entered a period of a — rather tentative — contentment.

Silly ass, Luthie!

Nim: (This is not a real letter.)
I've entered a period of an absolutely extravagant happiness!

•

A fragile extravagance? A delicate glass — goblet (do not think of goblets!) — poised on the edge of a . . . table? (I seem to have reached a plateau of sorts.)

Oh, in God's name!

The Germans come and bomb us.
(Life goes on.)

Nobody I knew *well* was killed today.
(One of the Hurri pilots: we had a pint together in the mess anteroom before dinner yesterday. Very blond hair; very, very blond eyebrows; blond eyelashes — not an albino, though. Had dunked his head in the bucket at the well at Dispersal once, I remember. His name: Morrison. Ted? Yes. Ted.)

. . .

Life goes on.
(Well, to work. To work. It is a workaday world out there.)

III

Work.
"Sergeant."
Sergeant Bennett. His polished shoes wet with dew, without their predatory gleam.
"A word with you, Sergeant. No. No. Quite all right. Carry on. Finish your work. *Then* would you see me at your earliest convenience?"

Fog. (Morning.) We're fogged in.
The ground crews: ghosts — on balloon-tired bicycles. They emerge, then recede again. The world is rather mysteriously beautiful. Fog.
The Germans cannot find us. Nobody can find us.
The Met. people say it should lift by ten or so.
(Well, catch up on your paperwork, Luthie. . . . To work. To work.)

I do wish Grenfeld were not so obsessed, by God! Sleeping in his kite — God in heaven! (I should say something, I think.)
And Cartwright . . . shot down not long ago. Has been *boisterous* ever since (had an adventure, so it seems, with a vicar's wife: a gorgeous creature!), but his face is pinched.
Peterson is dead, by the way. (No more violin playing.)
How he died (Hanmer saw it happen — yesterday afternoon): he bailed out; but as he hung there on his brolly, helpless between the sky and the earth, a German came and used him for target practice.
Makes sense, really, in its very own way: keeping Old Peterson from living to fight another day. Naturally, Hanmer made it a point of honor

in turn to send the Fritz to kingdom come. Did not help Peterson, of course. It is a dangerous world out there.

Well, to work. To work. Peploe-Webb . . . his logbook. . . . (I remember when they first arrived, I collected *all* the Wonders' logbooks.

He is at about the same point of readiness the rest of them were when they came to me.)

But Christ, what a supercilious little bugger, our good Peploe-Webb! (*St. Lawrence College.* And he chokes on his vowels.)

(Never mind.) Work. Here comes Sergeant Bennett: shoes dry of dew.

"Yes. Appreciate your promptness, Sergeant. Thank you."

. . .

Bloody hell! I will not stand for shoddiness!

. . .

"Sergeant, this has been the third time, I'm afraid. The third instance. The third incident."

(Do not say it *three* times! Once is enough.)

I will not tolerate shoddy work! (The hood of Brown's kite would not slide smoothly on the day we arrived here. Now . . . yesterday: they failed — they *forgot!* — to change oxygen bottles in Peploe-Webb's kite between sorties. The third time . . . the second time, actually — the *middle* incident — Grenfeld. A hammer(!) left on the floor of his kite. He discovered it purely by chance — pure luck — before taking off. Christ! A *big* hammer. A steep climb; a loop; a victory roll: that hammer could become as deadly as anything the Jerry throws at us. *I will not stand for shoddiness.*)

"Sergeant, you are responsible for the work of Corporal Lansing, Corporal Dunaway, and . . . and all the others."

Sergeant Bennett: his gingery tomcat's whiskers twitching. In displeasure. "I plead overwork, sir."

"Quite. I . . . understand." (But then I let a very long silence fall.)

Oh God! Oh, absolutely! Not enough of them; too much work. I know. (But I let a *very* long silence fall.)

Sergeant Bennett, in his best *sepulchral* butler's voice: "Sir . . . Nevertheless, I shall endeavor, sir —"

Endeavor. God in heaven!

"Try, Sergeant. *Try.* . . . Thank you. . . . That will be all, Sergeant. You may go, Sergeant. . . . Thank you."

One "thank you" too many. (But his whiskers twitching: in displeasure.)

. . .

(Well, and so things rather repeat themselves, don't they? I remember: I'd just rejoined the squadron; kept saying "thank you, thank you"; his whiskers had twitched, first in displeasure, and then in amusement.)

. . .

I will not stand for shoddiness!
. . .

Well, the ground crews like to work for winners. And that's God's truth! (One must watch them like a hawk.) Work.

Aunt Millicent. (Yesterday.) She is as good as new again. (Looks as good as new, at any rate.) Must have taken some doing, no doubt about it! (While she was being worked on, I had to fly a kite not my own. Did not like it.)

Well, yesterday. (I remember: standing on the catwalk in the hangar. The kite's wings dark in the semidarkness.) God, look at those wings!

The kite.

The Spit.

The Spitfire.

The aeroplane.

An enormous dark moth in the semidarkness. Dark. Beautiful. Dark. Dark. Oh, absolutely!

Stupid of me to call her *Aunt Millicent!* Creatures of darkness should not be made light of; subjected to whimsy. (Might they take revenge? Were my two close calls a . . . warning? Bloody hell!)
. . .

Am I, too, of darkness? (Bloody hell! . . . Never mind.)
. . .

I'm not superstitious.

All pilots are superstitious. "Superstitious as an RAF joker" — a saying.

Bloody hell!

"Better than a popsy, sir. Isn't she, sir? . . . Better than a judy any day or night. Don't you agree, sir?"

Corporal Dunaway: the *obsequious* one. The man gives me the shivers. And so I remain silent, of course.

I clear my throat. "I'd like to take her out. Put her through her paces . . . Armed, of course." And we both laugh, Corporal Dunaway and I. "Can you have her ready in thirty minutes, Corporal? . . . Thank you, Corporal."

Well, here she is!

Well, give it a good sprint — no, not a *sprint,* really — just a running step or two. . . . (Well, the brolly on one's backside makes one so bloody *bottom-heavy!*)

Left foot on the trailing edge of the wing; right hand makes a practiced grab for the back edge of the door. Now haul yourself up onto the wing root.

Step into the cockpit, the right leg first. Stand on the seat-mounting for the parachute. Grip the top of the wind screen with both hands. And slide down, feet first. A-a-ah!

"All comfy now, sir?" Corporal Dunaway the Obsequious tightening the shoulder straps. "The one on the left side, sir —"

"Yes. Oh, yes. . . . I'm fine. *Fine*. . . . Thank you."

. . .

And I slump down, adjusting the lap belt. Straighten up. The belt *tight* (not comfortably, but comfortingly tight). *Tighter*.

The cockpit drill: petrol gauge . . . altimeter to zero . . . the primer: a couple of strokes, with the throttle open ever-so-slightly. Left hand on the throttle; right hand on the ignition switches. The kite's nose *sniffing* the sky.

All clear of the airscrew, now?

"Contact!"

And press the starter button. And we go.

The aeroplane. The Spitfire. The Spit. The kite. *Aunt Millicent*.

Sheer bravado!

Oh, absolutely! Yes. Yes.

Sheer exuberance!

(Well, things do repeat themselves; but yet they are different.

. . .

I am the man I've always been?

Hush, Luthie. Hush. . . . I am myself.)

Aunt Millicent. Oh, they've done a wonderful job with her!

"Well done. . . . Bloody marvelous, actually."

And they all beam in happiness. The ground crews like to work for winners. And that's God's truth!

(Brown, Peploe-Webb, Grenfeld are not winners.)

(I do wish Grenfeld would not be so terribly . . . earnest.)

Work. Fog.

Victoria the Cat in the fog. (Today. In the morning. Quite early in the morning.) Ashley in the fog. Victoria watching the Spits in the fog. (Giant mice?: perhaps if I watch hard enough, am patient enough, they'll move.)

Ashley: his parachute over his shoulder. A metal mess-kit cup — tea? coffee? — in his hand. A piece of toast between his teeth: *a pirate dagger; a Gurkha's kukri?* (Oh, I remember: I was four, five, six, seven years old once! Auctions, and ginger squares, vanilla cream overflowing . . .)

. . .

Ashley: his ubiquitous camera about his neck. Comes to a sudden halt; watches Victoria watching the aeroplanes in the fog. Then he goes into a half-crouch.

Now let us watch Ashley juggle camera, cup, parachute, toast . . . oh, a true circus act! Cup in the grass; toast on top of it; parachute on his back, as he lowers himself on his belly into the grass . . . oh, cold grass, I'm sure. (The brolly precarious, unsupported: well, one must not get it wet — not even damp. And there is that dew — fog — on the grass!) Camera finally in hand.

Open the leather case; unscrew the lens cover.

In the picture, the grass will be gray. Victoria is gray. The planes will be gray, in the picture. The fog is gray. Can he do it?

There is a seriousness of purpose about his face.

. . .

Shall I ask, someday, to see some of his pictures? (Once I almost asked Stanhope for one of his peppermints. Did not ask, in the end. Have regretted it ever since, really.)

. . .

Ashley: selecting his angle. *Composing* the picture.
Well, hurry, hurry. . . . Victoria, don't move.
He snaps the picture. And I feel like cheering.
Another one? . . . *Well, hurry . . . in heaven's name!*

. . .

And now, the juggling act in reverse. The piece of toast between his teeth . . . the brolly over his shoulder . . . reach for the cup.

He bites down on the toast — not having meant to (apparently); the toast breaks. Falls into the grass. And Ashley, in a fit of anger — *too much anger?* or simply an act of childish pique? — he utters a most horrible oath (yes, all the way here I can hear it!) and then pours his tea (coffee?) — *throws* it — out of his cup.

Victoria runs. *And she an expectant mother!*

But Ashley, with fine adolescent unconcern, heads for the Ready Room.

. . .

"Good morning, Sergeant."

He jumps. "Good morning, sir." He'd had no idea I was there!

We stand, quiet. I'm put out with him, a bit. Now that he got what he wanted from Victoria — namely, the picture — he cares not one whit that he frightened her.

I pour some of my half-coffee, half-cocoa from my thermos into my own cup. His cup is empty.

I'm put out with him.

. . .

Is it proper for a flight commander to offer half-coffee, half-cocoa to one of the men under his command?

"Care for a drop, Sergeant? . . . Not bad, actually."

. . .

Well, he should not have *thrown* his out, like that.

. . .

Shall I ask to see some of his pictures?
(Ashley: a kindred spirit?)

. . .

Is it proper for a sergeant pilot to accept half-coffee, half-cocoa from an officer, his flight commander?
"Yes, sir. . . . Thank you, sir."
I grin at him. I'm put out with him, just a bit.

. . .

He hesitates. Ashley the Adolescent.
Is it proper — is it acceptable — for an adolescent to smile?
He smiles, grudgingly. Then . . . he smiles. (It is not a grin.) Ashley: squirrel teeth.
And we stand there, quiet, for a moment (out of the corner of my eye, from the window, I can see Farrell, Stanhope, Cartwright in the fog, heading our way); we stand there, friends together. Two living creatures together. Christ, life is good!

I have entered a period of contentment.
Will everything I do from now on turn out all right in the end?

. . .

The ground crews like to work for winners. What shall I do?
(Work. Fog.
The fog did lift shortly after ten; by a quarter to eleven we were in the air.)
(Written in the evening.)

The ground crews like to work for winners.
Oh, it's not deliberate — I hope. But there are not enough of them; and there is too much work. And they must work quickly.
They do not do it *consciously,* I hope; but they do make choices.
They give their attention to those they consider winners.

It is a dangerous workaday world.
I'll not stand for having danger added to the Wonders' lives! (And yet, not so long ago, I had . . . well, miscalculated; and then I led them . . .
Never mind.)

What shall I do?

4 5

And then the day came when Luthie — probably: very likely — saved Yellowbelly Brown's life. At twenty thousand feet or so — in the middle of a scrap! — Brown . . . well, things like this would happen only to Brown, wouldn't they? — no, he had not been wounded. He had come down with . . . food poisoning!

"Did you hear him? Did you hear?"

Ashley hadn't, at first. But then he had, over the R/T. Brown screaming, shrieking. No avoiding it. And so they all had assumed other things, of course: not food poisoning. But had no time to think about it, really. Once the initial attack had been delivered, it was every man for himself.

(*Go get the bombers. Concentrate on the bombers. Try to forget the fighters.*

Forget the 109s? Ha!)

Later, when they talked about it — examined the Brown incident from what they were satisfied must be every imaginable angle — the one thing that was not mentioned at all was each man's reaction to Brown's dreadful shrieking.

Ashley, for example, had been furious with Brown for carrying on so: Well, the screams added terror to the familiar fear, and Ashley in no way wanted more fear or terror.

God damn you, Brown! *Shut up   Shut up   Shut up.*

And Ashley was filled with fury . . . against the Germans.

Shut up   Shut up   Shut up. But then he realized that Brown was silent now and that the screams were his: Ashley's.

Shut up, for Christ's sake! Still the screaming went on, in Ashley's own voice — a voice now thin and reedy. And whether he was actually *saying* anything, he could not later remember.

God, he was *furious* with the Fritzes! Blood lust. Revenge. And all that. Yes. Yes. *Obsession.*

And . . . a 109 happened — just happened! — to come into his sights. And so Ashley gave him a good, long burst. Longer than he should have, really: longer than Luthie would have liked.

The Fritz spun out of sight, smoking.

And Ashley followed him down — though Luthie had told them they should not do so. Ashley saw a rather large dark speck separate from the now flaming Me. Then the Fritz's parachute opened.

Should Ashley go after the parachute?

But later, nobody talked about that.

•

So, Brown had come down with food poisoning and in one second seemed to have forgotten all he had ever learned about flying an aeroplane.

But — here came Luthie! He positioned himself on Brown's wing, almost wingtip to wingtip with Brown, who most definitely was out of control now: what might he do next? My God, Luthie was a brave man! Luthie: Brown's only defense against the 109s — well, against the whole miserable, terrifying, *awful,* frightening world!

And he talked Brown down. Calmly. Yes: most frightfully *gently.*

He and Buttercup. (Actually, her code name was different that day. But it was Buttercup: anyone would recognize the voice.)

Brown snuffling. Blubbering. Giving out little gasps of pain, every now and then. *Mewling* with pain. Snuffling. Blubbering. And then shrieking once again, yelling at Luthie, "No! No! I want *you!* You! You!" when Buttercup's voice had come on.

And so Luthie kept a good three-way (four-way?) conversation going: Luthie to ground; ground to Luthie; Luthie to Brown; and Brown to Luthie.

"He called him Tim. Timothy. Luthie did. Kept calling old Yellow Brown *Timothy.* Luthie did. Did you hear it?"

Ashley hadn't.

No one had ever heard Luthie call anyone of Flight B by his given name.

And Luthie — and Buttercup (not to forget Buttercup, so Ashley would think later): Luthie *and* Buttercup, then — lined Brown up calmly and gently for his finals. And Brown, seeming to feel quite a bit better now, thank you, came down smoothly and softly and gently, a perfect three-point landing (as nice as a midsummer morning — so those who saw him would say). A blood wagon was waiting. And Brown — protesting! — was taken away in the blood wagon.

Food poisoning. . . . *Poisoned strawberry jam?*
Yellow Brown.

By the time Ashley landed, Luthie had been on the ground for some time; and various Flight B people and others were clustered about him. (The men of Flight B: *each as if alone?* Ha! They were *Luthie's honor guard:* that was what Ashley saw.)
· · ·

Yellowbelly Brown.
Poisoned jam?
But Luthie had very likely saved Brown's life.

•

Luthie was gulping down tea. Big, big gulps. Uncivilized, no doubt about it. . . . Tea with milk? So sweet one could stand a spoon in it?

It is called gunpowder, that tea, because the British army fight on it. When all that sugar hits one's insides, one's knees stop feeling weak at once!

And Luthie looked tired. My God, exhausted past exhaustion! He lit a cigarette, and his hands were . . . shaking! (Yes, Ashley was close enough now. Ashley could see it.) Luthie's hands shook: Ashley had never ever seen them so unsteady — not even after that most ferocious scrap some time ago when Luthie had made . . . well, a mistake . . .

Luthie looked tired. And his hair was *soaked* with sweat, plastered to his forehead.

Then, quite abruptly, he looked up. For a moment he peered . . . past all those milling people. And he grinned, to himself — or perhaps at the world *in general:* the world beyond the milling people?

A big Luthie grin on his grimy face. An enormous grin. Huge teeth. A proud grin? No, not really. Not exactly, really.

But it almost was as if he had thoroughly enjoyed every minute of talking old Brown down, and then being yelled at: "I want you! You!" when Buttercup's voice had come on. Well, had he enjoyed it? Had he?

And so Ashley stood there and *observed* him.

They went out twice more that day — without Brown.

That was the day that Peploe-Webb made . . . well, an emergency landing on a beach. Uh oh. Well, my God! My God! On that *wet sand?*

But he was back in time for dinner, though with a nasty cut on his forehead and walking like a man whose muscles had been stretched and pulled all the wrong way.

The kite was a write-off.

And on that very same day, the replacement for the dead PO Peterson of Flight A — a man named . . . Driscoll? — was shot down: bailed out, but broke both his legs on landing.

Well, that was not bad at all, was it?

Brown remained at the Med. Section overnight.

46

I

My first thought: *appendicitis.* It was gas pains: our good Brown had had beans on toast for lunch. So the medicos inform me.

Christ! I think I know them; but even after all this time, I *still* do not know anything about them — my miserable Wonders, I mean. (Would it have occurred to me to warn them? God, there is nothing amusing about this: it very nearly tears one up inside, I understand.)

Well, *I*'d not think — not in a thousand years — to eat — ughh! — beans on toast for lunch.

(A *schoolmaster?* . . . Ha! A *schoolmaster?* The very idea! A man with a schoolmaster's instincts would anticipate . . . Well, wouldn't he?)

Brown feels *destroyed*. Completely. To protect him, I've made it be known about the squadron that it was food poisoning. My task: to let the others know they should not eat beans on toast before going upstairs — without making it obvious what happened to Brown. Good luck, Luthie! This certainly will not enhance Brown's reputation, even if I do manage to keep it to food poisoning. (Well, Hanmer and I spewed our scrambled eggs out into the grass once — the time of Dunkirk; the ground crews had watched us. It was only Hanmer's reputation, I think, that saved *my* reputation.)

. . .

What shall I do?

Mr. *St. Lawrence College* Peploe-Webb pranged this afternoon. The wretched wretch: under no circumstances will he admit to being shaken. *A piece of cake — I walk away from this sort of thing every day.* The kite: a write-off.

And one of Hanmer's people — the replacement for poor Peterson: he's out of the fray already. Hanmer is . . . in a *snit*.

Life goes on.

II

"Nim . . ." On the telephone. "I love you."
     "I love you."
     "I love you."
     "I love you."
     "I love you."
We can go on forever!

(Have just awakened.
     I dreamt: small pearl buttons on a white blouse.
     Oh, I'd like to fall asleep again, so that I might continue dreaming! But sleep will not come. The dream: she unbuttoned those small pearl buttons and opened that . . . *virginal* blouse, and she began to suckle our child.

Well, I saw it clearly, in the dream: a small head — very small — with dishwater blond fuzz on it, the color of my hair. Not the glorious copper of Nim's: it was like my hair.

"He is drinking," Nim said, her voice full of wonder.

In the dream, I thought: *A little son, then.* And then I thought, *One of each. A little son; a little daughter. It would be perfect.*

Then I could die.

No, then I'd want to live.)

Oh, life is so good!

(But it has just occurred to me that I've no letter for Nim *To Be Delivered in the Event of My Death.*

. . .

Never mind.)

Happiness.???

Being killed is what happens to other people.

4 7

They sprawled on their backs in the grass, the sun still summerlike on their faces. (*Still* summerlike: hot — *July*-hot, almost; but time was passing and now it was September!)

They had gathered for one of their regular discussions of tactics and such. But Luthie had said, "Well, let's not sit inside. Christ, this place is gloomy!"

(Well, he was balmy, wasn't he? It wasn't any gloomier than usual inside the Nissen hut.)

"Let's go. Let's go," he said. And he had taken them outside the base, to the river, and they had settled down and patiently waited for him to begin his *lecture;* but suddenly he'd toppled over, a blade of grass between his teeth. "Never mind. . . . Flight B, this is an order: *Enjoy.*"

And so they sprawled on their backs in the grass, and let the still-high afternoon — *summerlike* — sun bake their noses.

Luthie *was* balmy, wasn't he? But he was a thoroughly decent bloke, all in all. One could do worse for a flight commander, couldn't one?

They were accustomed to him now, and familiarity bred . . . well, not contempt (so Ashley thought, feeling wise and — under that hot sun — lazy); it bred *comfort.* (Oh, Ashley knew that the men of Flight B were quite comfortable with Luthie, now — wanted to be comfortable with him. . . . Well, did he, too, want to be accustomed to him, after all?)

•

The river flowed wide and muddy and deep. (Or was it shallow? No way of knowing.)

The sky — up, up, far away — was full of vapor trails: Spits and Me's, Hurricanes and Me's circling one another like . . . like snarling dogs. Well, that was why it was called a dogfight, wasn't it? But they were so high and so far away that one did not hear anything: no snarling. There only were the vapor trails. They looked . . . pretty. No, not *pretty,* really: interesting.

And there was Flight A taking off: Flight Lieutenant Acklington, PO Newby, and some of the others — the replacements — whom the men of Flight B hardly knew at all, just barely by sight. Over Flight B's sun-baked noses they came roaring.

After a while, Stanhope wandered off to the edge of the river. "Sir . . . Sir . . ." In his whiny voice. (It was hot: swimming weather.) "Sir, may we go swimming, sir?"

Luthie woke up. Yes, he had been asleep! (Well, Brown was asleep, too — not sprawled on his back but curled up like an unborn baby. Farrell also appeared to be dozing. Ashley . . . had even Ashley's eyes closed, for a moment?)

Cartwright sat up and took off his shirt. (They had shed their tunics or their short battle-dress jackets long ago.)

Stanhope went on: "Sir . . . Sir . . ." Whine. Whine. Whine. (But it *was* swimming weather, wasn't it?)

Luthie said, his voice fuzzy with sleep, "When you get hepatitis, send me a postcard from hospital." Then he said, "God knows what kind of filth the base empties into that water."

And so they continued to lie in the grass, feeling *limp:* sleepy; and it was swimming weather.

Farrell, awake now, resolutely peeled off his shirt.

Luthie's sleeves were rolled up past his elbows — his scars in plain view. (They frequently were in plain view, these days.) Luthie really seemed quite matter-of-fact about the scars now, didn't he? Sometimes he seemed to have forgotten all about them. When trying to explain something, when he *lectured,* his hands . . . well, rather painted pictures in the air: created things; built things. He made . . . *flying carpets* in the air (so Ashley thought).

It was swimming weather.

Flying Officer Luthie said, "All right. All right. But let's go upstream a bit, shall we?"

And so they gathered their shirts and their jackets . . . and formed a conga line. Now Luthie was balmy, wasn't he?: making them drag themselves all the way God knew where. It was a balmy thing to do; but rather happily they shuffled, singing!: *Doing the Lambeth Walk* and all that; and Luthie ran . . . pranced about, nipped at their heels like a . . . relaxed sheepdog.

They followed the gentle curve of the river, as first it hugged the perimeter of the base and then diverged from it; and a Hurricane was landing: making heavy weather of it!

Well, people about them — the Flight A people, and of course the men from the Hurri squadrons — people were *disappearing;* but they — Flight B — they were still together. Minus McGregor, of course. (But McGregor — that had been so long ago!)

Minus . . . what was his name: Randall? (But, of course, nobody'd known Randall, who had arrived for lunch to die by teatime.)

They were together.

Was being with Luthie *good luck?* (Farrell? — yes, Farrell — had mentioned it, yesterday: lightly, in passing, as if afraid that really talking about it might somehow prove a jinx. Farrell, who had worked so very hard to ingratiate himself with McGregor.)

(But the day was too hot and the sky too blue and too beautiful for Ashley to want to sit in judgment over people. He still *observed,* of course: he did not judge.)

"Sir, sir . . ." Damn Stanhope's whining!

But at last Flying Officer Luthie called a halt.

And yes, Stanhope was the first one out of his clothes. He fairly dashed to the water; then stopped, abruptly, and after a few moments of gathering courage, he very very cautiously dipped his toe.

"Is it cold?"

"It's warm."

"You bastard! It's *cold.*" And somebody — Cartwright — pushed Stanhope and then continued pushing him, driving him into the river. Stanhope fought back, until he lost his footing. The river was . . . shallow.

One by one they waded in, each and every one suntanned — sunburned, really — from the neck up, but pasty white from the neck down. And Ashley felt a bit sorry for them: so rather disgusting — *unsummerlike* — in their whiteness (one did not notice it in the showers, for example, so why was it that under the open sky it suddenly became so much more *pronounced?*) and then he looked down at himself and felt sorry for himself.

Grenfeld was hesitating. A Jew: he was different from the others; and he was *ever* self-conscious about it. He sat, his knees drawn up, chin resting on his knees, and . . . did he look *obsessed?* (Ashley observed him); but then at last he, too, took off his clothes (carefully) and folded them (neatly) and, stepping gingerly, he made his way to the riverbank.

They splashed and shouted; and then, quite suddenly, Peploe-Webb cried out and disappeared for a moment, head and all, and thus discovered a little pool where one could actually swim a few strokes; and so they swam, kicking — churning up the water; and they splashed and shouted.

"Sir . . . Sir . . . Come on in." Farrell: what courage! What cheek! (Well, Farrell had never before been known for his courage — at least not when McGregor was still alive.)

My God! What would Luthie do?

Was he *really* one of them or wasn't he? (That was the Luthie dilemma.)

Does an officer strip naked in front of the men under his command?

My God! Well, God damn it all!

Well, while they had splashed and shouted, Luthie had merely watched, looking sheepish. Now he grinned, and looked even more sheepish. And he . . . thought about it. (Clearly he was thinking about it.) What should he do?

Good God! Luthie: what courage!

Well, he stood up and stretched, (obviously) working rather hard at looking lazy. "Well, I don't mind if I do." He *sounded* lazy.

And then: he peeled off his clothes with a quite lightning speed *(quickly quickly — before I change my mind)*; and, unlike Grenfeld, he did not fold them neatly; and (obviously) working very hard at *not* looking sheepish, he sprinted to the water and ran through the water and dove into Peploe-Webb's pool.

There. That's . . . courage.

(Has he got hair on his chest?

What's he like between his legs?

Is he like Grenfeld: circumcised? . . . Well, he was a colonial, wasn't he? And the colonials are said to circumcise their male children, now aren't they?)

And Luthie came up for air, snorting like a walrus. He swam to the end of the little pool and stood up and stood there, the water reaching barely to his waist. Then he swam back, to the other end, and again he stood there, *enduring* rather patiently, the water just over his knees.

His back: not nearly so *unsummerlike* as the others'. He must have had a decent suntan once, not long ago; but it was fading. He, too, appeared more — well, *weather-beaten,* from the neck up.

And he was thin — God, painfully so! It clearly was the body of a man who had always been, and would always be, very thin. But something — Ashley couldn't quite put his finger on it — something about him gave one the impression that he had become even thinner recently: perhaps he had been losing weight slowly but steadily since . . . since when?

And thus one would have felt sorry for him, too, had it not been for the fact that the arms, for all their thinness, looked quite strong, really, and those miserable stork's legs had . . . well, a . . . a toughness about them: if he so chose, he could keep going forever, couldn't he?

Flight B — the *sheep:* were they disappointed? (Ashley observed them, as — working hard at being . . . what was the word?: *surreptitious* — they observed Luthie.) Yes, this definitely was a man older than anybody else in Flight B. (Was that what they were thinking?) Nothing unfinished — *un-grown-up* — about him. And he looked as if he had withstood . . . things. And could withstand more. (Was that what they were telling themselves?) The men of Flight B seemed satisfied. Comforted?

(Was Ashley, too, comforted?)

And they splashed and shouted and shouted and splashed, but nobody dared splash at Luthie. And Luthie splashed rather to himself and, after a while, he waded out; but, for all his aloneness, he, too, appeared satisfied: rather like a man who had proved something to them and to himself; and by and by he sprawled in the grass and let the sun dry him.

(Grenfeld was out of the water already. He sat there, knees again drawn up; arms folded on knees; chin resting on arms: did he *still* look *obsessed?* Impatient with the way the afternoon had turned out? Eager to get back to trying to kill the Germans?)

And, one by one, they all waded out and let the sun dry them.

The sun was hot. The sky high and blue, full of vapor trails.

Where was Acklington? And Newby . . . and the others? Had they come back? . . . In their search for the perfect bathing spot — following the course of the river — the men of Flight B had veered away from the base, were no longer directly under its glide path, and . . . yes, there were aeroplanes taking off and landing — yes, there were; but they had blocked it out: had really half-forgotten about it.

The sky was blue.

After a while, in a rather sleepy contentment, they began to tell filthy jokes — most of them known to all from many previous tellings — and they laughed, sleepily. And Luthie laughed with them, sounding relaxed and without a care in the world, but did not tell any jokes himself.

And Ashley . . . felt good. Oh my God, he felt good: to give up — for the moment: give up the struggle; stop wondering, worrying about who he was and who he should be and where he belonged . . . oh God, it felt good! Well, he did belong with all of them, didn't he? — for the moment: with Luthie . . . and Farrell . . . and Cartwright . . . Stanhope . . . and . . . Brown . . .

The sky was full of vapor trails.

•

And then somebody shouted: "A parachute!"

Somebody shouted, "A brolly! A brolly! A brolly!!!"

Cartwright jumped up. Luthie jumped up. And Farrell. "A brolly! Let's go!"

And they began to throw on their clothes. "Where is my bloody shirt?"

"You're standing on it."

"Will he go into the drink?" Into the river.

"There he is! Look, look, he's coming. Coming —"

"Wait! Wait for me! I haven't got my boots on!"

"Do without!"

And then — as one — they quite abruptly stopped and watched, for a moment — most of them still half-naked: well, Luthie himself was bare-foot and had only now shrugged into his braces, to hold up his trousers.

"He'll go . . . behind that little copse. There."

Somebody said, "It's . . . a Jerry."

"No, it is not."

"It is! It is! It is!"

And again they broke into a run — though somehow (at least that was what flashed through Ashley's mind) they suddenly did not really feel like breaking into a run again. "It *is* a Jerry. . . . It's a Jerry. A Jerry." A rather quiet voice, now: Cartwright's?

The parachute was down, behind the little copse.

And they ran and ran, through the tall, reedlike grass. Until Luthie stopped them.

Well, he was balmy, wasn't he?

He'd go alone, and he half-naked?!!! All unarmed and unprotected.

(They all were unarmed and unprotected.)

The Fritz will shoot him! Murder him . . . in cold blood!

(Luthie was balmy.)

And cautiously, stepping slowly, Luthie walked, barefoot, through the reedlike grass. Hands outstretched; empty palms outward. And he was talking: saying something . . . in German?

"Sir — Sir —" Somebody's voice: anxious.

(But Luthie had told them not to follow him; and so they did not follow.

Cowards? But Ashley, too, hung back.)

And then Luthie cried out. No words — nothing like that. Just a little cry. As if half-choking. Then he said, "Christ! . . . Somebody . . . please . . . help."

And *then* they were running. Running running . . .

Ashley got there first. Grenfeld was second.

Ashley took one look — and felt his lunch rising rising in his throat.

His eyes met Grenfeld's, and Grenfeld was as white as a freshly laundered sheet.

Brown said, quite unnecessarily, "It *is* a Jerry." That was what Brown said. Idiot!

Luthie said — a voice small and helpless — "Somebody . . . Ashley . . ." Not *Sergeant* Ashley. Just: *Ashley.* But he did not say: *George.* (It was peculiar what one noticed at a time like this!) "Ashley, would you please find a . . . a tree branch . . . a stick . . . something."

To put a . . . tourniquet on the German's arm?

Well, Luthie *was* balmy! As much of an idiot as Brown!

Sir . . . Sir . . . There is no arm! (There *almost* was no arm.)

And yet Luthie was holding on for dear life, pressing pressing where the tourniquet should go . . . and yes, he had managed to . . . to slow the bleeding — yes, to a trickle; but then his strength failed him, and at once a terrific — what was the word?: *geyser* — of blood gushed forth, and Luthie clamped down again . . .

But that was not the worst of it. That was not the worst. The German . . . had no face. The face was gone. Completely.

And the man — what was left of him — the man was shivering, shivering as if he were cold, and making little noises like . . . like a thing *blind,* searching, searching, trying to find the way — whatever the way was — and he was shaking, shivering . . .

"A jacket?" said Luthie. "A jacket? Anybody . . . a jacket?"

But nobody had a jacket: they'd left them on the riverbank. But Stanhope was taking off his shirt — and they all began to tear off their shirts — and they piled them on top of the German.

Luthie said, "Ashley . . . Ashley . . . Would you . . . would you please go —?"

And so Ashley went — ran — but there were no trees here, and there were no bushes, and where would he find a stick? And so he went back, and he was crying.

And somebody — *not* Brown, this time — Cartwright — was spewing into the grass not far away; and through his tears Ashley caught a glimpse of something: well, he saw that one of the German's boots had come off, and (Ashley could not help it: he was being drawn closer and closer!) the German had a hole in his sock . . . it had been darned once but the . . . stitches had all come apart . . . and the German's big toe was sticking through the hole.

And Ashley went on blubbering. He could see that the German . . . yes, the German had a belly wound.

Luthie said, "Christ, why doesn't the blood wagon come? They must have seen him . . . in plain view of the base . . . Somebody . . . Grenfeld. Grenfeld. Would you please run —" My God, he still said *please:* did not forget to say please! It was absolutely amazing! "Would you run try to see what is taking —"

And Grenfeld said: *"No."*
(Bloody Grenfeld said: *"No."* And he was white as a freshly laundered sheet.)
Grenfeld said: *"No."*
And then there was a terrible, horrible silence.
Even the German had stopped making his little noises. The German was dying.

Later, a rumor made the rounds of the base.
It went like this:
After the blood wagon had appeared at last and the German had been taken away, there had remained in the grass a piece of — ughhh! — flesh. And somebody from one of the Hurri squadrons — which Hurri squadron? Or maybe he was from a squadron based at the satellite field? Somebody came walking along — why? — and saw some chickens pecking at the . . . flesh.
Chickens?!! In that grass?!!!
And the man took out his Colt .45 and shot the chickens.
Good. Good.
But then the farmer to whom the chickens belonged appeared and began to shout at the man — his name was . . . Pilot Officer Stephens. (Now Ashley did not know a PO Stephens. Well, ask Farrell, or Stanhope, or Cartwright: nobody seemed to know a PO Stephens.)
And Stephens inquired very calmly how much chickens cost these days, with the price controls and all, and he paid the farmer. Then he began to walk away. He had barely taken a few steps when he fainted.

Well, Ashley did not remember any . . . flesh. He did not!
. . .
Ashley remembered — would never forget — Grenfeld saying "no."
Grenfeld said, "No. No no no no no." And he was screaming, screaming.
"He is a Nazi. I am a Jew. No. I said no!" And he was white, a *freshly laundered sheet* white?: well, he was pale as if there were not a drop of blood in his body.
The front of Luthie's shirt was soaked with blood: the German's blood. And Luthie's teeth were chattering as if he were colder than the German.
My God, Ashley would never forget Luthie's eyes: terrified eyes . . . stricken. And Luthie's Adam's apple: the man was swallowing, swallowing . . . and then he — well, so it seemed — he was just about to open his mouth . . .

Would he have taken back his request? Would he have sent somebody else?

But Grenfeld shrieked, "Everybody hates you!"

My God, what was it he was saying?! It was not true! It had never been true! They had never really hated Luthie! . . . Well, they had, but only for a little while — after McGregor had been killed. Mostly, they had felt . . . peculiar about him, in various ways — yes, they had: but really hate him?

My God, this was unlike anything McGregor had ever devised — unlike anything McGregor could have devised: this was . . . yes, different . . . in a rather *important* way . . .

And Grenfeld screamed again, "Everybody hates you!" in despair, and suddenly, in the voice of someone just realizing he is doomed.

And then there was a horrible, terrible, dreadful silence.

Even the dying German had stopped moaning.

But by that time, Flight B (and, well, even Luthie: Luthie, above all!) had forgotten about the German. They'd stopped paying attention to him as soon as Grenfeld had shouted that very first time: "Everybody hates you!"

They'd abandoned the dying German, so Ashley would always remember. They, Flight B, had abandoned the German for a — just then — more interesting show.

PART TWO

48

I

Nighttime thoughts. (Forsake all others.) Thoughts of . . . hurt.

Amritsar??? The town whose name sounds like paper being crumpled . . .
(Tell the story. The story wants out.)

Things that hurt:
   Grenfeld: "Everybody hates you."

Marshal your thoughts, Luthie.
   (A while ago I poured myself a large gin, and felt both worse and better at once.)

Christ, the things that are good about childhood!
   I was four, five years old: on the verandah a rocking chair just my size;
solemnly, I clutched my glass of lemon squash, and my father judi-
ciously sipped at his *sundowner.*
   · · ·
   Well, I belong in that dusty little town in the Punjab!
   I was born there.
   I belong there, by God!
   · · ·
   Thoughts that hurt.

Waiting for Grenfeld: in the Flight B office. Well, in the Flight A/Flight B
office: I share even the office with Hanmer.

My world, these days, ends at the gates of the base. An hour or so ago that
whole known world was having *their* sundowners: their whisky and sodas,
their brandy and sodas. I made my way to the showers: nobody there. I

let the water run. Leaned my face — my forehead — against the white-tiled wall; I let the hot *hot* water beat, sting, and pummel my back.

(A few of those tiles are loose; need regrouting. With my fingers I picked at those loose tiles.)

The world at dinner, now. I'm waiting for Grenfeld.

Is Grenfeld managing to eat his dinner? (Grenfeld is *under orders* to report to me at 2030.)

It is within my power to . . . destroy Grenfeld.

I destroy people every day.

(Luthie. Idiot!)

Amritsar. The name that sounds like paper being crumpled.

(My mother was about four months pregnant when the events of Amritsar happened.

From the time I was not quite two years old till the time I was almost seven — ready to be sent away to Simla — all that time my mother was not with us. All that time my mother was gone.)

(Nighttime thoughts.

Tell the story.)

II

There was a cot: the time of Dunkirk.

(Thoughts that hurt.)

There was a cot — oh, absolutely! And the building did not hold the heat of the day: the time of Dunkirk. Cold. I was so very cold.

But after a while, a blanket.

An interruption: a knock on the door. "Who is it?"

Hanmer.

"Acklington . . . for Christ's sake, go back and devour your roast beef and Brussels sprouts!"

(*Hanmer, you cannot help* — for all the ties that bind us.)

"Acklington . . . *nothing happened* this afternoon! A Fritz fell out of the sky, had the cheek to die at our feet — that's all. Now it is my right, well is it not, to request the presence of one of the pilots under my command. . . . I am *not* being pompous! It's a private matter. . . . *Ack-ling-ton, OUT!*"

End of interruption.

There was a cot: the time of . . . *(No. Not now.)*

Grenfeld: "He is a Nazi. I am a Jew."

   · · ·

Why did I go to war? (I close my eyes: I see that German's faceless face.)

Christ! Not even McGregor had dared defy me in such a way! . . . Grenfeld *refused*. I had made a request of him: he *refused!*

What shall I do when Grenfeld appears? I've no idea.
  . . .

"Everybody hates you."

III

The sky is burning. London. The city proper.

This afternoon London itself was bombed for the very first time.

As the Hun bastards were massing, we — Flight B — swam; stark naked we stretched out in the grass. The bastards: massing. *A thousand aircraft*. So people are saying. Hanmer and Flight A would take part in that dust-up.

But the Wonders and I — our afternoon off. We sprawled in the grass.

The air smells of brick dust after an air raid — so they say. I've never smelled the brick dust, yet, myself. *An innocent fighter pilot*. No doubt about it!
  . . .

(I destroy people every day.
Well, never mind.)

Waiting for Grenfeld. How much time left?

Grenfeld: he must report at 2030.
  . . .

Forty-seven minutes left. (My watch: on the desk in front of me.)
  . . .

Forty-three minutes and twenty-six seconds. . . . Twenty-four. Three . . . Two . . . One.

(Luthie. Idiot.)

IV

I had a happy childhood. (Tell the story.)
  (I am half-drunk.)

About my childhood:

Ali carried sun-fragrant towels; Ayah drew the water for my bath.
  . . .

Night: *coal's cuttles* lurked in the deepest darkness.

In the warm coolness of the morning, Ayah polished her bracelets and earrings. I helped her, sometimes. (Peculiar thoughts come to one when one is half-drunk. . . . Peculiar thoughts. Childhood.) About Surjit Chadha . . . Sir Prabhjot Chadha.

An interruption. Again!!!
Corporal Rossiter: he is one of the armorers. He who bought four potted plants from the plant-selling children; brought Victoria and Albert the cats here from Somewhere in Scotland in my dogshit Austin.
. . .
(*Is the gin bottle hidden, Luthie?* It was hidden.)
. . .
Corporal Rossiter: "Sir, Albert's been hurt, sir. Got in the way of a bowser, sir." A fueling van. "His leg may be broken . . . The bowser driver and I . . . we took him to the Med. Section — but they wouldn't help at all, sir. I . . . I need a chit, sir. To authorize the use of a motorcar to take Albert to the vet's in town. I thought perhaps you could help, sir . . ."
. . .
Oh, you childlike man! You . . . *unintelligent* cat, Albert!
. . .
I do not like Benzedrine. (Swallowed a Benzedrine tablet not long after I arrived here for my . . . vigil: all my movements are *darting.*)
. . .
He must be thirty, our Corporal Rossiter; he is childlike; he looked shrewd. He knew what I'd do. I did it: threw my car keys at him. But he looked startled when I giggled. "Report to me on Albert's condition . . . *tomorrow,* Corporal." *(Do not darken this door again tonight!)*
"I do hope the outcome is favorable," I said. "Well, Albert isn't very brainy, is he? But he does have his moments, doesn't he?"
And so the man laughed. Then he said, "Thank you very much, sir."
. . .
Everybody hates me? *Everybody?* . . . Ha!
Well, put *that* in your pipe and smoke it. *Grenfeld.*
End of interruption.

Sir Prabhjot Chadha. (Tell the story.)
Jolly, jowly: Sir Prabhjot Chadha. Toffees and jelly-babies from England in a scarlet silk pouch; scarlet drawstring. "Young Luthie, good for the tum, what?" (When he chuckled, his "tum" shook.)
Lady Chadha: betrousered; bejeweled. (Sikh women wear trousers, not saris.) She was driven about town in a very very black, very long-snouted motorcar. The syce's turban as white as . . . sugar; as spotless as Brunnhilde the Large Rabbit's cage (at home) is spotless after I've cleaned

it. (And Harriet of the Stout Heart — Harriet so often *tried* to walk the way Lady Chadha walked: head high . . . higher . . . highest! One was a bit afraid of Lady Chadha, no doubt about it. God, she was beautiful!)

Surjit: five months older than I. I first met him at an auction. Lady Chadha never came to auctions. (Surjit's task at *this* auction: *to make our acquaintance?*) No ayah with him (he had only an *English* ayah, anyway: her name was Nanny Winthrop); no ayah, then, but . . . not one, not two, but *three!* bearers. (They hovered, but not so close as to be . . . well, *bothersome.*) Surjit: alone. But he did not look lonely: he was pouting.

He had bright green knee-stockings on. *Green!* (I was six years old. My stockings: decently English. Tan . . . *Dull!*

Envy.)

I am a generous man. (I was six years old.) He was alone.

Uncertainty in my heart? (He did not seem lonely: he was pouting.)

"Luthie. W. R." And I offered my hand, sticky with jam.

Oh, Surjit was . . . five *years* older than I. *Twenty* years older! (Well, should I grow up *at once* and go and wash my hands *immediately?!* Not even Ayah ever looked at me like that when I had done something *ir-re-sponsible.*) (*Ir-re-sponsible!* . . . *Valise.* . . . *Grip. Gr-r-rip.* . . . *Port-man-teau.* Oh, I am a man in love with words!)

And I stood before him, and I brought my knees forward a bit, bent them a little, so as not to be so terribly double-jointed. (Ayah had taught me.) It makes one feel less vulnerable — oh, definitely!: not to look so terribly double-jointed (I had discovered).

Do they hate me because I am not . . . McGregor? Because I am not *a* McGregor? (That bastard will haunt me for the rest of my days!)

. . .

Well, I *did* mourn his passing, you miserable Wonders! I did. I did — after my own fashion.

The German: I've no idea, really, when exactly he breathed his last; I was so preoccupied.

What shall I do when Grenfeld arrives? (I should be *marshaling* my thoughts.)

But the stories go on. On on on on on.

. . .

Christ! My style of writing is . . . *inelegant!*

I was six years old. (A story about childhood: about Surjit.)

Defiantly, I slammed my knees back home. I am myself. (Not even then did I always do all that Ayah had taught me.) Anger rising in me.

But there . . . there came Dennis Kirby-Green. And Jimmy Clarke. And Harriet, of course.

And something almost like a veil dropped over Surjit's eyes.

He did not accept my jammy-sticky hand. But he said, "How do you do?" (God! His English: at that time probably better than mine. He never said "I am thinking" instead of "I think," I am sure. . . . Well, he had an *English* ayah!)

· · ·

Suspense. What would happen next?

· · ·

He looked at me. Me only. (Not at Dennis. Nor Jimmy. Nor Harriet.) "I'll race you to the gate," he announced, quite matter-of-factly.

And everyone relaxed. Green stockings or not — *he was one of us!*

· · ·

He wasn't one of us:

He clapped his hands, summoned the bearers. And one of them, an old Gujerati, drew a line in the dust with the heel of his sandal, at Surjit's command: oh, no pell-mell race, this; no shouting as we ran! Surjit, with clumsy fingers, untied his beautifully knotted tie — navy and green: to match his stockings? — and handed it to a second bearer. (Dennis snickered.) (Surjit, as haughty as his mother, opened his shirt collar.) Well, who would hold *my* tie? If Ayah should see me without my tie!

Said Harriet, solemnly: "Give it to me."

"Ready . . . Set . . ." said the Gujerati, in English. "GO!"

Oh, I remember running! ("Luthie-e-e! Luthie-e-e! Luthie-e-e!" yelled Dennis. And Jimmy Clarke. And Harriet.)

God, I remember running.

Surjit was five months older than I. I was the taller, by almost a head. (Truly, the taste of victory meant little to me even then. . . . But just this one time? Ha!)

"Ah, those stork's legs of yours," my father sometimes said. "Little son . . . *Tall* son." And he measured my growth on the door of his study: cut little marks into the frame with his pocketknife. And he once showed me a picture in a book of a stork sitting on a chimney-pot nest; and he showed me a picture of a stork walking on his stork's legs. But this was the time in my life when I was quite literal-minded: it didn't look to me much like my own legs. (Well, I tried it once: walking like a stork . . . It felt not right. . . . But I can keep going forever on those stork's legs of mine! . . . Running running running.)

It should have been no contest, really.

Surjit: compact. Determined. I have never seen anyone so determined.

I am not a sprinter. Have never been. Shall never be. Well, long distance — cross-country — that's what I can do.

I am twenty years old now. *Why did we run that race, Surjit and I?*

I am twenty years old now. *Surjit won.* No doubt about it. (If judged on effort and stout heart alone, he won. Oh, absolutely!)

But we thudded against the Holloways' gate together. Together. Not: one first, the other second. We were together.

I was taller, lighter; I had my stork's legs (though I have never been a sprinter). I should have left him far, far behind. But there we were. A tremendous thud.

Then, silence. Only our breath: gasping; rasping.

Torrents of sweat down my face. Down my back. And then, slowly, I turned my head: and sweat glistened in the little hollows about Surjit's nose, and it ran down onto his lip . . .

And, into the hush, the old Gujerati said, happily, "Two first." For him, the matter was most beautifully resolved. Everyone should be happy.

And, into the hush, Dennis said, "Bloody hell." (And, predictably, a grown-up somewhere said, "Dennis!!!")

And Surjit and I: murder in our hearts.

There we were, breathing to ourselves; but gradually, our breath quieted down.

Behind us, nobody spoke. Then Dennis said, not sounding convinced at all, "Luthie won." Jimmy Clarke mumbled, "Luthie won." And Harriet? Harriet the Stouthearted — her voice sad (spiteful?): "Chadha won." (But she still was clutching *her* prize: my miserable tie.)

And then Surjit did something terribly, terribly English. (Well, he had an *English ayah!* Bloody hell!) Surjit held out his hand, politely, for a sportsmanlike handshake. (Oh, it was infuriating!) His hand sticky with sweat.

(Mine, before, had been sticky with jam. Well, both our hands were disgusting now.)

So, there we were: a handshake, grudgingly. Very grown up. Looked at each other. No longer enmity between us. We both were tired, a bit; still out of breath, somewhat. (Oh my God, it was hot!)

We both were six years old. We knew: *one* of us should have won. In childhood, things ought not to remain unresolved. In childhood, things ought not to remain unclear.

Well, I am a man grown. In life, things become . . . resolved? Ha!

In that moment (I think) — *for* a moment — we left Dennis and Jimmy and Harriet behind: we were wise beyond our years. (And we stood there, and we still were out of breath.)

Thoughts that come when ghosts begin to walk . . .
. . .

Well, it isn't the proper time yet for ghosts to begin to walk!
. . .

What time is it? How much time is left?

Grenfeld. Grenfeld. Grenfeld. . . . Bugger Grenfeld.

(The power to destroy that I hold in my hands is staggering.)

•

I do not feel well. Too many cigarettes, I suppose.

And ... bad! Bad! Unwise — gin and Benzedrine, especially on an empty stomach: no dinner. All my movements — of the hands, the body — all my movements: *darting.*

Why did I go to war?

Oh yes, a coda:

About two months after our foot race — I heard this from my father — Surjit and Sir Prabhjot sailed for England.

Some three months later, Sir Prabhjot returned, without Surjit. Surjit, seven years old, would go to school in England.

I went to Simla, when my time came: a *colonial education.* Not quite the thing, even for only the first five years of one's schooling; but I'd not have cared then, had I known. And I do not care now.

I belong in that little town in the Punjab!

V

How much time left?

VI

Childhood:

"And the Chadha bloke gives money to Gandhi."

"Who?"

"*Sir* Prabhjot."

Sir Prabhjot? Sir Prabhjot Chadha?

"Dennis ... On your honor and hope to die?"

"Gandhi. ... Gandhi, you know: the bloke was behind Amritsar!"

Well, Dennis's father was the Political Agent: Dennis should know.

I remember a feeling of most dreadful powerlessness.

Nim   Do I want you to know how I lived?

Well, it occurred to me the other day that I had no letter ready for her *To Be Delivered in the Event of My Death.* No ... bequest. No ... legacy.

I'd truly disappear forever ...

(Oh, in God's name! This is *really morbid.*

  . . .

Dying is what happens to other people.)

Nim   Do I want you to know how I lived?

(I'll disappear: things private and hidden will remain hidden.)

VII

How much time left?

VIII

Grenfeld has been here; is gone.

Peace. Quiet.

Lorries — light armor, I think — rumbling on the road.

Silence falls.

The sound of a harmonica. Voices: singing. They must be sitting in the grass: a small gathering (there are female voices, too); sitting on the steps of a building . . .
  Switch off the light, Luthie. *Blackout: always the bloody blackout!* Open the door. The grass, for once, does not smell of petrol fumes. It is still scented with the sun of the day just past; underfoot — if I should step out — it would be quiet with the coolness of the evening . . .

The sky burning.

> *There Is a Tavern in the Town.*
> . . . Upon my breast a turtledove
> So they'd say that I died for love . . .

Nim
  I miss you terribly.

The Water Is Wide, I Cannot Cross Over.

Well, as a rule, we do not sing, "Oh Death Where Is Thy Stinga-linga-ling." We do not. Nothing so jauntily gruesome. We know better. Don't we?

Grenfeld has been here; is gone.
  Suddenly, I've a craving. *No more gin*. What I crave is a large glass of cool fresh milk. (How very odd. I've never been much of a milk-drinker.)

IX

"Han-mer —"
  Here he is again, God damn him!
  "Didn't I already tell you an hour ago — whenever — to bugger

off?... No, I do not want to go and get drunk. I *am* drunk. Was drunk.... Are *you* drunk, Hanmer?

"I do *not* want a good night's sleep. Hanmer, *I am ALL RIGHT.* You may go and get drunk or have a good night's sleep with a pristine conscience.

"What?! Grenfeld was seen ... on Ashley's motorcycle?... Leaving the base. *As if all the furies of hell were after him.* Quite. Quite. Picturesquely put. In his place I'd do the very same, I suppose.... Ackling-ton, this way to the door."

...

Grenfeld has been here; is gone.
Now ... *Waiting for Grenfeld (again).*
(No respite.... Bloody hell!)

(No milk.)

The singers are gone.
And now that night has truly fallen, the sky in the direction of London is *red.* No smoke, in the darkness; the sky is red. *Still* burning.
...

A thousand aircraft.
I am very frightened. (Hanmer is frightened. Hanmer went to get drunk.)

London's burning	London's burning
Look yonder	Look yonder
Fire fire	Fire fire
Pour on water	Pour on water

I'm singing to myself.
Grenfeld.
(No milk.)

X

So ... What to do now?
(Am I still half-drunk?... The bloody Benzedrine!: all my movements are ... darting.)

Did Grenfeld borrow the motorcycle with Ashley's permission or did he simply help himself?

There exists a photograph of my mother.
(Nighttime thoughts. Tell the story.)

An interruption, of sorts.

Under the window, a voice — one of the *guardians* of this place: hailing somebody, requesting that he should identify himself. . . . Not Grenfeld. . . . The *guardian* berating the culprit — sinner — criminal!!! for using an electric torch to light his way. *Blackout. Blackout.*

End of interruption.

As of ten minutes ago, the motorbikes in the base car park were the following: three Nortons, one Harley, one Matchless, two Triumphs. No Husqvarna. . . . What to do now?

Doodle, doodle. *Nim's face.* (Thoughts that are bright as sunshine!)
. . .

A motorcycle. A man on a motorcycle. The angle of the body is not right at all, though. Let us begin over.
. . .

Albert. A sketch similar to that I once made for the Wonders, on the blackboard. Albert — he of the Imbecilic Feats of Valor — inside a Spit; mangled ears sticking through the helmet, warlike . . . A drawing to make one smile: chuckle.

They do not hate me.

Nighttime thoughts:

A photograph. A plain snapshot of my mother.

Should win prizes in contests, though. (Eat your heart out, Ashley!? Or is Ashley too young to appreciate it? . . . He may not be.)

A private photograph . . . will never be in contests.

How I discovered it:

(Nighttime thoughts.)

God, there is a sweetness to a wartime homecoming! No other homecoming can match it. (I was home on leave for a few days after my wings exam.)

There is an anxiety to a wartime homecoming. (My father at that time: most terribly worried about the orchard. Well, the winter just past — one of the worst not only in living memory, but in the record books.)

I learned this later:

My mother woke up one night, during that winter: it was past midnight. My mother: "Philip . . . Philip . . . You are awake! What is it? Has the war really begun, then?" This was the time of the Phony War.
. . .

My mother, my father: meeting at the door between their bedrooms. A tug-of-war, for a moment?: both trying to open the door at the same time. My people haven't shared a bedroom since . . . well, since I was seven years old — at Simla — and she had come back after her five years' absence? Well, there is that connecting door, of course: here, in

England. At home. Does it ever get opened? Which of them opens it? . . .
None of my business? God Christ! . . . Well, never mind. . . . My father
is an old man, of course.

My mother: "Philip, Philip . . ."
  But it did not sound like shots, really, outside. Nor exploding bombs.
  And so, past midnight, my father gathered everybody — my mother,
Mrs. Simmonds, Mr. Parrish, and Janet — in the drawing room. Then
he put on layers upon layers of warm clothing, and, armed only with
an electric torch, he went to investigate. Found only in the morning
what had happened. Our apple trees, accustomed to the gentleness of
life — our apple trees had been exploding, shattering, in that dreadful
cold!
  Now again and again we went over the accounts. What options had we
should the harvest prove miserable and the rents — again! — *not on
schedule?* Scribble scribble (in my neat handwriting of those days); erase
erase . . . (The desk had been my grandfather's: no-nonsense; dark oak.)
Scribble scribble — my father in the big armchair by the window (close
to the mid-afternoon sunlight), black-bound ledgers on his knees.
"Wayne . . . Another pencil . . . Will you —?" (And another nitro tablet
under his tongue.)
  I opened the desk drawer, reached in: there was the photograph.
  And so, that night: well, W. R. Luthie — burglar??? Spy? Yes, spy!
Definitely!
  Everyone asleep. I made my way downstairs.
  And I studied — scrutinized — pored over — the photograph.

How my mother came home:
  It was a dark and stormy night. . . .
  It wasn't.

It is a very dark night now. Convoys out there: only their blackout headlamps on. Only a blackout headlamp on the bloody Husqvarna. I assume.

My mother.
  Well, I remember a morning when my father did not go off to St.
Joseph's as usual; instead, we went for a ride. A holiday! A *treat!* (Even
Apricot seemed to feel the joy of the occasion; my father rode Surya, a
glum old creature who never felt the joy of anything. . . . *Surya* means
radiant in Sanskrit. I think.) We headed out of town on the main road,
the road to Lahore . . .

Grenfeld is unfamiliar with the roads. . . . *What if he runs out of petrol?!*

•

Ah! Crowds crowds crowds, the road to Lahore, in the coolness of the morning: donkey carts; people walking, shuffling, carrying their luggage; horses; a bicycle, here and there; a motorcar, horn blaring — everybody scattered (only a cow, complacent, chewed her cud, in a nearby field, oblivious of the hubbub); a tonga rattled by; people walking, carrying their luggage . . .

Then we took a diverging road — a path, really. In a voice not quite his own my father asked me, after a while, whether I'd like to see my mother who now would at last like to return from England. Ha! Yes, ever since I was not quite two years old, she had been in England, caring for her parents — my other grandparents — who were old and ill. Ha!
. . .

Well, Dennis had accepted the story, for example; never asked questions. And little Jimmy Clarke. And Harriet.

After all, there was another small girl we knew — not of our circle, though; her name was Jennifer: her mother was dead. We all accepted that.

All the other children had mothers, of course.
. . .

The grown-ups: there must have been gossip! *Giggly* . . . *vicious?* (Or perhaps they all knew the truth. . . . I am almost twenty-one years old now: people were kind, in our Godforsaken little town. Nothing less than kindness had ever reached me . . . us, the children.)

Did I now want to see my mother?

(Ah, W. R. Luthie: a man of deep emotions!)

I was not quite seven years old, of course. Soon to be sent away to Simla. I shrugged, I think. "Yes. . . . Yes, I think," I said.

(Well, my father had told me once what he never told anybody else — I assume: that my mother surely must love me very much — only she did not know it yet because . . . well, because that was the kind of person she was; but one day she *may* realize just how much she missed me.)
. . .

Several weeks later we traveled by train to Lahore to meet her. She arrived from Bombay. The station, as usual, smelled of the engines: heat — hot metal; smoke; hot oil; and of the travelers' lunches — almost everyone carried a tiffin box! (And vendors hawked pungently fragrant roasted meats, sticky sweets, overripe fruit, and tea, bottled juices, and mango *lassis*.) Color. Squalor. Oh God, yes!

She was beautiful, quiet; did not touch me at first. She and my father did not touch: did not embrace; did not even shake hands. My father: quiet for a long, long time; then he talked too much in a voice not his own.

She was a lady in a hat. (A *cloche* hat — that's the word, I believe.)

(I have sharply etched memories of so many things! This one is a bit foggy, I must say.)

•

There is a photograph of my mother.

On the back of the photograph: *3 April '19,* in my father's hand.

My mother was about four months pregnant. At the time of Amritsar my mother was four months pregnant.

. . .

My mother: a girl. My mother: younger than I am now.

. . .

My mother, in a tentlike dress. Good God, there was no need for that dress yet!

The dress: white, with a collar of some darker fabric. The pockets of the dress: trimmed in the same dark fabric. My mother's hands: deep in the pockets of the dress. And the hands are stretching stretching the white dress over the as yet all-but-nonexistent swelling of the belly. And she is pushing pushing that all-but-nonexistent swelling of the belly at the camera.

> Well, world, here I am!
> Well, world, look at me!
> Oh, I am brazen!
> Oh, I am shameless in my pride!

On her head: a wide-brimmed straw hat. It covers her hair; all but covers her eyes. (My father once said that her hair — when he first met her — had been the hair of *a woman of character:* dark, not an insipid blond. It is a bit lighter now, of course: out of the hairdresser's bottle, no doubt.)

. . .

There is an *evenness* of feeling between them these days, I think — between my father and my mother. An affection? Yes. Oh yes. Small; peaceful.

. . .

My mother is a woman of some self-confidence, really.

She is a bit of a nag, actually.

In the photograph: a wide-brimmed straw hat on her head. Makes it somewhat difficult to see her eyes, of course.

My mother: standing in the garden of our house in that Godforsaken town in the Punjab. Pushing the swelling of her belly at the camera.

My mother: a stillness about her. And her eyes: she is looking, looking . . . within herself.

Christ God, she must have loved me then!

(Nighttime thoughts.)

About Grenfeld:

About . . . Beowulf?!:

. . .

Well God God God, how *disorganized!* How . . . *helter-skelter!*

An interruption, of sorts:
Somewhere — in the corner behind Hanmer's desk — rustle rustle.
Mice?
No Albert tonight.
. . .
Victoria . . . Hey, Vicky . . . puss puss . . . Where are you? . . . Victoria . . .
No, let the mice live.

(Written fifteen minutes later:
As of five minutes ago, the motorbikes in the car park were the follow-ing: *two* Nortons (the third one is gone); one Harley; no Matchless; *three* Triumphs.
No Husqvarna.)

XI

Beowulf was a dog.

Grenfeld.
You bastard, where are you?

Beowulf was a dog.
(And I was twelve years old, new to England; my grandfather still walked like a much younger man. But he said that he could never again do a vigorous dog justice. And thus a succession of Emmelines . . .)
I was new to England and felt lonely but would not let on: on my brand-new Raleigh, black and shiny, I made my rounds: *"Miss Odell . . . Miss Odell . . . Have you got any new John Buchan?"* And, full of wonder, I'd sit on a bench at the railway station as Mr. Mannington ushered in a duchess who had come to *tea.*
Sometimes I pedaled the five miles or so to visit the Cunnynghams — friends of my grandparents in a neighboring village — to watch Beowulf run.
Beowulf lumbering down the path.
Beowulf accelerating. Beowulf approaching takeoff speed. The earth shuddering.
Help me. Help. Concentrate. Let's all help Beowulf get off the ground.
Beowulf . . . airborne!!!
And . . . there he stayed. Defying all the laws of the universe. All four massive, hairy paws stretched out: Beowulf, light as a ballet dancer . . . Well, count the fractions of seconds: eternity . . . forever!
Beowulf's ears pinned back: ah, aerodynamic!
Beowulf . . . grinning? Ah, from ear to ear!
. . .

Beowulf coming down with a thud.

Beowulf: bewildered?

Poor Beowulf! (I used to let him lick my face, to make him feel better: I let him lick my face, in spite of his shockingly bad breath.)

Then my grandfather died and my father came Home. He stayed on for six weeks, and we worked most frightfully hard at learning to be two grown men together. His six weeks up, I went to see him off at Croydon.

The aeroplane: an HP-42, an ungainly looking brute.

My father: he did not want to leave — he did not want to leave me.

My father: he was anxious to be gone — though he dreaded the going.

But at last it was half past noon exactly by the control tower's big clock: the captain's head appeared in the flight deck hatch and he gave two blasts on his silver whistle (I'd read somewhere that the whistle was silver); the first officer scrambled through the hatch to furl up the Royal Mail pennant and the Civil Air ensign that had fluttered cheerfully from a mast behind the flight deck.

The aeroplane lumbering down the runway.

Beowulf (?!) accelerating. Beowulf (!) nearing takeoff speed.

Help me. Help me get off the ground.

And then . . . suddenly . . . ah, that enormous beast of an aeroplane: a thing of beauty, graceful in her own element! And, unlike Beowulf, she did not come down a few fractions of a second later: she continued to defy the laws of the universe. And I waved and waved, my heart in my throat, as she rose — free, free . . . God, what freedom!

And everything that I am went with her.

About Grenfeld, the little bastard: should be dead, by all rights. So . . . untalented. (He's like Vřešťala.) A lucky bastard. (Unlike Vřešťala.)

A man *obsessed,* and tall in *self-knowledge.* (In reality, a good bit shorter than I, of course.)

They are so *without knowledge,* the Wonders.

. . .

He probably is back, now. He is. I am sure of it.

Grenfeld:

I remember one of our *postmortems* — still Somewhere in Scotland. NAAFI tea; strawberry jam tarts. . . . We sat in the grass: the usual. The NAAFI always sold jam tarts in Scotland. "Sergeant," I said. "This is a suggestion. We're not at an air show, are we? Not trying to impress our grandmothers. Right? Absolutely! If you would . . . simplify your performance . . ."

. . .

Is he listening?

Grenfeld: well, chewing chewing on his jam tart. And chewing. *Well, swallow, in Christ's name!*
. . .

"A loop, for instance," I said. "The Jerry can just keep raising the nose of his kite and you are in his sights. . . . A slow roll: overdone. The Fritzes must have it posted somewhere by now: *watch the Tommies going for their slow rolls.* A half-roll is little better."
. . .

Grenfeld: serious of face? But ah, the fashion of the moment is *opaque!* The face: closed to me, against me. . . . He knows his purpose, by God! A man of *self-knowledge.*
I talked and talked. Talked myself hoarse. My tea got cold.
Grenfeld: terribly serious of face. Eager? To him, *the end is what matters, not the means.* . . . Oh you . . . child!
. . .

"Sergeant," I said, "make yourself familiar with a controlled spin. It gets you out of the fray. Quickly. And it just *might* make the Fritz think that you've been . . . incapacitated, and he'll not go after you again. You'll be alone. Time to gather your thoughts . . . Take all the time you need."
. . .

Well, *Grenfeld,* I've just handed you my head on a silver platter! One word from you to Old Hurry-up . . . Christ! W. R. Luthie, aiding and abetting the dreaded LMF — *lack of moral fiber* — in one of the men under his command!

(What would our squadron leader Hurry-up do *now* if he got wind of this *affaire Grenfeld?*
The entire Fighter Command — not just Hurry-up — knows about the German by now, of course! I cannot keep the Wonders from talking!
What would Hammett do to Grenfeld? What would he do to me?
Never mind. Well, where was I? . . . In Scotland, Yes. Yes.)

Grenfeld: *opaque.*
At last I let him go.
My jam tart: a rock in my stomach; I gulped down the rest of my cold tea in despair. I looked up. Grenfeld was quite far away from me now.
Grenfeld: he broke into a . . . trot. Big clumsy flying boots. He broke into a run. Grenfeld . . . gathering speed.
Beowulf (!!!) accelerating . . . (etc. etc.).
Grenfeld . . . airborne!!!
And there he was: blue (in his uniform) against the blue sky . . . Count the fractions of seconds: eternity! Forever!

All tensions released. (Grenfeld, in his big boots, as graceful as a ballet dancer!)

Joy!!! Happiness!!! Freedom!!!

(He is rid of . . . me? Of my earnest blathering — and so on?)

He is released from . . . what?

He came down with a thud. But, unlike Beowulf, he seemed to be . . . comfortable with coming back down to earth. Grenfeld: running through the grass. Grenfeld: trotting.

Grenfeld: walking. A man with a purpose.

I remember: I sat there for a while. The confounded wind had come up.

I was certain that Grenfeld would be the first of the Wonders to die.

And now he is out there — running running. Running from *his* thoughts that hurt? The bastard! (*Envy* . . . ?)

Bloody hell! The Husqvarna still isn't in the car park.

. . .

(Nor is my dogshit Austin back, by the way. Is our good Corporal Rossiter perchance careering about the countryside with a lady friend instead of taking Albert to the vet's?)

Ah, Luthie   Luthie

(Am I still half-drunk?)

XII

And we were running, Ayah and I. (Nighttime thoughts.)

No.

Tell the story. The story wants out.

(Nighttime thoughts.)

There was a cot: the time of Dunkirk . . .

(I do not want to think about it. *Somebody please come and interrupt me: my . . . lizardlike thoughts scurrying to and fro: my storytelling. Hanmer, you . . . bag of misery . . . come.*)

An interruption, of sorts: two men — drunk, quite loudly drunk — passing under the window. One of them — both of them? — urinating into the grass, loudly. (The *guardians* will collect them?)

Did Grenfeld go to get drunk?

And we were running, Ayah and I. (An explosion; smoke rising . . .)

Slap slap went Ayah's sandals, as we ran. Slap slap her heavy braid of hair against her back. She stopped, I remember, to gather her breath: sun and silence sat astride the rooftops. "Everyone is at home having their tea," I said, though of course I knew that it wasn't teatime; but it rather frightened me to see *her* frightened.

Then, at home: "The telephone is not working! Not a single telephone in town is working! We are cut off from the *whole world!*"

Outside agitators had done it. And it was . . . as disquietingly thrilling
as Ayah's stories of difficult childbirths: every ayah I knew had many sisters and cousins and aunts — and grandmothers! — all of them with difficult childbirths.

The explosion — *bang!* — had been exciting. But at the same time I
felt . . . as if I'd lost something: well, a place as important as St. Joseph's
Hospital, where my father was an important man — the telephone *there*
did not work! And it lasted for *weeks!* — well, so it seemed to me: it must
have been only a few days. I was six years old.

I remember: QUITT INDIA! painted in enormous red letters on a
wall.

My father: "Little son, remember: 'quit' is spelled with only one *t.*"

("Amritsar . . . Amritsar . . ." grown-ups whispering. "It will be another Amritsar . . ." Another Amritsar never came.)

Grenfeld is running from his thoughts that hurt . . . toward what?

XIII

Amritsar.

"There were trains." My father speaking.

Shall I summon Ashley — *question* him? What had Grenfeld's state of
mind been when he rushed off *as if all the furies* . . .

"There were trains." Amritsar. . . . My father speaking.

(But by then I was sixteen; he had come Home for my grandfather's
funeral — visited me at school at weekends. . . . I'd brought up the
subject.)

"I wasn't there, of course — at the station," he said. "I heard this
from . . . Ali. He was there, at the station."

. . .

Ali? Ali . . . of the (sun-warmed) towels?

. . .

"Women and children, mostly — I heard this from Ali." My father
speaking. "Ali said that, as the trains passed — did not stop — one
could see the faces in the windows, and some of the children were crying." Trains fleeing Amritsar. Heading for Lahore. But by then Lahore
was no longer safe, and so the trains were sent on to 'Pindi. Rawalpindi.

*Nim If you were here — if we had a glass of cold milk together — I'd
tease you: "Milk mustache! Milk mustache!" Then I . . . oh, I'd kiss away
the mustache!*

Nim, I miss you.
(This is not a real letter.)

Well. Yes. Where was I? (My thoughts come and go like . . . furtive fish: break the surface . . . a blink of an eye . . . they are gone.)

Several hours ago (how many? *This is my thought of the moment*): Grenfeld came about ten minutes before the appointed time. I *felt* them — sensed them — coming. All of them: my Wonders. Boots on the gravel; boots in the grass. (Quickly!: lights off, Luthie; and part the blackout curtains, slightly . . .) Shapes in the near-darkness. *Rhubarb . . . mutter mutter mutter.*

Grenfeld — in the middle? They flanked him. They were taking him . . . *to his execution. Rhubarb mutter mutter mutter.*

Then they stopped, a few yards away from the Flight A/Flight B office. Ashley . . . Was it Ashley? I peered: difficult to see. Ashley: what was he doing? — ah, with a *mother's hand,* with a *mother's gesture? Straightening Grenfeld's collar?!*

(It was some two or three minutes before the appointed time.
Rhubarb rhubarb mutter mutter mutter.)

I close my eyes now: I see that German — face without a face.
 . . .

Hallucinating, Luthie? Not just seeing things . . . hearing things? No, it just is that I keep repeating words in my mind. *Grenfeld: "Everybody hates you."*
 . . .

I am not drunk now. I am most dreadfully tired.

I remember:
Grenfeld: staring at the German. Grenfeld: his face white. Grenfeld: *snarling.*

Ah, Grenfeld, there are hatreds in the world!
(This is not a real letter. Why should I be writing a letter to Grenfeld?)

There is hatred of those who commit acts of <u>*wrongness.*</u> *And of those* <u>*perceived*</u> *as part of the wrongness. And hatred of those who try to do right. And of those trapped in the middle of those hatreds.*

Amritsar. (I'll not think of Grenfeld now.)
Amritsar. Gandhi. *Satyagraha.*
Ahimsa. Nonviolence. Sounds noble. It does.
But the man Gandhi is a lawyer by training, in heaven's name! A man

of shrewdness! Or has he changed, perhaps, over the years? People do change, of course. Some become better, and some become worse.
. . .

I am myself. Myself. I have not changed. (Oh, bloody hell!)

A history lesson is in order, I suppose.

Through the last two years of the war — the First War — things in India were unquiet. (My father: "But I wasn't there, of course.") The secretary of state for India had made a speech in the House of Commons, promising greater self-rule for the country once the war was over. "But those of the Muslim faith set to work at once to prevent those of the Hindu faith from ever becoming more self-governing than others. And vice versa. . . . Skirmishes. Terrorism. That sort of thing." My father speaking.

Well, such is India.
. . .

Such is the world, I suppose.
. . .

My father: "But I wasn't there." (Well, there was the war on. And my uncle Robert and my uncle George Henry died in that war; and my father saw — well, didn't see — my uncle Robert die.)

In January of 1919, an Emergency Powers Act was proposed to deal with the Indian . . . unrest. "But I paid it scant attention, really." That is what my father said. "My fault. We'd barely arrived then — I was so very new at the hospital. And we'd just found you were on the way. It was Rufus" — Mr. Kirby-Green — "he kept issuing *private* little warnings right and left. Oh, he so enjoyed being a — very *public,* you know — *secret agent!* Trouble. There would be trouble if the act was passed: all those former enemies would unite. Well, I may have said once or twice that perhaps the act was going too far. But I was so very, very tired from the war." My father the pacifist.

The act was passed in March, suspending civil liberties.

Satyagraha. Gandhi had tried it in South Africa: *passive resistance.*

Ahimsa. Nonviolence. Nothing could be more noble.

(In India, Gandhi had at that time but recently become a man of importance — a man of considerable influence and power. This is a history lesson.)

30 March: Gandhi had called for a *peaceful* general strike — a *hartal.*

A mob stormed the railway station at Delhi. And throughout North India there was rioting and looting. . . . "God, most of those people had no idea what *civil liberties* were!" (My father: helplessness in his voice?)

Gandhi called for another peaceful *hartal* to be held a week later.

But posters at street corners at Lahore and Amritsar screamed: PRE-PARE TO KILL AND DIE! GHADR! . . . Mutiny . . .

Bloody hell! The man Gandhi refused even to *try* to call off the *hartal;* nor did he consent to an announcement that he no longer was in support of it. Instead, he issued assurances that this time everything would truly be peaceful. (Well, one can read about it! In the newspapers. Well, I did: after my father told me. I read everything I could get my hands on.) Christ, the man Gandhi is a lawyer! Whatever else a lawyer may be, it is not *naive!* He knew what was about to happen. It happened.

(Is this getting too long? . . . But I cannot stop now!)

People dying. . . . Amritsar.

My father: "I wasn't there, of course. But they say the whole city seemed to be on fire." The town hall; the goods railway station; schools; banks; shops in the bazaar; a hospital; the telegraph office. And the Calcutta mail train was ambushed. And Englishmen and Englishwomen died, and Hindu men . . . women? . . . children? died; and Muslim men . . . women? and Sikh men . . . God!: for whose *civil liberties?* — they all died.

Jallianwalla Bagh. (A park of sorts; an enclosed place, near Amritsar.) Two hundred died there? on 13 April. (Some say two thousand!) Most of them trampled to death when troops fired into a crowd shouting *"GHADR!"* (Well, General Dyer — the man in charge: General Reginald Dyer, his name — he had not even bothered to learn that there was only one *narrow* way out of the place! Well, of all the —!)

At Lahore a mob sacked the treasury building . . . in retaliation?

Then *ghadr* was over. And the only result was that General Dyer's name was famous the world over, for a while . . .

And Gandhi's name became famous the world over — and remained famous. Was that what he'd set out to do from the beginning: make his cause, and himself, known to the world? *Ahimsa.*

Has the man changed, over these . . . more than twenty years? Some people become worse, and some become better.
· · ·

(I am forever myself? . . . Never mind.)

(Hatreds hatreds of those in the wrong; and those who become part of the *wrongness* . . . unwittingly? Well, not much they could do about it?! And hatreds of those who try to do right; and of those caught in the middle.)

My father the pacifist: helpless.

(And I remember: a column of smoke rising — and our town was cut off from the *whole world! I* remember a feeling of powerlessness.)
· · ·

Grenfeld, what do you know about the world?
I most definitely do not want to think of Grenfeld now!
· · ·

(Thoughts of . . . never mind. . . . Do not think others.)

About our dusty little town:
Little *groups* had collected at the station — the time of Amritsar: so my father told me. . . . Well, better than ogling a *nautch* girl in the bazaar — watching the trains: all new, never before seen . . . the English running for their lives; sending their women and children out of Amritsar.

"But only a few fists were raised at the trains." That is what my father told me. "Ali said that. I chose to believe him. . . . Well, the English in town . . . they were *their* English — that's what all those at the station seemed to think: I chose to believe it. Everybody knew *their English*. Why bother them, then, because of something happening at Amritsar?"

Until, suddenly, a mob — a *real mob?*: not the crowd gawking at the trains? — decided to storm the hospital. St. Joseph's!

"Well, Muslims. . . . Well, St. Joseph's treated Muslim women — with their husbands' . . . fathers' . . . permission. Oh, we accepted anybody! A human being in need — that was what mattered. I should have known better. Well, I was born in the Punjab!" That was what my father said. "But I left when I was eight years old. Came back after —" After his first wife's death. "And then it was appendectomies . . . that sort of thing; the patients mostly English . . ." (It was a lovely Sunday afternoon when he told me, on the towpath by the river near my school; I was sixteen years old — I'd brought up the subject of Amritsar: we were learning to be equals — men together.
. . .

Amritsar . . . Amritsar . . . Grown-ups whispering when I was a child . . .)

My father: "Out of the blue, these . . . people decided that the hospital was a source of corruption of all womanhood! Male doctors. Male patients. . . . You know, the Zenana Hospital at Amritsar — and it was for Muslim women only! — it was burned to the ground and an English woman doctor murdered. . . . But at the time I did not know about that, of course."

And so the mob came. My mother was at the hospital, that day, with my father: he did not want her to be separated from him because of the . . . uncertainty of things; she did not want him to be separated from her.

My mother: four months pregnant. My mother: nineteen years old.
My father: a pacifist.

(But by the time he finally offered the *ultimate elaboration* on the ending of the story, the present war was on: I'd joined up and then we waited . . . waited: five pounds a week for the waiting; and around and around and around we went, my father and I, through the orchard; leaned against the fence, stared at the apples.)
. . .

Now I set my burdens down on this piece of paper. Why was the coming of the new war the time for my father to try to unburden himself to me?

But unlike the morning when he told me about the dying of my uncle Robert, this time his voice was . . . impassive: no emotion to it, as if he were trying to be *Blind Justice:* objective.

"Your mother is a woman of great courage, you know. But she was very very young. . . . 'Philip, quickly! A rifle! Have you got a rifle?' She expected me to defend the place, heroically. She expected me to defend *her* . . . and you . . . heroically. *She* was ready to defend the place. Well, all the public buildings in town were under guard. And Major Rawlinson — he commanded the garrison — he'd offered . . . advised . . . protection for the hospital. But I refused. Well, I'd enough of all that: weapons, fighting. After all the events of the war, I was sick of it: all the dying. After all I'd seen in the war, I should have known better. . . . Actually, I feared that if there should be a . . . disturbance, the presence of armed soldiers might only make matters worse. Well, I did devise a plan of sorts to protect the patients, should the need arise. But now there was nothing anyone could do. Two of the nurses jumped out of a window at the back. But I could not leave, of course. And your mother: she refused to try to escape. And an idiotic idea struck me then: perhaps I could go and talk to those people. . . . Quite a number of them: perhaps a hundred. Then I simply resolved to shield her — and you — with my body as long as I could. . . . Ineffectual, I suppose."

. . .

And then what happened? Nothing. A detachment of soldiers came. In time. They fired over the crowd's heads. The crowd — no longer a mob — ran. Some of them ran and tried to set fire to the bank instead of the hospital but were quickly . . . dealt with.

Then things quieted down; and only the clusters of gawkers remained at the station. The clusters became smaller and smaller. And after a few days there was peace, in our little town.

My mother had married my father a few months before because the war — the First Great War — was over: there were no *young* men left.

She married him because the one young man of her acquaintance who still was among the living and with whom she was very much in love — that man had gone and married someone else.

My mother's pregnancy was on the difficult side, I understand.

But she had looked forward to coming to India: a new life! An adventure? (She was younger then than I am now.) But after the events of Amritsar, she conceived a hatred of the country — Christ, she hated it! (Did not fear it, though, so I understand: she is a woman of . . . boldness. . . . Well, she had been the one to ask my father to marry her — *she'd done the asking!*

But the marriage faded.)

And when the man had written to her one day — (do I bear that man's name? God! Surely my father had no idea at the time of my birth of the man's existence! He'd not have permitted it, I'm sure, for me to bear that man's name) — when the man had written, telling her that he was now divorced, she corresponded with him, without my father's knowledge, and then one day she left. Five years later — a woman grown? — she came back.

Do I blame Gandhi for the fact that my mother did not love me?
Why did I go to war?
· · ·

Ahimsa. It does not exist. Well, it becomes perverted. It *sounds* noble. I do not trust anything that *sounds* noble.
Gandhi . . . I reject his kind of *ahimsa.* Well, if necessary, I take up arms against those who, in my belief, do wrong: I do it honorably. (Well, that's what I thought then.)

Grenfeld . . . This in no way is a real letter!
Grenfeld, you stared at that dying Fritz, and you were as white as a blank sheet of paper, and you knew <u>absolutely</u> <u>nothing</u> about the world.

Before I went over Dunkirk, my father the pacifist had given me a knife.
· · ·

Ah, never before have I been so straightforward about naming those things that hurt!
· · ·

My father — being my father — had said, "Use it with good judgment."
I returned from Dunkirk. So far, my father has not asked what happened to his knife.
· · ·

Grenfeld . . . Why am I writing all this down?

My dogshit Austin is back. (Not the Husqvarna, though.)
Well, sod Grenfeld! I am going to bed, by God!
(But, what if . . . ? Ah, a fair number of us disappear from this world not courtesy of eager Fritzes! Our own doing: too much whisky, too much beer, too much brandy, too much gin, and a motorcar . . . motorbike?! . . . much much too fast . . .)
· · ·

Luthie, Luthie, Luthie . . . What time is it?

XIV

And so I started for "home." Turned back. (Had failed to lock the office. Left the key inside? . . . Switch the light on again . . . kick the lower left-

hand desk drawer shut properly. The wood didn't splinter, did it? My toes aren't bleeding, are they, inside my sock — inside my shoe?
. . .
    Pain.)
    I am tired.

There was . . . a cot: the time of Dunkirk. A cot.
    And I was cold.
    Pain.

Why am I writing all this down?
    I am *exorcising* thoughts that hurt!!! (Setting them in motion; letting them go.)
    Defiance? Resolve! . . . Do not think about Grenfeld.
    Courage?
    Bravery!
    . . .

    Ah, the *profligacy* of it! Never before so . . . no, not *extravagant,* but *profligate* with words in . . . naming hurts!
    (Never before so open about why I am writing all this down.)

Pain. But after a while, the sound of a key in the lock — the time of Dunkirk . . . A blanket came sailing into the room. A pillow. A real pillow! A cushion, actually. (Do I not want to think about it? . . . What shall I do if Grenfeld does not appear by eleven tomorrow? That is when we go on ops. . . . *Do not think about Grenfeld.*)

About that cushion:
    Late afternoon (that day the time of Dunkirk: five — six — seven? hours before): the coal's cuttles had dragged me — pushed and prodded me — to a village. The village: Germans Germans Germans came. Germans . . . with little tourists' cameras. Click, click. A nice snapshot of The Enemy *in extremis* to Send Home to Mother. Darkness closing in on me. . . . Well, I'd fainted once before already.
    I tried to look dignified.
    And chickens scratched in the dirt, I remember, under the Germans' feet; cared not a whit about my dignity.
    There was a building: the village school? A room. The headmaster's office? A sofa.
    And, suddenly, my hands were free: the pain of having my hands free so suddenly was unbearable. I cried out. And my knees were buckling.
    There was a cushion on the sofa. (The only brightness in that dark around me.) A child's head embroidered on the cushion — an angelic-looking child. Boy? Girl? . . . Well, God damn, who can tell, about

angels? The embroidered child appeared to be sleeping. *Em-broi-dered.*
(All those stitches! My, my! Small: tiny. Neat. Even. What *plenitude* of
stitches!

Plen-i-tude. Plen-i-tude. Very softly. As in *cu-ra-tor* — very softly.
Cu-ra-tor. Cu-ra-tor. And other words of childhood.)

Bloody hell!

Grenfeld: he is not running away *forever,* is he? He *will* be back. He
must. He has not done anything *really stupid,* has he? He is not . . . *de-
serting?!* Well, he cannot. He can't.

. . .

Somehow I must see this through. In the meantime, all the things that
hurt . . . well, as many of them as I can manage, as many as will pour out:
I am setting them in motion. The bastard Grenfeld and I: are we doing
the very same thing, really — each in his own way?

. . .

I spin stories; set their threads down one next to the other; I circle
around them: the circles tighter, tighter . . . one day I may reach the
core!

A ring of red (embroidered) roses framed the (embroidered) sleeping
child's head. Above the halo of roses, an invitation (embroidered): *Just
half an hour's rest* . . . (In French, of course.)

Well, I am English, damn it!

I drew myself up. *I am English.* "Sorry," I said. "May I have a bit of a
lie-down?"

I remember this very well: several pairs of hands caught me as I fell.
Yes, I remember being carried to the sofa. Then I . . . slept.

And afterward, the German officer — receding hairline, receding chin
— the commander of the unit — he did not know how to treat me, really.
With a quite *Prussian* correctness? ("Pilot Officer, tomorrow you will be
remanded to the Luftwaffe." God! Had he learned his English from detective stories?) With pity: compassion . . . and all that? ("Coffee, Pilot
Officer? It is newly brewed . . ." — his English: very good, indeed; the
coffee: awful.) As a father would treat a wayward child? ("Ach, my
young man, it is foolish, nicht wahr, to join to fight in a war which you
will of course lose.") Or as one man — one human being — would treat
another?

I was in pain. That is what I remember.

Do not think of Grenfeld.

Then . . . night: the cushion was back.

Loneliness? . . . No one, nothing, to feel lonely for! Nothing to make me feel lonely. A man alone. Oh, utterly alone! *Complete* desolation! (Thoughts of . . . desperate defiance?)

. . .

The blanket: standard army issue. Heavy. *Warmth. Warmth.*

. . .

Resourceful Luthie! Well, kick the blanket — and the cushion — toward the cot! (Those beautiful white bandages about my wrists, on my hands: they were the cleanest thing about me. . . . *Luthie, no bleeding permitted on the blanket!* But I kept stepping on the blanket. *Trip trip trip:* shall we dance? And the blanket was leading! That miserable blanket: a menace. Oh, the indignity of it!)

I lay on the cot: pain. (May have . . . lost myself for a few moments.)

A dead parrot staring at me: stuffed. (The room: a storage room of some sort. Ceiling-high shelves along the walls: copybooks, pencils in boxes — five dozen pencils to a box? A file cabinet. An artificial palm tree in the corner. And the parrot.

. . .

"Now, pupils, today we shall learn about faraway — *warm* — places."

. . .

(Plenitude. Plenitude of feathers. . . . Plen-i-tude.)

. . .

Just half an hour's rest . . . (And so I struggled; and, after a bit, I succeeded in wrapping myself in the blanket: warmth. And I laughed.)

. . .

The overhead light brought tears to my eyes. I tried to turn on my side: pain. (Bruises.)

Up again. I felt lightheaded (later, it would be that I'd feel lightheaded almost all the time: I had a fever).

Luthie, courage. Onward to *half an hour's rest.*

And, manfully, I set out on a search expedition for the light switch.

. . .

The switch must be outside, in the hall!

. . .

Thus, in a panic, I began to push, shove (not kick, really), *nudge* the cot toward the wall. Blanket warmth *warmth:* and a healing sleep . . . (Perhaps if I could wedge the cot between the file cabinet and the wall, the cabinet would shield me from that light . . .)

That brought them: the hellish noise I was making. They fell into the room: two of them. Their two big Walthers at the ready.

And I . . . stank. Of fear: past, present, and future. (I'd stopped noticing it long before, of course; but they — by God — they wrinkled their noses.) Stale sweat . . . that sort of thing. And my shirtsleeves: clammy, with my blood, of course. (Snip, snip. Skillful! Well trained!: the medicos; the Germans. They'd cut my shirtsleeves; then they bandaged me. Now what was left of my sleeves: the blood was drying. And blood has got a stench all its own.) I tried to look dignified. . . . Pain.

With some effort, I turned my clean, beautifully bandaged hands palms up: quietly, I showed those two my helplessness. . . . Pain.

And the younger of the two — not much older than I: he *liked* my helplessness.

What next?

I said, in German — my miserable, *unaccomplished* German, "I . . . move my bed." Is that what I said? I hope so. (I was cold.)

And the older of the two: he had a paunch against his belt — a bit like our IO, but he was about Sergeant Bennett's age (though I hardly knew Sergeant Bennett then). He said something to the other one. His eyes on me: cautious. He handed the younger one his Walther. So, Young Scrawny-neck: he had *two* of the big guns now. *Both* of them trained on me.

At my . . . belly. Low down on the belly.

. . .

He'd not kill me. No, not right away.

He'd simply . . . hurt me. He'd . . . hurt me. . . . Destroy me.

. . .

And Old Paunch picked up the cot and carried it over to the wall — dropped it with a thud between the cabinet and the wall: he'd guessed at once where I wanted it. He picked up the blanket . . . but did not *throw* it on the cot. Picked up the cushion . . . Gave it a few whacks.

Placed it on the cot. Picked it up again. Whacked it again.

He was fluffing the bloody thing up for me!

And we stared at each other. And there was a rather terrible silence.

. . .

I should have said thank you.

. . .

I looked down at my boots. (The floor: lino-covered; the lino, old.)

The boots looked old, too: did not look . . . nice. Well, that very morning they'd looked nice. Not as shiny as Sergeant Bennett's boots are shiny! But they'd been the kind of boots — in the morning — in which one can walk out with confidence — *op-ti-mism* — into the world.

And so now I stood there. Helplessness. Christ God, a sense of finality as great — almost — as . . . as when the coal's cuttles had held my own Colt .45 to my head! . . . Helpless feet. Feet slightly apart, to keep my balance: I felt lightheaded. I tried not to look so double-jointed.

(Two Walther pistols trained on me.)

Pain. I felt lightheaded.

Then Old Paunch himself said, "Thank you." In English. Butchering the "th." He said it in a hurt voice. A plaintive voice? A childlike voice, almost: a child . . . rejected? . . . Well, God in heaven!

"Thank you," he repeated. An offended voice.

And again. And this time, he flung it in my face: an insult.

He grabbed the Walther from Little Scrawny-neck.

(*No . . . No. Please don't . . .*)

But . . . the door slammed behind them. Key turning in the lock.

. . .

I should have said thank you.

. . .

The overhead light went out: a velvet-smooth, soothing darkness.

I should have said —

. . .

The light: on again. . . . I was in their power. Completely!

The younger one laughed. Then Old Paunch laughed. And they went on laughing. (The light: on and off, off and on. They were torturing me.)

. . .

But I slept then, in spite of the light. And when I woke up, I felt . . . much better. Without pain? No. But I could do . . . anything. *Anything!*

Walk out and keep walking and feel the grass under my feet . . . ?

My father: he has not asked me yet what happened to his knife.

(Thoughts that come with ghosts' whispers: set them in motion now; let them go. . . . Freedom! . . . It will not happen . . . ? Can it happen?)

What shall I do if Grenfeld does not appear by eleven in the morning?

XV

After Dunkirk — after hospital — I was at one of those RAF convalescent places.

Peace . . . I need a respite: peace. Now. Now. (I am tired.)

(Is the Benzedrine beginning to wear off at last? I am most desperately tired.)

I was at one of those convalescent places. Leather armchairs; green plants with tough leaves (the legless chap in love with Siobhan the physio was the one who said those leaves were as tough as boiled beef).

This is a . . . *wisp.* Yes, a *wisp* of a memory.

(God, I am so miserably tired!)

This . . . *wisp:* does it truly belong here in the *pattern* of the story? . . . Yes, it does. It does, by God! I know why it does. I think. . . . Well, does it, really? . . . Luthie. Idiot. (Tired.)

•

I could not sleep: nights at that convalescent place.

One night, I made my way downstairs (the beautiful Muriel on duty in the little sitting room which was the nurses' station) — this *was* a posh place. "Hullo, W.R.!" — I was known to all as W.R. — "Can't sleep? . . . Give a shout, will you, if you need anything."

Nim, I so very much wanted her to like me! She was so beautiful!

This is not a real letter.

I am being . . . straightforward. Nim, it is almost inevitable that in hospital one should fall in love with at least one of the nurses; then two days after leaving the hospital the "love" is gone.

I made my way downstairs: there, in the drawing room, an old charwoman was dusting (!) those boiled-beef-leaf plants. A well-worn gray smock on. As she bent forward — well, I could see . . . from here to there! Shocking. Shocking, because she was quite old. Bare legs. And there were varicose veins on her legs like . . . like little road maps of despair. Well, bloody hell!

Then she raised her head and saw me, and she looked startled but then she smiled: she had the whitest false teeth I have ever seen! They must have been brand-new. Her smile was . . . *wary,* though: was I . . . *mental?*

I gave her a small Luthie grin. Tightened the sash of my dressing gown: a modest man — W. R. Luthie! (The cuffs of my pajama bottoms showing.)

All her cleaning things: in a basket. Spray bottles, rags. And a little French maid dusting mop. Well, she created a delicate spray-mist about those tough leaves, delicately — quite as . . . as *Muriel* might, creating a mist of perfume about her . . . Then the old woman patted the leaves dry. (I may have dreamt this. Perhaps it never happened. A *wisp* of a memory — that is all.)

(At that time I was rather afraid of old women.)

Whatever possessed me! I picked up one of those spray bottles from her basket. (The mechanism itself looked like that on a perfume bottle: a rubber bulb on a little rubber tube . . .) I picked up a dusting cloth. . . . My right hand was not up to it yet, then. . . . Well, hold the bottle in the right hand; squeeze the bulb with the left. Dry the leaf, with the left hand. . . . Transfer the bottle to the *left* hand; squeeze . . . with the *right! The right hand!*

Sing! Dance! *The right hand! The right!* Celebrate! (It is possible that this never happened. It may have been a dream.)

She did not say anything. (That's why it rather seems as if it had never happened.) Well, her false teeth went clack clack every now and then, I remember. A warm night outside, I suppose. Inside, enclosed by the blackout, one felt as if . . . floating. (Perhaps it never happened.)

And upstairs, wounded men slept — or did not sleep.

. . .

At last all those big, tough leaves shone; glistened.

"Well, good night, lad," she finally said then; and this time her smile was not wary. She obviously was most dreadfully proud of those false teeth, which must have been brand-new! Her face: full of wrinkles. A scarf on her head — the ends tied into a knot on top of her head.

"Good night," I said. And then I went to bed. Well, perhaps it all was a dream? But Muriel was at the nurses' station; looked up from her paperwork. "Hullo, W.R. . . . Want to chat?"

I often came down to chat when I could not sleep.

"No, not this time. Perhaps . . . some other time. . . . Well, thanks."

And was there disappointment in her face?: well, did she enjoy those little dead-of-the-night chats of ours? *Oh, I so very much wanted her to like me!* But there was . . . oh yes: pleasure!, in that face: well, if I did not want to chat, then things must be . . . getting better, weren't they?

I went to bed.

And I slept.

Without dreams. Or without remembering those dreams in the morning.

(Birdlike steps . . . The old woman of birdlike steps: the old black raven of a woman . . . the time of Dunkirk.

The old raven-woman — her scarf had slipped, and her hair: like Ayah's bracelets just on the verge of needing a polish . . . A bit like . . . my grandmother's hair . . .

. . .

My grandmother: venom in her voice.

. . .

The old woman-raven . . .

Christ! More about that later? — one of these days. *The story goes on.*)

But — *peace, Luthie. Peace. Peace.*

(Thank you, Grenfeld. You little bugger.

Because of you I sit here, spinning stories; I've reached a — oh, not another *plateau!* I've reached a . . . watershed?)

Peace. *I am myself.* The time of that convalescent place: the boiled-beef leaves were dusted to within an inch of their lives. Conscientiously.

The bloody motorbike: will it be in the car park *now?*

London is still burning. (I got up from the damned desk a few minutes ago, for a minute: my legs trembling — with fatigue? or *still* the damned Benzedrine? I peered outside. The horizon: red.

London's burning
London's burning

Christ, what senselessness!)

Is Grenfeld . . . destroyed?

Why am I writing all this down?

THE HUSQVARNA IS IN THE CAR PARK!!!

XVI

And now at last I can write about it! At last I can manage to write about it!
Grenfeld came — how long ago was it? — at 2030 to the second. Oh, it is
no problem at all now to write about it!
    (I am most dreadfully tired.)

Grenfeld came. As quiet as . . . an owl's flight.
    The overhead lamp in the Flight A/Flight B office cast shadows. (A
green lampshade: not a bare lightbulb. The lampshade: green on top;
white on the underside. It casts shadows.)
    Grenfeld: he is quite extraordinarily handsome, really. (Makes the
WAAFS go: *oooh! A-a-ah!*)
    · · ·
    I am too thin for my height.
    My teeth are too large.
    · · ·
    Well, Nim *likes* me!
    Let us begin over.

Dear Uncle Dixon:
    In the Event of My Death, please do not make these pages public.
Please protect Grenfeld's privacy.

My Dear People:
    Today — yesterday — I had to deal with a situation —

No? No.

Nim. Under the window, I could hear: Suck suck, mutter mutter
mutter. Suck suck: Stanhope? Stanhope the Peppermint-Cruncher. Suck-
ing on a peppermint? Or on his thumb, again? Then there came a muted
squeal as if . . . as if a circumspect pig were dying. Somebody: "Shut up!"
A stage whisper. Silence. And then: mutter mutter mutter.

·

Grenfeld came.

Well, the door: it is opening . . .

Whose side are the Wonders on? Well, God in heaven! (Not even McGregor had dared defy me like this! Well, McGregor *et al.*: those were childish pranks!) What do the Wonders expect me to do?

(*I most certainly do not obey the Wonders!* I do *not* act according to *their* wishes!)

Grenfeld: there he was. In the room. Quiet . . . Quiet . . . (Not even his shoes squeaked.)

But outside, all the *mutter-muttering* was rather getting out of hand. I flung open the door Grenfeld had just shut behind him. "If anybody else wants to see me, form a queue. Take a number." Did my voice break?

Somebody please tell me what to do next.

And Stanhope . . . Stanhope: yes, yes! — he did drop a . . . peppermint wrapper into the grass, I think, as they retreated — melted — into the twilight. (Peculiar, the things one notices.) Somebody mumbled, hastily: "Good evening, sir." . . . Another voice: "Good evening, sir." . . . "Good evening, sir." (The things one notices: the large brown stain on the ceiling of the Flight B office, for example. The roof leaks, no doubt. It has not rained in a long time, of course.)

Grenfeld: "Sir." A voice that did not break.

Grenfeld: Dignified of face? (Well, it was rather difficult to tell.)

Grenfeld: "Sir . . . you asked to see me." *Unrepentant!*

(Quite. Quite. *I can destroy Grenfeld.*)

. . .

What shall I do next?

(The Benzedrine was just then beginning to take effect. I felt cheered, quite suddenly . . . and powerful. All my movements — the hands, body — *quick quick.*)

. . .

Somehow I must see this through.

Survival, Luthie. That is all that matters.

. . .

And I looked at him. Grenfeld . . . well, God in heaven! His collar open: his shirt collar unbuttoned! You . . . miserable . . . you, you —! This is not how one dresses in the RAF! (So, that was what Ashley had been doing, with such a *mother's hand!*: trying to button him up?)

Grenfeld's collar unbuttoned . . . What in the world —?

But there . . . on a golden chain — along with his identity disks, but separate from them — around his neck, in the V of the shirt, there flashed at me . . . a gold Star of David, by God!

(I did not close my eyes, then. They were wide-open, I remember.

But I saw the German's face — I did — for a span it takes one to draw a breath. I could not help it. . . . And I hated Grenfeld.)

Nim   Somebody
   Help me

Grenfeld, how can you do this! You bastard. How dare you! How dare you!
   (Grenfeld: *Mediterranean* good looks — that sort of thing. And all that.
   . . .
   Well, *Sergeant* Grenfeld. Do you know what you look like? Well, with that shirt open and that gold around your neck, you look like a Venetian gondolier, that's what!)
   Bloody hell! I've had enough Stars of David pushed at me in my time! (Took enough of the Wonders' *sassiness* from that bastard McGregor.)
   This is not how one reports to one's flight commander! (Grenfeld: *Unrepentant?* Ha! Well, I'll . . . I'll . . .
   . . .
   Survival!
   Oh yes: I destroy Grenfeld, and I survive.)
   I counted to ten, then. Twice. Very slowly.
   Blood pounding in my ears — but otherwise there probably was no other sound. What shall I do next? (I closed my eyes. I saw the German's face.)
   I took a deep breath. "Sergeant," I said. (And the Benzedrine was with me — oh, absolutely! I felt powerful . . . and nimble of thought . . . and yet I'd no idea how to proceed.)
   Grenfeld's head went up.
   Grenfeld: Unrepentant?
   Grenfeld's face: *contorted.*
   Grenfeld's face: *ugly* with . . . what?
   . . .
   And then . . . it happened in a fraction of a second: Grenfeld launched himself forward.
   (To my credit: I felt a rush of sadness.)
   Was he attacking me? Then nothing could help Grenfeld now! I could not overlook *this!* I could not.
   (A sense of . . . relief, at the very same time?: the matter had been taken out of my hands. I need not worry any longer how to proceed. Grenfeld himself had sealed his doom. Well, God in heaven!)
   In that first fraction of a second, it had not even occurred to me to try to defend myself — much less to fight back.
   . . .

Luthie, you idiot!

Well, now it is five — *six?!* — hours later. The Husqvarna is back!!!
Only now I can bring myself to write about it!
I am most desperately tired.

Grenfeld's head — how long ago was it: how many hours? — hit me
straight in the Adam's apple: he is quite a bit shorter than I. It knocked
the breath out of me. Sent me staggering back a few steps — into the
wall.
. . .
(Luthie . . . You idiot!)

But now it is *easy* to write about it!!!
. . .
I am tired.

Well, five hours ago — six? — at last I brought my arms up in front of
me, to push him away.
But Grenfeld's head had settled itself comfortably against my Adam's
apple, choking me; and *his* arms were up in front of him, his hands balled
up into fists against his chest. And against my chest.
And Grenfeld was . . . crying.

Dear Uncle Dixon:
Please protect the privacy of everyone concerned. Thank you.
W. R. Luthie

Grenfeld was weeping. Sobbing. *Hooting.* (Never before in my life had I
heard such a sound.) His whole body shaking shuddering with convul-
sive childish sobs.
What should I do next?
Well, of course I put my arms around him. Held him. Tight. Tighter.
. . .
God, what would happen if somebody should come in now and see us like
this . . . Grenfeld in my arms . . . What a dreadful scandal! . . . And would
they believe my explanation: our explanation? Oh, in God's name!
. . .
Grenfeld was seeking comfort with me.
I accepted it. It did not surprise me. My mind was *quick quick* . . . oh,
a squirrel's movements are like that! Quick. But *jerky.*
. . .
Nothing surprises me.
A memory swam out. It did not surprise me. . . . A memory: London.
I was walking down a street. A mother was scolding a child: the child, on

the verge of tears, peering about — trapped, trapped . . . Where to run, where to seek protection? Then, suddenly, with a small cry, he opened his arms and threw them about his mother's knees and buried his face in his mother's skirt . . . well, seeking protection from her *with* her . . . !

. . .

And so with Grenfeld. Nothing surprises me.

. . .

Grenfeld was crying.

His back is quite strong. Muscular. No longer an adolescent's back, really; and most certainly his body is not that of a child. (If he had chosen to attack me, it would have been an uneven match: I do not excel at hand-to-hand combat.)

We stood there. I held him. He was sobbing . . . like a child?

Grenfeld: a man in despair? A man newly come into recognition that adulthood . . . that coming into manhood . . . is altogether different from the way it should be, from the way one imagines it will be? . . . He'd always seemed somehow older than his age. Obsessed? Well, a man tall and somber in self-knowledge! Now he did not want to leave his childhood — he did not! In childhood, it seems *right* that things should be resolved. Grenfeld: a man suddenly possessed of the knowledge of all the things that *cannot* be resolved.

. . .

Yes, yes, there *is* "right" and "wrong" in the world.

Nim, is there? Is there? There must be. There must. Well, it is human to want it to be so. But . . . but . . .

You Little Bastard Grenfeld:
    Hatreds. Well, there are hatreds in the world. . . . One hates those who . . . do evil. Of course. But . . .

We stood, in understanding. After a while, I loosened my grip. But he burrowed deeper, yearning for more comfort, choking me. (His hair tickled my nose. His hair is very dark; rather coarse. It smelled of . . . Brylcreem? No, not Brylcreem; but a similar concoction.)

Then at last he took a half-step back. Would not look at me, in his dreadful shame.

I handed him my handkerchief. Good Irish linen: new just before Dunkirk. (My mother had sent me half a dozen good Irish linen handkerchiefs just before Dunkirk.) He stared at it as if he'd never seen a handkerchief before.

"Blow your nose," I said. He blew his nose. "Harder," I said. "Again . . ." Then I did not say anything.

But he would not look at me, in his shame.

I had a headache. The Benzedrine — or simply exhaustion? (or the

emotions of the moment? Oh, you miserable pompous ass, Luthie) —
the Benzedrine was making my heart labor.

At last I said, "You may leave whenever you wish."

And Grenfeld left.

Well, God Christ! He turned back — well, half-turned — just before
he reached the door. *Mumble mumble . . .*

· · ·

Shall I say, "You need not say anything"?

(It still is within my power to destroy Grenfeld.)

· · ·

Mumble mumble. "Sir . . . it's not true" — *mumble mumble mumble* —
"about . . . everybody hating you. It's not true, sir."

· · ·

Shall I say, "I'll *try* to forget it"?

· · ·

I did not say anything. I tried to nod. I said: "Sergeant, you may
leave." (*Sergeant. . . .* Well, was I once again but his flight commander;
he one of the pilots under my command?) I said, "Sergeant, please close
the collar of your shirt and your tunic."

· · ·

Grenfeld: "Sir, it is not true . . . about everybody hating you."

Dare I believe him?

I knew peace.

And so Grenfeld left. (He did not look handsome; and he was not *ugly*.
He was . . . ordinary. A man who'd been bawling.)

Outside: lorries rumbling, I remember.

Then: people singing.

The Water Is Wide, I Cannot Cross Over.

· · ·

Peace. Quiet.

· · ·

But then, of course, Hanmer's shark's teeth appeared in the door and
he informed me that Grenfeld had — borrowed? Ashley's motorcycle
and had left, driven by his . . . demons. (No business of mine to enumer-
ate them all. No business of mine even to try to guess at all of them.)

· · ·

Is hatred of me still one of those demons? Well, if it had not been for
me — for my role, rather by default, in today's . . . proceedings —
Grenfeld would not have been dragged into adulthood today. . . . Or
would he?

(Not humble of me to think such thoughts, is it? . . . Well, all's well
that ends well.)

•

But through that whole *vigil* of mine — through all my fears for Grenfeld's safety and all my terror of his demons (what might they do to
him?) — through that whole long night, I felt . . . well, God in
heaven! . . . smug. (Not humble of me, is it?)

But I'd acquitted myself creditably. No blame attaches to me. Right?
Right. Well done, Luthie. Well done. (All's well that ends well.)

"Hanmer . . . You bastard, not *you* again! . . . Yes. Yes, I'm coming. . . .
Hanmer, I'm not drunk. Hanmer, *you* are drunk. Don't breathe on me,
damn you!"

(Well, Hanmer had gone to get drunk because London is burning.)

"*I am coming.* . . . I'm coming down from On High. It's the miserable
Benzedrine. . . .I am not *giggling*. Acklington, you're drunk.

"I did not telephone Nim tonight. Will she be worried, do you
think? . . . Quite. Quite. I'll shut up. . . . A good night's sleep . . . Oh,
only half past four, isn't it? Well, I needn't haul myself out of bed till ten
tomorrow. Half *past* ten. Six hours: that's a good night's sleep. Oh, absolutely! *I am coming.* . . . I *am* getting into bed. . . . Acklington . . . God
damn! You need not unlace my shoes for me. Do you want me to unlace
your shoes for you?

"Hanmer . . . good night. You're drunk."
. . .

May Hanmer and his Belgian woman marry and be fruitful and
multiply!
. . .

We slept.

XVII

(Written the next day):

Well, life goes on.

There is a new section officer in Parachutes: a pert brunette creature.
Grenfeld: so very good-looking.

This afternoon (we were returning our brollies after a day's hard
work of Repelling The Enemy), the pert brunette creature said to me —
me! (Grenfeld was gone by then): "Who is that gorgeous child? Two
years from now, when he's a bit older, write me a letter, tell me where
he is."

"I'll write you a letter, tell you where *I* am." And my very best
Luthie . . . leer.

She made a face! Actually made a face, the creature! Then she recovered. Rapped my knuckles with her fingers, lightly. A small white hand:
should have held a folded fan, by God! "Oh, go on with you," she *sim-
pered*. No need to add "sir": she is an officer, too. The creature!
. . .

Well, Nim likes me.

Grenfeld.

I watched him all day today.

All the Wonders were quiet today. *They* watched Grenfeld.

Grenfeld — ah, business as usual!: took all his naps in the cockpit of his kite between sorties. *Obsessed:* it makes for a quicker getaway if there is no need to run for one's kite when the order comes to scramble.

When not sleeping, he looked . . . sullen? *Not* somber. *Do not let eyes stray in Luthie's direction.* Of course they kept straying in my direction.

The Wonders: *mutter mutter mutter.* And they, too, tried not to look at me. But they kept looking at me.

What do they know about me? What do I know about them? . . . What do I want for them?

What do they think of me?

Waiting. I am waiting.

A summons from Hurry-up. He'll get wind of *l'affaire Grenfeld* sooner or later, no doubt. . . . Or will he?

I cannot prevent the Wonders from talking.

Now, about my mother.

No, some other time. (I'll go telephone Nim now. Life goes on.)

PART THREE

49

They closed ranks.

"And the Old Man flattened him proper."

"Squish, Squash. . . . Gentlemen, he was nothing. Zero. Nil. Nought. A pancake." (Grenfeld had become nothing / zero / nil / nought / a pancake.)

(Ashley could not remember anybody *ever* calling Luthie the *Old Man* before.)

. . .

Ah, to see somebody — anybody — pounded into a fine white powder! (A Fritz, or Grenfeld: did it matter? Some things never changed.) But it was a joy — *oh, absolutely!* — the very *core* of their life, these days! — so Ashley thought as he watched: *bad things are happening to him* — to Grenfeld, in this case — *nothing bad is happening to me, for the moment* (the operative words: for the moment). It was a joy.

But were they still *obsessed* with killing Germans?

(Cartwright. Stanhope. Farrell. They were laughing. Even Brown: peering about — not peering about. "You see, I am just like everybody else," he seemed to be saying, mainly to himself. "You are *permitting* me to laugh with you. That means *you* think I am just like you."

And they *permitted* him to laugh with them.)

Then they dozed for a while, sheltered from the mid-afternoon heat by the wings of their aeroplanes. (Would the hell-cursed summer never end?

So, some things did change: only yesterday, the still-summerlike sun had seemed wonderful and smashing good fun all around, really! Ashley's nose now felt positively *roasted*. Grenfeld's nose looked *roasted*.) Where was Grenfeld? (They dozed, but kept an eye on Grenfeld.) Grenfeld: having a discussion with one of the kiwis. Corporal Lansing. About the tires on Grenfeld's kite? Then Grenfeld climbed into the cockpit, ignoring everybody, and closed his eyes.

A while later, the base was bombed, and they took the kites up. And when they came back, they learned that Corporal Lansing was dead. Pilot Officer Newby was missing, and Flight Lieutenant Acklington seemed in a bit of a state about it: because Newby had been one of the last *original* members of Flight A? And so Luthie went to talk to Acklington — even put his arm around Acklington's shoulders, briefly (consoling him?).

Well, what did it matter? (They went out four times that afternoon.)

"That Fritz . . . yesterday . . . do you think McGregor looked like that?"

The day over, it was a night full of stars beyond the blackout.

"Shut up!"

"Well, you shut up!" (Things unchanged and unchanging: somebody would always say "Shut up!")

And there would always be a silence, so Ashley thought. But silences do not last forever.

"Well, the Old Man *flattened* him." Good old Grenfeld.

(And Grenfeld's pillow, on the bed next to Ashley's, was white, smooth — it looked untroubled. Grenfeld was absent, again — in body, not just in spirit, as had usually seemed the case before. Grenfeld had disappeared directly after dinner.)

"What do you think Luthie did to Matzoh last night?"

Never before had anybody called Grenfeld "Matzoh." Grenfeld — mysterious! Had things of ordinary life *ever* concerned him, really? He had always seemed so different from the others: Grenfeld somehow was — what was the word? — *diminished* thereby. And Ashley . . . well, ever since the Fritz's death, yesterday — Ashley had had a great dark empty calm inside him. But now, suddenly, the calm was gone, and he felt wistful. As if they all had lost something.

Stanhope and Peploe-Webb blurted out, in unison, "What's *matzoh?*" Peploe-Webb's mind must have been on other matters, to slip up like this: he would rather . . . oh, crash-land his kite on a beach all over again than admit to ignorance of any kind!

Cartwright cackled in triumph, but did not hurry to explain what matzoh was. (Did *he* know?)

Well, Ashley knew that matzoh was something very Jewish — yes, food of some kind; but he was not quite certain what.

"Ashley . . . Hey Ashley! He didn't prang your motorbike last night, did he? Is the bike all right?"

"Uh-huh."

"Ashley, will you let *me* borrow the bike tomorrow?"

"No," Ashley said, tight-lipped. (No lies! — no excuses — this time about the Husqvarna being out of petrol: he would not do as he had that time, long ago, in Scotland! He was a . . . different man now? Was he?)

"You're a bastard, Ashley."

"When Matzoh came back last night, did you ask him where he'd been?"

"No."

"Ashley, you're a bastard." But they left him alone.

And by and by, they began to laugh again — one of those laughters-about-nothing. But was the room both too large and too small — simply *not right* — for that kind of laughter?

They stopped. Puzzled? Taken aback?

"Where is the bastard Grenfeld now?"

There was a small silence.

"Playing the piano. Gentlemen . . . 'The Minute Waltz.'"

They cackled. (Voices grating, after the silence.)

. . .

"What do you think will happen to Grenfeld?" (A voice choked off, cautious.)

"Well, nothing's happened to the bastard yet!" (A voice loud.)

"Luthie went and reported him to Hurry-up."

(And the silence that followed was big. Huge. *Enormous.* Some silences do go on forever. So Ashley thought.)

"How do you know? You don't. You don't. . . . You bastard."

It had been Farrell who had said Luthie had reported Grenfeld to Hurry-up. But at last Farrell was forced to admit that he'd . . . *surmised,* that's all. Farrell: an observer almost as keen as Ashley — yes, Ashley was jealous of him (sometimes). Farrell: he who had tried to ingratiate himself with McGregor by being a bringer of *interesting information* about Luthie. Farrell: the first one to suggest later (yesterday? the day before? . . . well, sometime after McGregor's death, anyway: what did it matter?) that perhaps Luthie was their good luck charm of sorts, that because of Luthie the rest of them were still alive while around them people were dying. Farrell: changeable as the weather. Farrell was . . . peculiar.

Now Farrell was shamed.

They heaped abuse on him; then there was a silence.

"Luthie *will* report it to Hurry-up." Stanhope's voice? "He must. . . . The only sensible thing to do, isn't it?" Well, it was, in a way. "*I* would." Tattle on Grenfeld? Would he? "Well, he can't let him get away —"

"And they'll come and put Grenfeld in handcuffs!"

"And there'll be a court-martial, and they . . . they'll sentence him to peeling potatoes in the mess kitchen for the rest of his life!"

"He'll peel potatoes and play the piano! Gentlemen . . . 'The Minute Waltz!'" They went on laughing.

"But . . . You know . . . Well, with *that* around his neck . . . after the war is over —"

They cackled. *After the war was over!*

"Well, when he grows up . . . He'll not be able to get a proper job or go to . . . to university or anything — with that hanging on his neck, you know." Cartwright: a voice of reason?

"Oh shut up!"

"Well, you shut up! Shut up! Shut up! Shut up!"

It was time to go to sleep. Tomorrow they'd have to be on the tarmac by seven in the morning.

Ashley tried to sleep.

Where was Grenfeld?

Playing the piano. (At least he was not out on the Husqvarna! Ashley was reasonably certain of that.)

Where *had* Grenfeld been last night, after his meeting with Luthie?

Ashley roiled up the covers with his feet. Threw off the blanket: hot. He was sweating. But his *portfolio* was under the mattress: be careful about tossing and turning. New pictures. Brand-new. My God, wonderful pictures! Better than anything he had ever done before!

But, should he ask Luthie's permission before sending them to magazines (for example)? Somehow, it would be — what was the word? — *unseemly* to make these pictures compete against others in a photo contest, for example. (And it did come to him — fleeting, a back-of-the-mind-thought, to vanish quickly — there had been a time once when he scarcely cared about the *seemliness* of anything.) He'd send the pictures to magazines. Newspapers? After all, the pictures were a *record.* . . . Or should he send them anywhere? (Well, two or three of them: he really should ask Luthie's permission. But Luthie probably would not give it.)

Would Luthie be angry with Ashley for taking the pictures at all?

Ashley shut his eyes tight. But sleep would not come.

(All day today Luthie had looked as if *he* hadn't slept at all. His nobody-can-tell-what-I-am-thinking sunglasses on, his hands winding and rewinding his dandyish silk scarf about his neck . . . *The standard Luthie disguise when he was uncertain of himself.* But, *secretive* sunglasses off, he had looked — Oh my God! My God!

What had passed between Luthie and Grenfeld last night?)

Ashley tried very hard not to think about Flying Officer Luthie. He tried to sleep.

Were the others asleep? There seemed to be something in the air . . .

•

"Now Luthie would not do that, would he now — go and babble to Hurry-up, would he?" Whose voice? In the corner. Muffled. Difficult to tell.

"No, he wouldn't ruin a bloke's life just because the bloke told him he hated him, now would he?"

And . . . an explosion! . . . An outburst! They *burst* out laughing! (Ah, for the first time in his life Ashley truly understood what it meant to burst out laughing!) They *exploded*. In . . . relief? (Had the *something* in the air been anger at Cartwright for having given voice to their fear for Grenfeld and his . . . future?)

And now that somebody had made an idiotic joke, in Christ's name! That's what it had been, a joke — giving voice to their hopes: had they a reason *not* to fear for Grenfeld's future? That was what Ashley thought.

"He's *fey*. Luthie." Peploe-Webb's voice.

Trust Peploe-Webb! (Did not know what *matzoh* was; but — probably — he knew what *fey* was. Hoped that nobody else knew what *fey* was.)

Not a single one of them asked, "What's *fey?*"

There. Served Peploe-Webb right.

"It'll be his birthday soon." Luthie's.

This time, Farrell sounded very sure of himself. (Obviously, Farrell knew *some* things. . . . How had he come by the knowledge?) "*Pukka gen.* He'll be old enough to vote."

"God help England!"

They were laughing. Laughing.

Companions. Friends. Together. (But this time — my God, why? why now? Just because somebody said that Luthie probably *would not ruin a bloke's life?!* — this time the companionship seemed to include Luthie.

There was . . . well, there was — my God! — *affection* for Luthie, in the air? Oh no, not mere tolerance. Not an amused — well, bemused — acceptance.

Affection, by God!)

"He flattened him proper." (Affection for Grenfeld? . . . And they were proud of Luthie! A pride even greater than when Luthie had — probably — saved Yellowbelly Brown's life? Gratitude, by God!)

"Well, time to go to sleep now," Farrell announced at last: the leader.

But Ashley still remained sleepless, in spite of having thrown off the blanket.

The sheep: Flight B. *For a complicated problem, a simple solution.*

Ah, Luthie — yesterday: for a complicated problem, a simple solution — *yell*. (And Ashley tried to forget — he knew he'd not forget.)

Oh my God, how Luthie had yelled at Grenfeld, yesterday afternoon, over that dying Fritz's body!

Grenfeld screaming, shrieking.

Luthie screaming, shrieking. "Sergeant Grenfeld . . . You . . . will . . . go . . . and . . . do . . . as . . . you . . . are . . . told! Or you will hate yourself! . . . I . . . do not . . . care that you are a . . . Jew! I . . . do not care . . . that he is a Nazi! . . . Go! . . . That . . . is . . . an . . . order!"

And Grenfeld: white as a freshly laundered sheet . . .

Two men hysterical. *(Break Grenfeld's will. Prevail.)* Was Luthie hysterical? Well, Ashley remembered — would never forget: as Luthie's voice rose, did Luthie himself seem to become taller and taller? Well my God! My God! Well, he did not *really* become taller! But his voice got steadier and steadier; and Grenfeld became so terribly small: a stupid quivering bowl of jelly? Well, Luthie proceeded to . . . *flatten* Grenfeld. Tore a strip off him proper — and all that.

And the German had died, in the meantime — while they paid no attention to his dying: so, in the end, there was no need for Grenfeld to go anywhere. But Luthie had *flattened* Grenfeld.

And the men of Flight B liked it. Companions; friends; together.

But then Luthie had decided to leave it at that, or so it seemed: he did not punish Grenfeld any further.

And the men of Flight B liked *that*.

Luthie had at last learned to *be forceful*. (But he had also learned to play the game: a stick; then a carrot. Clever Luthie!)

Ashley tossed and turned, mindful of his photographs under the mattress.

Was everybody asleep?

Somewhere — under the window? — somebody whispered, suddenly, "That Fritz — did McGregor . . . you know . . . ?"

And somebody else . . . well, the bed springs creaked.

And in his mind's eye, Ashley once again saw the German: well, the German had had no face, had he?; and there were voices inside Ashley's head: again he heard it all — the gossip, the rumors at dinner — about the chickens pecking. . . .

And he thought about Luthie: well, the gentleness about him, at first, toward that torn, bleeding rag that had been the German. And the men of Flight B liked that, too! The *lost* sheep: *panting* for a sheepdog. *The ripe apples:* Flight B. *Easy pickings* — ready to fall; be collected by Luthie. (Hadn't Luthie's family something to do with apples?)

Ashley lay in his bed and was terribly, terribly afraid — though he wasn't quite sure what it was he was afraid of this time: it did not seem to be death or dying, this time.

Was he afraid of becoming *too* grown up one day?

•

Grenfeld came in about ten minutes later. (Was *that* to be his "punish-ment," then — to be always *absent,* always *out* somewhere? That was what Ashley thought.) After some tiptoeing about, Grenfeld slid into the bed next to Ashley's. "Good night," Ashley said, after a while.

Grenfeld said, in a . . . noncommittal voice, "Good night."

Farrell seemed to be having a bad dream. Brown, in the corner, seemed to be having a bad dream.

It was too much, thought Ashley. Too much for all of them.

The next morning at breakfast Cartwright said, "You know . . . If Old Hurry-up ever hears what Matzoh Grenfeld did and said and if he hears that Luthie didn't *kill* him for it . . . it'd be bad for Luthie, you know."

They closed ranks: against the world; around Luthie.

(Oh yes — by the way: Pilot Officer Newby was not dead, after all. He had merely been shot down. He came back.)

50

Well, let us think pleasant thoughts.

Albert is recovering satisfactorily.

My Dear People:
   Albert is recovering satisfactorily.

Have the Wonders undergone a . . . sea change of sorts, overnight? The poor sods! My Wonders.

51

I

They sat on the steps of their sleeping quarters or in the dirty grass be-low; and once the sun had set, a wind came from the river.

Nothing out of the ordinary had happened all day, but they were tired.

After a while — dark *dark* by then: no moon — Luthie came. Folded his insect-legs; sat, cross-legged.

They were tired.

"Give here," Stanhope cried out suddenly.

"Shut up," Cartwright said: the predictable "shut up." Apparently,

Cartwright had somehow managed to . . . liberate Stanhope's sack of peppermints.

"But — but — but — but — give here, you bastard!"

"He said *shut up*," said Farrell the leader. He sounded tired.

Luthie did not say anything.

Rustle rustle. They passed the sack around.

Suck suck. Crunch crunch. Comforting slurping noises.

Ashley felt tired.

II

Then the day came when Ashley and Grenfeld became . . . friends.

How it came about:

Ashley had slept all afternoon and was on his way to tea, hungry enough to eat a wolf. The sirens began to wail. The ack-ack firing. Loud-speakers blaring: *All personnel not engaged in operations take cover.*

Cover? Where?! . . . There! Thank God! . . . Slam the trap door . . .

But was somebody pulling on the door from the outside? . . . Grenfeld. He fell in a heap on top of Ashley, and they huddled together. So, that was the beginning of how they became friends.

. . .

After that air raid:

"Digby's bought it!" Digby? (One of the Hurri pilots announcing it.) Oh! Digby: the yippy-yappy dog-dog — he who had had an . . . *unpleasant experience* with Victoria the cat . . . how long ago? (Time still was passing both slowly and quickly.)

Greasy-tasting black smoke hugged the ground, after that air raid. Well, things usually were on fire after an air raid, weren't they? But, for some reason, this smoke made Ashley gag.

"It's the brolly section burning! The bastards!" Pilot Officer Newby: was he speaking to Ashley? Unusual: had he forgotten that usually — well, since the episode of the deck chairs — he was not on friendly terms with the men of Flight B?

Where are we going to get our brollies? Fly without?

And a Jerry kite — a Ju-88 — had come down not far from Dispersal. *That* was not out of the ordinary, really.

"Now there was an He-111, once . . . before your time . . ." Ah, a Hurri armorer: fairly chafing at the bit to tell his story! (Chafing and coughing his lungs out — the smoke also made one cough.) "An He-111 —" *Oh, bugger off.* Yes, Ashley had heard the story before: the Fritz had . . . beheaded a few trees, then burned.

Now, the Ju-88: a . . . scattering. The guns and airscrew blades, wing spars and pieces of the undercarriage; finally, the rest of the plane.

"They're dead, the Huns inside. Dead. Took 'em away five minutes ago."

Dead. . . . And . . . faceless?

The living quarters of the pilots of one of the Hurricane squadrons had received a direct hit — that was where Digby had been napping, but nobody else was hurt. Ah, the usual — people dragging their possessions out. Ashley and Grenfeld stood together, watched. . . . A soggy, sooty mess of shirts and underclothes in the grass; two pairs of socks, neatly rolled up. A gramophone.

The unusual: on the second storey, a bit of the floor had remained — attached to a wall which had not caved in. On the floor, a small table. On the table, a fishbowl. Somebody's pet goldfish was swimming in the bowl.

The unusual: that had been the very first air raid Ashley had had to wait out on the ground.

Afterward, Grenfeld said, "Let's go get drunk."

"All right, let's," said Ashley. They were beginning to become friends.

Later, Ashley would remember: in the shelter, during the air raid, they had huddled. An electric torch had come on, spreading twilight into the blackness. And *one — two — three* — Ashley had counted without counting — *five* civilians: yes, some of those who repaired the runways and such.

Then the earth began to shake and tremble (the explosions muffled down here; but the sounds that were not muffled: one of the civilians . . . mewling; and Grenfeld — well, he was swearing, one horrible word after another, in a . . . monotone, so that it sounded almost like a prayer).

And little clumps of dirt fell into Ashley's hair, and dirt fine as sifted flour blinded his eyes; and behind his collar it felt like . . . well, it was as if *dead people's fingernails* were tickling him . . .

My mouth is full. I am suffocating. Help me. Get me out of here.

And the earth shook. . . . Half a lifetime before the all-clear sounded! But at last they scrambled out: Grenfeld first, and he pulled Ashley up. Grenfeld was shivering as if he were cold; and Ashley felt *pale,* but he held the trap door open for the civilians.

But the civilians — they did not move. Lungs full of the dead people's fingernails: coughing coughing, two or three of them; but they did not move. "Out! Out!" Ashley shouted.

Would they simply stay there forever? My God, there were craters in the runways to be filled in, weren't there?

"Out! Out!"

Well, God damn it all! These people: nobody paid attention to them, usually. They came and went. Oh, Ashley could remember one time, after an air attack: several civilians glaring at him — at all those in uniform — with . . . hatred: *they take their kites up, leave us here. . . .* But were these people terrified now of even the *good* things, up above: of the . . . the — and Ashley desperately tried to think of something good — the . . . sun, for example; the grass; the . . . *whittling* of little farm animals? (How many times had they sat through air raids? Would he become like them, if he were in their place: would he come to prefer the dead people's fingernails? My God!)

But there were craters in the runways to be filled in. "Well, come and help us," he said; and it came out pleading and thoroughly un-grown-up.

Still they huddled — did not move; and it was their silence that frightened Ashley, above all. Because quite suddenly he felt ashamed of sounding so terribly un-grown-up, and he turned on his heel and stalked away.

Did Grenfeld follow? He did.

Then, like wildfire, the news began to spread — though neither Ashley nor Grenfeld so much as breathed a word of it to anybody.

"They what —? They're on a *bloody strike?!*" (Were *more* civilians on strike?) "They say they can't take it anymore!"

"The buggers say they won't get out of the shelters?!"

"Says who?!" (Now this was one of the Flight A people: a middling-new chap. . . . What point was there in trying to remember people's names anymore?)

"They're *afraid?* Well, four of the bastards — they broke into stores. They're under guard now. I've seen them."

Four of the civilians had broken into stores — in the middle of the air attack!

"Well, the bloody Fritzes were bloody strafing them. *Strafing* them! The bloke guarding them now told me they were strafing them. But they were too busy even to notice the Fritzes. Dragging sacks of flour — this big! Sugar. They lobbed tins of peas like hand grenades over the fence. Two of their pals were waiting there — one with a child's wagon." A child's wagon! Such as the one the children in Scotland had pulled behind them — they who had come selling the little plants? . . . "The other one had a God-damned big bloody wheelbarrow. Bullets flying all around: the bloke guarding them said so. . . . *They can't take it?!* . . . Well, the ones that can't — the ones that won't get out — let's go and *drag* them out! Put them to work. They'll bloody well work!"

· · ·

And . . . and . . . there was no *rightness* to it, that's what: throwing tins of peas over the fence while others — well, some — probably had died trying to defend the base! (Or some had huddled, cold dirt tickling them.)

It was . . . *disrespectful,* that's what!: to be sitting in the shelter now, *consumed* by fear, not helping. Disrespectful to Ashley's brother John's memory, for example . . . (Oh, in heaven's name! Ashley had not really and truly thought of his brother in . . . weeks!)

Well, and so it was disrespectful to all those who were dead . . .

And here Ashley suddenly stopped. A wistfulness came over him once again — no: a terrible, bleak, black sadness, as if *he* had lost something (and, unlike everybody's loss when the men of Flight B began to call Grenfeld Matzoh, this loss was Ashley's alone and very, very private. . . . *Was there a rightness to anything?*)

. . .

"Won't work: dragging them out," somebody was saying. (A Hurricane squadron IO: he'd come . . . waddling. Was a potbelly one of the qualifications for becoming an IO?) "Ha! I had a shovel aimed at one of the bastards' heads — his own shovel. Was about to beat his brains out with it. But he wouldn't budge!"

Was there anything left to respect?

And not anger, but a peculiar sort of grief and helplessness seemed to have settled on everybody.

"Did you hear? Manston was abandoned." People whispering. "Nothing left of the runways, practically. The whole place — they left it. Not worth repairing it anymore."

A peculiar grief and helplessness.

It was only Ashley who shook with rage and with hatred. But no matter how strictly he tried to *examine* himself, he was not sure who the rage and the hatred were against. And because he wasn't sure, he simply turned on his heel and stalked away again, his throat still tight: full of . . . dust; dirt. (Dirt: not dead people's fingernails.)

Did Grenfeld follow? Did it matter? It did.

Oh, Ashley had felt lonely so many times before! (He was accustomed to feeling lonely, by God!) But still, for the first time since his brother's death (and he was a bit ashamed of himself, now — he was thoroughly ashamed of his need), he now very badly needed a companion.

III

Lorries rumbled about, bearing gravel.

Everyone talked at half-voice.

"Manston . . . Abandoned. . . ."

Lorries: driven by . . . *not* the civilians. But no one reviled the civilians anymore.

And Luthie appeared, after a while, looking haggard. Had he been counting heads? "Thank God! Everybody here. . . . No. Where is Cartwright?"

"Went to town after lunch, sir." Stanhope said it: he'd appeared out of nowhere.

"He'll be all right, then. They didn't want the town — they wanted us."

And Brown had been injured: had a small cut over the right eye. But the medicos had slapped a plaster on it; and Brown looked . . . rakish.

Luthie looked tired.

Lorries rumbled about.

Who was organizing the work? But there it was: shovels and so on. "Shovels, gentlemen. Take a shovel." . . . "Well, give the man a shovel."

And one of the kiwis — the replacement for Corporal Lansing — he was driving one of those huge machines that flattened everything: a steamroller. Looked like King of the Mountain up there, lording it over everybody. "Make way. . . . Out of the way, everybody." Well, he had a foul mouth that respected nobody, not even officers; and everybody got out of the way.

· · ·

"Did you hear? Manston . . . doesn't exist anymore." (And so on and so on.) *Are we going to be next?*

And the sun was setting.

They did not break for dinner: dinner was brought out. Mutton: the usual, the usual. Greasy, fatty, without taste — the usual. But they took big, savage bites — what did it matter what they were eating, really: the next lorry would be here any minute — no time to taste one's food; and when the lorry did come, somebody began to sing, as they worked. Off key, of course.

Everybody was there, working — except those *engaged in operations*. Ashley didn't feel like singing: Ashley felt like laughing, because with the coming of the lorries his mood had changed — well, for no reason at all, really! He could not understand it — and he felt so good.

Flying Officer Luthie looked most terribly tired. Rubbing the small of his back. "Ah, my poor bones!" he said; and he sounded thoroughly satisfied.

Then Luthie and Ashley and Grenfeld and a couple of other people Ashley did not know were assigned to transferring what was left of the contents of the brolly section to a *new* brolly section: a Nissen hut a quarter of a mile or so away. And so they fetched and carried, fetched and carried, and stumbled over the rubble, and they cursed when they stumbled. And they both sang and laughed. And then it was dark — too dark to see — and the work was not finished, and grief set in all over again.

"Let's go get drunk," Grenfeld said to Ashley.

They went to get drunk.

•

It was . . . unusual to hear Grenfeld say ordinary words. *Let's go get drunk.* (What *had* passed between Grenfeld and Luthie? What had happened during those hours Grenfeld had spent — going where — on the Husqvarna?)

Grenfeld had a bottle of brandy. Ashley would have preferred beer, actually. But they crawled out through the hole in the fence: ah, every airbase had one . . . two . . . or three! — common knowledge, really. They settled behind a cluster of bushes, and they drank, and Grenfeld began talking.

Long ago, it had been Ashley who would confide in Grenfeld, sometimes — only inside his head, of course — when he lay wide awake in the middle of the night. *Now Grenfeld was talking to Ashley! And aloud! Really talking to him!* Why to Ashley? Was he so very desperate — and lonely? Would he talk to anybody with whom he'd spent a quarter of an hour in an air raid shelter, dirt fine as sifted flour falling upon them?

Something about a popsy! A girl! Well, my God!

"Ruth. . . . Ruthie. She's a cousin. . . . Well, not a *real* cousin. Not a first cousin or anything. My grandfather's sister married somebody and . . . let's see . . . Ruth's people — Uncle Jacob and Aunt Hannah — they are the children — well, one of them, anyway: Aunt Hannah, I think . . . yes, Aunt Hannah is the daughter of the sister's husband's brother. . . . They escaped from Poland, just before the war: Ruth and so on. You see, my great-grandfather came here from Poland, long ago. Aimée says — Aimée is my mother. She wants *me* to call her Aimée — she's *progressive.*"

Ashley took a big gulp of the brandy. *A mother who wanted to be called by her given name?*

He took another big gulp of brandy. A new world was opening to Ashley!

"Pater calls her *Amy* when he's . . . peeved."

Somebody like Grenfeld would call his father Pater!

But oh, Grenfeld was so very ordinary! He had parent trouble, just like everybody else! Just as Ashley had had, once.

(But Ashley had not really given a thought to his old life in weeks. Well, it had . . . disappeared, that life. It seemed unimportant, now; irrelevant. Had he outgrown it? Was he now truly on his own: free? Free!?

Well, God damn it all! Ashley was grateful — oh yes, grateful — to Grenfeld for his companionship!)

And Grenfeld took *three* gulps of the brandy: he must like it better than Ashley.

After a while, Grenfeld said, "Aimée makes curtains. Well, she . . . designs fabrics. Had an exhibition once. Bloomsbury. Black walls, and drapes hanging everywhere — spotlights on them — and in the background water dripping. The water was . . . *timelessness.* The drapes were *inspired* by . . . by ancient civilizations — did not say which ones. And

Aimée walked about, wrapped in one of those curtains, and she struck poses. . . . Pater is in the City. Well, he's a banker, you know.

"Uncle Jacob and Aunt Hannah are a bit disgusting, really. Cook must make special meals just for them, you know, and keep a special set of dishes, and she finds it ever so confusing; and Uncle Jacob ever *must* have his applesauce at dinner. Applesauce all over his beard. Aunt Hannah wears a wig ridiculous beyond belief. About a week after they arrived, a chap . . . Sutherland Minor . . . well, we were at school together . . . he came visiting. His idea: to flush Aunt Hannah's wig down the loo, just to see what she'd do. Would be smashing good fun, he thought. We never managed it, though.

"Aunt Hannah . . . laments. Pretends to do it in secret, but she ever arranges it so that somebody sees her. She weeps for all the other relatives in Poland. . . . Well, nothing we can do about them now, can we?"

Well my God! My God!

(And Grenfeld was *really drinking* his brandy. Grenfeld did not seem accustomed to drinking.)

"Ruthie's got the most beautiful hair you have ever seen. It's so beautiful! And so one day I said, 'I say, Ruthie, is that a wig, too?' And I was hoping that it wasn't. And she . . . well, she looked as if I'd said 'bloody' in . . . in the presence of Queen Victoria! She blushed. She *blushed,* you know. 'When I get married, then I'll wear a wig,' she said. And I said, 'That's daft.' And Pater overheard it, and he called me into his study that evening, and he tore his hair and all and said I should start learning who I was. And later that night he had a proper row with Aimée — they didn't think I could hear them. He said to her I was a little savage — he said I was a *little Nazi!* He somehow knew all about the plan about Aunt Hannah's wig . . . And he said it was all Aimée's fault because she wasn't even a Jew anymore, and it is a man's mother who determines whether the man is a Jew or not . . . And Aimée said —"

Well my God, had Grenfeld told Luthie this, during their . . . meeting . . . whenever it was: two evenings ago?

Had Grenfeld defied Luthie, that afternoon before the evening, over the dying Fritz's body: had he put on that whole performance; well, had he been *a man with a purpose* all these weeks — months! — the whole past year?! just to prove to . . . oh, not to his father! (Ashley was quite certain of that) but to somebody named Ruthie that he knew who he was?

(And the brandy bottle — when Grenfeld passed it to Ashley — felt half-empty. Well, Ashley had only taken those few gulps: he still did not like brandy very much. But Grenfeld . . . There was no stopping Grenfeld!)

"Ruthie wears frocks ugly beyond belief. Pater once offered to buy some decent clothes for her, but Aunt Hannah said No, thank you. Well, one is embarrassed, nearly, to be seen in public with her!"

Oh, Grenfeld was ordinary! My God, had he been — was he still — *obsessed* with killing Germans simply to . . . to rid himself of guilt over being embarrassed to be seen in public with the woman he loved? Rid himself of guilt over finding Aunt Hannah and Uncle Jacob — who had escaped from the Germans — *a bit disgusting, really?*

"And then . . . was it a week ago? . . . ten days or so . . . I spoke to Pater on the blower, and he said he'd arranged passage to America for Ruthie and . . . so on. 'Better for everybody,' he said. Well, Aimée ever does go on, you know, about how *they* . . . well, Ruthie and all . . . they don't *fit in*. Well, Aimée calls *all* religion *mumbo jumbo,* you know; but she does ever go on about how her people came from Spain or wherever five hundred years ago or whenever. And one of her ancestors was famous . . . terribly wise, you know. And so he was counselor to the king of Spain. But then the king threw all the Jews out. Uncle Jacob and Aunt Hannah and all . . . they speak Yiddish. And they hardly learned any English at all this whole year! Most of the time we don't understand what they are saying. Now Ruthie is learning English. Pater sent her to a decent school last year. . . . Well, I didn't want Ruth to go to America!"

Grenfeld's voice was getting louder. Louder.

"And then, the other day . . . two days ago . . . whenever . . . in the morning, before we went on ops., I telephoned home again, and everyone was in a proper state — about to get on the blower to me. Well, Ruth had been staying for a few days with some people Pater knows, in the country. *In the country. Safe as houses!* But a bloody Dornier crashed into the house the night before. Ruthie is the only one who survived. The only one! She'll be all right. But she isn't . . . feeling well . . . Well, you know how it is! She could have been killed!"

Grenfeld was drunk.

Grenfeld wasn't drunk: somewhere in between.

But oh, he was desperate to justify his . . . outburst against Luthie!

Why was he telling all this to Ashley?

Had he told Luthie? (Probably not. Well, if he had, he would not be telling Ashley now. Probably.)

Grenfeld was *so very ordinary!* And . . . *young.* (The very way he talked — his voice, his words — it all seemed younger than the Grenfeld Ashley — and the rest of Flight B — used to know!) And yet now — suddenly — Ashley liked him better.

. . .

What in the name of the world *had* happened between Grenfeld and Luthie to make it possible for Grenfeld to pour all this out to Ashley?

Ashley sat. He did not know what to say.

The night was cold. Perhaps autumn was coming, after all; and he wished he could warm himself with the brandy, but the more he drank, the less he liked the taste of it.

A confidence — a *confession* — deserved a confidence in return. But what should he say?

Oh my God, he felt jealous! Jealous of that bastard Grenfeld: well, Grenfeld had his Ruthie in *frocks ugly beyond belief;* he himself had no one. Should he . . . pretend? Should he lie to Grenfeld, tell him that Buttercup was a real person — Ashley's girl, a *live girl* — not just a voice over the R/T? (A voice of someone who in Ashley's daydreams and night dreams looked a bit like the girl he had met at Campbell's, only he no longer could remember what the girl at Campbell's had really looked like.)

He did not say anything.

Well, he had made all the proper noises: astonished noises . . . and *yes-I-am-listening* kind of noises, and noises of sympathy and understanding . . . and the most difficult of all, noises of appreciation for Grenfeld's friendship . . .

He did not *say* anything.

. . .

And after a while, Grenfeld picked himself up and they went home.

Grenfeld was drunk. But, in the moonlight — for all his feet were a bit unsteady — he walked once again like somebody . . . no, not older than his age . . . and not even *grown up* . . . well yes, he was *grown up!* And yet he wasn't. He was somehow different from ever before. And Ashley liked him better.

What *had* passed between Grenfeld and Luthie? What *had* happened during that long ride — Ashley presumed it had been a ride — on the Husqvarna? But Ashley was well aware that he would probably never know.

He very badly needed to get drunk.

And so, after he saw Grenfeld to bed — Grenfeld needed to sleep — he made his way to the sergeants' mess. Walked in . . . almost collided with Luthie.

But this wasn't Luthie's territory! (As far as Ashley could remember, Luthie had never so much as set foot here before.) Had the men of Flight B invited him: *companions; friends; together?*

Luthie was on his way out.

Inside, the air felt *breathed out,* and it was hot and blue-gray with cigarette smoke. Luthie's face was flushed: with drink?

Ashley greeted him.

Instead of returning the greeting, Luthie seemed to study him for a fraction of a moment, and then he said, "Anything the matter?"

God! Face flushed with drink, the man still had the quietest eyes Ashley had ever seen! "Anything the matter beyond the usual, of course," said Flying Officer Luthie, and he grinned. The eyes . . . worried?

Well, Ashley had had an older brother once. Would never have another. (But suddenly it struck him that he had never known John terribly well, really. . . . Or perhaps he had, but no longer remembered. . . . Well, John had been the kind of person to whom things always had to be explained three times: that was what Ashley remembered.) And suddenly, Ashley wished more than anything in the world that he had known Flying Officer Luthie before John had died. . . . Or right *after* John had died, perhaps? Would things then have turned out . . . differently?

To tell the truth, Ashley wished most of all that Luthie had remained as he was . . . well, at the beginning of it all, before Flight B had — what was the word? — *encroached* upon him. Ashley wished that he could turn the clock back so that he himself could be as he was then. Could Luthie have been an older brother? . . . friend? . . . to him then?

But now Grenfeld would have to do.

IV

And again it was evening.

"Sir . . . Sir . . ." Stanhope whining: wheedling.

(Well, some days ago — the invasion expected any minute — all officers had been issued sidearms. And now what with *things* changed between the men of Flight B and Flying Officer Luthie: "Sir . . . Sir . . . May I, sir?" "May I try it, sir?")

Peploe-Webb, ever the expert: "It doesn't balance right."

"You're right. It doesn't terribly well."

The gun was the standard issue Colt .45.

It was a quiet evening.

"Sir . . . Please . . . May we have some target practice?"

The evening was quiet and rather early-autumn crisp, and Luthie was the kind of man who liked quiet evenings. Well, Ashley knew it. Everybody knew it!

"Oh, in God's name!" Luthie said.

"Sir . . . Sir . . ." It was Farrell: wheedling?

"Sir . . ." Flight B: wheedling? Farrell: wheedling, or — what was the word — *imperious?* Not really *threatening,* well was it? It wasn't — it really wasn't!

Flight B: "Sir . . . Sir . . ."

And Luthie stood there, *not* double-jointed.

The man was as still as the air is on a . . . troubled day.

Ashley watched.

"Sir . . ."

"Oh, all right."

And so they crossed the river and nailed a target to a tree and they tore the evening to pieces with the reports of the gun.

They shrieked and screamed and shouted and quarreled and laughed. Then, when it was too dark to see, they went back, satisfied.

52

I

Well, and so I pay a price for their . . . affection.

II

But let us think pleasant thoughts.

(No time? Did I not promise myself the other day to round out that mighty-as-the-river-Nile spate of confessions with a story about my mother?)

Ah, feet up on desk . . . Crunch crunch: one of Stanhope's peppermints. . . .

Yes, peppermints! I remember: crunch crunch, the Wonders and I, the other day. Comfort fragile: a single wave of the hand, and all happiness is gone.

If a man would have a serenity of mind in the present — and for the future, by God! — he must understand his past.

Exorcise the past! *Negotiate a truce* with the past. The thoughts that hurt: let them go . . . Will it ever happen?

But no time for any of that now.

Things to Do Tomorrow: 1) —

(The peppermints leave on the tongue a taste of Christmas.)

I pay for their . . . benevolence toward me.

III

About my mother:

When the infamous Air Ministry telegram arrived — the time of Dunkirk — Mr. Parrish presented it to my father, buff envelope and all; and my father read the message aloud, calmly, and then he fainted. *I was dead* (I must be dead); and his life was over.

My mother:

I may be dead . . . but far away; her husband at her feet . . . dying?
No time for grief. She had to cope.

These *are* pleasant thoughts.

But my father did not die, of course; and in the days that followed,
my mother *attacked* the garden: pruning, weeding — destroying? . . . or
putting in order? My father went for long walks: hobbled, leaning on his
walking stick (he'd begun to use a walking stick that past winter). I
learned most of this from Mrs. Simmonds; some from Mr. Parrish; some
from my father; not much at all from my mother.

My mother: "He is only missing . . ." *Presumed to have lost his life.*

My mother: "They . . . they'll give him a . . . decent burial, the Germans, will they not?"

My father: "Yes, Roberta." Ah, he had seen *decent burials!*

My mother: "He is only missing." My mother: "I . . . I wish I could
see the body, at least . . ."

"Roberta . . . You do not want to see the body. Roberta, remember
him as he was . . ." And all those other things people say. He did not
want to shout at her in rage, I suppose.

(Actually, was there much for my mother to remember? Did she know
me at all, really?

When I began to write this . . . memoir, I think I said once there was
nothing like a good war to make a mother realize that she loved her only
son, after all. . . . The course of events changes us.)

Only Grenfeld unchanged? . . . But he and Ashley have begun to tag
along together: never before had Grenfeld tagged along with anybody!

And his walk: a *sloppy,* loping stride?! No longer the grim step of a
man of purpose? . . . But I may be mistaken.
    · · ·

Oh, I remember! I remember:

Beowulf . . . Grenfeld . . . lumbering.

Beowulf accelerating. . . . Grenfeld breaking into a run.

Beowulf . . . airborne! . . . Grenfeld, in his blue uniform, outlined
against the blue sky; Grenfeld, on heavy-booted feet; Grenfeld: graceful
as a ballet dancer! All tensions released . . .

I'll never see *that* again, probably. A pity.
    · · ·

And I am *still* waiting waiting, to be summoned by Hurry-up. Will
unpleasant things happen then to Grenfeld and me? . . . Never mind.

About my mother:

Days passed; *the Miracle of Dunkirk* was over. The tatters of the

British Expeditionary Force were gloriously back in England, and those who were not would never be back now — or not for a long time.

My mother: "He may have been captured. Well, it says: *Inquiries will be made through the Red Cross* . . ."

And my father went for another walk. (God! Most of their married life — ever since my mother's return after her five years' absence — they had lived thus: side by side . . . amicably?; not really together. . . . I've no firm knowledge of their married life, of course.)

But then one morning my mother woke up; and after breakfast she put her hat on, and she put her gloves on, and she commanded Mr. Parrish to bring the *motor* around. (She calls it a *motor;* not a *motorcar;* not a *car.*)

And she drove herself . . . not to the village: she drove all the way to town. (My mother: not a terribly good driver. Our dusty town in the Punjab: *nobody* there drove — save for Lady Chadha, who was driven. . . .

Mr. Parrish drives my mother, usually.)

She drove. Parked on High Street in front of the library. (A Victorian building: red brick. Ugly. A stone lion guards the entrance.) She walked in. "I am Roberta Luthie." *The whole world knows Roberta Luthie.* (Such is my mother.) (My father once said that when he first met her her hair . . . not an insipid blond . . . was *the hair of a woman of character.*)

"Your telephone books, please," said my mother. "I am searching for my son. There is an . . . office here — private — is there not? With a telephone, I presume. May I have the use of it? You will be reimbursed, of course, for any charges incurred. . . . I am much obliged. Thank you so very much. . . . Most kind. . . ."

Well, it was after Dunkirk. Somehow, the librarian — Mrs. Darling: I'll remember that name forever — somehow she grasped my mother's plan. She *understood:* it being after Dunkirk. And so my mother — oh, she had known all along she'd prevail! — my mother ensconced herself in the little office, a pile of telephone books in front of her; she took off her hat; peeled off her gloves; and she began to dial.

All those trunk calls! First, hospitals in the south of England. (Waiting waiting for the calls to be put through.) No success? Well, she'd move a bit farther north. And farther. Farther. *She'd cover the whole bloody country — from the tiniest nursing home in . . . Upper-Toad-upon-Water to the big places in London!*

At half past five in the afternoon, Mrs. Darling let her take the telephone books home. "I shall return them tomorrow early in the morning," my mother promised. And she drove home. She had missed lunch. Now she refused tea. Refused dinner.

"Roberta . . ." (My father sat with her.) "Would you like to change — put on your dressing gown? More comfortable, you know."

"Philip . . . Hush."

(I learned this from my father.)

One trunk call after another. "Yes, it's L-U-T-H-I-E. . . . Pilot Officer, RAF. . . . Twenty years old. . . . He may be unconscious. Those . . . those *disks* about the neck . . . is it not possible for them to be . . . misplaced? Fair hair. Light brown eyes: hazel. But he may be . . . sleeping. It may not be possible to see the color of his eyes. . . . Not very good-looking. He is my son. Tall: six feet four inches. . . . His . . . face may be . . . disfigured. One may not be able to see his face. . . . L-U-T-H-I-E."

God, these definitely are pleasant thoughts!

(Well, it's better than thinking uneasy thoughts: the eternal bombings — the whole landscape of the base: rearranged. Manston had to be abandoned, they say. . . . The bloody civilians on a looting spree, the other day . . .

And the Wonders — they do extract a price, no doubt about it, for the regard in which they now — unexpectedly? — seem to hold me.)

Pleasant thoughts:

It was after Dunkirk — my mother on the telephone: and the people at all those hospitals were most frightfully busy, no doubt. But everyone — *everyone!* (so I heard later) — they all were gentle with her. Courteous. (It was after Dunkirk.) *No. He is not here. Very sorry. . . . I wish I had better news for you.*

. . .

And Mrs. Simmonds appeared in the door, by and by. *No dinner? Well, here is a bit of cold chicken, on a tray* . . . But my mother waved her away.

My father and my mother sat together. And he did not ask himself what in the world it was she was trying to prove; and he did not tell her that no proof was needed.

It was past midnight. Two o'clock past midnight.

Three o'clock: one *discussion* with an exchange operator over, another not yet begun, the telephone rang — into that exhausted silence.

A WAAF at the Air Ministry. I was at a hospital my mother had spoken to some two hours before: *they had told her I wasn't there.*

"Well, you people cannot do anything right!" my mother shouted. "Well, I've a mind . . . And the people at the hospital . . . how — disorganized! How . . . perfectly horrid! No wonder that villain Hitler is at our door! No wonder . . ." (Sometimes it is difficult to stop my mother.)

It was my father who took the receiver away from her, finally, and mumbled apologies at the startled — an understatement! — WAAF, and managed to extract from her all the particulars of my whereabouts.

"Roberta . . ."

My mother: "Well, I'll give that dreadful woman at the hospital a piece of my mind! Was she a nurse? I'll wager she wasn't!"

"Roberta . . . Roberta . . . Put on your shoes. . . . Pack a small case. Janet will help you pack, I'm sure. We may want to spend . . . several nights. . . . Roberta, let's go and see our son."

And it was only then that my mother suddenly went quiet.

(Well God in heaven! My mother: a stillness about her? Akin to the stillness in the photograph: my mother four months pregnant in the photograph: pushing pushing her not-yet-swollen belly at the camera: *I am shameless in my pride.*

. . .

Ah, W. R. Luthie: a man of an *extravagance* of emotion! I am unaccustomed to extravagant feelings for my mother.

. . .

But it was my father who mentioned that *stillness* of hers to me when later he told — and retold — this part of the story; though of course he did not say it in so many words.)

My mother finally breathed out: "Oh my God!"

And she threw her arms about my father's neck. Stood on tiptoes to do it, I'll . . . wager. (My father: even taller than I.)

And they began to laugh. (I learned this from Janet.)

And they danced . . . they danced! about the room. (I learned this from Mrs. Simmonds, I think.)

My father, who hobbles, danced with my mother. Whirled her, twirled her about the room.

And then they threw a few pieces of clothing together; and Mr. Parrish brought the *motor* around; and it was about four in the morning. . . . How safe was it for them to be on their way at that hour: only the blackout headlamps on, and all that?

There is an evenness of feeling between my mother and myself, these days. I think.

(We do not know each other very well.)

What else shall I say about my mother?

She knitted my beautiful roll-neck for me: the black yarn wool, and the white is silk — the very same roll-neck in which I went to call on Nim, that very first time.

. . .

Oh, it would feel wonderful against a woman's skin, should she choose to rest her head on my chest! (But Nim has not done so yet. . . . Well, not against *that* roll-neck!)

. . .

My mother: a bit of a struggle for her, to knit that roll-neck. Has not knitted anything, I'm sure, since she learned how as a young girl. Not terribly *domestic,* my mother. . . . Well, she gardens.

At school, years ago, she learned to draw — bowls of fruit, that sort of thing. Bowls of fruit: lovely drawings, really. Delicate. Bloody marvelous, some of them, actually!

My mother reads books. (My mother, knitting: her reading specs on.)

She dresses elegantly. Well, she is still very, very beautiful! (Quite young, really — only forty or so.) Her hair is lighter now, I understand, than when my father first met her: out of a hairdresser's bottle, no doubt. (A Newnham girl at Cambridge told me once, quite seriously, that as a woman aged, she should dye her hair a lighter color.)

. . .

My mother: knitting.

"Wayne, stand up. Is the back long enough? . . . Well, it is cold, isn't it, so very high in those aeroplanes. The pullover should cover the kidneys. One needs warmth over the kidneys. Mrs. Simmonds said so. Is it long enough?" Difficult for her to be domestic. She is oh-so-dreadfully shy about showing her maternal feelings for me.

She knitted that roll-neck — I suspect — as a means of coming to terms with the knowledge that I'd be leaving home again soon.

(And I did leave.)

My mother: a bit of a nag. *Voluble* on the subject of disorganized hospitals and the Air Ministry — how *horridly disorganized!*

I said once (trying to sound . . . teasing): "Well, why don't you join up? Show them how to do it right."

I sensed — did not see — my father stiffen, ever so slightly. Well, God in heaven, what an idea! *Son . . . Son, not a good idea. Not at all.* (He is an old man, of course, and quite ill. . . . Has never been much of a one for adventures. He is accustomed to her constant presence. . . . There is an evenness of feeling between them; and — since that time just after Dunkirk — something has . . . shifted: a bit like sunlight in the afternoon?

Yes, the course of events changes us.)

. . .

My mother: she was toying with the thought. *Ah, to strike terror in the hearts of air marshals!*

My mother: she was toying with the thought of . . . power over my father. (There is something flawed about my mother.)

. . .

She is a woman of elegance. "Those . . . WAAFs," she said. "Must one wear those *thoroughly unattractive* shoes?" she asked.

I laughed. "Yes. Yes, I suppose so."

My mother: lost in thought. Then she looked at my father.

And he relaxed: an . . . understanding between them. And with the tentative contentment of a weary man resting before resuming his struggle, he watched us — my mother and me — being friends together.

. . .

We do not know each other well, of course, my mother and I.

(Pleasant thoughts. Serenity of spirit.
Negotiating a truce with the past.)
. . .

(Grenfeld, you little bugger, I sat there, waiting for you — you out on the miserable motorbike . . . I reached what I called my *watershed*. Thank you, Grenfeld.)

Well, to bed, to bed — I suppose. Hanmer should be here very soon. (The last train for London — his Belgian woman's train — left about half an hour ago. . . . What is her name? Hanmer must have told me; I've forgotten.)

Things to Do Tomorrow:
1) Speak to Sergeant Bennett. *Again. . . . I will not stand for shoddiness!*
. . .

Well, bugger Sergeant Bennett! (Wonders. Ever the Wonders on my mind. *Another incident involving Brown!* The first time, the hood on his kite would not slide . . .
I will not have it! . . . But what shall I do?)
I am tired.
. . .

(Serenity of spirit?)

Now . . . *Where in the name of heaven and the other place is my toothpaste?* Has Hanmer been borrowing my toothpaste?

Nim said on the telephone tonight she had a surprise for me. A birthday present? (Pleasant thoughts.)

5 5

And Cartwright was shot down — his second time; but he came back. (Ashley and Grenfeld saw him walking from the railway station, dragging his parachute. Ah, no gorgeous vicar's wife to drive him, this time!)

Well, he seemed happy to be — no, not just alive — he seemed happy to be . . . home (that was what Ashley thought).

He ran toward Ashley and Grenfeld and threw his arms about them, and so that was how they went to report to Luthie that he was back: Cartwright in the middle, and they were laughing, and yes, they had left the parachute forgotten in the dust, and Cartwright's face — well, so

Ashley noticed, after a while — Cartwright's face was pale, in the mid-afternoon sunlight, and Ashley and Grenfeld were . . . helping him walk. Well, no wonder the man was all done in. After all, this was his *second time!* But they were laughing.

Cartwright's being shot down was not the only thing, though, to happen that day. In the morning — quite early in the morning — a bad German in a Ju-87 had come and deliberately — ah, maliciously! — he had made the base car park his target.

Luthie's dogshit Austin had disappeared in that — what was the word? — conflagration.

Flight Lieutenant Acklington's MG had vanished: only twisted metal remained.

Ashley's Husqvarna was one of the few survivors: at the fateful minute, Ashley had been on his way to fuel her up. (One hundred per-cent one-hundred-octane stuff — the very same they put in his Spit. The Husqvarna loved it. Illegal, but . . .)

The squadron leader's racing-green Jag had likewise escaped destruc-tion: the squadron leader had left for home even earlier that morning, before daybreak, because . . . because his children were gone. Dead. Both of them. His wife would *probably* live. He had no home.

What a horrid, horrid, horrid day!

Misfortunes always come in threes: not a quarter of an hour after Cartwright's homecoming the base was bombed yet once again and the WAAFs' living quarters received a direct hit. Women! Nine *women* were dead! *Nine!*

That night for the first time in a very long time Ashley slept without waking once: being awake would have been too horrible.

54

I

I pulled a tiny bottle of perfume out of the rubble. Unbroken.

I felt a . . . joy: *Nim was safe! Nim was not there! Nim was not among them!*

II

Let us remember Hurry-up Hammett's children. (Hammett: his bloody *immortality* is gone! *Little . . . uh-huh . . . Gloria who played the . . . uh-huh . . . piano and could span . . . uh-huh . . . an octave between her . . . uh-huh . . . thumb and her . . . uh-huh . . . second finger . . .*)

. . .

Let us remember Hammett's children. (The little boy: summer seashore sand — an enlargement of a snapshot; a sandcastle: turrets battlements and donjons drawbridges courtyards dungeons.)
. . .

Hammett: *salivating* into his unlit pipe.

III

In Hurry-up's absence, Hanmer — the senior flight commander — is squadron leader *pro tem.*
Has appointed me to oversee the administration of both flights.
For some reason, this has made Roy Newby surly. . . . Life goes on.
. . .

(*Negotiating* with the past?
The present intruding.)
I'd very much like to think pleasant thoughts.

IV

I bought my dogshit Austin not long after my wings exam, to celebrate.
"It says: 'Meticulously Maintained,'" I'd announced to my people on the telephone. "The advertisement says 'Meticulously Maintained.' . . . The chap . . . a retired schoolmaster, do you think?"
He wasn't. He was a bookkeeper. But his hobby was reading dictionaries! . . . After a sentence or two, I instinctively brought my knees forward a bit, bent them a little, so as not to be so double-jointed.
. . .

(Grief for a motorcar: *inappropriate,* under the circumstances?
. . .

Up yours! — should you choose to judge me.)

Christ, my hands are sore! Bleeding. Bruised. Fingernails broken. The skin of my palms torn, my knuckles scratched.
My wrists hurting: well, the scars are not supposed to hurt — something about nerve endings or whatever missing there; but they do hurt. I can hardly hold this bloody pen!
. . .

(We all tore at the rubble with our bare hands like maniacs.)
Nine women dead. Nine!

About Cartwright:
Went to see him at the Med. Section, after dinner. Saw him; forthwith put in an urgent request to speak to the medical officer in charge.
The MO looked me up and down: ah, his temples graying dandyishly; he pretended (? no way of knowing for certain!) to study Cartwright's

file. Humming: a surprisingly unfrivolous-sounding tune. "Well, we'll let him sleep tonight," he said.

They are letting Cartwright out tomorrow!

(Cartwright: every sound seemed to make him jump. *Every sound.* A door being shut: shut — *not* slammed: a trolley cart trundling-squeaking down the hall; when they brought his dinner, the clinking of the silverware made him shiver. And he blinked too often: eyelids fluttering . . .

They are letting him out tomorrow!)

· · ·

"You cannot do that," I said to the MO. He looked me up and down again. "Flying Officer . . ." he said. "My good man," he said. "Ah, my dear chap . . ." he said. "Son . . ." he said.

He chuckled; then he looked *unfrivolous.*

· · ·

They are letting Cartwright out tomorrow.

Powerlessness???

V

But at dinner we laughed. Hanmer and a newish Flight A chap named Jasper and one of the Hurri pilots were telling jokes; we laughed.

(When I was sixteen, my grandfather died; and then ancient relatives descended upon us; in the evening we sat — Mr. Parrish, Mrs. Simmonds, Janet, Tom, and I — we drank cocoa, told jokes. My grandfather was dead and we were laughing!

But it was different.

Was it different? Why was it different?

· · ·

Lately I seem obsessed with changes.)

VI

Last night I had a fantasy.

(But that was *last night!:* nothing to do with today?

For the roots of last night's fantasy please see under yesterday's entry: *Things to Do Tomorrow i) Speak to Sergeant Bennett. Again.*

· · ·

I'll return to it — explain it all — in a minute.

· · ·

Of course I did not speak to Bennett today. Too many things happened.)

Today's . . . reality:

Well, now what with Hammett gone and . . . preoccupied with other matters — Christ! — will *l'affaire Grenfeld* be truly forgotten: Grenfeld safe? Am I safe: never to be examined — *cross-examined;* called upon to defend my handling of the matter Luthie-fashion?

· · ·

Up yours! (And do not declare me callous, whoever you may be: should anyone decide to sit in judgment over me.)

· · ·

Hammett: ah, such a *dominant* type when I first rejoined the squadron! . . . *Will leave a mark on my life. On everybody: on Flight B? On my life.*

But it did not happen.

And I remember: we laughed about it once, Hanmer and I — laughed at his seeming retreat from our lives and from our dying.

(I seem obsessed with laughter.)

· · ·

Obsessed with changes:

Had Hammett at some point — when? where? why: mine not to be all-knowing! — slid into *acceptance* of powerlessness?

Little . . . uh-huh . . . Gloria who played the . . . uh-huh . . . piano.

(We laughed: I remember. Mourning little fat Geoff Thomas at the time, weren't we? Hanmer and I: Hanmer's sadness manifesting itself in a frightful bad mood; but we laughed at *Gloria's . . . uh-huh . . . thumb,* and at Hammett; and in our laughter did not feel powerless — yet.)

(Let us remember Hurry-up Hammett's children.)

Cartwright: they'll let him out tomorrow!

(They laughed this afternoon — Cartwright, Ashley, Grenfeld . . . Obsessed with laughter.)

And nine women are dead.

About last night's fantasy (please refer to: *another incident involving Brown!*):

Are the bloody ground crews trying to *kill* my Wonders?

Well, it is overwork, partly — definitely; but partly it is because of just *not caring.* . . . God! Well, the ground crews: they see people come and go . . . one more, one less . . . The replacement will be here tomorrow.

But they still work like madmen for winners. In the name of everything, aren't my Wonders winners?! They are!!! Haven't they lived longer now than any other group I know? They have! . . . Haven't they? Haven't they? Shouldn't that give them a . . . sliver of fame?! (But they have not killed enough Germans, I suppose.)

· · ·

I will not stand for shoddy work!

. . .

Powerlessness?

Yesterday's fantasy *(speak to Sergeant Bennett . . . etc. etc.)* —

Sergeant Bennett: his polished shoes brighter than suns orbiting an alien planet! (Am I getting fanciful?)

Flying Officer Luthie, in yesterday's fantasy: "Sergeant . . . Something wrong with my car, I'm afraid. An odd sort of sound . . ." Ah, nothing wrong with my dogshit Austin — yesterday. And he would have known it — yesterday, I'm sure. "Sergeant, would you or one of yours take a look at it? Much obliged. There will be remuneration involved, naturally."

(Bloody hell! I am beginning to sound the way he does: like a butler in a bad detective story.)

The next evening — in yesterday's fantasy: Sergeant Bennett presenting me with a bill, like any garage man.

Flying Officer Luthie: extracting a large amount of currency from his wallet — three or four times the amount required. "Sergeant . . . Well done. My appreciation. All those involved in this enterprise . . . please have a pint or two on me." (I talk the way he talks.)

Sergeant Bennett: "Thank you very much, sir."

Flying Officer Luthie: "Thank *you,* Sergeant. The next time your good offices are required, I shall take the liberty of calling upon you again."

(I sound like a butler in a detective story.)

And we look at each other — an understanding between us: *Take good care of mine, God damn you, a bit of real attention to their kites. Is that too much to ask?! And there will be something wrong with my Austin forever — well, as long as my Austin or I shall live.*

Sergeant Bennett: "Thank you very much, sir."

Flying Officer Luthie: "Thank *you,* Sergeant."

"Thank you, sir."

"Thank *you.*". . . *Too many thanks.* (And again we exchange looks. He knows: whatever has been between us — no, not enmity; not rivalry, exactly — this peculiar tug-of-war — he's won.)

But this was yesterday's fantasy! My Austin is no more! (I was quite fond of my Austin.)

(Powerlessness?)

I must have been absolutely mad! I actually considered it, by God! — thought it a clever idea, for a minute . . . for half an hour or so, last night, when I woke up with a start as usual at the time when ghosts walk: offering to *pay* the man for their lives . . .

God in heaven, what if he had thought that along with this . . . well yes, this bribe I was offering a payment for my own life?
· · ·

(Let us think pleasant thoughts.)

VII

Ashley. Came to see me this evening: waiting by the office door when I returned from my visit to Cartwright.
· · ·

"Yes. Yes. Of course I'll see you, Sergeant. Sit down."
(Ashley: squirrel teeth. Ashley: dark circles under his eyes.)

Christ, my hands are hurting! My wrists hurting.
(I washed all the abrasions — all the little wounds — carefully; applied antiseptic liberally. It looks disgusting. It hurts.)

Ashley's eyes: calm. (And the overhead lamp in the office cast shadows.)
"Sir . . . Sorry to bother you, sir. Would you please sign these, sir?"
Photographs. *Now?!*
I felt like throwing him out, I must say. ("Sergeant . . . You see, I am busy, I'm afraid." Should I say it?)
Well, one photo; but as many copies as there are Wonders. What in the world —? It is the photograph Peterson had taken on the day we left Scotland! McGregor in it. And I am *choking* McGregor . . .
· · ·

Oh you — how can you — you little beast! Ashley. *Out! Out with you!*
· · ·

Ashley: eyes calm. (Or merely old?) Ashley: handing me the pictures with a fine adolescent unconcern (with the same unconcern . . . he'd frightened Victoria the cat . . . how long ago? by *throwing* his tea out of the cup in a fit of childish pique!). Ashley: "Sir, Flight B have asked me to ask this favor of you . . ." (And he'd done their bidding!) Ashley: eyes not old: merely . . . wise?! Well, bloody hell: eyes *accepting* of the ways of the world?
Ashley: squirrel teeth. (And his hands: self-bandaged, so it seemed; a clumsy job. Well, he too had gone tearing at the rubble of the WAAFs' quarters like a maniac.)
Ashley the Adolescent.
Why did he come now? Why just now: why not yesterday; not tomorrow?

They had begun to sign the pictures already, the Wonders.
Peploe-Webb. (Well, he isn't even in the picture! He is McGregor's replacement! by way of that miserable wretch . . . Randall.)

Arse longa, vita brevis. W. S. D. H. Peploe-Webb. (And Know All Men By These Presents That He Is *St. Lawrence College:* educated!)
. . .

Frankly, my dear, I don't give a damn. Clark 'Gable' Cartwright. . . . Cartwright?!
. . .

Ah, the things that I would like to know about them! (I *still* know so little about them! Grenfeld, for instance: for all his *loping* — relaxed? — stride, is he still running from . . . whatever it was: his demons?)
. . .

Well, next to Grenfeld's signature: a few bars of music . . .
Ashley, obliging: "Must be what he sometimes sings in the shower, sir."
The Ride of the Valkyries.
. . .

Grenfeld?!
. . .

(Ah, Colin Kenley used to sing that on his way to terrify the Fritzes! Colin has been dead . . . for how many weeks now?)
(Grenfeld: his *sloppy* stride. Is he still obsessed?)

I wanted to throw our good child Ashley out.
. . .

Do not ever come back! (Or not for a long time.)
. . .

I began to sign.   W. R. Luthie   W. R. Luthie   W. R. Luthie
A big W, a slightly smaller R, and then the L in Luthie comes good and big and strong. (My hands hurting. Bugger my hands hurting! The L big and strong: I can do it!)
(And a muted sadness seems to lie on everything.)

I wanted to throw Ashley out.
But something had shifted between us. He looked as if a bit uncertain whether he liked me, but it seemed he quite desperately wanted me to like *him*. Ashley: eyes . . . trusting. . . . Well, God Christ in heaven!
He had a large brown envelope: more pictures. His pictures! "Sir . . ."
Ashley: tremendous courage.
Well, he wants to *publish them* — a bit muddled about how to go about *publishing them;* but that was why he had *really* come to see me: to get my permission to include a few of me in the selection! Tremendous courage. Oh, absolutely!
His trust rather did take my breath away. Had I passed a test of some sort by signing those innumerable copies of the wretched group photograph? . . . Yes, I pay a price for their . . . affection: I am learning the ways of *their* world. And in their world, the dead — for example — do

not matter. McGregor: erased from their minds . . . how long ago? Well, even in the picture he is now *invisible!:* replaced by Peploe-Webb. . . . Only I lag behind.

Will the faceless German be forgotten, too, soon?

All the dead become *invisible,* sooner or later.

. . .

Ashley's eyes: wise? . . . Well, the dying Fritz and I have dragged Grenfeld into adulthood, I think. . . . *Grenfeld. Yes, there is right and wrong in the world. There must be: it is human to want it to be so. But there are hatreds in the world. And one hates those who do evil, of course, but . . .* Has Ashley arrived by himself, though — alone — at an adulthood of . . . of muted sadness?

. . .

I sign the group photograph out of sheer . . . whatever it is I feel for them; and I play by the rules of their world.

About the permission: I said I'd have to think about it, let him know. "Tomorrow."

One of the pictures: I am asleep. Sprawled in a chair — a straight-backed — oh, uncomfortable! — chair; feet up on a second chair. Head thrown back — God, it looks uncomfortable! Mouth open, huge Luthie-teeth bared . . . how utterly, thoroughly unattractive! My hands folded across the abdomen, flying gloves on; I am clutching my helmet — R/T and oxygen leads dangling. I am dead to the world! Victoria the cat on my stomach, dignified in *her* sleep. The title: *Thus Sleep the Brave.* . . . Now which of us is meant to be the brave one? . . . But I vetoed the title outright.

The second picture: I must have just landed after a scrap. . . . I'd never noticed Ashley taking that picture.

. . .

God, here's a thought: I remember! I remember! Long, long ago — we were still Somewhere in Scotland — I sent my people a snapshot Hanmer had taken of me at the time of Dunkirk:

My Dear People,

Are my wrists really so very bony?

. . .

Now:

My Dear People,

I'm sure you'd never have thought it possible that my face — well, any human's face — could ever look like this.

God damn the Nosy Parker.

Ashley: what talent — oh good God, yes! The composition of his photographs: more interesting than any of my sketches; he is a better photographer than I'll ever be a writer.

. . .

Christ, I am jealous of the little bugger!

(And he does it all with that cheap little camera of his. And he is un-aware, I think, just how good he *really* is. God   God)

And so we sat together.

What shall I do?

(Well, I told him I needed some time to think about it.)

I mean: *What shall I do?*

(Cartwright: every sound made him jump. . . . They'll let him out tomorrow.

. . .

Ashley: he looked tired.

. . .

And there are eager Germans out there; and the ground crews: what do they care?)

. . .

What shall I do?

Not even my dogshit Austin exists anymore.

I did — and I do — feel jealous of Ashley. God damn him!

We sat there. "They're quite good," I said, after a while. The photo-graphs. "I am envious of you," I said, a few seconds later.

Ashley looked pleased.

. . .

We sat there, friends together.

Ashley's photographs will never be published. Not while the war is on, I mean: they are too truthful.

. . .

(My thoughts are once again *lizard-like:* darting . . .

The thought-of-the-moment: the WAAFs' quarters destroyed, this afternoon . . .

I have mourned men killed; but why is it a different grief when a woman is killed in a war?

. . .

Changes   Changes

. . .

Well, I remember, this afternoon: Roy Newby — tears running down his cheeks, this afternoon, after the bodies had been . . . removed. Uncle

Dixon and Jimmy the IO clutching at me: our arms linked; we comforted one another.)

We are *obsessed:*
  The Wonders are obsessed with killing Germans.
  Ashley: he is obsessed with making a record of . . . the truth.
  · · ·

By the way, what happened to the picture of Victoria the cat in the fog, watching our aeroplanes? Didn't it turn out well, after all? A pity.
  · · ·

  I am obsessed with being myself.
  · · ·

  Nobody can change me.
  · · ·

  I want to fly without killing people.
  · · ·

  The course of events changes us.
  (Pleasant thoughts: My mother and I — we have become friends of sorts . . .
  · · ·
  The course of events changes us.)

The old woman: the time of Dunkirk.
  The old raven-woman: her scarf had slipped . . .
  (A day will come: I must think about it. Nighttime thoughts.)
  · · ·
  Negotiating with the past.
  (The present intruding.)

Pleasant thoughts:
  Nim said she had a birthday present for me.

Let us remember Hurry-up Hammett's children . . .

Hanmer looks truly terrible tonight.
  The command of the squadron: too much responsibility of the kind he never wanted; too much Benzedrine . . .

55

Luthie was missing.
  "So, you thought you were *immune,* didn't you? You thought you'd become *famous,* didn't you?" Pilot Officer Newby . . . *grinning.* (Bastard bastard bastard spiteful bastard: so, he had *not* forgotten the episode of

the deck chairs! Well, he was like Farrell, a bit: changeable as the weather. That was what Ashley thought.) "Our world-renowned little Nine Days' Wonders with charmed lives . . ." (The bastard!)

"I'll kill him," said . . . Brown. Brown?!

"Shut up," said Farrell. "He'll hear you."

Then, for the next few hours, they went about their everyday business. Well, Luthie had disappeared on their last time-out for that day; they went about their business as usual — though nobody had gone off for the customary after-ops. nap. They planned how to kill Newby.

Torture him. Do horrible things to him.

Every fifteen minutes or so they took turns: one of them would go to ask Uncle Dixon whether there was any news.

After a while, Uncle Dixon became — what was the word? — *aggravated,* and began to shout at Stanhope. Dreadful words!!! *He did not want to be bothered anymore!*

They planned how to kill Pilot Officer Newby *and* Uncle Dixon; and it gave them a good amount of satisfaction. (It gave Ashley a good bit of satisfaction, anyway.)

. . .

Nobody said, "What will happen now?" *(They'd get another flight commander, wouldn't they?)* They went about their business as usual.

But how would it be — so Ashley wondered: did not want to wonder — how would it be once the evening closed in and the wind rose from the river?!

56

I

How one parachutes from an aeroplane:

(I'll not do it.

Did it once: the time of Dunkirk. Never again — if I can help it.)

(Well, all's well that ends well.)

How one parachutes from an aeroplane:

Slide the hood open. (And if she does not slide, that is that.)

Wrestle the crippled kite onto her back. (But if she will not do it, *that* is that.)

Fall out. (This is more difficult than it sounds: a hurricane-strength stream of air is rushing . . . no, not only past you, but at you and through you, and keeps slamming you back against the seat.)

Prevail and fall out, then. (But sometimes it happens that the configuration of man and plane is such that the kite's tail section moving past will slice the man in two — if fate so decrees.)

And after that, only the small matter of the brolly's opening remains. (Count calmly, calmly . . . Then pull on the ripcord ring. *It don't mean a thing / If you don't pull that ring* — and all that. . . . Shouldn't it have opened by now? What if it does not open? It is not opening . . . It will not open . . . And then the brolly wrenches at your shoulders with an absolutely horrifying force, makes your whole body snap . . .)

I'll not do it.

And most certainly not into that dark, *cold cold* water.

All was not well:

A cloud bank ahead of me; a cloud bank behind me; glimpses of the dark dark water below me. Where is land?

Can I trust the instruments: are they working? What if I am being led astray?

Aunt Millicent   Please   You bitch   Let's go

(And I was losing engine coolant: the temperature needle inching inching up toward red. Once it reaches red, the engine will seize up and I am finished.

. . .

My goggles were up on my forehead, and sweat of fear on my face.)

But all's well that ends well.

I was out of the cloud, suddenly, and . . . oh, God damn . . . Trees! God damn the trees! No end to them? Not soon enough? *I am finished.*

A gap in the trees? A field; meadows; pasture? . . . A barn: a shed of some sort. . . . Yes, I can do it.

And a wide, shallow, gentle, careful bank: peer down the wing . . . the world tilting: a sight so good, a feeling so familiar! *Aunt Millicent . . . you sweet wonderful girl . . . let's line you up with the gap in the trees.*

. . .

And then I saw the flames licking at the cowling.

. . .

Let's go. Let's go.

Undercarriage down . . . Is it? Is it? . . . Isn't it? . . . No warning klaxon sounding. But . . . what if the hydraulics *are* shot? . . . *Nothing I can do about it.*

Flaps down.

And I could hear myself breathing.

And the trees came rushing past, and I think I screamed but am not sure; and then poor Aunt Millicent was tearing through the earth, but somehow I managed to hold on; but then I could hold on no longer and I lost myself and found myself and lost myself again, and then the flames were high and seemed very close and I could smell petrol, and yes, the hood was miraculously open — had I opened it? I yanked at the harness release pin, and I was out and running running running.

And then I fell and wanted to lie there, face against the cool earth, forever. (All's well that ends well.)

But . . . But . . .

Running running, hadn't I glimpsed out of the corner of my eye —?

Children! And there they were: whooping, jumping up and down in excitement, because there was a plane burning behind Old Sam's — or somebody's — barn.

"Back!" I shrieked at them. "Back! She might blow!"

But they didn't seem to want to see me or hear me.

W. R. Luthie: hero. Ha!

. . .

Do not go back. I did not want to go back. Do not . . . (Self-preservation.)

. . .

Well, I learned only later that there had been five of the wretches: no time for a head count at the time. I grabbed two hands and ran ran ran ran ran, and thank God the other little beasts followed, and then the petrol tank did go — ah, spectacular!: terrible — but we were safe.

Then, out of the blue . . . homesickness. (???) . . . The utter surprise of it! (All is not well.)

Home. I wanted to go home. Home . . . to the base. (?) Be with my own. (Well, Cartwright had mumbled something about how good it was to be home, that time I visited him at the Med. Section.)

How long since I spent any length of time outside the base?

I wanted to be in splendid isolation from the . . . ordinary world!

(I had never felt like this before. Yearning: overwhelming yearning. . . . What to do now?)

Well, the barn — the shed — whatever — had caught on fire. And a village fire brigade came, by and by; but . . . hadn't they had *any* training?! Of course, they'd never had to put out a burning plane before.

My nose bleeding: I'd cracked it on the gunsights. A cut on my forehead. And sometime soon I'd begin to walk — I could feel it! — the very same way Peploe-Webb had that time he'd pancaked his kite on the beach: as if all my muscles had been pulled in all sorts of wrong ways.

But I more or less had to direct the fire brigade's efforts!

. . .

God, we'll never win this war!

. . .

Home. I do not want upon me that which should be dealt with by . . . the outside world.

(Yes, I'll do . . . my part: the . . . killing — et cetera et cetera — you do the rest.)

I've no idea what happened to the children. Some grown-up must have collected them: by the time I thought of them again, they'd disappeared.

A village bobby took charge of me after the firefighting.

"I must telephone. Now. Extremely urgent," I . . . shouted, I think.

"Easy, lad . . . Easy . . . Can't let you do anything. Must get my instructions first, you know." Or words to that effect. (Things were beginning to get a bit blurry at that point.) "No offense, lad" — or something like that — "but how do I know you are who you say you are? Might be a Jerry in disguise, now, mightn't you?" Or similar words. (*Everything* was blurry.)

And so we had an absolutely lovely row right there by the smoking remains of Old Sam's — or whoever's — barn and my poor Aunt Millicent.

Well, he . . . won: *the authority.* (If I do not *submit*, it will take longer still. And I was . . . tired.) And so we walked and walked — *slowly!* — toward the village, and my thoughts were of *Nim   My poor people   And my Wonders   My people   The Wonders   And Nim.* (If I do not get on the blower soon, a penciled line will be drawn through my name — and all sorts of events will be set in motion, culminating in the sending of the dreaded Air Ministry telegram.)

And around me and the stalwart constable: a throng. (A small throng: *mutter mutter mutter.*) Oh yes! *Reg* — the constable — *ah, he's clever as a fox, to be suspicious! . . . Reg is an idiot! . . . Can't you see the poor boy needs a cup of tea?* (I was the poor boy.) . . . And a good time was had by all. (But I never did meet Old Sam — or whatever his name — whose barn I'd burned down. At least I do not think I met him.)

I want to be with my own. (Homesickness.)
   . . .

(What I've in common with . . . Hanmer, for example; with the Wonders; with . . . Uncle Dixon or Jimmy the IO, for example: well, trivial things. Our nicotine-stained fingers, for example: they are browner than any I've seen anywhere!) (Homesickness.)

And then, at the police station, while the good Constable Reg was making certain everything would be by the book, the village doctor came to tend my . . . wounds; but by then I truly did not feel well, and so I simply put my aching head on his shoulder, to seek comfort with him.

The doctor: a man stooped with age, but accustomed mainly — well, so I surmised — to treating children's colds and old women's rheumatism.

I am young and strong; and nothing so terribly wrong with me, really: just a bumped nose. I think he found my need for comfort . . . surprising.

Well, all's well that ends well.

And so at last I was on the train for . . . home, my parachute my only luggage. I had a *surprising* checkered shirt on (not part of any uniform I know): well, my clothes had been rendered unappetizing by my nosebleed. (And it was Reg the constable had lent me the shirt, at the insistence of Mrs. Reg. She'd also done her best to clean up the rest of me; and she'd brought me . . . yes, a cup of tea, and a piece of something baked with tinned cherries on it. Delicious! . . . Let that be on record.)

The train was crowded, and I huddled in the corner of my compartment: *S R* on the little antimacassar on the seat opposite mine —

S R: Southern Railway?

S R   S R   S R . . . in time with the wheels.

Samantha Reilly . . . Who in the devil was Samantha Reilly?

Salt and Radishes . . .

S R   S R   S R . . . in time with the wheels.

When the needle reaches red, I am finished,
And my poor Aunt Millicent plowing up the earth.

. . .

And I had to put absolutely everything I had into not shivering as if I had a fever.

And there was a portly chap in my compartment . . . and also a rather determinedly *handsome* woman on the verge of middle age, in a black hat with a somewhat too-abundant veil . . . and her little daughter: ah, Harriet, of my childhood! Little-Gloria-who-played-the-piano! (Why do so many children look *stouthearted*? Did I, too, look *stouthearted* as I threaded my way through my childhood? . . . Most small girls remind me of Harriet. The little daughter had a cold: drew the snot up into her nose, now and then; kicked me in the shins as she fidgeted.) And yes, there also was a reverend with a rather giraffe-like neck . . . And one could . . . one could . . . Christ Jesus, yes! . . . one could positively drown in that river of . . . love? — adulation! — God in heaven! — that flowed from them. Toward me!

. . .

(Yes, there was a time, after Dunkirk: the RAF were . . . reviled. I remember. It was said we hadn't done our share at Dunkirk. God in heaven!

But things are different now. They are.)

. . .

The little daughter — little Gloria (and I sat there: missed Harriet; mourned Gloria; and felt homesick for my childhood) — the little daughter drew more snot up into her nose. "Where are you going?"

"Home," I said.

· · ·

Home. Home. I do not belong here. You people do not understand us.
(Things I've in common with my Wonders:
Well, yes . . . Ashley's eyes, for example: whatever it was in those eyes
when he came to see me yesterday about the photographs . . . There was
everything in those eyes he has seen and done since we left Somewhere
in Scotland!)

· · ·

"Where are *you* going?" I asked.
"To see Auntie. She had a bebby. His nabe is Beater." Beater? *Peter.*
(Her cold!) "My nabe is Susie. Beater's got hair. Mum said I hadn't got
any hair, hardly, when I was born. . . . How many *bandits* have you
killed?"

· · ·

And so our good Winnie-the-Pooh Churchill makes speeches about
us.
Can these people pay me what they owe me? Who will pay the Won-
ders? . . . Well, never mind. (I had never felt like this before.)

· · ·

The portly gent came to my rescue. "He's killed many, I'm sure."
And I gave Susie a good Luthie grin. (It made my nose hurt and almost brought tears to my eyes.) And she kicked me in the shin, as she
fidgeted.
And a river of . . . affection flowed toward me. (A much different
kind — oh, absolutely! — from the sort the Wonders exhibit toward
me!)
After a while I escaped to the Gents. But a few minutes later they apparently decided that perhaps I was not feeling well — and I wasn't —
and they sent the reverend to inquire whether I was all right. And he
dragged me back, triumphantly.
I want to go home, be with my own kind.
I want to live . . . die . . . in splendid isolation.

Bloody hell! *In some perverse fashion, I had enjoyed every minute of it, this*
afternoon! That whole afternoon: beginning with the sweat of fear on my
face . . .

I was tired. I did not want to go . . . home. I did not particularly want to
go anywhere: I wanted to remain in splendid suspension.
But in the end I did arrive.
(All's well that ends well.)

Everything is beyond my wildest expectations!!!

II

I trudged toward the base, carrying the miserable parachute. (At the gate they are accustomed to people coming back dragging their parachutes. The guardian let me through. Curiosity? He was blank of face. Compassion? He was blank of face. I walked, my *surprising* shirt on. Boots in the dust.)

A lorry rumbled past me, heading out.

Then a bright yellow MG: one of the handful of survivors of the infamous Stuka-attack inferno? A Hurri squadron pilot at the wheel, in a state of froth-at-the-mouth fury — *I will not crawl behind a lorry if it is the last thing I do!* His horn blaring. And again. Again.

A few seconds later there was another lorry, and I stepped aside to get out of the way.

I am home.

(Well, let's go to sleep. *In splendid isolation.*)

(All emotions spent — and all that.)

There, in the distance . . . in the middle distance . . . A small figure. A betrousered small figure.

Her cap on. (Too far away still for me to see the copper of her hair.)

Oh yes. I was most dreadfully tired, of course. (Emotions spent.) A . . . *mirage?* (Would there be copper hair?)

. . .

Happiness! Dance in the streets! Celebrate!

. . .

I was so tired. My heart took one wild leap into my throat and then . . . died.

N. M. Tunnard-Jones   Nim   Nim   Go back
They kill women here. Kill them. . . . Nine of them are dead.
Not your home. This is not your home.
Love   My only love   I cannot protect you.
I'll cherish you.
I cannot protect you. *Nim.*

She saw me, but she did not break into a run.

I did not break into a run. I've no idea why.

Slowly, we came together.

Go back.

Beautiful eyebrows. (In my dreams, before falling asleep every night, I see those eyebrows; in my waking hours I see those eyebrows. I've made

sketches of her face, of those eyebrows . . . And yet I've forgotten: this is how they *really* curve — I've forgotten that. I've forgotten!!!)
. . .

If I should lean closer, I'd catch a faint whiff of chamomile, wouldn't I?: her copper hair scented with chamomile. (But, standing a few steps away from her, I could not bring to my senses the scent of chamomile.)

Panic seized me. A terrible sorrow.

Nim   Please do not go.

(What if with time you would become but a voice on the telephone . . . *getting to know each other?* What if in all other respects you'd be nothing but a . . . dream: a memory? A . . . ghost? A ghost to whom I speak in my sleepless hours, in letters that are not *real letters: thoughts private and hidden.*)

Nim   Please stay.

Nim   Leave. Not your home. It is mine: a place of . . . peculiar emotions. It will make you think thoughts you have never thought before.
   Nim   Go. I want you to live.

Her face was . . . ravaged. That is the only way of putting it.

Well yes, she'd probably arrived here, only to be told that I was missing. Right? Right.
. . .

(*I want to be with my own kind.*

She is my own kind: one man — one lover: husband — dead, seven or eight months ago. . . . David. Her dead husband's name. David. Now she came here to be told I was . . . missing: *yes, she is a woman of knowledge.*)

She arrived here, and began to wait.

But I was back now.

How did *I* look? Well, for one, my nose was swollen. (The silly doctor had stuffed it full of gauze — or was it cotton wool? — but I'd pulled out the bloody wadding. Ah, bloody in more ways than one! A pun unintended!) I could breathe only through my mouth.

How did I look? Well, *the needle inching inching toward red . . . Aunt Millicent plowing up the earth . . . flames and the smell of petrol fumes:* no doubt I looked like a man who had seen all that.

I was most dreadfully tired.

Whatever possessed me?

No greeting. I did not say, "What in the world — what are you doing here? How did you get here?" Nothing like that.
. . .

(*This* was her "birthday present," then!)
. . .

I blurted out — it came rushing out of me — "Nim . . . I think I can get away from here tomorrow afternoon. For one night. One night. No more. . . . The squadron's being stood down. Must be back by two the next afternoon. One night. . . . Nim, will you come with me? Nim . . ."

There. *One night*.

Gray eyes: N. M. Tunnard-Jones.

(If she says yes, she must turn her back on the dead David forever.)

But she has barely arrived here! That can be her excuse: she cannot leave again so soon after arriving here!

Serious gray eyes.

Oh yes, she was . . . hesitating.

Time went by very slowly.

She was . . . assessing herself. And me. (Yes, that is her privilege. Oh, absolutely! *Take as much time as you need. Consider slowly. I'll wait patiently.*
. . .

I'll not wait patiently. Nim   Please   Please)

She said, "I'll see what I can do." And I knew she would: see what she could do, I mean. It was not an excuse.

N. M. Tunnard-Jones. You woman of character. (I'm most desperately in love with your eyebrows.)
. . .

Getting to know each other. . . . Celebrate!

I was tired.

But after a while I said, "Well, I'd better get rid of this brolly. Then may I see you . . . home?"

An ugly "home." Oh God, yes — a makeshift, hideous Nissen: now that the WAAFs' permanent quarters are no longer.

And she said — oh, that smile of hers: she is so absolutely lovely! "May I see *you* to the Med. Section?" she said. . . . A no-nonsense, practical woman!

Christ, I was tired! A headache. An absolutely blinding headache. (Once after Hanmer had been shot down, he'd had a headache like that; they'd kept him at the Med. Section overnight.)
. . .

I gave her the biggest — the very best — Luthie grin of my life: the Luthie grin of the century. "Right. . . . Right you are. . . . You're right."

"Oh, absolutely!" she said.

We burst out laughing. And the laughter made my nose hurt.
. . .

Getting to know each other???
We have known each other forever!

I deposited the brolly at the *new* Parachutes Section — another cramped Nissen: ah, nothing like the spacious — cavernous! — building we'd had before; then slowly we walked toward the Med. building.

My eyes on her. Hers on me.

We did not touch: people about. People. Too many people.

. . .

Go away, people.

. . .

"How . . . how did you . . . ? How did you manage to get here?" I said.

"I requested a posting. It took some doing." And she sounded smug. . . . *Nim, I love you. I love you.*

She said: "Remember . . . ? I told you once I'd gone to Edinburgh . . ."

Yes! Yes! "To see your . . . *uncle!*" Yes! (And the memory of it came: *And the uncle is bishop of Edinburgh and he will marry us. . . .* Obviously, he was not the bishop of Edinburgh.) "Nim, who are you? Who is the *uncle?* Air Marshal bloody Stuffy Dowding?"

"Hush."

. . .

Hush. (Nim and my mother: they say *hush.*)

. . .

"Well, he is a bit of an important man," she said, "and he and Daddy were at school together. And he *is* like an uncle to me. He did not want to do it at first. Said his conscience might get the better of him and he might ring Daddy up then and there and tell him what he was doing . . . putting me in harm's way and all that. But I begged and begged, and so at last he agreed to help without telling Daddy. And so my people do not know that this posting is at my own request . . ."

. . .

Ah, you woman . . . you woman of character.
(But there is nothing flawed about *her.*)

. . .

She is not beautiful. *But, Nim,* you *are so very lovely.*

We walked. We did not touch: all those people people!
(And I felt . . . well, humble before her.)

. . .

I was tired and had a blinding headache.

But life is so good!

And then again a most terrible fear took hold of me: *Nim, go back.* And I had to put absolutely everything I had into not shivering as if I had a fever.

•

"I'll be my usual bouncy self by tomorrow," I said when — at last, and yet all too soon — we reached our destination. "Right as rain! Fit as a fiddle! If they keep me here tonight for my beauty sleep, will you come to see me after dinner?"

She laughed. "You'll not believe it: I barely got here; tonight I'm working already. . . . I'll see you tomorrow," she said.

I remembered that once on the telephone I'd promised that the next time I saw her, I'd trace her eyebrows with my fingers.

And so we did touch at last. Well, I held out my hand . . . I did not trace her eyebrows with my fingers.

Her hand went out; our fingers touched, briefly.

. . .

Nim, you'll like me. You'll like me.
(I'll be a gentle lover to you.)

What had her David been like?

"I love you," I said.
And damn the people around us!
She said, "I love you."
"I'll kiss you tomorrow," I said. Suddenly, I was most painfully aware of how *unfresh* my breath was. And she smiled: that smile so *straightforward* — no female wiles and guiles! — a smile full of pleasure; and then the door of the Med. Section shut behind me.

5 7

That night Flight B celebrated: Luthie's birthday.

Well, it wasn't Luthie's birthday quite yet — but life was uncertain. (At least that was what Ashley thought.)

5 8

They did not keep me at the Med. Section overnight.

I even managed not to miss dinner (suddenly hungry in a quite unseemly fashion).

59

"Well, let's go. Let's go invite him." The news had spread quickly that the sawbones had not kept Luthie. Let the celebration begin!

"But what if he's with the popsy?" God damn the woman! Out of nowhere she had appeared, in the afternoon.

"He is not with her."

Farrell knew everything.

"They're going away together tomorrow."

Farrell knew *everything!*

"They're going to London. Acklington gave him the keys to his people's flat. Well, Acklington's people keep the flat to have a place to stay when they're in town . . . Nobody there now. At first Luthie said he didn't want to go to London. He said *London these days was like a French cemetery on All Hallows' Eve* . . ." My God, what a performance!: Farrell. Now he paused, though; did seem puzzled — *London: a French cemetery on All Hallows' Eve?* Well, Luthie would forever remain . . . fey.

But what a show! Had Farrell somebody in his *employ* to spy on Luthie?

The men of Flight B stared at Farrell in awe, and in envy: jealousy. But Ashley, this time, was not jealous — would never again be jealous? — of Farrell. Really, Ashley was a bit frightened by Farrell's terrible need to be a leader. (McGregor used to tease them with his knowledge. . . . Farrell came with naked information.)

Farrell: triumphant.

Luthie and the woman were going away together? (*With my body I thee worship* and so on and so on . . .)

Tomorrow? To London? Out of Flight B's grasp!

No lying in wait for them this time, as they had done that time in Scotland, the sun warming Stanhope's . . . Cartwright's . . . Ashley's . . . *all* their hides. No field glasses: "Give here. What are they doing *now?*"

Luthie had been theirs then — they had *owned* him — well, they'd tried to own him — in a manner that to Ashley now seemed both shameful and . . . nice.

He still was theirs, of course, but in a quite different way, because now, since the incident with Grenfeld, they also were his, body and soul. Weren't they?

God damn the woman! (If something should happen to her, it would be rather more than Ashley could bear.) Ashley was as jealous of Luthie as he was of Grenfeld, who had his Ruthie *in frocks ugly beyond belief.* (Although the girl from Campbell's had been much prettier — oh, prettier by far! — than the section officer from Signals, Ashley was a bit in love with the section officer from Signals, for Luthie's sake. God damn her!)

From now on, Luthie would never be theirs, ever again. He would be the woman's — would belong to her — for ever and ever.

Ashley watched the men of Flight B: slowly, slowly, the knowledge of it sank in.

. . .

"Well, let's go invite him. Let's go." In a . . . panic?

They woke Luthie up. Well, one of the Flight A officers went to wake him — a newish man — what was his name? It took two tries to wake him up: *grumble grumble,* the newish man grumbled, *messenger I am a bloody messenger . . . you want to do what? celebrate his BIRTHDAY?!* But at last Luthie did appear (had he taken an ice-cold shower? Well, he looked like a man who had *shocked* himself into wakefulness, and he looked like a man chilled to the bone, and his hair was wet — plastered to his forehead, but this time — for some reason — there was not the same . . . well, *aura* of cleanliness about him); and he said, "Right. A pint or two may make me feel a new man. . . . Or it may not. . . . I feel like an old man." And they went and got wonderfully drunk.

They drank and were merry because things were uncertain: they shouted and laughed; and, half-drunk, began to inspect one another's hands: the hands bruised — that was what they all shared — hands still full of little hurts from the time they'd gone tearing at the rubble that had been the WAAFs' quarters . . . ("D'you see? It's getting infected, I think. Here." Brown's voice, proud.) Well, it was a bit as if they all shared the scars that Luthie bore, wasn't it? Did it make them feel good? *The sheep,* thought Ashley, who did not like to get drunk *on command,* only when he himself wanted to.

Ashley and Luthie had many things in common, but Ashley could not remember what they were. (Yes, Ashley did feel like getting drunk, now. And so he drank and was satisfied. . . . Luthie had said that Ashley's photographs were *quite good!* Luthie had said that he was *envious* of Ashley!)

Finally, Luthie went to sleep. He was not watching over them, this time, as he had done the night after McGregor's death. He was not engineering their precise degree of drunkenness. Nothing like that! But he himself did not drink at all — my God, he must be too exhausted even to get drunk! — and then he went to sleep.

Well, here they were, celebrating his birthday, because they had wanted to do something nice for him: celebrate not only his survival this afternoon, but his very . . . existence?!

(But instead, they seemed to be . . . torturing him.)

Well, he was here because he knew that they were doing something nice for him. Ashley was sure of that.

And so the . . . the *atmosphere* — yes, that was the word! — the atmosphere was one of a quiet . . . coming together, for all the raucousness — and for all that nobody seemed to have noticed that Luthie was asleep, except Ashley — and Grenfeld? All the others were too busy celebrating. Luthie was sprawled in his chair, head thrown back, and he was snoring: he could not breathe through his nose.

Then he woke again, with a start, and stared around him; and, as their eyes met, it occurred to Ashley that what the two of them probably had in common were the kinds of dreams that woke them up at night.

And so they celebrated. Grenfeld — well, was he grown up or wasn't he? My God! — Grenfeld laughed only when Ashley laughed (imitating Ashley?); but his laughter sounded different from Ashley's. So, perhaps he was grown up after all.

They celebrated. But then at last they were homeward-bound, singing — shouting — at the top of their voices: "We wish you a merry Christmas, we wish you a merry Christmas, we wish you a merry Christmas . . . and a happy New Year!" And as they staggered toward the officers' quarters to see Luthie home, Ashley, too, felt suddenly at peace with all of them and *snugly* safe, and he was quite sure that nothing bad would ever happen to him or to anyone he liked.

Companions. Friends. Together.

Everything was all right, for the time being.

60

Sleep, Wonders. Sleep off your hangovers, silly Wonders.

Thank you for last night, silly Wonders.

(Morning. Fog. We're fogged in. Fire in the old potbellied stove: it is warm inside the Ready Room. Outside, the cold fog makes one blow on one's hands.)

Sleep, Wonders.

How I learned to fly:

No. . . . No? Yes.

It is the only momentous(!) . . . well, important . . . event of my life before the war that I have not put down on paper yet. If I do so now, will *something* have been completed *(half open a window; peer out)*?

. . .

Throw open the window! Lean out! (Make a truce etc. etc. That is why I am writing all this down, isn't it?)

I'll go to her . . . cleansed? (Luthie . . . Idiot! *Cleansed?* Things hidden; not hidden?)

I'll go cleansed and all new-day fresh and . . . hopeful?

(Today: this afternoon she is coming with me!)

(Yesterday: I suffered from a fatigue of the soul; today: let us feel hopeful.)

Dear Uncle Dixon

If one day I should find myself no longer among the living, I don't give a damn. Go ahead and read these pages to all and sundry!

I am in love with N. M. Tunnard-Jones!

Quite. (I am feeling hopeful. Thank you, Nim!!!)

How I learned to fly:

(About women:

Hanmer, this morning: "Buy her a *negligee*. . . . Hendrikje" — so, that is the Belgian woman's name! — "she's got a black lacy thing with shiny red ribbons here . . . and here . . ." Provocative! "Goes with my dressing gown, you know." The one that makes him look like a giant bat bleeding to death when he flaps about the room: black silk, lined in red-light-district scarlet.

Hanmer: "Are you taking pajamas at all?"

Where I am going, I'll not need pajamas!

She'll not need a negligee!

But I see her in cream silk. With lace like coffee with milk . . .)

. . .

Sleep, Wonders.

How I learned to fly:

I was sixteen, my grandfather dead, it was summer, my father back in India; upstairs, my grandmother lay: the tiny glass teardrops on the shade of her bedside lamp like the music of wind-bells heard from far away.

Oh, she was a beautiful old woman!

(*Robin. Robert.* She never again called me *Robert.* Her eyes on me sometimes full of reproach and sometimes baleful. Or perhaps, as the months went by, she simply conceived an unforgiving hatred of the world — of my father, again? — for *tormenting* her so by making her pretend that I was not my uncle Robert, when in fact she knew perfectly well that that was who I was.

She needed comfort; did not want it from me. I wanted comfort from . . . her? She would not give it.

We are a family blighted by war.

I was sixteen that summer and felt clumsy and so very thoroughly unaccomplished in my dealings with the world.

She died two years later.)

I am in love with N. M. Tunnard-Jones!!!

About Mr. Kennedy:
    He was manager and chief — and only — instructor of the local flying club. He was American and outrageously outspoken — rude! — to the club members, who actually rather encouraged this, I think: it proved his Americanness. (But I learned that only later. I never became a full-fledged member, really: most were young men far wealthier than I — though, with a fine adolescent unconcern, I was unaware then that we were not really truly wealthy; and they were older than I: one or two approaching thirty!)
    In the summer of my sixteenth year — my grandfather dead, my grandmother grieving, I the only male of the family in the house — I played God in the attic. (My great-aunt Maude's love letters, etc., etc.) In the summer of my sixteenth year, Mr. Kennedy the manager had somehow managed to obtain a Harvard. *The RAF use Harvards as trainers!*

About flying . . . I was sixteen:
    Beowulf lumbering down the path. Beowulf . . . accelerating. *Think thoughts of strength. Help him. Concentrate. See Beowulf defy all the laws of the universe: Beowulf airborne!!!*
    Poor Beowulf. Coming down.

(There is a small hill near our house. I first climbed it not long after I came to England. From the top: green as far as one could see.
    · · ·
    I do it still — and I am a man grown and have killed people.
    I spread my arms and launch myself down the hill   run run never stop   feel the ribbons of wind between my fingers . . . A yearning within me.
    · · ·
    I have grown into manhood and have killed people.)

When my father left for India again after my grandfather's funeral, I went to see him off. The plane: a big brute of an HP-42. *Concentrate. Think of Beowulf gathering speed. Observe the plane shuddering and shaking.* . . . And then there she was, in her element; but, unlike poor Beowulf, she continued, seemingly, to defy the laws of the universe.
    And I went with her.

Ah, W. R. Luthie, coming around Nanga Parbat!
    On his final approach into Gilgit!
    · · ·

Do I belong there?

I am not of India in the way that Ayah was, for example; not in the way that the vendor of sugared almonds was! Ali?: he who carried sun-fragrant towels? . . . Sir Prabhjot Chadha. Lady Chadha: head high higher highest.

Color . . . Squalor . . . Oh God yes! Crowds crowds crowds. All those people people: they *truly* belong there.

But I was born there: I belong there.

  . . .

When I was sixteen, my father told me the full story of Amritsar — *Amritsar whisper whisper when I was a child* . . . Thoughts of childhood suddenly then insistent upon me . . . *smoke rising: an explosion, Ayah and I running* . . .

Powerlessness.

  . . .

I am of a world which some people say should not be my home; and yet it is.

Flying transforms loneliness into solitude. (Well, that's what I thought when I was sixteen.)

Flying is teamwork, of course. (But teamwork at a . . . remove, so to speak. That is what I thought then.)

Flying transforms loneliness into solitude.

(It did then. It will do so again. It will!)

The Harvard:

I read about it in our local newspaper. Fired off a telegram to my father. (One does not telegraph lightly!) He telegraphed back: stern. "Be specific Stop Concise Stop Coherent" . . . Was I specific stop concise stop coherent in my reply?: "Modern aeroplane Stop Brakes Stop Flaps Stop Please Please"

Guilt? My father feeling guilty?

(Well, I'd gone to see him off at Croydon when he left for India again. And he did not really want to leave: he did not want to leave me.

But our eyes had met at one point: he was anxious to be gone, though he dreaded the going. . . . Christ! it must have been a hellish few weeks for him, after the funeral: I understand now — a man grown.

Having left, did he then feel guilty about having done so?)

He paid for the flying lessons. (And I gave no thought at the time to the fact that the lessons no doubt were most frightfully expensive.)

I went. Morning.

Mr. Kennedy: his Irish hair uncombed; his flying suit in need of a laundering . . . Chewing gum in his mouth!!! (All part of his . . . *act,* really: ah, the flying club asses paid him well *to be American!* When Mr. Kennedy was not *acting,* he was somebody different altogether; but I learned that only later.)

"Waddaya want, kid?"

I stood, *not* double-jointed. "I am W. R. Luthie."

Snort. He *snorted!* "The one whose daddy had me . . . investigated. Sending telegrams from *Inja* all over Creation. Checking up on my credentials." *Snort.* (That was the first I'd heard of it, of course: my father investigating him!)

. . .

Shame.

. . .

I stood, *not* double-jointed.

He glowered at me — and inwardly, I inspected myself: *unformed-looking* — knees and elbows too sharp in tweeds so decently English; my tie at half-mast (always at half-mast, in those days: *an affectation?* or *carelessness?* that was what he must be thinking — well, it was a bit of both, actually); my sinister sunglasses on, though it was quite early in the morning *(arrogance?);* leaning against the Bentley (*arrogance! definitely!* he must have decided).

(Actually, my sunglasses were hiding a terrible need not to be with people who were dying of the thirst for comfort, who did not want comfort from me.)

There, behind Mr. Kennedy on the grass, the Harvard stood, its cowling thrown open, its innards exposed.

. . .

Excitement. Uncertainty. (My sunglasses hid a yearning not to be sixteen. . . . They made me look mysterious, I hoped.)

. . .

Mr. Kennedy clearly did not like what he saw.

He had a filthy-dirty-oily rag in his filthy-dirty-oily right hand (well, *both* his hands were filthy-dirty-oily).

"Catch!" he shouted suddenly, and threw the rag at me. *This is a test.*

. . .

Nobody tests me!

. . .

(What shall I do?)

. . .

The thing coming at me: a second's decision. *Nobody tests me!*

. . .

I caught it; hugged it; held it against me *firmly,* by God! Well, it was DIRTY: an abomination. Then with one hand I pushed my sinister sunglasses up on my forehead. *Nobody tests me!*

. . .

Keep hugging the rag, Luthie.
. . .

And Mr. Kennedy stopped *being American.* Well, he still sounded like an American, of course. Blue eyes, I remember — light, as if . . . *washed clean?* Laugh lines in the corners of his eyes: crow's feet. (But later I came to know: he did not laugh often — not even when enjoying his *American act,* for example. When he did laugh, he did not squint: so much for *laugh lines.* Crows are dark creatures: *crow's feet.*) "Come on," he said. "Grab a cup of coffee. You can help me work on her." The Harvard! . . . Did I really hear him say it? *Dance in the streets!* "I'll tell you what I need, you hand me the right tool. Try not to mess up, O.K.? Then we'll see about the flying part."

He *lived* on coffee. An acquired taste — absolutely! My self-defense: half-coffee, half-cocoa — my very own invention, my own personal recipe. Three times a week the rest of that summer I drove to the airfield; a thermos flask: half-coffee, half-cocoa on the seat beside me.

Ah, W. R. Luthie, staring at the sun! (in pilots' parlance). (A very early sun: the world at peace.)

Flying is operating a machine.

The Spit: so many pounds of inanimate matter with wings.

(The Harvard was so many pounds of inanimate matter with wings.)

Not long ago, most aeroplanes were fabric-covered, not metal. (Even some of the Hurricanes at the start of the war were fabric-covered.) Delicate things. But not really fragile. Oh, tremendously sturdy, really!

Flying is operating a machine, paying attention to detail. Being precise. (Nim likes Bach. Now there's *precise* music! But I like the Romantics!)

Ah, W. R. Luthie: landing! *Coaxing* her, *gentling* her, *whispering* her over the fence.

Sheer bravado!

Through the blur-whir of the airscrew the earth coming up to meet me . . . And we touch, the earth and I; then I am off again.

Sheer exuberance!

Here I go, being *absolutely competent!*

(Well, I discovered that I was possessed of the right instincts; my reflexes are good. I pay attention.)

I first soloed before going back to school after the summer of my sixteenth year.

I received my pilot's license the following year — a Certificate of Competency, it is called. My photograph: *big* ears; two Air Ministry stamps; signature — in his own hand — by a Mr. James Bright, Deputy Minister for Civil Aviation.

•

Flying transforms loneliness into solitude.

I came to know Mr. Kennedy well, but not *very* well. For example: he had seen distinguished service in the war — the Great — now the First — War; but I learned this from . . . sources, not from him.

Snort: he always snorted when dissatisfied with my performance. A man shy in generosity: *mumble mumble;* but most certainly not niggardly in praise.

"Grab a cup of coffee, son." And we must have drunk gallons of the stuff together (later, at Cambridge, I actually came to like coffee, black as all the sins of the world); we drank out of mugs with filthy-oily-dirty smudges on the rim; but I never did learn — for example — whether he administered his *rag test* to everybody or whether it had been a whim of the moment.

I am in love with N. M. Tunnard-Jones.

A woman who studies the cello; a man who wants to fly around Nanga Parbat: how do they build a life together? . . . Never mind.

A . . . *schoolmaster?* I . . . a schoolmaster? Ha!

. . .

But a day will come: the duty of apple-growing will have been thrust upon me . . .

How do we make a life together? I've no idea.

One thing more. About women (how I came into manhood?) and flying:

I was at Cambridge for a year, before the war intervened — not a well-known college at all: for me, the best thing about being at Cambridge was the CU Air Squadron. (I've mentioned this before, haven't I?)

Women came to the airfield. Newnham women: long legs; *The Waste Land* and *The Love Song of J. Alfred Prufrock* tucked away under one arm; a tennis racquet under the other. Strawberries and bubbly in the afternoon . . . Oh, there were some Newnham women who liked pilots very much!

There was one: very large dark eyes. Serious: a bit like Nim's? Not really. *Different* from the others? (Actually, I professed to be singularly unimpressed by the Prufrock-and-tennis-racquet women. . . . Grinned at them desperately: not to let my . . . disdain show? . . . I grinned at them desperately: flattered. I am not good-looking. I was barely nineteen.)

She was . . . different. Her name was Joanna.

I no longer have the foggiest idea, really, how it came about that we found ourselves alone one day, away from the rest of the crowd.

"Catch!" I shouted, and threw a filthy-oily rag at her.

I watched her. Oh, she was magnificent! (I was nineteen.)

There she stood: *Nobody tests me! What shall I do? Nobody tests me!*
She caught the rag; hugged it.
She had a white skirt on.
I was most thoroughly ashamed of myself.
She held the thing. *Nobody tests me!* Then she dropped the rag at my feet, and walked away.
She never spoke to me again. Women are different from men.
How I grew into manhood?
(Why did I decide to tell this story just now?)
. . .

Oh, I am in love with N. M. Tunnard-Jones!

Sleep, Wonders.

Fog. We're fogged in. Nobody can find us.

You did not ask a price for your . . . benevolence toward me, last night. Thank you, Wonders.

(What if the fog is still with us at 1100, which is when we are to go off ops.? *Dance in the streets?* Well, *be cautiously optimistic,* actually.)

Now I cannot think of a single other tale about my before-the-war life — a single tale, that is, that has any bearing on all the things that happened once the war began. *Something* has been completed.

Oh — one thing more.
About Ayah: when my mother came back after her five years' absence, my father and I traveled to Lahore to meet her; returned the following day. Ayah: in the door. To welcome Memsahib my mother. Never before had I seen her with her head bowed in quite such a way; with her eyes downcast, *like this.* I was not yet seven years old then; did not think of it as *modesty* — I thought it peculiar.
Ayah: her hands clasped humbly in a . . . dignified *namaste.*
Ayah: as if barring the door against an intruder! And because there was then rather an absence of emotion in me for the lady in the bell-shaped hat, there was not yet even a confusion of feeling in me for the quiet lady who was said to be my mother: the sight of Ayah barring the door against an intruder cheered me.

Had she ever shared my father's bed? I am a man grown now. And I wonder.
She was dismissed not long after my mother's arrival.
Well, I missed her terribly, of course; and, for a while, the black nights seemed even blacker when bats were on the wing, large and

plump, and insects rubbed their legs together *Amritsar Amritsar,* and *coal's cuttles* lurked in the darkness. I missed her silver polish and . . . well, the way she hugged me: sweat and her rose perfume . . . But I was old enough by then to be sent away to Simla: a life not of freedom! Still, I had made do until then without a mother; now I must push Ayah into the back of my mind. . . . I was growing up.

Later — much later — my father told me that he had offered to find another situation for her, but she had been saving her wages and had also received a handsome settlement — that was how he put it: *a hand-some settlement* — upon her departure: a woman of a dowry, though an orphan without a family; and Mr. Rahul da Silva, the elderly half-Portuguese from Goa and carpet merchant in the bazaar — a kindly man — soon married her and kept her in honor. She was mission-educated; and though none of Mr. da Silva's associates — let alone competitors! — would ever learn this, my father said that she was shrewd in business. There were no children; and she became a barren widow of means.

We never saw each other again. But not long after the war began, I received a letter from her! In . . . English!!! — more or less.

Esteemed Sahib, the letter began. Oh, in heaven's name! A few sentences, no more: *There is news of war in your part of the world. May God protect you.*

I replied immediately: *O My Mother In All But Birth.* My letter was very very long, though I had never learned to write Hindustani well.

I haven't heard from her since.

Perhaps she cannot write Hindustani, only English?
. . .

She never could speak Punjabi well, for example.
. . .

I belong there. I was born there. I belong there.
Or does it matter, really, whether I belong anywhere?

I want to fly without killing people.

Now this is *truly, absolutely* all. My prewar life in an . . . *untidy* bundle.)

61

In near-sleep, almost-wakefulness, Ashley glanced at his watch: ten; the thought came to him again (he had been turning it over and over in his mind since yesterday): he had seen a notice — one of the Hurricane officers was selling a Hasselblad. My God! A Hasselblad! *A professional's camera!*

Then he drifted into sleep again, and dreamt . . . *not* about the girl from Campbell's, this time: God damn it all, why should he? — in his dreams the girl from Campbell's seldom looked like the real girl from Campbell's, anyway; this time, he dreamt about his brother. About the picture of his brother's last letter, actually. All as in real life: the letter on the breakfast table; Father had torn the envelope limb from limb; there was a plate with a half-chewed-up piece of toast; the napkin had marmalade stains on it. Utter . . . desolation. Well, John had disappointed *them;* and *they* had abandoned John.

And Ashley was terrified and wanted to run and *rescue* his brother.

But instead, in his dream he did as he had done that time so long ago in real life: he ran to fetch his camera and snapped the picture.

And he woke up.

At eleven they went off ops.: the fog had not lifted.

Into the fog — Luthie *bounding* away from them.

Somebody snickered. Somebody said one of those things one should not say about a man and a woman one *actually knew: knowing them* was what made it . . . not right. Yes, there was no rightness to it, that's what.

Ashley the Observer watched: were the men of Flight B staring into the fog with a sense of . . . leave-taking? Or with anger at being abandoned?

Well, the fog did begin to lift about fifteen minutes later — by noon it was the Hurricane squadrons that were in action.

62

I

This is a record of everything as it happened:

Nim looked tired.

(The railway station — early afternoon: we met. *We are Service colleagues, traveling together by chance:* the Royal Air Force are damnably — fussily! — Victorian about . . . carnal liaisons.

Do not let yourself be caught.)

. . .

She looked oh-so-miserably tired: well, she had been on duty all night — till four in the morning, to be exact, and then again from six till almost half past noon, to make it possible to come with me!

"Oh, hullo," I said.

"Good afternoon, Mr. Luthie," she said.

I grinned (restrained — grinning still made my nose hurt). I grinned: *we are sharing a secret.*

She gave me a small, very small smile: *we are sharing a secret.*

To look at her is most definitely like listening to the very last part of the last movement of the Dvořák cello concerto!

(This is a record of all that happened.)

SR   SR   SR? Ah, no *SR,* this time!
(And different people in our compartment, of course.)
. . .

Nim   Let's kiss now.
(But . . . *We must not let ourselves be caught.*)
. . .

And after a while, her eyelids drooped . . . *SR SR?* (no *SR,* of course!) and her head fell against my shoulder. Her cap askew. Thoroughly silly-looking. Definitely. What shall I do?
. . .

Tenderness.
. . .

What shall I do? Gingerly — *I do not want her to wake up* — I removed her cap. And she gave a comfortable little sigh: a woman liberated; and she snuggled up against my sleeve. A whiff of chamomile.

I sat there and felt *extravagantly* hopeful.

The night before, on our way from dinner — I could hardly put one foot in front of the other by then: the endurance of the body stretched to the limit; fatigue of the soul and all that — Hanmer had said, "No car, Luthie, remember? And you haven't got all the time in the world. How far can you get fast without a car?" And the man looked sage as an owl! "Luthie . . . Accept my kind offer," he said. "Take the flat!"

And so I did, thanking him profusely; and now I was feeling hopeful.
. . .

I do not like London. I did not want to go to London.

All my muscles sore, now, from crash-landing my poor, poor Aunt Millicent behind Sam's barn yesterday. . . . My nose hurting.

God, what a debauch last night! Those miserable wretches the Wonders. Thank you, Wonders.

Nim slept on.

We are Service colleagues. What shall I do? Slowly, very slowly, I put my arm around her, and held her . . . We belong together!

And the woolly grandmother-type in the seat opposite mine: well, she gazed into the distance — over my head? — and she seemed both happy and sad — both at once! God in heaven. Remembering her own young years?

And the tweedy gent with an umbrella next to her looked . . . scandalized: he was *so* jealous!

And a lieutenant of the artillery — about my age? or Hanmer's? — he gave me a . . . leer: no, it was a grin quite akin to my own; and silently he mouthed at me, "You lucky dog."

Chamomile.
. . .
SR   SR   SR. (It still was in my mind.) Soporific.
Nim slept.
. . .
I gave a passing thought to Hanmer . . . bloody hell! I *worried* about Hanmer.
. . .
Nim slept. And my eyes, too, closed, after a while. (I was quite giddy with hopefulness; but echoes of the day before were with me. Echoes . . . be gone!)
Where I am going I'll not need pajamas!
But I was tired. (Eyes heavy.)
And so . . . we slept together.
This was yesterday.

II

Why I was worried about Hanmer:
Noontime. Packing . . . one of those strap-over-the-shoulder canvas kit-bags: no pajamas! . . . But, other things . . . And I'll be straight-forward about it! I was prepared: *one* day we'll make a child together, Nim and I, but she may not want to do so just yet. . . . Never mind. Packing: toothbrush and toothpaste; clean socks; and I was polishing my shaving mirror . . .
Hanmer: morose.
"Acklington, what's the matter?" I said.
"Nothing." Hanmer: morose. Hanmer: "I've a . . . premonition."
Oh, in Christ's name! "What premonition? Acklington . . . No more of those thrice-cursed pills!"
"Something will happen to me today. I can feel it in my bones."
God damn him! Is he doing this on purpose? Trying — for some rea-son: whatever reason — to spoil my time with Nim?
No. No.
"Hanmer . . . Nothing will happen." For one, the whole squadron had been stood down till mid-afternoon the next day: somebody must finally have realized that we needed *some* rest! "And a new squadron leader will be here by teatime, probably, remember? In the meantime . . ."
"Well, the bloody Fritzes come and bomb us, all the time . . ."
In Christ's name!
What shall I do? "Well, *I* had a premonition, the other day. I'd over-slept, and then I was . . . well, less than polite to the waitress in the

mess . . . 'Two cups of coffee. Now. Both at once. At once! Didn't you hear?' And *then* I had a premonition, and so I made a . . . pact with God: 'God, . . . if you exist . . . God, if I live through this day I promise to apologize to the woman. God . . .' And I did live through the day, and the next morning I walked into the mess, and she . . . well, if looks could kill and all that . . . and so I did not apologize. And here I am. . . . So much for premonitions."

Hanmer: laughing. Hanmer: morose, for a moment. Hanmer: laughing. That was how I left him.

63

Afternoon:
When had an afternoon last stretched long and lazy before Ashley?

Luthie and the woman gone.
The men of Flight B scattered.
Grenfeld — obsessed?: *torturing* the piano in the sergeants' mess — the same six or seven notes over and over . . . Oh my God, how much more boring than trying to set up a picture!
It was the kind of music one got dressed up for — the kind Luthie liked — Ashley could tell that much: one of those Mozarts or Beethovens or whatnot . . . or perhaps the Sibbeh-What-Was-His-Name — *Sibelius!?*
Tedious! . . . (Well, no. Actually, Luthie's Sibelius had been like . . . like a dark river muttering angrily at night; but then it had broken through, triumphant, but without the true wildness of joy . . .)

Ashley: not the least bit lazy. Ashley: restless — decided to search out the notice about the Hasselblad again. Where had he seen it? What kind of a Hasselblad? And had a price been mentioned at all? He could not remember. It would be too much, of course. He knew it.

64

This is what happened:
We arrived: London was under air attack. Sirens and all that.
Puddles of water everywhere. ("Nim . . . Jump!" — holding out my hand.) Puddles: when had it rained last? Water: from a fire brigade's hoses?
A wall of rubble blocked the pavement. . . . Ah! And so we (and all the others picking their way around the rubble) . . . and the cars and buses and so on . . . we must compete for our . . . *Lebensraum.* (?!)
(God damn Hanmer! We should not have come here. . . . London under attack. *Grab Nim's hand and run. Hide.*

She looked . . . shocked. Well, how long has it been since she last was . . . home? She: a Londoner born and bred — she has said so. More than once, actually.)

I want to be with my own. (Echoes. Echoes of not only the previous day, but of . . . well, of all the months since the war began!)

Is she not one of us, after all? So newly arrived from Somewhere in Scotland . . . (Oh yes, she is. One lover — husband — dead not a year ago; and then yesterday she waited: I was missing . . .)

. . .

A woman suddenly so far away from me.
Her eyes were dark with grief.

French-cemetery gaudiness about London? A jauntily gay defiance of the ultimate darkness descending? Not in the daytime, by God! This defiance . . . well, it was not defiance, really:

Acceptance? *Acceptance of powerlessness?* No. . . . Endurance, I suppose. A city street in mid-afternoon: a mother with a fretting infant in a pram. . . . uniforms uniforms uniforms. . . . middle-aged men . . . women . . . children of various shapes and sizes, ages, and descriptions — not a soul looked up. Everyone stared straight ahead. Not a step quickened. No one ran to hide. . . . Avoidance? *If we pretend that there are no German bombers up in the sky, they will not be there?*

. . .

God damn the Fritzes!
(A flame of hatred. I doused it.
It sprang to life again — and frightened me.

. . .

All right. Let it burn itself out.

. . .

Uneasiness.)

The pavement resumed.

A building full of small offices of some kind appeared to have suffered chiefly smoke and water damage and broken windows, not long ago: only this morning? In front of the building, on the pavement: several typing tables; a typewriter on each — ah, here-to-stay, substantial-looking! ("Nim . . . Look . . . How much do you think one of those things weighs?") A gray-suited business type: dictating a letter to a secretary. (*"In reply to yrs. of 8th inst. —"* I intoned, trying to make Nim laugh. I tried to make us find joy in each other's presence.)

The secretary — blond hair — was a world champion of typists! *Business as usual.*

Nim did not laugh. Nor did I, of course.

. . .

And the air — vibrating; windows rattling. A passel of He-111s over-head, low in the high afternoon sky. Unopposed. God! No Spits . . . Hurricanes . . . no ack-ack harassing them! He-111s: dark   lumbering full of might   large . . . (Oh well, so many big dark cigars with wings.)

And the people in the street: *bracing themselves as if against inclement weather. Let us ignore the He-111s up in the sky.*

. . .

Suddenly — for no particular . . . no immediate . . . reason, really — I was most frightfully happy to be alive. I jumped up and waved at the German bastards. *Christ, am I glad I am not up there chasing you, you bas-tards.* "Hullo there!" I shouted.

And a stout bowler-hatted gent — graying mustache, big nose under the hat — he gave me a look: *you are a disgrace to your uniform.*

If not for Nim, I'd have given him the finger.

. . .

You people do not understand us. I want to be with my own.
(But I quite desperately wanted to be understood.

. . .

Nim and I: Do we understand each other?)

. . .

And the He-111s passed overhead — unopposed — on their way to wherever they had been told to go: to destroy. A factory? A bridge? If they can find it. . . . Well, they'll always find people.

"I'll hunt down a taxi," I said to Nim. (And oh yes, I had heard the hor-ror stories about trying to secure a taxi in London these days.)

Nim: the smallest of smiles. (Courageous.) And I remembered: our talk about London — that very, very first time in Scotland, just before I asked her to come for a walk with me. . . . Well, not a *talk:* just our thoughts like two streams flowing together, suddenly; but she had been the one then to say it aloud: "A bit like walking through a ghost story . . . London . . . these days."

Sorrow: to see the city enduring, I mean.
(But Nim   You are so very lovely.)

Have I made the least bit of difference in the events of the past few months? Well, I, too, have endured; and I have done things and things have been done to me. (I spin stories and try to find . . . not peace, but an . . . *accommodation* for myself amidst it all.)

And all those who are dead — has their dying made a difference? (Presumptuous of me, no doubt about it, to want to make a difference in the world.)

•

We walked, Nim and I.

W. R. Luthie: ready to break into a sprint at the sight of a taxi.

Down the street, on the corner, a chap in a tweed cap was hawking the afternoon *Daily Screamer* of some sort. On a large piece of paper — attached: glued?; nailed? to a wooden support — he had penciled in the headline of the day in huge letters:

TO-DAY'S SCORE

RAF 166   LUFTWAFE 42

Oh yes? And so we are a football score, are we?

. . .

You people do not understand us.
(The score: a lie, anyway. A deception — propaganda! — absolutely!!!)

. . .

LUFTWAFE — without the second *F* in the *WAFFE*.
I took my pen out of my breast pocket; wrote the second *F* in.

. . .

The bloody Luftwaffe. Give them some respect. They are not doing so very badly, are they, the bloody Luftwaffe.

. . .

And the chap pushed his frayed cap off his forehead and glared at me. For a moment. (I had spoiled his handiwork: different handwriting, blue ink instead of his sit-up-and-take-notice bright red, and the *F* was crowded in.) Then, suddenly, he chuckled. "T'anks, Guv," he said.

. . .

God, it definitely is a jauntily gay defiance of the darkness descending!

RAF 166   LUFTWAFFE 42

. . .

And I was happy to be alive.

In my pocket there was the key to Hanmer's people's flat and the directions, written out in Hanmer's self-confident hand.

. . .

Where I am going, I do not need pajamas!!!

. . .

Nim's eyes: she was not searching my face. We were very much aware, I think, of each other's fragility of feeling.

And so we looked at each other and . . . burst out laughing.

. . .

Nim   I love you.
(Echoes, go away.)

And we continued walking and my task was to be on the lookout for the taxi, but instead my eyes were on her and hers on me, and I walked straight into a pile of sandbags. A couple of urchins began to laugh at us and jeer — they fairly *hooted* with laughter! — and so we laughed again, too: trying to hold on to . . . something.

We are Service colleagues? Ha!

Happiness.

"Here . . . I'll buy some lavender," I said.

An elderly woman was sitting on a stool by a mess of concertina wire, which was there to barricade a crossing, I presume, should the need arise. Quite hoarse, the woman, from her shouting. (Or had she a very bad cold?) "Buy my lavender! Loverly lavender!"

"I'll put it on your pillow," I whispered in Nim's ear, and she . . . blushed. Her head down: in shyness.

· · ·

Yes, better than a negligee, by far.

· · ·

What did the lavender-seller look like? Well, I've no recollection, really (my eyes on Nim — and so on); I remember only the voice. But . . . *we understand each other, do we not? We are kin of sorts, are we not?:* she sitting there selling her lavender, surrounded by the rubble and grim grayness.

"Nim, I'll never manage to organize the miserable taxi," I said. "You're from here. This is your town." (I do not like London.) "Let's take the Underground. The bus. Whatever. You lead."

· · ·

(Kensington: Nim's people . . . they live in Kensington!!!

Hanmer's people's flat: in Kensington!!!

What if they are next-door neighbors? Christ!)

· · ·

Nim   You'll like me. I'll be a gentle lover to you.

· · ·

What had her David been like?

She took the lead.

Barrage balloons overhead. Well, they do not seem jaunty at all: a ponderous-looking defiance, at best.

· · ·

Life is good. (But I gave a passing thought to Hanmer: worried about Hanmer. . . . At least, I was away from the Wonders, wasn't I? Ever the Wonders on my mind. *And nothing will happen to the Wonders overnight.* May I permit myself a sigh: a man liberated? . . . But the city *is* like walking through a ghost story.)

This was yesterday.

65

Yes, the Hasselblad was much too expensive for Ashley.

66

The flat:
    The key stuck in the lock.
    (This is what happened.)
    I aimed a kick at the door — did not connect, of course: we stood, giggling laughing laughing. Quietly: into our cupped hands. (Are there neighbors: above? below? The house was tall and narrow: three floors, a flat on each.) The door looked heavy; the brass bell pull had not had a polishing since the beginning of the war, I was sure.
    "Shall I shoot out the lock?"
    · · ·

    (*Echoes.* Memories: Somewhere in Scotland. *Shall I shoot out the lock?* I had got in through the window, that time — the very first Flight B office. *Echoes, go away. . . . Echoes, stay with me.*)
    · · ·

    "No, of course I cannot shoot out the lock. Of course I haven't my trusty Colt with me. . . . If Hitler decides to invade tonight, I'll simply have to defend you and Mother England with my bare hands."
    And we giggled: laughter giggle laughter. Hysterical? Then I gave the door another tug: the key turned, the door opened.
    Shall I carry her across the threshold?
    I didn't: the flat beyond the door was small and dark and desolate.
    · · ·

    I should have brought roses, not lavender. Roses: flaming red.
    Or large yellow flowers of some kind: suns.
    · · ·

    Should I have carried her across the threshold?
    · · ·

    Her head down: in shyness.

The air inside was stale. Rooms meant to be cozy in their smallness, I suppose; our footsteps of course made them echo enormous.
    "Well, the . . . dining alcove over there," I said. (Not large enough to be a dining *room*.) "The kitchen here . . ." The bath. The . . . bedroom.
    Cobwebs. (And dust covers — old bed sheets — on the furniture: haphazard; un-neat. "Well, it bears Hanmer's stamp — oh, definitely!" I said. "He must have been the last one here."
    · · ·

Bloody hell! *Must he leave his and his . . . paramours'* — God in heaven! — *rubbish behind when he departs?* An ashtray full of cigarette stubs — how old? Some of them with ancient lipstick stains.)

I should have brought suns. (But there had been only the lavender.)
· · ·

Courageous Luthie! Now trace her eyebrows with your fingers. Kiss her.
· · ·

Getting to know each other? (What do I know about her? What does she know about me?)
Nim   Look at me.
· · ·

(I should not have listened to Hanmer. We should not have come here.)
· · ·

She said, "Well, let's make it habitable here." A no-nonsense, practical woman. And her head went up: her eyes were determined; yet she looked tired. Of course she looked tired! (I should not have brought her to London: the city braced against the darkness descending.)

"Habitable. You're right. Oh absolutely," I said, and I sounded cheery and enthusiastic. "Let's take this . . . shroud off the sofa, first." The sofa: dark leather. *Cold. Cold. . . . Our bare bodies on the cold, cold leather . . .*
· · ·

Well, we'll . . . cuddle. Shiver together. . . . Giggle giggle. "Nim, your toes are not toes — they're icicles!" *Giggle giggle.*
· · ·

Yes. Quite.
· · ·

She took off her cap, resolutely. We went to work.
(Copper hair in the late-afternoon sunlight.)
· · ·

We went to work. I tested the blackout curtains first, then the tape crisscrossing the windows. "It'll do." (If the windowpanes should go in a blast, the shattered glass would not go flying: it would simply cave in, and the shards would cascade down onto the floor.) I opened the windows: *city* air rushed in — not orchard-in-high-autumn fresh, of course; not really stale, though.

And Nim had disappeared somewhere; emerged with several dust cloths. "You dust this side of the room . . ."
Yes, ma'am.

She likes Bach: a woman of precision. I like the Romantics! I even dust in large, sweeping gestures. (But my miserable nose was hurting, and every muscle in my body felt sore. Ah, my poor *Aunt Millicent* burning behind Old Sam's barn, yesterday!)

I dust in large, sweeping gestures! (But, suddenly, I found her eyes on me: Pity? *Amusement?!* Compassion?! Bloody hell! *Aren't I doing it right?*)

Well, flying, for example, is precision; paying attention. I worked with precision.

. . .

(Memories: the convalescent place — the night of the old charwoman proud of her beautiful white false teeth which must have been brand-new . . . Boiled-beef-leaf plants: sprays and dust, spray and wipe the plants . . .)

Nim   You woman avoiding the touch of my hand.

Nim, I did not bring pajamas. Nim, I never wear pajamas, anyway. I sleep in my more-than-Oriental splendor, usually.

Nim   Why did you agree to come with me?

. . .

(Nim: small, sweet breasts underneath her crisp uniform shirt.)

. . .

I should have brought suns, to light up every room.

(Actually, the flat no longer seemed desolate. Still, it was empty, for all the rather massive furniture: I listened — no lingering . . . music of other people's happiness or cares. Good or bad, for us? *Fill it with our own happiness!(??)* Till tomorrow, as we pass through.

. . .

Yes. Quite.

. . .

And I gave a quick thought to Hanmer: could not help it. How was he getting on? I gave a quick thought to Hanmer's people, actually: well, this place . . . so temporary, really! Hardly *somebody's own* at all; but it was so very masculine, really: few traces, if any, of Hanmer's mother.

After all this time, what do I know about Hanmer?)

Getting to know each other.

I said to Nim, "I've an old gray lamb's-wool sweater at home, worn thin at the elbows. Well, one would look out of place in . . . in this chair, for example, in an old gray sweater worn at the elbows, don't you think?"

Getting to know *things* about each other. Desperately.

(But she was busy busy busy.)

. . .

What will become of me — what will become of both of us — if we pass through these rooms . . . touch . . . do not touch . . . then part again tomorrow: no lingering happiness . . . just silence?

Christ! Why did I ask her to come with me?!

Nim   Why did you come all the way from Scotland, rushing into danger, into a life uncertain: making me humble?
Nim   Nim   Tell me what you want.
. . .

Nim   Do not listen to your own . . . echoes. Send them away. . . . Keep only those that will give you pleasure.

And so, at last, the dining table . . . the this-and-that-table . . . *everything* was dusted and — good God! — the bath scrubbed (she'd said, "Well, look at it. Dreadful!"); and only the bedroom remained.
. . .

(Ah, thank you, Hanmer. God bless you, Hanmer!
Well, Hanmer had said — last night, on our way from dinner — Hanmer had said: "Luthie, accept my kind offer. Take the flat. You want to go to a hotel? Well, have you got a phoney wedding ring handy?" And the man looked *experienced* as . . . a graybeard! "Besides, hotels . . . well, they've got these damnably narrow beds," he said. "And you push them together . . . but then you go out — a spot of dinner or something — and the chambermaid will come and pull them apart."
. . .

Thank you, Hanmer!)
And so we . . . well . . . "Here's the linen cupboard," I said, bravely — *bravely*. Then I waited. . . . Pillows. Blankets. Eiderdowns. . . . I waited.
A stillness about her. *Nim   Love.*
But then, slowly slowly — arms *determined?* — she reached out and she picked up the pillows. Hugged them. Suddenly, she laid her cheek against one of those fluffy pillows: stood there . . . in comfort? *Something* in her eyes. . . . Thank you, Nim.
I brought the bed sheets, though my hands felt clumsy: starched, rustly, white sheets. And we made up the bed: she working efficiently; I felt . . . solemn.
Yes: single beds here, too. But we pushed them together. Nobody will pull them apart? Christ!
. . .

Nim   You needn't . . .
But she worked efficiently. . . . Shall I feel solemn?
The lavender. . . . Shall I put it on the pillow? I did.
Should I not have done it? No way to tell.
But I felt . . . defiant.
Nim did not blush, this time. (Serious gray eyes.)

Nim   Let's forget the world outside. Let's forget everything.
Nim   Will you like me? I am not good-looking.

•

And then I kissed her, at last. Long. Hard. Well, our very first kiss since our walk Somewhere in Scotland! . . . We went on kissing.

(Nim, I dreamt about this: small pearl buttons on a white blouse . . . But now it was a uniform shirt. . . . Never mind.

Nim   I dreamt: you were running toward me.

Give that little sigh of a woman liberated.)

I fumbled with her hair. Unpinned it — whatever. . . . Chamomile.

. . .

Buttons. Buttons, on her crisp blue shirt. But underneath the shirt, there was . . . yes, cream silk!!! . . . *Thank you, Nim!!! Ah, we have known each other for a long, long time!!!* (Somehow, she had known that that was how I saw her: creamy cream silk. Froth of lace like coffee with milk.

. . .

Thank you, love. My love. I love you. You are lovely.)

. . .

Beautiful collarbones.

Her arms had fallen by her sides. But something caught in her throat when at last I traced her eyebrows with my fingers; touched those lovely collarbones. *Ah, you woman who comes to a man in his dreams!*

(Eyes . . . trusting. Did she trust me — or did she trust herself? Did she trust whatever it was had made her draw in that tiniest of breaths and then hold it?)

Around her neck, the ugliness of the identity tags.

"Here, let's take these off," I said, and I removed them.

And she let me.

. . .

Thank you!!! *Nim   A woman far away? Not to be touched?!* Ha!

. . .

And thus, my fingers trembling with the daring of it, I . . . undressed her. The cool skin of her back; her shoulder blades: vulnerable under my hands.

Her breath: shallow. But her hands went up, and she covered herself.

Eyes . . . trusting. *Yes, you are a woman who wants to run toward me!* But her hands were shy.

"Nim . . . Here. . . . Let me look at you."

"Nim . . . You are so incredibly lovely."

And then, suddenly, her hands were on the buttons of *my* tunic: skillful hands quick, quick. Nimble, knowledgeable fingers — God in heaven! (Well, he . . . he . . . the man . . . her husband . . . he, too, had been in the RAF, well hadn't he?)

Her breath coming quickly, very quickly. Well, she wanted me. She wanted . . . a man.

. . .

She wanted *me* to lie between her legs.

. . .

And so we fell down on the bed and crushed the little bunch of lavender, and her arms were around me; and I closed my eyes against the overwhelming tide . . .

Nim   I dreamt about this. I dreamt: you were suckling our child.

One day we'll make a child together. One of each. A little son. A little daughter. It would be perfect. Then I could die.

No, then I'd want to live for ever and ever.

We belong together.

And it came tearing out of her: "David . . . Oh my God, David." A voice . . . What was in that voice?

And I wanted to stop myself, but could no longer; and so I emptied myself into her with a horrible, terrible cry of despair.

Then we lay there. I fumbled about in my clothes — in a heap on the floor — for cigarettes. Found them and lit one.

Nim: crying softly.

"I . . . apologize," I said.

She: crying softly.

After a while, I managed to say, "I'll take you to a hotel tonight. I'll take you wherever you want to go. Claridge's. The Connaught. I'll stay here. Don't worry about" — oh God Christ! — "don't worry about the . . . cost." God!

She had pulled the bed covers up to her neck; her shoulders were shaking with little sobs. "We can be friends," she said, and continued to weep: softly.

Friends!!!

And so I wanted to run. *I want to go home   Be with my own kind*

. . .

Friends. . . . Friends!!!

> Run and never stop
> Feel the ribbons of wind between my fingers
> Go down on my knees, somewhere
> Be small under the sky

. . .

> I want to be alone and lonely under the sky

But I am decently English. And so I lay there, quiet. And I rubbed my eyes with my fists — hard hard — so that my tears, when finally they came, would be those of purely bodily pain.

What happened after that, I am not quite sure.

Well, I was exhausted.

She was tired.

Well, and so we . . . slept together, I suppose.

This was yesterday.

6 7

In the middle of the night — everyone asleep: Stanhope snoring; Brown having a bad dream — Ashley reached a decision about the Hasselblad.

6 8

I

Eventually we had dinner.
(Could not part.)
Our pain bound us.
We withdrew — retreated: I wrapped myself around my pain, shielding it from her view. *N. M. Tunnard-Jones, are you doing the same?*
Yet, in a curious way, we put our pain on display for each other.
We wanted to hurt each other by not parting. (We could not part.)

Dinner: at a nondescript little restaurant.
The night before, when laying my plans, I'd had in mind a little place in Soho — North Indian, Kashmiri . . . or perhaps no dinner at all. *We'd so delight in each other's company that we'd forget dinner completely.*
Yes. Quite.

We ate. Hardly spoke. (Could not part.)
The restaurant was almost empty: only an elderly couple in the corner watched us, in a certainty (misguided!) that they were doing so in a discreet manner. *A lovers' quarrel,* they were obviously thinking.
The woman's eyes — when our gaze met — her eyes were . . . encouraging. Was she encouraging *me,* not Nim? God in heaven!
Nimuë   The downfall of Merlin the Magician
Nimuë   The downfall of all men
. . .

What a perfectly ridiculous name for parents to visit upon an unsuspecting child! What are her people like, anyway? Ridiculous.
Quite. Quite.

She could go home, of course, to spend the night.
(But I did not mention it. We could not part.)
. . .

"Would you pass the salt, please?"

"Here; let me refill your glass."

Well, we were being *friends* together! Weren't we? *Friends.* . . . Quite.

I hated her.

Dinner over. What to do now?

The streets: dark dark, as we walked back; the only lights those over the bomb-shelter entrances . . . small lights under little protective roofs . . .

. . .

London: the bomb-shelter lights like candles burning in a graveyard on All Hallows' Eve in remembrance of . . . something.

Walking through London: the excitement of fear. The pleasurable tingling feeling down one's spine — like listening to a scary story on a nasty, windy night in November; but after a while one begins to wish one had never heard the story.

It was all with me, now: our very first conversation, Somewhere in Scotland.

God damn it! *Echoes, go away.*

Or: *Echoes, stay with me?*

At last we reached the flat again. "Well, if you prefer, perhaps you should stay here," I said. "I'll go. You may be more comfortable here than at a hotel," I said. (Luthie. Idiot! More comfortable than at . . . Claridge's? The Connaught? *This* lonely place?)

"More private, I mean," I said. . . . *Lonely.* . . . "I'll go," I said.

And may you live in loneliness for the rest of your days, N. M. Tunnard-Jones!

You deserve your loneliness, N. M. Tunnard-Jones!

. . .

(But what if an air attack should come, as it had this afternoon? I'd have no away of knowing then whether she was safe!

Why should I care?

I'll go and get drunk.

I'll go with the first woman who offers herself to me.

. . .

I am not good-looking.

. . .

Bloody hell! *Women of a certain kind have offered themselves to me before!*

. . .

Where I am going, I'll not need pajamas!)

•

But in the end, we both stayed. (All emotions spent. We could not part — all emotions not spent? She looked small; confused; defiant (?!); rather desperately dignified.

Did we want to continue to hurt each other?)

I slept on the sofa. Cold cold leather . . .

. . .

We'll cuddle . . . Ha!

. . .

I had found an old dressing gown . . . of Hanmer's? of his father's? Not *flamboyant* enough for Hanmer, actually. It smelled of mothballs and of things abandoned. Nim remained in the bedroom: in a nightie of cream-colored silk? lace like coffee with milk? *I'll never know now.*

And so we stayed awake together. I presume: I know I stayed awake.

. . .

I want to be alone and lonely under the sky.

. . .

How am I going to explain all this to Hanmer? . . . Peculiar thoughts come to one.

God damn Hanmer! I'll not think about Hanmer!

. . .

I want to be small and lonely under the sky . . . Yes. Quite.

About an hour later: sirens. Well, I had known it would happen!

"Wayne . . ."

"Nim . . ."

"Wayne, I did not wake you, did I?"

Oh, in God's name! The sirens still wailing.

I laughed. We both laughed.

But: *I must cope.* I hated her. "Nim . . . Let's get dressed. Quickly. I'll take you to a shelter —"

"N-no. . . . No."

(Very well. And so we'll perish together.)

We listened; but could hear no engines — only the ack-ack: like the barking of dogs angry, but . . . helpless?

"I don't think they're coming here," I said. The Germans.

I was wrong.

. . .

Nim Let's go to the shelter. (But no doubt it was too late now.)

The whole house shaking. The earth shaking. . . . So many of them. So many. . . . At least this time somebody is going after them: the ack-ack, like dogs absolutely *furious.* "Well, they're past now," Nim said. "To the south. Southeast."

There always seems to be a straggler.

Lost in the darkness. Terrified of the darkness. Terrified of light — of the searchlights: ah, they pin one against the black sky as an insect is pinned in a collector's box!

My heart was beating for the bastard.

Nim, in a whisper: "Can you hear? His engines . . ."

Sounding sick. Deathly ill.

My heart: beating for him — though I hated him.

. . .

That is how I am.

I am myself.

. . .

God . . . if you exist . . . God   God   let him go.

Nim stood, hugging herself.

God, if you let him go, do not let him try to lighten his load here.

But he did: drop his bombs, I mean, to lighten the load.

I must cope. "Nim . . . Down!" I shouted. And we both fell down, I on top of her — shielding her with my body, though I hated her: *and so we'll perish together   I do not want to die   I do not want her to die* and then my breath was sucked out of me: a terrific concussion . . . *breathe . . . I cannot breathe . . .* and the lights went out, and the world ended.

. . .

(Nim's dressing gown: not silk; some thicker fabric: I could feel it against my cheek, after a while. That was how I knew I was alive.)

And sometime after that I said, "Well, that was not far."

We sat up, and I managed to find my cigarette lighter, and by and by I lit the huge paraffin lamp on the table by the sofa: yes, we had found the lamp during our afternoon housecleaning and I had placed it on the table for just such a possibility — W. R. Luthie: ready for anything! (and it had not even fallen off the table); and there was light.

. . .

Nim's dressing gown: yes, wool — a light wool, I think; tiny tartan checks of some sort. And she was barefoot: had lost her bedroom slippers; went searching, groping — for them; put them on; and then she stood . . . so desperately dignified!; but she was as frightened as I.

And we looked away from each other.

"Well, we'd better go and see what happened," I said. "Down the street a bit . . . on the corner, I think . . ."

And so we threw our clothes on — Nim first: "Here, you take the lamp," I said (and I felt *generous*), and then I stood there in the blackness, waiting (feeling sorry for myself: my pain had wrapped itself around me): I waited till she passed the lamp to me. And outside: shouting, and then fire engine bells . . . We went out — ran — *trying* to skirt broken glass (not being successful): several windows in the flat had given way.

(More *echoes.* . . . Oh yes!: *The WAAFs' living quarters destroyed.*

. . .

Little . . . uh-huh . . . Gloria who played the . . . uh-huh . . . piano.)

Christ, how utterly, terribly familiar! A house destroyed. (Two houses, this time.)

But in the newspapers — magazines — newsreels — when one sees, reads about it, the subject almost always is the East End, it seems: the *ordinary* — the *small* — people enduring. This was a woman of a well-bred accent. Keening. Her child was there. In the rubble. A boy? Yes, a little boy.

. . .

(Little . . . uh-huh . . . Gloria . . .)

. . .

Well, it all is very familiar.

The crowd made room for us. "Here are two more." Organized. Disciplined. The crowd, I mean. A middle-aged man: tin hat, an official-looking arm band; a somewhat younger woman in similar . . . attire: they seemed knowledgeable about these things and were directing the work.

And we worked. The child's mother keening. Then she stopped. She joined in the work, I think, but I am not sure: it was dark — not blackout-black, but no fire to light our way. The houses had not burned, only caved in; but somewhere in the distance the sky was burning — the all-clear had sounded not long before — and dust filled my lungs: brick dust — the air smelled of it. The air always smells of brick dust after an air raid, so I'd heard but had never before experienced an air attack in the city: *an innocent fighter pilot!!!* It all was so terribly familiar and yet it felt as if I were dreaming it all. And Nim was by my side.

And all the people worked almost silently: organized, disciplined. . . . All emotions spent?

We brought the child out alive. Horribly, dreadfully injured, though. But I only caught a glimpse. Perhaps the injuries merely *seemed* horrible. No, they were horrible. . . . Would he live?

An ambulance had come; now it sped away, bearing the mother away, too.

The crowd began to part: subdued; disciplined.

We walked back to the flat: Nim shivering. The night was not cool . . . but she had never ever done anything like this before! (But I had. The Wonders had. She had, too, now. So, we had even that in common, now, she and I. *Getting to know each other*. But what did it matter now?)

Once inside, I lit the lamp again. Our clothes: filthy; our hair: well, disheveled; hands full of little wounds: blood and dirt.

. . .

She is a musician. Plays the cello. She should not hurt her hands.

(Her hair falling in her forehead, full of dust.)

We laughed.

"How are we going to get home tomorrow?" I said. *Home*. To the base. Bloody hell! "On the train, looking like this . . ." (The skirt of her uniform had a tear in it.)

We laughed; then fell silent. (Our minds . . . touching. Well, all night we had taken care for our hands . . . our bodies . . . not to touch — though we *had* touched, of course, when I held her as the thrice-cursed bombs fell about us.)

She looked . . . disconsolate. Yes, that is the word: disconsolate.

. . .

Nimuë You downfall of all men.

(What a perfectly ridiculous name!)

. . .

We both mourned the child, I think. Oh, she was so absolutely drawn-into-herself quietly self-contained in her sorrow: her loveliness hurting me.

What to do now? (I pitied her. But I . . . reveled in my pain.)

What to do now?

And so I took a deep breath. . . . Shall I do it? . . . "What was he like?" *David.* (Our minds . . . touching.) "What was . . . David like?" (And I hated myself for my compassion for her. But what will become of me without her?) . . . (And what had been in her voice when that cry had come tearing out of her?)

Her head went up now: eyes full of terror, suddenly (terror?) — well, God in heaven! Or was it confusion? Shame. Shame in her face? Why?

Because she could no longer remember David? She had forgotten?!

And so I pitied David then, and I hated her:

Do not forget me, N. M. Tunnard-Jones — and all that.

Yes. Quite.

. . .

And her letter came into my mind:

Somewhere in Scotland . . . She had come running toward me on the day we left Somewhere in Scotland, the letter in her hand: in the letter she had said, among other things, *Am I capable of loving anybody?*

. . .

But I thought now, *God damn her thrice-confounded David!*

And I thought, *I should not have done this.*

. . .

She brought her hands up to her face as if to ward off a blow; but in the end she only covered her mouth. And her eyes . . . serious? ha! Her eyes so full of . . . yes, of *David* that I forced myself to lock my own eyelids shut against her remembering. And then silence stretched and stretched and stretched. *I should not have done this.* She went on remembering. "He . . . did not smoke," she finally said, slowly.

Just as slowly, I ground out the cigarette I had lit but a few seconds before. Left it smoldering . . . then it went out . . . in Hanmer's ashtray. (I'd emptied and washed the ashtray in the afternoon.)

And she truly began to laugh then. Threw her head back . . . A dreadful sort of laughter.

But then she began to talk and, for the next hour or so, there was nothing but the sound of her voice. *David David David. A universe full of David* (in fits and starts). No man should have so much knowledge inflicted upon him about his rival.

. . .

He is not a rival! He is dead!

. . .

(I myself had brought this down upon me! I had done the asking . . . because . . . because . . . Oh, bloody hell! Never mind.)

. . .

Intimate things. She talked. The most intimate things imaginable. She talked.

Tears in dirty smudges on her cheeks: she whispered through them. Laughter of remembrances — and all those other wonderful things: she talked through the laughter. And it poured and poured out of her even as this . . . this, my *memoir,* is pouring out of me. Could not be stopped.

Friends. I was a *friend. Friend.*

. . .

Would she be a *friend* to me?

(*Nim   Oh, all those letters I have written to you that are not real letters . . .*

Nim   Would you read all these pages once I've completed this record of my life?

And sadness wrapped itself around me: oh yes, quite unwittingly, she was . . . yes, *testing* me in a different and yet much the same way that . . . yes, Mr. Kennedy had tested me so deliberately how many . . . four, five years ago now? And, humbly — stupidly! — I held in my hands the hurt she had hurled at me . . .)

Friend. (And oh God, it tasted bitter! But I sat and listened, sat and listened; and, with each word, she . . . well, she drew back — she did! Farther farther she retreated into the *cave* of her mourning.)

Nim   I love you.

At last, when she was finished, it was . . . what time was it?

Time to sleep, anyway. I was exhausted past exhaustion.

"The bed is comfortable," she said. "The sofa isn't." A no-nonsense, practical woman! (Her voice still the voice of one who had been weeping.) But she is a no-nonsense, practical woman! (But then she opened her arms, suddenly, her palms outstretched: showing me her emptiness . . . helplessness; grief in her eyes . . . for me? for us? for David?

God in heaven! And she gave a *disconsolate* little shrug.) "I trust you," she said. Well, of course she *trusted* me! I was a *friend!* A . . . a *priest:* I had just heard her confession, hadn't I?

· · ·

Now, *a sword between us.*

Oh, absolutely! Definitely! No doubt about it! Yes. Quite. (And I rubbed my eyes with my fists — hard. Harder!)

You woman   What do you know about me?

But the bed *was* comfortable, and somewhere there was a faint whiff of lavender. And there was Nim's hair on the pillow next to mine: not chamomile — brick dust. (We had not even washed up — not even our faces.)

What kind of a nightie had she on?

I was past noticing. I slept.

At some point, I half woke up, and there was her head not on her own but on *my* pillow — well, nestled against my neck, as it had been earlier that day on the train; but once again she must have done it unaware: *Nim, instinct is guiding you: we belong together!* But her breath was deep; and when gently I slid my arm under and about her shoulders, she did not give a sigh of a woman liberated: she barely stirred; slept on. And I let my grief wash over me — the grief at what I had lost.

Then I, too, slept on.

II

And then it was morning — my watch said it was morning, though the blackout made it night still. I got up and got rid of the blackout, and sunlight poured in through one of the taped-up unbroken — windows; outside, sparrows quarreled.

In the bathroom, no water came out of the tap: the main must have broken last night. I stared at myself in the — cracked — mirror. I looked awful.

· · ·

I want to go home.

· · ·

Sleep-creases in her dirt-smudged face.

(Nim   I dreamt about this, in my waking hours: one day you'll wake up on my pillow. . . . I'll kiss away the sleep-creases from your face.)

· · ·

I want to go home.

· · ·

All is lost. My fault? (Should I have . . . waited?)
I have lost.
My fault? (I should not have . . . rushed.)

•

Then, for a long time, there was *nothing: nothingness: black nothing.* Stretched on the bed — carefully away from her — I lay, my mind floating . . .

That letter of hers: she had brought it on the day we left Somewhere in Scotland . . . a letter to haunt me — should I have reread it, now and again? Should I?
. . .

Ghosts were walking in the bright morning sunlight.
(I want to go home.)
. . .

(Nim   I still feel humble.)
. . .

Why, having forsaken that safe corner of Somewhere in Scotland — why had she now forsaken me? (Somewhere in Scotland: wind wind in the grass and in the heather and in people's bones: if you let it, it will sweep your soul cold and quiet).

Well, after all, we'd spoken on the telephone nearly every day since then — since that letter — Nim and I: well, almost every day since the time of her silence, when she had been trying to avoid me; and we had laughed then, happy together!
. . .

I have lost.
. . .

I seem obsessed with changes:

Well, something had . . . shifted within me since the days of Somewhere in Scotland — a shift like sunlight in the afternoon; changes fragile — a spider web in the morning: since the night I waited for Grenfeld out on the Husqvarna! And so I had assumed . . .

I should not have assumed. Well, the letter — it went something like this: "It seems unfair — to you more than to me, I suppose — that it should be a source of anguish to me that being with you made me feel just right."

(And so was it I who hurt her by not letting time take away the miserable David? How long a wait — God Christ! — till that anguish grew pale and cold and distant?

Well, there isn't time, *N. M. Tunnard-Jones.*)

All is lost. . . . Whose fault?
(Her face in the sunlight. Her face in the shadows. Her face full of shadows.

Hair: copper muted; dull with dust.)

I floated . . . Suddenly . . . I'd no idea, really, what it was that brought me to with such a start. My eyes shut. Shall I open them? I didn't. Shall I half-open them? I did. Shall I watch her through my eyelashes?

What was it had waked me up? (And I floated: did not want to go back into daylight, really: my sorrow was becoming a familiar refuge, a *friend!* But I was afraid of daylight and of sorrow added.)

Her hand was . . . tracing the line of *my* eyebrows!!! (And I almost shied away from her.)

Shall I watch her through my eyelashes?

Her face . . . was it the face of a child who had wished upon a star; but the wish had not come true?

Serious gray eyes. (*David.* Was *David* still in those eyes?)

(I almost shied away from her.)

Her hand light on my face. Her hand caressing my face. Fingers lighter lighter, then . . . withdrawing? (And sadness in the withdrawing? All the . . . helplessness! . . . of parting.) She was taking leave of me: *saying good-bye to her . . . wish.*

Tenderness in those eyes — in her hand. Well, not grief, really. Tenderness . . . for me! (And I lay still: well, my breath had stopped; but I had to put absolutely everything then into not trembling as if I had a fever. Whatever had ever been in those eyes, I had never before, I think, seen her look at me with the same kind of tenderness that I felt for her!)

. . .

We belong together.

Wherever else I may belong, we belong together. Yes. Quite.

She touched me one last time and then all was still. After a while, she spread her arms again — as she had done the previous night — and she looked down at her hands. Hands: empty . . . of me. Empty of everything.

. . .

All is lost.

. . .

Shall I watch her through my eyelashes?

Sunlight in her face. She shielded her eyes against it; but then she stared into the sunlight: in her eyes . . . terror of the emptiness? Terror of all *she* had lost?! God in heaven!

What to do now?

And so my eyes flew open; and we shied away from each other.

David in her eyes. Everything that happened yesterday, in her eyes.

(I remember that a thought came to me then, for whatever reason, about the injured child: Was he dead by now? Would he live? . . . And I almost shied away from her.)

•

We waited. What shall I do? Shall I give her . . . a small Luthie grin?
We waited.

I raised my hand; but did not touch her face. She, too, was waiting. Hesitating. . . . *Assessing* herself? . . . Silence. Empty hands.

Then — oh, a woman of tremendous courage! — she took both *my* hands and she kissed the scars on my wrists.

I do not want a woman to gentle my wounds.
I do not want a woman to be repelled by my wounds.

But it was a kiss of . . . acceptance?

A kiss . . . gentling *me* into acceptance — of what? Bloody hell!
Gray eyes. Resolute. (But her resolve . . . different from before?)

A woman far away   Coming to me
(Getting to know each other.)

Perhaps I need not make my own truce. Perhaps I can simply erase everything and start all over again: with her. (We'll live in *truce* with her own ghosts: a substitute? Ha!

All the thoughts that hurt . . . let them go . . . But I knew that would not happen. I knew I could not do it.)

Her eyes looking out into the world. (But *David* — and God knows what else — will be in them for a long time.)
. . .

We are two people blighted by war.
. . .

Getting to know each other.

"Nim . . . Do you really want this?" I said.

And she reached out, and she removed the ugly identity tags from around my neck. Then she reached out for me.

And so I took her and gave myself to her in . . . well, in bittersweet joy.

And she took me and gave herself to me in . . . well, there were those serious gray eyes . . . in joy.

It happened this morning!!!

III

And when, in the afternoon, we came back . . . home . . . to the base . . . home: God damn it! — Hanmer was waiting.

"Luthie . . . You hairy dog! You misery . . . How was it? *Tell me absolutely everything.* Is she red between her legs?"

"Acklington . . ." I said. "Another word from you . . ."

He was hale and hearty. So much for premonitions!

Hanmer: looking . . . shy?! "Luthie . . . Misery . . . Being engaged is not so terribly serious as actually being married, is it? I am thinking of becoming engaged."

"Congratulations."

And may the Almighty smite him on the spot! He wanted to . . . up-stage me!

(Will the wretch ever look adulthood in the face? . . . Well, I'd seen him do it once, actually — that time little fat Geoff Thomas died.)

But he seemed genuinely happy to see me — as if he had been lost(?) without me.

I told him that since last night there were cracks in the ceilings and walls of the flat — was the place safe? — and also broken windows and that we had tidied up the best we could, but there had not been enough time to find somebody to replace the glass.

That sent him scurrying off to telephone his people.

IV

The Wonders, too, were hale. Not really hearty.

Our evening session on tactics: "Sir . . . Sir . . . If Jerry comes from . . ."

Did they really care where Jerry came from? (An *atmosphere:* so thick one could cut it with a knife.)

Oh you little —! (Stripping me with their eyes: I could feel it.) *Well, you think you know what happened, don't you? You think you know it all, don't you? Well, you don't! Ha!* (An . . . atmosphere. They stared at me in envy/admiration, and were stewing in their adolescent juices.)

Poor Wonders!

V

My Dear People:

I am most extravagantly hopeful . . .

But home and they — my father and my mother — seem very far away.

Too much has happened.

6 9

I

Then, for Flight B (and Flight A, too, of course) things began to happen.

The new squadron leader arrived.

"Anybody seen him yet? What's his name?" (Nobody had seen him arrive.)

"What's he like?"

II

And also on that day, in the afternoon:

Ashley straddled his motorcycle, the engine idling.

The sky above was . . . muted: *lower,* somehow, than the skies of — for example — July; and some distance away there was the town: the church belfries — one two three of them, and the roofs of houses; from this far away they seemed such a wretched mournful black, really (though Ashley knew that when one got closer, they were a rather nice warm brown, most of them).

The road: tree-lined; and it stretched wide and, at the moment, empty. (At the crossroads, Ashley had had to let a convoy of lorries pass.) A roar overhead: a passel of Hurricanes taking off — quite high by now: the sound echoed, echoed, died away; then, silence. (Ashley had killed the engine; sat, straddling the motorcycle.)

In spring — how many months ago now? When they were still training — the chap named Grant had taken a picture of Ashley on his motorcycle. The motorcycle under a tree; the tree leafing out. *And I am on my way, my hair slicked down with Brylcreem. Where am I going? No idea, really. . . . And I look stupid, sitting here like this.* The chap named Grant had taken the picture on Ashley's request because (in a way that would be difficult to explain to people who *did not understand*) Ashley had wanted to show his dead brother that the motorcycle was in top condition.

Well, something had come full circle, then, hadn't it? *This* road was tree-lined. No. No. It was not a circle. And it was neither an end nor yet another beginning — it was a natural progression of things. Wasn't it?

And then, utterly surprising himself, Ashley put his head down on his arms folded across the handlebars and began to bawl — because now John was *truly* dead. Well, about an hour ago, mid-afternoon — the afternoon of the day the new squadron leader was scheduled to arrive; the afternoon of Luthie and the woman's return (and it had been Stanhope, this time — not Farrell-Who-Knew-Everything — who had been the bringer of the news that the two had been sighted, back from their London outing) . . . an hour ago, then, below the notice advertising the Hasselblad . . . one more pushpin in the cork of the notice board and it would be done . . . It was done: Ashley's Husqvarna was for sale.

III

"And Acklington said . . . Well, one of the Hurri armorers said he heard a Hurri pilot say Acklington said the *whole street* opposite the flat was *flattened.* Completely!" (The flat where Luthie and the woman had been staying.)

"Do you think they were naked when it happened? Well, was he in the middle of —"

But, suddenly delicate, Stanhope did not finish.

They laughed, though: hooting, chuckling, cawing, crowing. Ah, new squadron leader or no new squadron leader, the men of Flight B were in no way ready to let go of the *episode* of Luthie and the woman!

"Everything flattened. *Completely.*"

Then they fell silent: frightened? (So it seemed to Ashley.) Grateful, by God! Because it had been the *other* side of the street?

"A bloke saw them come from the station. Their clothes were *filthy!*"

And days would then again slip into nights; and summer was sliding into autumn. That was what Ashley thought, looking about him.

Well, only this past morning . . . Luthie and the woman still gone . . . Ashley, restless, wandering about, had made his way to Dispersal — had walked into the Ready Room. Now why in the name of God should he want to do that? He was still "on holiday" that morning! Out of sheer momentum? Could not stay away? Could not help it? He had walked in; and the children's drawings were gone.

There were new, different children's drawings! A new school year had begun.

Unsmudged, uncrumpled new paper. Well, yellowish paper: poor quality paper: wartime paper. But bright bright bright and unfaded colors.

Gone *My Dog Flufy*. No more *This Is My Cat Snowball; Mummy and I; My Angel Fish ~~There~~ Their Names Are Hark and ~~Harold~~ Herald.*

And a memory had come to Ashley: *"And so we know what we're fighting for."* Well, Luthie had said that: Ashley could remember. Luthie laughing — that odd little laugh: nobody knew Luthie! . . . who could understand him? — that very first day, the very first hour, after their arrival from Scotland.

These new drawings: they were of Spitfires and Hurricanes shooting down Messerschmitts, in garish colors — big scarlet flames and black smoke. A fat German — the color of the uniform was *almost* right; and besides, he had a huge swastika on his chest, so that nobody could mistake him for one of ours — a fat Fritz hung on a parachute, spewing *red* blood all over the *blue* sky.

And what else about the base was not now as it had been before?

The civilians were gone, for example — long gone: those who had refused to repair the bomb craters in the runways; those who during one of the air attacks had gone on a rampage looting stores, throwing sacks of sugar and potatoes over the fence to their waiting friends . . . they had been dismissed. Sent packing by . . . somebody: the station commander? Or had they been arrested by the police? It was the ground crews now who performed the essential bomb damage repairs. *Everybody* performed essential bomb damage repairs! — their various and sundry timetables and schedules permitting.

And so nights would continue to slide into mornings.

70

Nim   Nim   This is not a real letter.

Or perhaps it is. A real letter to you!

Nim   Nim   How much do you want to show the world? How much do you want me to show the world? Well, we meet in public — dinner in the mess tonight! — we'll continue meeting in pubic: I am both proudly bold and shy. Shy? On the alert for your feelings, I suppose.

How much of ourselves do we reveal to one another in times unprivate?

We must not let ourselves be caught — etc. etc. Ha! (We'll give ourselves away by and by. I know it.)

This is a very short letter. Sorry. To bed, to sleep I must go!: well, I expected the new CO to summon us — Hanmer and me, that is — upon his arrival; instead, he is meeting the whole squadron at seven hundred hours tomorrow: an early bird! (a man energetic?); ops. at eleven. (But I'll scurry to Signals before seven; leave this on your desk.)

Nim   I stand bold and proud and shy and hopeful before you.

And I do not want to die.

(Tomorrow: I do not want to die tomorrow.

Or the next day. Nor next week. Nor next month.)

Nim   I want to live to be a . . . great-grandfather!

(This is not a real letter.)

Now . . . Victoria the Gray-furred at my door.

Well, come in, Vicky! Puss Puss . . . My woman is not in my bed, and yes I feel lonely. I'll provide the warm sheets; you purr up my nose.

Victoria: *unqueenly,* these days; unsleek; almost clumsy. The middle drawer of the file cabinet in the Flight A/Flight B office is one of the favorite stops on her quest for a comfortable lying-in nest.

Our Emmeline, at home: God, how long since I'd given her a thought!?

Emmeline . . . Where have you been?

I've been to London to see the Queen,

And she says my hands are *perfickly* clean!

(The time she rubbed her head against my wrists: the cuffs of my shirtsleeves hid the scars. Now Nim has kissed the scars. Has she made them . . . disappear, thereby?)

Oh, Emmeline's tail must be thoroughly *adult* now!

The ginger-whiskered Albert, Victoria's *husband,* is missing, by the way: never quite recovered from his injuries. Had a splint on his leg for a while; it made him depressed and he stopped eating. So Corporal Rossiter tells me. One day Albert simply hobbled away.

Never to see his offspring . . .

. . .

Well, God Christ! Luthie, go to sleep!

. . .

Unlike the other Victoria, this Victoria does not seem to be in deepest mourning for her Albert.

. . .

Luthie . . . Go to sleep.

. . .

I am frightened. I do not want to die tomorrow.

(It *is* quiet here tonight. Even Hanmer: no puff puff puff in his slumbers; he is virtually silent.)

Nim   Dreams small and peaceful to you as the leaves of the old plum tree outside my window at home.

Yes, Victoria . . . I am stroking the little white widow's peak on your forehead.

. . .

Luthie   Go to sleep.

71

I

Perhaps a holiday was bad for one, Ashley thought as he tossed and turned in his bed that night. He had to get up and go to the bog.

Last night, he had tossed and turned without fear — had only worried: to sell or not to sell the motorcycle to buy the camera?; and so perhaps the very absence of fear yesterday was what tonight made one's insides squirm . . .

"Grenfeld . . . Hey, Jeremy. Are you awake? . . . Do you want to talk?"

"What do you want to talk about?"

"I don't know. . . . What do *you* want to talk about?"

Whisper whisper: about . . . Luthie and the woman, naturally. Talk talk talk talk talk.

Then, about . . .

"When I was little . . ." Ashley said, "I used to lie on the carpet in the hall and watch the sunlight on the antlers." (The glass-paneled door at home!: the two powerfully antlered stags etched into the glass.) "It made . . . patterns on the glass and on the carpet." (Couldn't he think of anything but *trivial* things just now? Or did it matter?)

The Husqvarna: the bloody Husqvarna for sale: that was what had made him think of home! (Did it matter?)

Grenfeld's house was much grander, probably. No doubt. But perhaps *that* did not matter, either: well, that time after they had sat in the shelter together — how long ago now? (ah, events ever seemed farther away in time than they really were!) — Grenfeld had revealed himself to Ashley as quite ordinary, really, with parent troubles like everyone else.

Had Ashley the Silent Observer ever *revealed himself* to anybody?

They talked. About nothing much. . . . Not about the Husqvarna and the Hasselblad.

"Ruthie is home from hospital now." Grenfeld: *obsessed* with his Ruthie in *frocks ugly beyond belief.*

But she was not well yet. She was . . . "Even quieter than usual!" . . . Suffered from nightmares. "She'll have to see a . . . psychiatrist!"

Thus, it was out of the question for Uncle Jacob, Aunt Hannah, etc., to leave for America anytime soon. Grenfeld was happy: *beyond belief,* no doubt.

And so Ashley told him about . . . yes! the girl from Campbell's (whom Grenfeld could barely remember) and about how he had . . . decided(?) not to think of her much anymore; but he did not mention Buttercup because . . . well, would Grenfeld understand it? He himself could not understand it — how somebody's voice heard only over the R/T could have such a hold over one and could become so mixed up in one's mind with the images of other people — with the image of the girl from Campbell's. But at last he did confide in Grenfeld — nonchalantly! (that was the word) — that he was just a bit in love with the section officer from Signals, for Luthie's sake. Now Grenfeld wouldn't laugh at him, would he?

He and Grenfeld were . . . mates now, surely. Weren't they? (As in schoolmates. . . . A new school year had begun. But then, the previous one would have been Ashley's last, if not for the war and his brother's dying.) Had he and Grenfeld become mates — *fast friends?* — because Ashley had — what was the word — *responded* to Grenfeld's *confidences* of how-long-ago? Were they equals? Was Grenfeld still different from other people? Or did it matter?

Then Stanhope woke up and began to scream at them — in a whisper — to shut up. "Shut up. Shut up. Shut up." And so they shut up.

(But Ashley had to go to the bog twice more that night. The fear was with him. He tried to forget the fear.)

Well, should he have mentioned the Husqvarna for sale or the Hasselblad to Grenfeld?

But Grenfeld himself had not mentioned it. (Grenfeld: he who had made his . . . *journey* on the Husqvarna!) Had Grenfeld missed the notice? And if so, how many other people would fail to see it?

Or had Grenfeld been merely waiting politely for Ashley to bring it up? But if he hadn't . . .

And what if *nobody* bought the motorcycle? (The whole matter taken out of Ashley's hands: he wouldn't have to make the final decision . . .) It would be dreadful.

Then it occurred to Ashley that perhaps he was worrying too much.

II

And the next morning the new squadron leader did not walk in; he did not stride in.

Force nine wind: Strong gale: Some structural damage occurs.

"Well, Luthie said that: *Force nine . . . Some structural . . .*" But Farrell would report this only later, of course. The brand-new Flight A bloke said he heard him say it — what's his name? Moriarty! Has the wart on his nose . . ."

Ah, Moriarty! They were like musical chairs, Flight A. And so — in spite of this being later, after they had met the squadron leader — it seemed to Ashley there was smugness in the air: Around them, people were dying; Luthie kept the men of Flight B alive . . . by magic.

"Moriarty said he heard Luthie say it to Acklington: *Force nine . . .*"

Moriarty should learn to keep his big mouth shut, Ashley thought.

The new squadron leader had blown in, then, like a force nine gale; both flight commanders in tow. He sat down; nodded at Luthie and Acklington to sit down. "You may sit," he said to the assembled squadron. (Everybody sat.)

. . .

Well, no rightness to it. All wrong. Here was a *beginning!* God damn it all! Well, for Ashley (for everybody?) things were . . . no, not coming to a close, exactly; but he did not want any *beginnings,* by God! (It was enough to deal with the *natural progression of things . . .*)

The new squadron leader: his face was as ordinary as — for example — Brown's. (See him once; you'll never remember him again.)

The new squadron leader. Nose: of an average size.

Teeth (he smiled before he began to speak): not Luthie-teeth (huge); nor as small and knife-sharp as Flight Lieutenant Acklington's.

Neck: no Adam's apple prominent above the collar of his shirt; neck: of an average length.

And hair: of an *average* color?

(His name was Johnson: the name was ordinary, of course.)

(And so his words, too, should be bland and safe.)

Blah blah blah blah. What was it he was saying?

While waiting for the man to appear, Ashley and Grenfeld had talked some: "Forty-five seconds left"; "Now he's two seconds late" — ordinary things; but Ashley's fear from the previous night was still with him . . .

Ops. at eleven. Again. Not quite four hours from now (he had thought). *Holidays: bad for one.* (Thoughts of the previous night.) *MY DOG FLUFY gone. . . . That is what we are fighting for.*

And then he'd thought that during a scrap one felt fine, really: the . . . oh yes! the danger excitement carried one through; but there was a tension . . . a competition . . . between the excitement and the necessity to concentrate on doing things right; and also at times the blind hatred-of-the-moment, which most of them had by now somehow learned to turn on and off almost at will: that carried one through! And after a successful scrap one felt on top of the world, really: well, full of elation — exultation! — though without true joy: now why and in what way was this . . . this joyfulness without joy different from . . . from — for example — the . . . music of Luthie's Sibbeh-Sibelius? And why had what's-his-name . . . the bloke Sibelius . . . been on his mind lately, anyway? Why was he going back to the beginning, if he did not want any beginnings?

Well, everything was fine, really, if only after ops. one could do away with the knowledge that soon one had to do it all over again!

"He is three minutes late." Oh yes. Reassuring, actually: a squadron leader who was three minutes late. (And now, look at him! He did seem reassuringly ordinary. *No beginnings. Things would go unchanged.*)

What was it he was saying? (Grenfeld seemed to be listening attentively.)

Blah blah blah blah. Morale morale . . . Well, squadron leaders — wing commanders — people like that: they usually talked about morale.

". . . A great deal of pushing and shoving in the NAAFI queue yesterday afternoon, I noticed."

Yes. Yes. *Pushing. Shoving.* (*The NAAFI van had sold apples, yesterday afternoon, after Ashley's return from his motorcycle ride: the first fresh apples of the season. Luthie would know what kind, probably. Cartwright had complained, "See the wormhole? . . . I want a new one." Pushing, shoving . . .*

And now Ashley was suddenly drowsy: it was airless in the room, and hot . . .)

· · ·

But but wait wait wait wait wait (and his eyes flew wide open). The new squadron leader — the man Johnson — hadn't been here yet yesterday afternoon! He hadn't!

· · ·

Or had he? My God!

•

"Pushing and shoving is indicative of lax discipline," Squadron Leader Johnson was saying.

. . .

Well, up yours!

Had he been here . . . all day yesterday? *Skulking about?* Roaming the base? *Sneaking: spying on them?* Spying!!!

(And only now Ashley quite abruptly became aware of little waves — ripples — in the . . . audience. And he — the Observer! — had missed it completely! Well, Grenfeld did not even return Ashley's *glance!* And as one man they all stared ahead: eyes at infinity . . . *regulation!* Unmoving. But still it was as if they were speaking to one another: ripples . . . waves . . . *an electric current of some sort.* My God!)

And the man was talking about . . . table manners. TABLE MANNERS?

"A pilot officer — at teatime — I shall not name names — *I heard him:* he slurped his tea. Extremely loudly. *Lost in himself. Satisfying a bodily need for liquid. No attention to anyone else: nothing else mattered.*"

. . .

Well, go and —! You — you . . .

(But: which pilot officer? "Newby?" whispered Cartwright, and Stanhope snickered. It would serve Newby right!

Well, you . . . how dare you! *Squadron Bloody Leader Johnson. Bastard.* How can you do this to us — sowing discord? That was what Ashley thought.)

. . .

"Then later, at dinner" — well, had Johnson been at dinner too? Nobody had seen him. And now he held them — trapped! they could not even discuss it! — "I caught a glimpse of a sergeant pilot," the madman continued — "no names. He was shoveling his dinner in, his chin almost on the table. *A voracious and desperate feeding.* Dispirited. Grim. His spirit turned inward. *I I I: I am getting my nourishment. My own survival the only thing in the world.*"

Were the Flight A people snickering, now? No.

(*Thank you. I'll never again think anything bad about Newby,* thought Ashley.)

Luthie: had he known about this? Any inkling what the man Johnson was like? . . . God damn him, couldn't he have warned them?

But no, Luthie clearly had not known. Luthie sat, stunned. (And Flight Lieutenant Acklington looked nervous. Acklington: nervous!)

Well, kill him. Both of you. Go and kill him: the bastard Johnson. Savage him.

Won't you defend us?

Luthie: those *reasonable* eyes. (Now staring over everybody's heads.

My God! Nothing else on his mind these days but his bloody *mistress?* Well, God damn him! *Mistress:* what a word!)

Luthie: a . . . drawn face. (Well, was he even thinner now than when they'd all gone swimming, just before the Grenfeld incident? Of course, Ashley's clothes, too, hung on him these days.)

Luthie: tired eyes. *Wonderment* in them? God damn him! (Well, that was what Luthie was like! Staring *beyond* the man Johnson — and yet somehow . . . *inside himself? His spirit turned inward!* That was Luthie.) Seeing them — Flight B, Flight A, everybody — as *they* had never seen themselves before — would not see themselves again — would not *want* to see themselves!: well, through the bastard Johnson's eyes; with an . . . outsider's eye? (That was what he was like.) God damn him.

(And so Ashley had known ever since the Grenfeld episode that in some ways Luthie would forever remain the same — even as in other ways he now was so very much changed; and how Ashley felt about it all was still most dreadfully complicated. It was only . . . only — and out of the blue it struck him — only when he took a really good picture that he was . . . well, in a way . . . explaining to himself all those things that he could not quite grasp otherwise: all the . . . contradictory things of living . . .

But did it matter?)

Sir . . . Sir . . . Go now and tell the bastard Johnson he is wrong. Go. Now.

In Luthie's eyes, though, there was only . . . understanding? And then, sadness? (My God! First he had abandoned them for the woman; would he now betray them to this bastard simply because he understood too much?) Despair in his eyes — because the man Johnson was both wrong and right in the way he saw them — well, right after his own fashion but so *terribly* wrong! (And Ashley, too, was dreadfully tired now: *dispirited? lost in himself?*)

Luthie: studying *himself* in despair? (Well, God damn him!)

Then: at last — at last! — something . . . akin to anger.

Yes. Anger. And a . . . *resolve.*

. . .

Well, it had taken long enough! (Or perhaps not so long, after all?)

. . .

Blah blah blah blah. "Actually, poor table manners —" the man Johnson was saying, "poor table manners have long been considered one of the . . . warning flags, if you will, of low spirits. Poor morale. You do not conduct yourselves as men of a keen edge. Gentlemen . . . What the times demand of us . . ."

Blah blah blah.

But *now* Luthie was halfway out of his chair . . .

But Flight Lieutenant Acklington looked terrified. (Acklington: terrified!) And then he threw Luthie a lightning-quick warning glance. My

God! Acklington: more *sensible* than Luthie? More *reasonable?* Well, at the moment, at least. My God! Incredible! Impossible! And Luthie subsided into his chair.

Thus it happened that Squadron Leader Johnson was permitted to smile then with . . . impunity (as he had before beginning his little speech).

He . . . smiled! (Ordinary teeth.) A friendly smile — how dare he! Not a *bastard's* — a *snake's* — smile? His face: well, the face of someone who was unaware that he was a *snake?* He did not *mean* to be a bastard? God damn him, who was he, anyway?

(*Compensating* — was that the word?: *compensating* — for looking so average by being a bastard? A smile — what was the word? — *conciliatory?* Or was he one of those blokes made of *stern stuff* and . . . Well, perhaps he was *admonishing* them, but did not really despise them.)

"We shall attack the problems of deficient morale together. Of course, I intend to lead you into action in person —"

He did?

"— more often than most of you have probably experienced with your former squadron CO, according to my information —"

According to his information! He *was* a snake!

Blah blah blah blah. He even managed to drag in . . . *one-oh-ninetis!*

The *miserable* snake. *One-oh-ninetis!!!* "A problem to be addressed throughout the entire Fighter Command, of course . . ." Throughout the entire Fighter Command! Was he accusing *them* of cowardice?

Was he suggesting that *they* were so afraid of the Me-109s that they'd swerve away, not deliver their attack? (And Grenfeld: he who had been — was still? — obsessed with killing Germans — he was almost out of his chair now; but Ashley slapped him down.) One-oh-ninetis. *Now who had told him? . . . Who had been blabbing?*

(And Acklington seemed ready either to burst or to faint with fury; and Luthie's eyes were wide . . . wide . . .)

. . .

"I particularly anticipate with pleasure the cooperation of both flight commanders . . ." Johnson said.

Bumph. All of it bumph!

"Together we shall prevail . . . Together we shall attain . . ."

Well, he'll let us go soon, now.

But then, out of the blue, the *new squadron leader* said: "You may smoke, by the way. I am sorry. I should have said so earlier."

And he produced a *real gold!* (was it? was it?) cigarette holder — look at the length of the thing: in no way average! — and he inserted a cigarette and proceeded to light it.

And the man Johnson continued talking, but he also smoked; and then — his arms *short:* not average — he pulled an ashtray within a comfortable reach . . . Such an everyday thing! ashes falling into an ashtray. And yet they all gaped as if . . . as if these were the very first cigarette ashes to fall since God created heaven and earth and hell! (Perhaps the man Johnson, short arms and all, was not ordinary, after all?!) Well, he had wanted to create a stir, by God! And had succeeded! Not a single one of them was *lost in himself,* now! And so now he was showing them . . . wasn't he? . . . that he could *take it:* the . . . commotion; could ride it all out . . .

He talked, and then he *squashed* the cigarette in the ashtray.

(But for all that, his neck still was of an average length.)

Then he dismissed them. "Happy hunting!" he said. . . . *Happy hunting!!!*

So, there they were.

They discussed it on the way to Parachutes to pick up their brollies.

"The bastard!" said Cartwright.

"The bastard!" said Brown.

"The bastard!" said Peploe-Webb.

"The bastard!" said Farrell.

"Yesterday . . . Anybody see a squadron leader's stripes?"

They'd have noticed an unknown squadron leader's stripes!

"The bugger hid his rank! Wore a *phony* uniform!"

Yes!!! Well, who would pay attention to him then, without his squadron leader's uniform? So many unfamiliar faces about the base, these days: a game of *musical chairs!* And so he had gone *spying* on them . . .

"If he fell into enemy hands in a uniform not of his own rank, the Fritzes would be perfectly justified to . . . to shoot the bastard!" (Farrell knew *everything.* Or did he?)

But after that they suddenly did not seem to know what else to say about Squadron Leader Johnson. They were tired. They did not seem to *want* to say anything else about Johnson.

. . .

"Well, Luthie and the popsy . . . where will they go now when they want to —?"

"To stores. . . . Which is softer to lie on: flour or sugar?"

"Flour!" They were laughing.

"Sugar!"

"Potatoes!" They were laughing.

"Well, aren't there parts of stores with spare blankets, you know, and pillows?" Why did Stanhope have to be so . . . practical?!

Oh, they hadn't wanted to let go of Luthie and the woman just yet! (But now they'd have to. Other things were happening.)

And it occurred to Ashley that there was a time once when he would have found the new squadron leader . . . well, interesting: a man whom it might be rather fun to *observe* — from afar. But it was too late now: too much had happened. *No more beginnings*.

And then again Ashley felt wistful — almost in the same way he had done that time after the air attack he and Grenfeld had sat out in the shelter together. He felt as if they all had lost something. Because it was . . . *disrespectful*, that's what!: all that *bumph* Squadron Leader Johnson had said. Disrespectful not to those who were dead; but to them — the men of Flight B, the Flight A people — the living! *Now* was there anything left to respect?

Somebody said, "Old Hurry-up Hammett . . . Do you think his wife will get well and they'll have more children?"

III

They went out three times that day.

And the third time — the last time — Stanhope's undercarriage would not come down on landing, and so around and around and around he went: circling circling, trying to gather courage; but then he did manage to ram the U/C home and he came in, unscathed . . . unharmed . . . not a scratch or bruise on him: well, some pulled muscles in the shoulder from battling the U/C handle, and his face not pale with terror but red as a beet from the effort — his neck flushed, too, and peculiarly *thick-looking:* not really swollen, but as if . . . strained; and so he knelt in the grass, no courage left, and he was bawling, and Luthie knelt by him (having waved away the blood wagon people). Luthie: whispering, whispering . . .

And Farrell, whom an identical . . . misfortune had befallen some time — a long time! — ago but who had not received an *exactly* identical treatment from Luthie: Farrell looked . . . jealous?

Shouldn't they have outgrown that by now? Ashley thought.

And what else happened that day? The base had not been bombed.

72

Nim   Lover   Friend

73

That evening a man came to see Ashley about the Husqvarna. He tested it, then said he'd let Ashley know.

74

Nim   Love

Went to see the man Johnson. Went in anger.
  Double-jointed before him! Oh, absolutely!

Nim   Love   <u>Getting to know each other</u> . . .
  No doubt you have noticed how I am when afraid, uneasy: knees for-
ward . . . mask the double-jointedness — I am invulnerable! (Correction:
it <u>used</u> to make me feel less vulnerable. Do I no longer need the <u>mask?</u>)

Nim   Love
  When it comes to matters which do not directly concern the two of us,
I'll continue to speak to you in <u>letters</u> <u>that</u> <u>aren't</u> <u>real</u> <u>letters.</u> Let us save
our private times for other words, other . . . deeds. No words: I'll listen to
your silences. Be patient with mine. And so we'll draw strength from each
other.

I sent Squadron Leader Johnson a note: "Sir: A minute of your time,
please"; did not wait for a reply: was on my way. (Ah, that very first time
I went to see Hammett, to beg him for a Miles Master for Stanhope!
How many "sirs"? Too many "sirs." . . . Not this time. Not with this man,
by God!)

Christ! Old Hurry-up Hammett: will he never be back, now? (An ex-
tended compassionate leave? A medical leave: has he . . . crumbled?)

Nim   I am not about to crumble. I will not crumble.
  Nim
  It has occurred to me that I never knew the name of Hammett's little
son: only little . . . <u>uh-huh</u> . . . Gloria's name. (And the child we pulled out
of the rubble the night before last is on my mind.)
  The photos behind Hammett's desk, back in Scotland: my thoughts al-
ways halt at the sandcastle, for some reason.

(The tide comes in: no more sandcastle? What a *profound* thought!
Luthie . . . Idiot!)

Well, our good old Hammett must have known that his *immortality*
would crumble! That poor sod: first *rejoicing* in his possession of . . . of
an insurance against *death complete;* then . . . *hoarding* and *guarding* his
joy: against the knowledge? . . . Foreknowledge (different from premoni-

tion! I think, foreknowledge). . . . Hammett: withdrawing from our lives and from our dying.

(The sandcastle: gone.

Hammett: gone from our lives and our dying.)

Nim   One day I'll rejoice in <u>*our*</u> *children!*

Nim   I rather dread the future. . . . The sandcastle: gone.

Well, that — that *wart* Johnson!

I took a deep breath. "Sir," I said, "I respectfully submit that you . . . do not understand us."

Ah! *Blue eyes:* the man Johnson. *Very* blue: like McGregor's eyes? God in heaven! . . . Have the Wonders noticed?

Do not stare at me so with those blue eyes, sir. You haven't got sinister eyebrows — like McGregor. Sir. I am not afraid of you. Sir.

. . .

Without those sinister eyebrows, Johnson's eyes *are* a bit more ordinary, of course.

Nim   Do you remember McGregor at all?

The man looked at me with those blue *blue* eyes; and I saw that they were . . . full of terror. Anguish! He: afraid of *me?*

. . .

Oh God, it felt good, for a moment!

. . .

No no no. Of course not. He did not fear *me!* Absolutely not! At least I do not think so. But was he afraid of . . . *not winning the war?*

Does he think *us* incapable of winning the war?

. . .

Would not winning the war be a death complete? A sandcastle gone?

Nim   One day I'll delight in our children! One of each: a little son, a little daughter. It would be perfect.

(This is not a real letter.)

Well, Johnson: he stared at me with those fearful eyes and said that he needed my cooperation, not my . . . fury. And I said yes, of course, sir, and let me explain. And he took out that cigarette holder of his; and his eyes: no longer fearful, now. Defiant? Well, *defensive.* And he said he needed my cooperation; but he said that he had heard about me (!!!) and that obviously I thought too much of myself because by luck or accident most of my men were still alive while all around people were dying as people usually die in war. . . . Well, God in heaven!

•

Nim   My only love   I'll see you tonight and it will be rather wonderful.

Nim,   I definitely must guard against the state of mind that descends upon one . . . sometimes. Well, the last time: Hammett's children; and the nine (!) women dead; and . . . and my poor Austin gone — all in one day . . . oh yes, and Cartwright crumbling, too — all in that one day. And on the day following: my poor Aunt Millicent plowing up the earth . . .
    Friend   Love   Your arrival that afternoon saved me.
    Nim,   I'll not crumble.

Nim   Is there to be no refuge, then? No . . . home? (I want to go home, be with my own kind.) Well, it is a bit as if being betrayed by one of one's own!: he does not understand us.

Or was he drunk?

(By the way, I never thought I'd miss old Hurry-up Hammett so! Well, after he was gone, I was glad, for a moment — relieved! L'affaire Grenfeld will be forever buried and forgotten, I thought. Am most thoroughly ashamed of myself now.
    But it has been buried and forgotten. The wart Johnson would have thrown both my and Grenfeld's unsoldierly behavior in my face, I am sure.)
    Nim   I'll see you tonight and it will be wonderful.

There are times: we simply go on killing and being killed. We do not think what we are doing it all for.
    (But I want to think pleasant thoughts and remain hopeful.)

Could I have said or done anything differently, though? How do I protect the Wonders from him?
    This should not have happened to us, at this point — well, not at any point.
    The man does not belong here.
    . . .

Helplessness.

7 5

I

And so, once again uncertain about . . . many things (as it had been at the beginning), everyone — Stanhope, Farrell — they *discussed* it: would Squadron Leader Johnson prove a real pain in the arse or merely an irritating thorn in their sides? *Would he stick his fingers into pies?*
    But for all that, life went on, of course: that evening there was an

all-ranks NAAFI sherry party (*sherry:* civilized — women would be present). "Well, that bastard *Snake* must have organized this before he even got here! *It will raise our bloody morale!*" And so they were laughing. (But it was not really laughter.)

(But Squadron Leader Johnson was not present. Good. Good. Excellent.)

Women in summer dresses, though the nights were no longer summer-like: bright yellow, delicate pink, pale blue, bold red, and all-sorts-of-colors-all-together-flowery frocks . . . bare arms; V-shaped necklines . . . (And too few of the women and too many men; and that rather made the men . . . well, *growl* at one another, after a while. The party: not a success, then, really?)

"Here they are!" Luthie and the section officer from Signals. (Now *that* raised the morale: something to talk about.)

Luthie and the woman were late: she still in uniform — must have just come off duty.

. . .

"Where are they now?"

"They're gone! They must've left!"

. . .

But they were back, by and by; and she too had changed into a dress. The color? Well, as blue-green as the sea is on a sunny day, with a white froth of foam! (A white collar on the dress.) "Not bad with that hair of hers," Stanhope said, and stuffed a peppermint in his mouth. The turquoise was *beautiful* with her hair! Oh yes, their spirits were lifted.

But . . . but . . . she and Luthie: they *clashed!* terribly! (that was what Ashley thought) — the green-blue of her frock and the blue of Luthie's uniform. She should have thought of it. She was not perfect. (That was what Ashley thought.) Well, she and Luthie looked ridiculous together, anyway: he so very tall and she so tiny.

And Ashley then admitted to himself that he was rather in love with her not just for Luthie's sake.

God damn it all! (The miserable girl from Campbell's . . . he had never even known her name, really . . . Buttercup: she was nothing but a voice from nowhere . . .)

Luthie and the woman dancing.

My God! *Now this was dancing!*

How in the world . . . ? The woman's skirts flying . . .

People always surprised one: neither Luthie nor the woman seemed the type, really . . .

Now the WAAF Mary Ann, for example — she of the abominable honey buns — she had surprised Ashley: knew how to pronounce Husqvarna!

Luthie always surprised one. Now one would almost not expect him to be good at *any* kind of dancing. . . . My God!

And the men of Flight B cheered Luthie and the woman on (and Luthie and the woman responded!); and yet (Ashley observed this) at the same time, Cartwright's, Farrell's . . . *everyone's* excitement was almost akin to anger (at Luthie? at the woman? or at both?: no way to tell) because there was no other woman there like the section officer from Signals and it made one feel so lonely one could howl. (Luthie had abandoned them. . . . Well, they would abandon *anybody:* for her. . . . Ashley looked about and knew they felt abandoned.) Only Grenfeld appeared unaffected: preoccupied with his own matters — with his Ruthie and so on and so on?

Was their — Luthie and the woman's — gaiety a bit too . . . frantic?

(But some time later Ashley saw them again, outside: all at once, he simply could not bear it to stay inside any longer; and there they were: the moon bright. But they did not see him: they'd probably not have noticed if a whole army of Ashleys had come (and then quickly ducked behind the bushes). The four-man band inside was *butchering* a mazurka — there always had to be a mazurka because of the downtrodden-though-gallant little Poland — and Luthie and the woman were conducting the band, there in the moonlight — not together but, facing each other, they waved their arms *at* each other; and they were chuckling — *chortling,* softly — together, at each other, comfortably: the comfortable voices of two people who knew each other very well, indeed: comfortable.

And then Luthie reached out for her, and she . . . flew to him; two or three steps: she *flew.* A fraction of a second's hesitation? But then . . . My God, what wonderful recklessness! Ashley had never seen anything like this in all his life. In her running steps there was . . . generosity? Ashley had never seen anything like it. It was as if she were giving something to the man; and there was in those few steps a need to be given something by him.

Under the huge moon one could see *everything.* Their kiss: not long, but fierce and hungry and almost desperate, but yet, at the same time — and Ashley now let his breath out at last because he was feeling faint — it was a kiss . . . oh yes, comfortable: an acknowledgment of a *pact sealed.* Comfortable. And her hands were . . . tracing the man's eyebrows! And there was something about Luthie . . . about the way he stood? — Ashley could see it: Luthie seemed to be at peace.

Well, that was what women were good at, of course: bringing peace. And God knows Luthie needed it! Probably.

But Luthie drew her to him again; she folded herself against him.

They looked ridiculous together. . . . What is it she's trusting him to do? . . . But the man held her, held her; did not do anything.

Ashley did not quite understand this.

This woman, she belonged to Luthie . . . and she wanted to belong to Luthie. (The girl from Campbell's: Ashley'd not known her name. Buttercup: a voice . . . Well, God damn it!)

This woman was too old for him anyway. (Must be as old as Luthie, perhaps even older. Though not so old as the WAAF Mary Ann.)

Ashley always somehow chose women — girls — he didn't have to *talk* to, really: did not have to *do anything about.*

Well, what would he say to this woman? He couldn't *chortle* at her, could he?

And it was then that despair truly seized him: even after all this time, he still felt *un-grown-up,* though sometimes he thought himself terribly *old;* and how much growing up must he still do?

Then, suddenly, there were voices somewhere in the darkness on the path, and almost at the same time the door behind Ashley flew open and a small crowd poured out, shouting and laughing: drunk, in spite of the *civilized* sherry? And Luthie and the woman sprang apart.

. . .

And the men of Flight B then saw Luthie one more time that day, after the dance. He must have escorted the woman *home,* and was on his way back.

Well, today was Luthie's birthday! He was twenty-one years old!

Well, they had already held a celebration for him: should they now say Happy Birthday again? "Happy birthday, sir," they said — Cartwright and Brown in unison, other voices chiming in: rising; falling.

"Oh! Thank you," he said; and then he stopped and stood there . . . and he stood there: as if wanting to be . . . close to them.

And then he said — he was confiding in them!!! (So, did that mean he still was one of them, in spite of everything? Ah, that ever-present *Luthie question!*) — he said, quietly: "The . . . the squadron leader . . ." — the bastard Johnson: for a few hours they had almost forgotten about him — "I . . . know nothing about him. It is possible he has seen too much; it is possible he has seen too little. If he has seen too little, he may change."

He was trying to offer them comfort.

But he sounded as if he himself did not believe what he was saying.

He *was* confiding in them, though. Even more quietly he said, "Well, it almost is as if one is being betrayed by one's own, isn't it?"

He was confiding. So, that *was* rather nice. Comforting. Comfortable.

Did he want comfort from *them?* My God!

But they couldn't give him any, of course.

•

And so Ashley went and got drunk. They all went and got drunk. Not a single one of them wanted to go back to the uncertainties of *the beginning*. (Then minutes would again flow into hours, and hours would make up a day. No matter what happened, time would pass both very slowly and very quickly.)

II

Moriarty — he of the big mouth and of the wart on the nose — was shot down; wounded in the leg — well, he would live.

Peploe-Webb went down: came back not much the worse for wear — he only seemed to blink too much, as Cartwright had done once, some days ago (well, on the day all those WAAFs had died and the Fritzes had bombed the base car park . . . Actually, Cartwright *still* blinked too much.)

And what else happened as hours and minutes passed to make a day?

A Messerschmitt landed at the satellite field!!! ("Let's go see it!" But how does one commandeer a lorry? And twenty-five miles is too far to walk . . . "Besides . . . Gentlemen, we must be at dinner, to use all the right forks!" Of course, Luthie had not said, "This is an order. Everybody must be at dinner, to use the right forks." But were they responsible only to Luthie? . . . There was tension in the air.)

Now the German bastard: *he* had had no trouble putting his undercarriage down (unlike Stanhope)!

Ah, putting one's U/C down in the presence of the enemy was just like raising one's hands in surrender! It meant one was willing to land on enemy territory. "But they say his arm was almost gone. Left arm. His throttle hand —"

"You're daft. The Fritzes use the right hand for the throttle hand!"

"Shut up. . . . Go on. Go on."

"Well, he was just holding the arm in place and the cockpit swimming in blood . . . But he landed the bloody kite! Landed her! But by the time they got to him, he was unconscious . . ."

They tried to feel sorry for the German bastard.

They tried to . . . hate him.

They tried to admire him — because what he had done *was* wizard! smashing! My God! Throttle hand useless and the cockpit swimming in blood! But none of these emotions seemed right or stayed with them long. Well, Ashley himself did not want to bother — at the moment — with anything besides excitement. (Too much trouble, really, these days, to work at feeling anything for anybody — except for oneself.)

Flying Officer Luthie said then (and he sounded tired but was grinning): "Be careful if you ever come across a Jerry with his U/C down. It may simply mean his hydraulics are shot." And so even Luthie — the cause, the *instigator,* of the Grenfeld brouhaha: so *terribly* far away now, the Grenfeld brouhaha: in another lifetime — not even Luthie chided them for their lack of feeling toward a fellow human being.

And what else happened? Well, the *Snake* — determined, obviously, to keep his promise about leading them into combat more often than Hammett had done — Squadron Leader *Snake* Johnson took Stanhope, Cartwright, and Farrell out. They came back — and Stanhope, Farrell, Cartwright were not talking.

"How was it? Have an . . . *interesting* trip? . . . *Slither slither* . . ."

"Bugger off, will you."

"Who are you saying *bugger off* to? Talk. Talk!"

"I said *bugger off.*"

And their eyes: they were such that people looked at one another and stopped asking questions.

What in bloody hell's name —?

Yes, there was tension in the air.

"Sir . . . Sir . . . Would you tell me . . ."

(Lately, when he couldn't sleep, Ashley had been talking to Grenfeld both aloud and inside his head: confiding in him. Now, suddenly, he was talking to Luthie — only inside his head, of course.)

"Morale . . . Well, what is morale, anyway, sir?

"Well, Moriarty, sir . . . the other day . . . before he had to go to hospital: he was so terribly new then . . . There was an air attack alarm, sir. And he came running into *our* sleeping quarters — not his own, sir. 'The shelter! Where is the bloody shelter?' And I was in bed — the only one in the room just then, sir — and I was as scared as Moriarty, but all at once it seemed too much of a bother to get up and run for the shelter, and so I just pointed outside: 'Over there — you'll find it.' And then I pulled the blanket over my head and said to myself, 'Nothing will happen to me. Nothing will happen to me.' — over and over.

"Well, sir . . . which is the *higher* morale? Moriarty's — my God, what an idiot! — because he was scared and wanted to run? Or mine: I was scared but I was too tired to run."

But he never did ask Luthie, of course.

. . .

God damn the man Johnson!

And then there was another — different — brouhaha involving Grenfeld . . . Not brouhaha, really. But the man Johnson was definitely sticking his fingers into pies.

76

I seem to be waiting for something.

Had meant to be *completely* finished with the storytelling by now — what with my prewar life revealed, described and analyzed, examined and inspected.

I am not finished. What in Christ's name *do* I expect to happen once the telling is done: the things that hurt — can one let them go etc. etc.?

Or must I wait till the end of the war to conclude the story — whichever way the war may turn out: *a sandcastle gone?* — only then to determine (but what if I no longer am among the living by then?) the worth of my life: *a sandcastle gone?*

. . .

(Thoughts one would keep private, secret, hidden.)

Oh, I am in love with N. M. Tunnard-Jones!

. . .

About my birthday:

On the telephone my father reminded me that now, being twenty-one, I get an income of my very own. *An income!* As well as my earnings. Christ, what to do with all that money?

1) An . . . engagement ring for Nim? . . . Too soon?

2) Be frivolous. Buy a box of chocolates! Prewar. Nim and I will eat them *all at once!*

3) Is my *income* sufficient to acquire another dogshit Austin? (When the day is done, Nim and I could leave this place behind so much more easily. . . . *I want to get out of here, by God!*)

About Nim: I must be very, very patient. One day *David* will disappear from her eyes completely . . .

(What am I waiting for? A *premonition?* God in heaven!)

Ah, there was a time once I'd have sat down and covered *reams* of paper giving an account of this latest uproar over Grenfeld! (But must get to sleep now. Spent every minute of the evening with Nim.

I want to think . . . gentle thoughts: be hopeful.)

I do not want to think about the Wonders, just now.

. . .

Oh, a man of tremendous dignity: Grenfeld. Absolutely! I told him he need not do anything he did not *want* to do.

He stood, dignified. "Yes, sir. I mean . . . no, sir. Thank you, sir."

Our first conversation *face to face* since his night out on Ashley's Husqvarna!

And I thought, *Sergeant Grenfeld . . . Well, do something . . . undigni-*

fied. Giggle. . . . Well, let's giggle together. Like . . . like two conspirators. Forget the night out on the Husqvarna!

But he would do no such thing, of course.

. . .

I do not want to think about the Wonders, at the moment. I am happy, and tired.

7 7

And the men of Flight B fought among themselves — fought each other — like . . . roosters, really: to inflict hurt, not just to heap scorn; to hurl insults, not just to squabble: did they fight because by now they knew little else? (That was what Ashley thought.)

The Grenfeld brouhaha: should Grenfeld *pose* — be a model — my God! — for a recruiting poster? Oh, it all was so utterly silly!

"Would be ripping good fun, actually!"

"You've the brains of a Jerry bowser."

There was discord. Yes, it did sound like the usual squabbling, but in truth, it was a battle.

Well, some time ago — so the story went — a passel of propaganda-wallahs (Luthie's word) had spotted Grenfeld —

"In a pub? . . . In town, walking?"

(Had the propaganda-wallahs been prowling about outside various bases? — as even the *snake* Johnson had gone on a prowl inside. . . . Actually, once or twice journalists and such had been allowed in, herded about cattlelike and kept on a tight lead like so many *untrustworthy* dogs.)

The propaganda-wallahs: on a search. *Cannot be an officer.*

Must be a sergeant pilot. (More appealing to the *masses,* no doubt.)

And so somehow they'd come across Grenfeld; and then through *official channels* the request had come (the rumor had it) to —

"To Hurry-up! And he let it sit there . . ."

On his desk: under piles of *stuff* important/unimportant; and not so much as a whisper of it had reached anybody, till the man Johnson's arrival (but this was not a rumor, really: that was how Luthie finally explained it to Grenfeld. . . . Grenfeld: handsome as a film star — not a single pimple of acne on him).

(Ah, meeting Grenfeld that very first time, in Scotland! Ashley remembered: a screen flickering . . . the names of the actors rolling . . . Jeremy Grenfeld as Don Diego de . . . Something . . . A castle burning, Grenfeld's rapier clink clink . . . and a swooned blonde's swooned breasts pointing at Grenfeld's teeth. That was how Ashley had seen Grenfeld then!)

But Grenfeld . . . on a poster? He was so un-English-looking! (That time of their first meeting Ashley hadn't known that Grenfeld was a Jew. Only that he had no acne and walked like a man with a purpose: more grown up — at that time — than Ashley, and Ashley had envied him.)

The Grenfeld brouhaha: Squadron Leader Johnson found the . . . documents on Hammett's desk; called Grenfeld in.

But Grenfeld — my God, what courage! what bravery! — refused to be a "monkey" (his word).

Squadron Leader "Snake" Johnson called in Luthie.

Half an hour later, Luthie requested Grenfeld's presence and told Grenfeld he need not do anything he did not want to do.
  . . .

("Well, he's cheeky, isn't he?" Luthie was. With Squadron Leader Johnson. Lately. There was tension in the air.)
  . . .

But "Snake" Johnson's birdbrain was fixed on the thought that having Grenfeld become famous would be wonderful for their . . . *cohesion.*

It caused a rift.

Now, *ordinary* life: it went on, too, of course. Squadron Leader Johnson took Ashley, Grenfeld, and Brown up. And so now they knew why the others hadn't talked after coming down: God, what a ride! A *dark* ride!

A man reckless: Squadron Leader Johnson. A man fearless.

A man . . . dangerous. But in what a . . . delicious way!

That afternoon, during his customary after-ops. nap, Ashley dreamed about it. He could not remember the dream by the evening — only that it had been about fear. In the dream he had been . . . well, would one call it that? . . . *in love* with fear.

And now that he was awake, he . . . well, missed it, suddenly; wanted more . . .

Was there something about the man's voice?

The voice: over the R/T . . . through the static . . . Ha! This was past danger excitement, this was a terror that grabbed one and held one . . . Would they dare *discuss* it later — or would they, too, say bugger off to anyone who asked?

"Luthie is always scared." Who said that? . . . What disloyalty!

But a strange exhaustion seemed to sit upon them that was quite different from the everyday fatigue of shooting at . . . at machines, of course — well, at people in the machines — and being shot at all the time. Ashley, for one, wanted very badly to be rid of the exhaustion. He longed to throw it off as one shrugs off a too-heavy blanket that stifles one's breath at night; and to achieve that he would run toward anything: toward an excitement that went beyond excitement . . .

"Now, about Luthie . . ." *Mutter mutter mutter.* To this day one could

hear the . . . not so much fear as the desperate *conscientiousness* underneath the calm *calm* surface of every command Luthie gave. But now he
no longer flirted with Buttercup — or anybody else — over the R/T!
He no longer sang

> Oh, it's home, dearie, home,
> Oh, it's home I want to be . . .

to make them laugh in *their* fear and thus make the prospect of facing
God-only-knew-how-many *bandits* a bit easier. Luthie was not as he had
been before.

He was cocky with "Snake" Johnson. Sure of himself. . . . Thought too
much of himself? How long would the man Johnson stand for it?

The man Johnson had caused a rift. They fought about Grenfeld —
purely for the sake of fighting? Because they were *falling in love* with the
tension?
    Only Grenfeld sat there, peered beyond them, as if it all did not con-
cern him, really. Then he got up, went off; left them to their quarreling.
    Going to *practice* his piano? The same idiotic six or seven notes over
and over. . . . My God!

And so Squadron Leader Johnson was proving to be both an irritating
thorn in their sides and a royal pain in the arse. Yes, he was . . . interesting. (*Mysterious,* as Luthie had been once, though in a vastly different
way, of course. Ashley conceded that.)
    But he was *poking his fingers into pies.*

And thus when the next day Squadron Leader Johnson went down while
on ops. with some of the Flight A people — disappeared; had gone for a
Burton; no parachute; would never be seen ever again — they celebrated. Danced: jumped about. Shouted for joy.
    Free! Free of the man! Liberated!!!
    . . .

    "Who's buying tonight? Gentlemen, let's drink — his health!"
    "Blotto. Definitely. Let's —"
    "Get drunk."

Force nine wind . . . Some structural damage . . .
    But no *damage* had occurred! They were intact! — though nobody
said so aloud. (But Ashley thought to himself he wouldn't peer just yet
into the corners of his mind: it seemed to him he was hiding a feeling
that they had escaped . . . something, just in the nick of time.)
    . . .

Now, sir . . . Luthie. *Give us one of your grins, will you now, sir?*
And Luthie was laughing. (He most certainly was one of them.)

"Get drunk."

Of course, without a squadron CO once again, Acklington and Luthie
would have to share the burden once again. . . . Well, good. Good. Wizard. Well, fate itself had brought things back where they should be: there
was that to be said for a war — it sometimes resolved matters beautifully.

"Let's get blotto."
(And then, as soon as Luthie was out of earshot: "Well, remember? Her
skirt's up here . . ." Luthie and the woman *dancing* at the sherry party.
"Nice legs."
"Too short."
"They're not too short. She's small. . . . You're daft."
Oh, and so they were liberated to return to the subject of Luthie
and the woman: when the Snake's arrival had forced them to turn their
minds to other matters, they had not been ready at all to let go of it yet!
But now Johnson was . . . history.)

Later that afternoon, Pilot Officer Newby was killed.
Had come home to die, actually; brought his kite in. (And most of the
Flight B men were still there to see it, though their day's work was done.
A perfectly ordinary landing: they had not noticed anything amiss.)
Newby had taxied up; cut the engine.
And the kite sat there. Sat there.
Somebody laughed. "Another bugger asleep!" (Well, it happened
with some frequency these days — people were *tired,* and nobody con-
sidered it noteworthy anymore, let alone alarming.)
But the kite sat. And sat.
And so the ground crew rushed forward to wake Newby up and begin
their work on the turnaround . . . And suddenly — at last! — the blood
wagon people seemed to wake up, too (there always was a blood wagon in
readiness); and the blood-wagon rushed forward, bell clanging . . .
Ashley and the other men of Flight B and the Flight A people ran.
Could not see much, though. (For a long time, they did not see anything.
They pushed and shoved. "What are they doing to him now?"
"Is it bad?"
"Can't see a bloody thing. . . . Let me see.")
Then, a stretcher. A shape on the stretcher: covered with a blanket.
The blanket pulled all the way up, over the shape's face: Newby was
dead. *And the cockpit swimming in blood* (as with the Fritz who had
landed on *enemy territory*).
. . .

Newby had never forgiven Flight B the episode of the deck chairs. But he had not deserved to die, really . . .

And *now* Ashley suddenly felt as if something were ending: Newby had been one of the last Flight A people they really knew, from back in Scotland. *No more beginnings*. Something was ending.

And so, instead of going off to sleep once the blood wagon was gone — bell *not* clanging — the men of Flight B sat in the grass and were together.

From somewhere Grenfeld's portable chessboard appeared.

Ashley watched Grenfeld and Stanhope playing chess. Ashley did not know much about chess. Some of the others began to play cards, but the game was over soon.

They were together.

And by and by, Flight A took off again, and this time Flight Lieutenant Acklington did not come back. Flight Lieutenant Acklington was overdue.

Somehow, news of it must have spread, because there was Luthie, quite out of the blue, in an RAF-painted Hillman (must have requisitioned it); at breakneck speed he dodged the tussocks of grass and the potholes; he braked, and his head almost went through the wind screen.

And so they all waited together. Grenfeld and Stanhope would give a chessman a push, every now and again, in silent concentration. They all passed Stanhope's peppermints around: rustle rustle.

And every ten minutes or so Luthie would go off to *bother* Uncle Dixon the Adj., to see whether there was any word — as even they, the men of Flight B, had done some days ago while waiting for Luthie.

And the woman came by, and she and Luthie went off together to speak to Uncle Dixon; and afterward they stood there, just the two of them, whisper whisper whispering together.

Well, did they know anything? What did they know?

They should not be whispering. It made people nervous.

But, in the end, the woman left: had to go to work, probably.

Thus the afternoon slipped into evening.

Ashley was hurting. He hurt for himself; and he hurt for Flight Lieutenant Acklington; and he hurt for Luthie.

He looked about — did not really *observe* the others: would not be right, somehow — but yes, they too seemed to be hurting.

Then . . . At last!!! Acklington was alive. He was in hospital.

Where? Some *nothing* little seaside town.

How bad was it? No news about that, yet.

•

And Ashley wished for his camera. . . . For the Hasselblad? God damn it all: any camera.

No, he did not wish for a camera!

But he knew he'd never forget the *potential* picture: Luthie outlined against the darkening sky, shoulders relaxed now, in relief; but his hands hanging empty by his sides; he was relieved and yet not relieved — not sure whether he should be relieved; the hands *empty:* a terrible emptiness, wanting to hold on to . . . hope.

Ashley would never forget that. (But it was too dark by then to take a picture, anyway.)

7 8

Hanmer   Come back   Live   Be well

7 9

That evening two people came to see about Ashley's motorcycle.

8 0

Friend   Nim

There is a false half-claim — a false half-kill — on my record because of Hanmer. I mean: for Hanmer's sake.

I've never told you this, now have I? I'm not sure that I'll ever tell you: getting to know each other???!

But that is how Hanmer and I became friends.

A human being burning to death sounds like a piece of bacon frying.

This is not a real letter.

Nim   Must I tell you?: sometime.

Nim   Did I ever tell you that Hanmer does not snore in his sleep: he puffs? Puff puff puff . . .

(And so I got down on my hands and knees, a while ago; looked under the bed. A stray sock? There must be a stray sock. But there wasn't.

Well, while I was at dinner earlier in the evening, *they* had scurried in — the effects people . . . Uncle Dixon? He *is* the effects officer — they had cleaned out Hanmer's half of the room.)

Nim   And we lost our respective breakfasts into the grass together, Hanmer and I — the time of Dunkirk; and then I tried to clean Hanmer up with my handkerchief, but he could not do the same for me because he does not carry handkerchiefs — a fop: oh, definitely! but disorganized; and then officially — well, it is on the record, I mean — I took upon myself one half of his guilt, though I did not want to do it, of course, and once it was done, he found of course it did not ease his conscience, anyway.

That is what binds us. . . . One should not have friends in wartime.

(I remember trying to make my bed *mine* when we arrived from Scotland. A dog-eared paperbound book half propped up against — half sliding off — the pillow, as if thrown there *very carelessly*. Dorothy Sayers, *Gaudy Night* — it takes place at Oxford.

And so now, my hand coming down: slowly, slowly . . . Shall I put the imprint of my palm on Hanmer's pillow? But it's not his pillow anymore.

And it would be *my* palm. . . . He's not here.)

Acklington   You miserable misery   Come back

I should try to let the Belgian woman know — she will not be notified officially: she is not next of kin. But I've no telephone number for her. No family name! *Hendrikje, London.* Well, God in heaven! God damn you, Hanmer!

. . .

I miss you. (He has been lung-shot: is fighting for his life. I learned an hour ago.)

Nim   Love
     That . . . that . . . wart Johnson: he is dead. The Wonders celebrated.

What do I want for them?

I suddenly felt hopeful again, I must say. Not just relieved or glad: I was happy! (And in no way ashamed of my happiness, I must say. . . . Only later did I try to find it within myself to pity him.)

I am myself.

I do think of his eyes: terrified (that first day when I went to see him). What was it he was afraid of losing?
     The silly man.
     A man of a dark-edged soul, though. I think.
     I never got to know him, of course. Well, that's how war is.
     I didn't want to get to know him: held him in contempt? He did not belong here. He should not have happened to us, at this point.

I cannot protect the Wonders from anything. And so they were begin-
ning to fall under his . . . spell: escaped just in time? Or has the inevitable
been merely postponed?

I seem to be waiting for something.

Hanmer's bed: smooth smooth *smooth* white sheets.
     He is not here. (It is as if he did not exist anymore.)

I want to make love to Nim on Hanmer's bed. Oh, absolutely!
     (Life exists.)

81

The Husqvarna roared into life, and down the road Ashley went. Faster.
Faster. Pouring on the speed. The beautiful loud *loud* sound of the engine in his ears; but it was the speed first and foremost that he craved, as
if wanting to leave something behind, so that it would never catch up to
him again. Damn it all! The road was too straight. His riding skill could
not be properly displayed here. And so he U-turned — the engine a sudden whine; the Husqvarna leaning, leaning into the turn *almost* dangerously; Ashley's foot on the ground, dragging on the rough paved surface,
briefly, to keep his balance . . . And then he jumped a ditch and was in
the fields: through the stubble fields he roared, zigzagging, twisting, a
cloud of dust surrounding him, little hard clods of earth hitting him in
the face and in the body; and he felt terribly, terribly lonely.
     But he would not bawl. He'd done that already. He was finished with
bawling.
     · · ·
     Tonight, the Husqvarna would go to its new rightful owner.
     · · ·
     And on and on he went, the wind in his face, making his cheeks burn
and his eyes water. God damn it all!
     What would his mother say . . . do? What would be inside her: what
would she feel when she learned John's motorbike was gone?
     "Bridget, put the kettle on." That was what she would say, of course.
     And Ashley saw his mother standing in front of the gilt-edged mirror
in the hall, and she stared: seeing anything at all? (Or was she seeing
John?)
     Would she now be angry with Ashley — angry enough to fly across
the room again (a plump little ball) and strike him in the face again? (Oh
my God, it had hurt!) That is: would she strike him should he happen to
be present? Because now John was really really dead.
     Well, she would cry in the end, of course. *Because John was really,*

really dead. (But of course the motorbike itself had at first meant but little to her, really. It was only after John was dead that it had become an object of value.) But mothers cried. Could not be helped. They were mothers.

And then Ashley saw her, in his mind's eye . . . waddling: she was not fat, really, only plump; but she rather waddled when she walked. He saw her sitting, her back terribly straight in a terrible resolve, and she was sipping her tea. Well, God damn it all!

And the wind was in his face.

Then he tried to think what his father would say or do when he heard, but try as he might, he could not think of anything. And that . . . rather terrified him. Suddenly, it seemed to him that perhaps he *should* know. But then again: Why should he? What did it matter? . . . Perhaps he should try to find out. . . . He could not ask him! Well, his father sometimes did write letters to Ashley: about . . . ordinary things. . . . Ashley addressed his own letters to *Dear Everybody:* that included Father, too, of course, and Bridget the scullery girl . . . Well, should he write a real letter to . . . ?)

(And Ashley braked hard, stopped, and killed the engine, and sat there straddling the motorcycle.)

Then he drove back toward the base at a sedate speed, still feeling lonely.

At the crossroads, he began to meet the base people and general traffic. Two Flight A men — he knew them slightly. Brown on a bicycle, leaning into the handlebars with determination, heading for the town; beyond the crossroads by now. Good. Good. Ashley felt lonely, but he did not want to be with anybody: did not want to have to wave, shout . . .

Luthie. Walking. From town. (Alone: the woman at work, probably; otherwise those two were as if glued together.)

Ashley did not want to be with anybody.

(Luthie must have been in town shopping: carried a smallish brown paper sack. And there was a rather hopeful spring to his step: well, the latest news was that Flight Lieutenant Acklington had survived the night, and surgery; was holding his own — even improving a bit, actually.)

But Ashley did not want to slow down.

Now he would have to, of course. He greeted Luthie; went on.

He was terribly alone; and suddenly, he did want to be with somebody. He pulled off to the side of the road, and waited.

Did a sergeant pilot offer a lift to his flight commander?

(Besides: were his eyes red, his eyelids puffed up, his nose swollen? Would Luthie recognize immediately that he had been trying not to bawl?)

"Sir . . . would you like a lift, sir?"

Would the man understand that this was a . . . ceremonial occasion?

(If anybody did, Luthie would. He would sense it. He would. He would. . . . Would he?)

And Luthie said: "Yes. All right. Thank you, Sergeant."

And so they proceeded toward the base, *sedately*. Another motorcycle — a dispatch rider's Norton — overtook them: then, a lorry. Luthie's package (a tin: biscuits? chocolates?) poked Ashley in the kidneys.

He parked the Husqvarna in what used to be and once again was the car park — only the ground was black, now: burnt; and there were fewer cars.

Excellent. Wizard. Good. Good, to have given Luthie a lift: with the man here, there could be no lengthy good-byes to the motorcycle.

And Luthie said once again, "Well . . . Thank you. Very kind."

God damn his *reasonable* eyes! Well, he knew, didn't he — he *understood!* It was there, in those eyes, the understanding — that for the camera Ashley was abandoning his . . . well, the thing that at one time had been *absolutely* precious to him! (But Ashley had wanted him to understand, hadn't he? And so why was he angry with the man now?)

Ashley was angry with Luthie.

Some time ago — for example — he had asked his permission to have the photographs published. (Still had but the vaguest of ideas how to go about it: where to send the pictures, etc., etc. Actually, he had been rather hoping that Luthie would suggest a likely . . . magazine?: *Life?* in America!) But Luthie had merely said he would think about the permission and would let Ashley know. But had he? He had not! Could not make up his mind? Had he forgotten? Too many things happening.

The woman had happened, that's what! God damn it all.

And so Ashley felt lonely.

Well, sir, what should I do now?

He was on his own. Would have to make his own decisions about . . . *everything:* the balance between making a *record* of events, for example, and carrying one's *observations* only within oneself, for example. And other things . . .

Or was there a balance?

He was . . . well, friends with people, maybe: he and Grenfeld were friends and all that; but still he was not a part of any crowd — and he was now neither proud of it nor wished for anything else. He was resigned, suddenly: accepting.

And then Luthie said, "Well, who is the lucky chap bought the Husqvarna?"

Ashley said, "The IO." The intelligence officer: he of the paunch tight against his belt. (And for some reason, it seemed rather silly just then to add *sir,* and so Ashley didn't.)

"Are you picking up the camera this evening, too, then?"

"Uh-huh."

For a while they chatted. Then Luthie said, "Well, good luck." And he grinned: one of those grins of his. And it was as if he were releasing Ashley.

From the war? No. No.

. . .

And Ashley wished with all his heart that the war had never happened, or that it could be after the war now, but with everything as before — except Ashley himself: he did not want to be as before. There was no going back, of course. Still . . .

Would there be welcome beginnings, after all?

And so they stood there, friends together.

8 2

I am hopeful.

I am feeling hopeful.

I permit myself to feel hopeful.

I hope Ashley will live to be a great-grandfather!

No, let us be *realistic* in our wishes: I hope he lives to use his camera.

I have neglected the Wonders a bit, lately. I think. Still, when I pause to think about it, I realize that, for some odd reason, they have come to mean as much to me as my own life. . . . Well, not quite. Almost.

. . .

Luthie. Idiot.

Go forth, Ashley the Nosy Parker . . . He still *is* an adolescent, in certain ways, isn't he? Ashley the Nosy Parker Adolescent!

. . .

I'm no less envious of his talents, though.

I've my own talents.

A few quick lines: Nim's eyebrows . . . a sketch of her face . . .

I've my own talents. Absolutely!

I sit here: scribble   scribble   scribble.

I am a man in love with words.

8 3

And then it all came crashing down.

A morning like any other, really — the morning it all came crashing down.

They came out on the tarmac about eight, though they were not up for ops. till eleven — one somehow could not stay away these days: it was as if sitting in the grass at Dispersal were *addictive*. The air was morning-cold and damp with dew. The Flight A people had already lit a fire in the Ready Room stove: used yesterday's *Times* and a magazine with naked women in it. Squabbling: should they have saved the naked women? (But everybody had seen them already. Many times.) And so they waited — the Flight A people were the ones waiting: by and by the Ready Room telephone would ring. (For the men of Flight B the wait would come later.)

The section officer from Signals came, and everybody quickly hid whatever naked women there remained. She had been on duty all night — looked tired and was on her way *home* to sleep; but she had fresh news about Flight Lieutenant Acklington. "He is . . . well, they call it *stabilized*. . . . *Stabilized* enough to be moved to an RAF hospital." From the *nothing* little town.

She was not speaking only to Luthie: everyone was included.

That copper hair of hers was truly magnificent (that was what Ashley thought; and Ashley was jealous).

Ah, she and Luthie: in public, they always stood at a polite distance from one another, didn't they? And, in public, they called each other *Mr. Luthie* and *Miss Tunnard-Jones* — even after that performance at the sherry party! My God! But Ashley had never ever in his life seen two people who were so . . . transparent about showing not only how much in love they were with each other but also how much they *liked* one another. Well, they were *shameless* about it, that's what!

What serious gray eyes! — the section officer from Signals. But when she looked at the man, she seemed joyful.

Luthie's eyes were utterly *un*reasonable! Utterly. *Grateful*. He was *grateful* to her, by God! And yet, there he stood: *his stork's legs double-jointed, proudly . . . And I'll never again be not double-jointed! By God!*

Well, it was . . . selfish of them, that's what, to show their happiness so much!

She yawned. Un-self-conscious. "Well, I'd better be off now. It's a long walk. I hope I can manage without falling asleep."

Practically the whole squadron laughed — not just politely, but as if she'd said something most wonderfully witty.

Out of the window, Ashley caught sight — they all must have caught sight — of a lorry coming. Bouncing on the unpaved path.

And Luthie went out and flagged the lorry down. Corporal Dunaway was driving — the one who always fawned on officers. Ashley knew that Luthie did not like him terribly much, really. Ashley himself did not like him. Who did? (He's the one always looks as if he's soaping his hands when he talks to officers — lathery-slathery: Farrell had said that once. . . . Farrell was a good observer, no doubt about it.)

Well, Corporal Dunaway did not seem to like Luthie's request much. He probably wanted to do his *fawning* on his own terms, that's what: *he* offered to do things; did not want to be asked to do them. But now he could not very well refuse, well could he? Served him right.

Luthie was back. "Ma'am . . ." He held the door open.

And he and the woman went out together.

And most of the squadron, both Flight A and Flight B, tagged along behind them. And so they all could see it — Ashley could see it! — Luthie handing her in. She hopped in: self-assured — *neat* — in every movement. And *self-contained*. (Had she run cross-country at school? Ashley remembered somebody asking that once.) And then . . . the two *lovers'* hands touching, for but a fraction of a second.

What had happened?
Nothing had happened. Everything had happened.
Well, that's how it always was with those two. God damn them!
(Ashley was jealous.)
· · ·

Luthie slammed the door shut. Waved to his *mistress.* . . . My God, what a word!

And she waved to him; and then to them. (My God, what a smile! No coyness about it: a smile like . . . a summer meadow . . .)

She looked tired; but she had taken off her cap, and her hair was *absolutely glorious*.

And the lorry was off.

Corporal Dunaway was cutting across the airfield. One should not do that: *it was forbidden;* but it was shorter that way: people did it all the time.

The rest of it Ashley would remember forever and ever; and yet it was all jumbled together . . . The siren: the siren first of all.

(Well, there almost never was enough warning.)

The Flight A people running for their kites, shouting. (Somebody Ashley did not know at all was leading them: Acklington was gone, after all — they had to have *somebody* to lead them.)

The loudspeakers blaring: "All personnel not engaged in operations take cover."

Shelter . . . Where is the bloody shelter?

But nobody ran for shelter: the men of Flight B did not run for shelter.

One two three Ju-87s — the bloody Stukas. What a sound! The . . . the furies from hell coming. Screaming. Screaming. *Cover your ears.*

Ashley covered his ears and hit the ground. Around him, everybody was hitting the ground.

But Ashley did not cover his head. . . . Did the others try to protect their heads? Did they cover their faces?

The lorry far away now: in the middle of the field — looking small. (Somehow, it had managed to dodge all the taking-off aeroplanes. Somehow, the aeroplanes had missed it.)

Luthie running.

Grenfeld . . . Grenfeld running!!!

One of the Stukas coming for another pass: at the lorry.

A second one coming for a pass: at Luthie and Grenfeld?

My God, who would have believed that Grenfeld could run so fast! *Faster than Luthie?* Faster . . . Catching up to him . . .

And then Grenfeld tackled Luthie — a wonderful rugger tackle: wizard! stunning! stunning! And they both went down, and around them the earth boiled, and — that boiling earth hiding them from view — they seemed . . . they seemed to be fighting: Luthie trying to fight off Grenfeld.

In the meantime, the lorry had exploded. And was burning.

And Grenfeld was crawling away now, like a whipped dog.

And Luthie was kneeling in the grass that was not grass at all any longer; and his hands were empty so terribly *empty;* and he . . . he looked as if he were confessing a . . . a dreadful sin of some sort.

Then he began to pound the ground with his fists in fury.

And then he crumpled like a rag doll and lay there.

That was how it all came crashing down.

Afterward:

Somebody — the wing commander himself! — said: "Take him to the Med. Section, for Christ's sake! Put him under. He needs an . . . injection."

Luthie said, "No, I am perfectly all right." (And on the *outside,* he did look all right: just filthy, with some scratches and — probably — later some bruises.)

The wing commander — a scarecrow of a man: they barely knew him, actually; hardly ever saw him — he said, "Flying Officer, this is an order."

Luthie said, "Do not touch me." And he said it in such a voice that Wings — a sensible man? — did not repeat the *order.*

•

In the afternoon — well, after 1100 hours — they went out as usual:
again and again. A day like any other.

It was not a day like any other. Were there even more Fritzes in the
sky than usual? And more killing. And there was a true joy in the killing — a frenzied scream-your-lungs-out-and-heart-in-the-mouth-and-
do-a-wild-dance joyfulness, and *no fear*.

A *dark* ride? Oh no, not at all.

Well, bugger the bastard Johnson! He was forgotten.

This was an afternoon's work never to be repeated: one could not —
would not — ever wish for another. Well, laugh and cry and kill . . . *No
fear*.

And Ashley got himself a Fritz who was hanging on a parachute. A
helpless bastard. And Ashley tore him into little pieces; and as he did so,
he could hear himself laughing; and sweat poured down his back . . .

Elation. Exultation. *Exaltation*. A grand victory with a true wildness
of joy.

Oh, not a *dark* ride! Oh, Ashley's head was filled with a *blinding light!*
He felt as if everything within him were about to explode. *No fear*.

And they were . . . doing it for Luthie. They were . . . *dedicating* this
to Luthie. *Laying it at his feet*. What else could they do for him?

What more could he want from them? God damn him!

And by the time the day was over, two of them were gone — dead —
had not come back; but the shock of *that* would come only later. Ashley
— for example — felt it at first merely around the edges.

Brown had crashed on takeoff sometime in the middle of the afternoon; and it was rumored — whispered — that it was the ground people's fault: they had done something wrong or had not done something at
all during that last turnaround because even they were ever so terribly
tired and besides, they didn't really give a damn about the Browns of this
world, did they? And so even in death Brown remained somehow . . . on
the fringes, because he had not died as he should have done: in battle,
slain by The Enemy.

But Cartwright had.

But the shock of that would come only later.

(In the meantime, it was rumored that there would be an *inquiry* into
Brown's death.

As if it *really* mattered how one died.)

About teatime — their work was done by then — there was yet another
air raid alarm: it turned out to be only an alarm, though (in the end the
Fritzes had decided to hit the satellite field instead); but this time they all
did run for the shelter, because by then the shock *was* beginning to seep
in: two of them were dead — Luthie's magic had broken down and could
never be put together again; and all of them were mortal. They sat in that

black hole, and a little rain of black earth fell on their heads (in spite of there being no explosions); and in the corner Luthie was weeping ever so softly: silently.

He was crying: blubbering. So now he would be all right.

And Grenfeld huddled in another corner: Grenfeld *undone, unmanned* — and all that — completely. Staring straight ahead.

Grenfeld: what a grand gesture! He had rushed forth to save Luthie's life (because by then nothing could be done to save the woman): he had done it to prove something . . . to himself? . . . to Luthie? But the war . . . and all that . . . and life itself; and everything: it was too enormous for Grenfeld — too enormous for everybody; and so one was helpless, could not do anything . . . God damn it all!

And then by and by it came to Ashley that he probably had not been in love with the section officer from Signals after all, because he did not think so much about her now as about Luthie.

Incredibly enough, the woman had survived. Must have jumped from the lorry at *absolutely* the last moment. But, of course, the fire did engulf her. Would she live? She was terribly burned, of course.

Would she live?

Usually, it was the men in war: they were maimed, burned . . . and so on. And what would their women do then?

Grown up. This was *grown up.* The kind of *grown up* that Ashley had never ever thought about before and would never ever want; and it was now Luthie's.

Luthie was crying.

That was how it all came crashing down.

8 4

When the war broke out — when I went off to war (only training, at first, but I was *going off to war:* this was before I'd got my dogshit Austin and so there we were, my people and I, at the station, and the stationmaster — not Mr. Mannington: old Mr. Mannington was retired by then — Mr. Mannington's nephew the stationmaster brought us a cup of tea to make the waiting easier; then the train did come; then, the train pulling out of the station), my father said — his very last words before the train pulled out, and he said them in the voice of someone who knows everything is lost — he said, "Come back unchanged."

My mother, who had never loved me: she gave him a *terrible* look and said to me, "Come back."

Nighttime thoughts.

PART FOUR

85

I

There was grass and sandy soil: the time of Dunkirk.

And I lay in the grass, in a darkness that did not come from a night sky; but then the darkness lifted, and the *coal's cuttles* came.
    . . .

I am a man who loves words.
Words shall be my nightmare.

I'll see Nim tomorrow.
    Tomorrow I'll go and see her.
    Her family will be there, no doubt. I have never met them.
    I don't know much about them. I know *nothing* about them.
    Do they know at all of my existence? Will they resent my presence?
    . . .

I am babbling.

Before I went over Dunkirk for the very first time, my father the pacifist had given me a knife.
    . . .

I must finish the story.
    I am telling the story.
    Things repeat themselves: the same, yet different, different, yet the same.
    . . .

Or is the story finished?

I am telling the story.
    I remember: I telephoned my people. "Do you think you'd want to meet me at Manchester, Central Station, six o'clock tomorrow morning?

I've an hour and a few minutes between trains. . . . Oh. Outside Platform Two."

I was not permitted to tell them where I was going. Strictly speaking, I should not have telephoned at all: they should not know till after the fact that I was going anywhere. They knew at once where I was going.

. . .

And the next morning: the sun barely rising; the world: innocent. (The little antimacassar on the headrest of the seat opposite mine: dirty.) On the way to Manchester, before I went over Dunkirk for the very first time.

I must not forget to bring flowers tomorrow: yellow suns.
Lavender.
Chamomile.

. . .

When I first saw her, she was a woman who *eats her dinner neatly*.

. . .

I'll bring yellow suns. Oh, definitely!

Hanmer   You misery   Come back   Be here with me   Help me

I am telling the story:
Nobody paid attention to me on the train to Manchester: so early in the morning, the sun barely rising.
Nobody reviled me: well, it would happen to RAF people *after* Dunkirk — they would be reviled, even accosted in the streets and all that, for not having done enough (that was how many people saw it). Well, nobody reviled me, but no one gazed at me in gratitude and adulation, as they do now. There was nothing for them to *understand* about me; I had no need to be understood by them, and no anger or despair within me because of not being understood.
I simply sat there, holding all my fears in the palms of my hands.
I remember that one of those many fears was that I might not be courageous enough in combat. Well God Christ!
The world: innocent.

The train: early arriving at Manchester; my people were late. Had they, too, taken the train (as a rule, trains are late in wartime) — or had they decided to drive?
Sit on a bench, Luthie. Pretend to be reading a magazine: *Granta,* I remember. (A Cambridge student effort: *Granta* . . . Once a Cambridge man, always a Cambridge man?)
Get up and wander about, scanning the crowd. Bump into people.
Look out! An old man. Very old. Shuffling shuffling shuffling. *Not*

carrying luggage. Well, how could he manage to carry anything? Shuffling shuffling shuffling.

. . .

God in heaven! There are times when I hope I die young.

. . .

I may be dead by tomorrow morning. By this afternoon.

. . .

Where *are* they? My parents.

(My mother who had never loved me.)

Well, here's a personable-looking female of approximately my age! Pretty. A *pert* hat. Nice legs. Breasts: *womanly* — absolutely! underneath her travel-crumpled jacket. Nice eyes: cheerfully looking out at the world. A suitcase *heavy*. . . . "Pilot Officer Luthie, ma'am.". . . I'll do it! I'll do it! (Have never done anything of the sort before.) I'll ask permission to carry the suitcase for her wherever it needs to be carried.

And then *they'll* come; and I'll not be there.

. . .

And I'll be dead by tomorrow; and they'll be sorry.

My mother running.

My mother never runs. She walks briskly: her *brisk* walk can be quite intimidating, sometimes. She does not run.

Her hat in her hand: it must have fallen off as she ran.

My mother is very small: like Nim.

She stopped: a stillness about her.

My mother is not like Nim at all: there is something flawed about my mother.

She seemed to take a deep breath and then she broke into a run again. We *collided;* I put my arms around her. Her hat between us: we were crushing it. "Well, that horrid policeman . . . Well, he said your father could not park the motor there . . ." They *had* driven, then!

And then she stood, rather *leaning* against me, a stillness about her.

And so I said, stupidly, "Don't worry. I'll be all right. I promise. I'll be careful. I'll telephone tonight, to tell you I am all right. I'll telephone again tomorrow evening . . ." What in the world was I getting myself into?

And then out of the corner of my eye I caught a glimpse of my father hurrying hurrying — limping quite badly: an old man . . .

. . .

Well, there are times when I hope I die young! (That was what I thought then. Later . . . Nim, I want to live to be a great-grandfather!)

. . .

And my father, too, stopped and — for a few moments — he looked . . . pleased: it always makes him happy to see my mother and me friends together; but I did not quite trust her love for me in those days yet.

Then we had breakfast in the station restaurant: I ate — did not know what I was eating — but I wolfed it down, I remember; and we talked — well, about the orchard, mostly; about the dreadful winter just past: had it damaged the orchard? My father was worried. "We should ease out the pearmains," I said, "concentrate on the pippins. The pearmains . . . the taste is wonderful, but they are so fragile, difficult to transport, hard to store . . ." I held forth: a practical man. And we talked talked could not stop.

Then it was time to go: another train; and then a bus, to a base in the Midlands. There I'd pick up a Spitfire for myself; fly her to Kent.

And in the Gents — this was still the station restaurant: we stood washing our hands, my father and I; then my father gave me the knife. Pushing this vicious thing at me (one of those: touch a spring, the blade comes out): "Here, take it, take it. Before somebody comes, sees us. It saved *my* life once. In the First War, you know."

Medical personnel are not supposed to carry weapons. But I did not say anything.

I'll bring flowers to Nim tomorrow.
I'll bring myself.

Somebody   Please   Help me
I am cold.

I am a just man in a just war.
(I went to war for the sake of people like Vřešťala's mother.)
(The Wonders, this afternoon . . .)

No, I think of yellow suns.
Lavender.

II

Foreknowledge:
I was four, five years old — coal's cuttles lurked in the deepest darkness.
And insects rubbed their legs together — their wings: *Amritsar, Amritsar,* they said: a word that sounds like paper being crumpled . . .
(Amritsar: There are hatreds in the world.)

There was grass, the time of Dunkirk; and the *coal's cuttles* came.
And so . . . slowly, slowly . . . I raised myself to my knees: a terrible way to be before one's childhood nightmare — on one's knees.
Slowly, slowly, I lifted my head and I looked at them, one after the other. Looked them in the face. Bravely. And I counted them, bravely: one two three four.
But it did no good.

On ran Dingo   Yellow Dog Dingo
Always hungry   Hungry in the sunshine
(Oh, a horrible thing!: to be *hungry in the sunshine*.)
Grinning   Grinning   Grinning like a coal's cuttle

And so . . . slowly, slowly . . . I got to my feet, and slowly I raised my hands above my head. *I am yours*.

(I should have finished my storytelling earlier. Long ago.
What would have happened had I finished earlier? Daylight: I'd have reached daylight, I think; brought up to daylight the things that would stay hidden in the . . . ghost-time: the hours when ghosts begin to walk.
Never mind.)

Slowly I raised my hands above my head.
Then I handed over my Colt .45 that I had in my boot.
 . . .

(When he had given me the knife, my father — being my father — had said, "Use it with good judgment.")
 . . .

(Come back unchanged . . .)

III

What did I want for my miserable Wonders?
(I'll not think about the Wonders now.)

IV

Nim: She'll live, of course.

(A pen: a piece of paper:
These are her eyebrows — yet again. Again. Hundreds of eyebrows.
These are her eyebrows when echoes of David are in her heart.
These are her eyebrows when she looks at me.
 . . .

Oh, I am good at drawing! I've talent, no doubt about it. . . . . Ha!
 . . .

These are her eyebrows when she is asleep.
These are her eyebrows when she is asleep after our lovemaking.
 . . .

The last time we made love, I'd crawled in through the window. A pebble against the windowpane; she'd opened the window quickly.
Christ! Dreadful things would happen to both of us should we be caught. Guards patrol the perimeter of the women's living quarters.

Her bed is as narrow as mine.

. . .

Beautiful eyebrows: N. M. Tunnard-Jones.
Serious gray eyes: N. M. Tunnard-Jones.
(Gray eyes: two spoonfuls of gray ashes?) . . .
(Is *that* what I was waiting for, then, to finish the story: foreknowledge?)

Father

She will live. Of course.

V

There was grass and sandy soil, the time of Dunkirk.
And the barest breath of wind stirred the treetops, and the coal's cuttles had forced me back to my knees — they had the knife: they'd found the miserable knife — I hadn't handed it over. I'd kept it hidden in the other boot.

. . .

"Use it with good judgment . . ."
"Come back unchanged . . ."
"It saved my life once . . ."

My Dear People

No.

Father
It was a hot day — unseasonably hot weather, the time of Dunkirk. Cold sweat poured from me; and blood ran down my palms, between my fingers — soaked the seat of my trousers.
My hands bound behind my back. With a piece of ordinary string. A thin string. And the string cut into the wounds in my wrists, and it sliced through the skin around the wounds: skin untouched yet — unharmed; well, they had pushed me at one point and I had fallen. I'd fallen, and my bound wrists had struck the ground — a rock? a pebble?

Five months later: I threw a pebble against Nim's windowpane; she opened the window quickly; we made love.

My wrists had struck the ground, and the blood had spurted — a jet of blood, a geyser of blood: I'd never have thought such a thing possible — a geyser.
Then I was on my knees, and I felt faint.
Father   It hurt quite badly.

Father   *It was a pain that cannot —* cannot *— be described in words. (I am a man who loves words.)*

Father   *I was in a great deal of pain.*

And they pressed the muzzle of my own Colt .45 — my very own — to the base of my skull. They pressed the gun — very firmly — where the hair ends and bare skin begins: it feels cool. It's as cool a feeling as . . . as a fresh pillow in the evening. Comfort.

Comfort perverted.

(And everything turns to blight.

We are a family blighted.)

There was silence. I sweated.

There was not silence. Click: and the gun was off safety.

Through the sandy soil, in front of my eyes, an ant was making its way purposefully, struggling with a burden of a crumb of bread.

And there was a darkness: a blackness within me.

An ant: alive.

I hated. Hated hated hated.

There was a darkness.

I hated . . . not *the ant.*

Nighttime thoughts.

Father

You've never asked me what happened to your knife.

VI

Both my uncles, both my father's brothers — my uncle George Henry and my uncle Robert: their lives ended on the Somme a long time — three years — before my life began.

My grandparents learned of both deaths on the same day: one telegram not long after breakfast; one in mid-afternoon.

My grandmother saved both telegrams. After she was dead — after my people came *home?* (would the house of his parents, his mother's house, ever again be a "home" to my father?) — after they came Home from India, my father found the telegrams one day in the "secret" compartment of her little spindly-legged, rosewood-and-ivory-inlaid writing desk. The message in both is written out by hand.

. . .

My father the pacifist.

My grandmother: her hair like Devon cream; like Ayah's bracelets, necklaces, and earrings just on the verge of needing more silver polish.

VII

Nim.
    She'll live, of course.
    (Foreknowledge.)

VIII

I am telling the story.
    I must finish the story. Why, in God's name? Reach for daylight. (Descend into darkness . . . ?)
    Nobody wants to know how I lived.
    Twenty, thirty, fifty years from now, nobody will know how I lived. . . . Do I want them to know how I lived?

I am telling the story of Dunkirk:
    The coal's cuttles: grinning. (This was before they'd pressed the gun to my skull. . . . I am telling he story as it happened. This is how it happened. I have left nothing out; I will leave nothing out.) Well, I'd handed the Colt over. (That was the only thing I'd handed over. I'd kept the miserable knife.)
    One of the four asked — indicated . . . whatever: "Anything else?"
    I hesitated: then shook my head in . . . feeble resolve.
    (Had I not hesitated, would they have believed me?)
    They were grinning, and their grins were evil.
    (It is almost five months later now.)
    · · ·

Their hands; their feet; ears; hair; the very shapes of their bodies: fairly ordinary, really. They were ordinary people, no doubt.

Father
    They were four ordinary men. Had I met each of them separately, the outcome would have probably been quite different.

There were four of them; and because there were four — four together — and I was alone and I was helpless and I was afraid, and because there was a war on (their rifles at the ready — definitely: looked a bit silly, actually, I suppose — four rifles against one frightened man), did it make them feel like . . . like a clutch of nine-year-olds daring one another to pull the wings off a fly?
    · · ·

    Grinning grinning
    · · ·

The nightmare of my childhood.

They were ordinary people.

. . .

(It is almost five months later now.)

. . .

When they searched me and found the knife (of course), they erupted in a rage self-righteous.

Father
Should I have given them the knife?
(The law — the law of war: a captive must always give up his weapons.

I was in their power — but I had attempted to keep a small piece of my own power to myself. *(Use it with good judgment.)*
(Their anger: righteous.)
(The wrong kind of power? . . . I'd broken the rules.)
And so, first they pressed the tip of the blade against my throat.
Dignity.
I must die with dignity.
Then . . . Well, they tortured me.
And they could feel my pain, I think: in their own bodies they could feel it, but yet they didn't feel it, of course; and because they both felt it and didn't feel it, my terror and my undignified howling . . . my suffering: it brought them joy.
Christ! The things they threatened to do to me with that knife! (It brought them joy.)
Their anger: righteous.
(There are hatreds in the world.)
They were ordinary people.

Father
You know what happened to your knife.
You've seen the scars.
(St. Joseph's: Cannas grew in front, big red red enormous hibiscus in the back.

Through all those years you never touched a patient with a surgeon's hand, but to this day your fingers are a surgeon's fingers.)
I remember: after Dunkirk; I was in hospital (before being sent to the convalescent place) — an Air Ministry WAAF had telephoned at last: you and Mother rushed to my bedside.
I remember: I was awake; weak as a kitten. My lungs still burning: I could not breathe. But I was awake.
A VAD in the door; Mother and you on her heels. And you looked at me — a lightning-quick glance! God yes — a physician's *eyes!!! For but a fraction of a second. I remember. I remember! A physician's eyes: first, foremost. Well, a physician's and a father's eyes. Then they simply became a father's eyes a fraction of a second later.*
You know what happened.

IX

Nim:
> She'll live. Of course.

Nim:
> She's not beautiful. She is lovely.

Nim:
> The very last part of the last movement of the Dvořák cello concerto.
> . . .
> I am telling the story.
> . . .
> She . . . was lovely.

Natural fingernails, N. M. Tunnard-Jones. . . . Never paints her finger-nails, N. M. Tunnard-Jones. Her fingernails are always clipped short, neatly neatly.
> She does not bite her fingernails.
> I bite mine. They're bitten to the quick.

I am babbling.

The quick and the dead.
> . . .
> Oh, in God's name, Luthie! I am babbling.

I am telling the story of Dunkirk!

X

The story:
> A cot, a blanket, and a cushion (not a pillow) — the time of Dunkirk; the building: made of stone; the stone: weeping. (The inside walls were painted: plastered and painted . . . whitewashed?; the paint: damp and stained with the stones' weeping.)
> The building did not hold the heat of the day.

Well, I've begun to tell this story once before, haven't I?
> Christ! I've told them all, now. All the stories. Hinted at them, at least: mentioned them. Not like this, though: I've told only one half of this story.
> I have not finished the whole story. (Are things rising to daylight, slowly?)

•

Pain. (The blood on my clothing drying slowly: it stank.)

Loneliness. (Stand very still. . . . It seemed to me that I did not take up any space. God in heaven, was I made up of nothing but thin air?

I told myself I did not exist; therefore there was no need for me to wish *not* to feel lonely.)
 . . .

Night.

(Earlier — afternoon: a village; Germans Germans Germans Germans *swarming*. . . . I have told about this once before. . . . *Take a snapshot to Send Home to Mother* with their tourists' cameras, the Germans. . . . Darkness closing in on me.) Now it was night.

Pain.

Nim   She is floating on the surface of her pain. (They've given her morphia, no doubt. I hope.)

I am telling the story of Dunkirk:

I was locked in the village school storage room. I was alone. (Pain.)

Plen-i-tude Plen-i-tude of stitches (On the cushion, an angelic-looking child embroidered: sleeping.)

Plen-i-tude. Plen-i-tude. (As in *Cu-ra-tor Cu-ra-tor — very softly;* and other words of childhood . . .)

(Oh, what homesickness for *Cu-ra-tor Cu-ra-tor very softly*, for everything that was good about childhood!)

My father is not an apple grower by choice or inclination.

After his first wife's death, he had resolved to give up his birthright in favor of my uncle Robert; but my uncle Robert died on the Somme.

Did my father's life, too, end on the Somme?
 . . .

I am babbling. Utter, utter nonsense!

But in some respects . . .

("And so I went out . . ." — well, he told me that, my father: on Sunday, 3 September, 1939: he told me . . . I remember! steam rising, the bathtub, an end-of-the-summer fly, undercarriage in poor working order — he said: "I went out" — out of the tent operating room — "and I rubbed my face against a tree trunk: I wanted to hate the tree for hurting me, so that my hatred of people would not overwhelm me."
 . . .

And my uncle Robert died.
 . . .

"Did you tell them?" My grandparents.

"She called me *her son's murderer*. She did." My grandmother. "Not my brother's; her son's."
 . . .

I was sixteen: my grandfather died. My grandmother: I wanted comfort from her; she could not give it.

"Grandmama . . . Lunch. Here's some nice curry."

I fed her. It was undignified.

"Robin . . . Robert . . . Read the obituary in the *Times* again."

The obituary was not long. My grandfather: not an important man. But how long before I ever told her that my name was not Robert?

· · ·

All this is part and parcel of the story of Dunkirk.)

Nim   I want to take your pain upon myself!
(Nim   Nim   You know this is not a real letter.)

I can feel that pain. I can feel it. Tearing at my flesh. . . . There.

· · ·

I cannot feel it, of course.

I . . . listen for it. Cannot feel it.

The story of Dunkirk:

I was cold (night: the time of Dunkirk).

I needed to rest. (On the cushion, over the child's head, an invitation was embroidered, in French: "Just half an hour's rest . . .")

The overhead light hurt my eyes. *Look for the light switch, Luthie.* (And a stuffed parrot watched my progress. The village school's storage room: copybooks and pencils in boxes; a file cabinet; globes — of the earth as well as of the heavens; an artificial palm tree in the corner . . .

· · ·

"Children, today we shall learn about faraway places.")

But the switch was outside, in the hall! (It must be.)

And thus, in a panic, I began to *nudge* the cot toward the wall: would the cabinet shield me? And that brought them: a young scrawny-neck; an old paunch. Their two big Walthers at the ready. (And I stank, and they wrinkled their noses.)

I said in German — my *unaccomplished* German, "I move my bed."

Father

It took some effort. But I turned my pristine, beautifully bandaged hands palms up. Father . . .

I showed those two my helplessness. Pain.

And the younger of the two: he *liked* my helplessness. . . . His gun trained on my belly.

· · ·

He'd not kill me. No, not at once, anyway.

He'd . . . hurt me. Destroy me.

. . .

But Old Paunch: he hesitated. Had he guessed at once where I wanted the miserable cot carried? And he thought about it, then handed the younger one his Walther. He dropped the cot by the cabinet: *thud.* Then he picked up the blanket . . . did not *throw* it. Grabbed the cushion. He whacked it. Placed it on the cot. Scooped it up again. . . . A few more whacks. (I have told this story before.) *He was fluffing the bloody thing up for me!*

And so we stared at each other.

. . .

I should have said thank you.

. . .

I remember that I glanced down then at my boots. Well, that very morning they'd looked nice. *Walk out into the world with op-ti-mism!*

Now I stood there. Feet helpless. Feet apart slightly, to keep my balance. I felt lightheaded. I had a fever.

Pain.

Knees forward . . . I tried not to appear so terribly double-jointed.

Helplessness. And I was very, very lonely.

Then Old Paunch himself said, "Thank you." In English. Not doing well with the "th." A plaintive voice? A child rejected? . . . God in heaven!

"Thank you," he said again. A voice of one offended.

And again. And this time, he flung it in my face: an insult.

He quickly retrieved his Walther from Young Scrawny-neck.

(No. . . . No. Please don't . . .)

But . . . the door slammed behind them. (Darkness soft as the old skin on my grandmother's old arms . . . I'd sought comfort from her once; she could not give it.)

I should have said thank you. I should have said . . .

. . .

The light: on again.

They laughed. They went on laughing. (The light: off and on; on and off. They were tormenting me.)

. . .

But I slept then, in spite of the light; and when I woke up, I felt . . . better. Pain? Oh good God, yes! But I could do . . . anything. *Anything!*

Walk out and keep walking and feel the grass under my feet!

. . .

Walk out and be shot. Walk out and die. So that I'd not feel so terribly lonely.

. . .

Walk out and become as a lowly homing pigeon: home home home home home.

(This is the end of the first part of this story.)

Nim   Home
   Nim   I've told you how to eat an apple, haven't I? Rub your palms around it, then sniff your palm. Only then *you bite into the apple.*

Dunkirk:
   There were pencils in boxes: Dunkirk. (How many pencils to a box?)
   . . .
   I'll create a . . . disturbance! I'll scream and shout. (Dunkirk. The second half of the tale: Dunkirk.)
   (And when somebody comes running, again — somebody; anybody! — I'll stab them with a pencil! Then I'll escape!!!)
   But I think I began to laugh then: the bloody pencils were not even sharpened! (Loneliness: *well, laugh to yourself, softly.* A man alone. On his own. Completely. A *man on his own:* not a *man independent.* . . . Christ! As abandoned as a man can be!)

(It is five months later now.
   I am telling the story as it happened: no ghosts with me yet, then. They came later.
   . . .
   I was a man *ordinary.*)

Defiance. A subdued defiance. (I had no one to feel lonely for! There was no one to make me feel lonely!)
   A flame of rage: I hated hated hated . . . Hated Hated Hated
   (But I was not sure at all, really, whom my hatred was for.)
   . . .
   (The coal's cuttles had pressed the gun to my head: I had hated hated hated *not* the ant.)

The Wonders   This afternoon
   (I'll not think about the Wonders.)

I looked about. (Dunkirk.)
   Bottles of ink, in boxes. (One, two . . . five ink bottles to a box.)
   . . .
   I'll shout and scream, and then when they come, I'll simply throw ink in their faces!
   . . .
   (Luthie . . . Unscrew the top of one of those bottles with those miserable hands of yours? . . . My right hand: the pain in it was different from the left. Well, a pain added! Had I sprained something? Bones broken?)
Cold. . . . And I shivered; my teeth chattered.

But I wanted to be free, the green grass under my feet . . .

I wanted to die, so that the blackness that I felt within me — the darkness of the soul I had never ever before known I was capable of carrying within me — would be gone . . .

I am telling the story:

I'll not think about the Wonders.

The dead parrot: watching me with his dead eyes.

The file cabinet: it contained . . . well, files. (The overhead light hurt my eyes. That electric light: where had it come from? Most of the houses in the village: nothing but rubble.

Ah, arrogant bastards, the Fritzes! Organized. *Wealthy*. . . . Bloody hell! *Self-confident* enough to light their way with a generator? And to light *my* way — and so hurt my eyes?

· · ·

Defiance. Hatred.

· · ·

But no one can stand up to them. Nobody!

Well, that was what I thought then. . . . I think so now.

· · ·

Desolation.)

· · ·

I want to go home   Home home home home home
I want to die at home

· · ·

(India is my home. . . . Loneliness. And I moved as if through a country covered with a mist. I had a fever, I think.)

The files (the pupils' files):

Vanderhoeven, Jacqueline . . . (People about Dunkirk speak Flemish, many of them.)

Mélançon. François-Pierre . . .

(And I had almost fainted with pain, struggling to open that uppermost drawer. Shall I bother with the middle one?)

More files. And . . . toys. Toys?! Confiscated by the *dour* teachers? Ah, the poor buggers: *fidgety* little scholars!

· · ·

(*Children, today we shall learn about how W. R. Luthie used to draw maps instead of doing his Latin prep. Spectacular maps — absolutely! Flights of fancy, but true to reality; faithful to the truth of my imagination* . . . Well, never mind.)

There was a spinning top. A small doll: the paint peeling off her porcelain (?) nose. A book: *La Prairie Flamboyante: Les Aventures Merveilleuses du Cowboy Jim*. A crumpled-up paper sack half-full of marbles . . . (Yes, Luthie! A nice read of *Les Aventures du Cowboy Jim* to help you go back to sleep. It's over, Luthie. Tomorrow the *boches* will hand you over to the Luftwaffe.)

(And: *Plen-i-tude Stitches* etc. etc. "Just Half an Hour's Rest". . .)

. . .

A knife. (In the corner of the file cabinet drawer.)

My heart stopped.

(Well, a small boy's pocketknife, in the corner of the file cabinet drawer.)

I felt no pain. Suddenly.

Cunning. . . . Triumph!!!

Touch the knife . . . Well, touch it: my soul light! (The very core of my being at peace. . . . Christ, the sweetness of hatred! The quiet satisfaction of revenge. I felt not righteous nor self-righteous, really — not at all, but *virtuous* in what I was contemplating.)

I'll not think about the Wonders — about anything that happened this afternoon.

The knife: a dark wooden handle, well worn; wood cool under my hot fingers, and smooth . . .

(But this was a *child's* knife!: not a weapon. Luthie . . .)

No pain, though. . . . Triumph. Victory. (And smugness.)

Use it with good judgment. (Touch the knife with joy. With gratitude. With reverence: the tool that would be my *redemption!* All the things that hurt . . . cut them loose. . . . Set all the wrongs right.

I felt lightheaded. I had a fever, I think.

I did not think. I did not plan, really. . . . I had a fever. . . . I only acted.

How do I open the knife — make the blade come out? (Oh, I was possessed of a strength superhuman! . . . Quite.) Well, at least I had enough sense to grasp the knife with my left hand. . . . I am right-handed. Can I strike with my left hand?

I did not think.

I . . . *created a disturbance.* I shouted and screamed.

That brought them: Young Scrawny-neck; Old Paunch. Eyes sleepy.

I said, "I must go to the toilet. W.C. . . . *Verstehen?*" I shouted, in English, "I have to piss, God damn you!" (They had not even provided me with a bucket for my bodily needs, God damn them.)

Young Scrawny-neck smirked. Old Paunch, rubbing the slumber from his eyes, said something to him; Scrawny-neck didn't like it much, it seemed. But Paunch motioned to me: "Let's go, then."

And carefully . . . *careful, Luthie, careful* . . . I kept my hands folded across the belly: hands raised slightly, as if keeping them down would make blood rush to my wounds and thus make the pain worse.

Father
I shielded the left hand with my right.
Father
I shielded the knife with the palm of the left hand. Father, I held the knife flat against me . . .

with . . . love. (And yet I was on my own. Oh, definitely!: a most wonderful feeling of *independence*.)
But I was afraid: this was only a *child's* knife.

Father   the pain was back.
· · ·
What shall I do now?

I was cold. . . . The building did not hold the heat of the day.
Young Scrawny-neck had stayed back. It was just Old Paunch propelling me along.
Where was the bloody bog, anyway? Inside the building? Outside?
The hallway: short. (A man passed: brushed against me. I stumbled: the knife almost slipped out! Christ! The man exchanged a word or two with Paunch, then laughed . . . at me? or not at me? In my face! Not in my face? He walked into one of the four (?) classrooms; the door slammed.)

They'll shoot me. I'll die.
I'll no longer be lonely.

I carried a blackness of the soul within me.
· · ·
Father
· · ·
(Old Paunch: he who had *fluffed up* the bloody cushion for me.
Old Paunch: he who had . . . tormented me: the light off and on . . . And he and Scrawny-neck: they had laughed about it.)
· · ·
We were outside.
The outhouse loomed large . . . menacing . . . God in heaven!
Somewhere . . . far? not far at all? the sky was burning. So that was the west. That was where I had to go. (And the sound of the guns was like a distant thunder.)
· · ·

Home home home home home

I am telling the story as it happened.

There must be sentries about.

But it was night, and The Enemy seemed to be sleeping. (Tomorrow they'll move on. The officer — a receding hairline; receding chin — had told me that. *Divulging military secrets.* Ha! Tomorrow . . .

The Enemy seemed to be sleeping now, though.)

They'll kill me.

And suddenly, the knife was in my hand, and my hand was . . . strong (?): not strong at all — I felt the pain: pain unbearable, but I . . . ignored it. Oh, I was possessed of a strength superhuman! . . . I spun around.

This was a *child's* knife: meant for carving one's initials into a classroom desk! for example. *François-Pierre Mélançon sat here.* It was not a weapon.

I struck wildly. Not aiming.

Well, I aimed for the face. For the . . . eyes.

. . .

The Old Paunch who had fluffed up the cushion for me. He screamed terribly.

I did not scream.

I ran.

This morning: I remember running running
The lorry a ball of flames Exploding

Nim . . .
My fault.

Nim:
She'll live, of course.

XI

I am telling the story of Dunkirk:

Well, they shot at me, and they almost got me: I still have my old flying jacket with the bullet hole in it to prove it.

They gave chase, but the merciful night swallowed me; and I ran and ran, but then I could run no longer; and so I . . . died. But then after some time I was alive again, though uncertain: how should a creature *un*dead feel?

•

> I'd rather stand around
> Piccadilly Underground

I sang to myself; and I traveled as if through a country covered with a mist. I walked and walked. The sky was burning.

And I cursed to myself. Horrible words, really.

I walked as if through a country covered with a mist.

Out of the night shadows the dog Shadow came. (Ghosts usually walk at about four in the morning. . . . It was about four in the morning by then, I suppose.)

And we traveled the road together, the dog Shadow and I; but he would not permit me to touch him. For some reason, it was most terribly important to me that the dog Shadow should permit me to touch him. "Well, it's not my blood you are smelling — it's another's," I said. . . . Both mine and the German's, actually. . . . "It will dry," I said. The blood would dry. And I said to the dog Shadow: "Don't be afraid of me. I'll take you home with me. We'll get home, you'll see. . . . And this will be as if it had never happened. I'll be the man I've always been."

A man *ordinary*.

(A man unchanged.)

(Ghosts:

They usually walk about four in the morning.)

Ahimsa. It does not exist.

Or it becomes perverted. Everything turns to blight.

. . .

Ghosts walk about four in the morning.

. . .

My father: the Great War — the First War — over . . . distant ghosts; he returned to India with his new wife, his second wife, my mother.

My father had married my mother because the First War — the Great War — was ending: both his brothers dead; he was *changed* — his soul changed: a fatigue upon him like . . . like snow at midnight falling, muffling everything — hope and love; but quite suddenly he wanted — in the name of heaven and hell, what was it he wanted?

Hampstead Heath. He and the girl who a year later would become my mother: they'd gone for a walk on Hampstead Heath. My mother: hair dark — a hairstyle unfashionable. *A woman of character*. She had asked him to marry her: she'd done the asking! . . . Hampstead Heath: little boys in sailor suits; little girls in coats with velvet collars.

Well, he must have known: *immortality* has a way of crumbling. I know now — I am a man wise: old Hurry-up Hammett's has crumbled. A sandcastle gone.

My mother married my father because the First War — the Great

War — was ending: one of the few young men left — he with whom she was very much in love — he had married someone else.

I probably was conceived on good old S.S. *City of Bagora* four months later: the events of Amritsar came. The mob came.

There are hatreds in the world.

Ahimsa: it does not exist.

. . .

There are hatreds which one can try to — is that the word? — *understand.*

There are hatreds one will never understand — does not want to understand.

. . .

My mother: ah, a woman of courage! My mother: "A rifle. . . . Is there a rifle?" My mother: a woman without *knowledge.*

My father: he'd not want to know slaughter again till the end of his days, the end of the world. A pacifist? Helpless. . . . "And so I resolved to shield her — and you — with my body as long as I could."

And from then on, my mother came to hate everything about India. And she left.

Do I hate Gandhi for the fact that my mother did not love me?

. . .

Goodness of the soul does not exist. Or it becomes perverted. Everything turns to blight.

Ghosts usually walk about four in the morning.

But then — the road: a country obscured by a mist — well, I somehow managed to keep the ghosts at bay. Because, as a rule, ghosts stay only with those clear-headed.

I was concentrating on my pain. "My hands hurt," I said to the dog Shadow. "My wrists hurt. . . . You see, I cannot even bring my fingers together; make a fist." This was the hand that had held the knife. Pain: my punishment.

Now: Nim's suffering — my punishment?

Ah, *ghost story!* Part . . . whatever.

The Old Paunch: he who had fluffed up the bloody cushion for me. *Well, ghosts . . . Off with you. Shoo. Go. Go away.* (Ghosts *not* distant. Ghosts: the time of Dunkirk.) "Oh, it hurts very badly!" I said to the dog Shadow. And once it was said, the pain lessened, and I began to feel hopeful. *Off with you, ghosts. Boo.* . . . And I was laughing, I think.

And the burning sky seemed beautiful.

And the dog Shadow would run ahead for a bit, but he always came back (though he would not permit me to touch him): he came back; so that must mean he needed me — as much as I needed him.

But then he died, suddenly, and I was left alone. (It did not surprise me, not at all, that he should die; that we all should die. But I was left without hope of . . . salvation.)

I traveled the road: *Home home home home home*. (Dead bodies along the road: in the ditches, in the middle of the road, and so on.)

And at last the sun rose: a fire ahead of me; a fire behind me. . . . Fever.

And then — the sun mid-morning high — I was strafed by a Stuka.
. . .

Then I came to a house. A house . . . untouched. A house: not a pile of rubble. Smoke curled from the chimney . . . from the chimney!

A lawn in the back of the house; laundry drying on the lawn.

And an old woman came out, picked up a watering can from the grass, and she began to sprinkle the laundry.
. . .

Oh God Christ, I was thirsty! And hungry.
. . .

An old woman dressed all in black: a black frock and apron; black stockings; a black scarf.

A black crow of a woman: birdlike steps. An old raven of a woman.

And then, suddenly, her black scarf slipped. She had beautiful white hair.

It is almost five months later now.

XII

I have been trying not to smoke so much lately. (Nim: Hanmer's flat, London — I remember she said that David . . . when he was alive . . . did not smoke.)

I have asked her, "Well, does it bother you, in general, when people smoke?" Christ, *everybody* smokes!

She said to me, sternly, *"You are not David." Do not try to be like David*. I am myself.

Serious gray eyes, N. M. Tunnard-Jones. Eyes: *not straightforward?* (Her eyes: no wile or guile — that is what she is like!) Now: lying? For my sake? N. M. Tunnard-Jones. It was so obvious — absolutely! — that when the man was still among the living, she was glad he did not smoke! But not because that was what made him David? . . . Well, she simply does not like people smoking: she was glad he did not smoke.

Getting to know each other. (Things are so terribly complicated, really.)

I have been quite desperately trying to be moderate about my smoking lately. To please her. Because I am myself. . . . Trying to be *unobtru-*

sive — unobvious — about it! (And so no one seems to have noticed, actually. . . . Nim has noticed. I think. Has not said a word.) (Things are complicated.)

Nim

She must live. Of course.

Nim
We'll become so that we never conceal from each other things truthful, for each other's sake . . .

This morning:
The lorry. I remember everything: the long scratch along the door; the dented mudguard; the spot of rust under the door handle.
And the bastard Dunaway: *ungracious.* Let's not forget Corporal Dunaway: *ungracious.* May God have mercy on his soul!
I opened the door; handed her in — she *hopped* in. . . . My fingers against hers; hers against mine. She waved.
No: she smiled first; then she waved.

The lorry burning.
. . .
No: Did she *wave* first? And *then* she smiled. . . . Christ!

The lorry burning.

My fault.
No salvation.

Her hands have been burned. (So I have learned. . . . Telephoned the hospital, said I was her brother. Well, they hadn't organized her paperwork yet — she has no brother: they believed me. Would never have told me otherwise, I suppose: I am not *family.*)
. . .
(The pressure of her fingers against mine . . .)

Her . . . her face: it has been burned.
My fault.
I remember:
Nim I'll trace your eyebrows with my fingers!
(And the time came: I traced her eyebrows with my fingers. I kissed away the sleep creases from her face.)
. . .
No salvation.

XIII

The alarm clock ticking on my beside table. (For the first time tonight I seem to have become aware of my surroundings.)

I should not do that: listen to the alarm clock ticking.

Nim   Yes   Yes   I do feel guilty because I am listening to the alarm clock ticking . . .

Silence outside: Nobody will come to my door.

  · · ·

I want to be with my own kind! They'll understand. (???)

  · · ·

Bloody hell! Nobody will come to my door.

Why do I want to finish the story of Dunkirk?

  · · ·

She will live. Of course.

XIV

I was thirsty; and hungry. (Dunkirk.)

(Yes, they'd fed me, the Germans — the night before. I hadn't touched that food, though — the night before. Well, how could I hold a spoon, etc.? Ah, the hand that later would hold the knife!)

Now I was most horribly thirsty.

And the woman . . . birdlike . . . was watering the laundry.

Water Water

Sprinkling the white laundry. . . . An old woman dressed all in black.

(I am telling the story as it happened:

Dehydrated, Luthie. De-hy-drat-ed. My kidneys had shut themselves down: Young Scrawny-neck; Old Paunch — I'd shouted at them: "I need to piss!" but I had not felt the urge to relieve myself in . . . ages!

Oh, I was so very thirsty! . . . That is how matters stood, then.)

Smoke curled from the chimney.

There were window boxes: flower boxes; red flowers in them.

A landscape as if obscured by a mist? Everything seemed in quite a sharp outline, suddenly! *(And ghosts would come.)*

What was she doing here? Daft? Senile?

  · · ·

There had been dead bodies along the road. *(Ghosts. Not mine.)* Men. Women. . . . Horses. (And a dog, of course. *A ghost: mine.* Bicycles abandoned. Wheelbarrows. Handcarts: suitcases, bundles. A horse-drawn wagon. Motorcars. . . . A . . . pram: a baby carriage. Oh, I had approached it . . . cautiously! I had to see — had to — must see; yet I did not want to see. Yes, there was a child: a baby in the carriage. How old? Small. A boy? Girl? Bloody hell, who can tell? Sleeping? "Are you dead?" I said. It was dead, of course.)

The guns in the distance — not in the distance: thunder.

A country of desolation. . . . What was the woman doing here?

. . .

She raised her head, and we stared at one another: old, old eyes that must have been blue once. The woman: unsurprised to see me. She appeared unafraid of me.

. . .

Move closer to the fence . . . closer, Luthie. (Now I was almost at the gate.)

. . .

White hair. But nothing like my grandmother's! (Well, I could see it now: hair thin — her very scalp showing. But the strands remaining *were* an old-ivory — no: buttery; soft . . . yellowish. She turned her head, as if listening for something: hair pulled at the back into the tiniest — but tidiest — old woman's bun I have ever seen in my life!

A birdlike neck, but like a plucked bird's: wrinkled.

Well God Christ, the horrible neatness of that hair! (The . . . ghostly neatness. . . . In God's name, who was she? And I think it was I who was afraid of her.)

(I had a fever.)

(I remember:

Silence. The guns booming. Silence.

Dead babies down the road. In the sky to the west: a blackness of the world burning.)

Did I want to protect her? Because she was so old. (I had a fever.)

Did I want comfort from her? (My grandmother had not been able to give it.)

I wanted to comfort *her*. (Did she need comfort?) . . . (Fever. I had some difficulty breathing.)

. . .

The tidy hair and those defiantly bright flowers in the window boxes. Two last stands against . . . Supply your own fear.

Nim: she'll be hideous in the eyes of the world.

She will be . . .

Well, those surgeons — plastic surgeons: they can perform veritable miracles, these days!

. . .

Fear: she'll be hideous in the eyes of the world.

I think I had a waking dream, then: the time of Dunkirk.
  . . .
  (I have left nothing out of the story; I will leave nothing out.)
  . . .
  A waking dream. (It probably lasted only a few seconds: the time of Dunkirk.)
  In the dream, she was sitting, the old woman: in a brown armchair (why a brown armchair?! — no idea, really), a velvety armchair, shabby at the armrests; and I was running toward her. The road: lined with poplars. (Now the road that I had traveled had most certainly *not* been lined with poplars. . . . Well, poplars: leaves . . . trembling. . . . God Christ, Luthie, what a *maudlin* dream!) But I was running. And she sat there, dark, at the end of a dark alley.

I've fallen asleep, now! (My forehead hit the surface of my desk.) W. R. Luthie: Famous Insomniac. Asleep!

Nim   Nim   I'm sorry.

(My writing hand hurts.)

Nim   I'm sorry.
  Nim   Forgive me.

(Why did I begin to write all this down at all, how many — two — months ago?
  1) Ah, the *coyness!* No: reticence . . . Fear? I said at first I had no idea why I was writing it all down.
  2) It was an exercise . . . physiotherapy — a means of strengthening my hand, bringing coordination back to my fingers!
  3) A rite of *exorcism?* (Well, *waiting for Grenfeld,* out on the Husqvarna . . . *nighttime thoughts,* etc.: I waited and waited; at last made an admission to myself. *Thank you, Grenfeld, out on the Husqvarna:* if not for your miserable *journey,* I'd not have made that admission?)
  4) But now I know why I am *finishing* the story! It drives me forward: tell the story and remain awake; and be with her, though I cannot be with her. I want to feel her pain.
  But I feel nothing, of course. . . . I pinch myself: then I can feel pain.

I said to the old woman, in my dream, "Please help me."
  And then, in my dream, I did what I hadn't done with the dog Shadow — not even after he was dead: I fell on my knees and hid my face in whatever warmth she had left. Not much: well, she was very cold.

(The dog Shadow — after he was dead: would it have seemed a *sacrilege* to touch him?) But after a while, the old woman touched *me:* the tips of her fingers on my hair; and that was absolutely wonderful. She said, "Well, close your eyes, and when you've opened them again, it'll all have gone away. And you'll be the same you've always been. . . . You *are* the man you've always been. Nobody and nothing can change you." . . . See? There!!!

Well, bugger the dog Shadow! (And I was feeling hopeful.) Well, I had *suggested* virtually these very words to the dog Shadow; but the dog Shadow had not responded, had not offered an . . . absolution.

To hell with the dog Shadow! (And I was hopeful.)

Who was this woman?

And so, in my dream, I closed my eyes; and when I opened them . . . we stood there.

She took a few steps toward me — those bobbing steps: no scent of dried apples about her (my grandmother: a scent of dried apples about her) — this woman smelled of old age and of an unwashed body.

Well, and so we belonged together: I, too, stank.

We were two people *ordinary.*

. . .

Thirsty. I was thirsty. And hungry. My throat: parched.

Well, open your mouth, Luthie. Speak up. But what if no words come? . . ."Madame," I said.

. . .

And smoke rose from the chimney. Everything was in a *very* sharp outline: focus. . . . Was she cooking something? Lunch? . . . Soup?

. . .

Doff your cap, Luthie. . . . I had no cap.

I . . . introduced myself. Mumbled my name.

(Old blank eyes staring at me: old blank eyes — blue once.)

Oh, it was difficult to gather my French together! "I . . . I am most dreadfully sorry." Did *that* sound French? "Madame . . . Please excuse me. I . . . I have been traveling since early this morning . . ." Well, this wasn't going well at all!

Crazily, I explained, "I ran away from the Germans . . . from the *boche.* But my hands —" And I showed her my hands, then, palms up: even as I'd shown them to the dog Shadow — and to Young Scrawny-neck; Old Paunch: helplessness. I did not so much as whisper a word of the story of the two knives, of course: oh, everything seemed very clear! Cunning, I was: *my own ghost.* "I am in some pain, I am afraid." . . . Now that did not sound *whiny,* did it? "It's a warm day," I said.

And in the meantime, while I was *conversing* (?) so, something like shrewdness had crept into her eyes. . . . Shrewdness?

I took a step back. "Well, the . . . unseasonable weather. . ." *(Unseasonable! Well done, Luthie. Well done!)* "And my . . . hurts . . . inju-

ries . . . my wounds . . . All that together . . . I am thirsty, Madame,"
I said, resolutely. "I'd be much obliged if you would offer me a drink of
water."

So, it was out.
. . .

What was it she was cooking? Soup? or stew? . . . Ah, lovely liquid
pouring down my throat!
. . .

I felt lightheaded. I had a fever.

(But: disappointment. *Disappointment*, Luthie — well, my *waking
dream* had not come true!: I'd opened my eyes, but we'd just . . . stood
there.)
. . .

Well, she had . . . promised: she'd promised to . . . end it. Everything
that was part and parcel of my living: well, all the threads — all the strands
— converging: they'd come converging at the railway station restaurant at
Manchester! and then rolled rolled yarn unrolling to the school storage
room at Dunkirk. . . . Well, what would she do? She'd gather those
threads. Roll them up again: a big ball of yarn. And then . . . then she'd
drop it into the black pocket of her black apron. . . . Who was this woman?
Life? Death? . . . A big ball of yarn as if ready for knitting things.
. . .

Well, and so my grandmother used to knit, too: I was four, five years
old — she sent me little knee-stockings, hand-knitted. "My Dearest
Darling Grandson, Our Emmeline is about to bring her Kittens into the
world. And do you know where she wants her little Nest to be? Why, in
the Library between *Mill on the Floss* and the Milton!". . . Well, God
Christ!
. . .

But this . . . this woman: she'd gather the yarn; and my grandmother's . . . ghost would be at peace, then. Everyone . . . well, my
father . . . released. We are a family blighted by war.
. . .

I am myself.
. . .

And this woman: she would *absolve* the whole world; and everything
would start over again: new; and the yarn would be ready for the knitting
of other stories — a new life for me. For everybody.
. . .

I am myself. I am a good man.
. . .

Was that what she had promised? I was not sure: probably not.
She had not kept her promise.
(But I had wanted to comfort *her*, now hadn't I? Did she need comfort?)
. . .

Thin hair. (Scalp showing — etc., etc.) That tidy tidy neat neat old woman's bun. And the hair was held in place with two combs: one on each side; and the one I could see — as she turned her head, then looked at me again — that comb: old, old, and no longer shiny black (as it must have been once); cloudy; with several teeth missing. . . . A pitiful comb.

Something rose in me, then.

I was caught by . . . not pity, really, but love.

She was a woman who could not offer promises.

. . .

And I could not begin a new story. (I was disappointed.)

I'd have to follow the threads of my living wherever they would take me. A man on his own: alone. (Would I ever manage to take *them* and lead them? *And ghosts would follow me.*) (Was I disappointed?)

. . .

She was a woman *ordinary*. Oh yes, we belonged together.

. . .

It is rather terrible to be caught by love.

. . .

And she opened her mouth. And words came pouring out.

God . . . if you exist . . . God, please . . . What words!

Her voice: like wind sighing in the trees; but *what words.*

Half of it in Flemish; half in French. I didn't understand the Flemish; I understood scarcely half of the French. But what I did understand, I *understood.*

"Don't," I whispered at her. "Please don't."

She wanted me dead. . . . Well, she would not give me any water. . . . She wanted me dead because I was English. She hated me because I was English. It was all my fault that the Germans were coming. All the fault of the English. . . . Dogs. *Dogs???* . . . My . . . my genitals, and dogs?! . . . Christ, I did not want to understand! I had never heard such horrible words from the mouth of anybody, man or woman. . . . She would not give me any water.

Numbness. A most dreadful numbness.

"Oh you bitch," I said.

The most terrible, horrible sense of betrayal. . . . No salvation.

"You bloody bitch." In English. "You bloody French bitch."

And so we hurled abuse at each other: she in her voice like wind in the trees, and I desperate and hoarse and breathless. "How dare you?" I screamed. And I leaned against the gate and pushed it open, and I was inside, on her patch of lawn.

Now she was the one to step back.

Well, afraid of me, are you? Are you, now? And I kept on coming; and she was . . . terrified: as terrified as I had been of the . . . coal's cuttles: well, I'd raised my hands in surrender to the coal's cuttles!: *I am yours.*

She was as terrified of me as I had been of the bloody Stuka. And oh God, it felt good to have somebody be as terrified of me as I had been of the bloody Stuka! The sweetness of power. I kept on coming — *well, I did not take up any space: a ghost* — oh, absolutely!; I kept on coming through her miserable laundry, through those white old woman's petticoats spread out on the lawn. . . . I was possessed of a strength *in*human! (This woman was Death: evil; and I had gone to war to conquer evil.)

. . .

Quite.

She tried to flee into the house, bar the door against me. We reached the door together.

Well, I was not quite so strong as I'd thought.

And she certainly was not senile. Oh good God no, not senile at all!

She went for my wounded hands. I deflected her just in time. She tried to drive her little fist between my legs. I squirmed around and caught the blow on the hip. Even so, it hurt.

I grabbed her in my arms, then — ah, not using my hands!: *trying* not to use those poor, poor hands: clever Luthie! — and I held her, as if in a dreadful lovers' embrace. Interesting to watch, no doubt about it — had a human soul been there to watch: well, I was not a ghost any longer — I was a half-dead twenty-year-old man. (A half-dead twenty-year-old man; a half-dead eighty-year-old woman engaged in hand-to-hand — mortal?! — combat.)

And all this time I was talking. Gasping for breath. Talking. "Well, if you won't give me any water . . . well, then I'll take it." Idiotic things like that I said. "Any food you have . . . I'll take as much as I want." Horrible things like that I said. "I . . . I hurt a man last night. I mean — this morning. I hurt him very badly. Cut him with a knife. . . . And I did it for you . . . for your sake . . ."

Why did I go to war? Well, to punish — inflict pain upon — those who had hurt people like Vřeštala's mother.

"And now I am thirsty . . . and I am feverish. And I can't piss."

I dragged her in the house.

An armchair . . .

. . .

A *brown* armchair? Oh God . . . please no.

. . .

In the kitchen: a straight-backed wooden chair. "Now sit there."

The tiny neck, yellow and wrinkled like a little plucked chicken's, that tiny neck snapped back.

Silence.

The house: dark.

Outside: the sun tiptoeing across the crumpled laundry.

I fainted, I think.

Then I sat on the floor, my head on my knees, my body shaking: well, not a *ghost* — a child weeping. Then, on my knees — a . . . supplicant? No: a hurting animal! — cannot stand up, cannot walk — I crept forward. I raised my good hand — the one that had held the knife; touched the birdlike neck: I felt a pulse.

I shivered with insane happiness.

Water. Yes, there was a pail. Cooking water. Washing-up water.

The kitchen: incredibly dingy. . . . Oh, quite at odds with her tidy hair; the bright flowers in the flower boxes! . . . The only towel I could find: *incredibly* filthy! Filthy, Luthie. God Christ!: *snot* on it? Had she used it instead of a handkerchief? (But as my stomach rose, I found I had nothing to bring up. . . . I was most dreadfully thirsty.)

Can I grasp the towel, hold on to it? Dip it in the water. . . . The water: quite warm — must have stood there for a long, long time. Frantic, I shook the towel, trying to cool it.

I dragged it back and forth across her face: I *bathed* her face. I pressed the cool cloth to her scrawny neck. Roll up her sleeves? Moisten her . . . wrists? Then moisten the place where the pulse is in the crook of the elbow? I did not manage to roll up her sleeves.

After a while, she opened her eyes. Old blank eyes that must have been blue once. She didn't know where she was, who I was.

I knew very well who I was, where I was. What I was.

"Are you better now?" I said. . . . Well, smooth her hair back into place, Luthie. (But my hands no longer obeyed me.) "I . . . I'm sorry," I said, and started laughing.

Slowly, very slowly, as if I had taken her age upon me, I got to my feet. (I was lightheaded: had a fever.) What . . . what *restitution* shall I make? . . . *Res-ti-tu-tion.*

Money? I had no money. Had had some francs, once; two ten-pound notes. A sizeable amount of money, really. The *coal's cuttles* had taken it. . . .

It would be sordid to leave money.

. . .

My watch? My watch was gone, too. My father's gift: my beautiful Rolex Oyster.

. . .

I had nothing of value. . . . My bandages: were they of value?

"Madame," I said. "My name is W. R. Luthie." (Well, I'd given her my name once before, hadn't I?) I recited my address, very carefully. Very slowly. "Please remember it." She wouldn't, of course. "If I do not come back, you'll know where to find me. I'll come back . . . when the war is over. I'll make a . . . restitution. After we have won." I was very cold.

Then I left.

I still was very thirsty. I needed water more than ever before.

All right, so I'll try the well. . . . Or . . . the watering can? No water in the watering can. I'd overturned the miserable watering can, trampling my way through her wretched laundry. . . . And I would not drink out of her pail! — I'd not have been able to do it even before I'd polluted it by dipping the filthy towel in that water: it was *her* water. But the water in the well — it came out of the ground, didn't it?: it belonged to everybody. . . .

The lid of the well was locked, though. Locked against all comers, against suffering Englishmen. Against the evil world.

I think I was still crying. "Oh, you French bitch," I whispered. (Flemish bitch, actually.) . . . We were two people *ordinary;* belonged together. Then I walked on.

And eventually, I found another house: a ruin of a house; but no water or food in that ruin; all I found was . . . a box of raisins. I took it.

(I remember that there was a chestnut tree near that house. A chestnut tree in full bloom. Tall pink clusters of blooms, like candles. . . . Candles in a cathedral. Oh, it was beautiful!)

Father

And some time later, a British tank crew — without a tank — found me. Caught up to me. . . . Whatever.

"Well, you look all done in, lad."

I stared blankly. No doubt. I do not remember.

"Chum . . . Have you got anything to eat, chum?"

I did not say anything.

They searched me. Thoroughly; with . . . expertise — exactly as the Germans had done: their paws on my person. I did not protest; could not resist.

They found the raisins. Ate them all. "Well, it's some fever you've got, lad. These things would only make it worse — make you more thirsty."

They had some water in a canteen; but said, quite sensibly, that they were saving those few drops against yet more dire times. They pushed a cigarette between my lips and lit it for me. The cigarettes were Woodbines, I remember. The cigarette made me sick at my stomach; it made me cough. And my chest hurt.

They helped me to my feet. "Lad . . . Chum . . . Sir . . ." Oh yes, I was an officer: they should call me *sir*. "RAF," one of them said. "RAF, wake up. Lean on me."

And so they took turns not carrying me, really; but dragging me along. I could not breathe.

But I got to the coast.

Goodness does not exist.

The story is finished.
    Since then, I have been afraid of old women.
    Twenty, thirty, fifty years from now: nobody will know how I lived.
    (Should these things remain private, secret, hidden: hidden in twilight
— ghosts on silent feet?)

Nim: She folds herself against me, trusting.
    We fit together. Her small naked back cool against my chest; her little
buttocks against my belly. I bring my legs up: the backs of her thighs
against my thighs. And I cross my hands over her breasts; she entwines
her fingers with my fingers. We sleep.
    Nim: trusting.

Nim   I am myself.

We sleep: comfortable.

Nim   I am a good man.

I am a just man in a just war.
    I went to war for the sake of people like Vřešťala's mother.
    (That is how I've grown into manhood — into adulthood: learning
that the goodness of intentions becomes twisted.
    The gentleness of spirit becomes perverted.)

Nim: Her arms have been burned; her back.
   · · ·
    I remember: her small shoulder blades against my chest.
    I remember the last time we made love: afterward, she lay facedown,
her cheek nestled in the pillow; I ran my finger down her backbone.
   · · ·
    A human being burning sounds like bacon frying.

Nim   Why am I writing all this down? Is it only to be awake with you?

Her pain: my ultimate punishment.
   · · ·
    I cannot feel the pain.

What did I want for my Wonders?
    (This afternoon: Their joy in the slaughter was their gift to me. Ah,

they enjoyed their killing! Happiness: it brought them happiness! — their hatred of those they were killing. And that hatred was their gift to me.

. . .

Thank you. Thank you, Wonders.)
I have failed.
(Their joy in the slaughter was their gift to me.

. . .

I have failed.

. . .

My gratitude to you, though, my dear dear Wonders. Thank you.
Well, it's the thought that counts, isn't it? Christ!
Thank you.)

. . .

You are men of . . . feelings.

This morning — early this afternoon: I killed without feelings.

No hatred, no revenge; no . . . fear; no *joy,* excitement; no sympathy or pity, or sorrow, later. I killed. And watched myself as if from the outside. No feelings. I was there, but did not *exist:* therefore there was no need for me to feel hatred, a thirst for revenge, fear, pity, or sorrow. No feelings.

. . .

I have failed.

. . .

Thank you, Wonders. You're not empty of . . . yes, *absolutely every-thing.*

But so it will be that one day you, too — my dear Wonders — you will become as I am now. I know it. Foreknowledge.

. . .

I have failed.
(Hatreds in the world.)

. . .

No foreknowledge: they've accepted the deaths of Cartwright and Brown without feelings, it seems.

The . . . fulfillment they found in the slaughter was their gift to me.

. . .

Two of them are dead: Cartwright, Brown. (I will think about that later.)

The alarm clock ticking. Silence outside.
Nobody will come to my door.

Nim will live.
She will be hideous in the eyes of the world.

XV

"Father . . ." On the telephone. (Well, from the Signals Section. God!)

My father *gulped.* (Had answered on the second ring: the *Air Ministry . . . the squadron adjutant phoning?* — in the middle of the night. He heard me; gulped down his terror. "Good to hear from you.") Voice firm. And far away.

. . .

My childhood (I was four, five years old once): a landscape in a mist?

. . .

I am letting go. All the things that hurt . . .
Bloody hell! I am not letting go. Father   Do something for me! Help me . . .

"Which is the very best hospital in the country for the treatment of burns?"

He said, "The Masonic. London, of course." Without hesitation. . . . And so he still knows!: he has kept abreast! And it has been so many years . . .

"Know anyone there?"

"N-no. Of course not." Probably did not know anyone there, ever. . . . *Homesickness* in his voice?: homesickness for things that never were and never would be? (But I had never before . . . identified it as such, had I? Had not named it, had I?: homesickness.)

Well, *I am letting go.*

Father   I was five years old; you scooped me up, held me aloft.

(And I remember: quietly, we surveyed our domain. Awfully brown, our domain, really. . . . A whiff of soap, warm water, and general well-being: my father's face. . . . In the distance, a large dark bird circled. A vulture? Oh quite far from us!)

. . .

I am letting go. Reach for daylight; descend into darkness. Well. Yes.

I was telephoning from the Signals Section; and I was there, of course: My body present; yet I was not there. (I was very much aware, though. A WAAF, bent over some calculations at the desk in the corner. She must stay: it is against the regulations to leave *anyone* alone with the phones! The WAAF pretending: I do not exist. The WAAF: *afraid of my grief?* Well, God in heaven! I noticed myself shivering. I was not cold, though.) I was a man very far away.

My father: helplessness in his voice?

It will always be so.

His voice *high-pitched,* breaking with terror once again. "Well, you are all right, aren't you?"

"My skin has not been burned, if that's what you mean."

(And another WAAF opening the door. The two women: whisper whisper. *Snuffling.* God in heaven! One of them patting her tears dry from the corners of her eyes with her fingertips, daintily; the other blowing her nose into a handkerchief, *un*daintily.)

On the telephone — my father: a breath of silence. Then, an *intake* of breath: a little moan? — as if cringing before . . . well, a blow; but one cannot tell which direction the blow will come from. "Why . . . are you asking, then?"

"For the woman I love. The woman whom I plan to marry. The woman I want to be the mother of my children."

. . .

Pompous ass, Luthie.

. . .

(And the WAAFs: as if a dam had broken. A *flood* of tears. . . . *Bloody hell!* . . . Oh, I was very much aware of my surroundings! The one sitting at the desk: reddish hair. Reddish. Red hair. . . . Nim's hair? Like watching a waterfall through a setting sun!

. . .

And I brought my knees forward a bit, bent them: I stood, not double-jointed. Makes one feel less vulnerable. . . . I felt most terribly cold.)

A *long* silence on the telephone. . . . Not a moan: a sigh?

Sadness. . . . Despair. Try to keep it within you; but it will rise to the surface — it will out, one day. The world is too horrible to live in. . . . He has carried his despair within him since . . . since . . ." *And so I hated the tree for hurting me, so that my hatred of people would not overwhelm me. . . ."*

. . .

Can *he* feel Nim's pain, and mine?

My mother, breaking in: "You are far too young to marry."

(The WAAFs: *staring* at me, now; terrified by my grief — it could be theirs; or their men's.)

. . .

Something flawed about my mother. It will always be so.

. . .

My mother: younger when I was born than I am now.

. . .

My mother: in possession of her own knowledge, wisdom! (I went to war. My father said, "Come back unchanged." She gave him a *terrible* look; said to me: "Come back." My mother who had never loved me.)

(My mother, after Dunkirk: dialing dialing . . . every hospital in the whole bloody country. ". . . Fair hair, hazel eyes. . . . Quite tall. Not very good-looking. He is my son." She loves me.

. . .

Something flawed about her, though.)
Somebody Help me

. . .

Everybody: helpless.
I accept the helplessness.

. . .

(The WAAFs: snuffling.)

My father: he has seen too much slaughter, did not want to see more till the end of his days. (But then — and I'd shriveled to nothingness under his love, oh absolutely! — he gave me the miserable knife.)

I am a just man in a just war.
Both of us: helpless. (We have been each other's ultimate failure, I suppose. It rather hurts, really, to have been a good man's ultimate failure.)

Now, my father on the telephone: "I'll see what I can do to help." His voice resolute, and determined.
His voice trailing off . . . (My father: *homesick* for a life in which he would not fail, not be helpless; a world in which a *gentleness of spirit* would prevail?

. . .

Is such a life possible? . . . What can I do? . . . Does such a world exist?)

Father They pressed my very own Colt .45 to my skull, where the hair ends and bare skin begins. And I hated hated hated not the ant.

Father Remember? Scotland: the squadron was still in Scotland. And Tom was killed and Mother telephoned to tell me about it and about Janet's miscarriage — she left a message for me . . .

and Christ! that was what then led to my first walk with Nim: she'd sent me a note from Signals. "Your immediate family all right, though there is bad news."
(Everything fits together so! But all those . . . threads: they still keep unrolling. The story, told in fits and starts: if I put my mind to it, some semblance of a whole will emerge. The story is not finished yet.)

Father My first thought had been that you were dead.

My thought was that now you'd never ever . . . well, <u>invite</u> me to tell you about the knife. And I'd never ever ask your . . . your forgiveness for hating hating hating not the ant . . .

Father   You coward.

Are you afraid of <u>my</u> forgiveness?

Well, it will always be so. I suppose.

Helplessness.

(*Now* the story is finished. . . . The story goes on.)

· · ·

Home is too far away: too much has happened. (Janet. Well, Janet, for example! I have not asked them about her in . . . ages!

Bloody hell! Not now: I'll think about that later.) (The refugee children from London . . . Yes, I'll ask about them later.)

· · ·

My parents are very far away: too much has happened.

Their shadows — the shadows of their lives — the shadow of my own life: are they *all* landscapes in a mist? Too much has happened.

I am letting go. Descend into darkness.
Reach for daylight.

· · ·

Descend into darkness.
Reach for daylight.

Nim. She is in pain.

She was lovely.

The alarm clock ticking. Silence.

Everyone asleep. Those wakeful: nobody will come to my door.

Ashley came to my door. (What time is it?)

"Sir . . . Sir . . . Grenfeld is gone again." Well, God in heaven!

What does he want me to do, Ashley the Nosy Parker? *Wait for Grenfeld,* again? In Christ's name! I'll not do it! How dare he disappear again! *Grenfeld the Rescuer.* Ha!

(Well, at least the bloody Husqvarna is out of his reach, now.)

· · ·

Ashley, leave me.

· · ·

Two of my Wonders are dead: Cartwright; Brown. (But I'll think about that later.)

· · ·

Ashley   Go forth, you miserable Nosey Parker. Alone. On your own. Alone. With your miserable camera. Good luck.

Ashley   Run. Run from me. You silly wretched little Wonders, you have come to be . . . well, close to my heart. But all of you have become . . . contaminated already; it might get worse. (I know that Ashley went after a parachute this afternoon. He tore a wounded German bastard to pieces. And it was his gift to me. . . . I heard him over the R/T. I knew it was his voice: shrieking, screaming. Calling the Germans names. Well, horrible names, naturally. No, he wasn't calling anybody names, really: it was a . . . chant. A *religious* chant. Well . . . ecstasy. And I recognized it as *ecstasy* because I myself was a man without feelings: viewed everything — heard everything — as if from the outside. Without feelings. . . . I am a man without feelings.)

· · ·

Ashley, leave.

But he stared at me. (Ashley: squirrel teeth.) His eyes are a nice, soft dark brown, actually. He stared at me as if he very much wanted to help me; did not know how.

· · ·

Two of them are dead. Brown's vanishing from this world: my fault? (But I'll think about it later.)

· · ·

Waiting for Grenfeld, again? I'll not do it.

· · ·

"Sergeant . . . Thank you for coming to tell me." (Yes, I want to be with my own kind! . . . They understand.) "Please go to sleep now."

Ashley . . . Thank you for coming to my door. I cannot protect you, but I'll remember you came to my door.

· · ·

And Ashley departed.

The alarm clock ticking.

Nim will live.
    What to do now?

XVI

And so . . . the hangar.

Semidarkness: voices somewhere in the near distance, muffled; a clattering of tools: somebody dropped something, is swearing.

A head in a sudden circle of light. "Sir . . . ?"

"Mind if I sit in my kite for a bit?"

"Right-o, sir. No problem at all, sir." An LAC of the fitters: I don't know him. But he knows me! He is both *tongue-tied* in self-consciousness and *hurried:* Since last morning I have become *famous.*

The hangar: Why?

Could not stand my room any longer. Hanmer's bed: clean sheets. His replacement will be here tomorrow.

. . .

Hanmer . . . You misery . . . Well, I'll come to see you in hospital! (But I must spend all my free time with Nim. You understand that, Hanmer, don't you?)

Hanmer . . . And so we'll see each other again. But it'll all be different. . . . Hanmer, good-bye???

Oh, for heaven's sake!

My Spit — ah, not good old *Aunt Millicent!* — my aircraft: a great dark moth in the semidarkness.

Take a few running steps . . . No parachute: it makes me light — feather-light! The left foot on the trailing edge of the wing, step on the seat with the right foot. Grasp the rim of the wind screen. Bring other foot in; slide down.

Quiet.

No feelings.

Indifference. . . . Indifference to everything around me; to myself.

No feelings.

Two of them dead. Brown. Cartwright.

Brown: Is it my fault?

Well, that absolutely *hare-brained* idea I'd had!: bribe good old Bennett and his cohorts into giving the Wonders — the Wonders' kites — the attention that should have been rightfully theirs all along. Remember, Luthie? Well, I'd have Bennett et al. work on my dogshit Austin — pretend that there was something wrong with it, then pay two, three times the amount of the bill for their services rendered!

When the Austin disappeared from Earth's surface, I . . . well, pushed the whole matter into the back of my mind.

Brown's death: my fault?

It doesn't seem to matter much right now, really.

Well, I want it to matter, by God! I do. I do. I do!!! (That is why I want to think about it later.)

Is this to be one of those occasions: *my life passes before my very eyes? . . .* Bloody hell!

•

Lean my head against the headrest . . .

Touch the undercarriage handle, idly. . . . It is cool. (It is not painted white. It's painted red. *Aunt Millicent*'s undercarriage handle was painted white.) I do not know this kite well.

And yet the inside of the cockpit has the smell about it of my fear — oh, definitely! Over the past few days: the fear . . . and the blood lust . . . etc. etc. . . . well, they all seep in, in the end. I remember — I recall! (but this was when *Aunt Millicent* was still with me) — I remember: hearing a Fritz breathing, once, over the R/T. *And so go home and breathe. . . . Go home and breathe. . . .* Well, all that becomes part of . . . of the polished wood on the instrument panel (for example), of the rudder pedals under the soles of one's boots . . .

Solace. . . . Am I seeking solace?

. . .

A dead calm about me.
There is no solace. No salvation.
No feelings.

. . .

Aunt Millicent — taking her out for the very first time: God, a fighter pilot's body takes a tremendous amount of punishment — absolutely! . . . I remember: *Streaming* upward. Up up up up up
Sheer bravado!
A controlled spin . . . Difficult to do in a Spit, no doubt about it.
Sheer exuberance!
A dead calm about me, now. . . . Indifference?
(Is this then *one of those occasions: one's life passing* . . . Well, God Christ in heaven! When it is over, am I then *truly* dead?)

Nim: when I first saw her, she was a woman who ate her dinner *neatly*.

Serious gray eyes: *a woman of character*. Her smile: *straightforward*. No female wiles and guiles. Her smile: a drink of water from a summer well!

. . .

She likes Bach. She is a precise person. She is so wonderfully self-contained.

. . .

She *hopped* in the lorry . . .

. . .

I remember:
Scotland. We were still in Scotland.
Nim. Hanmer. Nim pushing paperwork of some sort on Hanmer.
She made him take the papers. Hanmer: disgruntled.
And she turned on her heel. Leaning into the wind, calmly. (There

always was wind there: Scotland. Wind in the grass, and in the heather, and in people's bones.)

How will her life be now?

(I close my eyes:
   No salvation.)

I'll always remember her like that: leaning into the wind, calmly.
   . . .

   When this is over, am I then truly dead — or feeling curiously liberated?

Ashley: When I first met him . . . well, he had *spied* on me, the wretched Nosy Parker; had watched me *conducting* the Sibelius piece on the wireless. The Second Symphony. All about fate and-all that. . . . Pompous ass, Luthie.
   . . .

   Ashley: if not for the accursed war, which had made me his flight commander and him one of the men under my command — if not for that, we might have become fast friends a few years from now, when the difference in our ages ceased to matter.
   (This is one of *those occasions:* one's life passing. . . .)

The kite: a large dark moth in the semidarkness.
   I, too, am of darkness.

            Ah, W. R. Luthie coming around Nanga Parbat!
            On his final approach into Gilgit!

No feelings? Am I seeking solace?

Nim said once, "When this is over, will you be a schoolmaster?"
   Well, God in heaven, woman! I? A schoolmaster? Me?

            Ah, W. R. Luthie   Nanga Parbat

   Solace?

I went to war for the sake of people like Vřešťala's mother. (A just man in a just war.)
   And so it is . . . noble? for me to sacrifice my soul (pompous ass, Luthie!) — bloody hell! the Wonders' *gift* to me — the gift of their self-corruption, savagery: their sacrifice! — so that the souls of others might be saved.
   I have failed.
   Well, the children's drawings — *My Dog Flufy. This Is My Cat*

Snowball — remember? There have been new drawings, lately: they are of Spitfires shooting down Messerschmitts; dead bodies bleeding. Blood   blood   blood.

We've all failed.

I suppose. . . . Nobody remains *unchanged*. . . . Cannot be helped, I suppose. . . . I wanted the Wonders to remain *unchanged*. Have I failed them? . . . Nothing I can do.

In helplessness, we all slide toward *childhood*.

In childhood, things ought not to remain unresolved. (Well, Surjit Chadha and I: we'd run a race once — matters unresolved; and I remember: we then looked at each other and, for a moment, were wise beyond our years.)

. . .

In adulthood, things often remain unresolved.

. . .

Well, the dying German and I: we'd dragged good old Grenfeld into adulthood.

. . .

And we *grow up,* and the craving for adulthood is the very reason for our being. Still: now, in helplessness, we slide toward a . . . peculiar . . . well, childishness (?): the Wonders resolve things by finding the reason for *their* being in their gift of savagery to me; I resolve things by killing without feelings.

Semidarkness. Look in the rear-view mirror, in the semidarkness: I see my eyes in the rear-view mirror.

Nim said once my eyes were the best thing about my face.

. . .

I am not good-looking.

Nim   I am a good man.

Nim

   This is not a real letter.

   I was at a convalescent place — after Dunkirk: green plants everywhere; I helped an old charwoman one night dust the shiny tough green leaves of those plants. An old woman. And after that I slept without dreaming for the very first time since Dunkirk; and I was no longer afraid of old women.

   Is that enough? It is not enough.

   Nim   I am a good man.

   She will be . . . ugly.

   Well, what will happen now? How will she live her life?

N. M. Tunnard-Jones: the eyes of a woman of character.

. . .

Those serious gray eyes: two spoonfuls of gray ashes? Christ!
. . .

Her gaze: straightforward. N. M. Tunnard-Jones.
Her smile: a simple smile. Wonderful!
(I remember that very first walk: she lengthened her stride, I short-ened mine; our steps matched, and we walked together.
I remember she said, in her letter, that she painted pictures inside her head with music. . . . Does she then travel to places where I cannot fol-low her?
. . .

Getting to know each other.)

Waiting for Grenfeld. Again. . . . Bloody hell, where is the man?
How dare he do this to me again?
Grenfeld the Rescuer. Tried to save my . . . life. Yes. Quite.

Tired. I am very tired. No, I am not tired at all. Odd. . . . Well, I took a nap, a while ago: my head falling on the desk. . . . But I want to remain awake! I finally came to the end of my miserable storytelling trying to remain awake. I'll probably be tired tomorrow. . . . Well, I used to spin my stories *for my own sake:* for my own salvation? But now that I am done, for *her sake:* to be with her, though I cannot be with her; *to give her myself —*

Nim   Nim   It does not really matter why I began to write all this down. At some point, that <u>erstwhile</u> reason simply disappeared, and I began to write it for you.

Nim   These are real letters. I want you to know everything about me.

Nim   I stand humble and honest before you.

But what have I accomplished? She's *still* hurting. . . . Her pain: *my* ulti-mate punishment? Bloody hell, she is the one hurting!
What to do now? Nothing. . . . Helplessness.
I am awake not because I want to feel her pain, but because *she* is in pain. . . . I'll probably be tired tomorrow. . . . I am babbling: it has been tomorrow for . . . several hours.
Have not taken any Benzedrine; not a drop of brandy, whisky, gin.
. . .

Waiting for Grenfeld.
. . .

Lean my head against the headrest . . . My thumb on the Fire button on the stick. . . . Revulsion?
N-no. Indifference. (I am a man without feelings.)

Ah, W. R. Luthie coming around Nanga Parbat!

Reaching for daylight . . .
The threads have come together; the story is not finished.
The past does not matter . . . ? Oh yes, it matters. The things that hurt — etc. etc. . . . *I am letting go; ghosts will follow me.*
  . . .

Waiting for Grenfeld.
Ashley, thank you for coming to my door.
  . . .

My . . . tomorrow (God in heaven! Pompous ass, Luthie?): to make sure that a woman hideous in the eyes of the world knows she is lovely. (Very simple, really.)
  . . .

Yes. Quite.
  . . .

Actually, those plastic surgeons can perform miracles, these days! (I do not believe it. . . . Difficult times will be ours, I suppose.)
  . . .

Flowers. Must not forget flowers tomorrow.
I'll bring myself.
  . . .

Waiting for Grenfeld. (At least the accursed motorcycle is out of his reach. . . . The next time: a bare whiff of a . . . crisis — I'll confine him to quarters, I swear! . . . Bloody hell! I am babbling. . . . My sense of humor coming back? I am . . . myself?!)

Nim: She'll live. Of course.

What if she dies . . .
  . . .

Geoff Thomas — that little fat chap — long ago: he was burned; he died.

She will live. Of course.

(My life: a spider web in the morning, a little thing with dewdrops on it.)

PART FIVE

86

And a new day came, and it was afternoon; and as far as the men of Flight B knew, the woman was still alive.

The telephone in the Ready Room had done its ringing; the loud-speaker had spat and crackled: they had gone out and come back; Luthie was overdue. . . . Not *Missing*, yet: overdue.

They sat in the grass and waited.

And Ashley *examined* himself; Ashley *observed* the others, as they waited: it seemed to him they were waiting . . . without anxiety? — my God! — well, with acceptance.

Still: Who would lead them now?

They felt alone: Ashley felt alone.

Stanhope was sucking on his thumb — suck suck suck; but there was nobody there to laugh at him, make fun of him, tell him that he sounded like a fish in an aquarium at feeding time. Brown was gone.

Cartwright was gone.

They were tired.

Afternoon. In the morning, a Hurricane had crashed on landing — hadn't even made the runway: had come through the fence, flaming; had broken up, scattering parts of itself, burning. Now it was afternoon: the fire had been put out long ago, naturally. But the charred hulk was still there, naturally, in the not-too-distant distance.

They sat and waited. Tired.

Well, they had done all they could for Luthie.

They'd given him everything they could.

Was he dead? They did not want him to be dead. . . . Who would lead them?

They would miss him. . . . Oh, they would! They would! Ashley felt terribly alone.

Grenfeld lay sprawled in one of the lawn chairs, in a deep sleep; exhausted. Ashley had no idea — none — at what time Grenfeld had returned last night — this morning.

My God! My God! Where had the idiot been this time?

Victoria the Cat was sunning herself on the bonnet of a Hillman; her belly enormous. Well, her kittens would be born any day, now. Any hour? Any . . . minute?

Ashley observed her, and it came to him that human babies kicked inside their mothers' bellies. Kick kick kick. Did kittens kick, too? Tiny kitten-feet kicking. Kick kick kick. What would it feel like? And Ashley was . . . tired, but comfortable — well, he wanted to be comfortable: toying with the idea. Was he comfortable? Ashley felt *limp*. He felt as if he had drunk too much last night; but he had not been thoroughly drunk in . . . several days.

Luthie was overdue. He could not be dead!!!

They waited. And, waiting, they discussed the replacement for Flight Lieutenant Acklington: the man had arrived this morning.

Nobody liked him much, really.

Well, there would never ever be another Flight Lieutenant Acklington!
· · ·
There would never be another Luthie.

Luthie was not dead. He could not be. Could not.
· · ·
The sun-warmed grass smelled of petrol fumes; they stopped *discussing,* and silence hung over them.

And at last the Adj. came and wiped Luthie's name from the board. And told them that yes, Luthie was alive.

Wounded. On his way to hospital.

How bad was it? No word yet. But he must be conscious: at least, he had been conscious long enough to request that the people who had found him — a man and his wife: farmers — they should telephone the base.
· · ·

"Well, the bastard!" Farrell shouted, happy. "Now he's out of it! He'll leave us here. The bastard!" Happy.

"The bastard!" said Peploe-Webb.

"The bastard!" said Stanhope.

They reviled Luthie, in happiness. And Ashley's heart was somewhere where one's tonsils usually are, in happiness.

Then, of course, they had to settle down again; and they waited, again. Well, for the telephone . . . the loudspeaker . . . They were happy, of course.

. . .

Uncertain.

. . .

Grenfeld half-lay, half-sat in the grass, supporting himself on his elbow, *brooding*.

. . .

Victoria the Cat lumbered down from the bonnet of the Hillman and set off through the grass, her belly dragging, her broad gray back *heavy:* she was purposefully heading . . . somewhere.

Well, would *she* miss Luthie?

. . .

Ashley felt . . . accepting.

Oh yes, they had given Luthie everything they could; could not give more. And so it was . . . fitting — well my God! my God! — that he would not be back. Well, was it fitting? Was it? Whatever had been between him and Flight B was . . . ended? My God! Finished. Done. . . . Well, was it finished?

As far as anybody knew, the woman was still alive.

And so it seemed to Ashley that that, too, was . . . fitting: that these two people hurt — hurting — should . . . well, hurt together.

(But she could still die, of course.)

They sat and waited, the remaining men of Flight B; Ashley watched them and he watched himself; oh yes, they all were anxious about the future! But everything within them: their emotions — feelings — seemed to be . . . subdued. (Everything within Ashley was subdued.)

Luthie's thermos flask, in the grass. He'd left it behind when they'd scrambled. Liquid still sloshed in it: his famous half-coffee, half-cocoa. Peploe-Webb unscrewed the top, sniffed. "Still warm. . . . Coffee-and-cocoa, anyone?"

After a while, Stanhope said, "Give here." And he dipped his finger in the liquid; inspected the finger, but did not lick it; did not drink. Then they passed the thermos around; peered into its depths; did not drink. Then the thermos flask sat there, in the grass. The thermos — and Luthie's *sinister* sunglasses: he'd left those behind when they'd scrambled.

They sat and wondered: when would the various replacements be here? For Cartwright, Brown . . . and so on. What would they be like?
   (And everything within them was subdued.)

And then — the sirens. Again. Well, this was how it had been yesterday!
   Things repeating themselves? God damn it all
   What to do now? . . . One never got enough warning!
   . . .
   Let's go. Let's go. Let's get the kites off the ground . . .
   One never had enough warning!

The earth around them boiling.
   Hit the ground? Ashley hit the ground. Stanhope next to him: curled up against Ashley; Stanhope with his hands over his head.
   Farrell shouting. Screaming. Farrell screaming. Shouting. . . . Had they *got him,* or was it just fear?

In the distance — in the middle distance: Victoria the Cat.
   What was happening? Was she . . . injured? Confused? Well, *frozen* in her terror? (As . . . as a rabbit *freezes* before a snake.) No, she was not *frozen.* But she ran to and fro: frantic. Couldn't she escape?

The earth around them boiling.
   Grenfeld: Grenfeld running. That bloody idiot! The stupid idiot!
   Grenfeld: *obsessed* once with killing Germans; now . . . what an idiotic idiot! . . . *obsessed* with being a . . . savior?
   Grenfeld: *obsessed.*
   Did Ashley envy him?

What to do now?
   Let's go. Let's pick ourselves up and go get the Fritzes!

Grenfeld had reached Victoria; scooped her up.
   Victoria began to claw at Grenfeld, furiously. Was that what she was doing: clawing at him? Clawing at his . . . face?

The earth around Grenfeld and the cat boiling.
   Grenfeld dropped Victoria; Victoria the Cat ran. Limping?
   Grenfeld: his hands . . . were they bleeding? . . . covering his face.

•

"Well, God damn you! Get up   Get up   Get up! Go go go go go! I'll skin you alive, you little bastards!" This was the *new Flight Lieutenant Acklington:* the replacement for Flight Lieutenant Acklington. "Get in your bloody kites and take off!"

But was it all over, now?
   Well, let's go. Let's go and chase them.
   Would the Hun bastards dare come for another pass? (One of them had crashed and was burning.
   But two Hurricanes had collided on the ground, taking off, and were also burning.
   The . . . the officers' mess — was it the officers' mess? — was burning.)

Well let's go and chase them . . .
   And they ran for their kites. They left Grenfeld — the injured Grenfeld — on the ground.
   Ashley ran. And as he ran — and it felt a bit as if he were running but yet he wasn't: well, his legs were carrying him forward, but he didn't seem to be getting anywhere; as he ran, the thought came to him, all abruptly: should he tell Luthie, sometime, about the idiot Grenfeld and the stupid cat? . . . Visit Luthie in hospital? Sometime. Tomorrow. The day after. Sometime. One of these days. . . . Would Luthie be . . . pleased?
   If the woman should die (my God!) — or even if she lived — would he be . . . comforted?

(And Ashley envied Grenfeld terribly. Grenfeld . . . the admirable? Grenfeld: Ashley's friend. . . . God damn it all!)
   Well, perhaps not everything was finished between them and Luthie. . . . God damn it all!)

And then there Ashley was. Inside his kite. The ground people had started the engine for him.
   And so Ashley gave the ready-for-takeoff sign.
   And they went.
   And it was all wrong: Ashley did not really want to do it — he felt as if he were plunging into . . . well, into an *abyss;* but there they went, Ashley leading.

Let's go and chase them . . .
   (But it probably was too late by now, anyway.)

The next two days were foggy — a dense, cold cold fog: no flying — a much needed respite. And after that it sometimes almost seemed as if there were fewer enemy planes in the skies.